MYSTERIOUS VISIONS

MYSTERIOUS VISIONS

Great Science Fiction
by Masters of the Mystery

Edited by Charles G. Waugh, Martin Harry
Greenberg and Joseph Olander

St. Martin's Press, New York

Library of Congress Cataloging in Publication Data

Main entry under title:

Mysterious visions.

   1. Science fiction, American. 2. Science fiction, English. I. Greenberg, Martin Harry. II. Olander, Joseph D. III. Waugh, Charles.
PZ1.M99918 [PS648.S3] 823'.0876 78-3990 ISBN 0-312-55866-X

"The Angel of the Lord" by Melville Davisson Post, from *Uncle Abner: Master of Mystery*, copyright © 1918 by D. Appleton and Co. Reprinted by permission of Robert P. Mills, Ltd., 156 East 52nd St., New York, N.Y. 10022. Copyright renewed in the name of the author's estate, 1946.

"Music from the Dark" by Cornell Woolrich, as "Dark Melody of Madness," from *Dime Mystery*, copyright © 1935. Reprinted by permission of the author and the author's agents, Scott Meredith Literary Agency, Inc., 845 Third Avenue, New York, N.Y. 10022.

"The Legend of Joe Lee" by John D. MacDonald, from *Cosmopolitan*, copyright © 1964 by The Hearst Corporation. Reprinted by permission of the author and the author's agents.

"A Little Place off the Edgware Road" by Graham Greene, from *Collected Stories* by Graham Greene, copyright © 1975 by Graham Greene. Reprinted by permission of The Viking Press.

"The Man Who Loved the Shadow" by Bill Pronzini, from *The Magazine of Fantasy and Science Fiction*, copyright © 1971 by Mercury Press, Inc. Reprinted by permission of the author and the author's agents, Richard Curtis, 156 East 52nd St., New York, N.Y. 10022.

"The Red Signal" by Agatha Christie, from *The Witness for the Prosecution and Other Stories* by Agatha Christie, copyright © 1947 by Agatha Christie. Copyright renewed by Agatha Christie Mallowan in 1975. Reprinted by permission of Dodd, Mead & Company, Inc.

"The American's Tale" by Arthur Conan Doyle, from *London Society*, published in 1879. It is in the public domain.

"The Finger of Stone" by G. K. Chesterton, from *The Poet and the Lunatic*, copyright © 1929. Reprinted by permission of the Estate of the Late G. K. Chesterton and its agents, A. P. Watt, Ltd., 26/28 Bedford Row, London WC1R 4HL.

"The Strange Children" by Elisabeth Sanxay Holding, from *The Magazine of Fantasy and Science Fiction*, copyright © 1955 by Mercury Press, Inc. Permission granted by the Estate of Elisabeth Sanxay Holding.

"I Had a Hunch, and . . . " by Talmage Powell, from *Alfred Hitchcock's Mystery Magazine*, copyright © 1960 by H. S. D. Publications. Reprinted by permission of the author and the author's agents, Scott Meredith Literary Agency, Inc., 845 Third Avenue, New York, N.Y. 10022.

Acknowledgments

In preparing this book, several people were especially helpful. Robert Briney, Alan Hubin, and Francis M. Nevins, Jr. provided many suggestions and ideas. Gerry de la Ree, Pat Lannon, John Lutz, Robert A. Madle, and Mary Rand helped obtain copies of a number of stories. Alice Paris and Anne Todd spent many hours tracking down agents and handling correspondence. Larry Sternig sent us excellent background material on his clients. Thanks also to Denis Holler and Bob Miller for editorial assistance. And most of all, Frank D. McSherry, Jr., with his incredible encyclopedic memory of fantastic mysteries, gave us so many suggestions, stories, and sources that by all rights he should be considered an unnamed editor.

Contents

MYSTERIOUS VISIONS

Foreword

HOBGOBLIN

Isaac Asimov

I DON'T particularly value consistency, unless it is truly consistent.

Very often, it isn't truly consistent; it merely carries a varnish of lookalike; and to buy the nothing-content for the outside varnish is to fall prey to a foolish consistency. It is about that that, in 1841, Ralph Waldo Emerson gave us his best-known remark: "A foolish consistency is the hobgoblin of little minds, adored by little statesmen and philosophers and divines."

But let us not talk in abstractions and generalities; let's get down to specific examples.

I am reasonably well-known as a science fiction writer, and in my stories, at least in the person of my characters, I whizz along through outer space, visiting the far stars of the Galaxy.

In real life, I refuse to get on airplanes.

Come the little philosophers in many shapes and forms and say to me, "Isn't it strange that in your writing you visit the outermost corners of the Universe and yet in real life you will not fly."

It seems inconsistent, doesn't it?

Well, let's see if that's so. I compose all my fiction at my typewriter.

My typewriter has never crashed; it has never been skyjacked; it has never run out of fuel; its engines have never caught fire. In what way does it compare to an airplane? Why should anything I do at the typewriter force me to take an airplane? Why must I, in reality, mimic the actions of my characters, in fancy? Where does the consistency come in?

To bind fiction to reality, my fancy to my actions, my typewriter to an airplane is to insist on a *foolish* consistency, and thank you but I will not oblige.

If I decide to fly, I'll fly for good reasons; the fact that I write science fiction is not a good reason.

Second example, and more immediately to the point.

I'm a rationalist and I'm quite loud-mouthed about it. I stand resolutely against the faddish half-bakery of the world and why not? One thing of which I am quite certain is that a belief has only to be silly to attract the undying devotion of those millions whose brains match that belief in quality.

Sure, I'm ready to believe that UFOs are extraterrestrial spaceships as soon as the evidence is compelling. I'm even ready to consider that UFOs *may be* extraterrestrial spaceships as soon as the evidence is no more than suggestive. In fact, I'm ready to suspect that further investigation of UFOs may be worthwhile, as soon as the evidence is at least *interesting*.

As long as all the evidence concerning UFOs is, however, dished up in dreary anecdotes that offer no handles for further checking of even the most elementary sort, I won't even take the effort to yawn at it. If such an attitude arouses the UFO devotees to fury that makes me feel all the more comfortable, since I know that anger is the common substitute for evidence among those who have no evidence for what they desperately want to believe.

The same goes for Velikovskian catastrophes, for von Dänikenish ancient astronauts, for Gellerian spoon-bending, for mental powers of all varieties, for conversations with planets, for pyramid power—as well as for the more ancient notions of ghosts, spirits, fairies, angels, demons, astrology, necromancy, witchcraft and all the varieties of magic.

Surely, then, a rationalist like myself would *love* the hard-headed old-fashioned mystery in which all the clues are firmly on the table and in which a cold and inexorable chain of logic begins at the evidence and ends at the solution, skipping over all the red herrings and dodging round all the planted irrelevancies.

And I do, I do! I love all that logic! Isn't that consistent of me? You betcha!

And surely, then, a rationalist like myself would *hate* the fuzzy fantasies about ghosts and spirits and curses and voodoo and telepathy and ominous dreams and second sight and all the rest of that silly nonsense that has plagued the silly and nonsensical all through human history.

But I don't, I don't. I love all that fuzzy fantasy, *too*! I love to feel the cold chills and to shiver at the hint of things beyond and all that scary stuff.

Inconsistent? Me? Hell, no. If I rejected fantasy in fiction because I reject it in real life, I would be confusing fiction and reality and would be indulging in a foolish consistency, which is not my thing at all.

Consider! Why do I reject fantasy in real life? Because I accept the two basic assumptions that underlie the scientific view of the Universe: 1) that the Universe runs in accordance with a few very general and very powerful basic rules called "laws of nature" that do not change and cannot be subverted, and 2) that it is possible for the human mind slowly to work out those rules and interpret reality in their light.

Those are only assumptions and therefore can't be proved. I accept them on faith and in that sense the scientific view of the Universe is my religion.

However, I accept them for a reason. A Universe that is under the rule of Law and that is Comprehensible is a likeable Universe, and one that I find warm and comfortable to live in.

To be sure, the nature of the Law is as yet imperfectly understood and little by little it is being more deeply and broadly understood. Every inch of Comprehensibility must be fought for with every atom of our mind—but that makes it a fun Universe and one that I find exciting to live in.

Accept fantasy, though, and you have a Universe run by the whim of incomprehensible gods or demons. The Universe becomes a terrifying place in which ignorance is raised to the supreme virtue and blind obedience to the supreme act. Nothing is left for human beings to do but to fawn and beg. Not for me, thank you.

But what has all that to do with fiction? Must one refuse to read accounts of the climbing of Mount Everest, because one would refuse on any account to make the attempt oneself?

What pleasure it is to enter into the terrifying world of fantasy for a few moments and to live, vicariously, the kind of life in which the rules may be broken, where logic may be no sword and rationality no shield—just so long as it's not the real world, and you *know* it's not the real world.

There is no inconsistency in enjoying a temporary entrance into a world that you know doesn't exist—but fighting to the death any claim that it does exist.

And to my own taste, the most piquant flavor arrives when you mingle the opposites. If you can take the classic mystery, with its super-rationalisms; its creation of a small sub-Universe in which all the evidence is there and the logic is flawless; its evocation of a world in which there isn't even the real-life fuzziness of the incomplete—and then add to it not merely the incompleteness of the real, but the lawlessness of the fantasy, you've *got* to enjoy it.

Well, *I*'ve got to enjoy it, anyway, so I love this collection of piquancy and spice.

Introduction
THE FANTASTIC MYSTERY: A NEGLECTED GENRE
Charles G. Waugh

A BLEND of two popular literary genres, fantastic mysteries combine mystery, detective, crime, or suspense stories with elements of science fiction or fantasy. In the last one hundred years, virtually all of both fields' most important writers have produced at least one such tale. For example, this volume could have included stories by Edward S. Aarons, Samuel Hopkins Adams, Grant Allen, Margery Allingham, Michael Avallone, John Buchan, A. H. Z. Carr, Raymond Chandler, Wilkie Collins, Carroll John Daly, Robert L. Fish, C. S. Forester, Jacques Futrelle, Anthony Gilbert, Frank Gruber, F. Tennyson Jesse, Geoffrey Household, P. M. Hubbard, Dorothy B. Hughes, C. Daly King, Marie Belloc Lowndes, A. E. W. Mason, Phillip MacDonald, Helen McCloy, William P. McGivern, Edgar Allen Poe, Arthur B. Reeve, Dorothy Sayers, Dell Shannon, Vincett Starrett, T. S. Stribling, Lawrence Treat, Roy Vickers, Edgar Wallace, and Phyllis A. Whitney.

Yet, until recently, fantastic mysteries have received little acclaim or analysis. Why is this? Well, at least four reasons come to mind.

First, some people believe the two elements are incompatible. In the mystery field, eminent critic Monsignor Knox's second commandment of detection specifically ruled out "all supernatural or preternatural agencies" because "to solve a detective problem by such means would be like winning a race on the river by the use of a concealed motor-engine."[1] In the science fiction field, the *Golden Age's* leading editor, John W. Campbell, Jr., held similar views.[2] Presumably, he is the person who told Isaac Asimov "that 'by its very nature' science fiction would not play fair with the reader. In a science fiction story, the detective could . . . whip out an odd device and say, 'As you know, Watson, my pocket-frannistan is perfectly capable of detecting the hidden jewel in a trice.' "[3]

But Asimov was not impressed, nor should he have been, for to say a story is fantastic is not to say it has no limits, only that the limits are different from what most people think of as reality. As long as the writer plays fair by pointing out ground rules, there is no reason why a valid mystery cannot be constructed within them. For example, James Blish's *There Shall Be No Darkness* accepts the customary limitations of werewolves. So when his house guests barricade the windows and doors with garlic, readers should be able to surmise, as does the protagonist, that a subsequent murder must have been committed by a werewolf already in the house. Although this story is fantastic, it also is a legitimate mystery, since its solution is consistent with, and deducible from, its ground rules.

Second, mystery stories tend to emphasize deductive or convergent thinking, while fantastic stories emphasize creative, or divergent thinking.[4] And as Tchaikovsky and Bach seem to have different fans because of their differing emphases in music, mystery and fantastic stories seem to have different fans too. For example, the small amount of research done on mystery fans indicates the typical fan is a woman in her thirties, while

---

1. Ronald A. Knox, "Detective Story Decalogue," in Howard Haycraft (ed.), *The Art of the Mystery Story* (New York: Simon and Schuster, 1946), p. 194.

2. Quoted in Robert E. Briney, "Death Rays, Demons, and Worms Unknown to Science," in John Ball (ed.), *The Mystery Story* (Del Mar, Cal.: Publisher's Inc., 1976), p. 278.

3. Quotation in Isaac Asimov, *Asimov's Mysteries* (New York: Dell Publishing Co., Inc., 1968), p. 14.

4. The science fiction puzzle story (championed, ironically enough, by John W. Campbell, Jr.) is a notable exception to this rule. It is deductive and has many similarities to the mystery story. Indeed, Campbell even published a series of cop-and-robber puzzle stories by Ross Rocklynne. See Ross Rocklynne, *The Men and the Mirror* (New York: Ace Books: 1973). Also, Briney, op. cit., pp. 279-280.

several studies of science fiction fans indicate the typical science fiction fan is a man in his twenties.[5] Undoubtably, these demographic differences also reflect interest differences. Thus many mystery fans seem to have an active dislike for the out-of-the-ordinary. Ellery Queen admits "critics (and readers) have taken us sharply to task for some of the detective-science fiction selections we have published in *Ellery Queen's Mystery Magazine*"—and many fantastic fans could care less about who killed Roger Ackeroyd.[6] To be liked by *both* groups, therefore, a fantastic mystery would seem to need equally strong components of mystery, detection, crime, or suspense *and* science fiction, so that *each* group would find something to enjoy.

Considering the risks professional editors run by publishing these stories, much praise is due the heroic efforts of Anthony Boucher, Howard Browne, Hugo Gernsback, Alfred Hitchcock, Robert A. W. Lowndes, Ellery Queen, Dorothy Sayers, and Hans Stefan Santesson for their attempts at promotion and cross-pollination.*

Third, most readers have failed to develop the general concept of "fantastic mysteries." When mystery fans read one of these stories by a favorite author, they probably think of it as a mystery, or more particularly as a police procedural or a whodunit, rather than as a *fantastic* mystery. Similarly, when fantastic fans read one by a favorite author, they label it a fantastic story, or more particularly a ghost story, a space opera, and so forth. Lots of knowledge about fantastic mysteries is probably squirreled away, but since it is not stored under that general concept, it remains unintegrated and provokes little thought.

---

5. Marie Rodell, *Mystery Fiction* (New York: Hermitage House, 1952), p. 11; Charles G. Waugh and David Schroeder, "Here's Looking at You Kids: A Profile of Science Fiction Fans," *Anthro-Tech; A Journal of Speculative Anthropology*. Fall, 1978, pp. 12-19. Copies may be obtained from Darlene Thomas, Lockhaven State College, Lockhaven, PA 17745, for $1.00; and Dilys Winn, *Murder Ink: The Mystery Reader's Companion* (New York: Workman Publishing Company, Inc., 1977), p. 440.

6. *Ellery Queen's Mystery Magazine*, October, 1970, p. 142. See, also, Winn, op. cit., p. 44, and Anthony Boucher, "Recommended Reading," *The Magazine of Fantasy and Science Fiction*, May, 1957, p. 78.

*In fact, Howard Browne became so enthusiastic that he is said to have substituted ghost-writing for cajoling, and one of his supposed efforts on behalf of a famous mystery writer is such a marvelous job that it is included here as a challenge to all literary sleuths. So read carefully, and when you think you know, you can check your answer on page 321.

And because few fans from one group read the other's genre, widespread consciousness raising is not likely.

Finally, just as the lack of acclaim for science fiction discouraged formal critical analysis of that field until recently, so has the lack of acclaim for fantastic mysteries probably discouraged critical analyses of them. The most significant works appear to be Robert Briney's survey of science fiction mysteries in *The Mystery Story* (John Ball, ed.); Frank McSherry's discussion of Janus stories and future crimes in *The Mystery Writer's Art* (Francis M. Nevins, Jr., ed.), as well as several articles in *The Armchair Detective*; Sam Moskowitz's revised survey of the scientific detective in his book *Strange Horizons*; Larry Niven's "The Last Word about SF/Detectives" in his novel *The Long Arm of Gil Hamilton;* and Michael Parry's review of the supernatural detective in his anthology *The Supernatural Solution*. All are extremely good, but all are specialized studies, and none provide the reader with an overall history or typology.

Some materials even mislead. For example, Miram Allen deFord's introduction to *Space, Time, and Crime* first implies that Sam Moskowitz believes the science fiction detective story originated with *The Caves of Steel* (1953), and then misattributes Isaac Asimov's novel to Frederik Pohl and Cyril Kornbluth.

Actually, while Moskowitz refers to Asimov's work as "the supreme masterpiece" of the genre, he sees the science fiction detective story as originating at the beginning of this century with scientific detectives such as Arthur B. Reeve's extraordinarily popular Craig Kennedy; then developing through Hugo Gernsback's ill-fated *Scientific Detective Monthly* (1930) and series detectives such as David H. Keller's Taine of San Francisco, James Norman's Oscar, Martian detective, and Frank Belknap Long's John Carstairs, botanical detective; until it finally gained legitimacy in science fiction through "the first of the great masterpieces," Hal Clement's *Needle*, a novel which convinced influential John W. Campbell that this kind of story was possible.[7]

Our research clearly traced the fantastic mystery back to Charles Dickens, Robert Louis Stevenson, Wilkie Collins, Sheridan Le Fanu, and possibly, as a Janus story, Edgar Allen Poe's "The Tell-Tale Heart." Robert

---

7. John W. Campbell, "In Times To Come," *Astounding Science Fiction*, May, 1949, p. 51, and John W. Campbell, "The Analytical Laboratory," *Astounding Science Fiction*, August, 1949, p. 158.

Briney mentions penny dreadful serials such as *Varney the Vampyre* (1847) and *Wagner, the Wehr-Wolf* (1846-7), as well as some of the early Gothic novels such as Mrs. Radcliffe's *The Mysteries of Udolpho* (1794) and Horace Walpole's *The Castle of Otranto* (1764).[8] Even earlier, of course, there are folk tales, myths, and legends such as "Ali Baba and the Forty Thieves."

However, in assembling *Mysterious Visions*, our major concern was not investigating origins, it was to find good stories and develop an appropriate way to classify them. Eventually, we arrived at ten categories which seem to handle all the fantastic mysteries we could locate:

STEPPING BEYOND? These stories deal with mysteries that can be explained both naturally and supernaturally, and their final interpretation, like "The Lady and the Tiger," is left to the reader. Referred to by Frank McSherry as Janus or two-faced, they are written primarily by mystery authors, since fantastic fans consider them *passé*. Examples include Helen McCloy's *Through a Glass Darkly*, Ellery Queen's *And On the Eighth Day*, and Leslie H. Whitten's *Progeny of the Adder* and *Moon of the Wolf*.

STRANGE PHENOMENA These stories either deal with the natural occurrence of unusual experiences such as telepathy, precognition, and time travel, or with the appearance of seemingly unnatural, yet corporal beings such as doppelgangers, werewolves, and demons. Commonly written by both groups of authors, examples include Fredric Brown's *What Mad Universe*, John Dickson Carr's *Fear is the Same*, his *Fire, Burn*, and Cornell Woolrich's *The Night has a Thousand Eyes*.

BIZARRE DISCOVERIES These stories emphasize the discoveries of strange, but naturally explainable phenomena. For example, stories about telepathy and precognition that emphasize its discovery in others rather than its experience in oneself would be included here rather than under strange phenomena. Other potential subjects include monsters such as sea serpents and dinosaurs, strange plants or minerals, and lost lands. They are commonly written by both groups of authors and examples include Frank Herbert's *The Santaroga Barrier*, Frank Robinson's *The Power*, Vercours' *You Shall Know Them*, and Jules Verne's *Mysterious Island*.

SPECTRAL CREATURES These stories deal with incorporal beings such as ghosts, phantoms, spirits, and wraiths. They are commonly written by both groups of authors, although mystery writers may produce more. Examples

---

8. Briney, op. cit., p. 235.

include Manning Coles' *Come and Go*, Guy Cullingford's *Post Mortem*, Eric Frank Russell's *Sinister Barrier*, and G. M. Wilson's *I Was Murdered*.

MIRACLES AND MAGIC These stories deal with performing actions and acquiring knowledge by supernatural means. God, the devil, and other superior beings work directly through miracles, but lesser creatures usually need magical props, potions, or incantations to accomplish their ends. Commonly written by both groups of authors, examples include John Dickson Carr's *The Devil in Velvet*, Randall Garrett's *Too Many Magicians*, Fritz Leiber's *Conjure Wife*, and A. Merritt's *Burn Witch Burn!*

ALIENS These stories involve beings who are, though they may resemble humans, from other than earth stock. Written almost entirely by fantastic authors, examples include Hal Clement's *Needle*, Michael Crichton's *The Andromeda Strain*, Robert Heinlein's *The Puppet Masters*, and William Sloane's *To Walk the Night*.

INNOVATIONS These stories examine new ideas, new inventions, or new customs.

In recent years, many mystery authors have found the first to be a very successful theme, probably because it offers something that seems both startling and possible. Unfortunately, these exciting stories about kidnapping the president and blowing up the superbowl may ultimately inspire unstable readers to attempt to enact them, just as each showing of a film on airline extortion, the *Doomsday Flight*, leads to the phoning in of identical threats to local airports.[9]

Both groups have written about the second, new inventions, but usually the fantastic authors' proposals are more advanced and bizarre. They, for example, would be more likely to deal with matter transmitters than with an improvement in a missile guidance system.

Finally, the third type of innovation, the new custom, has been written about primarily by fantastic authors.

Examples include Piers Anthony and Robert E. Margroff's *The Ring*, Thomas Harris' *Black Sunday*, John D. MacDonald's *The Girl, The Gold Watch, and Everything*, and Alistair MacLean's *The Satan Bug*.

---

9. Leonard Berkowitz, *A Survey of Social Psychology* (Hinsdale, Illinois: 1975), pp. 4-5. Since the writing of this introduction, criminals have been arrested for attempting to carry out ideas suggested by the thrillers *Leviathan* (see *Newsweek*, September 18, 1978, p. 35) and *North Star Crusade* (see *Kennebec, Journal*, October 12, 1978, p. 23).

DANGEROUS MADMEN These stories involve super criminals or mad scientists.

The super criminal commits crimes with the aid of sorcery or scientific inventions and is usually interested in conquering the world or, if interstellar travel has been achieved, the galaxy. Both groups have written about super criminals, but science fiction authors commonly locate them in the future while fantasy and mystery authors usually locate them in the present or past.

The mad scientist commits crimes out of an obsession for an ideal, out of a desire to increase his or her knowledge through research, or out of revenge for having been scorned. Both groups have written about mad scientists, but among fantastic authors the theme is not as popular as it once was.

Examples include Agatha Christie's *So Many Steps to Death*, Robert Louis Stevenson's *Dr. Jekyll and Mr. Hyde*, Jules Verne's *Master of the World*, and H. G. Wells' *The Invisible Man*.

EXTRAORDINARY DETECTIVES There are three types.

There is the normal detective who often becomes involved in fantastic cases. Commonly written by mystery and fantasy (though not science fiction) authors, the interest in these stories springs from two sources. Is the case actually fantastic? And, if it is, how will the supernatural forces be defeated?

Next, there is the present-day scientific detective who uses futuristic laboratory devices to discover the culprit. Primarily written by mystery authors, these stories were extremely popular once, but are rarely written now.

Finally, there is the supernormal detective who possesses some extraordinary quality useful in solving crimes. Commonly written by both groups of authors, these stories have to avoid the problem of omniscient detectives. So special mental powers are usually presented as very limited or erratic, and often they are by-passed in favor of increased physical powers.[10]

Examples include Isaac Asimov's *The Caves of Steel*, William Hope Hodgson's *Carnacki, the Ghost Finder*, Seabury Quinn's *The Phantom Fighter*, and Sax Rohmer's *The Dream Detective*.

---

10. For an interesting discussion of this, see the foreword in F. Tennyson Jesse, *Solange Stories* (New York: Macmillan Company, 1931).

FUTURE VISIONS These stories portray a future world that differs substantially from the present. Thus, they are both the most advanced and the most difficult type of fantastic mystery that can be written. Written almost entirely by fantastic authors, examples include Alfred Bester's *The Demolished Man*, Frank Herbert's *Under Pressure*, Robert Sheckley's *The Status Civilization*, and Jack Vance's *To Live Forever*.

In summary, then, fantastic mysteries are frequently written by both groups of authors. But for reasons discussed above, there has been little analysis or acclaim. Hopefully, what we have just said will add to the understanding of this field, but in any case, the following twenty-six stories by great mystery writers certainly should add to its acclaim.

STEPPING BEYOND? _____

Melville Davisson Post *(1869–1930) deserves the Dr. Jekyll and Mr. Hyde award for mystery writers. First, he created Randolph Mason, a crooked lawyer who helped his clients commit legal crimes. Then after reforming Mason, he abandoned him in favor of Uncle Abner, a Bible-toting Methodist possessed with God's spirit. Indeed, this is a story which may very well match two forms of possession against each other.*

THE ANGEL OF THE LORD

Melville Davisson Post

I ALWAYS thought my father took a long chance, but somebody had to take it and certainly I was the one least likely to be suspected. It was a wild country. There were no banks. We had to pay for the cattle, and somebody had to carry the money. My father and my uncle were always being watched. My father was right, I think.

"Abner," he said, "I'm going to send Martin. No one will ever suppose that we would trust this money to a child."

My uncle drummed on the table and rapped his heels on the floor. He was a bachelor, stern and silent. But he could talk . . . and when he did, he began at the beginning and you heard him through; and what he said—well, he stood behind it.

"To stop Martin," my father went on, "would be only to lose the money; but to stop you would be to get somebody killed."

I knew what my father meant. He meant that no one would undertake to rob Abner until after he had shot him to death.

I ought to say a word about my Uncle Abner. He was one of those austere, deeply religious men who were the product of the Reformation. He always carried a Bible in his pocket, and he read it where he pleased.

3

Once the crowd at Roy's Tavern tried to make sport of him when he got his book out by the fire; but they never tried it again. When the fight was over Abner paid Roy eighteen silver dollars for the broken chairs and the table—and he was the only man in the tavern who could ride a horse. Abner belonged to the church militant, and his God was a war lord.

So that is how they came to send me. The money was in greenbacks in packages. They wrapped it up in newspaper and put it into a pair of saddle-bags, and I set out. I was about nine years old. No, it was not as bad as you think. I could ride a horse all day when I was nine years old—most any kind of a horse. I was tough as whit'-leather, and I knew the country I was going into. You must not picture a little boy rolling a hoop in the park.

It was an afternoon in early autumn. The clay roads froze in the night; they thawed out in the day and they were a bit sticky. I was to stop at Roy's Tavern, south of the river, and go on in the morning. Now and then I passed some cattle driver, but no one overtook me on the road until almost sundown; then I heard a horse behind me and a man came up. I knew him. He was a cattleman named Dix. He had once been a shipper, but he had come in for a good deal of bad luck. His partner, Alkire, had absconded with a big sum of money due the grazers. This had ruined Dix; he had given up his land, which wasn't very much, to the grazers. After that he had gone over the mountain to his people, got together a pretty big sum of money and bought a large tract of grazing land. Foreign claimants had sued him in the courts on some old title, and he had lost the whole tract and the money that he had paid for it. He had married a remote cousin of ours, and he had always lived on her lands, adjoining those of my Uncle Abner.

Dix seemed surprised to see me on the road.

"So it's you, Martin," he said; "I thought Abner would be going into the upcountry."

One gets to be a pretty cunning youngster, even at this age, and I told no one what I was about.

"Father wants the cattle over the river to run a month," I returned easily, "and I'm going up there to give his orders to the grazers."

He looked me over, then he rapped the saddlebags with his knuckles. "You carry a good deal of baggage, my lad."

I laughed. "Horse feed," I said. "You know my father! A horse must be fed at dinner time, but a man can go till he gets it."

One was always glad of any company on the road, and we fell into an idle talk. Dix said he was going out into the Ten Mile country; and I have always thought that was, in fact, his intention. The road turned south about a mile our side of the tavern. I never liked Dix; he was of an apologetic manner, with a cunning, irresolute face.

A little later a man passed us at a gallop. He was a drover named Marks, who lived beyond my Uncle Abner, and he was riding hard to get in before night. He hailed us, but he did not stop; we got a shower of mud and Dix cursed him. I have never seen a more evil face. I suppose it was because Dix usually had a grin about his mouth, and when that sort of face gets twisted there's nothing like it.

After that he was silent. He rode with his head down and his fingers plucking at his jaw, like a man in some perplexity. At the crossroads he stopped and sat for some time in the saddle, looking before him. I left him there, but at the bridge he overtook me. He said he had concluded to get some supper and go on after that.

Roy's Tavern consisted of a single big room, with a loft above it for sleeping quarters. A narrow covered way connected this room with the house in which Roy and his family lived. We used to hang our saddles on wooden pegs in this covered way. I have seen that wall so hung with saddles that you could not find a place for another stirrup. But tonight Dix and I were alone in the tavern. He looked cunningly at me when I took the saddle-bags with me into the big room and when I went with them up the ladder into the loft. But he said nothing—in fact, he had scarcely spoken. It was cold; the road had begun to freeze when we got in. Roy had lighted a big fire. I left Dix before it. I did not take off my clothes, because Roy's beds were mattresses of wheat straw covered with heifer skins—good enough for summer but pretty cold on such a night, even with the heavy, hand-woven coverlet in big white and black checks.

I put the saddle-bags under my head and lay down. I went at once to sleep, but I suddenly awaked. I thought there was a candle in the loft, but it was a gleam of light from the fire below, shining through a crack in the floor. I lay and watched it, the coverlet pulled up to my chin. Then I began to wonder why the fire burned so brightly. Dix ought to be on his way some time, and it was a custom for the last man to rake out the fire. There was not a sound. The light streamed steadily through the crack.

Presently it occurred to me that Dix had forgotten the fire and that I ought to go down and rake it out. Roy always warned us about the fire when he went to bed. I got up, wrapped the great coverlet around me, went over to the gleam of light and looked down through the crack in the floor. I had to lie out at full length to get my eye against the board. The hickory logs had turned to great embers and glowed like a furnace of red coals.

Before this fire stood Dix. He was holding out his hands and turning himself about as though he were cold to the marrow; but with all that chill upon him, when the man's face came into the light I saw it covered with a sprinkling of sweat.

I shall carry the memory of that face. The grin was there at the mouth, but it was pulled about; the eyelids were drawn in; the teeth were clamped together. I have seen a dog poisoned with strychnine look like that.

I lay there and watched the thing. It was as though something potent and evil dwelling within the man were in travail to re-form his face upon its image. You cannot realize how the devilish labor held me—the face worked as though it were some plastic stuff, and the sweat oozed through. And all the time the man was cold; and he was crowding into the fire and turning himself about and putting out his hands. And it was as though the heat would no more enter in and warm him than it will enter in and warm the ice.

It seemed to scorch him and leave him cold—and he was fearfully and desperately cold! I could smell the singe of the fire on him, but it had no power against this diabolic chill. I began myself to shiver, although I had the heavy coverlet wrapped around me.

The thing was a fascinating horror; I seemed to be looking down into the chamber of some abominable maternity. The room was filled with the steady red light of the fire. Not a shadow moved in it. And there was silence. The man had taken off his boots and he twisted before the fire without a sound. It was like the shuddering tales of possession or transformation by a drug. I thought the man would burn himself to death. His clothes smoked. How could he be so cold?

Then, finally, the thing was over! I did not see it for his face was in the fire. But suddenly he grew composed and stepped back into the room. I tell you I was afraid to look! I do not know what thing I expected to see there, but I did not think it would be Dix.

Well, it was Dix; but not the Dix that any of us knew. There was a certain apology, a certain indecision, a certain servility in that other Dix, and these things showed about his face. But there was none of these weaknesses in this man.

His face had been pulled into planes of firmness and decision; the slack in his features had been taken up; the furtive moving of the eye was gone. He stood now squarely on his feet and he was full of courage. But I was afraid of him as I have never been afraid of any human creature in this world! Something that had been servile in him, that had skulked behind disguises, that had worn the habiliments of subterfuge, had now come forth; and it had molded the features of the man to its abominable courage.

Presently he began to move swiftly about the room. He looked out at the window and he listened at the door; then he went softly into the covered way. I thought he was going on his journey; but then he could not be going with his boots there beside the fire. In a moment he returned with a saddle blanket in his hand and came softly across the room to the ladder.

Then I understood the thing that he intended, and I was motionless with fear. I tried to get up, but I could not. I could only lie there with my eye strained to the crack in the floor. His foot was on the ladder, and I could already feel his hand on my throat and that blanket on my face, and the suffocation of death in me, when far away on the hard road I heard a horse!

He heard it, too, for he stopped on the ladder and turned his evil face about toward the door. The horse was on the long hill beyond the bridge, and he was coming as though the devil rode in his saddle. It was a hard, dark night. The frozen road was like flint; I could hear the iron of the shoes ring. Whoever rode that horse rode for his life or for something more than his life, or he was mad. I heard the horse strike the bridge and thunder across it. And all the while Dix hung there on the ladder by his hands and listened. Now he sprang softly down, pulled on his boots and stood up before the fire, his face—this new face—gleaming with its evil courage. The next moment the horse stopped.

I could hear him plunge under the bit, his iron shoes ripping the frozen road; then the door leaped back and my Uncle Abner was in the room. I was so glad that my heart almost choked me and for a moment I could hardly see—everything was in a sort of mist.

Abner swept the room in a glance, then he stopped.

"Thank God!" he said; "I'm in time." And he drew his hand down over his face with the fingers hard and close as though he pulled something away.

"In time for what?" said Dix.

Abner looked him over. And I could see the muscles of his big shoulders stiffen as he looked. And again he looked him over. Then he spoke and his voice was strange.

"Dix," he said, "is it you?"

"Who would it be but me?" said Dix.

"It might be the devil," said Abner. "Do you know what your face looks like?"

"No matter what it looks like!" said Dix.

"And so," said Abner, "we have got courage with this new face."

Dix threw up his head.

"Now, look here, Abner," he said, "I've had about enough of your big manner. You ride a horse to death and you come plunging in here; what the devil's wrong with you?"

"There's nothing wrong with me," replied Abner, and his voice was low. "But there's something damnably wrong with you, Dix."

"The devil take you," said Dix, and I saw him measure Abner with his eye. It was not fear that held him back; fear was gone out of the creature; I think it was a kind of prudence.

Abner's eyes kindled, but his voice remained low and steady.

"Those are big words," he said.

"Well," cried Dix, "get out of the door then and let me pass!"

"Not just yet," said Abner; "I have something to say to you."

"Say it then," cried Dix, "and get out of the door."

"Why hurry?" said Abner. "It's a long time until daylight, and I have a good deal to say."

"You'll not say it to me," said Dix. "I've got a trip to make tonight; get out of the door."

Abner did not move. "You've got a longer trip to make tonight than you think, Dix," he said; "but you're going to hear what I have to say before you set out on it."

I saw Dix rise on his toes and I knew what he wished for. He wished for a weapon; and he wished for the bulk of bone and muscle that would have a chance against Abner. But he had neither the one nor the other. And he stood there on his toes and began to curse—low, vicious, withering oaths, that were like the swish of a knife.

Abner was looking at the man with a curious interest.

"It is strange," he said, as though speaking to himself, "but it explains the thing. While one is the servant of neither, one has the courage of neither; but when he finally makes his choice he gets what his master has to give him."

Then he spoke to Dix.

"Sit down!" he said; and it was in that deep, level voice that Abner used when he was standing close behind his words. Every man in the hills knew that voice; one had only a moment to decide after he heard it. Dix knew that, and yet for one instant he hung there on his toes, his eyes shimmering like a weasel's, his mouth twisting. He was not afraid! If he had had the ghost of a chance against Abner he would have taken it. But he knew he had not, and with an oath he threw the saddle blanket into a corner and sat down by the fire.

Abner came away from the door then. He took off his great coat. He put a log on the fire, and he sat down across the hearth from Dix. The new hickory sprang crackling into flames. For a good while there was silence; the two men sat at either end of the hearth without a word. Abner seemed to have fallen into a study of the man before him. Finally he spoke:

"Dix," he said, "do you believe in the providence of God?"

Dix flung up his head.

"Abner," he cried, "if you are going to talk nonsense I promise you upon my oath that I will not stay to listen."

Abner did not at once reply. He seemed to begin now at another point.

"Dix," he said, "you've had a good deal of bad luck. . . . Perhaps you wish it put that way."

"Now, Abner," he cried, "you speak the truth; I have had hell's luck."

"Hell's luck you have had," replied Abner. "It is a good word. I accept it. Your partner disappeared with all the money of the grazers on the other side of the river; you lost the land in your lawsuit; and you are to-night without a dollar. That was a big tract of land to lose. Where did you get so great a sum of money?"

"I have told you a hundred times," replied Dix. "I got it from my people over the mountains. You know where I got it."

"Yes," said Abner. "I know where you got it, Dix. And I know another thing. But first I want to show you this," and he took a little penknife out of his pocket. "And I want to tell you that I believe in the providence of God, Dix."

"I don't care a fiddler's damn what you believe in," said Dix.

"But you do care what I know," replied Abner.

"What do you know?" said Dix.

"I know where your partner is," replied Abner.

I was uncertain about what Dix was going to do, but finally he answered with a sneer.

"Then you know something that nobody else knows."

"Yes," replied Abner, "there is another man who knows."

"Who?" said Dix.

"You," said Abner.

Dix leaned over in his chair and looked at Abner closely.

"Abner," he cried, "you are talking nonsense. Nobody knows where Alkire is. If I knew I'd go after him."

"Dix," Abner answered, and it was again in that deep, level voice, "if I had got here five minutes later you would have gone after him. I can promise you that, Dix.

"Now, listen! I was in the upcountry when I got your word about the partnership; and I was on my way back when at Big Run I broke a stirrup-leather. I had no knife and I went into the store and bought this one; then the storekeeper told me that Alkire had gone to see you. I didn't want to interfere with him and I turned back. . . . So I did not become your partner. And so I did not disappear. . . . What was it that prevented? The broken stirrup-leather? The knife? In old times, Dix, men were so blind that God had to open their eyes before they could see His angel in the way before them. . . . They are still blind, but they ought not to be that blind. . . . Well, on the night that Alkire disappeared I met him on his way to your house. It was out there at the bridge. He had broken a stirrup-leather and he was trying to fasten it with a nail. He asked me if I had a knife, and I gave him this one. It was beginning to rain and I went on, leaving him there in the road with the knife in his hand."

Abner paused; the muscles of his great iron jaw contracted.

"God forgive me," he said; "it was His angel again! I never saw Alkire after that."

"Nobody ever saw him after that," said Dix. "He got out of the hills that night."

"No," replied Abner; "it was not in the night when Alkire started on his journey; it was in the day."

"Abner," said Dix, "you talk like a fool. If Alkire had traveled the road in the day somebody would have seen him."

"Nobody could see him on the road he traveled," replied Abner.

"What road?" said Dix.

"Dix," replied Abner, "you will learn that soon enough."

Abner looked hard at the man.

"You saw Alkire when he started on his journey," he continued; "but did you see who it was that went with him?"

"Nobody went with him," replied Dix; "Alkire rode alone."

"Not alone," said Abner; "there was another."

"I didn't see him," said Dix.

"And yet," continued Abner, "you made Alkire go with him."

I saw cunning enter Dix's face. He was puzzled, but he thought Abner off the scent.

"And I made Alkire go with somebody, did I? Well, who was it? Did you see him?"

"Nobody ever saw him."

"He must be a stranger."

"No," replied Abner, "he rode the hills before we came into them."

"Indeed!" said Dix. "And what kind of a horse did he ride?"

"White!" said Abner.

Dix got some inkling of what Abner meant now, and his face grew livid.

"What are you driving at?" he cried. "You sit here beating around the bush. If you know anything, say it out; let's hear it. What is it?"

Abner put out his big sinewy hand as though to thrust Dix back into his chair.

"Listen!" he said. "Two days after that I wanted to get out into the Ten Mile country and I went through your lands; I rode a path through the narrow valley west of your house. At a point on the path where there is an apple tree something caught my eye and I stopped. Five minutes later I knew exactly what had happened under that apple tree. . . . Someone had ridden there; he had stopped under that tree; then something happened and the horse had run away—I knew that by the tracks of a horse on this path. I knew that the horse had a rider and that it had stopped under this tree, because there was a limb cut from the tree at a certain height. I knew the horse had remained there, because the small twigs of the apple limb had been pared off, and they lay in a heap on the path. I knew that something had frightened the horse and that it had run away, because the sod was torn up where it had jumped. . . . Ten minutes later I knew that the rider had not been in the saddle when the horse jumped; I knew what it was that had frightened the horse; and I knew that the thing had occurred the day before. Now, how did I know that?

"Listen! I put my horse into the tracks of that other horse under the tree and studied the ground. Immediately I saw where the weeds beside the path had been crushed, as though some animal had been lying down there, and in the very center of that bed I saw a little heap of fresh earth. That was strange, Dix, that fresh earth where the animal had been lying down! It had come there after the animal had got up, or else it would have been pressed flat. But where had it come from?

"I got off and walked around the apple tree, moving out from it in an ever-widening circle. Finally I found an ant heap, the top of which had been scraped away as though one had taken up the loose earth in his hands. Then I went back and plucked up some of the earth. The under clods of it were colored as with red paint. . . . No, it wasn't paint.

"There was a brush fence some fifty yards away. I went over to it and followed it down.

"Opposite the apple tree the weeds were again crushed as though some animal had lain there. I sat down in that place and drew a line with my eye across a log of the fence to a limb of the apple tree. Then I got on my horse and again put him in the tracks of that other horse under the tree; the imaginary line passed through the pit of my stomach! . . . I am four inches taller than Alkire."

It was then that Dix began to curse. I had seen his face work while Abner was speaking and that spray of sweat had reappeared. But he kept the courage he had got.

"Lord Almighty, man!" he cried. "How prettily you sum it up! We shall presently have Lawyer Abner with his brief. Because my renters have killed a calf; because one of their horses frightened at the blood has bolted, and because they cover the blood with earth so the other horses traveling the path may not do the like; straightway I have shot Alkire out of his saddle. . . . Man! What a mare's nest! And now, Lawyer Abner, with your neat little conclusions, what did I do with Alkire after I had killed him? Did I cause him to vanish into the air with a smell of sulphur, or did I cause the earth to yawn and Alkire to descend into its bowels?"

"Dix," replied Abner, "your words move somewhat near the truth."

"Upon my soul," cried Dix, "you compliment me. If I had that trick of magic, believe me, you would be already some distance down."

Abner remained a moment silent.

"Dix," he said, "what does it mean when one finds a plot of earth re-sodded?"

"Is that a riddle?" cried Dix. "Well, confound me, if I don't answer it! You charge me with murder and then you fling in this neat conundrum. Now, what could be the answer to that riddle, Abner? If one had done a murder this sod would overlie a grave and Alkire would be in it in his bloody shirt. Do I give the answer?''

"You do not," replied Abner.

"No!" cried Dix. "Your sodded plot no grave, and Alkire not within it waiting for the trump of Gabriel! Why, man, where are your little damned conclusions?''

"Dix," said Abner, "you do not deceive me in the least; Alkire is not sleeping in a grave."

"Then in the air," sneered Dix, "with the smell of sulphur?''

"Nor in the air," said Abner.

"Then consumed with fire, like the priests of Baal?''

"Nor with fire," said Abner.

Dix had got back the quiet of his face; this banter had put him where he was when Abner entered. "This is all fools' talk," he said; "if I had killed Alkire, what could I have done with the body? And the horse! What could I have done with the horse? Remember, no man has ever seen Alkire's horse any more than he has seen Alkire—and for the reason that Alkire rode him out of the hills that night. Now, look here, Abner, you have asked me a good many questions. I will ask you one. Among your little conclusions do you find that I did this thing alone or with the aid of others?''

"Dix," replied Abner, "I will answer that upon my own belief you had no accomplice.''

"Then," said Dix, "how could I have carried off the horse? Alkire I might carry; but his horse weighed thirteen hundred pounds!''

"Dix," said Abner, "no man helped you do this thing; but there were men who helped you to conceal it.''

"And now," cried Dix, "the man is going mad! Who could I trust with such work, I ask you? Have I a renter that would not tell it when he moved on to another's land, or when he got a quart of cider in him? Where are the men who helped me?''

"Dix," said Abner, "they have been dead these fifty years.''

I heard Dix laugh then, and his evil face lighted as though a candle were behind it. And, in truth, I thought he had got Abner silenced.

"In the name of Heaven!" he cried. "With such proofs it is a wonder that you did not have me hanged.''

"And hanged you should have been," said Abner.

"Well," cried Dix, "go and tell the sheriff, and mind you lay before him those little, neat conclusions: How from a horse track and the place where a calf was butchered you have reasoned on Alkire's murder, and to conceal the body and the horse you have reasoned on the aid of men who were rotting in their graves when I was born; and see how he will receive you!''

Abner gave no attention to the man's flippant speech. He got his great silver watch out of his pocket, pressed the stem and looked. Then he spoke in his deep, even voice.

"Dix," he said, "it is nearly midnight; in an hour you must be on your journey, and I have something more to say. Listen! I knew this thing had been done the previous day because it had rained on the night that I met Alkire, and the earth of this ant heap had been disturbed after that. Moreover, this earth had been frozen, and that showed a night had passed since it had been placed there. And I knew the rider of that horse was Alkire because, beside the path near the severed twigs lay my knife, where it had fallen from his hand. This much I learned in some fifteen minutes; the rest took somewhat longer.

"I followed the track of the horse until it stopped in the little valley below. It was easy to follow while the horse ran, because the sod was torn; but when it ceased to run there was no track that I could follow. There was a little stream threading the valley, and I began at the wood and came slowly up to see if I could find where the horse had crossed. Finally I found a horse track and there was also a man's track, which meant that you had caught the horse and were leading it away. But where?

"On the rising ground above there was an old orchard where there had once been a house. The work about that house had been done a hundred years. It was rotted down now. You had opened this orchard into the pasture. I rode all over the face of this hill and finally I entered this orchard. There was a great, flat, moss-covered stone lying a few steps from where the house had stood. As I looked I noticed that the moss growing from it into the earth had been broken along the edges of the stone, and then I noticed that for a few feet about the stone the ground had been resodded. I got down the lifted up some of this new sod. Under it the earth had been soaked with that . . . red paint.

"It was clever of you, Dix, to resod the ground; that took only a little time and it effectually concealed the place where you had killed the horse; but it was foolish of you to forget that the broken moss around the edges of the great flat stone could not be mended.''

"Abner!" cried Dix. "Stop!" And I saw that spray of sweat, and his face working like kneaded bread, and the shiver of that abominable chill on him.

Abner was silent for a moment and then he went on, but from another quarter.

"Twice," said Abner, "the Angel of the Lord stood before me and I did not know it; but the third time I knew it. It is not in the cry of the wind, nor in the voice of many waters that His presence is made known to us. That man in Israel had only the sign that the beast under him would not go on. Twice I had as good a sign, and tonight, when Marks broke a stirrup-leather before my house and called me to the door and asked me for a knife to mend it, I saw and I came!"

The log that Abner had thrown on was burned down, and the fire was again a mass of embers; the room was filled with that dull red light. Dix had got on to his feet, and he stood now twisting before the fire, his hands reaching out to it, and that cold creeping in his bones, and the smell of the fire on him.

Abner rose. And when he spoke his voice was like a thing that has dimensions and weight.

"Dix," he said, "you robbed the grazers; you shot Alkire out of his saddle; and a child you would have murdered!"

And I saw the sleeve of Abner's coat begin to move, then it stopped. He stood staring at something against the wall. I looked to see what the thing was, but I did not see it. Abner was looking beyond the wall, as though it had been moved away.

And all the time Dix had been shaking with that hellish cold, and twisting on the hearth and crowding into the fire. Then he fell back, and he was the Dix I knew—his face was slack; his eye was furtive; and he was full of terror.

It was his weak whine that awakened Abner. He put up his hand and brought the fingers hard down over his face, and then he looked at this new creature, cringing and beset with fears.

"Dix," he said, "Alkire was a just man; he sleeps as peacefully in that abandoned well under his horse as he would sleep in the churchyard. My hand has been held back; you may go. Vengeance is mine, I will repay, saith the Lord."

"But where shall I go, Abner?" the creature wailed; "I have no money and I am cold."

Abner took out his leather wallet and flung it toward the door.

"There is money," he said "a hundred dollars—and there is my coat. Go! But if I find you in the hills tomorrow, or if I ever find you, I warn you in the name of the living God that I will stamp you out of life!"

I saw the loathsome thing writhe into Abner's coat and seize the wallet and slip out through the door; and a moment later I heard a horse. And I crept back on to Roy's heifer skin.

When I came down at daylight my Uncle Abner was reading by the fire.

Mother-dominated, introverted, living in hotel rooms, and drifting slowly into alcoholism, **Cornell Woolrich** *(1903–1968) still managed to become one of America's most popular and prolific mystery writers. From 1934 to 1948, for example, he produced 11 novels and over 150 shorter works of suspense, love, action, and the fantastic. Like virtually all his best work, "Music From the Dark" possesses elegant style and background, driving narrative, and an atmosphere of ironic fatalism. It is as intense and disturbing as fingernails on a blackboard, but once started it cannot be put down.*

MUSIC FROM THE DARK

Cornell Woolrich

AT FOUR in the morning, a scarecrow of a man staggers dazedly into the New Orleans Police Headquarters building. Behind him at the curb a lacquered Bugatti purrs like a drowsy cat, the finest car that ever stood out there. He weaves his way through the anteroom, deserted at that early hour, and goes in through the open doorway beyond. The sleepy desk-sergeant looks up; an idle detective scanning yesterday's *Times-Picayune* on the two hind legs of a chair tipped back against the wall raises his head; and as the funnel of light from the cone-shaped reflector overhead plays up their visitor like flashlight powder, their mouths drop open and their eyes bat a couple of times. The two front legs of the detective's chair come down with a thump. The sergeant braces himself, eager, friendly, with the heels of both hands on his desk-top and his elbows up in the air. A patrolman comes in from the back room, wiping a drink of water from his mouth. His jaw also hangs when he sees who's there. He sidles nearer the detective and says behind the back of his hand, "That's Eddie Bloch, ain't it?"

The detective doesn't take the trouble to answer. It's like telling him what his own name is. The three stare at the figure under the light, in-

17

terested, respectful, almost admiring. There is nothing professional in their scrutiny, they are not the police studying a suspect; they are nobodies looking at a celebrity. They take in the rumpled tuxedo, the twig of gardenia that has shed its petals, the tie hanging open in two loose ends. His topcoat was slung across his arm originally; now it trails along the dusty station-house floor behind him. He gives his hat the final, tortured push that dislodges it. It drops and rolls away behind him. The policeman picks it up and brushes it off—he never was a bootlicker in his life, but this man is Eddie Bloch.

Still it's his face, more than who he is or how he's dressed, that would draw stares anywhere. It's the face of a dead man—the face of a dead man on a living body. The shadowy shape of the skull seems to peer through the transparent skin; you can make out its bone-structure as though an X-ray were outlining it. The eyes are stunned, shocked, haunted gleams, set in a vast purple hollow that bisects the face like a mask. No amount of drink or dissipation could do this to anyone, only long illness and the foreknowledge of death. You see faces like that looking up at you from hospital-cots when all hope has been abandoned—when the grave is already waiting.

Yet strangely enough, they knew who he was just now. Instant recognition of who he was came first—realization of the shape he's in comes after that, more slowly. Possibly it's because all three of them have been called on to identify corpses in the morgue in their day. Their minds are trained along those lines. And this man's face is known to hundreds of people. Not that he has ever broken or even fractured the most trivial law, but he has spread happiness around him, set a million feet to dancing in his time.

The desk-sergeant's expression changes. The patrolman mutters under his breath to the detective, "Looks like he just came out of a bad smashup with his car." "More like a drinking-bout, to me," answers the detective. They are simple men, capable within their limitations, but those are the only explanations they can find for what they now see before them.

The desk-sergeant speaks. "Mr. Eddie Bloch, am I right?" He extends his hand across the desk in greeting.

The man can hardly stand up. He nods, he doesn't take the hand.

"Is there anything wrong, Mr. Bloch? Is there anything we can do for you?" The detective and the patrolman come over closer. "Run in and get him a drink of water, Latour," the sergeant says anxiously. "Have an accident, Mr. Bloch? Been held up?"

The man steadies himself with one arm against the edge of the sergeant's desk. The detective extends an arm behind him, in case he should fall backwards. He keeps fumbling, continually fumbling in his clothes. The tuxedo-jacket swims on him as his movements shift it around. He is down to about a hundred pounds in weight, they notice. Out comes a gun, and he doesn't even have the strength to lift it up. He pushes it and it skids across the desk-top, then spins around and points back at him.

He speaks, and if the unburied dead ever spoke this is the voice they'd use. "I've killed a man. Just now. A little while ago. At half-past three."

They're completely floored. They almost don't know how to handle the situation for a minute. They deal with killers every day, but killers have to be gone out after and dragged in. And when fame and wealth enter into it, as they do once in a great while, fancy lawyers and protective barriers spring up to hedge the killers in on all sides. This man is one of the ten idols of America, or was until just lately. People like him don't kill people. They don't come in out of nowhere at four in the morning and stand before a simple desk-sergeant and a simple detective, stripped to their naked souls, shorn of all resemblance to humanity, almost.

There's silence in the room for a minute, a silence you could cut with a knife. Then he speaks again, in agony. "I tell you I've killed a man! Don't stand there looking at me like that! I've killed a man!"

The sergeant speaks, gently, sympathetically. "What's the matter, Mr. Bloch, been working too hard?" He comes out from behind the desk. "Come on inside with us. You stay here, Latour, and look after the telephone."

And when they've accompanied him into the back room: "Get him a chair, Humphries. Here, drink some of this water, Mr. Bloch. Now what's it all about?" The sergeant has brought the gun along with him. He passes it before his nose, then breaks it open. He looks at the detective. "He's used it all right."

"Was it an accident, Mr. Bloch?" the detective suggests respectfully. The man in the chair shakes his head. He's started to shiver all over, although the New Orleans night is warm and mellow. "Who'd you do it to? Who was it?" the sergeant puts in.

"I don't know his name," Bloch mumbles. "I never have. They call him Papa Benjamin."

His two interrogators exchange a puzzled look. "Sounds like—" The detective doesn't finish it. Instead he turns to the seated figure and asks almost perfunctorily: "He was a white man, of course?"

"He was colored," is the unexpected answer.

The thing gets more crazy, more inexplicable, at every step. How should a man like Eddie Bloch, one of the country's best-known band-leaders, who used to earn a thousand dollars every week for playing at Maxim's, come to kill a nameless colored man—and then be put into this condition by it? These two men have never seen anything like it in their time; they have subjected suspects to forty-eight-hour grillings and yet compared to him now those suspects were fresh as daisies when they got through with them.

He has said it was no accident and he has said it was no hold-up. They shower questions at him, not to confuse him but rather to try to help him pull himself together. "What did he do, forget his place? Talk back to you? Become insolent?" This is the South, remember.

The man's head goes from side to side like a pendulum.

"Did you go out of your mind for a minute? Is that how it was?"

Again a nodded no.

The man's condition has suggested one explanation to the detective's mind. He looks around to make sure the patrolman outside isn't listening. Then very discreetly: "Are you a needle-user, Mr. Bloch? Was he your source?"

The man looks up at them. "I've never touched a thing I shouldn't. A doctor will tell you that in a minute."

"Did he have something on you? Was it blackmail?"

Bloch fumbles some more in his clothes; again they dance around on his skeletonized frame. Suddenly he takes out a cube of money, as thick as it is wide, more money than these two men have ever seen before in their lives. "There's three thousand dollars there," he says simply and tosses it down like he did the gun. "I took it with me tonight, tried to give it to him. He could have had twice as much, three times as much, if he'd said the word, if he'd only let up on me. He wouldn't take it. That was when I had to kill him. That was all there was left for me to do."

"What was he doing to you?" The both say it together.

"He was killing me." He holds out his arm and shoots his cuff. The wristbone is about the size of the sergeant's own thumb-joint. The expensive platinum wrist watch that encircles it has been pulled in to the last possible notch and yet it still hangs almost like a bracelet. "See? I'm down to 102. When my shirt's off, my heart's so close to the surface you can see the skin right over it move like a pulse with each beat."

They draw back a little, almost they wish he hadn't come in here. That he had headed for some other precinct instead. From the very beginning they had sensed something here that is over their heads, that isn't to be found in any of the instruction-books. Now they come out with it. "How?" Humphries asks. "How was he killing you?"

There's a flare of torment from the man. "Don't you suppose I would have told you long ago, if I could! Don't you suppose I would have come in here weeks ago, months ago, and demanded protection, asked to be saved—if I could have told you what it was? If you would have believed me?"

"We'll believe you, Mr. Bloch," the sergeant says soothingly. "We'll believe anything. Just tell us—"

But Bloch in turn shoots a question at them, for the first time since he has come in. "Answer me! Do you believe in anything you can't see, can't hear, can't touch—?"

"Radio," the sergeant suggests not very brightly, but Humphries answers more frankly: "No."

The man slumps down again in his chair, shrugs apathetically. "If you don't, how can I expect you to believe me? I've been to the biggest doctors, biggest scientists in the world—they wouldn't believe me. How can I expect you to? You'll simply say I'm cracked, and let it go at that. I don't want to spend the rest of my life in an asylum—" He breaks off and sobs. "And yet it's true, it's true!"

They've gotten into such a maze that Humphries decides it's about time to snap out of it. He asks the one simple question that should have been asked long ago, and the hell with all this mumbo-jumbo. "Are you sure you killed him?" The man is broken physically and he's about ready to crack mentally too. The whole thing may be an hallucination.

"I know I did. I'm sure of it," the man answers calmly. "I'm already beginning to feel a little better. I felt it the minute he was gone.'

If he is, he doesn't show it. The sergeant catches Humphries' eye and meaningfully taps his forehead in a sly gesture.

"Suppose you take us there and show us," Humphries suggests. "Can you do that? Where'd it happen, at Maxim's?"

"I told you he was colored," Bloch answers reproachfully. Maxim's is white only. "It was in the Vieux Carré. I can show you where, but I can't drive any more. It was all I could do to get down here with my car."

"I'll put Desjardins on it with you," the sergeant says and calls through the door to the patrolman: "Ring Dij and tell him to meet Humphries at the corner of Canal and Royal right away!'' He turns and looks at the huddle on the chair. ''Buy him a bracer on the way. It don't look like he'll last till he gets there.''

The man flushes a little—it would be a blush if he had any blood left in him. ''I can't touch alcohol any more. I'm on my last legs. It goes right through me like—'' He hangs his head, then raises it again. ''But I'll get better now, little by little, now that he's—''

The sergeant takes Humphries out of earshot. ''Pushover for a padded cell. If it's on the up-and-up, and not just a pipe dream, call me right back. I'll get the commissioner on the wire.''

''At this hour of the night?''

The sergeant motions toward the chair with his head. ''He's Eddie Bloch, isn't he?''

Humphries takes him under the elbow, pries him up from the chair. Not roughly, but just briskly, energetically. Now that things are at last getting under way, he knows where he's at; he can handle them. He'll still be considerate, but he's businesslike now; he's into his routine. ''All right, come on, Mr. Bloch, let's get up there.''

''Not a scratch goes down on the blotter until I'm sure what I'm doing,'' the sergeant calls after Humphries. ''I don't want this whole town down on my neck tomorrow morning.''

Humphries almost has to hold him up on the way out and into the car. ''This it?'' he says, ''wow!'' He just touches it with his nail and they're off like velvet. ''How'd you ever get this into the Vieux Carré without knocking over the houses?''

Two gleams deep in the skull jogging against the upholstery, dimmer than the dashboard lights, are the only sign that there's life beside him. ''Used to park it blocks away—go on foot.''

''Oh, you went there more than once?''

''Wouldn't you—to beg for your life?''

More of that screwy stuff, Humphries thinks disgustedly. Why should a man like Eddie Bloch, star of the mike and the dance-floor, go to some colored man in the slums and beg for his life?

Royal Street comes whistling along. He swerves in toward the curb, shoves the door out, sees Desjardins land on the running-board with one foot. Then he veers out into the middle again without even having stopped. Desjardins moves in on the other side of Bloch, finishes dressing by knotting his necktie and buttoning his vest. ''Where'd you get the Aquitania?''

he wants to know, and then, with a look beside him: "Holy Kreisler, Eddie Bloch! We used to hear you every night on my Emerson—"

"Matter?" Humphries squelches, "Got a talking-jag?"

"Turn," says a hollow sound between them and three wheels take the Bugatti around into North Rampart Street. "Have to leave it here," he says a little later, and they get out. "Congo Square," the old stamping-ground of the slaves.

"Help him," Humphries tells his mate tersely, and they each brace him by an elbow.

Staggering between them with the uneven gait of a punch-drunk pug, quick and then slow by turns, he leads them down a ways, and then suddenly cuts left into an alley that isn't there at all until you're smack in front of it. It's just a crack between two houses, noisome as a sewer. They have to break into Indian file to get through at all. But Bloch can't fall down; the walls almost scrape both his shoulders at once. One's in front, one behind him.

"You packed?" Humphries calls over his head to Desjardins, up front.

"Catch cold without it," the other's voice comes back out of the gloom.

A slit of orange shows up suddenly from under a windowsill and a shapely coffee-colored elbow scrapes the ribs of the three as they squirm by. "This far 'nough, honey," a liquid voice murmurs.

"Bad girl, wash y'mouth out with soap," the unromantic Humphries warns over his shoulder without even looking around. The sliver of light vanishes as quickly as it came.

The passage widens out in places into mouldering courtyards dating back to French or Spanish colonial days, and once it goes under an archway and becomes a tunnel for a short distance. Desjardins cracks his head and swears with talent and abandon.

"Y'left out—" the rearguard remarks dryly.

"Here," pants Bloch weakly, and stops suddenly at a patch of blackness in the wall. Humphries washes it with his torch and crumbling mildewed stone steps show up inside it. Then he motions Bloch in, but the man hangs back, slips a notch or two lower down against the opposite wall that supports him. "Let me stay down here! Don't make me go up there again," he pleads. "I don't think I can make it any more. I'm afraid to go back in there."

"Oh no!" Humphries says with quiet determination. "You're showing us," and scoops him away from the wall with his arm. Again, as before, he isn't rough about it, just businesslike. Dij keeps the lead, watering the place with his own torch. Humphries trains his on the band-leader's forty-dollar custom-made patent-leather shoes jerking frightenedly upward before him. The stone steps turn to wood ones splintered with usage. They have to step over a huddled black drunk, empty bottle cradled in his arms. "Don't light a match," Dij warns, pinching his nose, "or there'll be an explosion."

"Grow up," snaps Humphries. The Cajun's a good dick, but can't he realize the man in the middle is roasting in hellfire? This is no time—

"In here is where I did it. I closed the door again after me." Bloch's skull-face is all silver with his life-sweat as one of their torches flicks past it.

Humphries shoves open the sagging mahogany panel that was first hung up when a Louis was still king of France and owned this town. The light of a lamp far across a still, dim room flares up and dances crazily in the draught. They come in and look.

There's an old broken-down bed, filthy with rags. Across it there's a motionless figure, head hanging down toward the floor. Dij cups his hand under it and lifts it. It comes up limply toward him, like a small basketball. It bounces down again when he lets it go—even seems to bob slightly for a second or two after. It's an old, old colored man, up in his eighties, even beyond. There's a dark spot, darker than the weazened skin, just under one bleared eye and another in the thin fringe of white wool that circles the back of the skull.

Humphries doesn't wait to see any more. He turns, flips out and down, and all the way back to wherever the nearest telephone can be found, to let headquarters know that it's true after all and they can rouse the police commissioner. "Keep him there with you, Dij," his voice trails back from the inky stair-well, "and no quizzing. Pull in your horns till we get our orders!" The scarecrow with them tries to stumble after him and get out of the place, groaning, "Don't leave me here! Don't make me stay here—!"

"I wouldn't quiz you on my own, Mr. Bloch," Dij tries to reassure him, nonchalantly sitting down on the edge of the bed next to the corpse and retying his shoelace, "I'll never forget it was your playing *Love in Bloom* on the air one night in Baton Rouge two years ago gave me the courage to propose to my wife—"

But the Commissioner would, and does, in his office a couple hours later. He's anything but eager about it, too. They've tried to shunt him,

Bloch, off their hands in every possible legal way open to them. No go. He sticks to them like flypaper. The old colored man *didn't* try to attack him, or rob him, or blackmail him, or kidnap him, or anything else. The gun didn't go off accidentally, and he didn't fire it on the spur of the moment either, without thinking twice, or in a flare of anger. The Commissioner almost beats his own head against the desk in his exasperation as he reiterates over and over: "But why? Why? Why?" And for the steenth time, he gets the same indigestible answer: "Because he was killing me."

"Then you admit he did lay hands on you?" The first time the poor Commissioner asked this, he said it with a spark of hope. But this is the tenth or twelfth and the spark died out long ago.

"He never once came near me. I was the one looked him up each time to plead with him. Commissioner Oliver, tonight I went down on my knees to that old man and dragged myself around the floor of that dirty room after him, on my *bended knees*, like a sick cat—begging, crawling to him, offering him three thousand, ten, any amount, finally offering him my own gun, asking him to shoot me with it, to get it over with quickly, to be kind to me, not to drag it out by inches any longer! No, not even that little bit of mercy! Then I shot—and now I'm going to get better, now I'm going to live—"

He's too weak to cry; crying takes strength. The Commissioner's hair is about ready to stand on end. "Stop it, Mr. Bloch, stop it!" he shouts, and he steps over and grabs him by the shoulder in defense of his own nerves, and can almost feel the shoulder-bone cutting his hand. He takes his hand away again in a hurry. "I'm going to have you examined by an alienist!"

The bundle of bones rears from the chair. "You can't do that! You can't take my mind from me! Send to my hotel—I've got a trunkful of reports on my condition! I've been to the biggest minds in Europe! Can you produce anyone that would dare go against the findings of Buckholtz in Vienna, Reynolds in London? They had me under observation for months at a time! I'm not even on the borderline of insanity, not even a genius or musically talented. I don't even write my own numbers, I'm mediocre, uninspired—in other words completely normal. I'm saner than you are at this minute, Mr. Oliver. My body's gone, my soul's gone, and all I've got left is my mind, but you can't take that from me!"

The Commissioner's face is beet-red. He's about ready for a stroke, but he speaks softly, persuasively. "An eighty-odd-year-old colored man who is so feeble he can't even go upstairs half the time, who has to have his

food pulleyed up to him through the window in a basket, is killing—
whom? A white stumble-bum his own age? No-o-o, Mr. Eddie Bloch, the
premier bandsman of America, who can name his own price in any town,
who's heard every night in all our homes, who has about everything a man
can want—that's who!''

He peers close, until their eyes are on a level. His voice is just a silky
whisper. "Tell me just one thing, Mr. Bloch.'' Then like the explosion of
a giant firecracker, "How?'' He roars it out, booms it out.

There's a long-drawn intake of breath from Eddie Bloch. "By thinking
thought-waves of death that reach me through the air.''

The poor Commissioner practically goes all to pieces on his own rug.
"And you don't need a medical exam!'' he wheezes weakly.

There's a flutter, the popping of buttons, and Eddie Bloch's coat, his
vest, his shirt, undershirt, land one after another on the floor around his
chair. He turns. "Look at my back! You can count every vertebra through
the skin!'' He turns back again. "Look at my ribs. Look at the pulsing
where there's not enough skin left to cover my heart!''

Oliver shuts his eyes and turns toward the window. He's in a particularly unpleasant spot. New Orleans, out there, is stirring, and when it hears
about this, he's going to be the most unpopular man in town. On the other
hand, if he doesn't see the thing through now that it's gone this far he's
guilty of a dereliction of duty, malfeasance in office.

Bloch, slowly dressing, knows what he's thinking. "You want to get rid
of me, don't you? You're trying to think of a way of covering this thing
up. You're afraid to bring me up before the Grand Jury on account of your
own reputation, aren't you?'' His voice rises to a scream of panic. "Well,
I want protection! I don't want to go out there again—to my death! I won't
accept bail! If you turn me loose now, even on my own cognizance, you
may be as guilty of my death as he is. How do I know my bullet stopped
the thing? How does any of us know what becomes of the mind after
death? Maybe his thoughts will still reach me, still try to get me. I tell you
I want to be locked up, I want people around me day and night, I want to
be where I'm safe—!''

"Shh, for God's sake, Mr. Bloch! They'll think I'm beating you up—''
The Commissioner drops his arms to his sides and heaves a gigantic sigh.
"That settles it! I'll book you all right. You want that and you're going to
get it! I'll book you for the murder of one Papa Benjamin, even if they
laugh me out of office for it!''

For the first time since the whole thing has started, he casts a look of real anger, ill-will, at Eddie Bloch. He seizes a chair, swirls it around, and bangs it down in front of the man. He puts his foot on it and pokes his finger almost in Bloch's eye. "I'm not two-faced. I'm not going to lock you up nice and cozy and then soft-pedal the whole thing. If it's coming out at all, then all of it's coming out. Now start in! Tell me everything I want to know, and what I want to know is—everything!"

The strains of *Goodnight Ladies* die away; the dancers leave the floor, the lights start going out, and Eddie Bloch throws down his baton and mops the back of his neck with a handkerchief. He weighs about two hundred pounds, is in the pink, and is a good-looking brute. But his face is sour right now, dissatisfied. His outfit starts to case its instruments right and left, and Judy Jarvis steps up on the platform, in her street clothes, ready to go home. She's Eddie's torch singer, and also his wife. "Coming, Eddie? Let's get out of here." She looks a little disgusted herself. "I didn't get a hand tonight, not even after my rumba number. Must be staling. If I wasn't your wife, I'd be out of a job I guess."

Eddie pats her shoulder. "It isn't you, honey. It's us, we're beginning to stink. Notice how the attendance has been dropping the past few weeks? There were more waiters than customers tonight. I'll be hearing from the owner any minute now. He has the right to cancel my contract if the intake drops below five grand."

A waiter comes up to the edge of the platform. "Mr. Graham'd like to see you in his office before you go home, Mr. Bloch."

Eddie and Judy look at each other. "This is it now, Judy. You go back to the hotel. Don't wait for me. G'night, boys." Eddie Bloch calls for his hat and knocks at the manager's office.

Graham rustles a lot of accounts together. "We took in forty-five hundred this week, Eddie. They can get the same ginger ale and sandwiches any place, but they'll go where the band has something to give 'em. I notice the few that do come in don't even get up from the table any more when you tap your baton. Now, what's wrong?"

Eddie punches his hat a couple of times. "Don't ask me. I'm getting the latest orchestrations from Broadway sent to me hot off the griddle. We sweat our bald heads off rehearsing—".

Graham swivels his cigar. "Don't forget that jazz originated here in the South, you can't show this town anything. They want something new."

"When do I scram?" Eddie asks, smiling with the southwest corner of his mouth.

"Finish the week out. See if you can do something about it by Monday. If not, I'll have to wire St. Louis to get Kruger's crew. I'm sorry, Eddie."

"That's all right," broad-minded Eddie says. "You're not running a charity bazaar."

Eddie goes out into the dark dance-room. His crew has gone. The tables are stacked. A couple of old colored crones are down on hands and knees slopping water around on the parquet. Eddie steps up on the platform a minute to get some orchestrations he left on the piano. He feels something crunch under his shoe, reaches down, picks up a severed chicken's claw lying there with a strip of red-rag tied around it. How the hell did it get up there? If it had been under one of the tables, he'd have thought some diner had dropped it. He flushes a little. D'ye mean to say he and the boys were so rotten tonight that somebody deliberately threw it at them while they were playing?

One of the scrubwomen looks up. The next moment, she and her mate are on their feet, edging nearer, eyes big as saucers, until they get close enough to see what it is he's holding. Then there's a double yowl of animal fright, a tin pail goes rolling across the floor, and no two stout people, white or colored, ever got out of a place in such a hurry before. The door nearly comes off its hinges, and Eddie can hear their cackling all the way down the quiet street outside until it fades away into the night. "For gosh sake!" thinks the bewildered Eddie, "They must be using the wrong brand of gin." He tosses the object out onto the floor and goes back to the piano for his music scores. A sheet or two has slipped down behind it and he squats to collect them. That way the piano hides him.

The door opens again and he sees Johnny Staats (traps and percussion) come in in quite a hurry. He thought Staats was home in bed by now. Staats is feeling himself all over like he was rehearsing the shim-sham and he's scanning the ground as he goes along. Then suddenly he pounces— and it's on that very scrap of garbage Eddie just now threw away! And as he straightens up with it, his breath comes out in such a sigh of relief that Eddie can hear it all the way across the still room. All this keeps him from hailing Staats as he was going to a minute ago and suggesting a cup of java. But—"superstitious," thinks broad-minded Eddie. "It's his good-luck charm, that's all, like some people carry a rabbit's foot. I'm a little that way myself, never walk under a ladder—"

Then again, why should those two mammies go into hysterics when they lamp the same object? And Eddie recalls now that some of the boys have always suspected Staats has colored blood, and tried to tell him so years ago when Staats first came in with them, but he wouldn't listen to them.

Staats slinks out again as noiselessly as he came in, and Eddie decides he'll catch up with him and kid him about his chicken-claw on their way home together. (They all roost in the same hotel.) So he takes his music-sheets, some of which are blank, and he leaves. Staats is way down the street—in the *wrong direction*, away from the hotel! Eddie hesitates for just a minute, and then he starts after Staats on a vague impulse, just to see where he's going—just to see what he's up to. Maybe the fright of the scrubwomen and the way Staats pounced on that chicken-claw just now have built up to this, without Eddie's really knowing it.

And how many times afterwards he's going to pray to his God that he'd never turned down that other way this night—away from his hotel, his Judy, his boys—away from the sunlight and the white man's world. Such a little thing to decide to do, and afterwards no turning back—ever.

He keeps Staats in sight, and they hit the Vieux Carré. That's all right. There are a lot of quaint places here a guy might like to drop in. Or maybe he has some Creole sweetie tucked away, and Eddie thinks: I'm lower than a ditch to spy like this. But then suddenly right before his eyes, halfway up the narrow lane he's turned into—there isn't any Staats any more! And no door opened and closed again either. Then when Eddie gets up to where it was, he sees the crevice between the old houses, hidden by an angle in the walls. So that's where he went! Eddie almost has a peeve on by now at all this hocus-pocus. He slips in himself and feels his way along. He stops every once in a while and can hear Staats' quiet footfall somewhere way up in front. Then he goes on again. Once or twice the passage spreads out a little and lets a little green-blue moonlight part way down the walls. Then later, there's a little flare of orange light from under a window and an elbow jogs him in the appendix. "You'd be happier here. Doan go the rest of the way," a soft voice breathes. A prophecy if he only knew it!

But hardboiled Eddie just says: "G'wan to bed, y' dirty stay-up!" out of the corner of his mouth, and the light vanishes. Next a tunnel and he bangs the top of his head and his eyes water. But at the other end of it, Staats has finally come to a halt in a patch of clear light and seems to be looking up at a window or something, so Eddie stays where he is, inside the tunnel, and folds the lapels of his black jacket up over his white shirt-front so it won't show.

Staats just stands there for a spell, with Eddie holding his breath inside the tunnel, and then finally he gives a peculiar, dismal whistle. There's nothing carefree or casual about it. It's a hollow swampland sound, not easy to get without practice. Then he just stands there waiting, until without warning another figure joins him in the gloom. Eddie strains his eyes. A gorilla-like, Negro roustabout. Something passes from Staats' hand to his—the chicken-claw possibly—then they go in, into the house Staats has been facing. Eddie can hear the soft shuffle of feet going up stairs on the inside, and the groaning, squeaking of an old decayed door—and then silence.

He edges forward to the mouth of the tunnel and peers up. No light shows from any window, the house appears to be untenanted, deserted.

Eddie hangs onto his coat collar with one hand and strokes his chin with the other. He doesn't know just what to do. The vague impulse that has brought him this far after Staats begins to peter out now. Staats has some funny associates—something funny is going on in this out-of-the-way place at this unearthly hour of the morning—but after all, a man's private life is his own. He wonders what made him do this, he wouldn't want anyone to know he did it. He'll turn around and go back to his hotel now and get some shut-eye; he's got to think up some novelty for his routine at Maxim's between now and Monday or he'll be out on his ear.

Then just as one heel is off the ground to take the turn that will start him back, a vague, muffled wailing starts from somewhere inside that house. It's toned down to a mere echo. It has to go through thick doors and wide, empty rooms and down a deep, hollow stairwell before it gets to him. Oh, some sort of a revival meeting, is it? So Staats has got religion, has he? But what a place to come and get it in!

A throbbing like a far-away engine in a machine-shop underscores the wailing, and every once in a while a *boom* like distant thunder across the bayou tops the whole works. It goes: *Boom-putta-putta-boom-putta-putta-boom!* And the wailing, way up high at the moon: *Eeyah-eeyah-eeyah. . . !*

Eddie's professional instincts suddenly come alive. He tries it out, beats time to it with his arm as if he were holding a baton. His fingers snap like a whip. "My God, that's grand! That's gorgeous! Just what I need! I gotta get up there!" So a chicken-foot does it, eh?

He turns and runs back, through the tunnel, through the courtyards, all the way back where he came from, stooping here, stooping there, lighting matches recklessly and throwing them away as he goes. Out in the Vieux

Carré again, the refuse hasn't been collected. He spots a can at the corner of two lanes, topples it over. The smell rises to heaven, but he wades into it ankle-deep like any levee-rat, digs into the stuff with both forearms, scattering it right and left. He's lucky, find a verminous carcass, tears off a claw, wipes it on some newspaper. Then he starts back. Wait a minute! The red-rag, red strip around it! He feels himself all over, digs into all his pockets. Nothing that color. Have to do without it, but maybe it won't work without it. He turns and hurries back through the slit between the old houses, doesn't care how much noise he makes. The flash of light from Old Faithful, the jogging elbow. Eddie stoops, he suddenly snatches in at the red kimono sleeve, his hand comes away with a strip of it. Bad language, words that even Eddie doesn't know. A five-spot stops it on the syllable, and Eddie's already way down the passage. If only they haven't quit until he can get back there!

They haven't. It was vague, smothered when he went away; it's louder, more persistent, more frenzied now. He doesn't bother about giving the whistle, probably couldn't imitate it exactly anyhow. He dives into the black smudge that is the entrance to the house, feels greasy stone steps under him, takes one or two and then suddenly his collar is four sizes too small for him, gripped by a big ham of a hand at the back. A sharp something that might be anything from a pocketknife blade to the business edge of a razor is creasing his throat just below the apple and drawing a preliminary drop or two of blood.

"Here it is, I've got it here!" gasps Eddie. What kind of religion is this, anyway? The sharp thing stays, but the hand lets go his collar and feels for the chicken-claw. Then the sharp thing does away too, but probably not very far away.

"Whyfor you didn't give the signal?"

Eddie's windpipe gives him the answer. "Sick here, couldn't."

"Light up, lemme see yo' face." Eddie strikes a match and holds it. "Yo' face has never been here before."

Eddie gestures upward. "My friend—up there—he'll tell you!"

"Mr. Johnny yo' friend? He ax you to come?"

Eddie thinks quickly. The chicken-claw might carry more weight than Staats. "That told me to come."

"Papa Benjamin sen' you that?"

"Certainly," says Eddie stoutly. Probably their deacon, but it's a hell of a way to—The match stings his fingers and he whips it out. Blackness and a moment's uncertainty that might end either way. But a lot of savoir-faire, a thousand years of civilization, are backing Eddie up. "You'll make me late. Papa Benjamin wouldn't like that!"

He gropes his way on up in the pitch-blackness, thinking any minute he'll feel his back slashed to ribbons. But it's better than standing still and having it happen, and to back out now would bring it on twice as quickly. However, it works, nothing happens.

"Fust thing y'know, all N'yorleans be comin' by," growls the African watchdog sulkily, and flounders down on the staircase with a sound like a tired seal. There is some other crack about "darkies lookin' lak pinks," and then a long period of scratching.

But Eddie's already up on the landing above and so close to the *boom-putta-boom* now it drowns out every other sound. The whole framework of the decrepit house seems to shake with it. The door's closed but the thread of orange that outlines it shows it up to him. Behind there. He leans against it, shoves a little. It gives. The squealings and the grindings it emits are lost in the torrent of noise that comes rushing out. He sees plenty, and what he sees only makes him want to see all the more. Something tells him the best thing to do is slip in quietly and close it behind him before he's noticed, rather than stay there peeping in from the outside. Little Snowdrop might always come upstairs in back of him and catch him there. So he widens it just a little more, oozes in, and kicks it shut behind him with his heel—and immediately gets as far away from it as he can. Evidently no one has seen him.

Now, it's a big shadowy room and it's choked with people. It's lit by a single oil-lamp and a hell of a whole lot of candles, which may have shone out brightly against the darkness outside but are pretty dim once you get inside with them. The long flickering shadows thrown on all the walls by those cavorting in the center are almost as much of a protection to Eddie, as he crouches back amidst them, as the darkness outside would be. He's been around, and a single look is enough to tell him that whatever else it is, it's no revival meeting. At first, he takes it for just a gin or rent party with the lid off, but it isn't that either. There's no gin there, and there's no pairing off of couples in the dancing—rather it's a roomful of devils lifted bodily up out of hell. Plenty of them have passed out cold on the floor all around him and the others keep stepping over them as they prance back and forth, only they don't always step over but sometimes *on*—on prostrate faces and chests and outstretched arms and hands. Then there are others who have gone off into a sort of still trance, seated on the floor with their backs to the wall, some of them rocking back and forth, some just staring glassy-eyed, foam drooling from their mouths. Eddie quickly slips down among them on his haunches and gets busy. He too starts rocking back and forth and pounding the flooring beside him with his knuckles, but he's not in any trance, he's getting a swell new number for his repertoire at Maxim's. A sheet of blank score-paper is partly hidden under his body, and he keeps dropping one hand down to it every minute jotting down musical notes with the stub of pencil in his fingers. "Key of A," he guesses. "I can decide that when I instrument it. Mi-re-do, mi-re-do. Then over again. Hope I didn't miss any of it."

Boom-putta-putta-boom! Young and old, black and tawny, fat and thin, naked and clothed, they pass from right to left, from left to right, in two concentric circles, while the candle flames dance crazily and the shadows leap up and down on the walls. The hub of it all, within the innermost circle of dancers, is an old, old man, black skin and bones, only glimpsed now and then in a space between the packed bodies that surround him. An animal-pelt is banded about his middle; he wears a horrible juju mask over his face—a death's head. On one side of him, a squatting woman clacks two gourds together endlessly, that's the "putta" of Eddie's rhythm; on the other, another beats a drum, that's the "boom." In one upraised hand he holds a squalling fowl, wings beating the air; in the other a sharp-bladed knife. Something flashes in the air, but the dancers mercifully get between Eddie and the sight of it. Next glimpse he has, the fowl isn't flapping any more. It's hanging limply down and veins of blood are trickling down the old man's shrivelled forearm.

"That part don't go into my show," Eddie thinks facetiously. The horrible old man has dropped the knife; he squeezes the life-blood from the dead bird with both hands now, still holding it in mid-air. He sprinkles the drops on those that cavort around him, flexing and unflexing his bony fingers in a nauseating travesty of the ceremony of baptism.

Drops spatter here and there about the room, on the walls. One lands near Eddie and he edges back. Revolting things go on all around him. He sees some of the crazed dancers drop to their hands and knees and bend low over these red polka-dots, licking them up from the floor with their tongues. Then they go about the room on all fours like animals, looking for others.

"Think I'll go," Eddie says to himself, tasting last night's supper all over again. "They ought to have the cops on them."

He maneuvers the score-sheet, filled now, out from under him and into his side-pocket; then he starts drawing his feet in toward him preparatory to standing up and slipping out of this hell-hole. Meanwhile a second fowl, black this time (the first was white), a squeaking suckling-pig, and a puppy-dog have gone the way of the first fowl. Nor do the carcasses go to waste when the old man has dropped them. Eddie sees things happening on the floor, in between the stomping feet of the dancers, and he guesses enough not to look twice.

Then suddenly, already reared a half-inch above the floor on his way up, he wonders where the wailing went. And the clacking of the gourds and the boom of the drum and the shuffling of the feet. He blinks, and everything has frozen still in the room around him. Not a move, not a sound. Straight out from the old man's gnarled shoulder stretches a bony arm, the end dipped in red, pointing like an arrow at Eddie. Eddie sinks down again that half-inch. He couldn't hold that position very long, and something tells him he's not leaving right away after all.

"White man," says a bated breath, and they all start moving in on him. A gesture of the old man sweeps them into motionlessness again.

A cracked voice comes through the grinning mouth of the juju mask, rimmed with canine teeth. "Whut you do here?"

Eddie taps his pockets mentally. He has about fifty on him. Will that be enough to buy his way out? He has an uneasy feeling however that none of this lot is as interested in money as they should be—at least not right now. Before he has a chance to try it out, another voice speaks up. "I know this man, papaloi. Let me find out."

Johnny Staats came in here tuxedoed, hair slicked back, a cog in New Orleans' night-life. Now he's barefooted, coatless, shirtless—a tousled scarecrow. A drop of blood has caught him squarely on the forehead and been traced, by his own finger or someone else's, into a red line from temple to temple. A chicken-feather or two clings to his upper lip. Eddie saw him dancing with the rest, groveling on the floor. His scalp crawls with repugnance as the man comes over and squats down before him. The rest of them hold back, tense, poised, ready to pounce.

The two men talk in low, hoarse voices. "It's your only way, Eddie. I can't save you—"

"Why, I'm in the very heart of New Orleans! They wouldn't dare!" But sweat oozes out on Eddie's face just the same. He's no fool. Sure the police will come and sure they'll mop this place up. But what will they find? His own remains along with that of the fowls, the pig and the dog.

"You'd better hurry up, Eddie. I can't hold them back much longer. Unless you do, you'll never get out of this place alive and you may as well know it! If I tried to stop them, I'd go too. You know what this is, don't you? This is voodoo!"

"I knew that five minutes after I was in the room." And Eddie thinks to himself, "You son-of-a-so-and-so! You better ask Mombo-jombo to get you a new job starting in tomorrow night!" Then he grins internally and, clown to the very end, says with a straight face: "Sure I'll join. What d'ye suppose I came here for anyway?"

Knowing what he knows now, Staats is the last one he'd tell about the glorious new number he's going to get out of this, the notes for which are nestled in his inside pocket right now. And he might even get more dope out of the initiation ceremonies if he pretends to go through with them. A song or dance for Judy to do with maybe a green spot focussed on her. Lastly, there's no use denying there *are* too many razors, knives, and the like, in the room to hope to get out and all the way back where he started from without a scratch.

Staats' face is grave, though. "Now don't kid about this thing. If you knew what I know about it, there's a lot more to it than there seems to be. If you're sincere, honest about it, all right. If not, it might be better to get cut to pieces right now than to tamper with it."

"Never more serious in my life," says Eddie. And deep down inside he's braying like a jackass.

Staats turns to the old man. "His spirit wishes to join our spirits."

The papaloi burns some feathers and entrails at one of the candle-flames. Not a sound in the room. The majority of them squat down all at once. "It came out all right," Staats breathes. "He reads them. The spirits are willing."

"So far so good," Eddie thinks. "I've fooled the guts and feathers."

The papaloi is pointing at him now. "Let him go now and be silent," the voice behind the mask cackles. Then a second time he says it, and a third, with a long pause between.

Eddie looks hopefully at Staats. "Then I can go after all, as long as I don't tell anyone what I've seen?"

Staats shakes his head grimly. "Just part of the ritual. If you went now, you'd eat something that disagreed with you tomorrow and be dead before the day was over."

More sacrificial slaughtering, and the drum and gourds and wailing start over again, but very low and subdued now as at the beginning. A bowl of blood is prepared and Eddie is raised to his feet and led forward, Staats on one side of him, an anonymous colored man on the other. The papaloi dips his already caked hand into the bowl and traces a mark on Eddie's forehead. The chanting and wailing grow louder behind him. The dancing begins again. He's in the middle of all of them. He's an island of sanity in a sea of jungle-frenzy. The bowl is being held up before his face. He tries to draw back, his sponsors grip him firmly by the arms. "Drink!" whispers Staats. "Drink—or they'll kill you where you stand!"

Even at this stage of the game, there's still a wisecrack left in Eddie, though he keeps it to himself. He takes a deep breath. "Here's where I get my vitamin A for today!"

Staats shows up at orchestra rehearsal next A.M. to find somebody else at drums and percussion. He doesn't say much when Eddie shoves a two-week check at him, spits on the floor at his feet and growls: "Beat it, you filthy—"

Staats only murmurs: "So you're crossing them? I wouldn't want to be in your shoes for all the fame and money in this world, guy!"

"If you mean that bad dream the other night," says Eddie, "I haven't told anybody and I don't intend to. Why, I'd be laughed at. I'm only remembering what I can use of it. I'm a white man, see? The jungle is just trees to me; the Congo, just a river; the night-time, just a time for electric-lights." He whips out a couple of C's. "Hand 'em these for me, will ya, and tell 'em I've paid up my dues from now until doomsday and I don't want any receipt. And if they try putting rough-on-rats in my orange juice, they'll find themselves stomping in a chain-gang!"

The C's fell where Eddie spat. "You're one of us. You think you're pink? Blood tells. You wouldn't have gone there—you couldn't have stood that induction—if you were. Look at your fingernails sometime, look in a mirror at the whites of your eyes. Good-by, dead man."

Eddie says good-by to him, too. He knocks out three of his teeth, breaks the bridge of his nose, and rolls all over the floor on top of him. But he can't wipe out that wise, knowing smile that shows even through the gush of blood.

They pull Eddie off, pull him up, pull him together. Staats staggers away, smiling at what he knows. Eddie, heaving like a bellows, turns to his crew. "All right, boys. All together now!" *Boom-putt-putta-boom-putta-putta-boom!*

Graham shoots five C's on promotion and all New Orleans jams its way into Maxim's that Saturday night. They're standing on each other's shoulders and hanging from the chandeliers to get a look. "First time in America, the original *Voodoo Chant*," yowl the three-sheets on every billboard in town. And when Eddie taps his baton, the lights go down and a nasty green flood lights the platform from below and you can hear a pin drop. "Good-evening, folks. This is Eddie Bloch and his Five Chips, playing to you from Maxim's. You're about to hear for the first time on the air the Voodoo Chant, the age-old ceremonial rhythm no white man has ever been permitted to listen to before. I can assure you this is an accurate transcription, not a note has been changed." Then very softly and far-away it begins: *Boom-putta-putta-boom!*

Judy's going to dance and wail to it, she's standing there on the steps leading up to the platform, waiting to go on. She's powdered orange, dressed in feathers, and has a small artificial bird fastened to one wrist and a thin knife in her other hand. She catches his eye, he looks over at her, and he sees she wants to tell him something. Still waving his baton he edges sideways until he's within earshot.

"Eddie, don't! Stop them! Call it off, will you? I'm worried about you!"

"Too late now," he answers under cover of the music. "We've started already. What're you scared of?"

She passes him a crumpled piece of paper. "I found this under your dressing-room door when I came out just now. It sounds like a warning. There's somebody doesn't want you to play that number!"

Still swinging with his right hand, Eddie unrolls the thing under his left thumb and reads it:

You can summon the spirits but can you dismiss them again? Think well.

He crumples it up again and tosses it away. "Staats trying to scare me because I canned him."

"It was tied to a little bunch of black feathers," she tries to tell him. "I wouldn't have paid any attention, but my maid pleaded with me not to dance this when she saw it. Then she ran out on me—"

"We're on the air," he reminds her between his teeth. "Are you with me or aren't you?" And he eases back center again. Louder and louder the beat grows, just like it did two nights ago. Judy swirls on in a green spot and begins the unearthly wail Eddie's coached her to do.

A waiter drops a tray of drinks in the silence of the room out there, and when the headwaiter goes to bawl him out he's nowhere to be found. He has quit cold and a whole row of tables has been left without their orders. "Well, I'll be—!" says the captain and scratches his head.

Eddie's facing the crew, his back to Judy, and as he vibrates to the rhythm, some pin or other that he's forgotten to take out of his shirt suddenly catches him and strikes into him. It's a little below the collar, just between the shoulderblades. He jumps a little, but doesn't feel it any more after that. . . .

Judy squalls, tears her tonsils out, screeches words that neither he nor she know the meaning of but that he managed to set down on paper phonetically the other night. Her little body goes through all the contortions, tamed down of course, that that brownskin she-devil greased with lard and wearing only earrings performed that night. She stabs the bird with her fake knife and sprinkles imaginary blood in the air. Nothing like this has ever been seen before. And in the silence that suddenly lands when it's through, you can count twenty. That's how it's gotten under everyone's skin.

Then the noise begins. It goes over like an avalanche. But just the same, more people are ordering strong drinks all at once than has ever happened before in the place, and the matron in the women's restroom has her hands full of hysterical sob-sisters.

"Try to get away from me, just try!" Graham tells Eddie at curfewtime. "I'll have a new contract, gilt-edged, ready for you in the morning. We've already got six-grand worth of reservations on our hands for the coming week—one of 'em by telegram all the way from Shreveport!"

Success! Eddie and Judy taxi back to their rooms at the hotel, tired but happy. "It'll be good for years. We can use it for our signature on the air, like Whiteman does the Rhapsody."

She goes into the bedroom first, snaps on the lights, calls to him a minute later: "Come here and look at this—the cutest little souvenir!" He finds her holding a wax doll, finger high, in her hands. "Why it's you, Eddie, look! Small as it is it has your features! Well isn't that the clev—!"

He takes it away from her and squints at it. It's himself all right. It's rigged out in two tiny patches of black cloth for a tuxedo, and the eyes and hair and features are inked onto the wax.

"Where'd you find it?"

"It was in your bed, up against the pillow."

He's fixing to grin about it, until he happens to turn it over. In the back, just a little below the collar, between the shoulder-blades, a short but venomous-looking black pin is sticking.

He goes a little white for a minute. He knows who it's from now and what it's trying to tell him. But that isn't what makes him change color. He's just remembered something. He throws off his coat, yanks at his collar, turns his back to her. "Judy, look down there, will you? I felt a pin stick me while we were doing that number. Put your hand down. Feel anything?"

"No, there's nothing there," she tells him.

"Musta dropped out."

"It couldn't have," she says. "Your belt-line's so tight it almost cuts into you. There couldn't have been anything there or it'd still be there now. You must have imagined it."

"Listen, I know a pin when I feel one. Any mark on my back, any scratch between the shoulders?"

"Not a thing."

"Tired, I guess. Nervous." He goes over to the open window and pitches the little doll out into the night with all his strength. Damn coincidence, that's all it was. To think otherwise would be to give them their inning. But he wonders what makes him feel so tired just the same—Judy did all the exercising, not he—yet he's felt all in ever since that number tonight.

Out go the lights and she drops off to sleep right with them. He lies very quiet for awhile. A little later he gets up, goes into the bathroom where the lights are whitest of all, and stands there looking at himself close to the glass. "Look at your fingernails sometime; look at the whites of your eyes," Staats had said. Eddie does. There's a bluish, purplish tinge to his nails that he never noticed before. The whites of his eyes are faintly yellow.

It's warm in New Orleans that night but he shivers a little as he stands there. He doesn't sleep any more that night. . . .

In the morning, his back aches as if he were sixty. But he knows that's from not closing his eyes all night, and not from any magic pins.

"Oh my God!" Judy says, from the other side of the bed, "look what you've done to him!" She shows him the second page of the *Picayune*. "John Staats, until recently a member of Eddie Bloch's orchestra, committed suicide late yesterday afternoon in full view of dozens of people by rowing himself out into Lake Pontchartrain and jumping overboard. He was alone in the boat at the time. The body was recovered half an hour later.''

''I didn't do that,'' says Eddie grimly. ''I've got a rough idea what did, though.'' Late yesterday afternoon. The night was coming on, and he couldn't face what was coming to him for sponsoring Eddie for giving them all away. Late yesterday afternoon—that meant *he* hadn't left that warning at the dressing-room or left that death-sentence on the bed. He'd been dead himself by then—not white, not black, just yellow.

Eddie waits until Judy's in her shower, then he phones the morgue. ''About Johnny Staats. He worked for me until yesterday, so if nobody's claimed the body send it to a funeral parlor at my exp—''

''Somebody's already claimed the remains, Mr. Bloch. First thing this morning. Just waited until the examiner had established suicide beyond a doubt. Some colored organization, old friends of his it seems—''

Judy comes in and remarks: ''You look all green in the face.''

Eddie thinks: I wouldn't care if he was my worst enemy, I can't let that happen to him! What horrors are going to take place tonight somewhere under the moon? He wouldn't even put cannibalism beyond them. The phone's right at his fingertips, and yet he can't denounce them to the police without involving himself, admitting that he was there, took part at least once. Once that comes out, bang! goes his reputation. He'll never be able to live it down—especially now that he's played the Voodoo Chant and identified himself with it in the minds of the public.

So instead, alone in the room again, he calls the best-known private agency in New Orleans. ''I want a bodyguard. Just for tonight. Have him meet me at closing-time at Maxim's. Armed, of course.''

It's Sunday and the banks are closed, but his credit's good anywhere. He raises a G in cash. He arranges with a reliable crematorium for a body to be taken charge of late tonight or early in the morning. He'll notify them just where to call for it. Yes, of course! He'll produce the proper authorization from the police. Poor Johnny Staats couldn't get away from ''them'' in life, but he's going to get away from them in death, all right. That's the least anyone could do for him.

Graham slaps a sawbuck-cover on that night, more to give the waiters room to move around in than anything else, and still the place is choked to the roof. This Voodoo number is a natural, a wow.

But Eddie's back is ready to cave in, while he stands there jogging with his stick. It's all he can do to hold himself straight.

When the racket and the shuffling is over for the night, the private dick is there waiting for him. "Lee is the name."

"Okay, Lee, come with me." They go outside and get in Eddie's Bugatti. They whizz down to the Vieux, scrounge to a stop in the middle of Congo Square, which will still be Congo Square when its official name of Beauregard is forgotten.

"This way," says Eddie, and his bodyguard squirms through the alley after him.

" 'Lo, suga' pie," says the elbow-pusher, and for once, to her own surprise as much as anyone else's, gets a tumble.

" 'Lo, Eglantine," Eddie's bodyguard remarks in passing, "So you moved?"

They stop in front of the house on the other side of the tunnel. "Now here's what," says Eddie. "We're going to be stopped halfway up these stairs in here by a big orangoutang. Your job is to clean him, tap him if you want, I don't care. I'm going into a room up there, you're going to wait for me at the door. You're here to see that I get out of that room again. We may have to carry the body of a friend of mine down to the street between us. I don't know. It depends on whether it's in the house or not. Got it?"

"Got it."

"Light up. Keep your torch trained over my shoulder."

A big, lowering figure looms over them, blocking the narrow stairs, ape-like arms and legs spread-eagle in a gesture of malignant embrace, receding skull, teeth showing, flashing steel in hand. Lee jams Eddie roughly to one side and shoves up past him. "Drop that, boy!" Lee says with slurring indifference, but then he doesn't wait to see if the order's carried out or not. After all, a weapon was raised to two white men. He fires three times, from two feet away and considerably below the obstacle, hits where he aimed to. The bullets shatter both knee-caps and the elbow-joint of the arm holding the knife.

"Be a cripple for life now," he remarks with quiet satisfaction. "I'll put him out of his pain." So he crashes the butt of the gun down on the skull of the writhing colossus, in a long arc like the overhand pitch of a baseball. The noise of the shots goes booming up the narrow stairwell to the roof, to mushroom out there in a vast rolling echo.

"Come on, hurry up," says Eddie, "before they have a chance to do away with—"

He lopes on up past the prostrate form, Lee at his heels. "Stand there.

Better reload while you're waiting. If I call your name for Pete's sake don't count ten before you come in to me!''

There's a scurrying back and forth and an excited but subdued jabbering going on on the other side of the door. Eddie swings it wide and crashes it closed behind him, leaving Lee on the outside. They all stand rooted to the spot when they see him. The papaloi is there and about six others, not so many as on the night of Eddie's initiation. Probably the rest are waiting outside the city somewhere, in some secret spot, wherever the actual burial, or burning, or—feasting—is to take place.

Papa Benjamin has no juju mask on this time, no animal-pelt. There are no gourds in the room, no drum, no transfixed figures ranged against the wall. They were about to move on elsewhere, he just got here in time. Maybe they were waiting for the dark of the moon. The ordinary kitchen chair on which the papaloi was to be carried on their shoulders stands prepared, padded with rags. A row of baskets covered with sacking are ranged along the back wall.

"Where is the body of John Staats?" raps out Eddie. "You claimed it, took it away from the morgue this morning." His eyes are on those baskets, on the bleared razor he catches sight of lying on the floor near them.

"Better far," cackles the old man, "that you had followed him. The mark of doom is on yo' even now—" A growl goes up all around.

"Lee," grates Eddie, "in here!" Lee stands next to him, gun in hand. "Cover me while I take a look around."

"All of you over in that corner there," growls Lee, and kicks viciously at one who is too slow in moving. They huddle there, cower there, glaring, spitting like a band of apes. Eddie makes straight for those baskets, whips the covering off the first one. Charcoal. The next. Coffee-beans. The next. Rice. And so on.

Just small baskets that Negro women balance on their heads to sell at the market-place. He looks at Papa Benjamin, takes out the wad of money he's brought with him. "Where've you got him? Where's he buried? Take us there, show us where it is."

Not a sound, just burning, shriveling hate in waves that you can almost feel. He looks at that razor-blade lying there, bleared, not bloody, just matted, dulled, with shreds and threads of something clinging to it. Kicks it away with his foot. "Not here, I guess," he mutters to Lee and moves toward the door.

"What do we do now, boss?" his henchman wants to know.

"Get the hell out of here I guess, where we can breathe some air," Eddie says, and moves on out to the stairs.

Lee is the sort of man who will get what he can out of any situation, no matter what it is. Before he follows Eddie out, he goes over to one of the baskets, stuffs an orange in each coat-pocket, and then prods and pries among them to select a particularly nice one for eating on the spot. There's a thud and the orange goes rolling across the floor like a volley-ball. "Mr. Bloch!" he shouts hoarsely, "I've found—him!" And he looks pretty sick.

A deep breath goes up from the corner where the Negroes are. Eddie just stands and stares, and leans back weakly for a minute against the door-post. From out the layers of oranges in the basket, the five fingers of a hand thrust upward, a hand that ends abruptly, cleanly at the wrist.

"His signet," says Eddie weakly, "there on the little finger—I know it."

"Say the word! Should I shoot?" Lee wants to know.

Eddie shakes his head. "They didn't—he committed suicide. Let's do what we have to—and get out of here!"

Lee turns over one basket after the other. The stuff in them spills and sifts and rolls out upon the floor. But in each there's something else. Bloodless, pallid as fish-flesh. That razor, those shreds clinging to it, Eddie knows now what it was used for. They take one basket, they line it with a verminous blanket from the bed. Then with their bare hands they fill it with what they have found, and close the ends of the blanket over the top of it, and carry it between them out of the room and down the pitch-black stairs, Lee going down backwards with his gun in one hand to cover them from the rear. Lee's swearing like a fiend. Eddie's trying not to think what the purpose, the destination of all those baskets was. The watchdog is still out on the stairs, with a concussion.

Back through the lane they struggle and finally put their burden down in the before-dawn stillness of Congo Square. Eddie goes up against a wall and is heartily sick. Then he comes back again and says: "The head—did you notice—?"

"No, we didn't," Lee answers. "Stay here, I'll go back for it. I'm armed. I could stand anything now, after what I just been through."

Lee's gone about five minutes. When he comes back, he's in his shirt, coatless. His coat's rolled up under one arm in a bulky bulge. He bends over the basket, lifts the blanket, replaces it again, and when he straightens up, the bulge in his folded coat is gone. Then he throws the coat away, kicks it away on the ground. "Hidden away in a cupboard," he mutters. "Had to shoot one of 'em through the palm of the hand before they'd come clean. What were they up to?"

"Practice cannibalism maybe, I don't know. I'd rather not think."

"I brought your money back. It didn't seem to square you with them." Eddie shoves it back at him. "Pay for your suit and your time."

"Aren't you going to tip off the squareheads?"

"I told you he jumped in the lake. I have a copy of the examiner's report in my pocket."

"I know, but isn't there some ordinance against dissecting a body without permission?"

"I can't afford to get mixed up with them, Lee. It would kill my career. We've got what we went there for. Now just forget everything you saw."

The hearse from the crematorium contacts them there in Congo Square. The covered basket's taken on, and what's left of Johnny Staats heads away for a better finish than was coming to him.

"G'night, boss," says Lee. "Anytime you need any other little thing—"

"No," says Eddie. "I'm getting out of New Orleans." His hand is like ice when they shake.

He does. He hands Graham back his contract, and a split week later he's playing New York's newest, in the frantic Fifties. With a white valet. The Chant, of course, is still featured. He has to; it's his chief asset, his biggest draw. It introduces him and signs him off, and in between Judy always dances it for a high-spot. But he can't get rid of that backache that started the night he first played it. First he goes and tries having his back baked for a couple of hours a day under a violet-ray lamp. No improvement.

Then he has himself examined by the biggest specialist in New York. "Nothing there," says the big shot. "Absolutely nothing the matter with you: liver, kidneys, blood—everything perfect. It must be all in your own mind."

"You're losing weight, Eddie," Judy says, "you look bad, darling." His bathroom scales tell him the same thing. Down five pounds a week, sometimes seven, never up an ounce. More experts. X-rays this time, blood analysis, gland treatments, everything from soup to nuts. Nothing doing. And the dull ache, the lassitude, spreads slowly, first to one arm, then to the other.

He takes specimens of everything he eats, not just one day, but every day for weeks, and has them chemically analyzed. Nothing. And he doesn't have to be told that anyway. He knows that even in New Orleans, way back in the beginning, nothing was ever put into his food. Judy ate from the same tray, drank from the same coffeepot he did. Nightly she dances herself into a lather, and yet she's the picture of health.

So that leaves nothing but his mind, just as they all say. "But I don't believe it!" he tells himself. "I don't believe that just sticking pins into a wax doll can hurt me—me or anyone!"

So it isn't his mind at all, but some other mind back there in New Orleans, some other mind *thinking*, wishing, ordering him dead, night and day.

"But it can't be done!" says Eddie. "There's no such thing!"

And yet it's being done; it's happening right under his own eyes. Which leaves only one answer. If going three thousand miles away on dry land didn't help, then going three thousand miles away across the ocean will do the trick. So London next, and the Kit-Kat Club. Down, down, down go the bathroom scales, a little bit each week. The pains spread downward into his thighs. His ribs start showing up here and there. He's dying on his feet. He finds it more comfortable now to walk with a stick—not to be swanky, not to be English—to rest as he goes along. His shoulders ache each night just from waving that lightweight baton at his crew. He has a music-stand build for himself to lean on, keeps it in front of his body, out of sight of the audience while he's conducting, and droops over it. Sometimes he finishes up a number with his head lower than his shoulders, as though he had a rubber spine.

Finally he goes to Reynolds, famous the world over, the biggest alienist in England. "I want to know whether I'm sane or insane." He's under observation for weeks, months; they put him through every known test, and plenty of unknown ones, mental, physical, metabolic. They flash lights in front of his face and watch the pupils of his eyes; they contract to pinheads. They touch the back of his throat with sandpaper; he nearly chokes. They strap him to a chair that goes around and around and does somersaults at so many revolutions per minute, then ask him to walk across the room; he staggers.

Reynolds takes plenty of pounds, hands him a report thick as a telephone-book, sums it up for him. "You are as normal, Mr. Bloch, as anyone I have ever handled. You're so well-balanced you haven't even got the extra little touch of imagination most actors and musicians have." So it's not his own mind, it's coming from the outside, is it?

The whole thing from beginning to end has taken eighteen months. Trying to out-distance death, with death gaining on him slowly but surely all the time. He's emaciated. There's only one thing left to do now, while he's still able to crawl aboard a ship—that's to get back to where the whole thing started. New York, London, Paris, haven't been able to save him. His only salvation, now, lies in the hands of a decrepit colored man skulking in the Vieux Carré of New Orleans.

He drags himself there, to that same half-ruined house, without a bodyguard, not caring now whether they kill him or not, almost wishing they would and get it over with. But that would be too easy an out, it seems. The gorilla that Lee crippled that night shuffles out to him between two sticks, recognizes him, breathes undying hate into his face, but doesn't lift a finger to harm him. The spirits are doing the job better than he could ever hope to. Their mark is on this man, woe betide anyone who comes between them and their hellish satisfaction. Eddie Bloch totters up the stairs unopposed, his back as safe from a knife as if he wore steel armor. Behind him the Negro sprawls upon the stairs to lubricate his long-awaited hour of satisfaction with rum—and oblivion.

He finds the old man alone there in the room. The Stone Age and the Twentieth Century face each other, and the Stone Age has won out.

"Take it off me," says Eddie brokenly. "Give me my life back—I'll do anything, anything you say!"

"What has been done cannot be undone. Do you think the spirits of the earth and of the air, of fire and water, know the meaning of forgiveness?"

"Intercede for me, then. You brought it about. Here's money, I'll give you twice as much, all I earn, all I ever hope to earn—"

"You have desecrated the obiah. Death has been on you from that night. All over the world and in the air above the earth you have mocked the spirits with the chant that summons them. Nightly your wife dances it. The only reason she has not shared your doom is because she does not know the meaning of what she does. You do. You were here among us."

Eddie goes down on his knees, scrapes along the floor after the old man, tries to tug at the garments he wears. "Kill me right now, then, and be done with it. I can't stand any more—'' He bought the gun only that day, was going to do it himself at first, but found he couldn't. A minute ago he pleaded for his life, now he's pleading for death. "It's loaded, all you have to do is shoot. Look! I'll close my eyes—I'll write a note and sign it, that I did it myself—''

He tries to thrust it into the witch-doctor's hand, tries to close the bony, shriveled fingers around it, tries to point it at himself. The old man throws it down, away from him. Cackles gleefully, "Death will come, but differently—slowly, oh, so slowly!''

Eddie just lies there flat on his face, sobbing dryly. The old man spits, kicks at him weakly. He pulls himself up somehow, stumbles toward the door. He isn't even strong enough to get it open at the first try. It's that little thing that brings it on. Something touches his foot, he looks, stoops for the gun, turns. Thought is quick but the old man's mind is even quicker. Almost before the thought is there, the old man knows what's coming. In a flash, scuttling like a crab, he has shifted around to the other side of the bed, to put something between them. Instantly the situation's reversed, the fear has left Eddie and is on the old man now. He's lost the aggressive. For a minute only, but that minute is all Eddie needs. His mind beams out like a diamond, like a lighthouse through a fog. The gun roars, jolting his weakened body down to his shoes. The old man falls flat across the bed, his head too far over, dangling down over the side of it like an over-ripe pear. The bed-frame sways gently with his weight for a minute, and then it's over. . . .

Eddie stands there, still off-balance from the kick-back. So it was as easy as all that! Where's all his magic now? Strength, will-power flood back through him as if a faucet was suddenly turned on. The little smoke there can't get out of the sealed-up room, it hangs there in thin layers. Suddenly he's shaking his fist at the dead thing on the bed. "I'm gonna live now! I'm gonna live, see?'' He gets the door open, sways with it for a minute. Then he's feeling his way down the stairs, past the unconscious watchdog, mumbling it over and over but low, "Gonna live now, gonna live!''

The Commissioner mops his face as if he were in the steam room of a Turkish bath. He exhales like an oxygen tank. "Judas, Joseph and Mary, Mr. Bloch, what a story! Wish I hadn't asked you; I won't sleep tonight.'' Even after the accused has been led from the room, it takes him some time to get over it. The upper right-hand drawer of his desk helps some—just two fingers. So does opening the windows and letting in a lot of sunshine.

Finally he picks up the phone and gets down to business. "Who've you got out there that's absolutely without a nerve in his body? I mean a guy with so little feeling he could sit on a hatpin and turn it into a paper-clip. Oh yeah, that Cajun, Desjardins, I know him. He's the one goes around striking parlor-matches off the soles of stiffs. Well, send him in here."

"No, stay outside," wheezes Papa Benjamin through the partly-open door to his envoy. "I'se communin' with the obiah and yo' unclean, been drunk all last night and today. Deliver the summons. Reach yo' hand in to me, once fo' every token, yo' knows how many to take."

The crippled Negro thrusts his huge paw through the aperture, and from behind the door the papaloi places a severed chicken-claw in his upturned palm. A claw bound with a red rag. The messenger disposes of it about his tattered clothing, thrusts his hand in for another. Twenty times the act is repeated, then he lets his arm hang stiffly at his side. The door starts closing slowly. "Papoloi," whines the figure on the outside of it, "why you hide yo' face from me, is the spirits angry?"

There's a flicker of suspicion in his yellow eyeballs in the dimness, however. Instantly the opening of the door widens. Papa Benjamin's familiar wrinkled face thrust out at him, malignant eyes crackling like fuses. "Go!" shrills the old man, " 'liver my summons. Is you want me to bring a spirit down on you?" The messenger totters back. The door slams.

The sun goes down and it's night-time in New Orleans. The moon rises, midnight chimes from St. Louis Cathedral, and hardly has the last note died away than a gruesome swampland whistle sounds outside the deathly still house. A fat Negress, basket on arm, comes trudging up the stairs a moment later, opens the door, goes in to the papaloi, closes it again, traces an invisible mark on it with her forefinger and kisses it. Then she turns and her eyes widen with surprise. Papa Benjamin is in bed, covered up to the neck with filthy rags. The familiar candles are all lit, the bowl for the blood, the sacrificial knife, the magic powders, all the paraphernalia of the ritual are laid out in readiness, but they are ranged about the bed instead of at the opposite end of the room as usual.

The old man's head, however, is held high above the encumbering rags, his beady eyes gaze back at her unflinchingly, the familiar semicricle of white wool rings his crown, his ceremonial mask is at his side. "I am a little tired, my daughter,'' he tells her. His eyes stray to the tiny wax image of Eddie Bloch under the candles, hairy with pins, and hers follow them. ''A doomed one, nearing his end, came here last night thinking I could be killed like other men. He shot a bullet from a gun at me. I blew my breath at it, it stopped in the air, turned around, and went back in the gun again. But it tired me to blow so hard, strained my voice a little.''

A revengeful gleam lights up the woman's broad face. ''And he'll die soon, papaloi?''

''Soon,'' cackles the weazened figure in the bed. The woman gnashes her teeth and hugs herself delightedly. She opens the top of her basket and allows a black hen to escape and flutter about the room.

When all twenty have assembled, men and women, old and young, the drum and the gourds begin to beat, the low wailing starts, the orgy gets under way. Slowly they dance around the three sides of the bed at first, then faster, faster, lashing themselves to a frenzy, tearing at their own and each other's clothes, drawing blood with knives and fingernails, eyes rolling in an ecstasy that colder races cannot know. The sacrifices, feathered and furred, that have been fastened to the two lower posts of the bed, squawk and flutter and fly vertically up and down in a barnyard panic. There is a small monkey among them tonight, clawing, biting, hiding his face in his hands like a frightened child. A bearded Negro, nude torso glistening like patent leather, seizes one of the frantic fowls, yanks it loose from its moorings, and holds it out toward the witch-doctor with both hands. ''We'se thirsty, papaloi, we'se thirsty fo' the blood of ou' enemies.''

The others take up the cry. ''We'se hung'y, papaloi, fo' the bones of ou' enemies!''

Papa Benjamin nods his head in time to the rhythm.

''Sac'fice, papaloi, sac'fice!''

Papa Benjamin doesn't seem to hear them.

Then back go the rags in a gray wave and out comes the arm at last. Not the gnarled brown toothpick arm of Papa Benjamin, but a bulging arm thick as a piano-leg, cuffed in serge, white at the wrist, ending in a regulation police-revolver with the clip off. The erstwhile witch-doctor's on his feet at a bound, standing erect atop the bed, back to the wall, slowly fanning his score of human devils with the mouth of his gun, left to right, then right to left again, evenly, unhurriedly. The resonant bellow of a bull comes from his weazened slit of a mouth instead of papaloi's cracked falsetto. "Back against that wall there, all of you! Throw down them knives and jiggers!"

But they're slow to react; the swift drop from ecstasy to stupefaction can't register right away. None of them are overbright anyway or they wouldn't be here. Mouths hang open, the wailing stops, the drums and gourds fall still, but they're still packed close about this sudden changeling in their midst, with the familiar shriveled face of Papa Benjamin and the thick-set body, business-suit, of a white man—too close for comfort. Blood-lust and religious mania don't know fear of a gun. It takes a cool head for that, and the only cool head in the room is the withered cocoanut atop the broad shoulders behind that gun. So he shoots twice, and a woman at one end of the semicircle, the drum-beater, and a man at the other end, the one still holding the sacrificial fowl, drop in their tracks with a double moan. Those in the middle slowly draw back step by step across the room, all eyes on the figure reared up on the bed. An instant's carelessness, the wavering of an eye, and they'll be in on him in a body. He reaches up with his free hand and rips the dead witch-doctor's features from his face, to breathe better, see better. They dissolve into a crumpled rag before the blacks' terrified eyes, like a stocking-cap coming off some-one's head—a mixture of paraffin and fibre, called moulage—a death-mask taken from the corpse's own face, reproducing even the fine lines of the skin and its natural color. Moulage. So the Twentieth Century has won out after all. And behind them is the grinning, slightly-perspiring, lantern-jawed face of Detective Jacques Desjardins, who doesn't believe in spirits unless they're under a neat little label. And outside the house sounds the twenty-first whistle of the evening, but not a swampland sound this time; a long, cold, keen blast to bring figures out of the shadows and doorways that have waited there patiently all night.

Then the door bursts inward and the police are in the room. The prisoners, two of them dangerously wounded, are pushed and carried downstairs to join the crippled doorguard, who had been in custody for the past hour, and singlefile, tied together with ropes, they make their way through the long tortuous alley out into Congo Place.

In the early hours of that same morning, just a little more than twenty-four hours after Eddie Bloch first staggered into Police Headquarters with his strange story, the whole thing is cooked, washed and bottled. The Commissioner sits in his office listening attentively to Desjardins. And spread out on his desk as strange an array of amulets, wax images, bunches of feathers, balsam leaves, *ouangas* (charms of nail parings, hair clippings, dried blood, powdered roots), green mildewed coins dug up from coffins in graveyards, as that room has ever seen before. All this is State's Evidence, now, to be carefully labeled and docketed for the use of the prosecuting attorney when the proper time comes. "And this," explains Desjardins, indicating a small dusty bottle, "is methylene blue, the chemist tells me. It's the only modern thing we got out of the place, found it lying forgotten with a lot of rubbish in a corner that looked like it hadn't been disturbed for years. What it was doing there or what they wanted with it I don't—"

"Wait a minute," interrupts the Commissioner eagerly. "That fits in with something poor Bloch told me last night. He noticed a bluish color under his fingernails and a yellowness to his eyeballs, but *only* after he'd been initiated that first night. This stuff probably had something to do with it, an injection of it must have been given him that night in some way without his knowing it. Don't you get the idea? It floored him just the way they wanted it to. He mistook the signs of it for a give-away that he had colored blood. It was the opening wedge. It broke down his disbelief, started his mental resistance to crumbling. That was all they needed, just to get a foothold in his mind. Mental suggestion did the rest, has been doing it ever since. If you ask me, they pulled the same stunt on Staats originally. I don't believe he had colored blood any more than Bloch has. And as a matter of fact the theory that it shows up in that way generations later is all the bunk anyway, they tell me."

"Well," says Dij, looking at his own grimy nails, "if you're just going to judge by appearances that way, I'm full-blooded Zulu."

His overlord just looks at him, and if he didn't have such a poker-face, one might be tempted to read admiration or at least approval into the look. "Must have been a pretty tight spot for a minute with all of them around while you put on your act!"

"Nah, I didn't mind," answers Dij. "The only thing that bothered me was the smell."

Eddie Bloch, the murder charge against him quashed two months ago, and the population of the State Penitentiary increased only this past week by the admission of twenty-three ex-voodoo-worshippers for terms varying from two to ten years, steps up on the platform at Maxim's for a return engagement. Eddie's pale and washed-out looking, but climbing slowly back up through the hundred-and-twenties again to his former weight. The ovation he gets ought to do anyone's heart good, the way they clap and stamp and stand up and cheer. And at that, his name was kept out of the recently-concluded trial. Desjardins and his mates did all the states-witnessing necessary.

The theme he comes in on now is something sweet and harmless. Then a waiter comes up and hands him a request. Eddie shakes his head. "No, not in our repertoire any more." He goes on leading. Another request comes, and another. Suddenly someone shouts it out at him, and in a second the whole place has taken up the cry. "The Voodoo Chant! Give us the Voodoo Chant!"

His face gets whiter than it is already, but he turns and tries to smile at them and shake his head. They won't quit, the music can't be heard, and he has to tap a lay-off. From all over the place, like a cheering-section at a football game, "We want the Voodoo Chant! We want—!"

Judy's at his side. "What's the matter with 'em anyway?" he asks. "Don't they know what that thing's done to me?"

"Play it, Eddie, don't be foolish," she urges, "Now's the time, break the spell once and for all, prove to yourself that it can't hurt you. If you don't do it now, you'll never get over the idea. It'll stay with you all your life. Go ahead. I'll dance it just like I am."

"Okay," he says.

He taps. It's been quite some time, but he can rely on his outfit. Slow and low like thunder far away, coming nearer. *Boom-putta-putta-boom!* Judy whirls out behind him, lets out the first preliminary screech, *Eeyaeeya!*

She hears a commotion in back of her and stops as suddenly as she began. Eddie Bloch's fallen flat on his face and doesn't move again after that.

They all know, somehow. There's an inertness, a finality about it that tells them. The dancers wait a minute, mill about, then melt away in a hush. Judy Jarvis doesn't scream, doesn't cry, just stands there staring, wondering. That last thought—did it come from inside his own mind just now—or outside? Was it two months on its way, from the other side of the grave, looking for him, looking for him, until it found him tonight when he played the Chant once more and laid his mind open to Africa? No policeman, no detective, no doctor, no scientist, will ever be able to tell her. Did it come from inside or from outside? All she says is: "Stand close to me, boys—real close to me, I'm afraid of the dark."

Creator of Travis McGee, and author of over sixty novels,
John D. MacDonald *(1916–   ) is most highly regarded as a
mystery writer. But he has also written three science fiction
novels, including that delightful fantastic mystery,* The Girl, the
Gold Watch, and Everything. *Recently, a collection of his
shorter fantastic fiction,* Other Times, Other Worlds, *was
released, and perhaps the best of them is "The Legend of Joe
Lee," a touching portrayal of social crimes and generational
conflict.*

THE LEGEND OF JOE LEE

John D. MacDonald

"Tonight," Sergeant Lazeer said, "we get him for sure."

We were in a dank office in the Afaloosa County Courthouse in the flat
wetlands of south central Florida. I had come over from Lauderdale on the
half chance of a human interest story that would tie in with the series we
were doing on the teen-age war against the square world of the adult.

He called me over to the table where he had the county map spread out.
The two other troopers moved in beside me.

"It's a full moon night and he'll be out for sure," Lazeer said, "and
what we're fixing to do is bottle him on just the right stretch, where he got
no way off it, no old back-country roads he knows like the shape of his
own fist. And here we got it." He put brackets at either end of a string-
straight road.

Trooper McCullum said softly, "That there, Mister, is a eighteen mile
straight, and we cruised it slow, and you turn off it, you're in the deep
ditch and the black mud and the 'gator water."

Lazeer said, "We stake out both ends, hide back good with lights out.
We got radio contact, so when he comes, whistling in either end, we got
him bottled."

He looked up at me as though expecting an opinion, and I said, "I don't know a thing about road blocks, Sergeant, but it looks as if you could trap him."

"You ride with me, Mister, and we'll get you a story."

"There's one thing you haven't explained, Sergeant. You said you know who the boy is. Why don't you just pick him up at home?"

The other trooper, Frank Gaiders said, "Because that fool kid ain't been home since he started this crazy business five, six months ago. His name is Joe Lee Cuddard, from over to Lasco City. His folks don't know where he is, and don't much care, him and that Farris girl he was running with, so we figure the pair of them is off in the piney woods someplace, holed up in some abandoned shack, coming out at night for kicks, making fools of us."

"Up till now, boy," Lazeer said. "Up till tonight. Tonight is the end."

"But when you've met up with him on the highway," I asked, "you haven't been able to catch him?"

The three big, weathered men looked at each other with slow, sad amusement, and McCullum sighed, "I come the closest. The way these cars are beefed up as interceptors, they can do a dead honest hundred and twenty. I saw him across the flats, booming to where the two road forks come together up ahead, so I floored it and I was flat out when the roads joined, and not over fifty yards behind him. In two minutes he had me by a mile, and in four minutes it was near two, and then he was gone. That comes to a hundred and fifty, my guess."

I showed my astonishment. "What the hell does he drive?"

Lazeer opened the table drawer and fumbled around in it and pulled out a tattered copy of a hot-rodder magazine. He opened it to a page where readers had sent in pictures of their cars. It didn't look like anything I had ever seen. Most of it seemed to be bare frame, with a big chromed engine. There was a teardrop-shaped passenger compartment mounted between the big rear wheels, bigger than the front wheels, and there was a tail-fin arrangement that swept up and out and then curved back so that the high rear ends of the fins almost met.

"That engine," Frank Gaiders said, "it's a '61 Pontiac, the big one he bought wrecked and fixed up, with blowers and special cams and every damn thing. Put the rest of it together himself. You can see in the letter there, he calls it a C.M. Special. C.M. is for Clarissa May, that Farris girl he took off with. I saw that thing just one time, oh, seven, eight months ago, right after he got it all finished. We got this magazine from his daddy. I saw it at the Amoco gas in Lasco City. You could near give it a ticket standing still. 'Strawberry flake paint' it says in the letter. Damnedest thing, bright strawberry with little like gold flakes in it, then covered with maybe seventeen coats of lacquer, all rubbed down so you look down into that paint like it was six inches deep. Headlights all the hell over the front of it and big taillights all over the back, and shiny pipes sticking out. Near two year he worked on it. Big racing flats like the drag-strip kids use over to the airport.''

I looked at the coarse-screen picture of the boy standing beside the car, hands on his hips, looking very young, very ordinary, slightly self-conscious.

"It wouldn't spoil anything for you, would it," I asked, "if I went and talked to his people, just for background?"

"Long as you say nothing about what we're fixing to do," Lazeer said. "Just be back by eight-thirty this evening."

Lasco City was a big brave name for a hamlet of about five hundred. They told me at the sundries store to take the west road and the Cuddard place was a half mile on the left, name on the mailbox. It was a shacky place, chickens in the dusty yard, fence sagging. Leo Cuddard was home from work and I found him out in back, unloading cinder block from an ancient pickup. He was stripped to the waist, a lean, sallow man who looked undernourished and exhausted. But the muscles in his spare back writhed and knotted when he lifted the blocks. He had pale hair and pale eyes and a narrow mouth. He would not look directly at me. He grunted and kept on working as I introduced myself and stated my business.

Finally he straightened and wiped his forehead with his narrow arm. When those pale eyes stared at me, for some reason it made me remember the grisly reputation Florida troops acquired in the Civil War. Tireless, deadly, merciless.

"That boy warn't no help to me, Mister, but he warn't no trouble neither. The onliest thing on his mind was that car. I didn't hold with it, but I didn't put down no foot. He fixed up that old shed there to work in, and he needed something, he went out and earned up the money to buy it. They was a crowd of them around most times, helpin' him, boys workin' and gals watchin'. Them tight-pants girls. Have radios on batteries set around so as they could twisty dance while them boys hammered that metal out. When I worked around and overheared 'em, I swear I couldn't make out more'n one word from seven. What he done was take that car to some national show, for prizes and such. But one day he just took off, like they do nowadays.''

"Do you hear from him at all?''

He grinned. "I don't hear *from* him, but I sure God hear *about* him.''

"How about brothers and sisters?''

"They's just one sister, older, up to Waycross, Georgia, married to an electrician, and me and his stepmother.''

As if on cue, a girl came out onto the small back porch. She couldn't have been more than eighteen. Advanced pregnancy bulged the front of her cotton dress. Her voice was a shrill, penetrating whine. "Leo? Leo, honey, that can opener thing just now busted clean off the wall.''

"Mind if I take a look at that shed?''

"You help yourself, Mister.''

The shed was astonishingly neat. The boy had rigged up droplights. There was a pale blue pegboard wall hung with shining tools. On closer inspection I could see that rust was beginning to fleck the tools. On the workbench were technical journals and hot-rodder magazines. I looked at the improvised engine hoist, at the neat shelves of paint and lubricant.

The Farris place was nearer the center of the village. Some of them were having their evening meal. There were six adults as near as I could judge, and perhaps a dozen children from toddlers on up to tall, lanky boys. Clarissa May's mother came out onto the front porch to talk to me, explaining that her husband drove an interstate truck from the cooperative and he was away for the next few days. Mrs. Farris was grossly fat, but with delicate features, an indication of the beauty she must have once had. The rocking chair creaked under her weight and she fanned herself with a newspaper.

"I can tell you, it like to broke our hearts the way Clarissa May done us. If'n I told LeRoy once, I told him a thousand times, no good would ever come of her messin' with that Cuddard boy. His daddy is trashy. Ever so often they take him in for drunk and put him on the county road gang sixty or ninety days, and that Stubbins child he married, she's next door to feeble-witted. But children get to a certain size and know everything and turn their backs on you like an enemy. You write this up nice and in it put the message her momma and daddy want her home bad, and maybe she'll see it and come on in. You know what the Good Book says about sharper'n a sarpent's tooth. I pray to the good Lord they had the sense to drive that fool car up to Georgia and get married up at least. Him nineteen and her seventeen. The young ones are going clean out of hand these times. One night racing through this county the way they do, showing off, that Cuddard boy is going to kill hisself and my child, too."

"Was she hard to control in other ways, Mrs Farris?"

"No sir, she was neat and good and pretty and quiet, and she had the good marks. It was just about Joe Lee Cuddard she turned mulish. I think I would have let LeRoy whale that out of her if it hadn't been for her trouble.

"You're easier on a young one when there's no way of knowing how long she could be with you. Doc Mathis, he had us taking her over to the Miami clinic. Sometimes they kept her and sometimes they didn't, and she'd get behind in her school and then catch up fast. Many times we taken her over there. She's got the sick blood and it takes her poorly. She should be right here, where's help to care for her in the bad spells. It was October last year, we were over to the church bingo, LeRoy and me, and Clarissa May been resting up in her bed a few days, and that wild boy come in and taking her off in that snorty car, the little ones couldn't stop him. When I think of her out there . . . poorly and all . . ."

At a little after nine we were in position. I was with Sergeant Lazeer at the west end of that eighteen-mile stretch of State Road 21. The patrol car was backed into a narrow dirt road, lights out. Gaiders and McCullum were similarly situated at the east end of the trap. We were smeared with insect repellent, and we had used spray on the backs of each other's shirts where the mosquitoes were biting through the thin fabric.

Lazeer had repeated his instructions over the radio, and we composed ourselves to wait. "Not much travel on this road this time of year," Lazeer said. "But some tourists come through at the wrong time, they could mess this up. We just got to hope that don't happen."

"Can you block the road with just one car at each end?"

"If he comes through from the other end, I move up quick and put it crosswise where he can't get past, and Frank has a place like that at the other end. Crosswise with the lights and the dome blinker on, but we both are going to stand clear because maybe he can stop it and maybe he can't. But whichever way he comes, we got to have the free car run close herd so he can't get time to turn around when he sees he's bottled."

Lazeer turned out to be a lot more talkative than I had anticipated. He had been in law enforcement for twenty years and had some violent stories. I sensed he was feeding them to me, waiting for me to suggest I write a book about him. From time to time we would get out of the car and move around a little.

"Sergeant, you're pretty sure you've picked the right time and place?"

"He runs on the nights the moon is big. Three or four nights out of the month. He doesn't run the main highways, just these back-country roads—the long straight paved stretches where he can really wind that thing up. Lord God, he goes through towns like a rocket. From reports we got, he runs the whole night through, and this is one way he comes, one way or the other, maybe two, three times before moonset. We got to get him. He's got folks laughing at us."

I sat in the car half-listening to Lazeer tell a tale of blood and horror. I could hear choruses of swamp toads mingling with the whine of insects close to my ears, looking for a biting place. A couple of times I had heard the bass throb of a 'gator.

Suddenly Lazeer stopped and I sensed his tenseness. He leaned forward, head cocked. And then, mingled with the wet country shrilling, and then overriding it, I heard the oncoming high-pitched snarl of high combustion.

"Hear it once and you don't forget it," Lazeer said, and unhooked the mike from the dash and got through to McCullum and Gaiders. "He's coming through this end, boys. Get yourself set."

He hung up and in the next instant the C.M. Special went by. It was a resonant howl that stirred echoes inside the inner ear. It was a tearing, bursting rush of wind that rattled fronds and turned leaves over. It was a dark shape in moonlight, slamming by, the howl diminishing as the wind of passage died.

Lazeer plunged the patrol car out onto the road in a screeching turn, and as we straightened out, gathering speed, he yelled to me, "Damn fool runs without lights when the moon is bright enough."

As had been planned, we ran without lights, too, to keep Joe Lee from smelling the trap until it was too late. I tightened my seat belt and peered at the moonlit road. Lazeer had estimated we could make it to the far end in ten minutes or a little less. The world was like a photographic negative—white world and black trees and brush, and no shades of grey. As we came quickly up to speed, the heavy sedan began to feel strangely light. It toe-danced, tender and capricious, the wind roar louder than the engine sound. I kept wondering what would happen if Joe Lee stopped dead up there in darkness. I kept staring ahead for the murderous bulk of his vehicle.

Soon I could see the distant red wink of the other sedan, and then the bright cone where the headlights shone off the shoulder into the heavy brush. When my eyes adjusted to that brightness, I could no longer see the road. We came down on them with dreadful speed. Lazeer suddenly snapped our lights on, touched the siren. We were going to see Joe Lee trying to back and turn around on the narrow paved road, and we were going to block him and end the night games.

We saw nothing. Lazeer pumped the brakes. He cursed. We came to a stop ten feet from the side of the other patrol car. McCullum and Gaiders came out of the shadows. Lazeer and I undid our seat belts and got out of the car.

"We didn't see nothing and we didn't hear a thing," Frank Gaiders said.

Lazeer summed it up. "OK, then. I was running without lights, too. Maybe the first glimpse he got of your flasher, he cramps it over onto the left shoulder, tucks it over as far as he dares. I could go by without seeing him. He backs around and goes back the way he came, laughing hisself sick. There's the second chance he tried that and took it too far, and he's wedged in a ditch. Then there's the third chance he lost it. He could have dropped a wheel off onto the shoulder and tripped hisself and gone flying three hundred feet into the swamp. So what we do, we go back there slow. I'll go first and keep my spotlight on the right, and you keep yours on the left. Look for that car and for places where he could have busted through."

At the speed Lazeer drove, it took over a half hour to traverse the eighteen-mile stretch. He pulled off at the road where we had waited. He seemed very depressed, yet at the same time amused.

They talked, then he drove me to the courthouse where my car was parked. He said, "We'll work out something tighter and I'll give you a call. You might as well be in at the end."

I drove sedately back to Lauderdale.

Several days later, just before noon on a bright Sunday, Lazeer phoned me at my apartment and said, "You want to be in on the finish of this thing, you better do some hustling and leave right now."

"You've got him?"

"In a manner of speaking." He sounded sad and wry. "He dumped that machine into a canal off Route 27 about twelve miles south of Okeelanta. The wrecker'll be winching it out anytime now. The diver says he and the gal are still in it. It's been on the radio news. Diver read the tag, and it's his. Last year's. He didn't trouble hisself getting a new one."

I wasted no time driving to the scene. I certainly had no trouble identifying it. There were at least a hundred cars pulled off on both sides of the highway. A traffic-control officer tried to wave me on by, but when I showed him my press card and told him Lazeer had phoned me, he had me turn in and park beside a patrol car near the center of activity.

I spotted Lazeer on the canal bank and went over to him. A big man in face mask, swim fins and air tank was preparing to go down with the wrecker hook.

Lazeer greeted me and said, "It pulled loose the first time, so he's going to try to get it around the rear axle this time. It's in twenty feet of water, right side up, in the black mud."

"Did he lose control?"

"Hard to say. What happened, early this morning a fellow was goofing around in a little airplane, flying low, parallel to the canal, the water like a mirror, and he seen something down in there so he came around and looked again, then he found a way to mark the spot, opposite those three trees away over there, so he came into his home field and phoned it in, and we had that diver down by nine this morning. I got here about ten."

"I guess this isn't the way you wanted it to end, Sergeant."

"It sure God isn't. It was a contest between him and me, and I wanted to get him my own way. But I guess it's a good thing he's off the night roads."

I looked around. The red and white wrecker was positioned and braced. Ambulance attendants were leaning against their vehicle, smoking and chatting. Sunday traffic slowed and was waved on by.

"I guess you could say his team showed up," Lazeer said.

Only then did I realize the strangeness of most of the waiting vehicles. The cars were from a half-dozen counties, according to the tag numbers. There were many big, gaudy, curious monsters not unlike the C.M. Special in basic layout, but quite different in design. They seemed like a visitation of Martian beasts. There were dirty fenderless sedans from the thirties with modern power plants under the hoods, and big rude racing numbers painted on the side doors. There were other cars which looked normal at first glance, but then seemed to squat oddly low, lines clean and sleek where the Detroit chrome had been taken off, the holes leaded up.

The cars and the kids were of another race. Groups of them formed, broke up and re-formed. Radios brought in a dozen stations. They drank Cokes and perched in dense flocks on open convertibles. They wandered from car to car. It had a strange carnival flavor, yet more ceremonial. From time to time somebody would start one of the car engines, rev it up to a bursting road, and let it die away.

All the girls had long burnished hair and tidy blouses or sun tops and a stillness in their faces, a curious confidence of total acceptance which seemed at odds with the frivolous and provocative tightness of their short shorts, stretch pants, jeans. All the boys were lean, their hairdos carefully ornate, their shoulders high and square, and they moved with the lazy grace of young jungle cats. Some of the couples danced indolently, staring into each other's eyes with a frozen and formal intensity, never touching, bright hair swinging, girls' hips pumping in the stylized ceremonial twist.

Along the line I found a larger group. A boy was strumming slow chords on a guitar, a girl making sharp and erratic fill-in rhythm on a set of bongos. Another boy, in nasal and whining voice, seemed to improvise lyrics as he sang them. "C.M. Special, let it get out and *go.*/C.M. Special, let it way out and *go.*/Iron runs fast and the moon runs slow."

The circle watched and listened with a contained intensity.

Then I heard the winch whining. It seemed to grow louder as, one by one, the other sounds stopped. The kids began moving toward the wrecker. They formed a big, silent semicircle. The taut, woven cable, coming in very slowly, stretched down at an angle through the sun glitter on the black-brown water.

The snore of a passing truck covered the winch noise for a moment.

"Coming good now," a man said.

First you could see an underwater band of silver, close to the dropoff near the bank. Then the first edges of the big sweeping fins broke the surface, then the broad rear bumper, then the rich curves of the strawberry paint. Where it wasn't clotted with wet weed or stained with mud, the paint glowed rich and new and brilliant. There was a slow sound from the kids, a sigh, a murmur, a shifting.

As it came up farther, the dark water began to spurt from it, and as the water level inside dropped, I saw, through a smeared window, the two huddled masses, the slumped boy and girl, side by side, still belted in.

I wanted to see no more. Lazeer was busy, and I got into my car and backed out and went home and mixed a drink.

I started work on it at about three-thirty that afternoon. It would be a feature for the following Sunday. I worked right on through until two in the morning. It was only two thousand words, but it was very tricky and I wanted to get it just right. I had to serve two masters. I had to give lip service to the editorial bias that this sort of thing was wrong, yet at the same time I wanted to capture, for my own sake, the favor of legend. These kids were making a special world we could not share. They were putting all their skills and dreams and energies to work composing the artifacts of a subculture, power, beauty, speed, skill, and rebellion. Our culture was giving them damned little, so they were fighting for a world of their own, with its own customs, legends and feats of valor, its own music, its own ethics and morality.

I took it in Monday morning and left it on Si Walther's desk, with the hope that if it were published intact, it might become a classic. I called it "The Little War of Joe Lee Cuddard."

I didn't hear from Si until just before noon. He came out and dropped it on my desk. "Sorry," he said.

"What's the matter with it?"

"Hell, it's a very nice bit. But we don't publish fiction. You should have checked it out better, Marty, like you usually do. The examiner says those kids have been in the bottom of that canal for maybe eight months. I had Sam check her out through the clinic. She was damn near terminal eight months ago. What probably happened, the boy went to see her and found her so bad off he got scared and decided to rush her to Miami. She was still in her pajamas, with a sweater over them. That way it's a human-interest bit. I had Helen do it. It's page one this afternoon, boxed."

I took my worthless story, tore it in half, and dropped it into the wastebasket. Sergeant Lazeer's bad guess about the identity of his moonlight road runner had made me look like an incompetent jackass. I vowed to check all facts, get all names right, and never again indulge in glowing, strawberry-flake prose.

Three weeks later I got a phone call from Sergeant Lazeer.

He said, "I guess you figured out we got some boy coming in from out of county to fun us these moonlight nights."

"Yes, I did."

"I'm right sorry about you wasting that time and effort when we were thinking we were after Joe Lee Cuddard. We're having some bright moonlight about now, and it'll run full tomorrow night. You want to come over, we can show you some fun, because I got a plan that's dead sure. We tried it last night, but there was just one flaw, and he got away through a road we didn't know about. Tomorrow he won't get that chance to melt away."

I remembered the snarl of that engine, the glimpse of a dark shape, the great wind of passage. Suddenly the backs of my hands prickled. I remembered the emptiness of that stretch of road when we searched it. Could there have been that much pride and passion, labor and love and hope, that Clarissa May and Joe Lee could forever ride the night roads of their home county, balling through the silver moonlight? And what curious message had assembled all those kids from six counties so quickly?

"You there? You still there?"

"Sorry, I was trying to remember my schedule. I don't think I can make it."

"Well, we'll get him for sure this time."

"Best of luck, Sergeant."

"Six cars this time. Barricades. And a spotter plane. He hasn't got a chance if he comes into the net."

I guess I should have gone. Maybe hearing it again, glimpsing the dark shape, feeling the stir of the night wind, would have convinced me of its reality. They didn't get him, of course. But they came so close, so very close. But they left just enough room between a heavy barricade and a live-oak tree, an almost impossibly narrow place to slam through. But thread it he did, and rocketback onto the hard-top and plunge off, leaving the fading, dying contralto drone.

Sergeant Lazeer is grimly readying next month's trap. He says it is the final one. Thus far, all he has captured are the two little marks, a streak of paint on the rough edge of a timber sawhorse, another nudge of paint on the trunk of the oak. Strawberry red. Flecked with gold.

STRANGE
PHENOMENA _____

*A likely candidate for the Nobel Prize and the recipient of
honorary doctorates from Cambridge and Edinburgh, as well
as the Chevalier de la Légion d'Honneur,* **Graham Greene**
*(1904–   ) is the world's most celebrated writer of crimes and
intrigues. He has, however, also written a handful of short
fantasies and two very brief fantastic mysteries, of which "A
Little Place off the Edgware Road" is the longer.*

A LITTLE PLACE OFF
THE EDGWARE ROAD

Graham Greene

CRAVEN came up past the Achilles statue in the thin summer rain. It was
only just after lighting-up time, but already the cars were lined up all the
way to the Marble Arch, and the sharp acquisitive faces peered out ready
for a good time with anything possible which came along. Craven went
bitterly by with the collar of his mackintosh tight round his throat: it was
one of his bad days.

All the way up the Park he was reminded of passion, but you needed
money for love. All that a poor man could get was lust. Love needed a
good suit, a car, a flat somewhere, or a good hotel. It needed to be wrapped in cellophane. He was aware all the time of the stringy tie beneath the
mackintosh, and the frayed sleeves: he carried his body about with him
like something he hated. (There were moments of happiness in the British
Museum reading-room, but the body called him back.) He bore, as his
only sentiment, the memory of ugly deeds committed on park chairs.
People talked as if the body died too soon—that wasn't the trouble, to
Craven, at all. The body kept alive—and through the glittering tinselly
rain, on his way to a rostrum, he passed a little man in a black suit carrying a banner, 'The Body shall rise again.' He remembered a dream from

67

which three times he had woken trembling: he had been alone in the huge dark cavernous burying ground of all the world. Every grave was connected to another under the ground: the globe was honeycombed for the sake of the dead, and on each occasion of dreaming he had discovered anew the horrifying fact that the body doesn't decay. There are no worms and dissolution. Under the ground the world was littered with masses of dead flesh ready to rise again with their warts and boils and eruptions. He had lain in bed and remembered—as 'tidings of great joy'—that the body after all was corrupt.

He came up into the Edgware Road walking fast—the Guardsmen were out in couples, great languid elongated beasts—the bodies like worms in their tight trousers. He hated them, and hated his hatred because he knew what it was, envy. He was aware that every one of them had a better body than himself: indigestion creased his stomach: he felt sure that his breath was foul—but who could he ask? Sometimes he secretly touched himself here and there with scent: it was one of his ugliest secrets. Why should he be asked to believe in the resurrection of this body he wanted to forget? Sometimes he prayed at night (a hint of religious belief was lodged in his breast like a worm in a nut) that *his* body at any rate should never rise again.

He knew all the side streets round the Edgware Road only too well: when a mood was on, he simply walked until he tired, squinting at his own image in the windows of Salmon & Gluckstein and the A.B.C.s. So he noticed at once the posters outside the disused theatre in Culpar Road. They were not unusual, for sometimes Barclays Bank Dramatic Society would hire the place for an evening—or an obscure film would be trade-shown there. The theatre had been built in 1920 by an optimist who thought the cheapness of the site would more than counter-balance its disadvantage of lying a mile outside the conventional theatre zone. But no play had ever succeeded, and it was soon left to gather rat-holes and spider-webs. The covering of the seats was never renewed, and all that ever happened to the place was the temporary false life of an amateur play or a trade show.

Craven stopped and read—there were still optimists it appeared, even in 1939, for nobody but the blindest optimist could hope to make money out of the place as 'The Home of the Silent Film'. The first season of 'primitives' was announced (a high-brow phrase): there would never be a second. Well, the seats were cheap, and it was perhaps worth a shilling to him, now that he was tired, to get in somewhere out of the rain. Craven bought a ticket and went in to the darkness of the stalls.

In the dead darkness a piano tinkled something monotonous recalling Mendelssohn: he sat down in a gangway seat, and could immediately feel the emptiness all round him. No, there would never be another season. On the screen a large woman in a kind of toga wrung her hands, then wobbled with curious jerky movements towards a couch. There she sat and stared out like a sheepdog distractedly through her loose and black and stringy hair. Sometimes she seemed to dissolve altogether into dots and flashes and wiggly lines. A sub-title said, 'Pompilia betrayed by her beloved Augustus seeks an end to her troubles.'

Craven began at last to see—a dim waste of stalls. There were not twenty people in the place—a few couples whispering with their heads touching, and a number of lonely men like himself, wearing the same uniform of the cheap mackintosh. They lay about at intervals like corpses—and again Craven's obsession returned: the tooth-ache of horror. He thought miserably—I am going mad: other people don't feel like this. Even a disused theatre reminded him of those interminable caverns where the bodies were waiting for resurrection.

'A slave to his passion Augustus calls for yet more wine.'

A gross middle-aged Teutonic actor lay on an elbow with his arm round a large woman in a shift. The Spring Song tinkled ineptly on, and the screen flickered like indigestion. Somebody felt his way through the darkness, scrabbling past Craven's knees—a small man: Craven experienced the unpleasant feeling of a large beard brushing his mouth. Then there was a long sigh as the newcomer found the next chair, and on the screen events had moved with such rapidity that Pompilia had already stabbed herself—or so Craven supposed—and lay still and buxom among her weeping slaves.

A low breathless voice sighed out close to Craven's ear, 'What's happened? Is she asleep?'

'No. Dead.'

'Murdered?' the voice asked with a keen interest.

'I don't think so. Stabbed herself.'

Nobody said 'Hush': nobody was enough interested to object to a voice. They drooped among the empty chairs in attitudes of weary inattention.

The film wasn't nearly over yet: there were children somehow to be considered: was it all going on to a second generation? But the small bearded man in the next seat seemed to be interested only in Pompilia's death. The fact that he had come in at that moment apparently fascinated him. Craven heard the word 'coincidence' twice, and he went on talking to himself about it in low out-of-breath tones. 'Absurd when you come to think of it,' and then 'no blood at all'. Craven didn't listen: he sat with his hands clasped between his knees, facing the fact as he had faced it so often before, that he was in danger of going mad. He had to pull himself up, take a holiday, see a doctor (God knew what infection moved in his veins). He became aware that his bearded neighbour had addressed him directly. 'What?' he asked impatiently, 'what did you say?'

'There would be more blood than you can imagine.'

'What are you talking about?'

When the man spoke to him, he sprayed him with damp breath. There was a little bubble in his speech like an impediment. He said, 'When you murder a man . . .

'This was a woman,' Craven said impatiently.

'That wouldn't make any difference.'

'And it's got nothing to do with murder anyway.'

'That doesn't signify.' They seemed to have got into an absurd and meaningless wrangle in the dark.

'I know, you see,' the little bearded man said in a tone of enormous conceit.

'Know what?'

'About such things,' he said with guarded ambiguity.

Craven turned and tried to see him clearly. Was he mad? Was this a warning of what he might become—babbling incomprehensibly to strangers in cinemas? He thought, By God, no, trying to see: I'll be sane yet. I *will* be sane. He could make out nothing but a small black hump of body. The man was talking to himself again. He said, 'Talk. Such talk. They'll say it was all for fifty pounds. But that's a lie. Reasons and reasons. They always take the first reason. Never look behind. Thirty years of reasons. Such simpletons,' he added again in that tone of breathless and unbounded conceit. So this was madness. So long as he could realize that, he must be sane himself—relatively speaking. Not so sane perhaps as the seekers in the park or the Guardsmen in the Edgware Road, but saner than this. It was like a message of encouragement as the piano tinkled on.

Then again the little man turned and sprayed him. 'Killed herself, you say? But who's to know that? It's not a mere question of what hand holds the knife.' He laid a hand suddenly and confidingly on Craven's: it was damp and sticky: Craven said with horror as a possible meaning came to him, 'What are you talking about?'

'I know,' the little man said. 'A man in my position gets to know almost everything.'

'What is your position?' Craven asked, feeling the sticky hand on his, trying to make up his mind whether he was being hysterical or not—after all, there were a dozen explanations—it might be treacle.

'A pretty desperate one *you'd* say.' Sometimes the voice almost died in the throat. Something incomprehensible had happened on the screen—take your eyes from these early pictures for a moment and the plot had proceeded on at such a pace . . . Only the actors moved slowly and jerkily. A young woman in a nightdress seemed to be weeping in the arms of a Roman centurion: Craven hadn't seen either of them before. *'I am not afraid of death, Lucius—in your arms.'*

The little man began to titter—knowingly. He was talking to himself again. It would have been easy to ignore him altogether if it had not been for those sticky hands which he now removed: he seemed to be fumbling at the seat in front of him. His head had a habit of lolling sideways—like an idiot child's. He said distinctly and irrelevantly: 'Bayswater Tragedy.'

'What was that?' Craven said. He had seen those words on a poster before he entered the park.

'What?'

'About the tragedy.'

'To think they call Cullen Mews Bayswater.' Suddenly the little man began to cough—turning his face towards Craven and coughing right at him: it was like vindictiveness. The voice said, 'Let me see. My umbrella.' He was getting up.

'You didn't have an umbrella.'

'My umbrella,' he repeated. 'My—' and seemed to lose the word altogether. He went scrabbling out past Craven's knees.

Craven let him go, but before he had reached the billowy dusty curtains of the Exit the screen went blank and bright—the film had broken, and somebody immediately turned up one dirt-choked chandelier above the circle. It shone down just enough for Craven to see the smear on his hands. This wasn't hysteria: this was a fact. He wasn't mad: he had sat next a madman who in some mews—what was the name, Colon, Collin. . . . Craven jumped up and made his own way out: the black curtain flapped in his mouth. But he was too late: the man had gone and there were three turnings to choose from. He chose instead a telephone-box and dialed with a sense odd for him of sanity and decision 999.

It didn't take two minutes to get the right department. They were interested and very kind. Yes, there had been a murder in a mews—Cullen Mews. A man's neck had been cut from ear to ear with a bread knife—a horrid crime. He began to tell them how he had sat next the murderer in a cinema: it couldn't be anyone else: there was blood on his hands—and he remembered with repulsion as he spoke the damp beard. There must have been a terrible lot of blood. But the voice from the Yard interrupted him. 'Oh no,' it was saying, 'we have the murderer—no doubt of it at all. It's the body that's disappeared.'

Craven put down the receiver. He said to himself aloud, 'Why should this happen to *me*? Why to *me*?' He was back in the horror of his dream—the squalid darkening street outside was only one of the innumerable tunnels connecting grave to grave where the imperishable bodies lay. He said, 'It was a dream, a dream,' and leaning forward he saw in the mirror above the telephone his own face sprinkled by tiny drops of blood like dew from a scent-spray. He began to scream, 'I won't go mad. I won't go mad. I'm sane. I won't go mad.' Presently a little crowd began to collect, and soon a policeman came.

Bill Pronzini *(1943–   ) loves the pulps. He has collected over 3,000 of them and has even written a series of successful novels about a nameless detective who would rather read magazines than work. It seems obvious, therefore, that Mr. Pronzini must have enjoyed writing "The Man Who Collected 'The Shadow'." For it is a story of a pulp collector's dedication to his hobby and of the fantastic rewards such hobbies may bring.*

THE MAN WHO COLLECTED "THE SHADOW"

Bill Pronzini

MR. THEODORE Conway was a nostalgiac, a collector of memorabilia, a dweller in the simple, uncomplicated days of his adolescence when radio, movie serials, and pulp magazines were the ruling forms of entertainment, and superheroes were the idols of American youth.

At forty-three, he resided alone in a modest four-room apartment on Manhattan's Lower East Side, from where he commuted daily by subway to his position of file clerk in the archives of Baylor, Baylor, Leeds and Wadsworth, a well-respected probate law firm. He had no friends to speak of—certainly no one in whom he cared to confide, or who cared to confide in him. He was short and balding and very plump and very nondescript; he did not indulge in any of the vices, minor or major; nor did he have a wife or, euphemistically or otherwise, a girlfriend. (In point of fact, Mr. Conway was the rarest of today's breed, an adult male virgin.) He did not own a television set, did not attend the theatre, movies, or any other form of outside amusement. His one and only hobby, his single source of pleasure, his sole purpose in life, was the accumulation of nostalgia in general.

And nostalgia pertaining to that most ubiquitous of all superheroes, The Shadow, in particular.

Ah, The Shadow! Mr. Conway idolized Lamont Cranston, loved Margo
Lane as he could never love any living woman (psychologically, perhaps,
this was the reason why he never married, and seldom dated). Nothing set
his blood to racing quite so quickly or so hotly as The Shadow on the
scent of an evildoer, utilizing the Power which, as Cranston, he had
learned in the mysterious Orient, the Power to cloud men's minds so that
they could not see him. Nothing filled Mr. Conway with as much delicious
anticipation, as much spine-jellying excitement, as the words spoken by
The Shadow prior to the beginning of each radio adventure: *What evil lurks
in the hearts of men? The Shadow knows* . . . and the eerie, blood-curdling
laugh, the laugh of Justice triumphant, which followed it. Nothing filled
him with as much well-being and security as this ace among aces speaking
when the current case was closed, speaking out to all criminals everywhere, words of ominous warning: *The weed of crime bears bitter fruit.
Crime does not pay. The Shadow knows!* Nothing gave him more pleasure
in the quiet solitude of his apartment than listening to the haunting voice of
Orson Welles, capturing The Shadow like no other had over the air; or
reading Maxwell Grant's daring, chilling accounts in *The Shadow
Magazine*; or slowly, savoringly, leafing through one of the starkly drawn
Shadow comic books.

Mr. Conway had begun his collecting of nostalgia in 1944, with a wide
range of pulp magazines. He now had well over ten thousand issues, complete sets of *Black Mask* and *Weird Tales*, Vol. 1, No. 1 of 49 different
periodicals including *Adventure* and *Dime Detective* and *Detective Fiction
Weekly* and *Thrilling Wonder* and *Western Story* and *Doc Savage*. One entire room in his apartment was filled with garish reds and yellows and
blues, BEM's and salivating fiends, half-nude girls with too-red lips
screaming in the throes of agony, fearless hunters in the hearts of great
jungles, stagecoaches outrunning blood-thirsty bands of painted, howling
Indians. Then he had gone on to comic books and comic strips (*Walt Dis-
ney's Comics and Stories, Superman* and *Batman* and *Plastic Man, Mutt
and Jeff, Krazy Kat, The Katzenjammer Kids*, a hundred more), and to
premiums of every kind and description (decoders and secret-compartment
belts and membership cards and message flashlights, spy rings and shoulder patches, outdoor kits and compasses, microscopes and secret pens that
wrote in invisible ink so that you had to put lemon juice on the paper to
bring out the writing). In the 1950's, he began to accumulate tapes of radio
shows—some taken directly off the 16-inch discs upon which they were

originally recorded, some recorded live, some recorded off the air (Bob Hope and Jack Benny and Red Skelton and *Allen's Alley*, Ellery Queen and Charley Chan and *Mr. Keene, Tracer of Lost Persons*, Tom Mix and Hopalong Cassiday and The Lone Ranger, *Buck Rogers in the 25th Century* and Captain Midnight, *Jack Armstrong, The All-American Boy* and *I Love A Mystery*, Dick Powell as Richard Diamond and Howard Duff as *Yours Truly, Johnny Dollar, Bold Venture* with Bogie and Baby, *Fibber McGee and Molly, Inner Sanctum* and *The Whistler* and suspense).

But his favorite, his idol, from the very beginning was unquestionably The Shadow; the others he amassed happily, eagerly, but with none of the almost fanatical fervor with which he pursued the mystique of The Shadow. Hardly a week passed over the years that at least one new arrival did not come by mail, or by United Parcel, or by messenger, or by his own hand from some location in New York or its immediate vicinity. He pored over advertisements in newspapers and magazines and collectors' sheets, wrote letters, made telephone calls, sent cables, spent every penny of his salary that did not go for bare essentials.

And at long last, he succeeded where no other collector had even come close to succeeding. He accomplished a remarkable, an almost superhuman feat.

He collected the complete Shadow.

There was absolutely nothing produced regarding this superhero, not a written word, not a spoken sentence, not a drawing nor a gadget, that Mr. Conway did not claim as his own.

The final item, the one which had eluded him for twenty-six years—the last two of which, since he had obtained the final radio show on tape, had been spent in an almost desperate search—came to him, oddly enough, by virtue of blind luck (or, if you prefer, fate) on a Saturday evening in late June. He had gone into a tenement area of Manhattan, near the East River, to purchase from a private individual a cartoon strip of *Terry and the Pirates*. Having made the purchase, he had begun to walk toward the subway for the return trip to his apartment when he chanced upon a small, dusty neighborhood bookstore still open in the basement of one of the brownstones. On a whim, he entered and began to examine the cluttered, ill-lighted tables at the rear of the shop.

And there it was.

The October, 1931, issue of *The Shadow Magazine*.

Mr. Conway emitted a small cry of sheer ecstasy. He caught the

magazine up in trembling hands, stared at it with protuberant, almost dis-
believing eyes, opened it gingerly, read the contents page, read the date,
read it again, ran sweat-slick fingers over the rough, grainy pulp paper.
Near-mint condition. Spine unbroken. Colors only slightly faded. And the
price—

Fifty cents.

Fifty cents!

Tears of joy rolled unabashedly down Mr. Conway's plump cheeks as he
carried his treasure, his ultimate quest, to the bearded man at the cash register. The bearded man looked at him strangely, shrugged, and rang up
the sale. Fifty cents. Mr. Conway gave him two quarters, almost embarrassed at the incredibly small sum; he would have paid hundreds, he thought,
hundreds. . . .

As he went out hurriedly into the gathering darkness—it was almost nine
by this time—he cradled the periodical to his chest as if it were a child
(and in a manner of speaking, for Theodore Conway so it was). He could
scarcely believe that he had finally done it, that he now possessed the total
word, picture, and voice exploits of the most awesome master crime-
fighter of them all. His brain reeled dizzily. The Shadow was his now;
Lamont Cranston and Margo Lane (beautiful Margo!), his, all his, his
alone.

Instead of immediately proceeding to the subway, as he would normally
have done when circumstances caught him out near nightfall, Mr. Conway
impulsively entered a small diner not far from the bookstore and seated
himself in a rear booth. He could barely control his excitement, and his
fingers moved caressingly over the smooth surface of the magazine's
cover, tracing each letter of THE SHADOW slowly and rapturously.

When a bored waiter approached the booth, Mr. Conway ordered coffee
with cream and sugar in a perfunctory voice, and then he opened the
magazine. He had previously read, in reprint form, the story by Maxwell
Grant—*The Shadow Laughs!*—but that was not the same as this, no indeed; this was a milestone in the life of Theodore Conway, a day and hour
to be treasured, a day and hour of monumental achievement. He began to
read the story again, savoring each line, each page, the mounting suspense,
the seemingly inescapable traps laid to eliminate The Shadow, the
superhero's wits matched against those of archvillains Isaac Coffran and
Birdie Crull and their insidious counterfeiting plot, Justice emerging triumphant as Justice always did. *The weed of crime bears bitter fruit, crime
does not pay.* . . .

Mr. Conway lost all track of time, so engrossed was he in the magazine. When at last he came to the end, he sighed blissfully and closed the pages with a certain tenderness. He looked up, then, and was somewhat startled to note that the interior of the diner was now deserted, save for the counterman and the single waiter. It had been bustling with activity when he entered. His eyes moved upward to where a kitchen clock was mounted on the wall behind the service counter, and his mouth dropped open in surprise. Good heavens! It was past midnight!

He scrambled out of the booth, the pulp magazine pressed tightly under his right arm, and hurriedly paid for his coffee. Once outside, a certain apprehension seized him; the streets were very dark and very deserted, looking ominous and foreboding in the almost nonexistent shine from the quarter moon overhead.

Mr. Conway looked up and down both ways without seeing any sign of life. It was four blocks to the nearest subway kiosk, a short walk in broad daylight—but now, in what was almost the dead of night? Mr. Conway shivered in the cool breeze, moistening his plump lips; he had never liked the darkness, the sounds and smells of the city at night—and then there were the stories he had heard, substantiated by accounts in the papers every morning, of muggers and thieves on the prowl. In the evenings, he invariably remained indoors, surrounded by his memorabilia, his only friends.

Four blocks. Well, that really wasn't very far, only a matter of minutes if he walked swiftly. He took a deep breath, gathering his courage, and then he started off down the darkened street.

His shoes echoed hollowly on the empty sidewalk, and Mr. Conway could feel his heart pounding wildly in his breast. No cars passed, and his footfalls, except for the distant lament of a ship's horn on the East River, the sibilant whisper of the night wind, were the only sounds.

He had gone two blocks, walking rapidly now, his head darting furtively left and right, when he heard the muffled explosions.

He stopped, the hairs on the back of his neck prickling, a tremor of fear winding icily along his spine. He had drawn abreast of an alleyway—dark and silent—and he peered down it, poising on the balls of his feet preparatory to taking flight. At the end of the alley he could see a thin elongation of pale light, but nothing else.

Mr. Conway's brain was filled with a single thought: *Run!* And yet, curiously, he stood motionless, staring into the black tunnel. Those explosions: gunshots? If so, they meant that danger, sudden death, lurked in that alley, *run, run!*

But Mr. Conway still did not run. Instead, as if inexplicably compelled, he started forward into the circumscribed blackness. He moved slowly, feeling his way in the absolute ebon expanse, his shoes sliding almost noiselessly over the rough paving. *What am I doing?* he thought confusedly. *I shouldn't be here!* But he continued to move forward, approaching the narrow funnel of light, coming into its glare now.

He saw that it was emanating through the partially open side door to the brick building on his right, an electronics equipment firm, according to the sign over the street entranceway. Cautiously, Mr. Conway put out a hand and eased the door open wider, peering inside. The thudding of his heart seemed as loud as a drum roll in his ears as he stepped over the threshold and entered the murkiness beyond.

The light came from a naked bulb burning above a small, glass-enclosed cubicle across a wide expanse of concrete flooring. Dark, shadowy shapes that would be crates of electronics equipment loomed toward the ceiling on either side. He advanced with hesitant, wary steps, seeing no sign of movement in the gloom around him. At last he reached the cubicle, standing in the full cone of light. A watchman's office, he thought, and stepped up to look through the glass.

He stifled the cry which rose in his throat as he saw what lay on the floor within. It was an old man with white hair, supine next to an ancient desk; blood stained the front of his khaki uniform jacket, welling reddish-brown in the dim illumination. The old man was not moving.

He's dead, murdered! Mr. Conway thought fearfully. He had to get out of there, had to telephone the police! He turned—and froze.

The hulking figure of a man stood not three feet away, looking directly at him.

Mr. Conway's knees buckled, and he had to put out a hand against the glass to keep from collapsing. The killer, the murderer! His mind screamed again for him to run, flee, but his legs would not obey; he could only stare back at the man before him with horror-widened eyes, stare at the pinched white face beneath a low-brimmed cloth cap, at the rodent-like eyes and the cruel sneer on the thin-lipped mouth, at the yawning black muzzle of the huge gun in one tightly clenched fist.

"No!" Mr. Conway cried out then, in a strangled plea. "No, please! Please don't shoot!"

The man dropped into a low crouch, extending the gun out in front of him.

"Don't shoot!" Mr. Conway said again, putting up his hands.

Puzzled surprise, and a sudden trapped fear, twisted the killer's face. "Who is it? Who's there?"

Mr. Conway opened his mouth, and then closed it again abruptly. He could scarcely believe his ears; the man had demanded to know who was there—and yet, he was standing not three feet away from Mr. Conway, looking right at him!

"I don't understand," Mr. Conway said tremulously, before he could stop the words.

The gun in the killer's hand swung around and the muzzle erupted in brilliantine flame. The bullet was well wide of the spot where Mr. Conway was standing, but he jumped convulsively aside and hugged the glass of the cubicle. He continued to stare incredulously at the man—and suddenly, then, with complete clarity, he *did* understand, he knew.

"You can't *see* me," he said wonderingly.

The gun discharged a second bullet, but Mr. Conway had already moved easily aside. The shot was wild. "Damn you!" the killer screamed. His words were tinged with hysteria now. "Where are you? *Where are you?*"

Mr. Conway remained standing there, clearly outlined in the light, for a moment longer; then he stepped to one side, to where a board broken from a wooden pallet lay on the cement, and caught it up in his hand. Without hesitation, he walked up to the killer and hit him squarely on top of the head, watching dispassionately as he dropped unconscious to the floor.

Mr. Conway kicked the gun away and stood over him; the police would have to be summoned, of course, but there was plenty of time for that now. A slow, grim smile formed at the corners of his mouth. Could it be that the remarkable collecting feat he had performed, his devoted empathy, had stirred some supernatural force into granting him the Power which he now undeniably possessed? Well, no matter. His was not to question why; so endowed, his was but to heed the plaintive cry of a world ridden with lawlessness.

A deep, chilling laugh suddenly swept through the warehouse. "The weed of crime bears bitter fruit!" a haunting, Wellesian voice shouted. "Crime does not pay!"

And The Shadow wrapped the cloak of night around himself and went out into the mean streets of the great metropolis. . . .

The 20th century's most important mystery writer is **Agatha Christie** *(1890–1976). Not only did she outsell everyone else (400 million copies), but she was a compelling story teller with a flair for innovation (e.g.,* Who Killed Roger Ackroyd?) *and a talent for unexpected endings. A score of fantastic stories are among the cream of her shorter work, and one of the cleverest is "The Red Signal," a tale which might have been called "Sight Unseen."*

THE RED SIGNAL

Agatha Christie

"No, BUT how too thrilling," said pretty Mrs. Eversleigh, opening her lovely, but slightly vacant, blue eyes very wide. "They always say women have a sixth sense; do you think it's true, Sir Alington?"

The famous alienist smiled sardonically. He had an unbounded contempt for the foolish pretty type, such as his fellow guest. Alington West was the supreme authority on mental disease, and he was fully alive to his own position and importance. A slightly pompous man in full figure.

"A great deal of nonsense is talked, I know that, Mrs. Eversleigh. What does the term mean—a sixth sense?"

"You scientific men are always so severe. And it really is extraordinary the way one seems to positively know things sometimes—just know them, feel them, I mean—quite uncanny—it really is. Claire knows what I mean, don't you, Claire?"

She appealed to her hostess with a slight pout, and a tilted shoulder.

Claire Trent did not reply at once. It was a small dinner party—she and her husband, Violet Eversleigh, Sir Alington West, and his nephew Dermot West, who was an old friend of Jack Trent's. Jack Trent himself, a somewhat heavy, florid man with a good-humored smile and a pleasant lazy laugh, took up the thread.

"Bunkum, Violet! Your best friend is killed in a railway accident. Straight away you remember that you dreamed of a black cat last Tuesday—marvelous, you felt all along that something was going to happen!"

"Oh, no, Jack, you're mixing up premonitions with intuition now. Come, now, Sir Alington, you must admit that premonitions are real?"

"To a certain extent, perhaps," admitted the physician cautiously. "But coincidence accounts for a good deal, and then there is the invariable tendency to make the most of a story afterward."

"I don't think there is any such thing as premonition," said Claire Trent rather abruptly. "Or intuition or a sixth sense or any of the things we talk about so glibly. We go through life like a train rushing through the darkness to an unknown destination."

"That's hardly a good simile, Mrs. Trent," said Dermot West, lifting his head for the first time and taking part in the discussion. There was a curious glitter in the clear gray eyes that shone out rather oddly from the deeply tanned face. "You've forgotten the signals, you see."

"The signals?"

"Yes, green if it's all right, and red—for danger!"

"Red—for danger—how thrilling!" breathed Violet Eversleigh.

Dermot turned from her rather impatiently. "That's just a way of describing it, of course."

Trent stared at him curiously. "You speak as though it were an actual experience, Dermot, old boy."

"So it is—has been, I mean."

"Give us the yarn."

"I can give you one instance. Out in Mesopotamia, just after the Armistice, I came into my tent one evening with the feeling strong upon me. Danger! Look out! Hadn't the ghost of a notion what it was all about. I made a round of the camp, fussed unnecessarily, took all precautions against an attack by hostile Arabs. Then I went back to my tent. As soon as I got inside, the feeling popped up again stronger than ever. Danger! In the end I took a blanket outside, rolled myself up in it, and slept there."

"Well?"

"The next morning, when I went inside the tent, first thing I saw was a great knife arrangement—about half a yard long—struck down through my bunk, just where I would have lain. I soon found out about it—one of the Arab servants. His son had been shot as a spy. What have you got to say to that, Uncle Alington, as an example of what I call the red signal?''

The specialist smiled noncommittally. ''A very interesting story, my dear Dermot.''

''But not one that you accept unreservedly?''

''Yes, yes, I have no doubt but that you had the premonition of danger, just as you state. But it is the origin of the premonition I dispute. According to you, it came from without, impressed by some outside source upon your mentality. But nowadays we find that nearly everything comes from within—from our subconscious self.

''I suggest that by some glance or look this Arab had betrayed himself. Your conscious self did not notice or remember, but with your subconscious self it was otherwise. The subconscious never forgets. We believe, too, that it can reason and deduce quite independently of the higher or conscious will. Your subconscious self, then, believed that an attempt might be made to assassinate you, and succeeded in forcing its fear upon your conscious realization.''

''That sounds very convincing, I admit,'' said Dermot, smiling.

''But not nearly so exciting,'' pouted Mrs. Eversleigh.

''It is also possible that you may have been subconsciously aware of the hate felt by the man toward you. What in old days used to be called telepathy certainly exists, though the conditions governing it are very little understood.''

''Have there been any other instances?'' asked Claire of Dermot.

''Oh! yes, but nothing very pictorial—and I suppose they could all be explained under the heading of coincidence. I refused an invitation to a country house once, for no other reason than the 'red signal.' The place was burned out during the week. By the way, Uncle Alington, where does the subconscious come in there?''

''I'm afraid it doesn't,'' said Sir Alington, smiling.

''But you've got an equally good explanation. Come, now. No need to be tactful with near relatives.''

''Well, then, nephew, I venture to suggest that you refused the invitation for the ordinary reason that you didn't much want to go, and that after the fire, you suggested to yourself that you had had a warning of danger, which explanation you now believe implicitly.''

''It's hopeless,'' laughed Dermot. ''It's heads you win, tails I lose.''

''Never mind, Mr. West,'' cried Violet Eversleigh. ''I believe in your Red Signal. Is the time in Mesopotamia the last time you had it?''

''Yes—until—''

"I beg your pardon?"

"Nothing."

Dermot sat silent. The words which had nearly left his lips were: "Yes, until tonight." They had come quite unbidden to his lips, voicing a thought which had as yet not been consciously realized, but he was aware at once that they were true. The Red Signal was looming up out of the darkness. Danger! Danger close at hand!

But why? What conceivable danger could there be here? Here in the house of his friends? At least—well, yes, there was that kind of danger. He looked at Claire Trent—her whiteness, her slenderness, the exquisite droop of her golden head. But that danger had been there for some time—it was never likely to get acute. For Jack Trent was his best friend, and more than his best friend, the man who had saved his life in Flanders and been recommended for the V.C. for doing so. A good fellow, Jack, one of the best. Damned bad luck that he should have fallen in love with Jack's wife. He'd get over it some day, he supposed. A thing couldn't go on hurting like this forever. One could starve it out—that was it, starve it out. It was not as though she would ever guess—and if she did guess, there was no danger of her caring. A statue, a beautiful statue, a thing of gold and ivory and pale-pink coral—a toy for a king, not a real woman.

Claire—the very thought of her name, uttered silently, hurt him. He must get over it. He'd cared for women before. *But not like this!* said something. *Not like this*. Well, there it was. No danger there—heartache, yes, but not danger. Not the danger of the Red Signal. That was for something else.

He looked round the table and it struck him for the first time that it was rather an unusual little gathering. His uncle, for instance, seldom dined out in this small, informal way. It was not as though the Trents were old friends; until this evening Dermot had not been aware that he knew them at all.

To be sure, there was an excuse. A rather notorious medium was coming after dinner to give a seance. Sir Alington professed to be mildly interested in spiritualism. Yes, that was an excuse, certainly.

The word forced itself on his notice. An excuse. Was the séance just an excuse to make the specialist's presence at dinner natural? If so, what was the real object of his being here? A host of details came rushing into Dermot's mind, trifles unnoticed at the time, or, as his uncle would have said, unnoticed by the conscious mind.

The great physician had looked oddly, very oddly, at Claire more than once. He seemed to be watching her. She was uneasy under his scrutiny. She made little twitching motions with her hands. She was nervous, horribly nervous, and was it, could it be, frightened? Why was she frightened?

With a jerk he came back to the conversation round the table. Mrs. Eversleigh had got the great man talking upon his own subject.

"My dear lady," he was saying, "what *is* madness? I can assure you that the more we study the subject, the more difficult we find it to pronounce. We all practice a certain amount of self-deception, and when we carry it so far as to believe we are the Czar of Russia, we are shut up or restrained. But there is a long road before we reach that point. At what particular spot on it shall we erect a post and say, 'On this side sanity, on the other madness'? It can't be done, you know. And I will tell you this—if the man suffering from a delusion happened to hold his tongue about it, in all probability we should never be able to distinguish him from a normal individual. The extraordinary sanity of the insane is an interesting subject."

Sir Alington sipped his wine with appreciation and beamed upon the company.

"I've always heard they are very cunning," remarked Mrs. Eversleigh. "Loonies, I mean."

"Remarkably so. And suppression of one's particular delusion has a disastrous effect very often. All suppressions are dangerous, as psychoanalysis has taught us. The man who has a harmless eccentricity, and can indulge it as such, seldom goes over the border line. But the man—" he paused—"or woman who is to all appearance perfectly normal, may be in reality a poignant source of danger to the community."

His gaze traveled gently down the table to Claire and then back again.

A horrible fear shook Dermot. Was that what he meant? Was that what he was driving at? Impossible, but—

"And all from suppressing oneself," sighed Mrs. Eversleigh. "I quite see that one should be very careful always to—to express one's personality. The dangers of the other are frightful."

"My dear Mrs. Eversleigh," expostulated the physician, "you have quite misunderstood me. The cause of the mischief is in the physical matter of the brain—sometimes arising from some outward agency such as a blow, sometimes, alas, congenital."

"Heredity is so sad," sighed the lady vaguely. "Consumption and all that."

"Tuberculosis is not hereditary," said Sir Alington dryly.

"Isn't it? I always thought it was. But madness is! How dreadful. What else?"

"Gout," said Sir Alington, smiling. "And color blindness—the latter is rather interesting. It is transmitted direct to males, but is latent in females. So while there are many color-blind men, for a woman to be color blind, it must have been latent in her mother as well as present in her father—rather an unusual state of things to occur. That is what is called sex-limited heredity."

"How interesting. But madness is not like that, is it?"

"Madness can be handed down to men or women equally," said the physician gravely.

Claire rose suddenly, pushing back her chair so abruptly that it over-turned and fell to the ground. She was very pale, and the nervous motions of her fingers were very apparent.

"You—you will not be long, will you?" she begged. "Mrs. Thompson will be here in a few minutes now."

"One glass of port and I will be with you," declared Sir Alington. "To see this wonderful Mrs. Thompson's performance is what I have come for, is it not? Ha, ha! Not that I needed any inducement." He bowed.

Claire gave a faint smile of acknowledgement and passed out of the room with Mrs. Eversleigh.

"Afraid I've been talking shop," remarked the physician as he resumed his seat. "Forgive me, my dear fellow."

"Not at all," said Trent perfunctorily.

He looked strained and worried. For the first time Dermot felt an out-sider in the company of his friend. Between these two was a secret that even an old friend might not share. And yet the whole thing was fantastic and incredible. What had he to go upon? Nothing but a couple of glances and a woman's nervousness.

They lingered over their wine but a very short time, and arrived up in the drawing-room just as Mrs. Thompson was announced.

The medium was a plump middle-aged woman, atrociously dressed in magenta velvet, with a loud, rather common voice.

"Hope I'm not late, Mrs. Trent," she said cheerily. "You did say nine o'clock, didn't you?"

"You are quite punctual, Mrs. Thompson," said Claire in her sweet, slightly husky voice. "This is our little circle."

No further introductions were made, as was evidently the custom. The medium swept them all with a shrewd, penetrating eye.

"I hope we shall get some good results," she remarked briskly. "I can't tell you how I hate it when I go out and I can't give satisfaction, so to speak. It just makes me mad. But I think Shiromako—my Japanese control, you know—will be able to get through all right tonight. I'm feeling ever so fit, and I refused the Welsh rarebit, fond of cheese though I am."

Dermot listened, half-amused, half-disgusted. How prosaic the whole thing was! And yet, was he not judging foolishly? Everything, after all, was natural—the powers claimed by mediums were natural powers, as yet imperfectly understood. A great surgeon might be wary of indigestion on the eve of a delicate operation. Why not Mrs. Thompson?

Chairs were arranged in a circle, lights so that they could conveniently be raised and lowered. Dermot noticed that there was no question of tests, or of Sir Alington satisfying himself as to the conditions of the séance. No, this business of Mrs. Thompson was only a blind. Sir Alington was here for quite another purpose. Claire's mother, Dermot remembered, had died abroad. There had been some mystery about her—Hereditary—

With a jerk he forced his mind back to the surroundings of the moment.

Everyone took their places, and the lights were turned out, all but a small red-shaded one on a far table.

For a while nothing was heard but the low, even breathing of the medium. Gradually it grew more and more stertorous. Then, with a suddenness that made Dermot jump, a loud rap came from the far end of the room. It was repeated from the other side. Then a perfect crescendo of raps was heard. They died away, and a sudden high peal of mocking laughter rang through the room.

Then silence, broken by a voice utterly unlike that of Mrs. Thompson, a high-pitched, quaintly inflected voice.

"I am here, gentlemen," it said. "Yes, I am here. You wish to ask me things?"

"Who are you? Shiromako?"

"Yes. I Shiromako. I pass over long ago. I work. I very happy."

Further details of Shiromako's life followed. It was all very flat and uninteresting, and Dermot had heard it often before. Everyone was happy, very happy. Messages were given from vaguely described relatives, the description being so loosely worded as to fit almost any contingency. An elderly lady, the mother of someone present, held the floor for some time, imparting copybook maxims with an air of refreshing novelty hardly borne out by her subject matter.

"Someone else want to get through now," announced Shiromako. "Got a very important message for one of the gentlemen."

There was a pause, and then a new voice spoke, prefacing its remarks with an evil, demoniacal chuckle.

"Ha, ha! Ha, ha, ha! Better not go home. Take my advice."

"Who are you speaking to?" asked Trent.

"One of you three. I shouldn't go home if I were him. Danger! Blood! Not very much blood—quite enough. No, don't go home." The voice grew fainter. *"Don't go home!"*

It died away completely. Dermot felt his blood tingling. He was convinced that the warning was meant for him. Somehow or other, there was danger abroad tonight.

There was a sigh from the medium, and then a groan. She was coming round. The lights were turned on, and presently she sat upright, her eyes blinking a little.

"Go off well, my dear? I hope so."

"Very good indeed, thank you, Mrs. Thompson."

"Shiromako, I suppose?"

"Yes, and others."

Mrs. Thompson yawned.

"I'm dead beat. Absolutely down and out. Does fairly take it out of you. Well, I'm glad it was a success. I was a bit afraid something disagreeable might happen. There's a queer feel about this room tonight."

She glanced over each ample shoulder in turn, and then shrugged them uncomfortably.

"I don't like it," she said. "Any sudden deaths among any of you people lately?"

"What do you mean—among us?"

"Near relatives—dear friends? No? Well, if I wanted to be melodramatic, I'd say that there was death in the air tonight. There, it's only my nonsense. Good-by, Mrs. Trent. I'm glad you've been satisfied."

Mrs. Thompson in her magenta velvet gown went out.

"I hope you've been interested, Sir Alington," murmured Claire.

"A most interesting evening, my dear lady. Many thanks for the opportunity. Let me wish you good night. You are all going on to a dance, are you not?"

"Won't you come with us?"

"No, no. I make it a rule to be in bed by half past eleven. Good night. Good night, Mrs. Eversleigh. Ah, Dermot, I rather want to have a word with you. Can you come with me now? You can rejoin the others at the Grafton Galleries."

"Certainly, Uncle. I'll meet you there, then, Trent."

Very few words were exchanged between uncle and nephew during the short drive to Harley Street. Sir Alington made a semi-apology for dragging Dermot away, and assured him that he would only detain him a few minutes.

"Shall I keep the car for you, my boy?" he asked, as they alighted.

"Oh, don't bother, Uncle. I'll pick up a taxi."

"Very good. I don't like to keep Charlson up later than I can help. Good night, Charlson. Now where the devil did I put my key?"

The car glided away as Sir Alington stood on the steps searching his pockets.

"Must have left it in my other coat," he said at length. "Ring the bell, will you? Johnson is still up, I dare say."

The imperturbable Johnson did indeed open the door within sixty seconds.

"Mislaid my key, Johnson," explained Sir Alington. "Bring a couple of whiskies and sodas into the library."

"Very good, Sir Alington."

The physician strode on into the library and turned on the lights. He motioned to Dermot to close the door.

"I won't keep you long, Dermot, but there's just something I want to say to you. Is it my fancy, or have you a certain—*tendresse*, shall we say, for Mrs. Jack Trent?"

The blood rushed to Dermot's face.

"Jack Trent is my best friend."

"Pardon me, but that is hardly answering my question. I dare say that you consider my views on divorce and such matters highly puritanical, but I must remind you that you are my only near relative and my heir."

"There is no question of a divorce," said Dermot angrily.

"There certainly is not, for a reason which I understand perhaps better than you do. That particular reason I cannot give you now, but I do wish to warn you. She is not for you."

The young man faced his uncle's gaze steadily. "I do understand—and permit me to say, perhaps better than you think. I know the reason for your presence at dinner tonight.''

"Eh?'' The physician was clearly startled. "How did you know that?''

"Call it a guess, sir. I am right, am I not, when I say that you were there in your—professional capacity.''

Sir Alington strode up and down.

"You are quite right, Dermot. I could not, of course, have told you so myself, though I am afraid it will soon be common property.''

Dermot's heart contracted. "You mean that you have—made up your mind?''

"Yes, there is insanity in the family—on the mother's side. A sad case—a very sad case.''

"I can't believe it, sir.''

"I dare say not. To the layman there are few if any signs apparent.''

"And to the expert?''

"The evidence is conclusive. In such a case the patient must be placed under restraint as soon as possible.''

"My God!'' breathed Dermot. "But you can't shut anyone up for nothing at all.''

"My dear Dermot! Cases are only placed under restraint when their being at large would result in danger to the community.''

"Danger?''

"Very grave danger. In all probability a peculiar form of homicidal mania. It was so in the mother's case.''

Dermot turned away with a groan, burying his face in his hands. Claire—white and golden Claire!

"In the circumstances,'' continued the physician comfortably, "I felt it incumbent on me to warn you.''

"Claire,'' murmured Dermot. "My poor Claire.''

"Yes, indeed, we must all pity her.''

Suddenly Dermot raised his head.

"I say I don't believe it. Doctors make mistakes. Everyone knows that. And they're always keen on their own specialty.''

"My dear Dermot,'' cried Sir Alington angrily.

"I tell you I don't believe it—and anyway, even if it is so, I don't care. I love Claire. If she will come with me, I shall take her away—far away—out of the reach of meddling physicians. I shall guard her, care for her, shelter her with my love.''

"You will do nothing of the sort. Are you mad?"

Dermot laughed scornfully. "*You* would say so."

"Understand me, Dermot." Sir Alington's face was red with suppressed passion. "If you do this thing—this shameful thing—I shall withdraw the allowance I am now making you, and I shall make a new will leaving all I possess to various hospitals."

"Do as you please with your damned money," said Dermot in a low voice. "I shall have the woman I love."

"A woman who—"

"Say a word against her and, by God, I'll kill you!" cried Dermot.

A slight chink of glasses made them both swing round. Unheard by them in the heat of their argument, Johnson had entered with a tray of glasses. His face was the imperturbable one of the good servant, but Dermot wondered just exactly how much he had overheard.

"That'll do, Johnson," said Sir Alington curtly. "You can go to bed."

"Thank you, sir. Good night, sir."

Johnson withdrew.

The two men looked at each other. The momentary interruption had calmed the storm.

"Uncle," said Dermot. "I shouldn't have spoken to you as I did. I can quite see that from your point of view you are perfectly right. But I have loved Claire Trent for a long time. The fact that Jack Trent is my best friend has hitherto stood in the way of my ever speaking of love to Claire herself. But in these circumstances that fact no longer counts. The idea that any monetary conditions can deter me is absurd. I think we've both said all there is to be said. Good night."

"Dermot—"

"It is really no good arguing further. Good night, Uncle Alington."

He went out quickly, shutting the door behind him. The hall was in darkness. He passed through it, opened the front door and emerged into the street, banging the door behind him.

A taxi had just deposited a fare at a house farther along the street and Dermot hailed it, and drove to the Grafton Galleries.

In the door of the ballroom he stood for a minute, bewildered, his head spinning. The raucous jazz music, the smiling women—it was as though he had stepped into another world.

Had he dreamed it all? Impossible that that grim conversation with his uncle should have really taken place. There was Claire floating past, like a lily in her white-and-silver gown that fitted sheathlike to her slenderness.

She smiled at him, her face calm and serene. Surely it was all a dream.

The dance had stopped. Presently she was near him, smiling up into his face. As in a dream he asked her to dance. She was in his arms now, the raucous melodies had begun again.

He felt her flag a little.

"Tired? Do you want to stop?"

"If you don't mind. Can we go somewhere where we can talk? There is something I want to say to you."

Not a dream. He came back to earth with a bump. Could he ever have thought her face calm and serene? It was haunted with anxiety, with dread. How much did she know?

He found a quiet corner, and they sat down side by side.

"Well," he said, assuming a lightness he did not feel, "you said you had something you wanted to say to me?"

"Yes." Her eyes were cast down. She was playing nervously with the tassel of her gown. "It's difficult—"

"Tell me, Claire."

"It's just this. I want you to—to go away for a time."

He was astonished. Whatever he had expected, it was not this.

"You want me to go away? Why?"

"It's best to be honest, isn't it? I know that you are a—a gentleman and my friend. I want you to go away because I—I have let myself get fond of you."

"Claire."

Her words left him dumb—tongue-tied.

"Please do not think that I am conceited enough to fancy that you— would ever be likely to fall in love with me. It is only that—I am not very happy—and—oh! I would rather you went away."

"Claire, don't you know that I have cared—cared damnably—ever since I met you?"

She lifted startled eyes to his face.

"You cared? You have cared a long time?"

"Since the beginning."

"Oh!" she cried. "Why didn't you tell me? Then! When I could have come to you! Why tell me now when it's too late. No, I'm mad—I don't know what I'm saying. I could never have come to you."

"Claire, what did you mean when you said 'now that it's too late'? Is it—is it because of my uncle? What he knows?"

She nodded, the tears running down her face.

"Listen, Claire, you're not to believe all that. You're not to think about it. Instead, you will come away with me. I will look after you—keep you safe always."

His arms went round her. He drew her to him, felt her tremble at his touch. Then suddenly she wrenched herself free.

"Oh, no, please. Can't you see? I couldn't now. It would be ugly—ugly—ugly. All along I've wanted to be good—and now—it would be ugly as well."

He hesitated, baffled by her words. She looked at him appealingly.

"Please," she said. "I want to be good."

Without a word, Dermot got up and left her. For the moment he was touched and racked by her words beyond argument. He went for his hat and coat, running into Trent as he did so.

"Hallo, Dermot, you're off early."

"Yes, I'm not in the mood for dancing tonight."

"It's a rotten night," said Trent gloomily. "But you haven't got my worries."

Dermot had a sudden panic that Trent might be going to confide in him. Not that—anything but that!

"Well, so long," he said hurriedly. "I'm off home."

"Home, eh? What about the warning of the spirits?"

"I'll risk that. Good night, Jack."

Dermot's flat was not far away. He walked there, feeling the need of the cool night air to calm his fevered brain. He let himself in with his key and switched on the light in the bedroom.

And all at once, for the second time that night, the feeling of the Red Signal surged over him. So overpowering was it that for the moment it swept even Claire from his mind.

Danger! He was in danger. At this very moment, in this very room!

He tried in vain to ridicule himself free of the fear. Perhaps his efforts were secretly halfhearted. So far, the Red Signal had given him timely warning which had enabled him to avoid disaster. Smiling a little at his own superstition, he made a careful tour of the flat. It was possible that some malefactor had got in and was lying concealed there. But his search revealed nothing. His man, Milson, was away, and the flat was absolutely empty.

He returned to his bedroom and undressed slowly, frowning to himself. The sense of danger was acute as ever. He went to a drawer to get out a handkerchief, and suddenly stood stock still. There was an unfamiliar lump in the middle of the drawer.

His quick nervous fingers tore aside the handkerchiefs and took out the object concealed beneath them.

It was a revolver.

With the utmost astonishment Dermot examined it keenly. It was of a somewhat unfamiliar pattern, and one shot had been fired from it lately. Beyond that he could make nothing of it. Someone had placed it in that drawer that very evening. It had not been there when he dressed for dinner—he was sure of that.

He was about to replace it in the drawer, when he was startled by a bell ringing. It rang again and again, sounding unusually loud in the quietness of the empty flat.

Who could be coming to the front door at this hour? And only one answer came to the question—an answer instinctive and persistent.

Danger—danger—danger.

Led by some instinct for which he did not account, Dermot switched off his light, slipped on an overcoat that lay across a chair, and opened the hall door.

Two men stood outside. Beyond them Dermot caught sight of a blue uniform. A policeman!

"Mr. West?" asked one of the two men.

It seemed to Dermot that ages elapsed before he answered. In reality it was only a few seconds before he replied in a very fair imitation of his servant's expressionless voice, "Mr. West hasn't come in yet."

"Hasn't come in yet, eh? Very well, then, I think we'd better come in and wait for him."

"No, you don't."

"See here, my man. I'm Inspector Verall of Scotland Yard, and I've got a warrant for the arrest of your master. You can see it if you like."

Dermot perused the proffered paper, or pretended to do so, asking in a dazed voice, "What for? What's he done?"

"Murder. Sir Alington West of Harley Street."

His brain in a whirl, Dermot fell back before his redoubtable visitors. He went into the sitting-room and switched on the light. The inspector followed him.

"Have a search round," he directed the other man. Then he turned to Dermot. "You stay here, my man. No slipping off to warn your master.

What's your name, by the way?''

"Milson, sir."

"What time do you expect your master in, Milson?"

"I don't know, sir, he was going to a dance, I believe. At the Grafton Galleries."

"He left there just under an hour ago. Sure he's not been back here?"

"I don't think so, sir. I fancy I should have heard him come in."

At this moment the second man came in from the adjoining room. In his hand he carried the revolver. He took it across to the inspector in some excitement. An expression of satisfaction flitted across the latter's face.

"That settles it," he remarked. "Must have slipped in and out without your hearing him. He's hooked it by now. I'd better be off. Cawley, you stay here, in case he should come back again, and you can keep an eye on this fellow. He may know more about his master than he pretends."

The inspector bustled off. Dermot endeavored to get the details of the affair from Cawley, who was quite ready to be talkative.

"Pretty clear case," he vouchsafed. "The murder was discovered almost immediately. Johnson, the manservant, had only just gone up to bed when he fancied he heard a shot, and came down again. Found Sir Alington dead, shot through the heart. He rang us up at once and we came along and heard his story."

"Which made it a pretty clear case?" ventured Dermot.

"Absolutely. This young West came in with his uncle and they were quarreling when Johnson brought in the drinks. The old boy was threatening to make a new will, and your master was talking about shooting him. Not five minutes later the shot was heard. Oh, yes, clear enough."

Clear enough indeed. Dermot's heart sank as he realized the overwhelming evidence against him. And no way out save flight. He set his wits to work. Presently he suggested making a cup of tea. Cawley assented readily enough. He had already searched the flat and knew there was no back entrance.

Dermot was permitted to depart to the kitchen. Once there he put the kettle on, and chinked cups and saucers industriously. Then he stole swiftly to the window and lifted the sash. The flat was on the second floor, and outside the window was the small wire lift used by tradesmen which ran up and down on its steel cable.

Like a flash Dermot was outside the window and swinging himself down the wire rope. It cut into his hands, making them bleed, but he went on desperately.

A few minutes later he was emerging cautiously from the back of the block. Turning the corner, he cannoned into a figure standing by the sidewalk. To his utter amazement he recognized Jack Trent. Trent was fully alive to the perils of the situation.

"My God! Dermot! Quick, don't hang about here."

Taking him by the arm, he led him down a by street, then down another. A lonely taxi was sighted and hailed and they jumped in, Trent giving the man his own address.

"Safest place for the moment. There we can decide what to do next to put those fools off the track. I came round here, hoping to be able to warn you before the police got here."

"I didn't even know that you had heard of it. Jack, you don't believe—"

"Of course not, old fellow, not for one minute. I know you far too well. All the same, it's a nasty business for you. They came round asking questions—what time you got to the Grafton Galleries, when you left, and so on. Dermot, who could have done the old boy in?"

"I can't imagine. Whoever did it put the revolver in my drawer, I suppose. Must have been watching us pretty closely."

"That séance business was damned funny. 'Don't go home.' Meant for poor old West. He did go home, and got shot."

"It applies to me, too," said Dermot. "I went home and found a planted revolver and a police inspector."

"Well, I hope it doesn't get me, too," said Trent. "Here we are."

He paid the taxi, opened the door with his latchkey, and guided Dermot up the dark stairs to his den, a small room on the first floor.

He threw open the door and Dermot walked in, while Trent switched on the light, and came to join him.

"Pretty safe here for the time being," he remarked. "Now we can get our heads together and decide what is best to be done."

"I've made a fool of myself," said Dermot suddenly. "I ought to have faced it out. I see more clearly now. The whole thing's a plot. What the devil are you laughing at?"

For Trent was leaning back in his chair, shaking with unrestrained mirth. There was something horrible in the sound—something horrible, too, about the man altogether. There was a curious light in his eyes.

"A damned clever plot," he gasped out. "Dermot, you're done for."

He drew the telephone toward him.

"What are you going to do?" asked Dermot.

"Ring up Scotland Yard. Tell 'em their bird's here—safe under lock and key. Yes, I locked the door when I came in and the key's in my pocket. No good looking at the other door behind me. That leads into Claire's room, and she always locks it on her side. She's afraid of me, you know. Been afraid of me a long time. She always knows when I'm thinking about that knife—a long, sharp knife. No, you don't—"

Dermot had been about to make a rush at him, but the other had suddenly produced a revolver.

"That's the second of them," chuckled Trent. "I put the first in your drawer—after shooting old West with it—What are you looking at over my head? That door? It's no use, even if Claire were to open it—and she might to you—I'd shoot you before you got there. Not in the heart—not to kill, just wing you, so that you couldn't get away. I'm a jolly good shot, you know. I saved your life once. More fool I. No, no, I want you hanged—yes, hanged. It isn't you I want the knife for. It's Claire—pretty Claire, so white and soft. Old West knew. That's what he was here for tonight, to see if I were mad or not. He wanted to shut me up—so that I shouldn't get at Claire with a knife. I was very cunning. I took his latch-key and yours, too. I slipped away from the dance as soon as I got there. I saw you come out of his house, and I went in. I shot him and came away at once. Then I went to your place and left the revolver. I was at the Grafton Galleries again almost as soon as you were, and I put the latchkey back in your coat pocket when I was saying good night to you. I don't mind telling you all this. There's no one else to hear, and when you're being hanged I'd like you to know I did it. There's not a loophole of escape. It makes me laugh—God, how it makes me laugh! What are you thinking of? What the devil are you looking at?"

"I'm thinking of some words you quoted just now. You'd have done better, Trent, not to come home."

"What do you mean?"

"Look behind you."

Trent spun round. In the doorway of the communicating room stood Claire—and Inspector Verall.

Trent was quick. The revolver spoke just once—and found its mark. He fell forward across the table. The inspector sprang to his side, as Dermot stared at Claire in a dream. Thoughts flashed through his brain disjointedly. His uncle—their quarrel—the colossal misunderstanding—the divorce laws of England which would never free Claire from an insane husband—"we must all pity her"—the plot between her and Sir Alington which the cunning of Trent had seen through—her cry to him, "Ugly—ugly—ugly!" Yes, but now—

The inspector straightened up.

"Dead," he said vexedly.

"Yes," Dermot heard himself saying, "he was always a good shot."

BIZARRE
DISCOVERIES _____

Sir Arthur Conan Doyle's *(1859-1930) chronicles of Sherlock Holmes brought worldwide popularity to the mystery story. But Sir Doyle also wrote several fantastic mysteries. Indeed, the first, which was "The American's Tale," preceded the great detective's adventures by almost a decade. A brief but hearty story, it concerns evidence both circumstantial and planted.*

THE AMERICAN'S TALE

Arthur Conan Doyle

"IT AIR strange, it air," he was saying as I opened the door of the room where our social little semi-literary society met; "but I could tell you queerer things than that 'ere—almighty queer things. You can't learn everything out of books, sirs, nohow. You see, it ain't the men as can string English together, and as has had good eddications, as finds themselves in the queer places I've been in. They're mostly rough men, sirs, as can scarce speak aright, far less tell with pen and ink the things they've seen; but if they could they'd make some of you Europeans har riz with astonishment. They would, sirs, you bet!"

His name was Jefferson Adams, I believe; I know his initials were J. A., for you may see them yet deeply whittled on the right-hand upper panel of our smoking-room door. He left us this legacy, and also some artistic patterns done in tobacco juice upon our Turkey carpet; but beyond these reminiscences our American story-teller has vanished from our ken. He gleamed across our ordinary quiet conviviality like some brilliant meteor, and then was lost in the outer darkness. That night, however, our Nevada friend was in full swing; and I quietly lighted my pipe and dropped into the nearest chair, anxious not to interrupt his story.

"Mind you," he continued, "I haven't got no grudge against your men of science. I likes and respects a chap as can match every beast and plant, from a huckleberry to a grizzly, with a jaw-breakin' name; but if you wants real interestin' facts, something a bit juicy, you go to your whalers and your frontiersmen, and your scouts and Hudson Bay men, chaps who mostly can scarce sign their names."

There was a pause here, as Mr. Jefferson Adams produced a long cheroot and lighted it. We preserved a strict silence in the room, for we had already learned that on the slightest interruption our Yankee drew himself into his shell again. He glanced round with a self-satisfied smile as he remarked our expectant looks, and continued through a halo of smoke:

"Now, which of you gentlemen has ever been in Arizona? None, I'll warrant. And of all English or Americans as can put pen to paper, how many has been in Arizona? Precious few, I calc'late. I've been there, sirs, lived there for years; and when I think of what I've seen there, why, I can scarce get myself to believe it now.

"Ah, there's a country! I was one of Walker's filibusters, as they chose to call us; and after we'd busted up, and the chief was shot, some of us made tracks and located down there. A reg'lar English and American colony, we was, with our wives and children, and all complete. I reckon there's some of the old folk there yet, and that they hain't forgotten what I'm a-going to tell you. No, I warrant they hain't, never on this side of the grave, sirs.

"I was talking about the country, though; and I guess I could astonish you considerable if I spoke of nothing else. To think of such a land being built for a few 'Greasers' and half-breeds! It's a misusing of the gifts of Providence, that's what I calls it. Grass as hung over a chap's head as he rode through it, and trees so thick that you couldn't catch a glimpse of blue sky for leagues and leagues, and orchids like umbrellas! Maybe some of you has seen a plant as they calls the 'flycatcher' in some parts of the States?"

"Dionœa muscipula," murmured Dawson, our scientific man *par excellence*.

"Ah, Die near a municipal,' that's him! You'll see a fly stand on that 'ere plant, and then you'll see the two sides of a leaf snap up together and catch it between them, and grind it up and mash it to bits, for all the world like some great sea squid with its beak; and hours after, if you open the leaf, you'll see the body lying half-digested, and in bits. Well, I've seen those flytraps in Arizona with leaves eight and ten feet long, and thorns or teeth a foot or more; why, they could—But darn it, I'm going too fast!

"It's about the death of Joe Hawkins I was going to tell you; 'bout as queer a thing, I reckon, as ever you heard tell on. There wasn't nobody in Arizona as didn't know of Joe Hawkins—'Alabama' Joe, as he was called there. A reg'lar out and outer, he was, 'bout the darndest skunk as ever man clapt eyes on. He was a good chap enough, mind ye, as long as you stroked him the right way; but rile him anyhow, and he was worse nor a wildcat. I've seen him empty his six-shooter into a crowd as chanced to jostle him a-going into Simpson's bar when there was a dance on; and he bowied Tom Hooper 'cause he spilt his liquor over his weskit by mistake. No, he didn't stick at murder, Joe didn't; and he weren't a man to be trusted further nor you could see him.

"Now, at the time I tell on, when Joe Hawkins was swaggerin' about the town and layin' down the law with his shootin'-irons, there was an Englishman there of the name of Scott—Tom Scott, if I rec'lects aright. This chap Scott was a thorough Britisher (beggin' the present company's pardon), and yet he didn't freeze much to the British set there, or they didn't freeze much to him. He was a quiet, simple man, Scott was—rather too quiet for a rough set like that; sneakin', they called him, but he weren't that. He kept hisself mostly apart, and didn't interfere with nobody so long as he were left alone. Some said as how he'd been kinder ill-treated at home—been a Chartist, or something of that sort, and had to up stick and run; but he never spoke of it hisself, an' never complained. Bad luck or good, that chap kept a stiff lip on him.

"This chap Scott was a sort o' butt among the men about Arizona, for he was so quiet an' simple-like. There was no party either to take up his grievances; for, as I've been saying, the Britishers hardly counted him one of them, and many a rough joke they played on him. He never cut up rough, but was polite to all hisself. I think the boys got to think he hadn't much grit in him till he showed 'em their mistake.

"It was in Simpson's bar as the row got up, an' that led to the queer thing I was going to tell you of. Alabama Joe and one or two other rowdies were dead on the Britishers in those days, and they spoke their opinions pretty free, though I warned them as there'd be an almighty muss. That partic'lar night Joe was nigh half drunk, an' he swaggered about the town with his six-shooter, lookin' out for a quarrel. Then he turned into the bar, where he know'd he'd find some o' the English as ready for one as he was hisself. Sure enough, there was half a dozen lounging about, an'

Tom Scott standin' alone before the stove. Joe sat down by the table, and put his revolver and bowie down in front of him. 'Them's my arguments, Jeff,' he says to me, 'if any white-livered Britisher dares give me the lie.' I tried to stop him, sirs; but he weren't a man as you could easily turn, an' he began to speak in a way as no chap could stand. Why, even a 'Greaser' would flare up if you said as much of Greaserland! There was a commotion at the bar, an' every man laid his hands on his wepins; but before they could draw, we heard a quiet voice from the stove: 'Say your prayers, Joe Hawkins; for, by Heaven, you're a dead man!' Joe turned round, and looked like grabbin' at his iron; but it weren't no manner of use. Tom Scott was standing up, covering him with his derringer, a smile on his white face, but the very devil shining in his eye. 'It ain't that the old country has used me over-well,' he says, 'but no man shall speak agin it afore me, and live.' For a second or two I could see his finger tighten round the trigger, an' then he gave a laugh, an' threw the pistol on the floor. 'No,' he says, 'I can't shoot a half-drunk man. Take your dirty life, Joe, an' use it better nor you have done. You've been nearer the grave this night than you will be ag'in until your time comes. You'd best make tracks now, I guess. Nay, never look back at me, man; I'm not afeard at your shootin'-iron. A bully's nigh always a coward.' And he swung contemptuously round, and relighted his half-smoked pipe from the stove, while Alabama slunk out o' the bar, with the laughs of the Britishers ringing in his ears. I saw his face as he passed me, and on it I saw murder, sirs— murder, as plain as ever I seed anything in my life.

"I stayed in the bar after the row, and watched Tom Scott as he shook hands with the men about. It seemed kinder queer to me to see him smilin' and cheerful-like; for I knew Joe's bloodthirsty mind, and that the Englishman had small chance of ever seeing the morning. He lived in an out-of-the-way sort of place, you see, clean off the trail, and had to pass through the Flytrap Gulch to get to it. This here gulch was a marshy, gloomy place, lonely enough during the day even; for it were always a creepy sort o' thing to see the great eight- and ten-foot leaves snapping up if aught touched them; but at night there were never a soul near. Some parts of the marsh, too, were soft and deep, and a body thrown in would be gone by the morning. I could see Alabama Joe crouchin' under the leaves of the great Flytrap in the darkest part of the gulch, with a scowl on his face and a revolver in his hand; I could see it, sirs, as plain as with my two eyes.

" 'Bout midnight Simpson shuts up his bar, so out we had to go. Tom

Scott started off for his three-mile walk at a slashing pace. I just dropped him a hint as he passed me, for I kinder liked the chap. 'Keep your derringer loose in your belt, sir,' I says, 'for you might chance to need it.' He looked round at me with his quiet smile, and then I lost sight of him in the gloom. I never thought to see him again. He'd hardly gone afore Simpson comes up to me and says: 'There'll be a nice job in the Flytrap Gulch tonight, Jeff; the boys say that Hawkins started half an hour ago to wait for Scott and shoot him on sight. I calc'late the coroner'll be wanted tomorrow.'

"What passed in the gulch that night? It were a question as were asked pretty free next morning. A half-breed was in Ferguson's store after daybreak, and he said as he'd chanced to be near the gulch 'bout one in the morning. It warn't easy to get at his story, he seemed so uncommon scared; but he told us, at last, as he'd heard the fearfulest screams in the stillness of the night. There weren't no shots, he said, but scream after scream, kinder muffled, like a man with a serape over his head, an' in mortal pain. Abner Brandon, and me, and a few more was in the store at the time; so we mounted and rode out to Scott's house, passing through the gulch on the way. There weren' nothing partic'lar to be seen there—no blood nor marks of a fight, nor nothing; and when we gets up to Scott's house out he comes to meet us as fresh as a lark. 'Halloo, Jeff!' says he, 'no need for the pistols after all. Come in an' have a cocktail, boys.' 'Did ye see or hear nothing as ye came home last night?' says I. 'No,' says he; 'all was quiet enough. An owl kinder moaning in the Flytrap Gulch—that was all. Come, jump off and have a glass.' 'Thank ye,' says Abner. So off we gets, and Tom Scott rode into the settlement with us when we went back.

"An all-fired commotion was on in Main Street as we rode into it. The 'Merican party seemed to have gone clean crazed. Alabama Joe was gone, not a darned particle of him left. Since he went out to the gulch nary eye had seen him. As we got off our horses there was a considerable crowd in front of Simpson's, and some ugly looks at Tom Scott, I can tell you. There was a clickin' of pistols, and I saw as Scott had his hand in his bosom, too. There weren't a single English face about. 'Stand aside, Jeff Adams,' says Zebb Humphrey, as great a scoundrel as ever lived; 'you hain't got no hand in this game. Say, boys, are we, free Americans, to be murdered by any darned Britisher?' It was the quickest thing as ever I seed. There was a rush an' a crack; Zebb was down, with Scott's ball in his thigh, and Scott hisself was on the ground with a dozen men holding him. It weren't no use struggling, so he lay quiet. They seemed a bit uncertain what to do with him at first, but then one of Alabama's special chums put them up to it. 'Joe's gone,' he said; 'nothing ain't surer nor that, an' there lies the man as killed him. Some on you knows as Joe went on business to the gulch last night; he never came back. That 'ere Britisher passed through after he'd gone; they'd had a row, screams is heard 'mong the great flytraps. I say ag'in, he has played poor Joe some o' his sneakin' tricks, an' thrown him into the swamp. It ain't no wonder as the body is gone. But air we to stan' by and see English murderin' our own chums? I guess not. Let Judge Lynch try him, that's what I say.' 'Lynch him!' shouted a hundred angry voices—for all the ragtag an' bobtail o' the settlement was round us by this time. 'Here, boys, fetch a rope, and swing him up. Up with him over Simpson's door!' 'See here, though,' says another, coming forward; 'let's hang him by the great flytrap in the gulch. Let Joe see as he's revenged, if so be as he's buried 'bout theer.' There was a shout for this, an' away they went, with Scott tied on his mustang in the middle, and a mounted guard, with cocked revolvers, round him; for we knew as there was a score or so Britishers about, as didn't seem to recognize Judge Lynch, and was dead on a free fight.

"I went out with them, my heart bleedin' for Scott, though he didn't seem a cent put out, he didn't. He were game to the backbone. Seems kinder queer, sirs, hangin' a man to a flytrap; but our'n were a reg'lar tree, and the leaves like a brace of boats with a hinge between 'em and thorns at the bottom.

"We passed down the gulch to the place where the great one grows, and there we seed it with the leaves, some open, some shut. But we seed something worse nor that. Standin' round the tree was some thirty men, Britishers all, an' armed to the teeth. They was waitin' for us, evidently, an' had a business-like look about 'em as if they'd come for something and meant to have it. There was the raw material ther for about as warm a scrimmidge as ever I seed. As we rode up, a great red-bearded Scotchman—Cameron were his name—stood out afore the rest, his revolver cocked in his hand. 'See here, boys,' he says, 'you've got no call to hurt a hair of that man's head. You hain't proved as Joe is dead yet; and if you had, you hain't proved as Scott killed him. Anyhow, it were in self-defence; for you all know as he was lying in wait for Scott, to shoot him on sight; so I say ag'in, you hain't got no call to hurt that man; and

what's more, I've got thirty-six-barreled arguments against your doin' it.'
'It's an interestin' p'int, and worth arguin' out,' said the man as was
Alabama Joe's special chum. There was a clickin' of pistols, and a loosenin' of knives, and the two parties began to draw up to one another, an' it
looked like a rise in the mortality of Arizona. Scott was standing behind
with a pistol at his ear if he stirred, lookin' quiet and composed as having
no money on the table, when sudden he gives a start an' a shout as rang in
our ears like a trumpet. 'Joe!' he cried, 'Joe! Look at him! In the flytrap!'
We all turned an' looked where he was pointin'. Jerusalem! I think we
won't get that picter out of our minds ag'in. One of the great leaves of the
flytrap, that had been shut and touchin' the ground as it lay, was slowly
rolling back upon its hinges. There, lying like a child in its cradle, was
Alabama Joe in the hollow of the leaf. The great thorns had been slowly
driven through his heart as it shut upon him. We could see as he'd tried to
cut his way out, for there was a slit on the thick, fleshy leaf, an' his bowie
was in his hand; but it had smothered him first. He'd laid down on it likely
to keep the damp off while he were a'waitin' for Scott, and it had closed
on him as you've seen your little hothouse ones do on a fly; an' there he
were as we found him, torn and crushed into pulp by the great, jagged
teeth of the man-eatin' plant. There, sirs, I think you'll own as that's a
curious story.''

"And what became of Scott?" asked Jack Sinclair.

"Why, we carried him back on our shoulders, we did, to Simpson's bar,
and he stood us liquors round. Made a speech, too—a darned fine
speech—from the counter. Somethin' about the British lion an' the 'Merican eagle walkin' arm in arm forever an' a day. And now, sirs, that yarn
was long, and my cheroot's out, so I reckon I'll make tracks afore it's
later''; and with a ''Good-night!'' he left the room.

"A most extraordinary narrative!" said Dawson. "Who would have
thought a diancea had such power!"

"Deuced rum yarn!" said young Sinclair.

"Evidently a matter-of-fact, truthful man," said the doctor.

"Or the most original liar that ever lived," said I. I wonder which he
was.

Besides writing two fantastic novels, The Flying Inn *and* The
Napoleon of Notting Hill, **Gilbert Keith Chesterton**
*(1874–1936) was the creator of one of the world's three most
famous detectives and the master of paradoxical stories.
Though sometimes criticized because Father Brown always
found mundane explanations for seemingly impossible events, in
other stories, such as "The Finger of Stone," Mr. Chesterton's
resolutions could be shattering.*

THE FINGER OF STONE

G. K. Chesterton

THREE young men on a walking tour came to a halt outside the little
town of Carillon, in the south of France; which is doubtless described in
the guide books as famous for its fine old Byzantine monastery, now the
seat of a university; and for having been the scene of the labors of Boyg.
At that name, at least, the reader will be reasonably thrilled; for he must
have seen it in any number of newspapers and novels. Boyg and the Bible
are periodically reconciled at religious conferences; Boyg broadens and
slightly bewilders the minds of numberless heroes of long psychological
stories, which begin in the nursery and nearly end in the madhouse. The
journalist, writing rapidly his recurrent reference to the treatment meted out
to pioneers like Galileo, pauses in the effort to think of another example,
and always rounds off the sentence either with Bruno or with Boyg. But
the mildly orthodox are equally fascinated, and feel a glow of agnosticism
while they continue to say that, since the discoveries of Boyg, the doctrine
of Homoousian or of the human conscience does not stand where it did;
wherever that was. It is needless to say that Boyg was a great discoverer,
for the public has long regarded him with the warmest reverence and
gratitude on that ground. It is also unnecessary to say what he discovered;

105

for the public will never display the faintest curiosity about that. It is vaguely understood that it was something about fossils, or the long period required for petrifaction; and that it generally implied those anarchic or anonymous forces of evolution supposed to be hostile to religion. But certainly none of the discoveries he made while he was alive was so sensational, in the newspaper sense, as the discovery that was made about him when he was dead. And this, the more private and personal matter, is what concerns us here.

The three tourists had just agreed to separate for an hour, and meet again for luncheon at the little café opposite; and the different ways in which they occupied their time and indulged their tastes will serve for a sufficient working summary of their personalities. Arthur Armitage was a dark and grave young man, with a great deal of money, which he spent on a conscientious and continuous course of self-culture, especially in the matter of art and architecture; and his earnest aquiline profile was already set towards the Byzantine monastery, for the exhaustive examination of which he had already prepared himself, as if he were going to pass an examination rather than to make one. The man next him, though himself an artist, betrayed no such artistic ardour. He was a painter who wasted most of his time as a poet; but Armitage, who was always picking up geniuses, had become in some sense his patron in both departments. His name was Gabriel Gale; a long, loose, rather listless man with yellow hair; but a man not easy for any patron to patronize.

He generally did as he liked in an abstracted fashion; and what he very often liked to do was nothing. On this occasion he showed a lamentable disposition to drift towards the café first, and having drunk a glass or two of wine, he drifted not into the town but out of it, roaming about the steep bare slope above, with a rolling eye on the rolling clouds; and talking to himself until he found somebody else to talk to, which happened when he put his foot through the glass roof of a studio just below him on the steep incline. As it was an artist's studio, however, their quarrel fortunately ended in an argument about the future of realistic art; and when he turned up to lunch, that was the extent of his acquaintance with the quaint and historic town of Carillon.

The name of the third man was Garth; he was shorter and uglier and somewhat older than the others, but with a much livelier eye in his hatchet face; he stepped much more briskly, and in the matter of a knowledge of the world, the other two were babies under his charge. He was a very able medical practitioner, with a hobby of more fundamental scientific inquiry; and for him the whole town, university and studio, monastery and café, was only the temple of the presiding genius of Boyg. But in this case the practical instinct of Dr. Garth would seem to have guided him rightly; for he discovered things considerably more startling than anything the antiquarian found in the Romanesque arches or the poet in the rolling clouds. And it is his adventures, in that single hour before lunch, upon which this tale must turn.

The café tables stood on the pavement under a row of trees opposite the old round gate in the wall, through which could be seen the white gleam of the road up which they had just been walking. But the steep hills were so high round the town that they rose clear above the wall, in a more enormous wall of smooth and slanting rock, bare except for occasional clumps of cactus. There was no crack in that sloping wilderness of stone except the rather shallow and stony bed of a little stream. Lower down, where the stream reached the level of the valley, rose the dark domes of the basilica of the old monastery; and from this a curious stairway of rude stones ran some way up the hill beside the watercourse, and stopped at a small and solitary building looking little more than a shed made of stones. Some little way higher the gleam of the glass roof of the studio, with which Gale had collided in his unconscious wanderings, marked the last spot of human habitation in all those rocky wastes that rose about the little town.

Armitage and Gale were already seated at the table when Dr. Garth walked up briskly and sat down somewhat abruptly.

"Have you fellows heard the news?" he asked.

He spoke somewhat sharply, for he was faintly annoyed by the attitudes of the antiquarian and the artist, who were deep in their own dreamier and less practical tastes and topics. Armitage was saying at the moment:

"Yes, I suppose I've seen today some of the very oldest sculpture of the veritable Dark Ages. And it's not stiff like some Byzantine work; there's a touch of the true grotesque you generally get in Gothic."

"Well, I've seen today some of the newest sculpture of the Modern Ages," replied Gale, "and I fancy they are the veritable Dark Ages. Quite enough of the true grotesque up in that studio, I can tell you."

"Have you heard the news, I say?" rapped out the doctor. "Boyg is dead."

Gale stopped in a sentence about Gothic architecture, and said seriously, with a sort of hazy reverence:

"*Requiescat in pace*. Who was Boyg?"

"Well, really," replied the doctor. "I did think every baby had heard of Boyg."

"Well, I dare say you've never heard of Paradou," answered Gale. "Each of us lives in his little cosmos with its classes and degrees. Probably you haven't heard of the most advanced sculptor, or perhaps of the latest lacrosse expert or champion chess player."

It was characteristic of the two men, that while Gale went on talking in the air about an abstract subject, till he had finished his own train of thought, Armitage had a sufficient proper sense of the presence of something more urgent to relapse into silence. Nevertheless, he unconsciously looked down at his notes; at the name of the advanced sculptor he looked up.

"Who is Paradou?" he asked.

"Why, the man I've been talking to this morning," replied Gale. "His sculpture's advanced enough for anybody. He's no end of a chap; talks more than I do, and talks very well. Thinks too; I should think he could do everything except sculpt. There his theories get in his way. As I told him, this notion of the new realism—"

"Perhaps we might drop realism and attend to reality," said Dr. Garth grimly. "I tell you Boyg is dead. And that's not the worst either."

Armitage looked up from his notes with something of the vagueness of his friend the poet. "If I remember right," he said, "Professor Boyg's discovery was concerned with fossils."

"Professor Boyg's discovery involved the extension of the period required for petrifaction as distinct from fossilization," replied the doctor stiffly, "and thereby relegated biological origins to a period which permits the chronology necessary to the hypothesis of natural selection. It may affect you as humorous to interject the observation 'loud cheers,' but I assure you the scientific world, which happens to be competent to judge, was really moved with amazement as well as admiration."

"In fact it was petrified to hear it couldn't be petrified," suggested the poet.

"I have really no time for your flippancy," said Garth. "I am up against a great ugly fact."

Armitage interposed in the benevolent manner of a chairman. "We must really let Garth speak; come, Doctor, what is it all about? Begin at the beginning."

"Very well," said the doctor, in his staccato way. "I'll begin at the beginning. I came to this town with a letter of introduction to Boyg himself; and as I particularly wanted to visit the geological museum, which his own munificence provided for this town, I went there first. I found all the windows of the Boyg Museum were broken; and the stones thrown by the rioters were actually lying about the room within a foot or two of the glass cases, one of which was smashed."

"Donations to the geological museum, no doubt," remarked Gale. "A munificent patron happens to pass by, and just heaves in a valuable exhibit through the window. I don't see why that shouldn't be done in what you call the world of science; I'm sure it's done all right in the world of art. Old Paradou's busts and bas-reliefs are just great rocks chucked at the public and—"

"Paradou may go to—Paradise, shall we say?" said Garth, with pardonable impatience. "Will nothing make you understand that something has really happened that isn't any of your ideas and isms? It wasn't only the geological museum; it was the same everywhere. I passed by the house Boyg first lived in, where they properly put up a medallion; and the medallion was all splashed with mud. I crossed the marketplace, where they put up a statue to him just recently. It was still hung with wreaths of laurel by his pupils and the party that appreciates him; but they were half torn away, as if there had been a struggle, and stones had evidently been thrown, for a piece of the hand was chipped off."

"Paradou's statue, no doubt," observed Gale. "No wonder they threw things at it."

"I think not," replied the doctor, in the same hard voice. "It wasn't because it was Paradou's statue, but because it was Boyg's statue. It was the same business as the museum and the medallion. No, there's been something like a French Revolution here on the subject; the French are like that. You remember the riot in the Breton village where Renan was born, against having a statue of him. You know, I suppose, that Boyg was a Norwegian by birth, and only settled here because the geological formation, and the supposed mineral properties of that stream there, offered the best field for his investigations. Well, besides the fits the parsons were in at his theories in general, it seems he bumped into some barbarous local superstition as well; about it being a sacred stream that froze snakes into ammonites at a wink; a common myth, of course, for the same was told about St. Hilda at Whitby. But there are peculiar conditions that made it pretty hot in this place. The theological students fight with the medical students, one for Rome and the other for Reason; and they say there's a sort of raving lunatic of a Peter the Hermit, who lives in that hermitage on the hill over there, and every now and then comes out waving his arms and setting the place on fire.''

"I heard something about that," remarked Armitage. "The priest who showed me over the monastery; I think he was the head man there—anyhow, he was a most learned and eloquent gentleman—told me about a holy man on the hill who was almost canonized already.''

"One is tempted to wish he were martyred already; but the martyrdom, if any, was not his,'' said Garth darkly. "Allow me to continue my story in order. I had crossed the marketplace to find Professor Boyg's private house, which stood at the corner of it. I found the shutters up and the house aparently empty, except for one old servant, who refused at first to tell me anything; indeed, I found a good deal of rustic reluctance on both sides to tell a foreigner anything. But when I had managed to make the nature of my introduction quite plain to him, he finally broke down; and told me his master was dead.''

There was a pause, and then Gale, who seemed for the first time somewhat impressed, asked abstractedly:

"Where is his tomb? Your tale is really rather strange and dramatic, and obviously it must go on to his tomb. Your pilgrimage ought to end in finding a magnificent monument of marble and gold, like the tomb of Napoleon, and then finding that even the grave had been desecrated.''

"He had no tomb,'' replied Garth sternly, "though he will have many monuments. I hope to see the day when he will have a statue in every town, he whose statue is now insulted in his own town. But he will have no tomb.''

"And why not?'' asked the staring Armitage.

"His body cannot be found,'' answered the doctor; "no trace of him can be found anywhere.''

"Then how do you know he is dead?'' asked the other.

There was an instant of silence, and then the doctor spoke out in a voice fuller and stronger than before:

"Why, as to that,'' he said, "I think he is dead because I am sure he is murdered.''

Armitage shut his note book, but continued to look down steadily at the table. "Go on with your story,'' he said.

"Boyg's old servant," resumed the doctor, "who is a queer, silent, yellow-faced old card, was at last induced to tell me of the existence of Boyg's assistant, of whom I think he was rather jealous. The professor's scientific helper and right-hand man is a man of the name of Bertrand, and a very able man, too, eminently worthy of the great man's confidence, and intensely devoted to his cause. He is carrying on Boyg's work so far as it can be carried on; and about Boyg's death or disappearance he knows the little that can be known. It was when I finally ran him to earth in a little house full of Boyg's books and instruments, at the bottom of the hill just beyond the town, that I first began to realize the nature of this sinister and mysterious business. Bertrand is a quiet man, though he had a little of the pardonable vanity which is not uncommon in assistants. One would sometimes fancy the great discovery was almost as much his as his master's; but that does no harm, since it only makes him fight for his master's fame almost as if it were his. But in fact he is not only concerned about the discovery; or rather, he is not only concerned about that discovery. I had not looked for long at the dark bright eyes and keen face of that quiet young man before I realized that there was something else that he is trying to discover. As a matter of fact, he is no longer merely a scientific assistant, or even a scientific student. Unless I am much mistaken, he is playing the part of an amateur detective.

"Your artistic training, my friends, may be an excellent thing for discovering a poet, or even a sculptor; but you will forgive me for thinking a scientific training rather better for discovering a murderer. Bertrand has gone to work in a very workmanlike way, I consider, and I can tell you in outline what he has discovered so far. Boyg was last seen by Bertrand descending the hillside by the watercourse, having just come away from the studio of Gale's friend the sculptor, where he was sitting for an hour every morning. I may say here, rather for the sake of logical method than because it is needed by the logical argument, that the sculptor at any rate had no quarrel with Boyg, but was, on the contrary, an ardent admirer of him as an advanced and revolutionary character."

"I know," said Gale, seeming to take his head suddenly out of the clouds. "Paradou says realistic art must be founded on the modern energy of science; but the fallacy of that—"

"Let me finish with the facts first before you retire into your theories," said the doctor firmly. "Bertrand saw Boyg sit down on the bare hillside for a smoke; and you can see from here how bare a hillside it is; a man walking for hours on it would still be as visible as a fly crawling on a ceiling. Bertrand says he was called away to the crisis of an experiment in the laboratory; when he looked again he could not see his master, and he has never seen him from that day to this.

"At the foot of the hill, and at the bottom of the flight of steps which runs up to the hermitage, is the entrance to the great monastic buildings on the very edge of the town. The very first thing you come to on that side is the great quadrangle, which is enclosed by cloisters, and by the rooms or cells of the clerical or semi-clerical students. I need not trouble you with the tale of the political compromise by which this part of the institution has remained clerical, while the scientific and other schools beyond it are now entirely secular. But it is important to fix in your mind the fact itself: that the monastic part is on the very edge of the town, and the other part bars its way, so to speak, to the inside of the town. Boyg could not possibly have gone past that secular barrier, dead or alive, without being under the eyes of crowds who were more excited about him than about anything else in the world. For the whole place was in a fuss, and even a riot for him as well as against him. Something happened to him on the hillside, or anyhow before he came to the internal barrier. My friend the amateur detective set to work to examine the hillside, or all of it that could seriously count; an enormous undertaking, but he did it as if with a microscope. Well, he found that rocky field, when examined closely, very much what it looks even from here. There are no caves or even holes; there are no chasms or even cracks in that surface or blank stone for miles and miles. A rat could not be hidden in those few tufts of prickly pear. He could not find a hiding place; but for all that, he found a hint. The hint was nothing more than a faded scrap of paper, damp and draggled from the shallow bed of the brook, but faintly decipherable on it were words in the writing of the Master. They were but part of a sentence, but they included the words, 'will call on you tomorrow to tell you something you ought to know.'

"My friend Bertrand sat down and thought it out. The letter had been in the water, so it had not been thrown away in the town, for the highly scientific reason that the river does not flow uphill. There only remained on the higher ground the sculptor's studio and the hermitage. But Boyg would not write to the sculptor to warn him that he was going to call, since he went to his studio every morning. Presumably the person he was going to call on was the hermit; and a guess might well be made about the nature of what he had to say. Bertrand knew better than anybody that Boyg had just brought his great discovery to a crushing completeness, with fresh facts and ratifications; and it seems likely enough that he went to announce it to his most fanatical opponent, to warn him to give up the struggle."

Gale, who was gazing up into the sky with his eye on a bird, again abruptly intervened.

"In these attacks on Boyg," he said, "were there any attacks on his private character?"

"Even these madmen couldn't attack that," replied Garth with some heat. "He was the best sort of Scandinavian, as simple as a child, and I really believe as innocent. But they hated him for all that; and you can see for yourself that their hatred begins to appear on the horizon of our inquiry. He went to tell the truth in the hour of triumph; and he never reappeared to the light of the sun."

Armitage's far-away gaze was fixed on the solitary cell halfway up the hill. "You don't mean seriously," he said, "that the man they talk about as a saint, the friend of my friend the abbot, or whatever he is, is neither more nor less than an assassin?"

"You talked to your friend the abbot about Romanesque sculpture," replied Garth. "If you had talked to him about fossils, you might have seen another side of his character. These Latin priests are often polished enough, but you bet they're pointed as well. As for the other man on the hill, he's allowed by his superiors to live what they call the eremitical life; but he's jolly well allowed to do other things, too. On great occasions he's allowed to come down here and preach, and I can tell you there is Bedlam let loose when he does. I might be ready to excuse the man as a sort of a maniac; but I haven't the slightest difficulty in believing that he is a homicidal maniac."

"Did your friend Bertrand take any legal steps on his suspicions?" asked Armitage, after a pause.

"Ah, that's where the mystery begins," replied the doctor.

After a moment of frowning silence, he resumed. "Yes, he did make a formal charge to the police, and the Juge d'Instruction examined a good many people and so on, and said the charge had broken down. It broke down over the difficulty in most murders. Now the hermit, who is called Hyacinth, I believe, was summoned in due course; but he had no difficulty in showing that his hermitage was as bare and as hard as the hill-side. It seemed as if nobody could possibly have concealed a corpse in those stone walls, or dug a grave in that rocky floor. Then it was the turn of the abbot, as you call him, Father Bernard of the Catholic College. And he managed to convince the magistrate that the same was true of the cells surrounding the college quadrangle, and all the other rooms under his control. They were all like empty boxes, with barely a stick or two of furniture; less than usual, in fact, for some of the sticks had been broken up for the bonfire demonstration I told you of. Anyhow, that was the line of defence, and I dare say it was well conducted, for Bernard is a very able man, and knows about many other things besides Romanesque architecture; and Hyacinth, fanatic as he is, is famous as a persuasive orator. Anyhow, it was successful, the case broke down; but I am sure my friend Bertrand is only biding his time, and means to bring it up again. These difficulties about the concealment of a corpse—Hullo! Why here he is in person."

He broke off in surprise as a young man walking rapidly down the street paused a moment, and then approached the café table at which they sat. He was dressed with all the funereal French respectability: his black stove-pipe hat, his high and stiff black neckcloth resembling a stock, and the curious corners of dark beard at the edges of his chin, gave him an antiquated air like a character out of Gaboriau. But if he was out of Gaboriau, he was nobody less than Lecocq; the dark eyes in his pale face might indeed be called the eyes of a born detective. At this moment, the pale face was paler than usual with excitement, and as he stopped a moment behind the doctor's chair, he said to him in a low voice:

"I have found out."

Dr. Garth sprang to his feet, his eyes brilliant with curiosity; then, recovering his conventional manner, he presented M. Bertrand to his friends, saying to the former, "You may speak freely with us, I think; we have no interest except an interest in the truth."

"I have found the truth," said the Frenchman, with compressed lips. "I know now what these murderous monks have done with the body of Boyg."

"Are we to be allowed to hear it?" asked Armitage gravely.

"Everyone will hear it in three days' time," replied the pale Frenchman. "As the authorities refuse to reopen the question, we are holding a public meeting in the market place to demand that they do so. The assassins will be there, doubtless, and I shall not only denounce but convict them to their faces. Be there yourself, monsieur, on Thursday at half-past two, and you will learn how one of the world's greatest men was done to death by his enemies. For the moment I will only say one word. As the great Edgar Poe said in your own language, 'Truth is not always in a well.' I believe it is sometimes too obvious to be seen.''

Gabriel Gale, who had rather the appearance of having gone to sleep, seemed to rouse himself with an unusual animation.

"That's true," he said, "and that's the truth about the whole business."

Armitage turned to him with an expression of quiet amusement.

"Surely you're not playing the detective, Gale," he said. "I never pictured such a thing as your coming out of fairyland to assist Scotland Yard."

"Perhaps Gale thinks he can find the body," suggested Dr. Garth, laughing.

"Why, yes, in a way," he said; "in fact, I'm pretty sure I can find the body. In fact, in a manner of speaking, I've found it."

Those with any intimations of the personality of Mr. Arthur Armitage will not need to be told that he kept a diary; and endeavoured to note down his impressions of foreign travel with atmospheric sympathy and the *mot juste*. But the pen dropped from his hand, so to speak, or at least wandered over the page in a mazy desperation, in the attempt to describe the great mob meeting, or rather the meeting of two mobs, which took place in the picturesque market place in which he had wandered alone a few days before, criticizing the style of the statue, or admiring the sky-line of the basilica. He had read and written about democracy all his life; and when first he met it, it swallowed him like an earthquake. One actual and appalling difference divided this French mob in a provincial market from all the English mobs he had ever seen in Hyde Park or Trafalgar Square. These Frenchmen had not come there to get rid of their feelings, but to get rid of their enemies. Something would be done as a result of this sort of public meeting; it might be murder, but it would be something.

And although, or rather because, it had this militant ferocity, it had also a sort of military discipline. The clusters of men voluntarily deployed into cordons, and in some rough fashion followed the command of leaders. Father Bernard was there, with a face of bronze, like the mask of a Roman emperor, eagerly obeyed by his crowd of crusading devotees, and beside him the wild preacher, Hyacinth, who looked himself like a dead man brought out of the grave, with a face built out of bones, and cavernous eye-sockets deep and dark enough to hide the eyes. On the other side were the grim pallor of Bertrand and the rat-like activity of the red-haired Dr. Garth; their own anticlerical mob was roaring behind them, and their eyes were alight with triumph. Before Armitage could collect himself sufficiently to make proper notes of any of these things, Bertrand had sprung upon a chair placed near the pedestal of the statue, and announced almost without words, by one dramatic gesture, that he had come to avenge the dead.

Then the words came, and they came thick and fast, telling and terrible; but Armitage heard them as in a dream till they reached the point for which he was waiting; the point that would awaken any dreamer. He heard the prose poems of laudation, the hymn to Boyg the hero, the tale of his tragedy so far as he knew it already. He heard the official decision about the impossibility of the clerics' concealing the corpse, as he had heard it already. And then he and the whole crowd leapt together at something they did not know before; or rather, as in all such riddles, something they did know and did not understand.

"They plead that their cells are bare and their lives simple," Bertrand was saying, "and it is true that these slaves of superstition are cut off from the natural joys of men. But they have their joys; oh, believe me, they have their festivities. If they cannot rejoice in love, they can rejoice in hatred. And everybody seems to have forgotten that on the very day the Master vanished, the theological students in their own quadrangle burnt him in effigy. In effigy."

A thrill that was hardly a whisper, but was wilder than a cry, went through the whole crowd; and men had taken in the whole meaning before they could keep pace with the words that followed.

"Did they burn Bruno in effigy? Did they burn Dolet in effigy?" Bertrand was saying, with a white fanatical face. "Those martyrs of the truth were burned alive for the good of their Church and for the glory of their God. Oh, yes, progress has improved them; and they did not burn Boyg alive. But they burned him dead; and that is how they obliterated the traces of the way they had done him to death. I have said that truth is not always hidden in a well, but rather high on a tower. And while I have searched every crevice and cactus bush for the bones of my master, it was in truth in public, under the open sky, before a roaring crowd in the quadrangle, that his body vanished from the sight of men."

When the last cheer and howl of a whole hell of such noises had died away, Father Bernard succeeded in making his voice heard.

"It is enough to say in answer to this maniac charge that the atheists who bring it against us cannot induce their own atheistic government to support them. But as the charge is against Father Hyacinth rather than against me, I will ask him to reply to it.''

There was another tornado of conflicting noises when the eremitical preacher opened his mouth; but his very tones had a certain power of piercing, and quelling it. There was something strange in such a voice coming out of such a skull-and-crossbones of a countenance; for it was unmistakably the musical and moving voice that had stirred so many congregations and pilgrimages. Only in this crisis it had an awful accent of reality, which was beyond any arts of oratory. But before the tumult had yet died away Armitage, moved by some odd nervous instinct, had turned abruptly to Garth and said, ''What's become of Gale? He said he was going to be here. Didn't he talk some nonsense about bringing the body himself?''

Dr. Garth shrugged his shoulders. ''I imagine he's talking some other nonsense at the top of the hill somewhere else. You mustn't ask poets to remember all the nonsense they talk.''

''My friends,'' Father Hyacinth was saying, in quiet but penetrating tones. ''I have no answer to give to this charge. I have no proofs with which to refute it. If a man can be sent to the guillotine on such evidence, to the guillotine I will go. Do you fancy I do not know that innocent men have been guillotined? M. Bertrand spoke of the burning of Bruno, as if it is only the enemies of the Church that have been burned. Does any Frenchman forget that Joan of Arc was burned; and was she guilty? The first Christians were tortured for being cannibals, a charge as probable as the charge against me. Do you imagine because you kill men now by modern machinery and modern law, that we do not know that you are as likely to kill unjustly as Herod or Heliogabalus? Do you think we do not know that the powers of the world are what they always were, that your lawyers who oppress the poor for hire will shed innocent blood for gold? If I were here to bandy such laywer's talk, I could use it against you more reasonably than you against me. For what reason am I supposed to have imperilled my soul by such a monstrous crime? For a theory about a theory; for a hypothesis, for some thin fantastic notion that a discovery about fossils threatened the everlasting truth. I could point to others who had better reasons for murder than that. I could point to a man who by the death of Boyg has inherited the whole power and position of Boyg. I could point to one who is truly the heir and the man whom the crime benefits; who is known to claim much of the discovery as his own; who has been not so much the assistant as the rival of the dead. He alone has given evidence that Boyg was seen on the hill at all on that fatal day. He alone inherits by the death anything solid, from the largest ambitions in the scientific world, to the smallest magnifying glass in his collection. The man lives, and I could stretch out my hand and touch him.''

Hundreds of faces were turned upon Bertrand with a frightful expression of inhuman eagerness; the turn of the debate had been too dramatic to raise a cry. Bertrand's very lips were pale, but they smiled as they formed the words:

"And what did I do with the body?''

"God grand that you did nothing with it, dead or alive,'' answered the other. "I do not charge you; but if ever you are charged as I am unjustly, you may need a God on that day. Though I were ten times guillotined, God would testify to my innocence; if it were by bidding me walk these streets, like St. Denis, with my head in my hand. I have no other proof. I can call no other witness. He can deliver me if He will.''

There was a sudden silence, which was somehow stronger than a pause; and in it Armitage could be heard saying sharply, and almost querulously:

"Why, here's Gale again, after all. Have you dropped from the sky?''

Gale was indeed sauntering in a clear space round the corner of the statue with all the appearance of having just arrived at a crowded At Home; and Bertrand was quick to seize the chance of an anticlimax to the hermit's oratory.

"This,'' he cried, "is a gentleman who thinks he can find the body himself. Have you brought it with you, monsieur?''

The joke about the poet as detective had already been passed round among many people, and the suggestion received a new kind of applause. Somebody called out in a high, piping voice, "He's got it in his pocket''; and another, in deep sepulchral tones, "His waistcoat pocket.''

Mr. Gale certainly had his hands in his pockets, whether or no he had anything else in them; and it was with great nonchalance that he replied:

"Well, in that sense, I suppose I haven't got it. But you have.''

The next moment he had astonished his friends, who were not used to seeing him so alert, by leaping on the chair, and himself addressing the crowd in clear tones, and in excellent French:

"Well, my friends,'' he said, "the first thing I have to do is to associate myself with everything said by my honorable friend, if he will allow me to call him so, but the merits and high moral qualities of the late Professor

Boyg. Boyg, at any rate, is in every way worthy of all the honor you can pay to him. Whatever else is doubtful, whatever else we differ about, we can all salute in him that search for truth which is the most disinterested of all our duties to God. I agree with my friend Dr. Garth that he deserves to have a statue, not only in his own town, but in every town in the world.''

The anticlericals began to cheer warmly, while their opponents watched in silence, wondering where this last eccentric development might lead. The poet seemed to realize their mystification, and smiled as he continued:

"Perhaps you wonder why I should say that so emphatically. Well, I suppose you all to have your own reasons for recognizing this genuine love of truth in the late professor. But I say it because I happen to know something that perhaps you don't know, which makes me specially certain about his honesty."

"And what is that?" asked Father Bernard, in the pause that followed.

"Because," said Gale, "he was going to see Father Hyacinth to own himself wrong."

Bertrand made a swift movement forward that seemed almost to threaten an assault: but Garth arrested it, and Gale went on, without noticing it.

"Professor Boyg had discovered that his theory was wrong after all. That was the sensational discovery he had made in those last days and with those last experiments. I suspected it when I compared the current tale with his reputation as a simple and kindly man. I did not believe he would have gone merely to triumph over his worst enemy; it was far more probable that he thought it a point of honor to acknowledge his mistake. For, without professing to know much about these things, I am sure that it was a mistake. Things do not, after all, need all those thousand years to petrify in that particular fashion. Under certain conditions, which chemists could explain better than I, they do not need more than one year, or even one day. Something in the properties of the local water, applied or intensified by special methods, can really in a few hours turn an animal organism into a fossil. The scientific experiment has been made; and the proof is before you."

He made a gesture with his hand, and went on, with something more like excitement:

"M. Bertrand is right in saying that truth is not in a well, but on a tower. It is on a pedestal. You have looked at it every day. There is the body of Boyg!"

And he pointed to the statue in the middle of the market place, wreathed with laurel and defaced with stones, as it had stood so long in that quiet square, and looked down at so many casual passers-by.

"Somebody suggested just now," he went on, glancing over a sea of gaping faces, "that I carried the statue in my waistcoat pocket. Well, I don't carry all of it, of course, but this is a part of it," and he took out a small object like a stick of grey chalk; "this is a finger of it knocked off by a stone. I picked it up by the pedestal. If anybody who understands these things likes to look at it, he will agree that the consistency is precisely the same as the admitted fossils in the geological museums."

He held it out to them, but the whole mob stood still as if it also was a mob of men turned to stone.

"Perhaps you think I'm mad," he said pleasantly. "Well, I'm not exactly mad, but I have an odd sort of sympathy with madmen. I can manage them better than most people can, because I can fancy somehow the wild way their minds will work. I understand the man who did this. I know he did, because I talked to him for half the morning; and it's exactly the sort of thing he would do. And when first I heard talk of fossil shells and petrified insects and so on, I did the same thing that such men always do. I exaggerated it into a sort of extravagant vision, a vision of fossil forests, and fossil cattle, and fossil elephants and camels; and so, naturally, to another thought: a coincidence that somehow turned me cold. A Fossil Man.

"It was then that I looked up at the statue; and knew it was not a statue. It was a corpse petrified by the curious chemistry of your strange mountain stream. I call it a fossil as a loose popular term; of course I know enough geology to know it is not the correct term. But I was not concerned with a problem of geology. I was concerned with what some prefer to call criminology and I prefer to call crime. If that extraordinary erection was the corpse, who and where was the criminal? Who was the assassin who had set up the dead man to be at once obvious and invisible; and had, so to speak, hidden him in the broad daylight? Well, you have all heard the arguments about the stream and the scrap of paper, and up to a point I have entirely followed them. Everyone agreed that the secret was somewhere hidden on that bare hill where there was nothing but the grass-roofed studio and the lonely hermitage; and suspicion centered entirely upon the hermitage. For the man in the studio was a fervent friend of the man who was murdered, and one of those rejoicing most heartily at what he had discovered. But perhaps you have rather forgotten what he really

had discovered. His real discovery was of the sort that infuriates friends
and not foes. The man who has the courage to say he is wrong has to face
the worst hatred; the hatred of those who think he is right. Boyg's final
discovery, like our final discovery, rather reverses the relations of those
two little houses on the hill. Even if Father Hyacinth had been a fiend instead of a saint, he had no possible motive to prevent his enemy from
offering him a public apology. It was a believer in Boygism who struck
down Boyg. It was his follower who became his pursuer and persecutor;
who at last turned in unreasonable fury upon him. It was Paradou the
sculptor who snatched up a chisel and struck his philosophical teacher, at
the end of some furious argument about the theory which the artist had
valued only as a wild inspiration, being quite indifferent to the tame question of its truth. I don't think he meant to kill Boyg; I doubt whether anybody could possibly prove he did; and even if he did, I rather doubt
whether he can be held responsible for that or for anything else. But
though Paradou may be a lunatic, he is also a logician; and there is one
more interesting logical step in this story.

"I met Paradou myself this morning; owing to my good luck in putting
my leg through his skylight. He also has his theories and controversies;
and this morning he was very controversial. As I say, I had a long argument with him, all about realism in sculpture. I know many people will tell
you that nothing has ever come out of arguments; and anyhow, if you want
to know what has come out of this, you've got to understand this argument. Everybody was always jeering at poor old Paradou as a sculptor and
saying he turned men into monsters; that his figures had flat heads like
snakes, or sagging knees like elephants, or humps like human camels. And
he was always shouting back at them, 'Yes, and eyes like blindworms
when it comes to seeing your own hideous selves! This is what you *do*
look like, you ugly brutes! These are the crooked, clownish, lumpish attitudes in which you really do stand; only a lot of lying, fashionable por-
trait painters have persuaded you that you look like Graces and Greek
gods.' He was at it hammer and tongs with me this morning; and I dare
say I was lucky he didn't finish that argument with a chisel. But anyhow
the argument wasn't started then. It all came upon him with a rush, when
he had committed his real though probably unintentional killing. As he
stood staring at the corpse, there arose out of the very abyss of his disappointment the vision of a strange vengeance or reparation. He began to see
the vast outlines of a joke as gigantic as the Great Pyramid. He would set

up that grim granite jest in the market-place, to grin for ever at his critics and detractors. The dead man himself had just been explaining to him the process by which the water of that place would rapidly petrify organic substances. The notes and documents of his proof lay scattered about the studio where he had fallen. His own proof should be applied to his own body, for a purpose of which he had never dreamed. If the sculptor simply lifted the body in the ungainly attitude in which it had actually fallen, if he froze or fixed it in the stream and set it upon the public pedestal, it would be the very thing about which he had so bitterly debated; a real man, in a real posture, held up to the scorn of men.

"That insane genius promised himself a lonely laughter, and a secret superiority to all his enemies, in hearing the critics discuss it as the crazy creation of a crank sculptor. He looked forward to the groups that would stand before the statue, and prove the anatomy to be wrong, and clearly demonstrate the posture to be impossible. And he would listen, and laugh inwardly like a true lunatic, knowing that they were proving the utter unreality of a real man. That being his dream, he had no difficulty in carrying it out. He had no need to hide the body; he had it brought down from his studio, not secretly but publicly and even pompously, the finished work of a great sculptor escorted by the devotees of a great discoverer. But indeed, Boyg was something more than a man who made a discovery; and there is, in comparison, a sort of cant even in the talk of a man having the courage to discover it. What other man would have had the courage to undiscover it? That monument that hides a strange sin, hides a much stranger and much rarer virtue. Yes, you do well to hail it as a true scientific trophy. That is the statue of Boyg the Undiscoverer. That cold chimera of the rock is not only the abortion born of some horrible chemical change; it is the outcome of a nobler experiment, which attests for ever the honor and probity of science. You may well praise him as a man of science; for he, at least, in an affair of science, acted like a man. You may well set up statues to him as a hero of science; for he was more of a hero in being wrong than he could ever have been in being right. And though the stars have seen rise, from the soils and substance of our native star, no such monstrosity as that man of stone, heaven may look down with more wonder at the man than at the monster. And we of all schools and of all philosophies can pass it like a funeral procession taking leave of an illustrious grave and, like soldiers, salute it as we pass."

SPECTRAL CREATURES

A pioneer of the psychological suspense novel, **Elisabeth Sanxay Holding** *(1889–1955) was also one of its most skillful practitioners. Noted for her characterization and style, she can perhaps best be seen to advantage in a number of excellent short stories written late in her career for* Ellery Queen's Mystery Magazine *and* Anthony Boucher's The Magazine of Fantasy and Science Fiction. *Certainly one of the most powerful is "The Strange Children," a story of baby-sitting, ghosts, and betrayal.*

THE STRANGE CHILDREN

Elisabeth Sanxay Holding

Mᴀʀᴊᴏʀɪᴇ Smith sat up very straight in the car. When they swerved sharply round a corner, it sent her lurching against the side wall; when they made a sudden stop, it jerked her forward.

And it seemed to her that this was as it should be. Her blue corduroy raincoat was bulky, the collar rubber her chin, and to her stern young conscience, this was right. Right and fitting to be uncomfortable, when you were doing something that you knew was wrong.

It *is* wrong, she told herself. I've always said I'd never do it. Never go to sit with children I hadn't met. It's not fair to them, or to yourself. If anything goes wrong, if they wake up, and call, it's a shock for them to see a complete stranger. And you can't do your best for them, if you don't know them at all.

But this Mrs. Jepson had been so insistent on the telephone, a few hours ago. Do *please* help us out, Miss Smith! We're more or less obliged to go to this thing at the Country Club; we engaged a table there, and invited these people to a late supper ages ago. And Katie, the maid who's been with us for years, was suddenly called away to a sick sister. Do, please, manage it somehow, Miss Smith! I've heard such wonderful things about you from Myra Williams. At half past 8?

I'd like to come earlier, to meet the children before they go to bed, Marjorie had said. But, my dear, the chauffeur's gone on an errand. I couldn't send the car for you until 8. I'll take a taxi, Marjorie had said. But, my dear, it's not *necessary!* Mrs. Jepson had cried. It's a perfect maelstrom here, without Katie. I'll have to get some sort of dinner for my husband and myself, and then we'll have to dress. . . . Really, it's not necessary. The children *never* wake up at night.

You never know when they may, though, Marjorie had said. And if there was a stranger there . . . My dear! Mrs. Jepson had said, my children don't mind strangers the least bit! They're the friendliest children— almost *too* friendly, I sometimes think.

And then she had said, Miss Smith, my husband and I both realize how bothering this is for you. Being asked at the last moment, and such a bitter cold night, and not knowing us, and so on. We're going to make out a check for twenty-five dollars—

No, thank you! Marjorie had said. It will be my usual rate. If I come. Oh, well! We can argue about that later, Mrs. Jepson had said. There are stacks of new books here, my dear, and magazines, and Katie's left all sorts of things in the icebox—cold chicken, and chocolate cake, and salad. . . .

Then she must have realized that she was off on the wrong track, and getting nowhere. The chauffeur says he can get this woman he knows, she had gone on. But I've seen her once, and I hate the idea of leaving the children with her. I'm quite sure she drinks—and suppose she set the place on fire, with a cigarette? That's always my great terror. Do, please, manage to come, Miss Smith, so that I won't have to get that woman.

I was a fool to say yes, Marjorie told herself. This woman who drinks might very well be just an invention of Mrs. Jepson's, to get me there. But if she wasn't an invention then I don't think much of this Mrs. Jepson. No matter how important her engagement was, to leave her little children with someone she didn't trust . . .

But people do things like that. You read about them in the newspapers. If I do decide to marry Johnny, and we have children of our own, I don't see how I could ever bear to leave them with anyone, unless it was Mother, or my own sister, or some old friend. . . . Because—I like children.

The car turned off the highway into a side road that seemed to plunge into a forest, black and frozen. The bare trees creaked in the wind; here and there stood a big old house, some with a light in a window, some in darkness. I suppose it's mostly a summer place, Marjorie thought. They always look rather forlorn in the winter.

Then, as they turned a corner, she saw ahead of them a bungalow, brightly lighted, trim and cheerful as a little launch in a harbor among grim old freighters. The car stopped; the chauffeur, who had not said one word, had not once turned his head, jumped out nimbly and opened the door of the car. Marjorie got out, went along the path and up the two shallow steps to the veranda. I'm glad the house is like this. It's cosy.

She rang the bell, and the door was opened almost at once by a big, heavy man in shirt-sleeves and braces.

"Miss Smith?" he said. "I'm Jepson. Carl Jepson. This is very good of you. Very good."

His big shoulders sloped, his arms hung down in front of him, giving him a clumsy air. He was handsome, after a fashion, with butter-colored hair slick on his skull, good features, but marred by a curious expression of unhappy and almost stupid confusion. He looked at Marjorie, his light brows drawn together.

"You're very young. . . ." he said, in a loud tone.

"I'm twenty-two," she said, a little nettled at what she thought a criticism. "And I've had quite a lot of experience with children."

"Ralph, *darling!*" cried a gay, clear voice. "Let poor Miss Smith come in and get her coat off, do!"

It was the voice Marjorie had heard on the telephone that afternoon, a lovely and very persuasive voice. And Mrs. Jepson herself was like that: dark-eyed, slender, and tall, she persuaded you with a glance that she was your friend, your well-wisher, that you would be happy in her company. She wore a black dinner dress, a necklace of shining silver leaves and earrings to match, and she was charming.

"Ralph, darling, hurry up and finish dressing!" she said. "While I brief Miss Smith." She raised her arms in a gesture of shoving him away, and led Marjorie into the long, softly lit sitting room. "It's a weird little house," she said. "The children's rooms are down here—those two doors. And here's their bathroom. And here's the kitchen. You'll find lots of things in the icebox; just please take anything you like. And there's a radio, and a television, and a phonograph, and stacks of records. And don't worry about waking the children. *Nothing* bothers them. And here are books, and magazines, and cigarettes. And here's the telephone number where you can reach us, and the doctor's number. Will you be all right?''

"Yes, thank you," said Marjorie, a little stiffly. For, in her New England fashion, she found Mrs. Jepson a little too nice, too eager. "And the children's names?''

"There's Ronald; he's seven, and Jean, five. We won't be very late, Miss Smith. *Au revoir!*''

When she had gone, and the door closed after her, it was as if some fresh breeze had suddenly died, leaving the air stagnant; the little house was very still. The wind blew against the windows; an electric clock ticked, with a sort of purr; the refrigerator buzzed and whirred for a moment, and then was silent.

Ronald and Jean, Marjorie said to herself. Two little children here, in my care, and I've never seen them. If they don't wake up, I suppose I'll go home without having seen them, and they'll never know I've been here. I don't like it.

She took up a magazine, but she could not read. She was waiting. For the sound of a car going by outside, for the telephone to ring, for the icebox to start up again? For a board to creak, for a tap to drip, for a rustle, a sign? But there was only the wind, and the rain outside.

And then she heard it, a sound that should not frighten anyone: a low chuckle of laughter. It's one of the children, she thought. Still asleep, probably. And then a soft murmur, another soft laugh. She rose, and as she stood by the chair, she heard the patter of bare feet running. They're up, she thought. I'll have to see.

She went to the nearest door and turned the handle gently. But the door was locked. She tried the next one, and that, too, was locked. She knocked.

"I'm Marjorie Smith," she said. "I've come to see you. Open the door, will you?''

"No, thank you!" answered a little boy's voice, very resolute. "Go away, please.''

"Go away!" echoed a little girl's voice.

"I just want to come in and say good-evening—''

"No, thank you!" said the little boy. "We *never* let *anybody* come in at night, *never*.''

"Just for a moment.''

"Go away!" cried the little girl.

Marjorie stooped, and looked through the keyhole. The light was on in there; she could see a pink wall, a bed on which a little fair-haired girl in a blue dressing gown was sitting beside a dark-haired young man in a gray suit.

"Let me in!" she called, knocking more loudly.

"Go away!" said the little boy.

The young man in there said nothing, did not stir. I'm afraid! Marjorie thought. Who is he? What is he doing there? How did he get in? *I'm afraid*.

All right! Be afraid, then. It doesn't matter. Those children are in my care, and I'm going to get into that room. I'm going to find out who that man is. And I'm going to get rid of him.

She put on her raincoat; she fixed the front door on the latch and left it held ajar by a telephone book. Better to let the house grow chill than for her to take any chances of being shut out, away from the children.

The cold caught her by the throat, took her breath away. If only the house next door had one lighted window; if only there were some sound from the street, a car going by, a radio; if only there were someone . . .

The light from the children's room shone across the gravel path; she went close to it, and looked in. A dark little boy in a plaid dressing gown sat on the floor, hands clasped round his knees; the little girl still sat on the bed, and now the young man had his arm about her shoulders. Both the children were looking up into his face; they were listening to him.

With an effort, Marjorie pushed up the window from the bottom.

"Who are you?" she cried.

He turned his head and looked at her, with desperate, dark eyes. And then he was gone. He had not risen, or moved, but he was gone.

For a moment she held tight to the window sill, and it seemed to her that the wind went roaring through her head, so that she could see nothing, hear nothing. But the little girl's voice came to her, high and wild.

"Georgie! Georgie! Come back! Come back, Georgie!"

She climbed in over the sill; she stood in the room, dripping wet, her hair blown across her forehead.

"That's a fine way to treat me!" she said, laughing. "The very first time I come to see you, too. Making me go out in the pouring rain and climb in the window."

She had struck the right note.

"Well, you see," the little boy said. "Georgie won't stay if anybody else comes. Even Mommie. He doesn't want *any*body to see him but us."

"Katie sawed him, and she went away," said the little girl.

"Do you like him?" Marjorie asked.

They both looked at her, surprised, wondering.

"We like him the *best*," said Ronald. "He tells us stories, and he sings songs."

"And he stays here in the dark, too," said the little girl. "You go away now, and he'll come back."

"I can't go away," said Marjorie. "I promised your mommie I'd stay with you till she came home."

"We'd rather have Georgie, thank you," said Ronald.

"Some other time," said Marjorie. "I thought we'd all go out to the kitchen, and make some cocoa, have a little party."

It was nearly two hours before she could get them back to sleep. She made cocoa for them, and toast; she read to them, she played the phonograph records they wanted; she told them stories. They were, she thought, unusually attractive children, intelligent, reasonable, mannerly, and the little girl was beautiful, with great dark eyes and thick, fair hair, as fine as silk. But they were, both of them, curiously tense and excited; again and again they would turn their heads, they would look, they would listen.

"I thought it was Georgie," the little girl said.

Marjorie ignored that. She asked them no questions; she tried, in every way she could, to distract their attention from Georgie, to quiet them. When they had fallen asleep, she opened both their doors, and sat down in the living room. I got chilled when I went out, she told herself. That's why I'm so cold. The heat's not very good in this house. It's—there seems to be a draft somewhere. A very cold draft.

Almost all children invent imaginary playmates who seem absolutely real to them. When they're pretending they're one of these imaginary creatures, their voices change, and their expressions. If *they* feel absolutely sure they see one of those imaginary creatures, it might . . . Thought-transference? People can be made to believe they've seen things, and heard things. . . .

No, I did see him. I did hear him. And he—vanished. Is it my duty to tell Mrs. Jepson? Oh, how *can* I?

"Please don't be frightened," he said. "I'd very much like to come and talk to you for a few moments, but if you'd rather I didn't, I'll stay away."

The comfortable lamp-lit room was empty, but the voice was near.

"Where—are you?" she asked.

"I'll clear out, if you'd rather."

"Where are you?" she demanded, so loudly that she felt a sudden worry about waking the children.

"Well, I'm here," he said. "If you want to see me, I can fix it. But if you don't—"

She was silent for a moment, trying not to breathe so fast, so loudly.

"Yes. I do want to see you," she said.

Then he was there, standing at the other side of the table. He was young, and he was handsome, in a way, but his gray suit was shabby, and he looked tired to exhaustion, his dark eyes hollow.

"Who—are you?" she asked.

"My name is George Stewart," he said. "Or it was. But, you see. . . . It's hard to explain. . . . You see, I was murdered five years ago."

"No!" Marjorie said. "Things like that—aren't true."

"I didn't believe things like this, myself," he said, "until it happened to me. It's—you can't think how bad it is."

"Then why do you do them? Why do you—come back?"

"Well . . ." he said, in his gentle, tired voice, "we don't 'come back,' you know. We've never been able to get away. When you've been murdered, when you die—*at the wrong time*—you're caught here in this world."

"You mean—you're alive?"

"No," he said. "Not alive. And not dead."

"I don't understand," she said curtly.

"I don't think anyone does, quite," he said. "Some of the others like me have worked out theories—"

"You mean other ghosts?" she asked, and because of the dreadful confusion within her, she spoke in a scornful, sneering tone she had never used before in her life.

"That's what you call us," he said. "I've gone to see others I've heard about, in England, Ireland, Hungary. They'd all been murdered, even though sometimes it wasn't suspected. And one woman who'd been in a castle in Ireland for four hundred years told me it was because if you're murdered, it's not the *right time* for you to die. So that you *can't* die. You can't go on to the next world."

"And what's the 'right time' to die, may I ask?"

"This woman believed it was all predestined. You're born, she thought, with a natural life-span, whether it's one day, or ninety years, depending upon the constitution you've inherited. Your inherited constitution will determine what diseases you'll avoid, and what ones will finish you."

"What about accidents?"

"She thought they were predestined, too. And it's true that if you go to a place where there's been some great disaster, a flood, a volcanic eruption, a train-wreck, anything of that sort, no ghosts have ever been heard of there. No. It's only murder that makes us—as we are. Because murder, she said, doesn't *have to* happen. Nobody is born destined to be murdered, because nobody is born obliged to become a murderer."

"So if you've been murdered, you stay on earth, and try to hurt and terrify people?"

"I've never found a genuine case of anyone's being really hurt by a ghost," he said, with a faint sigh. "If people are terrified at the sight of us, that's not our fault. We go on and on, in a sort of despair, and nobody will listen to us, nobody will help."

"Why do they want people to listen to them? What sort of help do they want?"

"We want to be killed," he said.

"But you *have* been killed!"

"No," he said. "It wasn't the right time for us to die, so we couldn't."

"And when is this 'right time' supposed to come again?"

"Any time after we're murdered," he said. "We're ready then. Our life here is finished. We're longing, every minute, to get out of this world, and on to the next one."

"Well? Can't ghosts kill themselves?"

"I don't know," he said. "But they never do. They never even try. It's—I couldn't tell you how bad—how shocking the idea seems to us. No. We wait. We feel we *must* wait. Until we're taken."

"What do you mean by 'taken'?"

"We're killed," he explained, earnest and patient. "A building collapses, there's a stroke of lightning, a fire; in the war, some of us were killed by bombs. But often it's a long time. Such a long time . . . That's why we're always looking for someone who'll be merciful enough to set us free. Even to listen to us, as you're listening to me."

"Why should the murdered people, the victims, be punished, and not the murderers?" she demanded.

"I don't know what happens to the murderers," he said. "But I'm certain that our waiting isn't meant as a punishment. I suppose—'' He paused for a moment. "I suppose," he went on, "that if life is eternal, one hundred years, five hundred years, of waiting hasn't much significance. The way I see it, it's part of a plan, an order of things that we can't grasp. But . . . If you'll help me . . . If I give you the gun . . ."

"No! I couldn't! I couldn't! What happened to you, to turn you—into this?"

"Nella killed me," he said, casually.

"Nella?"

"Mrs. Jepson."

"*What!* What are you saying?"

"I was her lover," he said. "I suppose that's the word for it. Anyhow, that autumn, five years ago, she was sure Jepson suspected what was going on, and she wanted to get rid of me. She tried to bribe me—with Jepson's money—to go away somewhere. When I wouldn't do that, she got into a panic. She believed I was going to make a scandal, ruin her, make her lose Jepson's money, her social position, everything she valued."

"Were you going to do that?"

"No," he answered, simply. "I've never been like that. Never wanted to injure anyone. But she couldn't believe that; literally *couldn't*. She thought everybody was vindictive—and dangerous. She asked me to talk things over with her, and we drove in her car up to the lake. She was very quiet and serious; more reasonable, I thought. She'd brought along some drinks in a thermos, and she poured out one for each of us. I don't know how she managed it, but mine was poisoned. I wasn't watching her, particularly. I was smoking. I was looking out at the lake, at the autumn leaves floating on it. I was starting to tell her, once more, that she needn't worry, but that I wasn't going to give up my job here, my friends, everything, and go to Seattle, as she wanted, when the pain came.

"It was—like a thread spinning up and up, round the blade of the sharpest knife. Then it was cut into ribbons, and it was over. . . . She'd got me out of the car, onto the ground, when Jepson came. I don't know what made him come, or how he knew. But he was—overwhelmed, that's the word. Sick, with horror.

"Nella was stunned, for a moment. But only for a moment. Then she had her story for him. She said she'd never imagined the stuff she gave me would be fatal. She said she'd only wanted to knock me out for a few moments, so that she could get back some foolish letters she'd written to me. I'm sure Jepson didn't believe her. But he helped her. He tied a heavy stone on my ankles and another round my neck, and together they dragged me down to the lake and into the water, where it was deep.

"I stayed there, at the bottom of the lake, for a while, two or three days. But I knew, all the time, what had happened to me. I knew I could get out when I wanted."

"But how?" Marjorie cried.

"I don't know how to explain it," he said. "It doesn't seem strange to me. I can be anywhere I want, and it's no trouble, no effort. I can be here, or not here."

"You can disappear?" she said, unsteadily. "Vanish?"

"It doesn't seem like that, to me," he said. "To me, it's simply going away, somewhere else. It's hard for me to realize that I frighten anyone. I don't eat or drink, of course, because we don't need to. Nothing in us breaks down or wears out; nothing needs building up. But I'm just what I was, five years ago; the same blood, and bones, and muscles, the same mind. I can see, I can hear, I can speak. Why am I—terrible?"

"You're not!" she said, and it was true; all her cold horror and confusion had gone. "But why do you come back here? Is it to—make them remember what they did?"

"No," he said. "I don't care about Nella any more. And I'm only sorry for Jepson. He doesn't need any reminding. He's never got over it. He's—you can see it in his face, poor devil. . . . No, I've never let him see me here. No. It's Jean. You see, she's my child."

Marjorie began to cry, and that seemed to trouble him.

"I'm sorry," he said. "But I don't know where else to turn. It won't take a moment. If I give you the gun—"

"I couldn't! I couldn't! Please don't ask me! Can't you stay here—with Jean?"

"But don't you see?" he cried. "That's the worst of it. If anything should happen to her, if she should die, she'd go on, to the next world. And I couldn't. She'd be gone, and I couldn't find her. I beg of you—!"

The wind shook and rattled the front door; a freezing blast streamed in as it opened and Jepson stood there. Marjorie's lips parted, but before she could make a sound, there was a streak of yellow light, the crack of a shot, and George Stewart fell at her feet.

"I saw the whole thing from my window," said the woman who lived across the street. "And I called up the police at once. I saw Mr. Jepson go up on the veranda and look in at the window. I saw him open the door and when he was in the room, I saw him take out his gun and fire."

"I didn't mean to," said Jepson. That was what he had said to Marjorie, over and over, before the police came.

"Sure," said the police lieutenant. "You didn't know the gun was loaded. Only how did you get rid of the body so fast? Or was there a body? Did he—"

"No, he was dead, Lieutenant. There wasn't any doubt," said Jepson. "This time," he added.

"Yes," said the woman from across the street. "I can identify the dead man. His name is George Stewart, and I used to see him here—" She paused. "*A lot*," she said, with malicious significance.

"Did you see Mrs. Jepson?"

"Yes. She got out of the car, and she went into the house right after he did."

"Mrs. Jepson, will you tell us—?"

"No," said Nella Jepson. "I have nothing to tell you. I'm not obliged to give evidence against my husband."

She could not have said anything more fatal to him, and, thought Marjorie, she knew that, and intended it to be so.

"I didn't mean to," said Jepson. "I didn't think he was . . . I didn't think there was anyone here."

"Do you wish to state that you did not see this man, when you fired a shot directly at him?"

Jepson wiped his forehead with a handkerchief. His heavy face was dazed and stricken.

"I didn't know I *could* see him. . . . I've thought about him, night and day. . . . I thought he was—gone."

"Come now, Mr. Jepson. Pull yourself together. Do you admit that you fired that shot?"

"Yes, I did. But I didn't think it would—do any harm."

"Why did you think that?" The police lieutenant waited. "Come now!" he said. "Why did you think it wouldn't 'do any harm' to fire a bullet in the man's back?"

Bear witness to the truth. . . . Marjorie was saying to herself. Never mind about your pride. Never mind what people will think of you. Never mind how hard it is. Mr. Jepson *can't* say it. But I can. I must.

"The man was dead before Mr. Jepson came in," she said.

"Why, he was not!" cried the woman from across the street. "I saw him, with my own eyes, standing there, talking to you!"

"He was a ghost," said Marjorie, with an effort that made her voice husky and deep.

Jepson turned to her, his blurred eyes brightening with gratitude.

"Yes!" he said. "Yes! You're—very kind. . . ."

"McGraw," said the lieutenant, "take Miss Smith home in your car."

"I'd rather stay—"

"You're not doing any good here, Miss Smith," said the lieutenant. "We'll want to ask you some questions, later on. *Will* we want to ask you questions! Perfect eyewitness testimony to a murder, plus a virtual confession—and no body to tie it to. The corpus delicti without a corpus . . . You're the one who should be able to straighten it out; but just now you're—overwrought. Drive her home, McGraw."

"Overwrought," Marjorie said to herself. Hysterical, does he mean? Or crazy? Raving? She could imagine the spiteful woman from across the street telling this story with delight. A *ghost*, that Smith girl said. *Imagine!* The story would spread through the little suburban town; perhaps it would reach the ears of people who liked her and respected her, but wouldn't want to leave her in charge of their children any more.

She could not save Jepson. His wife would not help him. He was doomed. He would go from here to a jail, if he was quiet, or a madhouse, if he insisted on the truth. She looked at him, and he smiled, and the blurred misery in his face had gone. It was as if his monstrous burden had at last been lifted, and he was at ease.

"Thank you!" he said, again.

Since **Talmage Powell** *(1920–   ) is a respected professional who has produced ten novels and over five hundred short stories and screenplays during his thirty-seven year career, it is unlikely that he has pointed the finger at the butler very often. Still, if any of his other butlers chose victims like the spirited heroine of this story, we know the poor fellows hadn't a ghost of a chance.*

I HAD A HUNCH, AND...

Talmage Powell

AFTER a strangely timeless interval, Janet realized she was dead.

She experienced only a little shock, and no fear. Perhaps this was because of the carefree way she had conducted her past life.

She had never felt so free. A thought wave her propulsion, she zipped about the great house, then outside, toward the great, clean open sky. Above, the stars were ever so bright and beautiful. Below, the lights of the suburban estate where she had been born and reared shone as if to answer the stars.

Janet was delighted with the whole experience. It confirmed some of the beliefs she had held, and it is always nice for one to have one's beliefs confirmed. It also excited the vivacious curiosity which had always been one of her major traits. And now there were ever so many more things about which to be curious.

She returned to the foyer of the house and looked at her lifeless physical self lying at the base of the wide sweeping stairway.

Whillikers, I was a very good-looking hunk of female, she decided. *Really I was.*

The body at the foot of the stairway was slender, clad in a simple black

137

dinner dress. The wavy mass of black hair had spilled to rest fanwise on the carpet. The soft lovely face was calm—as in innocent, dreamless sleep.

Only the awkward twist and weird angle of the slim neck revealed the true nature of the sleep.

A quick ache smote Janet. *I must accept things. This—this is really so wonderful, but I do wish I—she—could have had just a little more time. . . .*

The great house was silent. Lights blazing on death, on stillness.

Janet remembered. She had returned unexpectedly to change shoes. Getting out of the car at the country club, she had snagged the heel of her left shoe and loosened it.

"I'll only be a little while," she had promised Cricket and Tom and Blake.

"We'll wait dinner," Blake had said, after she'd waved aside his insistence that he drive her home.

At home again, she had reached the head of the stairs when she heard someone in her bedroom.

She'd always possessed a cool nerve. She'd eased down the hallway. He'd been in there. Murgy. Dear old Murgy. Life hadn't begun without the memory of Murgy. He was ageless. He had worked for the family forever. Murgatroyd had been as much a part of Janet's life as the house, the giant oaks on the lawn, the car in the garage, over which Murgy lived in his little apartment.

She simply hadn't understood at first. Crouched in the hallway and peering through the crack of the partially opened door, she had seen a brand-new Murgy. This one had a chill face, but eyes that burned with determination. This one moved with much more deftness and decisiveness than the Murgy she'd always known.

He was stealing her jewelry. He was taking it from the small wall safe and replacing paste replicas. They were excellent replicas. They must have cost Murgy a great deal of money. But whatever the cost, it was pennies compared to the fortune he was slipping under his jacket.

She saw him compare a fake diamond bracelet with the real thing. The fakes were so good, she might have gone for years without knowing a large portion of her inheritance had been replaced by them.

As she saw the genuine diamond bracelet disappear into his pocket, she had gasped his name.

He had responded like a man jerking from a jolt of electricity. Frightened, she had turned, run. He had caught her at the head of the stairs.

She had tried to tell him how much his years of service meant, that she would have given him a chance to explain, a chance to straighten the thing out.

But he had given *her* no chance. He had pushed savagely at her with both arms. She had fallen, crying out, trying to grab something to break the fall.

She had struck hard. There had been one blinding flash, mingled with pain.

Murgy had followed her down. He had stood looking at her, wiping his hands on a handkerchief. He had listened, and heard no sound. She had come alone. Everything was all right. Even the heel on her left shoe had come off during her fall.

Murgy's decision was plain in his face. He would go to his quarters. Let her be discovered. Let her death be considered an accident.

Janet broke away from the study of what had once been her body.

Murgy, you really shouldn't have done it. There is a balance in the order of things and you have upset it. There is only one way you can restore the balance, Murgy. You must pay for what you have done. Besides, my freedom won't be complete until you do.

Janet was aware of a presence in the foyer.

Cricket had entered. Cricket and Tom and Blake, wondering why she hadn't returned, beginning to worry, deciding to see what was keeping her.

A willowy blonde girl, not too intelligent, but kind and eager to please, Cricket saw the body at the base of the stairway. She put her fists to her temples and opened her mouth wide.

Janet rushed to her side. In her world of silence, she couldn't hear Cricket screaming, but she knew that was what she was doing. Cricket's merry blue eyes were not merry now. They strained against their sockets with a terrible intensity.

Poor Cricket. I'm not in pain, Cricket.

She tried to touch Cricket with the touch of compassion.

Cricket wasn't aware of this effort, Janet knew instantly. She wasn't here, as far as Cricket was concerned. She would never again be here for Cricket, or for any of the others.

Blake and Tom were beside Cricket now. Tom was helping her to a deep couch. Blake was taking slow, halting steps toward the body at the foot of the stairs.

Blake kneeled beside the young, dead body. He reached as if he would touch it. Then his hands fell to his sides. He rose, his dark, handsome face pained.

He turned, stumbled to Tom and Cricket. Cricket had subsided into broken sobs. Tom sat with his arms about her shoulders. Shock and fright made the freckles on Tom's lean, pale face stand out sharply.

They were discussing the discovery. Janet could feel their horror, their sorrow. She could sense it, almost touch it. It was as if she could almost reach the edges of their essence, of their being, with her own essence and being.

Blake was picking up the telephone now. This would be for the doctor.

Before the doctor arrived, Murgy came in. Janet strained toward him. Then she recoiled, as from a thing dark and slimy.

He was speaking. *Saying he had heard a scream, no doubt.*

Then Blake stepped from in front of Murgy. And Murgy looked toward the stairs.

Cosmic pulsations passed through Janet as she slipped along with Murgy to the body at the stairway.

She could feel the fine control deep within him, the crouching of the dark, slimy thing as, in its wanton determination to survive, it braced the flesh and ordered the brain and arranged the emotions.

The emotions were in such a storm that Janet drew back.

Murgy went to his knees beside the body and wept openly. *There was Blake now, helping Murgy to a chair. Everything was so dreadfully out of balance.*

She tried to get through to Blake. She strained with the effort. She succeeded only in causing Blake to look at Murgy a little strangely, as if something in Murgy's grief struck a small discord in Blake.

Blake went to fetch Murgy a glass of water. Janet turned her attention to Cricket and Tom. Tom's mind was resilient and strong. She battered at the edges of it, but it was too full of other things. Memories. Janet could vaguely sense them. Memories that somehow concerned her and the good times their young crowd had had.

Cricket was simply blank. Shocked beyond thinking.

Janet perched over the front doorway and beheld the scene in its entirety.

Look, people. He did it. Murgy's a murderer. He mustn't be allowed to get away with it.

Doctor Roberts came into the house. He spoke briefly with the living and turned toward the dead. He stood motionless for a moment. His grief spread like a black aura all about him. It spread until it had covered the whole room. He had delivered Janet, prescribed for her sniffles, set the arm she'd broken trying to jump a skittish horse during a summer vacation from college. He had sat by her all night the night he'd broken the news to her that her parents had been killed in a plane crash, that now she would have to live in the great house with Murgy and a housekeeper to look after her wants.

She flew to Doctor Roberts, remembering the way the big, square face and white goatee had always symbolized strength and intelligence to her.

You must understand, Doctor. It was Murgy. He was ever so lucky; everything worked devilishly for him, my arrival alone, the broken shoe heel.

Then she fell back, appalled. It was as if she had bruisingly struck a solid black wall, the walls of a crypt where Doctor Roberts had shut away a part of himself. *She would never reach him, because he didn't believe. When a man died, he died as a dog or a monkey died. That's what Doctor Roberts maintained.*

Janet moved to a table holding an assortment of potted plants. She studied the activities before her.

She saw Doctor Roberts complete his examination. He talked with Blake. He looked at the broken shoe heel and nodded.

He put a professional eye on Cricket. He reopened his bag, took out a needle, and gave her a shot. Then he spoke with Tom, and Tom took Cricket out.

The doctor was explaining something to Blake. At last, Blake nodded his consent.

Janet felt herself perk up.

Of course, they'll phone the police. It's a routine, have-to measure when something like this happens.

She felt the dark, slimy thing in Murgy gather and strengthen itself, felt its evil smugness and confidence.

This was her last chance, Janet knew. The balance simply to be restored. Otherwise, she was liable to be earthbound until Murgy, finally, died and a higher justice thus restored the cosmic balance.

But what if they send someone like Doctor Roberts?

The policeman came at last.

He was a big man, had sandy hair and gray eyes and a jaw that looked as if it had been hacked from seasoned oak. His nose had been broken sometime in the past and reposed flagrantly misshapen on his face.

Janet hovered over him.

Look at Murgy!

For Pete's sake, one second there, when you walked in, it was naked in Murgy's eyes!

Intent on his job, the policeman walked to the stilled form at the foot of the stairway. He looked at the left shoe, then up the stairs.

After a moment, he walked up the stairs, examined the carpet, the railing. He measured the length of the stairs with his eyes.

Then he came slowly down the stairs.

He paused and looked at the beautiful girlish body.

His compassion came flooding out into the room. Janet felt as if she could ride the edges of it like a buoy.

It was a quiet, unguarded moment for him. Janet threw her will into the effort.

It was Murgy. Look at Murgy, the murderer!

He glanced at Murgy. But then, he glanced at the others too.

He began talking with Doctor Roberts.

Janet stayed close to the policeman.

If she could have met him in life, she knew they would have enjoyed a silent understanding.

I met a lot of people like that. Everybody meets people whom they like or distrust just by a meeting of the eyes.

You're feeling them out, forming opinions right now, by looking into their eyes, talking with them, letting the edges of your senses reach out and explore the edges of theirs.

I feel your respect for the doctor.

I feel you recoil now as you talk with Murgy. The dark, slimy thing is deep down, well hidden, but somehow you sense it.

But for Pete's sake, feeling it isn't enough. You must pass beyond feeling to realization.

Murgy killed me.

The balance simply has to be restored.

The policeman broke off his talk with Murgy. More official people had arrived. They took photographs. Two of them in white finally carried the body away on a stretcher.

Except for the policeman, the official people went away.

Blake went out. The doctor departed. Murgy was standing with tears in his eyes. The policeman touched Murgy's shoulder, spoke.

Janet was in the doorway, barring it. But Murgy didn't know she was there. He went across the lawn, to his apartment over the garage.

Only the policeman was left. He stood with his hat in his hands, looking at a spot at the base of the stairs with eyes heavy with sadness.

He was really younger than the rough face and broken nose made him appear.

Young and sad because he had seen beauty dead. Young and sad, and sensitive.

Janet pressed close to him. *It's all right, for me. You understand? There's no pain. It's beautiful here—except for the imbalance of Murgy's act.*

It wasn't an accident. You mustn't believe that. Murgy did it. You didn't like him. You sensed something about him.

Think of him! Think only of Murgy!

Don't leave yet. Ask yourself, are you giving up too easily. Shouldn't you look further?

He passed his hand through his hair. He seemed to be asking himself a question. He measured the stairway with his eyes.

She could sense the quiet, firm discipline that was in him, the result of training, of years of experience. The result of never ceasing to question, never stopping the mental probe for the unlikely, the one detail out of place.

Yes, yes! You feel something isn't quite right.

The shoe—if a girl came home to change it, would she go all the way upstairs and then start down again without changing it?

Oh, the question is clear and nettlesome in your mind.

It's a fine question.

Don't let it go. Follow it. Think about it.

He stood scratching his jaw. He walked all the way upstairs. Down the hallway. He looked in a couple of rooms, found hers.

In her room, he opened the closet. He looked at the shoes.

He stood troubled. Then he went back to the head of the stairs. Again he measured them with his eyes.

But finally, he shook his head and walked out of the house.

Come back! You must come back!

She couldn't reach him. She knew he wasn't coming back. So she perched on the roof of his speeding car as it turned a corner a block away.

He went downtown. He stopped the car in the parking lot at headquarters. He went into the building and entered his office.

Another man was there, an older man. The two talked together for a moment. The older man went out.

The policeman sat down at his desk. He picked up a pen and drew a printed form toward him.

Janet hovered over the desk.

You mustn't make out the form. You must not write it off as an accident. Murgy did it.

He started writing.

It was murder.

He wrote a few lines and stopped.

Go get Murgy. He was the only one on the estate when it happened. Can't you see it had to be Murgy?

He nibbled at the end of the pen.

Think of the shoe. I went up, but I didn't change shoes.

He ran his finger down his crooked nose. He started writing again.

Okay, bub, if that's the way you want it, go ahead and finish the report. Call it an accident. But I'm not giving up. I'm sticking with you. I'll throw Murgy's name at you so many times you'll think you're suffering combat fatigue from being a cop too long.

Ready? Here we go, endlessly, my friend, endlessly. Murgy, Murgy, Murgy Murgymurgymurgy . . .

He drove home. He showered. He got in bed. He turned the light off.

After a time, he rolled over and punched the pillow. After another interval, he threw back the covers with an angry gesture, turned on the light, sat on the edge of the bed, and smoked a cigarette.

There was a telephone beside the bed and on the phone stand a pad of paper.

While he smoked, he doodled. He drew a spiked heel. He drew the outlines of a house. He wasn't a very good artist. He looked at the drawing of the house and under it he wrote: "No sign of forced entry. Only that servant around . . ."

He drew a pair of owlish eyes, and ringed them in black. He added some sharp lines for a face.

Then he ripped off the sheet of paper, wadded it and threw it toward the wastebasket. He snubbed out his cigarette, turned off the light for a second time, punched his pillow with a gesture of betokening finality, and threw his head against it.

He reached the curtain of sleep. He started through it. Cells relaxing, the barriers began to waver, weaken.

She pressed in close.

MurgymurgymurgyMURGY!

He tossed and pulled the covers snug about his shoulders. Then he threw them off, got out of bed, and snapped on the light.

He was still agitated as he dressed and went out.

He sat in the dark car for many long minutes before starting it. He drove aimlessly for a couple of blocks, his mind a pair of millstones grating against themselves. He stopped before a bar and went in.

He sat down at the end of the bar, alone. He had one, two, three drinks. His face was still troubled by nagging questions.

Two more drinks. They didn't help. The creases deepened in his cheeks.

Janet balanced atop a cognac bottle. *Better give Murgy a little more thought. Why not follow him, shadow him? He isn't resting easy. He'll want to get rid of those jewels in a shady deal now and be ready to run if the fakes are spotted.*

The policeman raised his gaze and looked at the television set over the bar. He stopped thinking about the long stairway, the broken heel, Murgy, and various possibilities. His mind snapped to what he was seeing on the TV set.

A local newscaster with doleful face was talking about her, her death. He was only a two dimensional image and she could sense nothing about him from this point. He was taking considerable time, and she could only guess that he was talking about her background, her family. There were some old newspaper pictures, one taken when she'd been helping raise money for the crippled children's hospital. She hadn't wanted any publicity for that, and she wished the newscast were less thorough.

There was a sudden disturbance down the bar. A fat man with a bald head and drink-flushed face was giving the TV set the Bronx cheer.

Janet felt quick displeasure. *Really, I was never the rich, degenerated hussy you're making me out, mister.*

The force of the mental explosion back down the bar caused Janet to rise to the ceiling. She saw that the fat man's exhibition had also disturbed her young policeman. He slammed out of the bar. And he was so mad he started across the street without looking.

Janet became a silent scream.

He looked up just in time to see the taxi hurtle around the corner. He tried to get out of the way. He'd had a drink too many.

Instantaneously, he became an empty shell of flesh and blood, shortly destined to become dust, lying broken in the middle of the street. A terrified but innocent cabbie was emerging from his taxi, and a small crowd was pouring out of the bar to join him.

This was defeat, Janet knew. Never had a defeat of the flesh been so agonizing. The stars could have been hers. Now the stars would have to wait, for a long, long time. For as long as Murgy lived. It wasn't the waiting that would be so hard. It was this entrapment in incompleteness, this torture, this unspeakable pain of being inescapably enmeshed in cosmic injustice.

She took her misery to the darkest shadow she could find and lurked there awhile, until the scene in the street had run its course, from arrival to departure of the police.

A bitter thought wave her propulsion, she returned to the estate. She filtered through the roof and hovered in the foyer.

While there had been hope, the foyer's full capacity for torture had not reached her. Now she felt it.

"Hello, Beautiful."

Where had the thought come from? She swirled like a miniature nebula.

"Take it easy I'm right here."

He swirled beside her. *Her policeman.*

"You!"

"Sure. I was so amazed at where I found myself I didn't get to you while you were hiding near the accident. You know, you *feel* even more beautiful than you looked."

"Why, thanks for the compliment. And your own homeliness, fellow, was all of the flesh. But don't you concern yourself with me."

"Why not?"

"I'm stuck here. You didn't catch Murgy."

"I had a hunch about that guy . . ."

"Hunch? Hah! It was me trying to get the guilt of the old boy across to you."

"Really? Well, I was going to keep an eye on him."

"I was after you to do that, too. See, I caught him stealing my jewels."

"I had to go and ruin everything!"

"But you didn't mean to barge in front of that cab."

"Just the same, I'll spend eternity being sorry. Sure you can't come with me?"

"Nope. Just go quickly."

He was gone. She felt his unwilling departure. It was the final straw of torture.

"Look, honey, my name's Joe."

He was back.

"I got this idea. It's worth a try at least."

It was so good having him back.

"My superior officer, Lieutenant Hal Dineen. He's the sharpest, most tenacious cop ever to carry a badge. That report of mine, to start with, is going to raise a question in his mind. The same facts you were trying to get over to me are there for him to find. I just bounced over to headquarters and back. Just a look told me my fray with that taxi has knocked his mental guards to smithereens. He was at his desk, reading that last report of mine. If you alone could do what you did, consider what the two of us trying real hard can do if we hit Dineen, in his present state, with full thought force."

Janet bounced to the rooftop. Joe was beside her.

"Janet, Dineen is razor-sharp at playing hunches. He believes in them. All set to hit him with the grandfather of all hunches, the results of which he'll talk about for a lifetime?"

"Let's." *Let's, darling.*

Lieutenant Hal Dineen was talking to a fellow officer, "I dunno. Just one of those things. Comes from being a cop, I guess, from having the old subconscious recognize and classify information the eyes, ears, and hands miss. Just a hunch I had about this old family retainer. We all get 'em— these hunches. Me, especially, I'm a great one for 'em. And this one I couldn't shake and so I figured . . ."

Prolific master of the locked room mystery, **John Dickson Carr** *(1906–1977) wrote stories in which things were seldom what they seemed to be. Like Dorothy Sayers, he frequently introduced elements of the macabre, but while she usually dispelled them, he often embraced them. Novels such as* The Devil in Velvet, Fear is the Same, *and* Fire, Burn! *are classics, and shorter works such as "New Murders for Old" are almost as good.*

NEW MURDERS FOR OLD

John Dickson Carr

Hargreaves did not speak until he had turned on two lamps. Even then he did not remove his overcoat. The room, though cold, was stuffy, and held a faintly sweet odour. Outside the Venetian blinds, which were not quite closed, you saw the restless, shifting presence of snow past street-lights. For the first time, Hargreaves hesitated.

"The—the object," he explained, indicating the bed, "was there. *He* came in by this door, here. Perhaps you understand a little better now?"

Hargreaves' companion nodded.

"No," said Hargreaves, and smiled. "I'm not trying to invoke illusions. On the contrary, I am trying to dispel them. Shall we go downstairs?"

It was a tall, heavy house, where no clocks ticked. But the treads of the stairs creaked and cracked sharply, even under their padding of carpet. At the back, in a kind of small study, a gas-fire had been lighted. Its hissing could be heard from a distance; it roared up blue, like solid blue flames, into the white fretwork of the heater; but it did little to dispel the chill of the room. Hargreaves motioned his companion to a chair at the other side of the fire.

"I want to tell you about it," he went on. "Don't think I'm trying to be"—his wrist hesitated over a word, as though over a chesspiece—"highbrow. Don't think I'm trying to be highbrow if I tell it to you"—again his wrist hesitated—"objectively. As though you knew nothing about it. As though you weren't concerned in it. It's the only way you will understand the problem he had to face."

Hargreaves was very intent when he said this. He was bending forward, looking up from under his eyebrows; his heavy overcoat flopped over the sides of his knees, and his gloved hands, seldom still, either made a slight gesture or pressed flat on his knees.

"Take Tony Marvell, to begin with," he argued. "A good fellow, whom everybody liked. Not a good business man, perhaps: too generous to be a good business man; but as conscientious as the very devil, and with so fine a mathematical brain that he got over the practical difficulties.

"Tony was Senior Wrangler at Cambridge, and intended to go on with his mathematics. But then his uncle died, so he had to take over the business. You know what the business was then: three luxury hotels, built, equipped and run by Old Jim, the uncle, in Old Jim's most flamboyant style: all going to rack and ruin.

"Everybody said it was madness for Tony to push his shoulder up against the business world. His brother—that's Stephen Marvell, the former surgeon—said Tony would only bring Old Jim's cardhouses down on everybody and swamp them all with more debts. But you know what happened. At twenty-five, Tony took over the business. At twenty-seven, he had the hotels on a paying basis. At thirty, they were hotels to which everybody went as a matter of course: blazing their sky-signs, humming with efficiency, piling up profits which startled even Tony.

"And all because he sneered at the idea that there could be any such thing as overwork. He never let up. You can imagine that dogged expression of his: 'Well, I don't like this work, but let's clean it up satisfactorily so that we can get on to more important things'—like his studies. He did it partly because he had promised Old Jim he would, and partly *because* (you see?) he thought the business so unimportant that he wanted to show how easy it was. But it wasn't easy. No man could stand that pace. London, Brighton, Eastbourne; he knew everything there was to know about the Marvell Hotels, down to the price of a pillow-case and the cost of grease for the lifts. At the end of the fifth year he collapsed one morning in his office. His brother Stephen told him what he had to do.

" 'You're getting out of this,' Stephen said. 'You're going clear away.

Round the world, anywhere; but for six or eight months at the shortest time. During that time, you're not even so much as to think of your work. Is that clear?'

"Tony told me the story himself last night. He says that the whole thing might never have happened if he had not been forbidden to write to anybody while he was away.

" 'Not even so much as a postcard,' snapped Stephen, 'to anybody. If you do, it'll be more business; and then God help you.'

" 'But Judith—' Tony protested.

" 'Particularly to Judith,' said Stephen. 'If you insist on marrying your secretary, that's your affair. But you don't ruin your rest-cure by exchanging long letters about the hotels.'

"You can imagine Stephen's over-aristocratic, thin-nosed face towering over him, dull with anger. You can imagine Stephen in his black coat and striped trousers, standing up beside the polished desk of his office in Harley Street. Stephen Marvell (and, to a certain extent, Tony, too) had that overbred air which Old Jim Marvell had always wanted and never achieved.

"Tony did not argue. He was willing enough, because he was tired. Even if he were forbidden to write to Judith, he could always think about her. In the middle of September, more than eight months ago, he sailed by the *Queen Anne* from Southampton. And on that night the terrors began."

Hargreaves paused. The gas-fire still hissed in the little, dim study. You would have known that this was a house in which death had occurred, and occurred recently, by the look on the face of Hargreaves' companion. He went on:

"The *Queen Anne* sailed at midnight. Tony saw her soaring up above the docks, as high as the sky. He saw the long decks, white and shiny like shoe-boxes, gleaming under skeins of lights; he saw the black dots of passengers moving along them; he heard the click-rattle-rush of winches as great cranes swung over the crowd on the docks; and he felt the queer, pleasurable, restless feeling which stirs the nerves at the beginning of an ocean voyage.

"At first he was as excited as a schoolboy. Stephen Marvell and Judith Gates, Tony's fiancée, went down to Southampton with him. Afterwards he recalled talking to Judith; holding her arm, piloting her through the rubbery-smelling passages of the ship to show her how fine it was. They went to Tony's cabin, where his luggage had been piled together with a basket of fruit. Everybody agreed that it was a fine cabin.

"It was not until a few minutes before the 'all-ashore' gong that the first pang of loneliness struck him. Stephen and Judith had already gone ashore, for all of them disliked these awkward, last-minute leave-takings. They were standing on the dock, far below. By leaning over the rail of the ship he could just see them. Judith's face was tiny, remote and smiling; infinitely loved. She was waving to him. Round him surged the crowd; faces, hats, noise under naked lights, accentuating the break with home and the water that would widen between. Next he heard the gong begin to bang: hollow, quivering, pulsing to loudness over the cry: 'All ashore that's going ashore!'; and dying away in the ship. He did not want to go. There was still plenty of time. He could still gather up his luggage and get off.

"For a time he stood by the rail, with the breeze from Southampton Water in his face. Such a notion was foolish. He would stay. With a last wave to Judith and Stephen, he drew himself determinedly away. He would be sensible. He would go below and unpack his things. Feeling the unreality of that hollow night, he went down to his cabin on C Deck. And his luggage was not there! He stared round the stuffy cabin with its neat curtains at the portholes. There had been a trunk and two suit-cases, gaudily labelled, to say nothing of the basket of fruit. Now the cabin was empty.

"Tony ran upstairs again to the purser's office. The purser, a harassed man behind a kind of ticket-window desk, was just getting rid of a clamouring crowd. In the intervals of striking a hand-bell and calling orders, he caught Tony's eye.

" 'My luggage—' Tony said.

" 'That's all right, Mr. Marvell,' said the harassed official. 'It's being taken ashore. But you'd better hurry yourself.'

"Tony had here only a feeling of extreme stupidity. 'Taken ashore?' he said. 'But why? Who told you to send it ashore?'

" 'Why, *you* did,' said the purser, looking up suddenly from a sheet of names and figures.

"Tony only looked at him.

" 'You came here,' the purser went on, with sharply narrowing eyes, 'not ten minutes ago. You said you had decided not to take the trip, and asked for your luggage to be taken off. I told you that at this late date we could not of course, refund the—'

" 'Get it back!' said Tony. His voice sounded wrong. 'I couldn't have told you that. Get it back!'

" 'Just as you like, sir,' said the purser, smiting on the bell, 'if there's time.'

"Overhead the hoarse blast of the whistle, that mournfullest of all sounds at sea, beat out against Southampton Water. B Deck, between open doors, was cold and gusty.

"Now Tony Marvell had not the slightest recollection of having spoken to the purser before. That was what struck him between the eyes like a blow, and what, for the moment, almost drove him to run away from the *Queen Anne* before they should lift the gangplank. It was the nightmare again. One of the worst features of his nervous breakdown had been the conviction, coming in flashes at night, that he was not real any longer; that his body and his inner self had moved apart, the first walking or talking in everyday life like an articulate dummy, while the brain remained in another place. It was as though he were dead, and seeing his body move. Dead.

"To steady his wits, he tried to concentrate on familiar human things. Judith, for instance; he recalled Judith's hazel eyes, the soft line of her cheek as she turned her head, the paper cuffs she wore at the office, Judith, his fiancée, his secretary, who would take care of things while he was away; whom he loved, and who was so maddeningly close even now. But he must not think of Judith. Instead, he pictured his brother Stephen, and Johnny Cleaver, and any other friends who occurred to him. He even thought of Old Jim Marvell, who was dead. And—so strong is the power of imaginative visualisation—at that moment, in the breeze lounge-room facing the purser's office, he thought he saw Old Jim looking at him round the corner of a potted palm.

"All this, you understand, went through Tony's mind in the brief second while he heard the ship's whistle hoot out over his head.

"He made some excuse to the purser, and went below. He was grateful for the chatter of noise, for the people passing up and down below decks. None of them paid any attention to him, but at least they were there. But, when he opened the door of his cabin, he stopped and stood very still in the doorway.

"The propellers had begun to churn. A throb, a heavy vibration, shook upwards through the ship; it made the tooth-glass tinkle in the rack, and sent a series of creaks through the bulkheads. The *Queen Anne* was moving. Tony Marvell took hold of the door as though that movement had been a lurch, and he stared at the bed across the cabin. On the white bedspread, where it had not been before, lay an automatic pistol.''

The gas-fire had heated its asbestos pillars to glowing red. Again there was a brief silence in the little study of the house in St. John's Wood. Hargreaves—Sir Charles Hargreaves, Assistant Commissioner of Police for the Criminal Investigation Department—leaned down and lowered the flame of the heater. Even the tone of his voice seemed to change when the gas ceased its loud hissing.

"Wait!" he said, lifting his hand. "I don't want you to get the wrong impression. Don't think that the fear, the slow approach of what was going to happen pursued Tony all through his trip round the world. It didn't. That's the most curious part of it all.

"Tony has told me that it was a brief, bad bout, lasting perhaps fifteen minutes in all, just before and just after the *Queen Anne* sailed. It was not alone the uncanny feeling that things had ceased to be real. It was a sensation of active malignancy—of hatred, of danger, of what you like—surrounding him and pressing on him. He could feel it like a weak current from a battery.

"But five minutes after the ship had headed out to open sea, every such notion fell away from him. It was as though he had emerged out of an evil fog. That hardly seems reasonable. Even supposing that there are evil emanations, or evil spirits, it is difficult to think that they are confined to one country; that their tentacles are broken by half a mile's distance; that they cannot cross water. Yet there it was. One moment he was standing there with the automatic pistol in his hand, the noise of the engines beating in his ears and a horrible impulse joggling his elbow to put the muzzle of the pistol into his mouth and—

"Then—snap! Something broke: that is the only way he can describe it. He stood upright. He felt like a man coming out of a fever, shaken and sweating, but back from behind the curtain into the real world again. He gulped deep breaths. He went to the porthole and opened it. From that time on, he says, he began to get well.

"How the automatic had got into his cabin he did not know. He knew he must have brought it himself, in one of those blind flashes. But he could not remember. He stared at it with new eyes, and new feeling of the beauty and sweetness of life. He felt as though he had been reprieved from execution.

"You might have thought that he would have flung the pistol overboard in sheer fear of touching it. But he didn't. To him it was the part of a puzzle. He stared much at it: a Browning .38, of Belgian manufacture, fully loaded. After the first few days, when he did keep it locked away out of sight in his trunk, he pondered over it. It represented the one piece of evidence he could carry home with him, the one tangible reality in a nightmare.

"At the New York customs-shed it seemed to excite no surprise. He carried it overland with him—Cleveland, Chicago, Salt Lake City—to San Francisco, in a fog, and then down the kindled sea to Honolulu. At Yokohama they were going to take it away from him; only a huge bribe retrieved it. Afterward he carried it on his person, and was never searched. As the broken bones of his nerves knitted, as in the wash of the propellers there was peace, it became a kind of Mascot. It went with him through the blistering heat of the Indian Ocean, into the murky Red Sea, to the Mediterranean. To Port Said, to Cairo in early winter. To Naples and Marseilles and Gibraltar. It was tucked away in his hippocket on the bitter cold night, a little more than eight months after his departure, when Tony Marvell—a healed man again—landed back at Southampton in the S.S. *Chippenham Castle*.

"It was snowing that night, you remember? The boat-train roared through the thickening snow. It was crowded, and the heat would not work.

"Tony knew that there could be nobody at Southampton to meet him. His itinerary had been laid out in advance, and he had stuck to the bitter letter of his instructions about not writing even so much as a postcard. But he had altered the itinerary, so as to take a ship that would get him home in time for Christmas; he would burst in on them a week early. For eight months he had lived in a void. In an hour or two he would be home. He would see Judith.

"In the dimly lighted compartment of the train, his fellow-passengers were not talkative. The long voyage had squeezed their conversation dry; they almost hated each other. Even the snow roused only a flicker of enthusiasm.

" 'Real old-fashioned Christmas!' said one.

" 'Hah!' said another appreciatively, scratching with his fingernails at the frosted window.

" 'Damn cold, I call it,' snarled a third. 'Can't they ever make the heat work in these trains? I'm damn well going to make a complaint!'

"After that, with a sympathetic grunt or mutter, each retired behind his newspaper; a white, blank wall which rustled occasionally, and behind which they drank up news of home.

"In other words (Tony remembers that he thought then), he was in England again. He was home. For himself, he only pretended to read. He leaned back in his seat, listening vaguely to the clackety-roar of the wheels, and the long blast of the whistle that was torn behind as the train gathered speed.

"He knew exactly what he would do. It would be barely ten o'clock when they reached Waterloo. He would jump into a cab, and hurry home—to his house—for a wash and brush-up. Then he would pelt up to Judith's flat at Hampstead as hard as he could go. Yet this thought, which should have made him glow, left him curiously chilly round the heart. He fought the chill. He laughed at himself. Determinedly he opened the newspaper, distracting himself, turning from page to page, running his eye down each column. Then he stopped. Something familiar caught his eye, some familiar name. It was an obscure item on a middle page.

"He was reading in this paper the news of his own death. Just that.

" 'Mr. Anthony Dean Marvell, of Upper Avenue Road, St. John's Wood, and owner of Marvell Hotels, Ltd., was found shot dead last night in his bedroom at home. A bullet had penetrated up through the roof of the mouth into the brain, and a small-calibre automatic was in his hand. The body was found by Mrs. Reach, Mr. Marvell's housekeeper, who . . . '

"A suicide!

"And once again, as suddenly as it had left him aboard ship, the grasp fell on him, shutting him off from the real world into the unreal. The compartment, as I told you, was very dimly lighted. So it was perhaps natural that he could only dimly see a blank wall of upheld newspapers facing him; as though there were no fellow-passengers there, as though they had deserted him in a body, leaving only the screen of papers that jiggled a little with the rush of the train.

"Yes, he was alone.

"He got up blindly, dragging open the door of the compartment to get out into the corridor. The confined space seemed to be choking him. Holding his own newspaper up high, so as to catch the light from the compartment, he read the item again.

"There could be no possibility of a mistake. The account was too detailed. It told all about him, his past and present . . .

" '. . . His brother, Mr. Stephen Marvell, the eminent Harley Street surgeon, was hurriedly summoned. . . . His fiancée. Miss

Judith Gates . . . It is understood that in September Mr. Marvell suffered a nervous breakdown, from which even a long rest had not effected a cure. . . .'

"Tony looked at the date of the newspaper, afraid of what he might see. But it was the date of that day: the twenty-third of December. From this account, it appeared that he had shot himself forty-eight hours before. And the gun was in his hip-pocket now.

"Tony folded up the newspaper. The train moved under his feet with a dancing sway, jerking above the click of the wheels; and another thin blast of the whistle went by. It reminded him of the whistle aboard the *Queen Anne*. He glanced along the dusky corridor. It was empty except for someone, whom he supposed to be another passenger, leaning elbows on the rail past the windows and staring out at the flying snow.

"He remembers nothing else until the train reached Waterloo. But something—an impression, a subconscious memory—registered in his mind about that passenger he had seen in the corridor. First it had to do with the shape of the person's shoulders. Then Tony realized that this was because the person was wearing a greatcoat with an old-fashioned brown fur collar. He was jumping blindly out of the train at Waterloo when he remembered that Old Jim Marvell always used to wear such a collar.

"After that he seemed to see it everywhere.

"When he hurried up to the guard's van to claim his trunk and suitcase, the luggage-ticket in his hand, he was in such a crowd that he could not move his arms. But he thought he felt brown fur press the back of his shoulders.

"A porter got him a taxi. It was a relief to see a London cab again, in a coughing London terminus, and hear the bump of the trunk as it went up under the strap, and friendly voices again. He gave the address to the driver, tipped the porter, and jumped inside. Even so, the porter seemed to be holding open the door of the taxi longer than was necessary.

" 'Close it, man!' Tony found himself shouting. 'Close it, quick!'

" 'Yessir,' said the porter, jumping back. The door slammed. Afterwards, the porter stood and stared after the taxi. Tony, glancing out through the little back window, saw him still standing there.

"It was dark in the cab, and as close as though a photographer's black hood had been drawn over him. Tony could see little. But he carefully felt with his hands all over the seat, all over the open space; and he found nothing."

At this point in the story, Hargreaves broke off for a moment or two. He had been speaking with difficulty; not as though he expected to be doubted, but as though the right words were hard to find. His gloved fingers opened and closed on his knee.

For the first time his companion—Miss Judith Gates—interrupted him. Judith spoke from the shadow on the other side of the gas-fire.

"Wait!" she said. "Please!"

"Yes?" said Hargreaves.

"This person who was following Tony." She spoke also with difficulty. "You aren't telling me that it was—well, was—?"

"Was what?"

"Dead," said Judith.

"I don't know who it was," answered Hargreaves, looking at her steadily. "Except that it seemed to be somebody with a fur collar on his coat. I'm telling you Tony's story, which I believe."

Judith's hand shaded her eyes. "All the same," she insisted, and her pleasant voice went high, "even supposing it was! I mean, even supposing it was the person you think. *He* of all people, living or dead, wouldn't have tried to put any evil influence round Tony. Old Jim loved Tony. He left Tony every penny he owned, and not a farthing to Stephen. He always told Tony he'd look after him."

"And so he did," said Hargreaves.

"But—"

"You see," Hargreaves told her slowly. "You still don't understand the source of the evil influence. Tony didn't, himself. All he knew was that he was bowling along in a dark taxi, through slippery, snowy streets; and whatever might be following him, good or bad, he couldn't endure it.

"Even so, everything might have ended well if the taxi-driver had been careful. But he wasn't. That was the first snowfall of the year, and the driver miscalculated. When they were only two hundred yards from Upper Avenue Road, he tried to take a turn too fast. Tony felt the helpless swing of the skid; he saw the glass partition tilt, and a black tree-trunk rush up huge at them until it exploded against the outer windscreen. They landed upright against the tree, with a buckled wheel.

" 'I 'ad to swerve,' the driver was crying. 'I 'ad to! An old gent with a fur collar walked smack out in front of—'

"And so, you see, Tony had to walk home alone.

"He knew something was following him before he had taken half a dozen steps. Two hundred yards don't sound like a great distance. First right, first left, and you're home. But here it seemed to stretch out interminably, as such things do in dreams. He did not want to leave the taxi-driver. The driver thought this was because Tony doubted his honesty about bringing the luggage on when the wheel was repaired. But it was not that.

"For the first part of the way, Tony walked rapidly. The other thing walked at an equal pace behind him. By the light of a streetlamp Tony could see the wet fur collar on the coat, but nothing else. Afterwards he increased his pace to what was almost a run; and, though no difference could be seen in the gait of what was behind him, it was still there. Unlike you, Tony didn't wonder whether it might be good or evil. These nice differences don't occur to you when you're dealing with something that may be dead. All he knew was that he mustn't let it *identify* itself with him or he was done for.

"Then it began to gain on him, and he ran.

"The pavement was black, the snow dirty grey. He saw the familiar turning, where front gardens were built up above the low, stone walls; he saw the street sign fastened to one of those corners, white lettering on black; and, in sudden blind panic, he plunged for the steps that led up to his home.

"The house was dark. He got the cold keys out of his pocket, but the key-ring slipped round in his fingers, like soap in bath-water, and fell on the tiled floor of the vestibule. He groped after it in the dark—just as the thing turned in at the gate. In fact, Tony heard the gate creak. He found the keys, found the lock by a miracle, and opened the door.

"But he was too late, because the other thing was already coming up the front steps. Tony says that at close range, against a streetlamp, the fur collar looked more wet and moth-eaten; that is all he can describe. He was in a dark hall with the door open. Even familiar things had fled his wits and he could not remember the position of the light-switch.

"The other person walked in.

"In his hip-pocket, Tony remembered, he still had the weapon he had carried round the world. He fumbled under his overcoat to get the gun out of his pocket; but even that weak gesture was no good to him, for he dropped the gun on the carpet. Since the visitor was now within six feet of him, he did not stop. He bolted up the stairs.

"At the top of the stairs he risked a short glance down. The other thing had stopped. In faint bluish patches of light which came through the open front door, Tony could see that it was stooping down to pick up the automatic pistol from the carpet.

"Tony thinks—now—that he began to switch on lights in the upper hall. Also, he shouted something. He was standing before the door of his bedroom. He threw open this door, blundered in, and began to turn on more lamps. He had got two lamps lighted before he turned to look at the bed, which was occupied.

"The man on the bed did not, however, sit up at the coming of noise or lights. A sheet covered him from head to feet; and even under the outline of the sheet you could trace the line of the wasted, sunken features. Tony Marvell then did what was perhaps the most courageous act of his life. He had to know. He walked across and turned down the upper edge of the sheet, and looked down at his own face; a dead face, turned sightlessly up from the bed.

"Shock! Yes. But more terror! No. For this dead man was real, he was flesh and blood—as Tony was flesh and blood. He looked exactly like Tony. But it was now no question of a real world and an unreal world; it was no question of going mad. This man was real; and that meant fraud and imposture.

"A voice from across the room said: *'So you're alive!'* And Tony turned round, to find his brother Stephen standing in the doorway.

"Stephen wore a red dressing-gown, hastily pulled round him, and his hair was tousled. His face was one of collapse.

" 'I didn't mean to do it!' Stephen was crying out to him. Even though Tony did not understand, he felt that the words were a confession of guilt; they were babbling words, words which made you pity the man who said them.

" 'I never really meant to have you killed aboard that ship,' said Stephen. 'It was all a joke. You know I wouldn't have hurt you; you know that, don't you? Listen—'

"Now Stephen (as I said) was standing in the doorway, clutching his dressing-gown round him. What made him look round towards the hall behind, quickly, Tony did not know. Perhaps he heard a sound behind him. Perhaps he saw something out of the corner of his eye. But Stephen did look round, and he began to scream.

"Tony saw no more, for the light in the hall went out. The fear was back on him again, and he could not move. For he saw a hand. It was only, so to speak, the flicker of a hand. This hand darted in from the darkness out in the hall; it caught hold of the knob on the bedroom door, and closed the door. It turned a key on the outside, locking Tony into the room. It kept Stephen outside in the dark hall—and Stephen was still screaming.

"A good thing, too, that Tony had been locked in the room. That saved trouble with the police later.

"The rest of the testimony comes from Mrs. Reach, the housekeeper. Her room was next door to Stephen's bedroom, at the end of the upstairs hall. She was awakened by screams, by what seemed to be thrashing sounds, and the noise of hard breathing. These sounds passed her door towards Stephen's room.

"Just as she was getting out of her bed and putting on a dressing-gown, she heard Stephen's door close. Just as she went out into the hall, she heard, for the second time in forty-eight hours, the noise of a pistol-shot.

"Now, Mrs. Reach will testify in a coroner's court that nobody left, or could have left Stephen's room after the shot. She was looking at the door, though it was several minutes before she could screw up enough courage to open the door. When she did open it, all sounds had ceased. He had been shot through the right temple at close range; presumably by himself, since the weapon was discovered in a tangle of stained bed-clothing. There was nobody else in the room, and all the windows were locked on the inside. The only other thing Mrs. Reach noticed was an unpleasant, an intensely unpleasant smell of mildewed cloth and wet fur."

Again Hargreaves paused. It seemed that he had come to the end of the story. An outsider might have thought, too, that he had emphasised these horrors too much, for the girl across from him kept her hands pressed against her eyes. But Hargreaves knew his business.

"Well?" he said gently. "You see the explanation, don't you?"

Judith took her hands away from her eyes. "Explanation?"

"The natural explanation," repeated Hargreaves, spacing his words. "Tony Marvell is not going mad. He never had any brainstorms or 'blind flashes.' He only thought he had. The whole thing was a cruel and murderous fake, engineered by Stephen, and it went wrong. But if it had succeeded, Stephen Marvell would have committed a very nearly perfect murder."

The relief he saw flash across Judith's face, the sudden dazed catching at hope, went to Hargreaves' heart. But he did not show this.

"Let's go back eight months," he went on, "and take it from the beginning. Now, Tony is a very wealthy young man. The distinguished Stephen, on the other hand, was swamped with debts and always on the thin edge of bankruptcy. If Tony were to die, Stephen, the next of kin, would inherit the whole estate. So Stephen decided that, if he was to continue living himself, Tony had to die.

"But Stephen, a medical man, knew the risks of murder. No matter how cleverly you plan it, there is always *some* suspicion; and Stephen was bound to be suspected. He was unwilling to risk those prying detectives, those awkward questions, those damning post-mortem reports—until, more than eight months ago, he suddenly saw how he could destroy Tony without the smallest suspicion attaching to himself.

"In St. Jude's Hospital, where he did some charity work, Stephen had found a broken-down ex-schoolmaster named Rupert Hayes. Every man in this world, they say, has his exact double. Hayes was Tony's double to the slightest feature. He was, in fact, so uncannily like Tony that the very sight of him made Stephen flinch. Now, Hayes was dying of tuberculosis. He had, at most, not more than a year to live. He would be eager to listen to any scheme which would allow him to spend the rest of his life in luxury, and die of natural causes in a soft bed. To him Stephen explained the trick.

"Tony should be ordered off—apparently—on a trip round the world. On the night he was to sail, Tony should be allowed to go aboard.

"Hayes should be waiting aboard that same ship, with a gun in his pocket. After Stephen or any other friends had left the ship conveniently early, Hayes should entice Tony up to the dark boat-deck. Then he was to shoot Tony through the head, and drop the body overboard.

"Haven't you ever realized that a giant ocean-liner, just before it leaves port, is the ideal place to commit a murder? Not a soul will remember you afterwards. The passengers notice nothing; they are too excited. The crew notice nothing; they are kept too busy. The confusion of the crowd is intense. And what happens to your victim after he goes overboard? He will be sucked under and presently caught by the terrible propellers, to make him unrecognizable. When a body is found—if it is found at all—it will be presumed to be some dock-roisterer. Certainly it will never be connected with the ocean-liner, because there will be nobody missing from the liner's passenger list.

"Missing from the passenger list? Of course not! Hayes, you see, was to go to the purser and order Tony's luggage to be sent ashore. He was to say he was cancelling the trip, and not going after all. After killing Tony he was then to walk ashore as—''

The girl uttered an exclamation.

Hargreaves nodded. ''You see it now. He was to walk ashore *as Tony*. He was to say to his friends that he couldn't face the journey after all; and everybody would be happy. Why not? The real Tony was within an ace of doing just that.

''Then, Hayes, well coached, would simply settle down to play the part of Tony for the rest of his natural life. Mark that: his natural life; a year at most. He would be too ill to attend to the business, of course. He wouldn't even see you, his fiancée, too often. If ever he made any bad slips, that, of course, would be his bad nerves. He would be allowed to 'develop' lung trouble. At the end of a year, amid sorrowing friends . . .

''Stephen had planned brilliantly. 'Murder'? What do you mean, murder? Let the doctors examine as much as they like! Let the police ask what questions they like! Whatever steps are taken, Stephen Marvell is absolutely safe. For the poor devil in bed really has died a natural death.

''Only—well, it went wrong. Hayes wasn't cut out to be a murderer. I hadn't the favour of his acquaintance, but he must have been a decent sort. He promised to do this. But, when it came to the actual fact, he couldn't force himself to kill Tony: literally, physically couldn't. He threw away his pistol and ran. On the other hand, once off the ship, he couldn't confess to Stephen that Tony was still alive. He couldn't give up that year of sweet luxury, with all Tony's money at his disposal to soothe his aching lungs. So he pretended to Stephen that he had done the job, and Stephen danced for joy. But Hayes, as the months went on, did not dance. He knew Tony wasn't dead. He knew there would be a reckoning soon. And he couldn't let it end like that. A week before he thought Tony was coming home, after writing a letter to the police to explain everything, Hayes shot himself rather than face exposure.''

There was a silence. ''That, I think,'' Hargreaves said quietly, ''explains everything about Tony.''

Judith Gates bit her lips. Her pretty face was working; and she could not control the twitching of her capable hands. For a moment she seemed to be praying.

''Thank God!'' she murmured. ''I was afraid—''

''Yes,'' said Hargreaves; ''I know.''

''But it still doesn't explain everything. It—''

Hargreaves stopped her.

"I said," he pointed out, "that it explains everything about Tony. That's all you need worry about. Tony is free. You are free. As for Stephen Marvell's death, it was suicide. That is the official record."

"But that's absurd!" cried Judith. "I didn't like Stephen; I always knew he hated Tony; but he wasn't one to kill himself, even if he were exposed. Don't you see, you haven't explained the one real horror? I must know. I mean, I must know if you think what I think about it. Who was the man with the brown fur collar? Who followed Tony home that night? Who stuck close by him, to keep the evil influences off him? Who was his guardian? Who shot Stephen in revenge?"

Sir Charles Hargreaves looked down at the sputtering gas-fire. His face, inscrutable, was wrinkled in sharp lines from mouth to nostril. His brain held many secrets. He was ready to lock away this one, once he knew that they understood each other.

"You tell me," he said.

MIRACLES
AND MAGIC _____

In the following story (which might also be called "Jinn Runner"), **Maurice Procter** *(1906–1973) draws upon his nineteen years of police experience to humorously suggest why an ordinary constable might come to decide that a police force has "No Place for Magic."*

NO PLACE FOR MAGIC

Maurice Procter

STUDENTS of enchantment will be interested to learn that as recently as this year the Lamp was located in the British Isles, in the industrial town of Utterborough, England.

The circumstances of its appearance were not auspicious. The English are temperamentally opposed to any sort of enchantment, and their industrial regimen is quite destructive to it. The Lamp was in serious danger until it was rescued by a police constable and eventually restored to its custodian.

The invaluable object had been thrown away by a young woman when she was sorting the property of a recently deceased maiden lady, whose only heir she was. For many years the lady had lived in comfort, apparently with no income at all, in a flat above some offices in King Street, Utterborough. She left no money, but the furnishings of her flat were priceless. Her disappointed niece, an uncultured person, thought that they were too old-fashioned to be of any value. She hastily packed the articles that seemed to be salable and sent them to an auctioneer, and threw the remainder into the back yard. The Lamp lay on a pile of rubbish in a bin without a lid. But for the action of P. C. Wade it would certainly have been collected by the dustmen, to be pressed and melted as scrap brass.

Wade was on night duty, examining lock-up property around King Street, when he found the Lamp. The electric beam of his own Wootton Lantern seemed to linger upon it. He picked it up and observed its arabesque design. Like the girl who had discarded it, he thought that it was "old-fashioned." But, though he was what is called an uneducated man, he was endowed with natural good taste and he rather liked the look of it.

He began to clean the Lamp with a sheet of newspaper. He held the paper crushed in his hand, and the tip of one of his fingers rubbed against the metal. There was the usual swirl of aromatic dust, and the Slave of the Lamp materialized. He greeted his new Master with a deep salaam.

Since the Slave is ten feet tall by English measurement, and powerfully built, there can be no doubt that the policeman received a shock. It is reported that he ran backwards for quite several paces, and that the way in which his baton appeared in his hand was itself almost magical. Of course the Slave bade him fear not his faithful servant.

Occult sources from which this account is largely obtained state that when Wade had recovered his poise he thought—since it was the only non-magical conclusion possible—that he was momentarily sleeping and dreaming while habit and necessity kept him balanced on his feet.

"I'm surprised at you, George," he heard himself saying with mock severity. "Going about in bathing drawers with a towel round your head. You're improperly dressed. Go and get some clothes on."

"I hear and obey," said the Slave. He vanished, and Wade supposed that he was now fully awake. "Coo," he breathed. "That *was* a nightmare."

Then he remembered a story that he had seen in pantomime at a theater, and he perceived that the object in his hand was indeed an ancient lamp. He shivered suddenly as he felt that cold unearthly wind which all true magicians know. He rubbed the Lamp cautiously, and the Slave reappeared, splendidly attired in the full uniform of a chief constable.

"Here," Wade said nervously, as he began to realize what an extraordinary thing was happening to him, "you can't wear that uniform. It's an offense. You'll get locked up."

"The Master is displeased?" asked the Slave in his deep voice.

"Er, not exactly. But I'd rather you went and changed into plain clothes. A decent suit and a trilby hat, like."

The Slave became a whirling dust-devil; then he reappeared in the required dress.

"That's right," said the constable approvingly. "My word, you're a smart figure of a man."

"The Master is pleased," said the genie with satisfaction. "What is his further wish? Doth he desire a guarded palace and a harem such as the caliphs only dreamed about? With many musicians and dancing girls, and much fruit and wine?"

Wade was considering this traditional offer when he heard the impatient tapping of Inspector Hostler's stick out in King Street. He looked at his watch and realized that he ought to have made his point five minutes ago. He made a certain wish concerning the inspector, but he remembered, just in time, not to utter it. The tapping came nearer. Wade peeped round the corner of the yard and saw Hostler standing in the light of a street lamp at the entrance.

"I wish Inspector Hostler was up at the Cattle Market, tapping his stick for somebody else," he said carefully. The Slave vanished, and so did Hostler.

Wade put the Lamp in his tunic pocket and wandered round his beat, smoking his pipe and meditating upon the things that are not dreamed of in man's philosophy. He realized that he would have to be careful how he spoke in the presence of the genie. A few minutes ago he had nearly dispatched the inspector to hell, and Hostler was a decent man with a wife and three children. Then again, he saw the need to be explicit. The creature did not seem to know his business with regard to the police. It was tactless of him to show up in a chief's uniform like that. He would have been in serious trouble if Hostler had seen him.

Then there was the offer of a palace and dancing girls. That was impossible. Where could it be built? Every square inch of England was owned by somebody. There would be some awkward business about trespass and ground rent, and a Ministry investigation to find out where all the building material had come from, and sightseers and newspaper photographers. Somebody would peep inside and see the girls in their muslin pants, and then it would be raided as a disorderly house. Mrs. Wade might find out about it, and that would be terribly awkward.

The constable's thoughts turned—as they often did—to the question of his own promotion, which he considered to be overdue. He doubted if the genie could help him with that, because it would have to be decided by the chief constable and the Watch Committee. Still, there was no harm in asking. He looked up and down the street, then went into the opening be-

tween the Midland Bank and the Prudential Chambers. He rubbed the
Lamp, and the Slave appeared.

"George," said Wade, "can you alter people's minds?"

"I have no control over the souls of men, O Master," was the reply.

"I didn't think you would have. Thanks, I just wanted to know."

The inspector's stick sounded again. Wade nearly said: "Blast the
man."

"Take Inspector Holster to the Cattle Market again, if you please, and
come back here," he said.

"I hear and obey," answered the Slave. He vanished, and returned.

"I could do with some money," said the P.C. "Go and put a hundred
one-pound notes into the pocket of my best greatcoat. It's in a wardrobe in
the front bedroom of my house. And mind you don't waken the wife.
She'd die of fright if she saw you."

The rest of the night's tour of duty was uneventful. Wade was not an
imaginative or demanding person, and he did not touch the Lamp again.
He was only visited once by his sergeant, and once by Inspector Hostler,
who seemed annoyed and upset about something.

When he went home in the morning he stood on a stool in the scullery
and put the Lamp on the highest shelf, among his paintbrushes and tins of
patent fertilizer. Upstairs, he felt in his greatcoat pocket to make sure of
the money, and went to bed.

He awoke at 2 o'clock in the afternoon. When he was dressed he went
down into the living-room, where his wife and his dinner awaited him.

Mrs. Wade was buxom and thoroughly domesticated. "Eeh," she said,
"I've had a funny feeling all morning. As if there were somebody else in
the house besides you."

"Johnny's at school, isn't he?" Wade inquired.

"Course he's at school."

"Well, then," said Wade.

"I know," she replied. "But it's a funny feeling."

He wondered if the Slave remained near the Lamp, invisible, when he
was not wanted. He would be able to watch everything. It was an embarrassing thought. "I'll have to stop that caper," he decided.

After dinner he went into the garden, where he sat on an old chair in the
sunshine, smoking and pondering. The Lamp was a handy thing, he concluded, but the possession of it had certain disadvantages. For instance, he
dared not take his wife into his confidence. She would pester him until he

summoned the genie for her to see, and when he appeared she would scream the house down. Her distrust in the creature would be unshakable, and she would be unhappy about every one of the benefits that he brought. It was awkward, very awkward. Wade put aside a dream of a handsome new car, because his wife knew that he could not afford any sort of car.

At that moment a car did stop at his gate, and his wife called out to him: "C.I.D."

It was Detective-Sergeant Brown from headquarters.

"We thought we'd let you have your sleep out," he said with a smile. "There was a break-in on your beat last night. The Midland Bank. Did you notice anything unusual?"

Wade immediately thought about the genie. His dismay must have shown in his face, but Brown expected that. Any policeman is dismayed when he has failed to find a break-in.

"Don't you worry," the detective said. "There are no marks which you should have noticed. We think it's a duplicate-key job, and we're interrogating the staff. It's the rummest job you ever saw. The strong-room left wide open, but only a hundred quid missing. Somebody must have disturbed the thieves. Inspector Hostler perhaps. He says he had a feeling there was something queer going on around there last night."

"I'm sorry," said Wade. "I saw nothing. I can't help you at all."

Brown went away. Wade waited until his wife was upstairs, then he went into the scullery and rubbed the Lamp. The genie appeared, almost filling the tiny room.

"You stole that hundred pounds." Wade accused.

"The Master required it," the Slave answered simply. "Gold and jewels can be conjured, but not the wealth that is made of paper. Such paper is but a token of riches, but each piece hath a number. If your Slave made it, it would not be even a token." He sighed unhappily.

"I see your point," said the policeman. "But you mustn't steal. You'd better nip back to the Midland Bank and push those tokens through the letter box."

"I hear and obey," said the Slave, fading rapidly.

Wade went upstairs. The money was no longer in the wardrobe. He sighed with relief.

That incident was not without good results. It gave the constable an idea. He decided that he would have a super-policeman to keep his beat clear of crime. He took the Lamp on duty with him that night, and when he had turned out on his beat he called the Slave and gave him his instructions.

"George," he said. "I want you to float around my beat all the time I'm on duty. I'll contact you regularly. You can report to me everything that happens, but I don't want you to interfere in anything unless I seem to be in difficulties. Is that clear?"

"It is clear, O Master," the genie replied.

Master and Slave worked together for the remainder of that fortnight's spell of night duty. Wade was lucky—normally he would have thought he was unlucky—in having a case of shopbreaking on his beat. The vigilant genie called him to the shop just as three men were escaping with hundreds of pairs of nylon stockings. The men dropped their parcels and attacked Wade. He overpowered one of them without much trouble, and the other two never knew what had hit them. He was complimented by the bench, and his name appeared in the newspapers under such headlines as: LONE P.C. KNOCKS OUT THREE.

During those nine or ten nights he also had several less important captures, due to the genie's assistance. He arrested a man who had broken a plate-glass window in drunken exuberance, and he caught a man driving away a motor car without the owner's permission. Also, he reported the licensee of the Fighting Cocks Inn for supplying intoxicating liquor during non-permitted hours, and sundry customers for consuming the liquor. The licensee still believes that there was a spay among the customers, because *somebody* must have unbarred the door for the police to enter.

The Slave quickly acquired a basic knowledge of police work, and he increased it by reading over Wade's shoulder as he wrote his reports. There is proof that he was susceptible to environment, because one night at the end of those two weeks he completely changed his form of address. He appeared before Wade and saluted in the correct military manner, and said: "Sir, I beg to report that there is a blue Morris saloon, CYK 3979, proceeding towards us from the direction of Sisters Road. There appears to be an offense of failing to display two obligatory white lights to the front, under the Road Vehicles Lighting Regulations, 1936, Section One."

"Now, that's a lot better than bowing and scraping, George," replied Wade with approval. "But we won't bother with the car. Is there aught else?"

"There is the man James Smith, alias Jimmy the Jumper, loitering in the alley behind the Jubilee Wine Stores. He appears to be considering the possibility of climbing to an upper window."

"Good work, old boy," said the policeman. "We'll go and investigate."

It will be seen that the genie, though intelligent, had certain deficiencies. He could not tell the difference between a minor offense and a serious crime. Until he had listened to the court proceedings a few times, he seemed to think that all offenders, from highway robbers to keepers of dogs without licenses, were summarily strangled by bowstring and thrown into the Utter. Nevertheless, he was invaluable to Wade. The policeman even used him on day duty, though he had to be very careful about his appearances. A few people saw him, looked again and saw nobody, and believed that they had been mistaken.

When Wade had been using the genie as an auxiliary policeman for two months there was a Watch Committee meeting at which several promotions were to be made. There were many eligible officers, and Wade was not among those chosen. But someone mentioned his name, and soon it was on every committeeman's lips. After much discussion his name was put on the list and he was promoted.

As a sergeant Wade had half the town to patrol, and with the Slave's help he could have made many arrests. But he was discreet enough to put many of his cases into the hands of keen young constables. At that time, too, he employed the genie at home. In a piecemeal and unobtrusive way he had curtains and carpets renewed, and furniture repolished. His wife thought that the gloss on the furniture was the result of her chronic efforts with beeswax and a cloth.

With the magic of the Lamp Wade could perhaps have heaped benefits upon mankind. But he lacked imagination, and though he was not unduly selfish his outlook was limited by years of police routine. So he confined his kindnesses to people with whom he came in contact. Poor people, elderly people, needy widows, and mothers of large families discovered stocks of food or small amounts of silver money which they thought they must have overlooked. At no cost to himself, he enjoyed the satisfaction of giving.

Wade's personal demands remained moderate. When he needed tobacco or money—never more than a handful of silver—he summoned the Slave and asked for it. The latter, under the iron—or rather brass—discipline of the Lamp's enchantment, made no protest about having to materialize for such trivial reasons, though he did once shed angry tears when he was called upon to supply a box of matches in the middle of the night. It must be remembered that he was a jinni, a devil. He constantly hoped that Wade would ask him to produce a lovely troublesome houri, or order the violent death of an enemy, and Wade constantly disappointed him. When he wept, the policeman thought that he was tired because he had been handling boxes of groceries all day, so he gave him a two day leave.

About a week later, at 5:45 one sunny morning, there occurred one of those incidents which can happen to policeman at any time. A man entered Utterborough Police Headquarters and complained that he had lost a wallet containing twenty pounds while he was rushing to the station to catch the first train. He had seen nobody except a few policemen, and he remarked, rather apologetically, that he felt sure one of the policemen must have picked up the wallet.

Wade was alone in the sergeants' office at the time, making up the following nights' postings, and through the letter-hatch to the inspectors' office he heard Hostler receive the complaint. The worthy inspector was extremely proud and jealous of the force's reputation, and he was infuriated by the mere suggestion that a policeman might dishonestly keep the wallet.

"When the men come in at 6 o'clock," he boomed, "we'll ask every one of them, including myself, to submit to a search. I hope that will satisfy you."

Wade immediately thought of the Lamp in his pocket. He could not put it in his drawer because that would be searched too. If Hostler found the Lamp he would rub it to see what it was made of. He would see the genie and make shrewd guesses about Wade's smart captures, his own transportation to the Cattle Market, everything. That would be awful. In a panic, Wade looked around for a place to hide the Lamp. But the little office was too tidy. A police station has no place for magic.

At any moment, he knew, the inspector might come striding indignantly into the room. He took the Lamp from his pocket and summoned the Slave.

"Here," he whispered urgently. "Take this and hide it somewhere."

The Slave took the Lamp in his hands and smiled enigmatically.

"Go on," whispered Wade in a fright. "Fade!" And the genie faded.

It was a pity really, because it was afterwards discovered that the complaining civilian had left his wallet at home. Not until the search was over did Wade realize that he would never see the Lamp again. He went into a quiet corner of the police-station yard and called for the genie as loudly as he dared. For answer, he heard a sound that began like a chuckle and ended like a roll of thunder in the clear morning sky. He was afraid to call again. He went away, trying to convince himself that he would be better without the Lamp. He had always been rather uncomfortable about it, he remembered. There was no place for magic in his world.

With an unsurpassed ear for dialogue, and an enormous talent,
Evan Hunter *(1926–   ) burst upon the mystery field in 1954*
with a starkly realistic look at juvenile delinquency called
Blackboard Jungle. *Then, donning the mask of* **Ed McBain***, he*
started America's most popular police procedural series—the
87th precinct. But before beginning his successful life of crime,
he had written three fantastic novels, and had deftly combined
both genres in short stories such as this.

THE FALLEN ANGEL

Evan Hunter

HE FIRST came in one morning while I was making out the payroll for
my small circus. We were pulling up stakes, ready to roll on to the next
town, and I was bent over the books, writing down what I was paying
everybody, and maybe that is why I did not hear the door open. When I
looked up, this long, lanky fellow was standing there, and the door was
shut tight behind him.

I looked at the door, and then I looked at him. He had a thin face with a
narrow mustache, and black hair on his head that was sort of wild and
sticking up in spots. He had brown eyes and a funny, twisted sort of
mouth, with very white teeth which he was showing me at the moment.

"Mr. Mullins?" he asked.

"Yes," I said, because that is my name. Not Moon Mullins, which a lot
of the fellows jokingly call me, but Anthony Mullins. And that is my real
name, with no attempt to sound showman-like; a good name, you will
admit. "I am busy."

"I won't take much time," he said very softly. He walked over to the
desk with a smooth, sideward step, as if he were on greased ball bearings.

"No matter how much time you will take," I said, "I am still busy."

"My name is Sam Angeli," he said.

"Pleased to meet you, Mr. Angeli," I told him. "My name is Anthony Mullins, and I am sorry you must be running along so quickly, but . . ."

"I'm a trapeze artist," he said.

"We already have three trapeze artists," I informed him, "and they are all excellent performers, and the budget does not call for . . ."

"They are not Sam Angeli," he said, smiling and touching his chest with his thumb.

"That is true," I answered. "They are, in alphabetical order: Sue Ellen Bradley, Edward the Great, and Arthur Farnings."

"But not Sam Angeli," he repeated softly.

"No," I said. "It would be difficult to call them all Sam Angeli since they are not even related, and even if they were related, it is unlikely they would all have the same name—even if they were triplets, which they are not."

"*I* am Sam Angeli," he said.

"So I have gathered. But I already have three . . ."

"I'm better," he said flatly.

"I have never met a trapeze artist who was not better than any other trapeze artist in the world," I said.

"In my case it happens to be true," he said.

I nodded and said nothing. I chewed my cigar awhile and went back to my books, and when I looked up he was still standing there, smiling.

"Look, my friend," I said, "I am earnestly sorry there is no opening for you, but . . ."

"Why not watch me a little?"

"I am too busy."

"It'll take five minutes. Your big top is still standing. Just watch me up there for a few minutes, that's all."

"My friend, what would be the point? I already have . . ."

"You can take your books with you, Mr. Mullins; you won't be sorry."

I looked at him again, and he stared at me levelly, and he had a deep, almost blazing, way of staring that made me believe I would really not be sorry if I watched him perform. Besides, I could take the books with me.

"All right," I said, "but we're only wasting each other's time."

"I've got all the time in the world," he answered.

We went outside, and sure enough the big top was still standing, so I bawled out Warren for being so slow to get a show on the road, and then this Angeli and I went inside, and he looked up at the trapeze, and I very sarcastically said, "Is that high enough for you?"

He shrugged and looked up and said, "I've been higher, my friend. Much higher." He dropped his eyes to the ground then, and I saw that the net had already been taken up.

"This exhibition will have to be postponed," I informed him. "There is no net."

"I don't need a net," he answered.

"No?"

"No."

"Do you plan on breaking your neck under one of my tops? I am warning you that my insurance doesn't cover . . ."

"I won't break my neck," Angeli said. "Sit down."

I shrugged and sat down, thinking it was his neck and not mine, and hoping Dr. Lipsky was not drunk as usual. I opened the books on my lap and got to work, and he walked across the tent and started climbing up to the trapeze. I got involved with the figures, and finally he yelled, "Okay, you ready?"

"I'm ready," I said.

I looked up to where he was sitting on one trapeze, holding the bar of the other trapeze in his big hands.

"Here's the idea," he yelled down. He had to yell because he was a good hundred feet in the air. "I'll set the second trapeze swinging, and then I'll put the one I'm on in motion. Then I'll jump from one trapeze to the other one. Understand?"

"I understand," I yelled back. I'm a quiet man by nature, and I have never liked yelling. Besides, he was about to do a very elementary trapeze routine, so there was nothing to get excited and yelling about.

He pushed out the second trapeze, and it swung away out in a nice clean arc, and then it came back and he shoved it out again and it went out farther and higher this time. He set his own trapeze in motion then, and both trapezes went swinging up there, back and forth, back and forth, higher and higher. He stood up on the bar and watched the second trapeze, timing himself, and then he shouted down, "I'll do a somersault to make it interesting."

"Go ahead," I said.

"Here I go," he said.

His trapeze came back and started forward, and the second trapeze reached the end of its arc and started back, and I saw him bend a little from the knees, calculating his timing, and then he leaped off, and his head ducked under, and he went into the somersault.

He did a nice clean roll, and then he stretched out his hands for the bar of the second trapeze, but the bar was nowhere near him. His fingers closed on air, and my eyes popped wide open as he sailed past the trapeze and then started a nose dive for the ground.

I jumped to me feet with my mouth open, remembering there was no net under him, and thinking of the mess he was going to make all over my tent. I watched him falling like a stone, and then I closed my eyes as he came closer to the ground. I clenched my fists and waited for the crash, and then the crash came, and there was a deathly silence in the tent afterward. I sighed and opened my eyes.

Sam Angeli got up and casually brushed the sawdust from his clothes. "How'd you like it?" he asked.

I stood stiff as a board and stared at him.

"How'd you like it?" he repeated.

"Dr. Lipsky!" I shouted. "Doc, come quick!"

"No need for a doctor," Angeli said, smiling and walking over to me. "How'd you like the fall?"

"The . . . the fall?"

"The fall," Angeli said, smiling. "Looked like the real McCoy, didn't it?"

"What do you mean?"

"Well, you don't think I missed that bar accidentally, do you? I mean, after all, that's a kid stunt."

"You fell on purpose?" I kept staring at him, but all his bones seemed to be in the right places, and there was no blood on him anywhere.

"Sure," he said. "My specialty. I figured it all out, Mr. Mullins. Do you know why people like to watch trapeze acts? Not because there's any skill or art attached. Oh, no." He smiled, and his eyes glowed, and I watched him, still amazed. "They like to watch because they are inherently evil, Mr. Mullins. They watch because they think that fool up there is going to fall and break his neck, and they want to be around when he does it." Angeli nodded. "So I figured it all out."

"You did?"

"I did. I figured if the customers wanted to see me fall, then I would fall. So I practiced falling."

"You did?"

"I did. First I fell out of bed, and then I fell from a first-story window, and then I fell off the roof. And then I took my biggest fall, the fall that . . . But I'm boring you. The point is, I can fall from any place now. In fact, that trapeze of yours is rather low."

"Rather low," I repeated softly.

"Yes."

"What's up?" Dr. Lipsky shouted, rushing into the tent, his shirttails trailing. "What happened, Moon?"

"Nothing," I said, wagging my head. "Nothing, Doc."

"Then why'd you. . . ?"

"I wanted to tell you," I said slowly, "that I've just hired a new trapeze artist."

"Huh?" Dr. Lipsky said, drunk as usual.

We rolled on to the next town, and I introduced Angeli to my other trapeze artists: Sue Ellen, Farnings, and Edward the Great. I was a younger man at that time, and I have always had an eye for good legs in tights, and Sue Ellen had them all right. She also had blond hair and big blue eyes, and when I introduced her to Angeli those eyes went all over him, and I began to wonder if I hadn't made a mistake hiring him. I told them I wanted Angeli to have exclusive use of the tent that afternoon, and all afternoon I sat and watched him while he jumped for trapezes and missed and went flying down on his nose or his head or his back or whatever he landed on. I kept watching him when he landed, but the sawdust always came up around him like a big cloud, and I never could see what he did inside that cloud. All I know is that he got up every time, and he brushed himself off, and each time I went over to him and expected to find a hundred broken bones and maybe a fractured skull, but each time he just stood up with that handsome smile on his face as if he hadn't just fallen from away up there.

"This is amazing," I told him. "This is almost supernatural!"

"I know," he said.

"We'll start you tonight," I said, getting excited about it now. "Can you start tonight?"

"I can start any time," he said.

"Sam Angeli," I announced, spreading my hand across the air as if I were spelling it out in lights. "Sam An—" I paused and let my hand drop. "That's terrible," I said.

"I know," Angeli answered. "But I figured that out, too."

"What?"

"A name for me. I figured this all out."

"And what's the name?" I asked.

"The Fallen Angel," he said.

There wasn't much of a crowd that night. Sue Ellen, Farnings, and Edward the Great went up there and did their routines, but they were playing to cold fish, and you could have put all the applause they got into a sardine can. Except mine. Whenever I saw Sue Ellen, I clapped my heart out, and I never cared what the crowd was doing. I went out after Edward the Great wound up his act, and I said, "Ladeeeees and Gentulmennnn, it gives me great pleasure to introduce at this time, in his American première, for the first time in this country, the Fallen Angel!"

I don't know what I expected, but no one so much as batted an eyelid.

"You will note," I said, "that the nets are now being removed from beneath the trapezes, and that the trapezes are being raised to the uppermost portion of the tent. The Fallen Angel will perform at a height of one hundred and fifty feet above the ground, without benefit of a net, performing his death-defying feats of skill for your satisfaction."

The crowd murmured a little, but you could see they still weren't very excited about it all.

"And now," I shouted, "the Fallen Angel!"

Angeli came into the ring, long and thin, muscular in his red tights, the sequins shining so that they could almost blind you. He began climbing up to the bars, and everyone watched him, a little bored by now with all these trapeze acts. Angeli hopped aboard and then worked out a little, swinging to and fro, leaping from one trapeze to another, doing a few difficult stunts. He looked down to the band then, and Charlie started a roll on the drums, and I shouted into my megaphone, "And now, a blood-chilling, spine-tingling double somersault from one moving trapeze to another at one hundred and fifty feet above the ground—*without a net!*"

The crowd leaned forward a little, the way they always will when a snare drum starts rolling, and Angeli set the bars in motion, and then he tensed, with all the spotlights on him. The drum kept going, and then Angeli leaped into space, and he rolled over once, twice, and then his arms came out straight for the bar, and his hands clutched nothing, and he started to fall.

A woman screamed, and then they all were on their feet, a shocked roar leaping from four hundred throats all together. Angeli dropped and dropped and dropped, and women covered their eyes and screamed, and brave men turned away, and then he hit the sawdust, and the cloud rolled up around him, and an *Ohhhhhh* went up from the crowd. They kept standing, shocked, silent, like a bunch of pallbearers.

Then suddenly, casually, the Fallen Angel got to his feet and brushed off his red-sequined costume. He turned to the crowd and smiled a big, happy smile, and then he turned to face the other half of the tent, smiling again, extending his arms and hands to his public, almost as if he were silently saying, "My children! My nice children!"

The crowd cheered and whistled and shouted and stamped. Sue Ellen, standing next to me, sighed and said, "Tony, he's wonderful," and I heard her, and I heard the yells of "Encore!" out there, but I didn't bring Angeli out again that night. I tucked him away and then waited for the landslide.

The landslide came the next night. We were playing in a small town, but I think everyone who could walk turned out for the show. They fidgeted through all the acts, crowding the tent, standing in the back, shoving and pushing. They were bored when my aerial artists went on, but the boredom was good because they were all waiting for the Fallen Angel, all waiting to see if the reports about him were true.

When I introduced him, there was no applause. There was only an awful hush. Angeli came out and climbed up to the bars and then began doing his tricks again, and everyone waited, having heard that he took his fall during the double somersault.

But Angeli was a supreme showman, and he realized that the value of his trick lay in its surprise element. So he didn't wait for the double somersault this time. He simply swung out one trapeze and then made a leap for it, right in the middle of his other routine stunts, only this time he missed, and down he dropped with the crowd screaming to its feet.

A lot of people missed the fall, and that was the idea, because those same people came back the next night, and Angeli never did it the same way twice. He'd fall in the middle of his act, or at the end, or once he fell the first time he jumped for the trapeze. Another time he didn't fall at all during the act, and then, as he was coming down the ladder, he missed a rung and down he came, and the crowd screamed.

And Angeli would come to me after each performance and his eyes would glow, and he'd say, "Did you hear them, Tony? They want me to fall, they want me to break my neck!"

And maybe they did. Or maybe they were just very happy to see him get up after he fell, safe and sound. Whatever it was, it was wonderful. Business was booming, and I began thinking of getting some new tops, and maybe a wild-animal act. I boosted everybody's salary, and I began taking a larger cut myself, and I was finally ready to ask Sue Ellen something I'd wanted to ask her for a long, long time. And Sam Angeli had made it all possible. I spoke to her alone one night, over by the stakes where the elephants were tied.

"Sue Ellen," I said, "there's something that's been on my mind for a long time now."

"What is it, Tony?" she said.

"Well, I'm just a small-time circus man, and I never had much money, you know, and so I never had the right. But things have picked up considerably, and . . ."

"Don't, Tony," she said.

I opened my eyes wide. "I beg your pardon, Sue Ellen?"

"Don't ask me. Maybe it could have been, and maybe it couldn't. But no more now, Tony. Not since I met Sam. He's everything I want, Tony; can you understand that?"

"I suppose," I said.

"I think I love him, Tony."

I nodded and said nothing.

"I'm awfully sorry," Sue Ellen said.

"If it makes you happy, honey . . ." I couldn't think of any way to finish it.

I started work in earnest. Maybe I should have fired Angeli on the spot, but you can't fire love, and that's what I was battling. So instead I worked harder, and I tried not to see Sue Ellen around all the time. I began to figure crowd reactions, and I realized the people would not hold still for my other aerial artists once they got wind of the Fallen Angel. So we worked Farnings and Edward (whose "great" title we dropped) into one act, and we worked Sue Ellen into Angeli's act. Sue Ellen dressed up the act a lot, and it gave Angeli someone to kid around with up there, making his stunts before the fall more interesting.

Sue Ellen never did any of the fancy stuff. She just caught Angeli, or was caught by him—all stuff leading up to Angeli's spectacular fall. The beautiful part was that Sue Ellen never had to worry about timing. I mean, if she missed Angeli—so he fell. I thought about his fall a lot, and I tried to figure it out, but I never could, and after a while I stopped figuring. I never stopped thinking about Sue Ellen, though, and it hurt me awful to watch her looking at him with those eyes full of worship, but if she was happy, that was all that counted.

And then I began to get bigger ideas. Why fool around with a small-time circus? I wondered. Why not expand? Why not incorporate?

I got off a few letters to the biggest circuses I knew of. I told them what I had, and I told them the boy was under exclusive contract to me, and I told them he would triple attendance, and I told them I was interested in joining circuses, becoming partners sort of, with the understanding that the Fallen Angel would come along with me. I guess the word had got around by then because all the big-shot letters were very cordial and very nice, and they all asked me when they could get a look at Angeli because they would certainly be interested in incorporating my fine little outfit on a partnership basis if my boy were all I claimed him to be, sincerely yours.

I got off a few more letters, asking all the big shots to attend our regular Friday night performance so that they could judge the crowd reaction and see the Fallen Angel under actual working conditions. All my letters were answered with telegrams, and we set the ball rolling.

That Friday afternoon was pure bedlam.

There's always a million things happening around a circus, anyway, but this Friday everything seemed to pile up at once. Like Fifi, our bareback rider, storming into the tent in her white ruffles.

"My horse!" she yelled, her brown eyes flashing. "My horse!"

"Is something wrong with him?" I asked.

"No, nothing's wrong with him," she screamed. "But something's wrong with José Esperanza, and I'm going to wring his scrawny little neck unless . . ."

"Now easy, honey," I said, "let us take it easy."

"I told him a bucket of *rye*. I did *not* say a bucket of oats. JuJu does not eat oats; he eats rye. And my safety and health and life depend on JuJu, and I will not have him eating some foul-smelling oats when I distinctly told José . . ."

"José!" I bellowed. "José Esperanza, come here."

José was a small Puerto Rican we'd picked up only recently. A nice

young kid with big brown cow's eyes and a small timid smile. He poked
his head into the wagon and smiled, and then he saw Fifi and the smile
dropped from his face.

"Is it true you gave JuJu oats, José, when you are told to give him
rye?" I asked.

"_Si, señor,_" José said, "that ees true."

"But why, José? Why on earth . . ."

"José lowered his head. "The horse, _señor._ I like heem. He ees nice
horse. He ees always good to me."

"What's that got to do with the bucket of rye?"

"_Señor,_" José said pleadingly. "I did not want to get the horse drunk."

"Drunk? Drunk?"

"_Si, señor,_ a bucket of rye. Even for a horse, thees ees a lot of
wheesky. I did not theenk . . ."

"Oh," Fifi wailed, "of all the stupid—I'll feed the horse myself. I'll
find him myself. Never mind!"

She stormed out of the wagon, and José smiled sheepishly and said, "I
did wrong, _señor?_"

"No," I said. "You did all right, José. Now run along."

I shook my head, and José left, and when I turned around Sam Angeli
was standing there. I hadn't heard him come in, and I wondered how long
he'd been there, so I said, "A good kid, José."

"If you like good kids," Angeli answered.

"He'll go to heaven, that one," I said. "Mark my words."

Angeli smiled. "We'll see," he said. "I wanted to talk to you, Tony."

"Oh? What about?"

"About all these people coming tonight. The big shots, the ones coming
to see me."

"What about them?"

"Nothing, Tony. But suppose—just suppose, mind you—suppose I
don't fall?"

"What do you mean?" I said.

"Just that. Suppose I don't fall tonight?"

"That's silly," I said. "You have to fall."

"Do I? Where does it say I have to fall?"

"Your contract. You signed a . . ."

"The contract doesn't say anything about my having to fall, Tony. Not
a word."

"Well . . . say, what is this? A holdup?"

"No. Nothing of the sort. I just got to thinking. If this works out to-night, Tony, you're going to be a big man. But what do I get out of it?"

"Do you want a salary boost? Is that it? O.K. You've got a salary boost. How's that?"

"I don't want a salary boost."

"What, then?"

"Something of very little importance. Something of no value what-ever."

"What?" I said. "What is it?"

"Suppose we make a deal, Tony?" Angeli said. "Suppose we shake on it? If I fall tonight, I get this little something that I want."

"What's this little something that you want?"

"Is it a deal?"

"I have to know first."

"Well, let's forget it then," Angeli said.

"Now wait a minute, wait a minute. Is this 'thing'—Sue Ellen?"

Angeli smiled. "I don't have to make a deal to get her, Tony."

"Well, is it money?"

"No. This thing has no material value."

"Then why do you want it?"

"I collect them."

"And I've got one?"

"Yes."

"Well, what. . . ?"

"Is it a deal, or isn't it?"

"I don't know. I mean, this is a peculiar way to . . ."

"Believe me, this thing is of no material value to you. You won't even know it's gone. But if I go through with my fall tonight, all I ask is that you give it to me. A handshake will be binding as far as I'm concerned."

I shrugged. "All right, all right, a deal. Provided you haven't misrep-resented this thing, whatever it is. Provided it's not of material value to me."

"I haven't misrepresented it. Shall we shake, Tony?"

He extended his hand, and I took it, and his eyes glowed, but his skin was very cold to the touch. I pulled my hand away.

"Now," I said, "what's this thing you want from me?"

Angeli smiled. "Your soul."

I was suddenly alone in the wagon. I looked around, but Angeli was gone, and then the door opened and Sue Ellen stepped in, and she looked very grave and very upset.

"I heard," she said. "Forgive me. I heard. I was listening outside. Tony, what are you going to do? What are *we* going to do?"

"Can it be?" I said. "Can it be, Sue Ellen? He looks just like you and me. How'd I get into this?"

"We've got to do something," Sue Ellen said. "Tony, we've got to stop him!"

We packed them in that night. They sat, and they stood, and they climbed all over the rafters; they were everywhere. And right down front, I sat with the big shots, and they all watched my small, unimportant show until it was time for the Fallen Angel to go on.

I got up and smiled weakly and said, "If you gentlemen will excuse me, I have to introduce the next act."

They all smiled back knowingly, and nodded their heads, and their gold stickpins and pinky rings winked at me, and they blew out expensive cigar smoke, and I was thinking, *Mullins, you can blow out expensive cigar smoke, too, but you won't have any soul left.*

I introduced the act, and I was surprised to see all my aerial artists run out onto the sawdust: Sue Ellen, Farnings, Edward, and the Fallen Angel. I watched Angeli as he crossed one of the spotlights, and if I'd had any doubts they all vanished right then. Angeli cast no shadow on the sawdust.

I watched in amazement as the entire troupe went up the ladder to the trapezes. There was a smile on Angeli's face, but Sue Ellen and the rest had tight, set mouths.

They did a few stunts, and I watched the big shots, and it was plain they were not impressed at all by these routine aerial acrobatics. I signaled the band, according to schedule, and I shouted, "And now, ladies and gentlemen, the Fallen Angel in a death-defying, spine-tingling, bloodcurdling triple somersault at one hundred and fifty feet above the ground, *without a net!*"

Sue Ellen swung her trapeze out, and Angeli swung his, and then Sue Ellen dropped head downward and extended her hands, and Angeli swung back and forth, and the crowd held its breath, waiting for him to take his fall, and the big shots held their breaths, waiting for the same thing. Only I knew what would happen if he did take that fall. Only I knew about our agreement. Only I—and Sue Ellen, waiting up there for Angeli to jump.

Charlie started the roll on his snare, and then the roll stopped abruptly, and Angeli released his grip on the bar and he swung out into space, and over he went, once, twice, three times—and *slap*. Sue Ellen's hands clamped around his wrists, and she held on for dear life. I couldn't see Angeli's face from so far below, but he seemed to be struggling to get away. Sue Ellen held him for just an instant, just long enough for Edward to swing his trapeze into position.

She flipped Angeli out then, and over he went—and *wham*. Edward grabbed his ankles. Angeli flapped his arms and kicked his legs, trying to get free, but Edward—Edward the Great!—wouldn't drop him. Instead, he swung his trapeze back, and then gave Angeli a flip and Farnings grabbed Angeli's wrists.

Farnings flipped Angeli up, and Sue Ellen caught him, and then Sue Ellen swung her trapeze all the way back and tossed Angeli to Edward, and I began to get the idea of what was going on up there.

Edward tossed Angeli, and Farnings caught him, and then Farnings tossed him to Sue Ellen, and Sue Ellen tossed him right back again. Then Farnings climbed onto Sue Ellen's trapeze, and they both swung back to the platform.

Edward took a long swing, and then he tossed Angeli head over heels, right back to the platform, where Sue Ellen and Farnings grabbed him with four eager arms.

I was grinning all over by this time, and the crowd was booing at the top of its lungs. Who cared? The big shots were stirring restlessly, but they'd probably heard that Angeli sometimes fell coming down the ladder, and so they didn't leave their seats.

Only tonight, Angeli wasn't doing any falling coming down any ladder. Because Sue Ellen had one of his wrists and Farnings had one of his ankles, and one was behind him, and the other was ahead of him; and even if he pitched himself off into space, he wouldn't have gone far, not with the grips they had on both him and the ladder. I saw the big shots get up and throw away their cigars, and then everybody began booing as if they wanted to tear down the top with their voices. Angeli came over to me, and his face didn't hold a pleasant smile this time. His face was in rage, and it turned red, as if he would explode.

"You tricked me!" he screamed. "You tricked me!"

"Oh, go to hell," I told him, and all at once he wasn't there any more.

Well, I'm not John Ringling North, and I don't run the greatest show on earth. I've just got a small, unimportant circus, and it gives me a regular small income, but it's also a lot of trouble sometimes.

I still have my soul, though; and, what's more, I now have a soulmate, and she answers to the name of Sue Ellen Mullins, which is in a way most euphonic, you will agree.

THREE DAY MAGIC

Charlotte Armstrong

Do you believe in magic? Old-fashioned magic? That which can twang the threads of cause and effect, take a swipe right across the warp and woof of them, and alter the pattern?

If you ask George this question, he will get a look on his face, a certain look, as if he were remembering a time, an hour, maybe only a certain feeling that once he had. He'll answer, yes, he believes in magic. But he won't explain.

You'll concede he has the right to mean whatever he means by that. You'll like George.

The Casino at the Ocean House, up in Deeport, Maine, was a long room with windows to the sea. Its tables and soft lights, the dance music, gave the hotel's guests something to do in the evening. It was a huge success. Even the village oldsters were proud of it. "Beth'z down to the Casino, last night," they'd say. "George'z got a new trumpet. Fellow from Bath. Ayah. Pretty good, she says."

George Hale and his band played in the Casino every summer, but George, himself, belonged to Deeport, as had his Pa and his Grandpa and many other Hales before him. Tourists exclaimed over the old Hale house, up on the slope, when they saw it glimmering behind the lilacs, under the elms. But George always thought it was most beautiful in the winter when the flouces and ruffles of green fell away and it stood forth, bared and exquisite, etched by delicate shadow, white on white.

Here, also, lived his mother and two of her sisters, all three of them widows, all three doting on George, but each pretending, with a native instinct towards severity, that this was not so. Nor did Nellie Hale, Aunt Margaret or Aunt Liz ever admit that the way he earned a living was "work" at all. George had too much fun. George knew he had fun and he knew the Casino was a success. But he did not suspect what a huge success *he* was.

He was perfect for the Casino. For George felt he was in the middle of a party, any night; therefore, when he took up his saxophone as if he *had* to join, something better than the seabreeze blew across the floor. George's music may have been a little bit corny. He liked all kinds, George did, but whatever he, himself, touched, came out with a jig quality, a right foot, left foot, whirl-me-around-again ta-ra-a-boom-de-ay effect. But he was right for the Casino. He kept the customers remembering that here they were, up on the coast of Maine, breathing deeper than they breathed in town, and in touch for two weeks, more or less, with some simple source of joy.

The Casino paid George well, in fact, enough to last him a frugal winter. But it never occurred to George to push onward. Winters, he went right on enjoying himself. Then the band, and at local fees, would play for the Elks, or the High School prom. In fact, for some miles around, wherever people gathered together for fun and society, George was usually right there, beating out the festive rhythm of their mood. Deeport was proud of him, for in the winter, like the streets and the shore, he was theirs alone.

George was nearly 29, and unmarried. The neighbors speculated about this, sometimes. But his mother and the Aunts, if they speculated, said nothing. Aunt Liz darned his socks exquisitely. Aunt Margaret ironed his shirts to perfection. And his mother, without seeming to do so, based the menus on his preferences.

Naturally George had his secrets. For one thing, he played some pretty highbrow records when he was alone. For another, he believed in true love. He wasn't so naïve as to think it happened to everybody, but he did hope it was going to happen to him. There were certain volumes of English poetry, never caught off the shelves in the old Hale house, which grew, nevertheless, dog-eared and loose at the bindings. Oh, George had his secrets.

One evening in August, George was leading the boys through a waltz, when a red-haired girl in a white dress floated out of the dimness in somebody's arm. Something about the line of her back, the tilt of her head as she took the turns (George played a fast bright waltz, nothing dreamy) pleased him very much for no reason he could trap by taking thought. When later, she danced by with John Phelps 3rd, an old-timer among the summer people, George gave the baton to his second fiddle, climbed down, and sought Phelps out.

She was sitting at a table with an elderly bald-headed man, who had a long sour face and cold gray eyes over which horny lids fell insolently. She was Miss Douglas. He was Mr. Bennett Blair. George didn't know who Bennet Blair was and didn't care. He invited Miss Douglas to dance.

The music happened to be another waltz. George held her off, the prettiest way to waltz, and somehow, on the crowded floor there was plenty of room. They flew along, dipping like birds. Her long white skirt fanned and flared. Her bright hair swung. Her brown eyes smiled at George and he smiled gently down.

She had no "line." Neither did George, of course. They exchanged a little information. They told each other where they lived. She lived in New York with Mr. Blair who was no kin but her guardian. She liked Maine very much. George said he'd been to New York twice and he liked it very much. It was a wonderful city. She said it was wonderful up here, she thought. And they waltzed.

When it was over, there was a small warm spot, somewhere under George's dress shirt, a little interior glow, perhaps in the heart.

The next morning George was hanging around the drugstore when she came in. It wasn't much of a coincidence, because all the summer people went to the drugstore at least twice every day. She came in alone. She wore a blue dress that was solid in the middle. He'd known she wouldn't come down to the drugstore with her ribs bare. He felt very close to her, having known this in advance as he had.

Her name was Kathleen. After she accepted his invitation to a coke so graciously, it seemed all right to ask her.

She said she was called Kathy. He said there wasn't any nickname for

George, except Georgie, but he'd outgrown that of course, by the time he was six. Then he was telling her about his mother and the Aunts. Pretty soon, George and Kathy were walking up High Street towards the old Hale house, and inside, against their coming, Aunt Liz was wiping the pink hobnail pickle dish, Aunt Margaret was straightening the antimacassars in the sitting room, and Nellie Hale was adding just a little more milk to the chowder.

Kathy stopped at the gate and said the exact right thing. She said, "It must be just beautiful in the winter time!" George's hand on the gate shook a little as he opened it. There was a meaning to the time. It would be remembered, this moment in which Kathy Douglas stepped through his front gate.

Nellie Hale and the Aunts, for all one could tell, were absolutely hardened to George's well known habit of bringing strange and beautiful red-haired girls home for dinner. They thought nothing of it at all. But in a little while they began to unbend from this stiff proud nonchalance. For Kathy talked about old things and she understood them, too. Old things that had belonged here a long long time. She asked about Captain Enos Gray, whose cherry table they sat around. And about Captain Mark, who'd brought the china home. She listened, bemused, while the ships went out again and some went down . . . the tales were spun . . . the worn rosary of family legend was told out, bead by bead.

It was after three o'clock before George took her back to the Ocean House. They laughed a lot, skipping along the afternoon streets, her hand in his arm.

They were a little giddy, both of them.

Phelps 3rd was on the veranda, looking concerned. Mr. Blair, in a formidable beach outfit, was waiting in the lobby. He shooed Kathy upstairs. He looked at George from under his horny lids and grunted and walked away.

George came, blinking, out on the veranda again and now, too late, Phelps 3rd told him.

Kathy Douglas had as her inheritance about $5,000,000 of her own. Bennett Blair had about $10,000,000 of his own and was a power in the land. Also, upright and cold, he was a guardian who really guarded. Nobody would get Kathy except the crème de la crème in blood, character, business ability and financial standing.

She was a flower, a lovely lovely flower, but not a wild flower, nor one that had grown under amateur culture in a suburban garden. No, delicately and expensively nurtured, precious and unobtainable was Kathy. She was not, admitted Phelps 3rd, for such as he, who was heir to only half a million from Phelps 1st, toothpaste.

She was not . . . oh, heavens, never! . . . for such as George!

For a dashed moment or two, it seemed to George that he must give her up. But then his vision cleared. By definition it was no solution to give her up. So he dismissed the notion from his mind.

The aroma of millions clung to Mr. Blair and around Kathy, too. It wafted along the harsh Maine sand to the beach, where Kathy and her Fraulein spent most of the day. Naturally, George took to the beach. Afternoons, he would greet Mr. Blair, back from his morning golf to stretch his knobby white knees to the sun. But George couldn't for the life of him dig up any mutual interests. Mr. Blair looked wearily down from an eminence of age and experience and nothing George had to offer seemed worth his response. Yet George knew he was not ignored. He felt, in the afternoons, the weight of that cold glance. He felt himself being labeled and filed in some compartment of that shrewd old brain. Mr. Blair was a guardian who really guarded. Phelps 3rd had known what he was talking about, all right.

But, somehow, seeing Kathy every day, the problem postponed itself and hung suspended in a golden time. For Kathy wasn't discouraging at all.

A golden week went by and then, one morning, Kathy came running to tell him. "George, we're leaving. We have to go!" Clouds fell over the day. "Mr. Blair had planned another week, but something has come up."

"Gosh," said George from the bottom of his heart, "I'm sorry to hear that." And yet, somewhere inside his head a little lick of triumph told him that nothing had come up at all.

George folded himself up and sat down where he was and Kathy knelt beside him. "When, Kathy?" he asked bleakly.

"This afternoon." She was frankly full of woe.

George bit his lip thoughtfully. "Back to New York?"

"Yes."

George looked at the ocean and something closed in his mind. Something said 'goodbye' to it. "Me, too," he said. "Right after Labor Day, when the Casino closes, I'm coming down."

"Oh, George! You'll come to see me!" She was all vivid and glad. Her hand moved on the sand towards his.

"I can't say anything, Kathy. I can't ask you anything, yet."

"Ask me what?" Her eyes were shining.

But George, in the bottom of his soul, agreed with Mr. Blair. Nothing was too good for Kathy. Of course, she was infinitely precious and she must have the best, the very best of everything. So he put his lips on her hand, just once, and let it go. "I'm going to be able to ask Mr. Blair," he said grimly, "the very same day."

Yet, here on the beach in the sunshine, with Kathy near and the dark blue sea and the whole world sparkling around them, the future cleared before him. H'd go down to New York and settle himself and make about a million dollars in some sound respectable way and then he'd ask her. It seemed not only clear and simple, but certain that all this must come to pass.

For Kathy wasn't discouraging at all.

George's decision was the result of a marching logic. Now, in the blood and character departments, George was fine. What he lacked was in the success department. So he must abandon this easy-going life. He must acquire the proof, that is to say, the money. Nothing he could do in Deeport would lead to the kind of money Mr. Blair probably had in mind. So . . .

The boys in the band were disconsolate. The manager of the hotel set up such a pained and frantic howl that George fled his office, with bitter reproaches of ingratitude, pleas for mercy, predictions of the Casino's ruin, ringing in his ears. George thought this was shock. He was sorry.

He arranged to leave the bulk of his earnings in the bank for his mother and the Aunts where it would, as it always had, take them nicely through the winter. "So you see," George explained to them hopefully, "it's not going to make any difference to you."

The three ladies tightened their mouths and agreed. Aunt Margaret, although plump, was the one who tended to fear the worst, but, of course, she didn't weep. Aunt Liz, tiny and angular, chose to look on the bright side, and smiled mysteriously to herself as if she'd been tipped off by a private angel. Nellie Hale, a blend of both temperaments, simply tightened her mouth. "George is grown," she said, and that was all she would say.

So, darned and mended, cleaned and pressed, and fed to the utter limit,

George, with $200 in his pocket and his saxophone in his hand, took the train one September evening, without the faintest conception of the gap his departure tore in the whole fabric of the town's life. All hints of this he took for kindliness and so he was spared. He suffered only the wrench of his own homesickness.

New York received George and his saxophone with her customary indifference. Yet he was lucky in the first hour, for he walked by Mrs. McGurk's four-story brownstone on West 69th Street just as her hand in the front window hung up the vacancy sign.

George, trained all his life to pretend that only cleanliness mattered, saw that the square ugly room on the fourth floor was clean and so said he'd take it. Mrs. McGurk sniffed. Take it, indeed! She said she'd take him. Rent by the month, in advance. That was her rule. George paid and looked about him. The room had no charm but George, although he had always lived in the most charming surroundings, knew not the word or its definition. The place felt queer. He imagined, however, that it was only strange.

Mrs. McGurk was a widow, 40-odd, toughened by her career. The poor woman had a nose that took, from head-on, the outline of a thin pear, and was hung, besides, a trifle crookedly on her face. Her character, though scrupulously honest, was veiled by no soft graces. Like the room, she was clean but she had no charm.

What other roomers might hole up, two to a floor, below him in this tall narrow house, George did not know. He tried to say "Good day" to a man who seemed about to emerge from the other door on his landing, but he got no answer. All he saw was a brown beard, a narrow eye, and the door, reversing itself, closing softly to wait 'til he had gone by.

George shrugged. He had other matters on his mind. First, he had to get a job. This was not very difficult since he was a member of the union in good standing. Pretty soon George had hired himself and saxophone out to Carmichael's Cats, a small dance band, playing in a small night club. It wasn't such a wonderful job, but George felt that, in this great city, first one got a toehold and then one took the time to look around.

His first night off, he called on Kathy. She lived only just across the Park in Bennett Blair's gray stone house that looked to George exactly like a bank building. He was received in a huge parlor, stuffed full of ponderous pieces, dark carving, stifled with damask in malevolent reds and dusty greens, lit by lamps whose heavy shades were muddy brown.

Kathy was glad to see him. Bennett Blair was not.

George walked home through the Park and on its margins the tall buildings glittered, high and incredible in the dark. " 'Tisn't going to be so darned easy!'' George thought to himself. And he tightened his mouth.

George, from his toehold, had no time to look around because the toehold gave way. Carmichael's Cats were sorry but they couldn't use him. He wasn't right.

George had to stir himself and get another job with Barney and his Bachelors. They played, as had the Cats, a jagged and stylized kind of music, full of switches and turns. Barney liked to ambush himself, to leap on a sweet passage with an odd blue interruption, to fall from a fast blare to a low whimper with shock tactics. These tricks were no ingredient of George's bag. It wasn't that he didn't like the effect. He admired it. But he couldn't do it. Barney could jerk and shake up the whole band, but not George. George would try, but first thing he knew, there he'd be, tootling along in his own jig time, following one note with the probable next at the probable interval. Being obvious! Barney was disgusted!

So George left the Bachelors, unhappily, and approached Harry and his Hornets.

Each new month, Mrs. McGurk waited for dawn to crack, but no longer. Pay in advance was her rule and her system had no flaws. Rarely, indeed, did the sun go down upon a deficit, or a roomer escape to carry his debt unto the second day.

On the fourth floor, George, occupationally a late riser, was just getting up when she sang out, "First of the month, Mr. Hale." Her initial assault was always blithe and confident.

"Why, sure," drawled George. "Come in a minute." He fumbled under his handkerchiefs in the top drawer. "Hey," cried George in honest surprise, "I don't seem to have much money!"

The landlady's nostrils quivered, scenting battle.

"Gosh," said George reasonably, "I can't give you all of this!" In the midst of turmoil, changing jobs, George had not noticed how low his capital funds were getting. He stared at calamity. He had been here a month and a half, now, and he had not only had made no progress toward his million dollars, he dared not pay the November rent!

Mrs. McGurk was nagging monotonously. "Month in advance. Told you my rule. Took the room, didn't you?"

Up in Deeport, of course, money lay in the bank. But it was not his.

"Rent's due," shrilled Mrs. McGurk. "You've got it!"

George pulled himself together. "How about taking half of it?"

She looked at the bills he offered and on her lop-sided face there was no recognition. "Half of it now," urged George. "I've just got a new job. All I want to do is see the man and get an advance." George was not going to let next week's meals out of his fingers. He couldn't. This crisis had sneaked up on him but his instinct was to meet it with caution and compromise. There was a sense, here, in which Greek met Greek.

Mrs. McGurk snorted. "Why don't you pay me and *then* go get this advance?"

"Because I'd rather do it the other way around," said George.

"Nope," said Mrs. McGurk.

"Yup."

"Nope."

"Do you think I'm trying to cheat you?" George was really curious.

"I got my rules, young man, and nobody's talked me out of them for twenty years."

George sat down on the bed and ran his hand through his hair. "I wish a little bird would tell me where the money's gone," he said ruefully.

"Either pay up or get out!" Mrs. McGurk wanted no persiflage. "I'll take two weeks notice money. You want it like that? Eh?"

George said, "The first of the month lasts 'til midnight. Take half. If I bring you the rest before midnight, it's my rent on time. If I don't, then this is notice money." Her face, if possible, hardened. "That's fair," said George.

"That's not the way I do business."

"But it's fair," he insisted.

"You got it, right there, and I want it!"

"You're not going to get it," said George quietly. He put the bills on the bed.

Mrs. McGurk was wild. George swung around. "Of course, there's another way that's just as fair. Give me back a half, tonight, if things go wrong. Want *me* to trust *you?*" George smiled. "O.K."

Head down, she glowered at him. Her hand snatched at the money on the bed and stuffed it furiously into her old brown handbag. Mrs. McGurk was fit to be died. During the years of shortages, what with rent ceilings and rising costs, she had not grown rich and avarice was not her trouble. But she had acquired a taste for power, and she was not going to be jockeyed out of position. "You gimme the rest before midnight," she cried, "or I'll rent the room out from under you tomorrow." She flung herself out the door and pounded across the hall. "Mr. Josef! Mr. Josef!"

George closed his door gently. He had to think, what to do. As a matter of fact, Harry, the bandleader, hadn't been absolutely definite about taking George on. And no use looking for Harry this early. George sat down on the bed and removed all artificial props from under his spirits. Promptly they sank, way down. This ugly room was more unfriendly, uglier than ever.

But the mood was one George had been taught to cast off. He thought he'd go across the Park and see Kathy for a minute.

Kathy came in a little girl's hop down the great stairs, seeming, as always, glad to see him. But she said, "Oh, George, Mr. Blair is home. He wants to have a talk with you and I promised. . . ." George felt a chill of foreboding. "Maybe," she added hopefully, "he's too busy."

But Mr. Blair was not too busy. George was taken from Kathy's side and ushered through the high rooms to the library where Mr. Blair, entrenched behind his desk, frostily received him.

Mr. Blair was old and cold and his past lay around him here in this sanctum, relics of past enthusiasms, the accumulations of his mind. The total effect was overwhelming. There was so much, and everywhere each single item in the mass reeked of its expense. The smell of money rose like dust. George nearly choked.

Mr. Blair massaged the vague arthritic pains in his knuckles. "Mr. Hale," he said crisply, "am I correct in guessing that your reason for transplanting yourself to this city is your interest in my ward?"

"Correct," croaked George.

A faint sigh came out of Mr. Blair. It seemed to set the dust dancing. "I envy you your youth," he said in his rusty voice. George thought of the knobby old knees that had never tanned, in all that Maine week, though he had held them so faithfully to the sun, and felt, oddly in this place, a brief pang of pity. "But," the tough old lids lowered, "I must ask you to consider my point of view."

"I recognize your point of view, sir. I wouldn't think of asking for Kathy . . . yet."

Mr. Blair pushed out his lower lip. George had jumped the interview several steps ahead. "You expect to be in a position to ask for her, ever?"

"Yes, sir. I do."

Mr. Blair went into a fast rhythm. "What is your work?" He barked.

"I . . . uh . . ."

"You play a saxophone." Mr. Blair knew the answers, too. "How much do you earn?"

"Uh . . ."

"Not very much. What prospects for the future?"

"Well . . ."

"Few," said Blair. "As a matter of fact, you are just floundering. And even if you had a job, at this moment, what prestige, what standing in the community are you aiming for?"

"But . . ."

"When can you hope to ask for Kathleen?"

George wilted. "I don't know," he admitted.

Mr. Blair took another tack. "Now, if," he purred, "you point out to me that Kathleen already has enough mere money, I would agree with you. But I'll ask you this. Have you had any business training? Have you the slightest idea how to watch over and guard her estate?"

"I intend to learn," said George desperately.

Mr. Blair let his lids fall in pure disdain. "Let me speak plainly. If you were to defy my expressed opinion, I am empowered to divert her estate into charitable channels . . ."

"No, sir," said George promptly. "That won't happen."

Bennett Blair's lids lifted and he stared a moment. "I don't accuse you of fortune hunting," he said stiffly. "I merely say, that since it will take you many years to achieve the standing I consider necessary, will you ask her now, to fix her affections on you? Can't you see that's unfair?"

George leaned back. "It certainly is," he answered steadily. "I shouldn't even risk her liking me, now. Somebody better for *her* than I am might be shut out. That's what you mean, sir, isn't it?" Mr. Blair's fish mouth remained a little open. "It does me a lot of good to see her," said George wistfully. "But I'll have to get along without that."

"Quite right," snapped Mr. Blair. "You realize what it means?"

"Yes," said George sadly.

"I cannot," said Mr. Blair crossly, "be so swayed by my admiration for your handsome attitude that I will forget to insist upon a strict accord between your principles and your actions."

"Did you think I was just talking?" asked George forlornly. He got up. "Is there some back way out?"

Mr. Blair caught his tongue between his teeth and around this physical arrangement crept a reluctant grimace verging on a smile. "Oh, no, no, no," he waved a hand. "You may speak to Kathleen, of course. You might tell her," he added ruthlessly, "how we agree."

Kathy was waiting in the parlor. George took her hands. "Goodbye," he said.

She scrambled out of the chair in alarm.

"Mr. Blair's been explaining some things and he's right, Kathy. I'd better not see you any more. Until maybe . . . someday."

Kathy's hair gleamed as if it brightened with her temper. "I won't be seeing you at all? Because Mr. Blair says you mustn't?"

"But he's right, Kathy. Maybe you don't realize . . ."

"You haven't asked me what I realize."

"I know *you* never think about money or success or things like that," groaned George. "But they have a meaning, just the same. I . . . I have a lot to do." He stepped away from her. "In the meantime, don't wait."

"What!"

"Don't . . . don't wait . . ." said George, ready to bawl.

Kathy flung out her hands in a gesture that might have been despair.

"There's only one thing to do," babbled George.

Kathy cocked her head. "Are you sure you know what it is, George?"

George's eyes were storing up the sight of her.

"I haven't any intention of waiting for you!" said Kathy boldly.

George was beyond heeding. "Then . . . Kathy, goodbye," he groaned. She looked so lovely, so tempting, so perfect, George felt he couldn't bear it another minute. He blurted out, "I hope I'll be seeing you . . . but if I never do, it was wonderful to have seen you at all. Goodbye. Goodbye."

He turned and fled.

Kathy began to breathe very quickly, in angry little gasps. She ran after him. She cried out, to the door that had already closed behind him, "Aren't you going to ask me what I mean?" The last word went up in an outraged wail. But Kathy took her hand from the door and drew away.

It was a black morning. George walked along, staggering under a succession of blows. He was about as far down as he could get. But, gradually, the bottom began to feel solid under his feet.

He wouldn't be seeing Kathy, so he must use every moment to claw and fight his way back to her. Definitely, he must kick away the toehold of his musical background. That meant no Hornets. That meant no advance! That meant raising the rest of his rent some other way.

Well, he'd sell his saxophone. So much was settled. George's spirits began to bounce. He would close his mind to what Kathy had said. Whether she waited or not, nothing could keep him from hoping, from *trying*.

By sheer luck, he caught the landlady off guard and ran up the long stairs. On the last flight he overtook the bearded figure of his fourth floor-mate. "Pardon," said George. The man flattened himself against the wall, palms in, head turned, eyes furtive. He stood as if he felt himself to be invisible against the protective coloration of the wallpaper.

George paid him no mind. He knew what he had to do. When his hand went cozily around the handle of his instrument case, he beat down the sentimental pang. He reconnoitered. Mrs. McGurk's voice was raised, back in her kitchen regions, so he fled past the last newel post and es-caped.

He tramped along the street, west, his mind busy solidifying plans. Sell the sax, pay the rent, read the ads, go to employment agencies, poke and pry, wedge himself in, somewhere. His imagination glanced off miracles of one kind or another, bouncing, steadying.

There probably weren't going to be any miracles, George reminded him-self. He mustn't expect any magic.

He didn't believe in magic, at this time.

Something told him to stop walking. He saw that he stood before a pawnshop, looking into a very dirty window at a jumble of stuff that gleamed in the dust, whether jewelry or junk, he couldn't tell. But deeper within he could discern the dim shapes of larger objects, among them the unmistakeable curve of a violin. Musical instruments? Well, he could ask.

George opened the door and went in. A bell made a flat clank over his head. Out of the shadowy back regions, the proprietor approached, a very small man, humped and telescoped with age, his face netted with a million wrinkles. He had a dark eye, this little man, dark, liquid and gleaming.

"Yess?" he said.

George lifted his case. "How much for this?" he asked, speaking dis-tinctly in case these ancient ears were deaf.

The proprietor fluttered back of the counter. He moved silently and somehow weightlessly. "Sixteen dollarsss," he said in a dry wisp of sound.

"Not enough," said George's Yankee blood promptly.

The old man moved his shoulders in light indifference. But the dark eyes swam to look up, as if to suggest a hesitation. So George stood still, although his urgency, the glow of his resolution, the steam George had up, tumbled and churned around him.

The old man said, "I've got things I give you to boot."

"What things?" said George. "Look, I don't want to swap, you know. I want . . ."

"Yesss . . . but come. . . ." The whole little man was nodding, now.

George followed him along a dark lane that led to the darkest interior corner. The proprietor paused in a clearing in the jungle of objects, picked up something and set it on a low table. "If you wish," said the proprietor, "sixteen dollarsss and thisss. . . ." "Thisss" was an old carpet bag.

"What's in it?"

"See . . ."

George pulled at the double handle. "Nuh-uh. What would I want with. . . ? Hey, what's that?" He reached in. There was an old sword wedged diagonally in the bag. George had a fancy for old things and a small-boyish love for swords. He fondled the hilt of this one. The scabbard was some worn crimson stuff.

George waked himself out of a dream. The old man's bright eyes were avid and sly. "No, no," said George.

"Maybe isss antique. . . ."

"Looks antique, all right," George fished into the bag and found a small carved box. The lid opened by sliding. There was nothing in it but a flower. A rose. Artificial, he supposed. He dropped the box and rummaged again. There were soft cloth masses. There was a piece of flat metal, framed with a wrought design, burnished in the center. Old, very old. There was a small dark leather pouch. "What's this?"

"Open," said the proprietor softly.

George pulled the thong fastenings. Inside, he found a single piece of metal. Flat, lopsided, with some worn engraving on it, perhaps it was gold. "Hey," said George, "did you know this was in here?" The old man made his butterfly shrug. "Is it a coin? Is it gold?"

"Maybe . . ."

"This might be worth something," George said honestly. "Old coins, y'know."

"May be . . ." said the proprietor indifferently. "You take?"

"Wait a minute," said George, "how do you know this isn't gold? How do you know it isn't worth a lot of money?"

"I am tired," said the old man.

George looked dubious. He chewed on his lip. The whole thing was queer. Queer shivery feeling to this place. "I certainly don't want this bagful of junk. Give me $25 and the coin. How about that?"

"I give twenty and all thisss. So no more, not less." The sibilants sighed on the dusty air.

"You seem to want to get rid of it," murmured George. His imagination was jumping. Maybe the coin was worth a lot. Maybe the sword would sell for something to a man who knew about swords.

"I am going," said the proprietor softly, "to California."

Ah! George relaxed. He had a sense of satisfaction, and clearing of confusion. Of course! Anyone who was going to California flung off the winter garments of old caution. *He* wouldn't want to bother, this old fellow whose bones were promised to the sun!

But George was young and full of beans, and George could spare the energy that lurks at the bottom of most strokes of luck. George said, "It's a deal."

The old man's hands came up as if he would rub them together, but cautiously, he did not. He simply nodded, all over, as before, and fluttered towards his till.

When George lugged his new property out into the street, he felt perhaps he'd been had. One thing led him to hope he'd done well. The queer stark look with which the old man's eyes clung to the carpet bag, there at the last . . . as if there were something . . . something unusual . . . about this carpet bag.

As a matter of fact, it was old-fashioned, ungainly, misshapen, distended ridiculously at one bottom corner because the sword inside was really too long, and it made George feel foolishly conspicuous. The only thing to do was dump it in his room.

Even as he gained the second floor, he heard a hen-like flutter in the lower hall. He went up fast, anyway, shut himself in and began to empty the carpet bag out on his bed. Might as well see what he had here.

Across the hall, Mr. Josef held his ear against the inside panel of his own door. His eyes rolled, relishing this pose. His fat hand, on which the nails were chewed away, caressed the inner knob with delicious stealth.

Down below, Mrs. McGurk muttered to herself and began to climb.

Outside, the city roared.

George looked at what he had here. There was the pouch. He tossed it aside. The box that held a rose, the sword . . . George balanced it a moment in his hand and it felt alive. He had a terrible suspicion that he could never sell it.

There was that flat metal oval. Then there was a strange object, in metal that resembled a teapot and yet was not a teapot. Baffled, George put it down. He fished out a queer old flask. It seemed to be made of pinkish stone, with a stony stopper, the whole bound in an intricate metal lattice. Something swished inside. George could not get the stopper out to sniff at whatever was in there. He put it down and delved deeper.

Now he came to the fabric. First, he drew out an odd garment, made of a black, rather porous cloth that was opaque and yet so soft it seemed to melt under his fingertips. The thing was designed to be worn. The top of it was cut, obviously, to fit around ones shoulders. George blinked and put it by.

He certainly did not understand what kind of person packed this bag, nor of what kind of household these things could be the relics. There must be some rhyme or reason to this conglomeration. True, all these things were old. But what other quality they had in common he couldn't . . . at this time . . . imagine.

Rolled tightly at the bottom of the bag there now remained a small thin, old, and shabby Oriental rug. As George extracted it, something else dropped. The last object of all in the bag was a ring.

Very old. Not gold, however. Perhaps it was blackened silver. On a plain band, a wrought setting in the same dark metal held an uncut lumpish stone of a bluish gray color. This stone was curiously filmed over. George put his thumb on it. It wasn't dusty. Nothing rubbed off. It was certainly a queer looking ring. He held it in his palm, thinking suddenly of Kathy.

Mrs. McGurk rapped sharply, opened the door, and stepped in. She loosened the set of her mouth long enough to let out a "Well?"

George dropped the ring and felt for the coin in his pocket. "It's not midnight yet," he said mildly. It occurred to him that he had better hunt up an old coin man as soon as possible.

"Lying, weren't you?" she sneered. "You got no new job, and no man to see!"

George didn't answer. He just met her steady glare with a steadier look of patience and regret. Mrs. McGurk's eyes fell away. They spied the bed. "I'd thank you to keep that junk off my bedspread," she snapped.

"Sorry," said George gently. "I've got to go out again, now."

Mrs. McGurk said venomously. "Don't hurry. I've decided not to accept your full month's rent. I'm giving *you* notice, Mr. Hale."

"All right," said George patiently. "Excuse me?" He went out, past her, leaving her there.

He felt stiff and sad. There was no need for such unpleasantness. It served no purpose except to sadden and embitter the innocent day.

Mr. Josef stood in the hall. When George appeared, he turned his back and pretended to be entering his room. George started downstairs. He looked back. Mr. Josef was in a ridiculous position. He seemed to be staring into the blank wood, a foot and half from his face. He was not, of course. His eyes, sidewise, were watching George.

"Who," wondered George, "does he think he is, anyway?"

Mrs. McGurk, having been rude, ugly and unjust, was of course furious. She stalked about George's room, looking for something to pin her fury on. George, however, kept his things clean and orderly as effortlessly as he breathed. There was nothing for his landlady to pounce on, except the bed and its array of strange objects.

Mrs. McGurk approached it then, with nostrils dilated. But, dusty and old as many of these things appeared, nothing, no dust of any kind, had been transferred to the bedspread. Mrs. McGurk's fury began to give way to sheer curiosity.

The cloak she made nothing of. It couldn't belong usefully to a personable young man like George. The metal things she shook her head over. Junk. She wouldn't, she huffed to herself, give them houseroom.

What quiet there was, existing under the constant flow of sound from the city, was being broken hideously by a cat, down below. He was a displaced feline who lived by his wits in the deep yards in the heart of the block. He was sitting on a fence, wailing his heart out. Mrs. McGurk winced at the piercing pain of his cries.

She picked up the pinkish stone flask and shook it, but she couldn't get the stopper out, either. She opened the pouch and drew her mouth down at the sight of the flattened lump of gold that lay within in. She could not know that George, even now, was taking a similar coin out of his pocket to show it to a man behind a counter, two blocks south. Nor could she know that George had not the slightest idea of the existence of this second coin. No thief, she merely drew the thongs tight and cast the pouch down, impatiently.

The cat wailed as if the world's end were at hand. Mrs. McGurk moved to the window and joined the neighbors in a lively exchange of shouted despair. The cat had no mind for the troubles of humans. It wailed on.

Shaking her head, Mrs. McGurk drew it into the room again. She picked up the ring. A curious piece of work. She slipped it on her finger, where it fit with a pleasant weight to it and looked, for all its queerness, rather well on her work-bitten hand.

The cat thought of something particularly outrageous and screamed in an ecstasy of self-pity. "I wish to goodness," said Mrs. McGurk out loud, "that cat would stop its yowling!"

On her hand, the dull bluish lump of stone in the ring began to catch light. For a brief moment, it gleamed. The dusty look of it seemed to burn away.

The cat stopped it. Abruptly. His current yowl, in fact, was cut off in the middle and never finished. Silence poured down like water and extinguished the noise.

Mrs. McGurk blinked. The precipitous quiet was just a trifle uncanny. She listened with a curious eagerness for the cat ro resume, but it did not. She took off the ring and dropped it back on the bed, vaguely sorry, in an inexplicable way, that she had ever touched it.

For just a moment, the things lying on the bed up here in George's room were more than queer. Their antiquity was worse than puzzling.

"Fifty?" said the old coin man, casually. His thumb came up in a caressing pinch. His junior clerk wasn't breathing.

George made a low mirthful sound. "You've certainly been helpful," he said cheerfully. "May I see your classified directory?"

"One hundred dollars," said the man.

"Two hundred," said George gaily.

"It's a deal," snapped the man and now George staggered. In a tense silence, the junior took the coin, the money was fetched and George signed something.

Then the little office bloomed with three wide smiles.

"I'm satisfied, you know," said George. "But I wish you'd tell me . . ."

"Rare!" babbled the man. "Rare? Not even listed. And indisputably genuine. The inscriptions, the feel of the gold . . ." he rubbed his fingers, "greasy with time . . ." He slapped the counter jubilantly. "Now tell me. Where *did* you get it?"

"Found it, like I told you," said George cheerfully. "I'm certainly glad you liked it. Tell you what, if I ever run across another one, I'll let you know. So long."

George went off jauntily. The boss's mouth curled. "He'll bring us another one! Ha!"

"Ha ha!" echoed the clerk.

Mrs. McGurk had shaken off her funny feeling. She went on examining this queer collection, and at last she picked up the little carved box with the sliding lid and looked sourly at the rose inside. Artificial, she presumed. Yet . . . no . . . Or, if it were, it was a marvel! Her woman's eye could see as much. She touched it and the petals were sweet and cool. Mrs. McGurk raised the box to her crooked nose. To her senses came the unmistakeable fresh rich fragrance of the living rose.

Just then, George opened his door.

Rose to nose, Mrs. McGurk looked full at him.

Until this day, Mrs. McGurk's impression of George had been mild. Her trained gaze had gone over him and not finding the mark of the complainer, or the destroyer of rented property, or the innocent stare of the deadbeat, she had looked no more.

This morning, however, he had offered her good faith and fair play and she had been obliged to turn them down. Under her tough protective crust still existed an uneasy heart that knew and recognized her losses. George had what she had no more . . . the capacity for trusting. Something about him was sweet to the core. and it hurt! So, of course, she had been stubbornly angry.

But now, as the perfume of the rose penetrated her senses, something very strange happened to Mrs. McGurk. This crust of hers seemed suddenly and for no cause to dissolve. Her bosom swelled as if some withered seed, lying dormant in her heart, had been touched by magic moisture so that it sprang into life and began to grow. Looking full at George, the light in her eye grew suddenly tender. How was it she had not noticed before the gentleness of his eyes, the sweetness of his smile? This was such a boy as one could be fond of, as if he were one's own, almost. Mrs. McGurk had the sensation of melting. She swayed a little. She put the rose, in its box, down on the bed and she smiled.

Even in its best day, Mrs. McGurk's smile had been rather terrifying, involving her long teeth bared to the upper gums and somehow the illusion that the bulbous end of her nose had taken a sudden twitch farther off center. "I'm sorry, Mr. Hale," said she contritely. And her inner being swooned and swam in the luxury of this humility. "I was rude and unjust to you and I'm terribly sorry."

George realized at last what she thought she was doing with her face. However, to him a kindly feeling was the most natural thing in the world and he accepted it immediately. "That's all right, Mrs. McGurk. I was probably irritating. I've got the money, now," he added gently. "Do I owe you anything?"

"My dear boy!" cried Mrs. McGurk, "of course not! You paid me for two full weeks ahead! And you must stay! This room is yours. I want you to feel at home!"

It was the first time the sweet sense of home had come to her mind for years and years. Mrs. McGurk's eyes filled. She wanted to do more for George. She felt a compelling urge to make him happy. "Please let me show you my second floor front," she snuffled. "Such a lovely room it is, Mr. Hale. It would just suit you! Only one flight up and a private bath."

"That's mighty nice of you," said George, somewhat bewildered. "But you know I can't afford . . ."

"Same price!" cried she. "And handy to the phone!"

"Well, I . . . uh . . . if you say so," said George weakly. "It's very nice of you. But I want to pay my full month ahead. Please. I know it's your rule."

"One has to have rules, Mr. Hale. The people I meet . . ."

"Sure, I know. I don't bla—"

"But I should have *seen*," said his landlady, "that *you* are *different!*"

George realized, with some dismay, that Mrs. McGurk was trying to be charming. There she stood, in her shapeless print dress, with her hair piled up in the usual slapdash coiffure, the same woman . . . and yet . . . The head was cocked, now, in a kind of old-fashioned coquetry, the curled lip bared the long teeth; the glance came sideways from under arched brows, with the left eye not quite in focus. It was a formidable sight!

George swallowed. But, being George, he gave her full marks for effort. He thanked her.

"Oh, you will stay?" cried she. "I'll go right down. And freshen up the room a bit. Don't bother about your things. I'll move them. It's no trouble. I feel," said Mrs. McGurk "so happy to have someone like you in the house, I can't tell you. . . !" The brows ached with sweetness. She went out with a bob and a flirt of her skirt.

George sank down on the bed. He rubbed the back of his head. The money was in his hand. He stared down at it. It occurred to him that this was one of the strangest days of his life.

But here was $200, here in his hand. He began to wonder if there was more, disguised in the heap of stuff beside him. He shoved the money into a pocket and reached for that flat oval . . . But his thoughts drifted off to

Kathy. Now that he had $200, was he any nearer? When would he see her again, her sweet pretty face, the red gold of her hair, the enchanting lights in her tawny eyes?

Kathy was standing in the middle of a dainty bedroom . . . on a thick white rug . . . near a soft green chair . . .

George inhaled a great gasp.

He *was* seeing her!

He had been looking absently into the burnished metal and now it was acting like a mirror but what it reflected was not here! He could see Kathy!

He lifted the thing in both trembling hands. The vision did not go. It trembled a little, but the tiny Kathy began to fumble at the fastenings of her dress!

George's hair rippled on the back of his neck. He'd heard there were people who could see things in a crystal ball. Now he, George Hale, of Deeport, Maine, was seeing things! Why, the strength of his love was so great. . . !

Kathy began to wiggle out of her dress. She stood in her slip, bare shouldered, adorable. Another figure crossed the little reflected scene. Fraulein!

Now, George knew darned well he wasn't in love with Fraulein!

He breathed. He had to. The image in the Magic Mirror shook with his body but did not fade.

Magic?

Kathy pushed the straps of her slip down and took hold of it at the hem. She was going to take it off. No doubt of it. Right now, across the Park, Kathy was undressing!

But George, in spite of his state of absolute astonishment, was yet a gentleman, and, above all, he adored her. So he tore his gaze away from the enchanted bit of metal, turned it over, dull side up, and slid it away from him, under the pillow.

He put his reeling head in his hands.

In a little while, he lifted his face. It was rather white. Not everyday does a man run into old-fashioned magic! Slowly, he drew the pouch to him, opened it, and observed with only a dull thud of verified suspicion the presence therein of another golden coin. He took this out and put it in his pocket, drew the thongs together for a moment, and looked inside again. Sure enough. There lay the third coin. George left it there. This was the Magic Purse that never stayed empty!

Here? On 69th St.?

But what else? Suddenly he was in a frenzy to know what else. That carpet. Well, of course! He had no doubt it was the one that could fly! He got up and began to paw over his strange loot. He took up the soft black cloak, put it over his shoulders, and vanished.

That is, of course, George remained standing right where he was, but when he looked down along his body, he couldn't see it! This was the Cloak of Darkness! The very one!

He shuddered out of the thing. Cold chills were racing in his spine. He hung the Cloak in his closet, aimlessly, without thought.

Ah, the thing like a teapot! He recognized it now! He'd seen it drawn, in a hundred illustrations. It was the Lamp, the only Lamp that could qualify for this collection! Aladdin's! Must be! Must be! But George wasn't going to rub it. Not now. He didn't want to meet the Slave of the Lamp! Not this afternoon!

George inched it aside. He was excited and he was scared. He daren't stop and think. That ring? Ah, but all the old tales were full of rings, with one magic property or another. He slipped it on his finger, where it seemed to fit comfortably. Nothing happened.

His eye lit on the pink stone flask and he picked it up. He was convinced, now, that this, too, was magically endowed. Somehow, he had here the strangest of all collections.

(The little old proprietor must have known! How old? How old was that man? A thousand? Five thousand? He'd said he was tired! George trembled. Never mind. Don't think of it!)

Oh yes, everything here, logic insisted, must be magical.

The pink flask was heavy in his right hand. He rubbed his head. "I wish," he murmured, "a little bird would tell me what's in here."

In the Ring, forgotten on his left hand, and back of his head, the dull stone brightened. It lit, like an eye that saw, suddenly.

"Water from the Fountain of Youth." This sentence came into the air. It was like a line of music, high and full of flats. George turned his head in sharp alarm. Had he heard it? Or thought it? No sound now, certainly. Only beyond the window sill, the flutter of wings . . . Some sparrow . . .

Water from the Fountain of Youth! George loosened his fingers. He wanted none of that! Suddenly, he wanted none of any of it. He stripped off the Wishing Ring and threw it down. He understood that one might wish to get rid of these things.

It wasn't . . . well, it wasn't right! He wanted to crawl back within the safety of the possible, the steadiness and order of the natural world, the sane and simple world of splitting atoms, of nebulae, of radar and penicillin.

It is not so easy to believe in magic.

George paced up and down, conquering his fright, assimilating his wonder.

There remained the Rose and the Sword. He mistrusted the Rose. He had a shadowy recollection of the Rose and the tale of the Rose. He picked up the Sword and drew it from the scabbard.

It leaped in his hand. What a piece it was! George swung his wrist over and sliced off the top of the bedpost. The hard brass separated, clean and sharp. The upper six inches fell off on the floor.

It was impossible not to take another swipe at something. George brought his arm around. The Sword leaped and flashed down through the back, the seat, the springs of his tough, hard-cushioned leather chair. Clattering, it fell apart in two perfectly neat sections. Wood, fabric, metal, anything! Lord, lordy, what a sword! The Sword of Swiftness, or maybe Excalibur itself! He whirled the blade around his head. Whistling sweetly, it descended and cleaved the washbasin as if it were butter. A chunk of the hard porcelain came clean away and dropped with a bang on the floor. Lucky he'd missed the plumbing, for heaven's sakes! George realized he'd better restrain himself. This thing was dangerous! Much, much too dangerous to play with.

He flicked the Sword at the window sill, cutting a swift notch with the bare tip. He took a neat triangle delicately out of the mirror. He fought temptation. Sweating, he made himself take up the crimson scabbard and insert therein the wicked and utterly fascinating blade.

(Outside, in the hall, Mr. Josef stood quivering. His beard was agitated. His eye yearned for George's keyhole.)

But George sheathed the Sword and put it away from him. He puffed out his breath. What to do now? Anybody else might have run for a good stiff drink, but to George came the thought that he'd had no lunch! No wonder he felt queer. Besides, he'd think better on a full stomach.

Oh, he hadn't forgotten what he was really after. It would take more than a bag of magic to make George forget what he'd wrapped his whole life around. Now, somehow, he was going to be able to ask for Kathy! All he had to do was calm himself, and think it out!

He shoved all the stuff back into the carpet bag, or thought he did. He hadn't counted the nine objects. He was too excited to check. He forgot the Mirror, still under his pillow, and the Cloak, in his closet.

The rest he packed and then he shoved the bag under the bed with the instinct to hide it. He felt of his money. He was whistling a Georgish version of *Tonight We Love* as he slammed out of his door, and went downstairs with swift heels beating out the jig time of his tune.

No sooner did George depart, in the very backwash of the sound of his going, Mr. Josef oozed across the hall. His ears shadowed George out the door far below, checked the finality of its slam. Then, softly, he put his own key into George's lock. It yielded. Mr. Josef poured himself around the edge of the door and inside.

He stared at the empty room as if he would hypnotize this space to remain empty. The closet door was half open. Mr. Josef went slinking along the wall towards it, his right hand in his pocket. Finally, he took a leap and a whirl and brought himself up sharp with the closet door wide open and he confronting and threatening George's blue serge and other garments.

Mr. Josef watched the blue serge closely for a moment. Then he took his hand out of his pocket, arranged the muscles around his eyes, and began to rake the place methodically with a narrowed glance. When he spied the chair, lying so absurdly in two pieces, his eyes rounded. In fact, they popped.

But he moved coolly to examine it. He saw the washstand and blinked incredulously at the thick raw edge where George had sliced it, at the hunk of the outer curve that lay like a piece of melon on the floor. As he crept over and touched it, gingerly, there came from deep in the house the thump of feet on the stairs.

It was, in fact, Mrs. McGurk, coming up.

Mr. Josef rolled himself a glance of dark warning, via the mirror. He took long crouching steps across to the door. He skated down the hall.

When Mrs. McGurk, humming *My Wild Irish Rose* in a gay wobbly soprano, had gone into George's room, Mr. Josef slipped like a shadow in soft pell-mell down the stairs to the telephone.

"X?"

"Y."

"Z!" breathed Mr. Josef. "Listen, I have stumbled on something terrific! I must have help at once! Something bigger even than A. You know what I mean?"

"Frankly, no," said Y, wearily.

"A, I say!"

"A for apple?"

"No, no, no. Nuclear Fission," hissed Mr. Josef. "Send Gogo, At once! I tell you, they have a secret weapon!"

"Yeah?"

"I saw results with my own eyes, you fool! This is of desperate importance! *Mother must know!*"

"Hm? Oh, yeah," mumbled Y. "Mother Country, that is."

"Stupid!" Mr. Josef spat into the phone. "Send Gogo. At all costs, I will secure for us this secret!"

"O.K." said Y. "Keep your shirt on. O.K. O.K."

"I will expect him here in five minutes," said Mr. Josef silkily. He hung up, silkily.

Y looked across the plain office toward the other desk. "Josef. That clown. He's got a spy complex."

"He *is* a spy," said the other man, placidly. "We all are, I suppose." He wrote down a neat numeral.

"I'd better send somebody around, if only to keep an eye on him. It's embarrassing. Why doesn't the FBI pick him up?" frothed Y. "We've betrayed him, six times over."

The other man shook his head, went on totalling some figures, compiling information received.

Y got on the phone again, angrily.

Mrs. McGurk stopped humming for a moment, when she saw the broken chair, the washbasin, the bedpost. But the warm flood of happy activity on which (under the spell of the Rose) she was floating bore her right by such details. If George had done the damage, he, being George, would of course make it right. They would talk it over, once he was snug downstairs.

She found his empty suitcase under the bed, beside an old carpet bag, already packed. Mrs. McGurk opened George's dresser drawers and began to fill the suitcase. At last, staggering a little, she lugged both pieces to the top of the stairs and started down.

The second floor front was a room of pleasing proportions. Mrs. McGurk felt proud of it. Into the clean paper-lined drawers of her best dresser she put George's clothing, fussing daintily with the arrangement. She was an absolutely happy woman. She was creating, with love. She was Making a Home.

She closed the drawers. The top of the dresser was bare. Ah, but his own things . . . all the little touches . . . She dove into the carpet bag. This flask, now, was a pretty thing. But the metal lattice work seemed dull. Mrs. McGurk fetched a rag and some scouring paste. Snatches of old tunes came humming out of her as she worked. Her fingers felt tireless. She was so light of heart that she wondered, intermittently, if she were not coming down with something.

At last the flask shone as bright as she could make it and she set it on the dresser and cocked her head. It looked well, but certain artistic instincts were stirring in Mrs. McGurk today. It needed balancing. She dug into the carpet bag and came out with the lamp.

Naturally, at the first swipe of her cleaning rag across its surface, the Genie materialized. It seemed for a moment that steam was pouring out of the spout-like protuberance on the lamp, but the cloud fell away rapidly to reveal a rather pleasant looking man, whose skin was on the dark side, and who wore, of course, an Oriental costume of Aladdin's day. He was standing in the air about a foot above the floor.

Mrs. McGurk leapt. She screamed! The lamp rolled off her lap. Before the Genie had time to make his set speech about being the Slave of the Lamp and so forth (which perhaps he delayed in the process of translating it from the Arabic) Mrs. McGurk cried, "Eek! Go away!"

The Slave of the Lamp, of course, obeyed her.

Mrs. McGurk stood trembling in an empty room. Then she fled that place. Ricocheting from wall to wall, blindly, she raced for the sanctuary of her kitchen.

George munched his lunch, considering ways and means. The thing was, he concluded, to show the old man that Kathy would be safe and sound as George's wife, even without her inheritance. That George, all by himself, with his own resources, could take care of her.

At last, George rose and paid for his meal and sloped his course towards

Mrs. McGurk's stepping jauntily, trying to beat down a persistant little twinge of uneasiness. He told himself that with the Lamp, with the bottomless Purse, all *must* be magically smooth. There was a legless man, begging in the street. George put two fingers on the old gold coin in his pocket, tossed it into the cup and went swiftly on. It made him feel a trifle better to do this.

He had forgotten about his new quarters. He proceeded up the stairs, as usual, put his key in the lock of the door, and waltzed blithely in. Something hard jabbed him in the ribs. A thousand motion pictures, from childhood on, had conditioned him to know, at once, exactly what it was. His arms began to go up.

The voice behind him said, "My dear Mr. Hale, won't you . . . sit down?"

George saw the mocking eye of Mr. Josef, gleaming with pleasure. A second man came from behind the door, a large creature with a flat impassive face. George recognized the type. A henchman!

"Close the door," hissed Mr. Josef. The henchman kicked it shut.

George let the tail of his eye explore the room. The bedspread had been flung up over the pillow. He could see the curls of dust on the bare floor under the bed. The carpet bag was not where he had left it.

"Now, if you please," said Josef sternly, "the secret, and quickly!"

"What secret?"

"Come now, Mr. Hale. Surely we needn't pursue the childish course of torture?"

"I don't know what you're talking about," said George. "My money's in my pocket." He pointed with his elbow.

Mr. Josef put his head to one side. "Gogo, he is going to be stubborn."

"What did *that?*" said Gogo suddenly in a reasonable tone of curious inquiry.

"Did what? Oh . . ." George saw that he meant the cut up the washbasin. "Why . . . uh . . ." He swallowed hard. "Accident," he croaked. It did not seem possible to answer this question. George realized he was in quite a spot. The fourth floor was well removed from a policeman. The house had been so quiet, no help could be in it. And there were two of them.

"What kind of accident?" asked Gogo skeptically.

Josef shoved himself between them. The gun looked wicked and unsafe in his gloved hand. "Mr. Hale, naturally you are loyal to your government. But we will, you know, by one means or another, possess this new ray."

"Huh?" said George.

Mr. Josef chuckled. "So it *is* a ray!" he purred triumphantly.

"Ray!" said George in perfect astonishment.

"You would never," teased Mr. Josef, "make your fortune on the stage."

George simply goggled.

"Can we bribe you, Mr. Hale?" inquired Josef suddenly.

"Bribe me to do what?"

"Oh, give us specifications. We wish to know the source of this ray's power, how it is controlled, all about it. Come now."

"There is no such thing!"

Mr. Josef smiled.

"I don't know what you mean!" cried George.

Mr. Josef's eyebrows rose, pityingly.

George knew, now, he had to get away. There wasn't anything he could say. They had in their heads an explanation for the damage in his room that was just about as preposterous as the real one. They weren't going to listen to his old-fashioned stuff. And torture wasn't going to get anybody anywhere, especially George. He said, in an artful whimper, "Don't hurt me." He stumbled back a little farther. "I can't tell you anything."

"A hero," said Mr. Josef regretfully. "Ah, well, we have our little ways. No one regrets these necessities more than I do," cried Mr. Josef, frothing a bit at the mouth, "but we must know what you know, and know it now! And if we pay eventually with our lives for what we do . . . be it so!" The gun quivered with his fervor.

George made up his mind and leaped backward into the closet. He wound himself into the Cloak and leaped out again as the gun in Mr. Josef's startled hand went off. The bullet got George's blue serge in the heart, but George, in his gray, invisible and whole, slid along the wall away from danger.

"A secret passage!" screeched Mr. Josef, tearing his beard. He staggered towards the closet, eyes bulging. George lifted an invisible foot and kicked Gogo hard on the seat. The shock on the toe of his shoe felt wonderful. He only wished it had been Mr. Josef.

His visitors did not notice the door apparently open by itself, for Gogo was growling in his throat, looking on all sides for what had hit him. And

Mr. Josef, with his eyes so narrowed that he could hardly see at all, was frantically clawing the inside closet wall.

George, still in the Cloak, flitted down to the second floor. The carpet bag was there, all right. He had deduced as much. Furthermore, it had been opened. George spotted the Flask. Then he saw the Lamp, on the floor. When he also saw the cleaning rag, where Mrs. McGurk had let it fall, George deduced the rest.

He sighed. He supposed the poor lady had been frightened out of her wits. He hated to sneak out on her now, especially since she had been so kind. But he could not stay in the same house with Mr. Josef's obsession. And his new plans involved leaving here, anyhow.

So George scribbled a note. "Inclosed please find a full month's rent . . . also what I hope will pay for the damages . . . Many thanks for your kindness . . . All best wishes . . ."

Then he listened to the house. There was a muted, though furious, buzzing still going on upstairs. He guessed he was safe here for a few more minutes.

George slid out of the Cloak and packed it. He took up the Lamp. Gently and somewhat fearfully, he brought his palm to its side and rubbed.

When the Genie appeared, George, having been braced for this, found himself unalarmed. This Genie looked like a nice fellow. Nothing ferocious about him. Little bit up in the air, of course, George smiled cordially.

"I am the Slave of the Lamp," said the Genie slowly. "What are your commands?" He used the broad A, George noticed.

"Uh, how about getting me a reservation at the Waldorf for the night?" asked George a bit nervously. "Single room, with bath, of course. Name of Hale."

The Genie bowed his turbanned head. "I hear and obey," he murmured.

"Wait a minute," said George, more easily. "As long as you're here, listen. You could build me a house, I suppose? A real nice house, furnished, and with pretty grounds? Fix it, with servants and all, so I could invite some people, say, to lunch?"

The Genie bowed.

"Lessee," said George. "About how long would it take you? Could I count on that by the middle of November?" The Genie looked simply scornful. "By next week then?" The Genie's expression remained haughty. "Tomorrow!" cried George joyfully.

The Genie drew air whistling in through his teeth. "I hear and obey," he said, as before.

"Wait a minute. Don't be in a hurry," George wished this fellow would relax and chat. "Fix it up . . . say . . . uh . . . in one of the nice parts of Westchester County. I want it to look rich, you know. Maybe there should be a swimming pool. But everything the best quality. Nothing flashy. How will I know my address?" demanded George, who liked things clear.

"I will return, Master."

"Call me . . . uh . . . Mr. Hale," said George, shuddering. "And, by the way, the servants should be regular. Not . . . uh . . . slaves, y'know. O.K.? Then, tomorrow morning, I'll be seeing you."

The Genie appeared to shimmer in the air. George didn't say any more. The Genie quietly vanished. George took up the Lamp and packed it. He felt exhilarated, with something of the sensation of one who defies the laws of gravity on a tight rope and walks on the wings of mere balance. Things were moving fast, all right.

He got out of the house without any trouble. The spies must have still been rooting around in the upstairs closet, and poor Mrs. McGurk was nowhere to be seen. George hefted the carpet bag and set off down the street. Whatever way he was going, he knew he was headed for Kathy.

He went by way of the Waldorf. George's natural caution . . . just common sense, after all . . . told him he'd better check on this Genie's powers, before assuming too much. But everything was fine. The great hostelry swallowed him in without a ripple in its digestion. George looked around the room they gave him, which was extremely handsome, and he decided the Genie must be the McCoy.

The time had come, here, now, and on the same day. He could call up Kathy. His throat all but closed up when he heard her voice. He managed to say, "It's George."

"Oh, George!" Kathy wasn't anything but glad. "Where are you?"

"At the Waldorf."

"What?"

"Kathy, I . . . did you miss me?" He knew it was ridiculous, but he couldn't help it.

"Oh, George," she said, "I've missed you terribly!" Then they both knew that they meant the long vista of empty days ahead of them, not the mere afternoon behind.

"Kathy, darling," cried George, in spite of himself. "Will you marry me?"

"I certainly will!" said Kathy. "Oh, George, I'm so glad you called!"

"I love you, I love you, I love you," he said.

"I'm so glad . . . so glad you c-called. . . ."

George felt like crying, too.

"Are we going to run away?" she was asking. "Shall we go to Maine? Oh George, let's! Mr. Blair can't do anything that matters."

"Kathy, I'm going to ask him for you and he's going to be glad about the whole thing . . ."

"But . . ."

"Listen, I want you and Mr. Blair to come to lunch tomorrow at my house . . ."

"Your house? Do you mean in Maine?"

"No, no . . . my new house."

"But . . ."

"Tomorrow, Kathy. I'll call him up myself. You'll come to lunch and you'll see. Because I can take care of you, Kathy. And I can prove it. You're going to be surprised."

"George, are you coming over?"

He said, "Kathy, I'd better not, because I promised. Sweetheart, until I can *ask* him . . . and I can, tomorrow . . . Don't you see?"

"George, are we engaged to be married?"

"I meant to wait," he groaned.

"But you didn't and I said, 'Yes.' So we are!"

"We sure are!"

"Well, then," said Kathy, "I don't see what difference anything else makes. Honestly, I don't. But do it your own way. I'll *give* you 'till to-morrow."

"Kathy, don't be mad! Kathy, would you like an emerald?"

"I've got an emerald," she wailed.

George said, "I can't stand it! Will you meet me in the tearoom on Madison, right now?"

"No," said Kathy, female that she was. "You promised. Besides, I'm all dressed for the evening. Tomorrow, dear . . . dear George . . ."

"Until tomorrow," said George, "Oh, dearest Kathy . . ."

He loved her, he loved her, he loved her!

Most of Mrs. McGurk's roomers were in their rooms on Sunday morning.

Ordinarily, therefore, this was Her Day, to which Mrs. McGurk looked forward as quite the liveliest day in the week. But this Sunday, she was not in the mood.

She was, in fact, disconsolate.

The evening before, having finally conquered her fright, she had gone up to the second floor and found George's note. It seemed to her to be the sweetest letter she'd ever had, and it broke her heart. Mrs. McGurk did not see how she could Go On.

Mysteriously, he had left his clothing behind in the drawers. She puzzled all night long over this. She hoped it meant he would return, if only for a few minutes . . . Oh, she could not rent his room! No, indeed! It would remain as it was, yearning for him, and maybe . . . someday . . . She took to comforting herself with dreams.

Came the dawn, she realized that there was no sense maintaining two shrines to George's memory, on two different floors. So, rather early Sunday morning, Mrs. McGurk climbed up to his old room. She let herself in. Yes, she thought sadly, here was the real shrine, after all. For had it not been George, himself, who had broken that washbasin? Mrs. McGurk saw other traces of his being, and she flung herself on his bed for a good cry. Dimly, she perceived the luxury of this, how even her tears were a bath and a refreshing. Still, she wept with all her heart, until her nose, burrowing against the pillow, met something hard.

She explored with her hand and drew out the Mirror.

Mrs. McGurk sat up and wiped her eyes. This, whatever it was, had been His. Her hands caressed it. Oh, if he had only told her where he had gone! She could let him know. She could get in touch with him. But he had disappeared into the outer world and she had no clue. Oh, would she ever again see his dear face or his darling smile?

Mrs. McGurk was ready to fling herself howling into the pillow once more, when she noticed a moving image on the burnished metal surface she held in her hands. This was odd! Stony with shock, Mrs. McGurk watched the magic scene. She had been thinking of George, so, of course, it was George she saw.

George was walking on grass, looking up at the façade of a magnificent house. He moved beside beds of gorgeous flowers, chrysanthemums in white and bronze masses. He strolled on the edge of a great pool that lay like a jewel in the leaf strewn lawn.

But it was George! George, with his hands in the pockets of a new tweed suit . . . Mrs. McGurk clutched the Mirror. She was over 40. In her day, Bluebeard had murdered all his wives but one without benefit of Dick Tracy. Ah, Mrs. McGurk had known the old tales, the classics! Furthermore, just yesterday, she had seen a Genie! Now, two and two whirled together in her head. She didn't understand, but she recognized, and her heart began to beat in wild elation.

Even as she stared, George was strolling down a long curving drive. Where was he? Where? Ah, if he kept on as he was going, she might find out! Since it was the Magic Mirror and her thought controlled it, the image shifted, running ahead of George. Yes, there it was, on a stone pillar there at the end of the drive. She began to mutter, over and over again, "2244 Meadow Lane . . . 2244 Meadow Lane . . ." Now George strolled into the scene and stopped, with that look on his face, that dear baffled look he was wearing, to touch his own name on the handsome mailbox.

Mrs. McGurk sighed in a flood of peace and joy. George was at a place of his own and she had the address. She pressed the Mirror to her heart. It should never leave her!

Away down below, somebody was leaning on her doorbell. Mrs. McGurk, light as a girl, flew downward. She thrust the Mirror inside the bosom of her dress, where it was extremely uncomfortable, flung open her front door, and lavished one of her toothiest smiles on a perfect stranger who was teetering, in an obvious rage, on the stoop.

"George Hale live here?" yelped this man.

"He isn't here right now," trilled she.

"You can tell him from me, eh's a dirty crook!" cried the caller. "Look at that!" In his trembling palm lay two old gold coins, exactly alike. "You can tell him from me," stormed the rare coin dealer, for it was he, "that he needn't send any more beggars around to my competitors with any more of this junk! He can't kid around with the Law of Supply and Demand! Maybe he tricked me once! But you tell him, if any more of these show up, I'll get the Government after him for hoarding gold! And I mean it! Good day!"

"Good day," said Mrs. McGurk. She closed the door. Her surprise gave way to a belated but loyal anger. She was about to open and shout defiance at the enemy's back when she realized that she was not alone. Somebody was breathing on her neck.

It was Mr. Josef, who had crept close behind her in his furtive way. He fingered his beard. His eyes were sly.

"Morning," said his landlady shortly.

"Oh, Mrs. McGurk," said the spy, "could you supply me with Mr. Hale's forwarding address?" She looked at him sourly. "I am rather anxious to get in touch with him," drawled Mr. Josef. "Something to his advantage . . ."

The end of Mrs. McGurk's nose twitched thoughtfully. "You don't happen to have a street map, do you?"

"Many. Many." He rubbed his hands together. "Of what district?"

"Well . . . uh . . . I don't know. You see, I . . . happen to have the street number, but not the . . . uh . . . community," blushed Mrs. McGurk.

"Quite a pretty little problem!" cried Mr. Josef, in great delight. "Come, we shall solve it. This," said he happily, "is just the sort of thing I am rather good at. Ah, fear not! We shall ferret him out, you and I!"

George had, somehow, envisioned a larger or perhaps fresher copy of the old Hale house, when he had given his orders. He had certainly expected something simpler in line and decor than this! But the Genie, naturally, George supposed, would have more Oriental ideas of what luxury was. Anyhow, George conceded, it was sure some house! It would certainly impress Mr. Blair. Since that was the point, George felt he should be satisfied.

It was still quite early Sunday morning. He had come up by Genie. That is, as soon as he'd shaved and had breakfast, he'd rubbed the Lamp. The Genie had materialized somewhat tardily. He'd seemed rather out of breath, too, and there had been definite beads of sweat on his coffee-colored brow. George had asked him, in all sympathy, if anything was the matter, but the fellow had only rolled his eyes in a stiff unfriendly way. George didn't wish to offend by insisting. He'd let himself be whisked up here.

In fact, George didn't know exactly where he was.

He'd gone through the whole place, picked out a suit he liked, up in the master chamber, and put it on. He'd given orders to the butler about luncheon. Now he was restless. He was anxious to get Bennett Blair out here and impress him and get it over with.

He'd drive himself back into town, he decided, incidentally finding out where he was and how to get back again. He'd call for Kathy and her guardian in the . . . lessee . . . the Cadillac.

As he drove out the gate, a state cop stopped him. "You live here?"

"Guess so," said George cheerfully. "Hale's my name."

"O.K.," said the cop mildly. He spat at the pavement.

"Say," said George, "what's the best way to get to New York from here?"

The cop told him and George rolled smoothly off, waving his thanks. In a mile or two, he wondered whether he had a license plate. If so, was it on the records, somewhere in the vast recesses of the Bureau of Motor Vehicles? George shook off the thought. It made his head ache. He began to experiment with the throttle. He felt, all of a sudden, that he'd better hurry.

The cop, left behind, stayed where he was for a while, rubbing his chin on his palm, gazing thoughtfully at the house.

The funny thing was, he'd been by here, yesterday, and there'd been no house.

His head was aching a little, too.

Mr. Blair sat like an old toad, motionless, in the tonneau. The sweet air blew on him in vain. When they turned in at the gates, however, he roused. They bowled up to the front entrance. A man servant came to hand them from the car. The butler stood respectfully in the great doorway.

Within, sunshine sifted through splendid drapery to glow on the polished floor. This entrance hall, alone, would knock the old man's eye out, thought George to himself. The great stairs winding up, the rich dark paneling, the white cockatoo in his silver cage, adding that one exotic note . . .

Kathy said, "Oooooh!"

Mr. Blair said nothing. George led them into the drawing room. It was baronial. On the vast floor lay a rug of such exquisite color and pattern, such size, such texture, that Mr. Blair was forced to cover a covetous gasp with a fake clearing of his throat. George bit on his own smile. Blandly, he ordered cocktails in the library. Then, with the tail of his eye on the old man's face, George ushered them through the green and silver music room (with its silver piano) to the colossal coziness of the library. A soft fire bloomed in the grate. Cocktails came at once in a gold and crystal shaker.

The somber beauty of the room was absolutely still. Kathy, since her first gasp, had made no sound. Mr. Blair was stricken dumb. But he was not paralysed. He walked to and fro. He went over to the bookshelves and drew out a volume or two. Then he began to pat his hand along the shelf and mutter in his throat. He went close to a painting, peering at the corner of it. He turned on George.

"You inherited this place!"

"Well, in a way," said George. "Anyhow, it belongs to me, sir."

"Furnished, as it *is?*"

"Oh, yes. Sure."

"Did you know," demanded Mr. Blair, going so far as to point, vulgarly, with a forefinger, "that whole shelf, there, is ALL first editions?"

"Is that so?" said George pleasantly.

"That rug in the other room . . . Where did it come from?"

"It was just here," said George.

"You realize this is a Matisse?" snapped Mr. Blair, indicating the painting.

"I'll be darned," said George feebly. "I guess I hadn't noticed."

What there was of hair on Mr. Blair's head seemed to stir as if it would rise on end. He fell into a chair and seized his drink, thirstily.

Kathy went over to look out of the window. George stood behind her. "It's pretty . . . uh . . . big . . ." he murmured. Kathy nodded. "Too big," said George quietly.

Kathy leaned back just enough to seem to say, "Thou art my shield . . . in thee I trust . . ."

"Don't worry," he whispered. "We don't have to live here." She turned her cheek against his lips.

Meanwhile, Mr. Blair had picked up a small china bowl from the table. Now he looked at the under side of it and began to curse softly.

"Looking for an ashtray, sir?" George gave a host-like leap. "I guess that will do, won't it, sir?"

Mr. Blair cast George a wild glance and leaned back and blew his breath in puffs toward the ceiling.

Luncheon was served in the 40-foot dining room where they gathered like two kings and a queen in great carved chairs. At once, Mr. Blair began to examine the lace in the tablecloth.

"Kinda pretty, isn't it?" George beamed innocently. "My Aunt Liz used to crochet a lot."

"Your Aunt Liz," exploded Mr. Blair, "never crocheted this!"

"Well, no, of course she didn't."

"Came with the place, eh?"

"Oh, yes . . ."

"Don't know much about lace, do you?".

"Well—uh—no."

"No," said Mr. Blair.

Kathy was looking blankly at the china, the crystal. Her puzzled eyes kept coming back to George's face, to say "It's all right, of course. Because it's you."

George squirmed a little. He felt, himself, that the food was, well, astonishing. He had tried to tell the butler what he would like served for this meal, but he must have been vague, or left a lot of leeway somehow, because he didn't recognize one single dish. Although it tasted fine. Mr. Blair seemed to think so.

Also, the butler kept filling wine glasses with different kinds of wine and each time, Mr. Blair would sip and then close his eyes as one in pain. George didn't drink much wine. It all tasted alike to him, anyhow, he explained cheerfully. Kathy sat, hardly eating anything but a little of the cucumber mousse, and George couldn't really eat, either.

Just so Mr. Blair had a good lunch. Because, after lunch would be the time to ask him.

In the drawing room, George's man servant brought cigars and coffee.

George cleared his throat. "Mr. Blair, I wanted you to come today because . . ."

"Yes," Mr. Blair's attention came away from the furnishings with a snap.

"Because I want to marry Kathy," said George. "I wanted to show you that I can take care of her. So now I . . . uh . . . ask your permission to . . . uh. . . ." George forgot the sentences he had made up ahead of time. "I love her so darned much!" he cried, "And she . . ."

Kathy's hand was in his. It had flown there. "Me, too," said Kathy. Their hands, holding each other tight, lifted between them, entreating him.

Suddenly Mr. Blair looked very old and very patient. He said gently, "I take it all this magnificence is supposed to impress me."

"It does," said George, sharply, for him.

"Oh, it does. It does, George," conceded Mr. Blair. He leaned back and said, coldly, "I would like very much to meet what friend of yours so kindly loaned you this place for the day."

George said, "Nobody loaned it to me, sir. It's mine."

"You will produce certain proofs?"

"Proofs?"

"A deed to the property, perhaps. The inevitable records of ownership. My dear chap, this is rather astonishing, you know. For Kathleen's sake, I must see the proof and you cannot afford to be offended that I ask for them."

"Well, of course not," stammered George. "Gosh, I . . ."

"However," said Mr. Blair, "granting the existence of such proof, if you then think you have proved your capacities in such a way as to satisfy me, I am sorry you are so deceived. What you have done," said Mr. Blair, opening his eyes wide with an effect of pouncing, "is exactly the opposite! You've proved yourself a perfect ignoramus!"

"Huh?"

"You have no more idea what is in this house than a Hottentot!" rasped Mr. Blair. "You offer me a bowl of priceless porcelain for an ashtray! You never heard of Matisse! Don't tell me! How you imagine that I will permit . . ."

"Just a minute," said Kathy, very quietly. "George and I are engaged to be married."

"I'm sorry to hear that, Kathleen," said her guardian levelly and coldly.

"Wait," cried George. "Maybe I don't know very much, but I can learn, and anyhow, it doesn't matter!"

"It matters," snarled Mr. Blair. "Kathleen's fortune will never pass into the hands of . . ."

"I don't *need* Kathy's fortune!"

"I don't *care!*" said Kathy.

"Sit down, Kathleen," barked Mr. Blair. "There is a good deal that must be explained. I want to know, and so should you, my dear, exactly how a saxophone player without a penny to his name, yesterday, claims to be in possession of a place like this, today. If, as I all along suspected, he's only borrowed it, then he is a cheat. And you'd better know it. So sit down."

With an expression of disdain on her face, an expression that signified her perfect faith in George, Kathy sat down.

"Now," snapped Mr. Blair. "Do one of two things, George, if you please. Produce your papers and explain how you got them. Or name the real owner." Suddenly Mr. Blair's toe rubbed across the soft silk of the rug, as if it had been wanting to do so for minutes. "In a way," he said, with genial brutality, "I hope you can prove yourself the owner, because, if you do, George, I intend personally to swindle you out of several things you don't *yet* know you've got here."

George looked about him, wildly. It was if his fairy godmother had turned and bit him.

But then the butler, at George's elbow, said, "I beg pardon, sir."

"Hm?"

"People are approaching the house, sir. In fact, there are persons at the door. I don't quite know what you wish in the matter . . ."

They all became aware of crowd noises. George strode to the window. Men were milling around, out there.

"Excuse me," said George. He walked down the long drawing room to the hall and he opened the front door. The first face he saw was that of the cop he had spoken to, that morning. "Say, what is all this?" asked George, in his friendly fashion.

Everybody began to talk at once. The group converged on the door. It advanced and invaded. George was soon surrounded. Competing voices rose louder and louder.

"Who inspected your wiring here?" "Permit?" "Fire law says . . ." "Why didn't the Building Department get an application?" "I'm from the union . . ." "Who put in the plumbing here?" "Zone . . ." "You can't put up a pre-fab unless . . ." "My client . . ." "Second mortgage . . ." "Title." "Tax . . ."

Somebody was snapping the lights off and on. It seemed that others were darting off in all directions, into the depths of the house. "Hey!" said George.

"Electricians local won't . . ." "Painters and Paperhangers got a beef if you . . ." "Where's your meter?"

Some were returning and screaming, now.

"My God, he's into the gas lines!" "Who inspected . . ." "What about the sewers? He can't . . ." "Wait 'till the water company . . !" "Slap a summons on him . . ." "Wrong type construction . . ." "Have to tear it out . . ." "Permit . . ."

George, in the center of the mass, struggled.

A little dark man screeched, "Telephone!" He fought his way towards the instrument. "Can't be a telephone," he whimpered. Now the state cop was braying down the noise. He achieved an uncertain quiet. He said, in it, "O.K. Mr. Hale. Your turn." The whole house vibrated.

The little man could be heard moaning low into the phone. "You're wrong. Operator! There *is* no such number!"

George clutched his hair. "Listen, I . . . I don't know what to say." A wordless growl rose from the pack. "I didn't mean to break the regulations."

The state cop said, sourly, "I figgered, when I saw this place, which wasn't here, yesterday . . . I figgered you mighta forgot a few dee-tails."

"This ain't no pre-fab!" said one. "Moved it in?" "Say, listen, you can't move a house . . ." "Permit?" "Wait till the office opens . . ." "Jeese," said one, furiously, "who does this guy think he is!" "Yeah," they cried, "who do you think y'are?"

Kathy, cowering in the sofa, murmured, "Oh, please, Mr. Blair!" Her guardian, who had sat stonily through the beginning of it, now rose.

"Not here YESTERDAY!" said the gas man, suddenly, with distended eyeballs. They grew quiet. All grew quiet. Mr. Blair stood still.

"Not here!" screamed the white cockatoo, from his silver cage. "Not here!" Something like a shudder passed through the crowd. They moved closer to each other. They seemed to press in on George, now, silently. Their breathing alone was very loud.

"Yesterday! Yesterday!" squawked the pink-eyed bird.

George threw out his arms, thrusting them back. "Now, listen, whatever I have to do to make this right, I'll do. So go away. Write me letters, will you?"

"Will you?" said the cockatoo.

Sound began to swell again from their throats. It was working up.

"My name is Blair," said that gentleman. "Bennett Blair." The perfume of his wealth, the strong odor of much money, was wafted on the heated air. "I think my young friend," said Mr. Blair with the faintest accent on the significant noun, "is right. I fear his impetuous haste has cut a lot of red tape. But," his fish mouth closed, his cold eye held them. "Red tape doesn't bleed, you know." They gave him their murmuring chuckle, on cue. They shifted their feet in soft confusion on the carpet. "So suppose we go about this in some orderly fashion. Tomorrow is a business day . . ."

"Yeah, that's right . . ." "Good enough for me, Mr. Blair." "Sure, let the office handle it." "I wouldna come out here, only Joe called me." "Proper channels . . ." "Sure . . ."

The little man at the phone had dropped his head on his arm.

"Ah . . . no . . ." he kept moaning. He was cursed with imagination. He contemplated the System, the ramifications, the delicate, vast, and incredibly dainty complexity . . . He stared starkly into the floor with white eyes.

"I'm afraid," said Mr. Blair, with distaste, "this man is unwell . . ."

"Come on, Riley." Somebody scooped up the telephone man. "Give him air." "Come on, you guys. Get him outa here."

Thus, Mr. Blair by a potent and rather frightening magic of his own, got them all out of there. George wiped his face. The jittery butler closed the door. Then, Mr. Blair allowed himself to tremble.

"George," he said, with a fearful quaver. "Was this house here, yesterday?"

"No," said George, and sent Mr. Blair tottering.

"For the love of heaven, boy!"

"I was *going* to explain," said George. "I will. Gee! Now I understand! Poor fellow! No wonder he looked pale! Things must have gotten a little complicated since his day." He pulled himself together and smiled at Kathy. "Wait," he said, " 'till I get my carpet bag. Let's go into the library, shall we?"

So George explained.

Now, Mr. Blair lay back on the leather sofa. His hooded eyes were brooding. Kathy, beside him, rested her cheek on her hand. George was sitting on the floor, the other side of the low table on which he'd spread his bagful of uncanny property. The big room was filled with somber light. Outside, it had come on to rain. Leaves rattled in the wet wind. But the high thick book-lined walls around them were ramparts of silence.

Kathy said, dreamily, "I suppose when he built a palace, in the old days, it would stand all by itself."

"Sure," said George. "No . . . uh . . . connections," He looked sadly at his collection. "I guess this stuff is kinda out of date. I wish I had the Mirror, though. It was wonderful."

Kathy smiled. "Was it something like television?"

George smiled back at her. "But without any sound. Doesn't it seem as if a lot of things people have wished for, they've got?"

"I guess you tend to get what you wish for," dreamed Kathy, "more or less like magic."

"Too bad . . ."

"Yes, too bad," she mused. "People wished for ways to kill and yet be far away . . . Can you un-wish? What if there gets to be too much of some kinds of magic?''

"Well," said George stoutly, "look . . . magic *can* go out of date and get outgrown. Men go past it. People change the way they think and the day comes . . . we just have no use for some kinds.''

Kathy smiled very sweetly upon him.

"Of course," said George, louder, "You'd be able to live pretty comfortably with these things to fall back on.''

Mr. Blair raised his head.

"Anyhow, sir," said George to him directly, "now you see why, if there's anything in this house you want, you're welcome to it.''

The old man looked around the room. "No," he said. "Not now. I don't want *these* first editions, George. Or that painting. God knows what it is. It isn't human! So what does it mean?'' He fidgeted. "The aroma's gone. The patina . . . Do you know what I mean?''

"It's kind of phoney," said George sadly. "Then, I can't bribe you, hm?''

Mr. Blair said nothing for a long moment. His crabbed hands massaged his knees. "Maybe you *can* bribe me," he said at last. "Maybe you can.''

George was very quick. "Any of this stuff?'' He gestured towards the table. "Because I'd rather have Kathy.''

Kathy said quickly, "I'd rather, too.''

"Money and power," mused the old man, staring at the table, "I have. I've had a long time. Furthermore, I worked for it. I carved it out. No, there's only one of your little gadgets, George that . . . tempts me, somewhat.''

Slowly, George reached out. "You're welcome to this Flask.''

Mr. Blair grunted his admiration. "Yes," he said, "I . . . thank you, my boy. I somehow feel you are going to be . . . right for Kathleen. You may take it that I withdraw any objections.''

George looked at Kathy joyfully and she smiled like a rosy angel.

Mr. Blair's gnarled hand closed softly on the pink stone Flask. He rested it on his knee. His head dropped forward. Chin on breast, the old man sat dreaming.

George snatched at the Ring. "Would you wear this . . . temporarily?''

Kathy said, "If you want me to.''

He put it on the proper finger. He drew her up out of the seat. They skipped off together, out of the amber-colored room entirely. Her shoulder tucked under his, they slipped around the dreaming old man. They closed the door between. In the green and silver music room, they kissed, and then, George, holding her, could not speak, so filled was he with happiness.

In a little while, they sat down on a window bench in a nook behind the silver piano. George just could not say a word. He just kept looking at her . . . dear, darling, delicious Kathy!

Kathy smiled and then her eyes grew moist and then she smiled again. She looked down at the Ring. She twisted it. She put her head on George's shoulder and out of George came a soft sound like a purr, wordless, and not even chopped into thoughts at all.

Kathy sat up a little straighter and blinked her eyes. "I . . . I wish it would stop raining," she said, just aimlessly, groping for the earth.

It stopped raining.

"George," she said, "this Ring winked at me!"

"Hmmmmmmmmmmmmmm?"

"It seemed to. Oh, I suppose it caught the sun." The sun was shining. Kathy turned her wondering head to look out and George kissed her. She pushed him away a little, laughing. "I feel so funny," she admitted. "Do you? As if it all happened so suddenly. Oh, dear, I wish I hadn't eaten those cucumbers."

The prompt distress on George's face was comical. "Oh, never mind, silly," laughed Kathy. "It isn't import . . ." Lips parted, she looked down with quick suspicion at her left hand. For the taste of cucumbers had vanished. She said, in a funny little voice, "George . . ."

"Hmmmmmmmmmmmmmm?" He was still in a state.

"Oh . . ." she burst out, "I wish you'd *say* something!"

"I love you," said George immediately. "I love you so much I can hardly talk. Wheeee! Kathy, darling, I thought I'd lost my voice."

But Kathy was staring at the Ring. "It winked again. George, do you suppose. . . ?" She looked around the room. "George, wouldn't you like to be up in Maine, right now?"

"I don't care where we are," he babbled.

Kathy said, rather slowly, quite deliberately, "I wish we were in Deeport, Maine."

Nothing happened.

The stone in the Ring remained dull and lifeless. It felt heavy on her finger.

"Oh," said George, catching on, "you thought it was a Wishing Ring! Say, maybe it is!"

"Maybe," said Kathy thoughtfully. "One person gets just three wishes. Isn't that so?"

"That's the rules and regulations, the way I heard it," babbled George. "The heck with them." He kissed her.

But Kathy's fingers moved. The forefinger . . . rain! The middle finger . . . cucumbers! The ring finger . . . yes, indeed! George *had* said something!

"It's a bad habit," said Kathy, when she could, "to go around saying 'I wish' all the time."

There was a middle door of this room and now the knob turned, the door cracked. "Beg pardon, sir. A Mrs. McGurk is here to see you. Are you engaged, sir?"

"Darned tooting, I am!" replied George happily. "Mrs. McGurk here! For heaven's sakes! Come on, Kathy. I want you to meet her. Let's tell her! Gee, I've got to tell somebody!"

Mrs. McGurk was waiting in the drawing room. She was dressed as for church. Her hat was last Easter's madness, and under it her hair was crimped violently. Her face was stiff with peach-colored kalsomine, and she'd left a little lipstick on her long teeth.

It wasn't in George to rebuke the surge of affectionate pleasure that brought her two hands reaching out to him. The hat and the kalsomine did not obscure, from him, the real moisture in her eye. "It's nice to see you," said he cordially, and bent to pick up her handbag off the floor. It was one of those soft suitcases. There was something hard and heavy in it. "Did you get my note?"

"Oh, I did! I did!" She gave him a Look.

But George didn't notice. "Kathy."

Mrs. McGurk became aware of Kathy, graceful in a soft blue wool frock, moving up within George's arm, with her red gold mane so near his shoulder. "Mrs. McGurk, this is Kathy Douglas. Kathy . . . Mrs. McGurk . . ."

The landlady's head, which had frozen in mid-nod, went on with the gesture it had begun. Then she swerved and tapped George on his forearm. "But oh . . . please, George, 'Constance?' My name, you know?"

"Uh . . . very pretty name," said George feebly. He took a step back.

He had a horrid suspicion.

"Have you come far, Mrs. McGurk?" said Kathy politely.

"Just from the city," said Mrs. McGurk with a lofty sniff. "A friend with a car drove me."

"But how did you. . . ?"

Mrs. McGurk cut George's question off. It could only lead to her surrender of the Mirror. So she ducked it. "Oh, George," she cried. "I thought you should know! A man called. He made the nastiest threats. Something about gold . . ."

"Gold?"

"Coins, you know. He had two of them. He seemed to think you had deceived him."

"Oh, gosh!" said George. In his mind he ticked off the bottomless Purse. Obsolete! "Well, it was kind of you to bother." George whipped back to his main concern. "Mrs. McGurk, what do you think? I'm going to be married. Kathy's promised!"

"I'm so glad," said Mrs. McGurk, with fingers turning white on the handbag. "It isn't going to make any difference," she blurted.

"What?" said Kathy.

"I want you to go on thinking of my house as home," wailed Constance. "And if ever . . ." she now shot a hard suspicious look at Kathy, "you are troubled and need a friend . . ."

"I beg your pardon," said Kathy. "George, dear, is this a relative of yours?"

"No, no. Mrs. McGurk runs a rooming house where I . . . she was very kind," said George desperately. He backed away.

"I understand!" cried Constance, dramatically. "Now, you have all this! The world is at your feet! Only remember, my dear, glitter isn't everything. Kind hearts do count . . ."

"Glitter?" said Kathy, a bit tensely.

"And a pretty face and a hank of red hair," went on the landlady, quite carried away, "may not take the place of . . ."

"What place?" asked Kathy ominously.

"Of one who . . . boo hoo hoo . . . oh . . . hoo . . ."

"George," said Kathy, smouldering, "if you'll excuse me, please . . ."

"Don't, Kathy. Mrs. McGurk, now, you mustn't cry."

Mrs. McGurk's hat was askew. So was her nose, even more than normally. "George, she isn't right for you! Forgive me! But I think of you and you only. See how cold she is! George, think!Before it is too late!"

In Kathy a dam busted. "I'm sorry, but she can't come in here and say things like that!"

"She doesn't know what she's saying," said George in anguish. "Just . . . just bear with it . . ."

"Wouldn't it be simplest if she . . . left?" asked Kathy brightly.

"You see!" The landlady clung to George's hand. "She'd turn me out of your life! Your true friend, George . . . the truest friend . . ."

"Now, wait a minute." George held out his other hand to Kathy. "She's not to blame, Kathy. She can't help it. I realize what must have happ . . . I can explain."

But Kathy's mane rippled and flared with the swing of her body. "Maybe you'd better take this back." She pulled off the Ring and smacked it into his palm, "until you do!"

"KATHY!"

"Oh, evil temper!" cried Mrs. McGurk.

"Mr. Blair," called Kathy, as she ran. "I want to go home. Mr. Blair, please . . ."

George ripped his hand from Mrs. McGurk's moist grasp and rounded on her. "Now see here! Rose or no Rose, you're going to have to understand, Mrs. McGurk. As far as I'm concerned you were kind . . . sometimes . . . and that's all! You can't insult my girl and I won't . . . WHAT'S THAT!"

At the window there was a profile, pressed against the glass. Its eyes squinted to peer through its own shadow. Like a strange outlandish piece of vegetation, the hair of its beard hung there.

It was Mr. Josef's face of course.

George said, "How. . . ? He. . . ? Who. . . ?" He shoved the Ring on his finger. His hands curled into fists.

"Mr. Josef brought me," wailed Mrs. McGurk. "Oh George, don't be mad at me! I can't bear it!" She burst into tears.

"Excuse me," said George. He dashed off towards the music room, the way Kathy had gone.

The old man sat dreaming. Memory, flowing like water, gently exploring the vast fields of past time. Ah, the long, long days of his life! How various they had been. How . . . after all and on the whole . . . he had enjoyed them! How wise he felt! How vividly he could now see the interplay of influences, how he had been deflected, in what ways, and why.

He should be tired. Well, he was tired, the old man thought, often and often. But the fatigue was in his body, his bones, his sinew. Not in the mind. A mind, fortified with so much experience, could play the game of life on a different level. All was illuminated, now. He saw further ahead, further behind. If it were not for the weariness of his flesh . . . what fun! What fun!

Young in spirit, he thought complacently, I have kept, for I have only refined my taste, not lost my appetite.

He roused from his reverie to realize he was alone. They'd gone, the young pair. Gone to embrace, to murmur plans. He knew. He knew. It was a shame and a pity and a waste . . . yes, waste! . . . that all he knew, all he remembered, all he had learned with such difficulty, so many pains . . . all this was tied to a declining body, chained to the span of a creature who must, at the appointed hour, long since struck for him, begin to die.

Mr. Blair took the stopper out of the Flask. He'd seen old flasks of this type. He knew the trick. It was one of the little barnacles of knowledge that had accumulated to him. He sniffed at the neck of the Flask and detected no smell. He looked about him for a vessel. There was his coffee cup. He emptied the dregs into a saucer. He drew out his handkerchief and wiped the cup quite dry.

There were no printed instruction on any label. He shook the Flask. Then he tipped it up and poured a little liquid out into the cup. A fleeting fear of poison or . . . worse . . . flat disappointment (for perhaps it was plain water) crossed his mind. But he faced the chances. Lips touched the rim. He drank.

It was perfectly tasteless.

He put down the empty cup and sat quietly where he was. He closed his eyes. A tree, in early spring, before it pushes forth its buds, must feel a deep interior thrill . . .

Mr. Blair had a moment to think this gentle thought and then he experienced a kind of personal earthquake, a sensation so entangled with that of speed that he was out in the clear at the other time-side of the whole shaking experience before he could tell himself *what* it felt like!

He opened his eyes and the room leapt into clarity. He could see, but how marvelously well! He'd forgotten how it was to see with a depth of focus, without glasses, with young eyes!

He bounded off the sofa. Oh, the spring in his legs! The freedom to move quickly! The strong responding pump of the willing heart!

But his clothes were all askew. His trousers were far, far too loose at the waist. His coat was tight on the edge of his shoulders. Its tail was out like a bustle in the back. Mr. Blair unbuttoned his vest. He had to. He flexed his biceps. He held out his hands before him and saw that they were young.

He felt of his face, patting it with loving frantic fingers. He felt of his hair. Ah, the warm plenty of it! The soft thatch, the crisp wave at the temples! (It was blond and parted in the middle.)

George's butler crossed, with grave mien, the kitchen of George's house and said to the cook, who was his wife, "Marie, we've decided right. We give notice."

She nodded. "I don't like it, Edgar. It's odd. Those men running in . . ."

He leaned closer. "It is *very* odd. For instance, the master has a woman by each hand, in the drawing room."

"Tch. . . !"

"There is, also, a man with a beard going around the house, looking in at the windows."

"My!"

"Also . . . don't be alarmed, Marie . . . there is another man, a big fellow, watching this back door."

"Ooh . . ." said Marie. "That is odd, isn't it?"

"And," said the butler, "a strange young gentleman I never saw before is standing on his hands in the library."

"Standing on his hands!"

"As I breathe! Feet in the air!"

"Odd," she said. "No place for us, Edgar."

"Oh, no," he said. "Certainly not!"

Kathy ran through the music room. She fell against the door to the library. "Mr. Blair!"

Mr. Blair, enjoying the sweet coursing of his blood, nevertheless realized that he must stop this mere jumping about. There were bound to be certain problems. He must face them. He must contrive to avoid the hurrah and the vulgarity of public knowledge, and blend this miraculous renaissance into a prosey world without an uproar. He would, somehow, arrange for old Bennett Blair to fade away. Yes, and he would substitute himself as his own . . . what? Grandnephew! Bennett Blair 2nd! He fancied that! He would, for instance, change his signature.

Wait. . . ! Mr. Blair took out his pen, snatched a book, and scribbled his name on the margin. Good heavens! Not so! On the contrary, he must learn to forge his own signature and force this smooth young script into the former crabbed scrawl of his ripened personality.

He laughed out loud. It didn't worry him.

Somehow, Mr. Blair's wise old mind (and it saw and knew and didn't care) was being subtly altered by the vigor of his new young body. That Cloak, for instance. He'd been indifferent to it. Might be a lot of sport, though, it now occurred to him. He chuckled. He picked up the little box. George had warned them not to touch it, or he would have put the Rose in his lapel out of sheer exuberance.

Good fellow, George! They could be friends, pals, sidekicks, buddies . . . Amused at the layers of slang that lay like strata in his memory, Mr. Blair, just exercising another of his five rejuvenated senses, lifted the box and smelled the Rose.

He drew in the perfume. Ah. . . !

He heard his name. Kathy turned the knob. She opened the door.

Dead silent astonishment held them both.

Kathy caught on quickly. She got her voice back. "M-Mr. Blair?"

"Call me Bennett!" he said in a rich tenor. "Oh please, Kathleen. Oh, how lovely you are! I have never seen you before. Kathleen, do you know me? I am young again, and oh, my dear . . . I am young again for you! Kathleen, beautiful darling, this miracle is ours!"

"OH!" she screamed. "OH NO!" She slammed the door between them. George tore in from the drawing room.

"What's the matter?"

"He's yuh-yuh-young! He's talking about l-love!"

"That damned Rose!" said George at once. "Mrs. McGurk, too. It *is* the Rose of Love. It makes you fall . . ."

"Oh!" She was enlightened. "Oh, George, forgive me, I didn't understand. But oh, take me away from here." She was unnerved and trembling with shock.

"Wait, there's a spy . . . that crazy Josef . . ."

She started blindly toward the drawing room. "Not in there," warned George. He whisked her through the middle door to an elbow of the great hall. They were together, and this was good. This was, however, about the only factor that could be called good or even fair among all the existing circumstances, as George soon discovered.

He peered toward the front door. The big Cadillac was still standing in the drive. They might pass swiftly across the arch, ignore Mrs. McGurk . . . "Wait a minute," said George. "Nope. He's right out there. Joseph. He's dangerous, believe me. We can't go that way, not that way."

They stood, arm and arm, in a quandary.

Mr. Blair moved swiftly through the empty music room. At the drawing room door he came face to face with Mrs. McGurk.

"Where is she?" "Where is he?" they cried.

"Whoops!" said George, in the hall. He drew Kathy into the morning room on the opposite side of the house.

Mr. Blair strode over the great silky rug, his young feet spurning its fabulous beauty. He burst into the hall, flung open the front door. He cried into Josef's startled beard, "Hey, have you see a beautiful red-haired girl?"

Mr. Josef, confounded, tried to look as if he were waiting for a street-car. But Mr. Blair, seeing the Cadillac still there, slammed the door and stood with his back to it. If only he could find her! He'd done wrong. He'd frightened her. Great tides of potential gentleness, deep wells of soothing charms surged restless in his breast. If only he could find her!

George and Kathy slipped from the morning room to the dining room, through the butler's pantry to the kitchen to the back door. The servants might have been so many cupboards. George saw no way to explain this spectacle of the master and his lovely luncheon guest simply flying by, hand in hand.

On the brink of an exit, George reversed them again. "Gogo," he said. "We better not go this way."

"Why don't we use the magic? George, why can't we get the Genie?"

"Say!" said George. He pulled Kathy, another way, into the hall again, the hall that lay like the hole in a doughnut, at the center of everything.

Mrs. McGurk was in the library!

"Wait," said George. "Wait, Kathy." He was most reluctant to face the poor woman. He hesitated. He drew Kathy behind the dining room door to think.

This was an error.

Mr. Blair stood over the second maid. "Went out the back door, did they?"

"No, sir."

"Didn't?" Following a reflex, he chucked her under the chin. "Where then?"

"That way."

Mr. Blair heaved at his sagging trousers and pursued.

The butler peered palely from the pantry.

Mr. Blair rushed into the hall, dug his heel into the carpet to brake himself, heard breathing in the library, and veered that way.

Someone was breathing. It was Mrs. McGurk. "Seen them?" She shook her head. "They're in the house. They haven't left it." Her woebegone face brightened a little. "How about giving me a hand?" suggested Mr. Blair. "Otherwise we can run circles in this squirrel cage for days."

"I want to talk to George," she quavered.

"Good. Fine." Mr. Blair's legs had temporarily given over to the jurisdiction of his wise old brain. Now he remembered to pick up the Flask and shove it into his pocket. He said, "You come and stand where you can watch the front door and the stairs while I go around again."

Mrs. McGurk nodded. But she was full of suspicion. That was George's flask! She knew it. Had she not polished it with her own two hands? Who was this odd-looking young man? And what right had he to put George's property into his pocket?

When he had gone ahead, through the music room, then quietly, before she followed, Mrs. McGurk took up the Lamp. She knew its value. George should not lose it! Not while his Constance lived! Yes, it was HIS, and she would defend it! One day he would thank her devotion for this!

When George and Kathy eased into the library, it was too late. The Lamp had gone! George sucked a tooth. His collection was sure getting scattered and it wouldn't do. He had a dreadful sinking feeling, a foreboding. This was just going to lead to all kinds of trouble. He bundled into the carpet bag all of the magic objects that remained.

Kathy whimpered. George said, "Honey, this is just awful! But I can't take you outside with those thugs hanging around.'' They had reached the hall's elbow again.

"Can't we try upstairs?"

George said, "Upstairs is a dead end, Kathy. You put on the Cloak. Slip out . . .''

"I want to stay with you."

"But—uh—they might shoot!"

"Then *you* must wear the Cloak!"

"No, because if they should grab YOU, I'd . . . I'd . . . I'd . . .''

Kathy pulled herself together. "Why don't I just face Mr. Blair.'' Her pretty mouth grew firm. "I've been silly . . . yes, I've been silly.''

"Honey . . .'' George ached to protect her. "There must be a way out of this, if I had the sense . . . I wish,'' he murmured unhappily, "a little bird would tell me how I could get out of here.''

"On the Flying Carpet,'' said the white cockatoo, tartly.

"Eh? What's that?'' said George.

He was wearing the Ring. He had slipped it on his finger, long ago. At his words, of course, the stone in the Ring had become quite clear and shining. George wasn't noticing, however. He was gazing, astonished, at the cockatoo, and the cockatoo stared back, insolently, as if to say, "You dope! You shoulda thought of that!''

"George!'' Kathy was jolted out of her nervous reaction. "The Ring! Oh, give me that Ring!''

"Wha. . . ?''

"Quick! I can't expl . . . Oh, quick, before you say another word!''

George gave it to her. "What's the matter?'' he said. "By golly, it's the perfect solution! Come on. Upstairs.''

Mr. Blair heard Mrs. McGurk give tongue, but too late. George and Kathy scrambled out a window to a flat roof. He spread out the Carpet and they sat down on it.

"Take us to Maine, if you please,'' said George firmly. "Deeport, Maine.'' And then they rose. They fell giggling into each other's arms. It was so wonderfully absurd and delightful. Here they were, together. The mad afternoon was over. They floated, free. The sun was sinking behind a band of red . . .

"Well, they're gone,'' said Mr. Blair.

"Yes,'' sighed Mrs. McGurk. Her face was calm.

Mr. Blair thought he knew whither the fugitives were flying. He saw no reason to tell this old harridan what he had guessed.

Mrs. McGurk, for her part, knew exactly what she was going to do and how she was going to find them. But she didn't intend to let this wild young man in on her secret.

"I shall go back to town," said he. "I shall just borrow George's car. May I give you a lift?"

"Oh no, thank you," she said. "I have a car."

They parted. It didn't occur to either to wonder why the other was so calm.

The rose and the gold withdrew, leaving a thin gray sky. They huddled together in the very center of the Carpet, because it was quite small, for two, and steep and empty air was most vividly near, on all sides. Their vehicle was rolling along through chilly space with an undulating flutter that had been a little trying, at first.

Also, there was nothing between them and the stellar distances to keep off draughts. Ah, it was bitter up here! Bitter! Finally, George had hauled the Cloak out of the bag and wrapped it around them both. This helped a great deal, although it was rather frightening and bleak to be invisible. They had to hang on to each other very close to be sure each was not utterly alone, in the middle of the air.

Irritably, George said he wished he knew who the dickens had swiped that Lamp.

Kathy said, "Don't wish, George."

He stretched a cramped leg very cautiously lest a shoe fall into New England. "Say, Kathy, why did you make me take off the Ring? What happened?"

She explained. George found her freezing hand and felt of the Ring with a numb thumb. "Kathy, if it is a Wishing Ring, I can't have used all mine up." He straightened and the Cloak fell back. "Let me get you a sandwich!"

"A sandwich! Of all things, George!"

"But you're hungry! You're starving!"

"I'm not starving," said Kathy. "I just feel as if I were starving. No!" She sat on the hand that wore the Ring. "You know," she went on, thoughtfully, pulling a corner of the Cloak up and vanishing, "you and Mr. Blair make the same mistake. You both want to take care of me. You forget I'm alive . . . and thinking and doing! I have some sense!'' She squirmed indignantly. ''Whatever made Mr. Blair think I'd let *you* throw my fortune around foolishly? *I'd* be there, wouldn't I? If anybody was going to throw it around foolishly, it would be both of us! You men!'' Her body leaned on his. It wasn't as mad as her voice sounded.

''Honey, give me the Ring. This darned thing is too darned draughty and slow . . .''

''First you're going to have to think back. One wish you wasted, I know. That silly bird.''

''Bird!'' said George feebly.

''You've got a pet phrase. You said . . .'' George groaned. ''Oh, George, how many times?''

''Once before, in my room. I remember, now. It was a sparrow.''

''Two wishes gone!'' wailed Kathy. ''And all of mine! That certainly settles it! No sandwich, and we'll proceed to Maine the way we're going.''

''Honey, please . . . I don't like you to be cold . . .''

''I'm thinking of both of us. We just can't afford . . .''

''I know and you're wonderful and I love you but . . .''

Kathy said she loved him, too, and the point of their dispute got lost, somehow. After a while, Kathy laid her head snug on his shoulder. The Carpet kept rolling along, and miserable as they were, it was peaceful there in the silent sky.

Suddenly, it wasn't silent. George heaved his shoulder. He pointed with an invisible hand.

It was an airliner, a silver thing, speeding the way they were going with a steady roar. It pursued. It caught up. It passed. The Carpet tossed its invisible passengers, as it bucked and staggered in the backwash.

Through the little windows they could see where the dim light bathed the warm upholstered scene. Leaning at his ease in the deep cushioned seat was a young man with blond hair (parted in the middle). He'd been dining. Now he was smoking. A pretty hostess bent to remove his tray. Mr. Blair (for it was he) knocked, as he whisked by in the sky, his lazy ashes off, and smiled up into the pretty face with a quaint turn-of-the-century wolf-ishness, the image of which persisted on the gray cold air when he had gone.

The Carpet kept lumbering along.

The night wore on. Mrs. McGurk took the Mirror, once more, out of her bag. She was tired and bruised from bouncing through the night in Mr. Josef's old rattletrap of a car, which he pushed so recklessly at a speed beyond comfort. At times, she'd been about to ask him to slow down, but she hated to tamper with his absorption.

"Still east?" he asked.

"Still east, I judge. They seem to be nearing Narragansett."

She and Mr. Josef were, she feared, far, far behind. Mrs. McGurk sighed. She was weary and her heart was sore, and she began to suspect that this was ridiculous. She hardly knew, any more, what she hoped. At first, it was only to see George, face to face once more, but now her resolution flagged. She was discouraged. She was . . . and her heart ached . . . growing old. Oh, she'd known *that*, all along. Still, she had hoped that even her middle-aged heart could hold the luxury of devotion. A secret spring of joy, it might have been! Ah, that devil, jealousy, had undone everything!

She had wept already. In her distress, she'd babbled. She'd mentioned magic.

But Mr. Josef didn't believe. He thought they were pursuing a helicopter. He didn't even believe in the Mirror. He'd said, scornfully, that Mrs. McGurk was guilty of reactionary thinking. No doubt, he said, it was simple radar. But when she swore she could lead them to George, he'd been perfectly willing, even eager to go on.

The other one, that Gogo, had left them flat. He'd given a brief total opinion of the whole matter. He'd said, "Nuts!" Mr. Josef had screamed something after him, something like "Traitor!" Traitor to what? she wondered sleepily. She thrust her precious Mirror back into the depths of her bag and this time her fingers stumbled on the Lamp!

For heaven's sake! What a fool she was!

"Mr. Josef," she cried. "Stop, please!"

"At the next gas station, Madame," he said patiently.

Mrs. McGurk bit her tongue. She forbore to correct him. She really could not imagine what the sight of the Genie might do to Mr. Josef. She decided she had better not rub the Lamp until she was alone.

A mangy little roadhouse lay just beyond the next bend. It looked and was a dump. But Mrs. McGurk cried, "Stop here, Mr. Josef. Maybe," she fluttered, "you would care for something to drink? I might take a little myself."

"Ah, perhaps so." They pulled up. Mr. Josef's hand under her arm, and he looking suspiciously on all sides, they went in.

Behind the bar a hairless man with a roll of fat at the back of his neck looked up without expression. The stale smelling twilight seemed otherwise deserted.

Mrs. McGurk asked the bartender and he told her. There was the usual anteroom, the powder table. She took the Lamp out of her bag, pulled herself together, summoned courage. So, in the lady's room of Joe's Bar and Grill, Cocktails, French fries, she met, for the second time, the Slave of the Lamp. This time Constance McGurk did not flinch. She waited calmly while he introduced himself with his formula, until he had asked the conventional question. "What are your commands?"

"Bring George Hale to me," she said.

"I regret, Madame," he replied, "it is not within my power."

"What's that!" Mrs. McGurk was outraged.

"Magic cannot cross magic," the Genie told her.

"Is that so! You mean to tell me, just because he is riding around on that Carpet. . . ?"

The Genie bowed.

"Well!" said Mrs. McGurk in a huff. "A fine thing! Look here, you can do it if he gets off, can't you?"

The Genie bowed.

"Very well," she snapped. "The minute he does get off that thing, *then* bring him to me."

"I hear and obey."

"Wherever I am," she added sharply.

"I hear and obey."

"And never mind that girl. Do you understand? I don't care . . ." The knob on the door behind was rattling. "That's all," she said quickly. "Shoo . . . go on, now."

The Genie vanished. A sullen looking blonde in a fur jacket was entering this sanctuary. Her black eye flickered on the big handbag in Constance's hands. Or did it remark her ruby (relic of Mr. McGurk) solitaire?

The blonde passed on to the inner sanctum. Mrs. McGurk slipped off her ruby and hid it, too, in her bag, which she swung by its long strap over her shoulder. It had occurred to her that she might be among thieves.

Mrs. McGurk was suspicious all over, but she had her own brand of toughness. She demanded a piece of string from the bartender, and she tied the strap of her bag to her slip strap . . . no silken wisp, this, but a broad band of strong cotton. She even tied the clasp of the bag with several loops of cord. Now! To rob her would involve more serious crime. Let them try it if they dared!

Now she turned commandingly. She said to Josef, "I want to go home."

His beard tipped up. "Dear lady," he soothed, "you must not lose heart."

"I want to go back."

"No, no, we go on!"

"It isn't necessary," she snapped.

"Ah," he purred, "I am afraid, dear lady, you don't quite understand. We . . . Go on!" Mr. Josef, locking eyes with the bartender, reached out and grasped her hand.

"Take your hand off me!" said Constance in shrill alarm.

"You see," said Mr. Josef, silkily, "you are to lead me to Hale."

"Lead *you!*"

"Did you think," Mr. Josef laughed nastily, "I've taken so many pains with no motive of my own? Ah, come," he chided. Then he barked. "To the car!"

"Help," said Constance feebly.

"Not in here, Mac," said the bartender. "Outside." He jerked his chin. He turned his back.

"Help! Murder!" cried Constance. She ran.

"Ah, no, my chickadee," said Josef merrily. As she fell out the door he caught her by her arms. He forced them back. With some of the bartender's cord, he was binding her wrists together. Joe's Bar and Grill remained indifferent. Only the neon fluttered over their heads. In this dead of night, the road lay bare.

Josef marched her to the car, forced her to the seat. "My dear woman," he said righteously, "let me assure you, you are only a means to an end. Function as that means and you are perfectly safe." He walked around and got in at her side. "East?" he inquired, calmly.

"East," quavered Mrs. McGurk. "Oh," prayed she, "George! Oh, George!"

When the sun rose, George at last threw off the protecting Cloak and peered over the edge. Below was Maine, and all around was morning, and suddenly George wanted the world to be as clear and crisp as it looked.

"Kathy, let's dump all this stuff! It's no good!" He held up the Rose in its box. "We don't want this around, do we?"

"I don't think you ought to dump it," said Kathy thoughtfully. "You just can't tell. It's not the fault of the *things*, George." She was sitting with her legs crossed, her brown eyes serious. "It's just that the more power you've got in your hand," mused Kathy, "the more careful you have to be how your hand turns."

George took out the Purse. "Gold sure ain't what it used to be."

"But we'll keep it." Kathy put it and the Rose in a deep pocket of her dress.

"Let's see. Mrs. McGurk must have the Mirror. Mr. Blair's got the Flask. One of them's got the Lamp. We're sitting on the dumb Carpet. And you're still wearing the Ring."

"Yes," she said, "I must remember. And here's the Cloak." She folded it over her arm, as one might put on her gloves when the train is entering the station.

"One thing left." George drew out the Sword. The hilt snuggled into his hand as if the blade were begging to dance. "I'd kinda like to . . . uh . . . hang on to this," said George sheepishly. "But I'm darned tooting going to get rid of this bag!" He buckled the sword belt around his waist. Then he lifted the carpet bag and heaved it over into space. "There!"

He felt better. He lay down on his belly and inspected the terrain. He thought he could spot the Congregational spire. George bet Kathy a dollar his mother would make him shave on an empty stomach. So they lay, giggling, peering down, kicking their heels, and the sun was warm on their backs. They forgot they'd been miserable. They were almost home.

Mr. Blair touched earth long before dawn, hired a car, and drove himself to Deeport. At the Ocean House, he registered, unchallenged, as Bennett Blair 2nd. He reserved a suite for Miss Douglas. He had her luggage put there.

Oh, he was a fox! He chuckled, looking down at George's suit that he had filched from the vast array in the upstairs wardrobe at George's fabulous house. All his own suits were hopeless. He was a fox! He'd thought of this!

Oh, it had been jolly, whipping down the parkways in George's Cadillac, sneaking into his own house, commanding Fraulein in an imitation of his own old voice, over the house phone, to pack for Kathy. Maneuvering the servants out of the way before he made his dash to the streets again. He was postponing, he was evading. First and foremost came Kathleen.

The darling girl had run away and he could not blame her for that. He had overwhelmed her too suddenly, pouring out such talk! Well, he could not blame himself for that, either. That glorious surge of the heart had overwhelmed him. He did not regret it.

All would be well, yet. Mr. Blair felt absolutely invincible.

He breakfasted in his room, alone. This was his first free time with a looking glass. He tried to part his blond hair on the side, but it refused. How old was he, he wondered. A scar, there, at the hairline. He remembered the occasion of it. He must be at least twenty-five. A good age! Just the right age for Kathleen!

Kathleen! Mr. Blair was, actually, in a state of civil war, his physical youth resisting his foxy old brain, so that he swayed between dreams of love and the cooler strategy of conquest.

At last, he realized that even that ancient decrepit Carpet would be ambling into port, soon. So he tore his gaze from the fascinating face in the glass, borrowed binoculars, drove off to an unpopulated stretch of beach. He would take up a post. He would meet the morning Carpet. Mr. Blair chuckled. What a glorious morning! He frisked on the pebbly strand.

Mr. Blair's wise old mind, bouncing, willy nilly, while the rest of him danced, remarked that Wall Street had never been like this!

The Carpet began to lose altitude. It was coming in for a landing on a deserted potato field. George peered anxiously over. He saw a car draw up, the figure of a man got out and run, arms waving. "Oh, my gosh!" said George in dismay.

"It's Mr. Blair, isn't it?" said Kathy calmly. "Never mind." George squeezed her hand.

The Carpet came softly, softly down. George stepped off, turned to hold his hand to his lady, and vanished.

Mr. Blair came bounding up. "Hello, hello."

"Hello," said Kathy coolly. The fact that George had vanished didn't perturb her at once. After all, they had both been vanishing, off and on, all night long. She was perfectly accustomed to the idea.

"Have a nice trip?" said Mr. Blair pleasantly.

"Not very," she answered severely. "George . . ." She missed the feel of his hand, the sense of his near shoulder, even more . . . "Shall we go home?"

No answer came.

"Where'd he go?" said Mr. Blair, looking about them. But Kathy began to walk straight ahead of her. She was so very tired, so very hungry . . . And George . . . Why didn't his arm come around her weary shoulders? Tears stung her eyes. She lifted her own arm to mop at them with fabric.

The Cloak hung on her arm!

But then. . . ! "Oh!" cried Kathy. "Oh! Oh!" The Lamp! Now she remembered its lost and terrible power!

"I don't understand what's happened to George," said Mr. Blair, rather angrily, "but if this is the way he takes care of you. . . !"

"I'm afraid . . . there was something," she said forlornly, "he *had* to do."

Mr. Blair's brain beat his body down in a short sharp struggle, for it knew an opportunity when it saw one. He became the soul of tender kindness. *He* would take care of her. He brought her to her room at the Ocean House. Ah, the sweet warm comfort of it, after the vast chill inhumanity of the sky! He commanded them to bring coffee . . . Oh, blessed liquid!

Thus he comforted her with the civilized arts. Now, she must bathe and rest, he said, and then take lunch, perhaps? Mr. Blair's breath grew a trifle gaspy. "Kathleen, won't you call me Bennett, now?"

He was being so kind. Kathy couldn't be ungracious. She smiled and said she'd try.

Mr. Blair's wise old mind fought like a maddened hornet in his skull against his urge to grab her. "Rest well," he counseled, and withdrew.

Sore and bewildered, Kathy nevertheless bathed and dressed herself in fresh clothing. What to do? George was gone! And she could not think how, except by the power of the Lamp. And who, then, had invoked its power but that fatuous old Mrs. McGurk? But what to do? She turned over what magic she had in stock. The Rose and the Purse? She put them in the handbag Fraulein had supplied. George was right. These things were no good. Neither could the Cloak help her. It lay on the bed. The Carpet?

Oh, heavens! It lay abandoned in the field, and what mad adventure waited now for some Yankee farmer, she dreaded to imagine. Oh, George had been so right! This troublesome, troublesome magic . . . She wished . . .

Wished! Wished, indeed! Kathy threw herself down to weep. Here hung the Ring on her finger, and she with no wishes left!

"Oh, George," wept Kathy, "George . . ."

When the sun rose and people began to appear, Mr. Josef abandoned the highways. He made the car slink through back alleys and lanes. It seemed to put one wheel cautiously ahead of the other, like pussy feet. Even the engine whispered along.

He had not gagged Mrs. McGurk. The poor woman was nearly speechless anyhow with misery. She had kept saying, "East . . . North . . ." at random, and he followed her directions with a queer blindness.

He kept talking. He expounded his philosophy, explaining how, by stealth, treachery, and violence, he would help make a fairer world. "No more slaves!" cried Mr. Josef, pounding the steering wheel with his fist. Mrs. McGurk's enslaved ear heard all this, but her unregenerate mind was going furiously around the same old circle. How to get free?

The Lamp was here, still tied to her person. What if Mr. Josef should open her handbag. How could she benefit? If he should accidentally rub the Lamp and summon the Genie! Of course, Mr. Josef could not, on principle, acquire a Private Slave. No, no, all must be chained alike to the wheel of the State! Mrs. McGurk wondered to herself if there was an Amalgamated Brotherhood of Oriental Genii with a closed shop. She felt hysterical. She fought down the feeling.

They were slinking along a country lane. "North?" asked Mr. Josef.

"A little east," she answered wearily, as she had been answering for hours, quite at random.

He stopped the car. There was a glade at their right; an old crabapple tree stood among wild grasses. On the left a little wood and the curve of the lane closed them in.

"We have been here before," said Mr. Josef and he turned and behind his eyes there burned a reddish anger.

Mrs. McGurk closed her eyes. He'd come out of his state. He'd noticed they weren't getting anywhere. And what to do or say now, she did not . . . did not . . . know.

Then, suddenly, George . . . George himself . . . was there, standing beside the car, leaning on the sill at her side, looking reproachfully into her face. "You shouldn't have done this, Mrs. McGurk," he said, more in sorrow than in anger.

She screamed, "George! Be careful! He . . . Gun . . . Mad . . . Oh. . . !"

"Huh?" said George.

Mr. Josef got nimbly out on his side and raced around the hood. A gun was in his hand.

George backed away from the car in confusion and surprise. His feet slipped among the sweet-scented tall grasses of the glade. His hand went, with an ancient instinct, to the hilt of the Sword.

Mr. Josef, gun in hand, charged at him. "Ha!" cried the spy. "Haha! Haha!" His face went into its most menacing leer. His beard wagged. "We shall continue," purred Mr. Josef, "our little chat. I will have the secret of the ray, please. And now! I'll give you two minutes, 120 seconds to explain the process verbally or turn over documents . . ."

"Secret! Documents!" cried George. "You dumb bunny! Listen, I cut up that stuff in my room with this old sword."

"Impossible," said Mr. Josef calmly.

George said, "Let me show you! Maybe you'll believe it when you see it. Maybe you'll stop this idiotic Grade-B nonsense!" He pulled the Sword half out of the scabbard.

"Nonsense," said the spy thickly. "That's typical of you stupid Americans!"

Then George really did get mad. "Now, wait a minute," he said. "Shut up a minute, you with the beard! Suppose I had a secret ray? What in hell," cried George, "makes you think I'd give it to such as you? What makes you think I'd let a mutt like you, waving a gun around, steal a better weapon? You're not fit to be trusted with a bow and arrow. I wouldn't give you *any* secret *any* time *any*where for *any* reason . . . You and your corny threats!" cried George. He drew the Sword out all the way. "You obsolete old bully! Get out of the way!"

Mr. Josef raised the gun. The rules of his craft did not permit him to kill dead somebody with a secret. Ideology said, torture. His eyes narrowed calculating pain.

The Sword leapt in George's hand. It glittered across the air like a fork of lightning. It cut the gun . . . and a fingertip . . . from Josef's hand.

Blood flowed.

Mr. Josef looked down. He often had thoughts of blood, but not often was the blood in his thoughts *his* blood. Mr. Josef turned very pale. Holding the wounded hand before him, he tipped, fainting, forward. Fascinated, George watched him fall . . . against the blade! The wicked blade, still poised in George's hand!

Mr. Josef expired at once.

George loosened his hand from the hilt of the terrible toy. It fell on the ground beside the body. His hand was stinging. It was divorced from the rest of him by its independent guilt.

George sunk his face in his hands and groaned aloud.

Mrs. McGurk said, "George, dear George, don't you mind! You couldn't help it! Untie me," she begged. "Oh, George, you don't know! When you hear, you won't feel quite so bad about him. It was self-defense, George. You had to do it."

"Untie you!" said George stupidly. He came to the car. He worked at her wrists. He would not touch that Sword again, even for Mercy's sake. He cut the cord with a dull penknife from his pocket.

Mrs. McGurk, in spite of the pain, moved her hands to her handbag. "Don't worry . . . don't worry . . . you and I will be far far away. See what I have!" she cried, as to a hurt baby. (See! See the pretty Lamp!)

But George shook himself. What's done is done, he thought in some hard sturdy core. Never meant to kill him. Was a kind of accident and in self-defense, besides. I'm not, probably, going to prison. He looked down the long vista of his days, every one of which the memory of this day would mar. No, he would not go to prison, he thought bleakly.

Mrs. McGurk cried out, trying to work her fingers. "Open my bag, George. The Lamp!"

"No," he said. "I can't do that." He put his hand on the bag's tied-up clasp. "This isn't the way, Constance . . . I've got to go straight through everything, now. Or always be sorry. Sorrier, I mean, than I am already. We'll have to notify the police. You'll . . . help me, won't you?"

"I will! I will!" sobbed Mrs. McGurk. "Oh, George, dear George, I'll tell them how it was. You've saved me!"

A brown animal broke out of the woods. It was a mule. A stout old woman in a dirty gingham garment . . . an old woman with a face like the gray bark of an ancient tree, was holding a rope attached to the animal.

"How do?" she said. "Had a little trouble?"

"Yes, we . . . Yes . . ."

"Seen it," she said. "Sent a kid up to the main road. He'll be back wid somebody," she continued. She leaned on the mule and scratched her tousled gray head with a twig she now took out of her mouth.

"With somebody? You mean, the police?"

"Ay-ah."

"Oh," said George. "Well, thanks very much."

There was a tableau, minutes of no sound and no motion, except the mule's gentle cropping at the grass. Then sound and motion were approaching. George left Mrs. McGurk's side and went to meet the man in uniform.

"What goes on here?" said the Law. "That a dead man over there?"

"Oh, officer!" cried Constance. "He was trying to kidnap me! He had a gun! This young gentleman was forced to . . . do it!"

"He was trying to kidnap you, you say!" said the cop, focusing on her face. Her nose was violently askew, after all she had been through. The cop blinked and looked about him.

"You know me," said the woman with the mule, putting the twig back into her mouth.

"Say! Sure. You're the woman who keeps a bunch of pigs down there in the hollow. You see what happened here?"

"Ay-ah."

"He kill him?" The cop indicated George.

"He killed him, all right. Sliced into him. I seen it."

The cop stepped over the tall grass, looked down, looked up. "Why'd you do it?" said he suddenly, savagely, to George.

"It was . . . more or less . . . an accident . . ." George was feeling sick.

"Nah," said the woman with the mule, spitting out the twig.

"No?" said the cop. "What would you say it was, hey?"

"Murder. That's what it was," said the pig woman, not violently at all. Her dull eyes rested indifferently on George.

About noon, Kathy and Bennett Blair were settled snugly in the bar, sipping sherry. Kathy was the prisoner of inaction. Mr. Blair had agreed that, no doubt, George must have been kidnaped (in a sense that was the word) by Mrs. McGurk. But, he suggested gently, if George did not, now, care for the situation in which he found himself, then, being grown and responsible, he would make his own efforts to change it. Let, hinted Mr. Blair, George do it. While they were waiting for him, in this pleasant meantime, he and she might just explore each other's friendship a little.

Ah, he was a fox! Kathy relaxed. There was nothing else to do. And she was warm and not very hungry any more, and there was the old beauty of the sea, outside, and she snug beside a friend who knew her well.

The manager came into the bar. "Say, Frank, I just heard something over the air. Fellow name of George Hale got picked up over to Snowden." His voice was low, but at that name Kathy was clutching the edge of the table.

"Picked up!" said the bartender. "What for?"

"Homicide. That's murder, to you."

"Murder!"

"Coincidence, eh?" chuckled the manager. "I bet you Miz Hale's phone is going to be ringing."

"Nah," said the bartender. "Nobody's going to think that's *George!* Wouldn't hurt a fly, for gossake. Besides, he's still down to New York."

"Lots of fools in this world," said the manager cheerfully. "Seems this fellow ran a man through with a sword."

"Sword, eh? Kinda unusual. I wonder if somebody hadn't oughta tip George off," mused the bartender. "Tell him to call up his folks and say it ain't him. You think Miz Mar-gret is liable to worry any?"

"Miz Liz and Miz Nell won't let her," soothed the manager. "Just the same, I'd certainly like to talk to George. It could help to talk to George."

"He oughta come back home."

"Frank, nobody knows . . . nobody knows how I wish he'd come back home!" mourned the manager.

"Boys in the band feeling pretty sick, too."

"Going to be a lo-ong winter."

"Sweet guy, that George." The bartender's was a sentimental trade. "I dunno what it was about him . . . Gee, wouldn't I like to see him walk in. . . !"

The manager stifled a sob.

Kathy leaned over. "We have to go there," she whispered fiercely. "Now!"

"Suppose," said Mr. Blair cautiously, "I . . . er . . . see what I can find out."

"Just let's go," said Kathy and she rose.

"Kathy, please listen, my dear . . ." He caught up to her. "You can't go there!"

"But of course I can!"

"No, no, dear." His hands were kind but they held her. "It's a nasty mess. Didn't you hear him say homicide? George is evidently in jail. You can't go there."

"Why not?" she blazed.

"Because you mustn't be involved. Think of the newspapers! The whole moronic public licking its lips . . . Kathy, consider. George wouldn't *want* you to go through all that. You are too precious. *I* don't want . . ."

"What you want," said Kathy coldly, "and even what George would want, is not the point exactly. *I want!* Did you ever think of that? You don't even consider I'm alive! Also," her hair swung in a gleaming arc, "you don't mean 'precious.' You mean delicate and breakable! Well, I'm not breakable! I'm me! And if *I* want to be there when George is in trouble, I am going to be there!

"Oh, no," said Mr. Blair, losing his head.

"Oh, yes," said Kathy, turning her back.

"Oh, no," he cried, seizing her arm.

"Oh, yes," she cried, twisting away.

"Kathy," he blurted. "He isn't worth it!"

"Oh, isn't he?" said Kathy, very, very dangerously.

Mr. Blair groaned, regretting error. He let her run up the one flight of stairs. He followed. She ran to her room. He took a stand in the corridor.

He tried to think what to do or say now. If she insisted, why, he'd better take her to Snowden, defend her from what annoyance he could, regain what ground he had just lost, so foolishly. He wouldn't lose his head again!

Kathy opened her door, wearing her jacket, purse under her arm. She was so beautiful! Mr. Blair's head went looping away from him like a collar button under the dresser.

"Kathy!" he cried in his throbbing tenor. He took a step as if he would surge on one knee with hands up to plead . . .

She slipped back behind the half closed door. She picked the Cloak off the bed.

Had Mr. Blair not been so furiously occupied, retrieving his head for the second time and jamming it fiercely back in place, he might have noticed certain dainty depressions, dotting alone along the padded floor.

It was a crude little jail, but George was tight in a cell just the same, the only prisoner at the moment.

Beyond a thick door, he knew there was a kind of anteroom, and that there, side by side on hard straight chairs, Mrs. McGurk and the pig woman were waiting. He knew this because every now and then someone connected with the law would walk through this corridor. Whenever the end door at the left swung in, he could see that bare and dusty place, and the two of them.

George stared at the wall. The cell block smelled dismally of antiseptics. He felt anesthetized. He would rouse himself and his thoughts would go spinning around the circle of his anxieties. Kathy . . . whether Mr. Blair was being a problem . . . whether to insist that his people be notified . . . His mother and the Aunts, he knew, would march in close formation, right beside him, heads up, mouths firm, right through this trouble. Yet, if he could spare them any confusion before it was clear just what kind of trouble this was going to be, George felt he must.

Then there were the pig woman and Mrs. McGurk, both problems, and his legal status at their oddly assorted mercies. And there were the complications he'd left behind, about the big house . . . And other complications ahead. There was Mr. Blair. So his thoughts went around and came out at the same place and meanwhile, there arose about him the carbolic flavored, dreary, and somehow official smell of delay.

An attendant of some kind pushed the end door inward. Mrs. McGurk sailed around his bulk. She cried, "George!"

George rose politely. "What's happening?"

"They're waiting. As soon as somebody or other comes back, then they'll start asking questions. Oh, George! Her strange nose was pink from weeping and wrangling. "Remember," she whispered, "remember we can still get away."

George roused in alarm. "No, no. Don't do that, Constance, please!"

"We can leave all this behind," she breathed. There was a light in her eye he groaned to see. "Everything behind us! Some desert isle . . . far, far away . . ."

George felt the impulse of his hair to stand on end. He could look right into her dream. He could see the hibiscus in her hair.

"That would be the worst thing you could possibly do," said George in a stern desperate whisper. "No, please. You'd better give me the Lamp."

"They'd only take it away from you. George, you must trust me!"

George tried very hard not to look as frightened as he felt. "I do," he said. "I know *you* know I can't spend the rest of my life a fugitive. I must clear my name. *You* understand!"

"I suppose so," she sniffled. It was on the tip of George's tongue to point out that he'd been whisked into that strange duel. It had been *her* doing. But he dared not. "Don't you know," he pleaded, "every time that trick is worked it only causes trouble?"

"Trouble for you, but oh, George, it wasn't trouble for me. It was my salvation!"

Mrs. McGurk had it all twisted around. She'd forgotten that Josef had been after George. She saw herself in the juiciest role, naturally. She was the Heroine. George was, of course, Her Hero. It was maddening.

George changed the subject. "Could you do anything with that pig woman?"

"Pig woman!" spat Constance. "I've talked and talked! She won't listen. We know she's lying. They'll have to believe us. They'll have to!"

But George thought to himself, No, they won't either have to. It was a queer thing, but Mrs. McGurk's obvious partisanship was going to make the truth sound like a lie, while the pig woman's lie, because she told it without heat, was going to shine forth as a simple impersonal objective statement of fact.

He shook his head. "There'll be some way to prove the truth," he soothed, trying to sound serene and confident. "Don't worry. Don't do anything. Nothing to do, but wait till they ask for our story."

Mrs. McGurk nodded. She straightened her tired back. "We'll tell our story," said she. But George saw right through to the female squirm of her judgment. "But if they don't believe it," Mrs. McGurk was saying darkly to herself, "I shall act! I, Constance, shall save him, in spite of himself!"

George stifled a groan. And as Mrs. McGurk, not entirely without realizing the drama of it all, let herself be led away, he beat his head on the bars. Tell their story, eh? Including one thing and another? George closed his eyes and winced all over.

Kathy's voice said, "Hello."

The end door was swinging shut. He seemed alone. "Kathy, where are you?"

"George, have you had any food?"

"No," he said. "Yes. I mean, no. Kathy!"

"I brought you a couple of sandwiches," said she in business-like tones.

He felt the package in his hand. As she let go of it, it became visible.

"Ham! Cheese! Darling!"

"And a thing of coffee." The hot carton came out of the air.

"Kathy, how. . . ?"

"I'll tell you while you eat." He could feel her presence, just outside his bars. "Golly, George, do you know something? Being invisible isn't what it's cracked up to be. I'm so battered. I took a bus and five people nearly sat on me. I was leaping from seat to seat the whole time. And it's 70 miles. You see, I didn't have any money, except this old gold, and it would have just caused a commotion. And Mr. Blair had the keys to his car in his pocket. George, I stole the food. Is it good? The only advantage when you're invisible is that you really can steal things quite easily."

George, even among the sandwiches, was a grin all over. He felt so much better he could hardly believe it. "Kathy, this coffee is delicious!"

"Did I sugar it right?"

"Oh, perfectly! Just perfectly!" How dear and close they were, even in so small a thing! Oh how much cosier was even trouble when it was built for two! "Kathy," he said, "we can get through this, somehow, if she only won't . . . take us apart."

Kathy said, "I want you to tell me. I'm trying to wait till you're not so hungry."

Angel! thought George, and washed down a big bite. Then he told her.

"Oh, dear!" said Kathy at last.

"Honey, was Mr. Blair . . . uh. . . ?"

"Well, not very," she said. But George knew the problem of Mr. Blair was not diminished. "Well." He could feel her brace up as she spoke. "What *can* we do? Let's see. George, I think I'll go and steal the Lamp."

"Say!"

"That would help, wouldn't it?"

"Boy, would it!"

"All right. That's one thing we can do. Of course, there's this." He felt the warm metal circle slip into his palm. The Ring! "We're pretty sure you've got one wish left," she reminded him. "The only trouble is . . . George, what should you wish?"

"Oh, Kathy, I w . . . "

Her warm hand muffled his mouth. "Sssssh . . . Sssssh! For goodness sakes! This time, we've got to figure it out carefully."

"I guess that's right."

"Don't even speak," warned Kathy, "because . . . for instance, you could wish we had the Lamp, but it would be silly not to try to steal it first. Because maybe you'll need the wish to make the pig woman stop lying . . . but then . . . There are so many angles . . ." she wailed. "I think we better try everything else first and save the Ring for an emergency."

George wondered, for a moment, what she called an emergency. Then he pressed his lips tight. He agreed. For if, he thought, Mrs. McGurk were to whisk him off to a desert isle, *that* sure would be the emergency of all time!

Kathy's hand touched his goodbye. "Call the man, so he'll open the door." George diverted the attendant for a moment or two. Oh, wonderful Kathy!

Say!

What if he and she . . . George and Kathy . . . were to be magically transported to a flowery isle? There was an idea. George stared at the wall. He knew right away it wasn't any good. A man can't leave what life is, in the name of life. No, if they were not to be with their kind, to mix in, to take part, to struggle humanly in the great complicated mesh that made the world of men, then what was life for? No . . . no good.

The Ring hung heavy on his hand. One magic wish! Just one! Darned if George could think what it ought to be.

In the anteroom, an unseen Kathy hovered over the ladies in their chairs. Mrs. McGurk was cross-examining. "Now," she said, "when you first caught sight of the car, what was happening?"

"You was screaming," said the pig woman readily.

"Why was I screaming?"

"Because the fella wid the sword just come outa the woods at ya."

"No, no, no," protested Mrs. McGurk.

"Fella wid the beard goes running around to get rid of him."

"Exactly! So it was self-defense."

"Sure it was. Fella wid the beard was defending the both of ya."

"No," screeched Mrs. McGurk. "Listen . . ." she began again.

Kathy saw no lamp-shaded bulges in the landlady's print dress. The Lamp must be in that fat handbag. And it, she discovered, was tied tight to Mrs. McGurk. No way to steal the handbag. Kathy touched the clasp with a careful forefinger. Alas, the clasp itself was tied around and around with cord.

Kathy drew back to think it over. Very well. Attack the problem another way. Ah, suppose Mrs. McGurk were not so sentimentally attached to George? Then, would she even think of whisking George and herself away where they couldn't be found? No, of course she wouldn't! Kathy took the Rose, invisibly, out of her own purse. It was worth trying, she thought in excitement. If only she could induce Mrs. McGurk to sniff the Rose a second time and then let her eye light on another, *not* George . . .

On whom? Kathy looked about her. Why, on the fat attendant, of course. He would do quite well. Kathy crept closer on quiet feet.

A great loop of Mrs. McGurk's hairdo had come loose and it bobbed and dipped with the vehemence of her continuing arguments. She paid no attention to the Rose, as Kathy tossed it into her lap.

"My wrists were tied behind my back!" she fumed. "Tied, mind you! I can prove it! Was it George who tied them?"

"I dunno," said the pig woman. "Was it?" Her flesh sagged all around the inadequate surface of the narrow chair. Her coarse hands were folded across her stomach. Her bulk was inert. Mrs. McGurk, in comparison, bounced like a pingpong ball. The Rose bounced in her rayon lap. Just then the attendant got up and went to the door, off on one of his mysterious strolls down George's corridor. Kathy reached for the Rose.

So, yawning, did the pig woman. Her big hand closed. Her thick fingers were in possession. Now the dainty blossom (Kathy watched it, helpless with dismay) moved in that coarse grasp towards the stub of her nose.

"Purty flower," said the pig woman. "Where'd this come from?" She sniffed. The hulking bosom heaved a sigh.

The attendant was returning!

He swung the door inward, as it must go, against himself. The pig woman's little eyes rested, naturally, on the opening gap. Her gaze passed through it, to where, snug in his cell, smack in the line of her sight, sat George.

The blob of flesh in the pig woman's chair began to surge. Somehow, it organized itself roughly into the figure of a woman. Kathy snatched back the Rose but . . .

"Say!" said the pig woman. "How long do they think they can keep that kid in this lousy clink, hey?"

"What!" Constance's jaw dropped.

The pig woman heaved to her feet. "You, Fatso, take me in there. I wanna see if he needs anything. Somebody oughta take care of him."

Constance gasped.

"Lissen, sister," said the pig woman, turning. The air churned like water under the Queen Elizabeth. "How come you're so innerested? Old enough to be his grandmaw, ain't you?"

"Whose grandma?"

"HIS grandmaw. George's. George . . ." repeated the pig woman with a holy softness. Her weatherbeaten face was warm . . . nay, sunny . . . with affection. "Nothing bad is going to happen to a nice kid like HIM. I'll see to that!"

"YOU will!"

"Shuddup!" said the pig woman. "You been making a fool outa yourself long enough."

"Well, I. . . ! You old fat pig!"

"Rather be fleshy than a scrawny old crow," said the pig woman, ominously. "You let HIM alone."

"Who?"

"George."

"Oh?"

"Ay-ah."

"Hah!"

The pig woman's big mitt made a feint at the McGurk puss. The McGurk clawed for the scant and scrambled coiffure of the enemy. But the pig woman got a firm grip in return and Mrs. McGurk's switch left her.

By now, the attendant, with loud male shouts, had interposed himself. Reinforcements poured in from another room. With huffing and puffing, with yelps from their victim, with contributing screeches from Mrs. McGurk, at last they dragged the pig woman away. One of them humanely opened the door to reassure a frantic George that there had been only a little bloodshed.

Kathy slipped back to him. "Oh George . . . " she sobbed. "Oh . . . oh . . . look!"

The door had become wedged open. They could see Mrs. McGurk, settling her ruffled feathers. Pale with outrage, she perched on the edge of her chair. The cops were all busy, elsewhere, subduing their billowing witness. Mrs. McGurk was alone. Through the door, George and Kathy, watching with a horrid fascination, saw the landlady's hands and teeth begin to work on her handbag. She undid the cord. She dove into the bag. She took out the Lamp.

"Kathy . . . Kathy . . ." Their hands clung.

"Wish!"

"But what'll I wish?"

"Call to her . . . Stop her. . . !"

"Constance!"

Bosom heaving, eyes flashing, Mrs. McGurk was in no state to respond.

She didn't hear. She was lifting the Lamp to . . .

There came a sharp rap on the outer door.

It was a reprieve. "I beg your pardon," said a familiar tenor. "Oh, I say, it's you, isn't it?"

"How do?" said Mrs. McGurk, unenthusiastically.

"My name is Blair," He cleared his throat. "Is Miss Douglas here, anywhere, do you know?"

"Douglas? Oh, you mean that red-headed girl? No, no, she is not." Mrs. McGurk was brusque.

"But Hale is here?"

"In there," said Constance and her eyes blazed.

"Yes, I . . . er . . . see . . ." Mr. Blair swept the cell block with enough of a glance to see how empty it seemed of Kathy. He brushed by George with a formal little nod. (George, who stood with his hands held through the bars in so odd, so tense a position.) "Ah . . . I see you have the Lamp there," said Mr. Blair pleasantly.

Her hand tightened.

"Powerful little gadget, isn't it?" He gave her a magnetic smile and sat down beside her.

"Y'know, I have an idea."

He had, too. Kathy's hands writhed, if possible, closer to the hands of George. Their four hands were all bruised on the Ring . . .

"*I* could use that Lamp," drawled Mr. Blair, "whereas *you* might have some use for . . . this!" He took the Flask from his pocket. "This," he said and no salesman ever spoke with softer lure, "is water from the Fountain of Youth . . ." The last syllable fell on the sanitary air like the serpent's whisper in Eden. "You see, Mrs. . . . er. . . ?"

"McGurk," she murmured, hypnotically.

"I am *Bennett* Blair, you know."

Her gaze slid on the pink stone bottle. "Thought he was an older man . . ."

"He was," came the seductive voice. "I *was* old. Now, it appears to me that you . . . are fond of George? Isn't that so?"

"I am," she snuffled. "Oh, Mr. Blair, he is in such trouble and that horrible woman, she . . . bahoo!"

"My dear lady, there is nothing to worry about. Not now that I am here."

"You mean you can help?" she quavered. "He killed a man!"

"I'm sure he never meant to," soothed Mr. Blair. "Why, of course, I'll help. I would like so much to have that Lamp," he continued with a glide of tone that pointed up the connection. "And you'd rather like to be . . . young again?"

"Young?" *Pig woman*, thought Mrs. McGurk, *ha ha!*

"George, George, he mustn't have it!"

A series of futile wishes paraded in George's head. Futile . . . futile . . . inadequate all.

"I can't find Kathleen, you see," Mr. Blair was murmuring. "I want so much to find her and . . . er . . . keep her."

"I see," said Mrs. McGurk, eyes riveted on the Flask. *Redhead, ha ha!*

"Wish, George! Wish!"

"But *what?* Oh Kathy, what will I wish?"

"I'm not so sure," said Mrs. McGurk, suddenly recalling her best self. "Now, I can use this Lamp to take George right out of this. But . . . er . . . the thing I had in mind . . . We'd need the Lamp, there. I won't," she said with stubborn devotion, "have George doing without well-balanced meals and the comforts of civilization."

"Oh, my dear girl!" cried Mr. Blair, reading her dream. "Don't do that! Pray don't! How much better to clear him of these charges, simply clear him. And then, both of you so young . . ."

She raised her tempted swimming eyes to his face. "How do I know you can get him free?"

"It will be simple. I happen to know certain officials of this state rather well. I believe I could exert certain pressures on people in even higher places, if necessary . . ."

"You're sure, now!" said Mrs. McGurk, lifting the Lamp in both hands.

"I am Bennett Blair," he laughed, reaching for it.

"But . . . Bennet Blair's an *old* millionaire. How will. . . ?"

"Exactly," said he, very quickly indeed. "Think of it! Only the day before yesterday, I was an old millionaire!" He dazzled her with a smile. "You, too," said Mr. Blair with the flawless technique of the radio commercial, "can be young again . . ."

Her mind was paralyzed. Her hands began to loosen.

But so did George's. He pulled them free. Now he knew what the wish must be!

Out there in the anteroom, the Lamp and the Flask hung in the air, passing. George spoke aloud in a shaking but solemn voice.

"I WISH," said George, "THIS WAS THE DAY BEFORE YESTERDAY."

The Ring winked. "But in the morning!" cried George belatedly. (Oh, was it adequate, after all?) Their hands were locked again. The Ring blazed in the tangle of their fingers. "And oh . . . don't . . . don't . . ." pleaded George "don't let me forget! Not again! Don't let me forg . . ."

Time swirled in a kind of stew. All dissolved.

Thus, it became the day before yesterday.

"If you wish," said the proprietor, "sixteen dollarss and thiss. . . ."

"What's in it?" said George.

"Ssee?"

"Nuh-uh. What would I want with. . . ? Hey, what's that?" George spied the hilt of the Sword. What a magnificent old thing! He was attracted. Maybe . . . his mind was reaching for a good reason . . . maybe he ought to consider this deal. There might be something valuable in this carpet bag.

As he touched the hilt, something thrilled through to his hand. This blade in the crimson scabbard was old, very old. It was evil.

"No, no," murmured George mechanically.

"Maybe iss antique?" said his tempter. George didn't answer. Evil? The shadows all around him were drawn over evil unknown. He looked at his hand, where it merely touched the sword. There was no reason for this shiver, this ghost of horror.

George took his hand away and rubbed it on his trousers. He shook his head slightly to dispel this misty fright that was growing up around him.

Silly! Nothing to be afraid of! Just a lot of old junk. He fished into the bag to see what else it held.

He drew out a little box with a sliding lid. George looked down at the rose. What was it, anyhow?

"You take?" whispered the old old man.

George stared at him dumbly. Time rustled by, like feathers dragging. There was something wrong. Something was pricking on his nerves.

But, in George's upbringing, there was no tradition of nerves. One went ahead and did the right thing, regardless of how one felt. That was his training and it stiffened him, now. Maybe this was a chance . . .

He stood, hesitating. It was strange how time hung, as if the unwinding ribbon of it snagged on a point. As if George was balanced between two futures. And was it real? Were there two real futures? Does it matter, when we try? Are we free to choose? Looking back, we think we see . . . we *seem* to learn.

George thought, Yes, it matters. What we do, how we choose, where we push, how we aim . . . Being men, we must, to call ourselves alive, believe it matters. Dreaming, he swayed on the point of decision, teetering there, held in this whirling gust of strange unbidden thoughts.

Then the proprietor chose to push at the balance. "Thiss," he said, shifting closer. "thiss rose . . ." His ancient finger gave it a sly poke. He turned his wrinkled face up and it broke into a smile George didn't like, "iss Rose of Luff!" said the man with hideous glee.

(It was glee for George. George didn't need anybody's glee. George didn't like it.)

"You let girlss smell thiss . . . they luff!"

George closed the box. He felt a little ill of his distaste. "No, thanks," said George quietly. "I don't think I need anything of this sort."

He turned and burst back through the heaps of stuff towards the light. He ran out into the street and gulped the fresh air. He was shaking a little, as if he'd just almost had an accident. "Don't *need*," he heard himself saying. Well, now, how true that was!

He came to a drugstore; he found the phone booth; he put in his nickel. His throat all but closed up when he heard her voice.

She wasn't angry. He could tell.

"Kathy," said George, slowly and clearly, "when you said you wouldn't wait, *what did you mean?*"

"I thought you'd never ask!" Her voice was strong and fresh and glad.

"I meant I don't *want* to wait. *I want* . . ."

"Kathy," cried George, "Darling! Marry me! Right away!"

"I certainly will! I certainly will! That's it! That's what I meant! Oh, George I'm so glad you c-called . . ."

"If Mr. Blair keeps back all your money," groaned George.

"You don't want it, do you?"

"Who? Me!" cried George, horrified.

"Well, I thought not. So, pooh!" She switched in the most enchanting way. "We'd better run away," she said practically, "to Maine, I think. The cheapest way. We'll take a bus, George."

"Oh," said George, "dearest Kathy, meet me . . . oh darling . . . meet me on the corner!"

Mrs. McGurk stood behind her front room curtains with the sign in her hand, savouring this moment of delicious power. George was off, bag and baggage, and a cute red-headed trick, besides. Sister? Mrs. McGurk thought, cynically, not. Bride? Well, if so, *she* wanted no newly-weds in her house. Always so much in love . . . never had any leverage on them.

Now, she thought, take him. This one, coming up the steps to the stoop. Very prompt with the rent, he was. And serious minded. "How do, Mr. Josef," she greeted him pleasantly.

He bowed. "Good afternoon, Madame." He fingered his beard. His eyes slanted to the card. "Someone has left us?" He implied that he deduced it.

"Hale. Fourth floor."

"Ah," said Mr. Josef. "And the next occupant?" He watched her face slyly for any hint of a plot.

"I'll tell you one thing about the next occupant," said Constance cheerfully. "He will have a full month's rent in advance."

She raised her hand. She put the sign, the symbol of her power, in the window. That simple, potent, magic word, "Vacancy."

Fraulein stood in Mr. Blair's lair, twisting unhappy hands. "So I pack for her, Mr. Blair. What else can I do? Oh, sir, do you think . . . once they marry . . . that she will want me?"

He grunted.

"Can she afford me?" asked Fraulein boldly.

Mr. Blair looked up over his glasses. He took them off. He rubbed the vague persisting ache in his knobby knuckles. "Of course she can afford you," he said irritably. "I can't keep the child's fortune from her. I used all the pressure I could bring to bear," he continued waspishly, "but the young won't listen, they'll make mistakes." He brooded. "Sometimes," he said to Fraulein's listening face, and knew not why he said it, "I shudder to think of the mistakes one makes, being young." He shook his own (bald) head.

"I am glad if she is happy," said Fraulein stoutly. "This George is a good man?"

A thin, reluctant smile approached the old fish mouth. "As a matter of fact," he admitted, "this George . . . and I have checked . . . *is* a good man."

"And they love!"

"That, of course, makes everything rosy!" said Mr. Blair sourly.

But not as sourly as he might have.

Darkness gathered over New England. The chill sky pressed down.

Inside, the bus reeked of gasoline, tired people, old candy bars. Gum wrappers and scratchy little gobs of cellophane grated under shifting feet. There was a baby, of course, and a man with a rasping snore. Now and then, the bus screamed to a stop. Clumsy folk blundered in and out, stirring the stale air with piercing draughts. Again, they would slam on through the night.

But Kathy was snug in a seat by the window. Her hair was a pool of gold on George's shoulder. ". . . know what you'd call success," she murmured sleepily, "when everybody in the whole town, probably the whole state of Maine, adores you. And me, too, besides . . ."

George filled his soul with the sweet warm scent of her hair. He wasn't really worried about success, right now. For him, the bus was flying, gossamer light, through the soft cool night. It was a dear chariot, carrying ALL. And all within . . . the baby fretting pinkly up ahead, the old man, sleeping in noisy peace across the aisle, the middle-aged wife with the beautiful worry lines on her mother-face, the work-soiled, black-nailed, strong man's hand on the back of the next seat, all, all he knew and loved. All their pale faces in the weak light yet were aglow and gilded with something more.

For he loved her, loved them, loved all.

"Why it's like Magic! thought George. It *is* Magic! And he saw the world, and all its knots and problems, transformed, illuminated, and the pattern changed, by the beautiful blaze of the magic enchanting his eyes.

The bus winged on.

ALIENS _____

Under the pen names of Anthony Boucher and H. H. Holmes,
William Anthony Parker White *(1911–1968) did much to link
mysteries and the fantastic. As award winning critic for* The
New York Times Book Review *and* Ellery Queen's Mystery
Magazine *he called attention to fantastic mysteries by science
fiction writers. As first editor of* The Magazine of Fantasy and
Science Fiction *he published appropriate stories by major
mystery writers. Finally, as author, he gave us* Rocket to the
Morgue, *an ingenious mystery novel about science fiction
fandom, and a host of shorter hybrids such as the witty
how-done-it, "Nine-Finger Jack."*

NINE -- FINGER JACK

Anthony Boucher

JOHN Smith is an unexciting name to possess, and there was of course no
way for him to know until the end of his career that he would be forever
famous among connoisseurs of murder as Nine-finger Jack. But he did not
mind the drabness of Smith; he felt that what was good enough for the
great George Joseph was good enough for him.

Not only did John Smith happily share his surname with George Joseph;
he was proud to follow the celebrated G.J. in profession and even in
method. For an attractive and plausible man of a certain age, there are few
more satisfactory sources of income than frequent and systematic widower-
hood; and of all the practitioners who have acted upon this practical principle, none have improved upon George Joseph Smith's sensible and un-
patented Brides-in-the-Bath method.

John Smith's marriage to his ninth bride, Hester Pringle, took place on
the morning of May 31. On the evening of May 31 John Smith, having
spent much of the afternoon pointing out to friends how much the wedding
had excited Hester and how much he feared the effect on her notoriously
weak heart, entered the bathroom and, with the careless ease of the practiced professional, employed five of his fingers to seize Hester's ankles and

271

jerk her legs out of the tub while with the other five fingers he gently pressed her face just below water level.

So far all had proceeded in the conventional manner of any other wedding night; but the ensuing departure from ritual was such as to upset even John Smith's professional bathside manner. The moment Hester's face and neck were submerged below water, she opened her gills.

In his amazement, John released his grasp upon both ends of his bride. Her legs descended into the water and her face rose above it. As she passed from the element of water to air, her gills closed and her mouth opened.

"I suppose," she observed, "that in the intimacy of a long marriage you would eventually have discovered in any case that I am a Venusian. It is perhaps as well that the knowledge came early, so that we may lay a solid basis for understanding."

"Do you mean," John asked, for he was a precise man, "that you are a native of the planet Venus?"

"I do," she said. "You would be astonished to know how many of us there are already among you."

"I am sufficiently astonished," said John, "to learn of one. Would you mind convincing me that I did indeed see what I thought I saw?"

Obligingly, Hester lowered her head beneath the water. Her gills opened and her breath bubbled merrily. "The nature of our planet," she explained when she emerged, "has bred as its dominant race our species of amphibian mammals, in all other respects superficially identical with *homo sapiens*. You will find it all but impossible to recognize any of us, save perhaps by noticing those who, to avoid accidental opening of the gills, refuse to swim. Such concealment will of course be unnecessary soon when we take over complete control of your planet."

"And what do you propose to do with the race that already controls it?"

"Kill most of them, I suppose," said Hester; "and might I trouble you for that towel?"

"That," pronounced John, with any hand-craftsman's abhorrence of mass production, "is monstrous. I see my duty to my race: I must reveal all."

"I am afraid," Hester observed as she dried herself, "that you will not. In the first place, no one will believe you. In the second place, I shall then be forced to present to the authorities the complete dossier which I have gathered on the cumulatively interesting deaths of your first eight wives, together with my direct evidence as to your attempt this evening."

John Smith, being a reasonable man, pressed the point no further. "In view of this attempt," he said, "I imagine you would like either a divorce or an annulment."

"Indeed I should not," said Hester. "There is no better cover for my activities than marriage to a member of the native race. In fact, should you so much as mention divorce again, I shall be forced to return to the topic of that dossier. And now, if you will hand me that robe, I intend to do a little telephoning. Some of my better-placed colleagues will need to know my new name and address."

As John Smith heard her ask the long-distance operator for Washington, D.C., he realized with regretful resignation that he would be forced to depart from the methods of the immortal George Joseph.

Through the failure of the knife, John Smith learned that Venusian blood has extraordinary quick-clotting powers and Venusian organs possess an amazingly rapid system of self-regeneration. And the bullet taught him a further peculiarity of the blood: that it dissolves lead—in fact thrives upon lead.

His skill as a cook was quite sufficient to disguise any of the commoner poisons from human taste; but the Venusian palate not only detected but relished most of them. Hester was particularly taken with his tomato aspic *à l'arsénique* and insisted on his preparing it in quantity for a dinner of her friends, along with his *sole amandine* to which the prussic acid lent so distinctively intensified a flavor and aroma.

While the faintest murmur of divorce, even after a year of marriage, evoked from Hester a frowning murmur of "dossier . . ." the attempts at murder seemed merely to amuse her; so that finally John Smith was driven to seek out Professor Gillingsworth at the State University, recognized as the ultimate authority (on this planet) on life on other planets.

The professor found the query of much theoretical interest. "From what we are able to hypothesize of the nature of Venusian organisms," he announced, "I can almost assure you of their destruction by the forced ingestion of the best Beluga caviar, in doses of no less than one-half pound per diem."

Three weeks of the suggested treatment found John Smith's bank account seriously depleted and his wife in perfect health.

"That dear Gilly!" she laughed one evening. "It was so nice of him to tell you how to kill me; it's the first time I've had enough caviar since I came to earth."

"You mean," John demanded, "that Professor Gillingsworth is . . ."

She nodded.

"And all that money!" John protested. "You do not realize, Hester, how unjust you are. You have deprived me of my income and I have no other source."

"Dossier," said Hester through a mouthful of caviar.

America's greatest physiologist took an interest in John Smith's problem. "I should advise," he said, "the use of crystallized carbon placed directly in contact with the sensitive gill area."

"In other words, a diamond necklace?" John Smith asked. He seized a water carafe, hurled its contents at the physiologist's neck, and watched his gills open.

The next day John purchased a lapel flower through which water may be squirted—an article which he thenceforth found invaluable for purposes of identification.

The use of this flower proved to be a somewhat awkward method of starting a conversation and often led the conversation into unintended paths; but it did establish a certain clarity in relations.

It was after John had observed the opening of the gills of a leading criminal psychiatrist that he realized where he might find the people who could really help him.

From then on, whenever he could find time to be unobserved while Hester was engaged in her activities preparatory to world conquest, he visited insane asylums, announced that he was a free-lance feature writer, and asked if they had any inmates who believed that there were Venusians at large upon earth and planning to take it over.

In this manner he met many interesting and attractive people, all of whom wished him godspeed in his venture, but pointed out that they would hardly be where they were if all of their own plans for killing Venusians had not miscarried as hopelessly as his.

From one of these friends, who had learned more than most because his Venusian wife had made the error of falling in love with him (an error which led to her eventual removal from human society), John Smith ascertained that Venusians may indeed be harmed and even killed by many substances on their own planet, but seemingly by nothing on ours—though (his) wife had once dropped a hint that one thing alone on earth could prove fatal to the Venusian system.

At last John Smith visited an asylum whose director announced that they had an imnate who thought he *was* a Venusian.

When the director had left them, a squirt of the lapel flower verified the claimant's identity:

"I am a member of the Conciliationist Party," he explained, "the only member who has ever reached this earth. We believe that Earthmen and Venusians can live at peace as all men should, and I shall be glad to help you destroy all members of the opposition party.

"There is one substance on this earth which is deadly poison to any Venusian. Since in preparing and serving the dish best suited to its administration you must be careful to wear gloves, you should begin your campaign by wearing gloves at all meals . . ."

This mannerism Hester seemed willing to tolerate for the security afforded her by her marriage and even more particularly for the delights of John's skilled preparation of such dishes as spaghetti *all'aglio ed all'arsenico* which is so rarely to be had in the average restaurant.

Two weeks later John finally prepared the indicated dish: ox tail according to the richly imaginative recipe of Simon Templar, with a dash of deadly nightshade added to the other herbs specified by The Saint. Hester had praised the recipe, devoured two helpings, expressed some wonder as to the possibility of gills in its creator, whom she had never met, and was just nibbling at the smallest bones when, as the Conciliationist had foretold, she dropped dead.

Intent upon accomplishing his objective, John had forgotten the dossier, nor ever suspected that it was in the hands of a gilled lawyer who had instructions to pass it on in the event of Hester's death.

Even though that death was certified as natural, John rapidly found himself facing trial for murder, with seven other states vying for the privilege of the next opportunity should this trial fail to end in a conviction.

With no prospect in sight of a quiet resumption of his accustomed profession, John Smith bared his knowledge and acquired his immortal nickname. The result was a period of intense prosperity among manufacturers of squirting lapel flowers, bringing about the identification and exposure of the gilled masqueraders.

But inducing them, even by force, to ingest the substance poisonous to them was more difficult. The problem of supply and demand was an acute one, in view of the large number of the Venusians and the small proportion of members of the human race willing to perform the sacrifice made by Nine-finger Jack.

It was that great professional widower and amateur chef himself who solved the problem by proclaiming in his death cell his intention to bequeath his body to the eradication of Venusians, thereby pursuing after death the race which had ruined his career.

The noteworthy proportion of human beings who promptly followed his example in their wills has assured us of permanent protection against future invasions, since so small a quantity of the poison is necessary in each individual case; after all, one finger sufficed for Hester.

*Filled with action, sex, and violence, "The Veiled Woman" is
typical of the small but potent collection of hard-boiled
mysteries* **Mickey Spillane** *(1918–   ) has churned out over the
past thirty years. Invariably panned by reviewers, they are
gobbled up by the public at an astounding rate. Indeed, at one
time, his first 7 novels were all among the top 10 fiction best
sellers of this century.*

THE VEILED WOMAN

Mickey Spillane

Lodi's soft warm hand shook me awake. "Sh-h-h, Karl. Don't say anything." I could barely hear her. "There's someone downstairs."

The .45 I kept under my pillow was in my hand before I had my eyes
fully open. The bedroom was in total darkness because of the heavy curtains covering the windows, and the only sound was the almost inaudible
purr of the air-conditioning unit. I pressed the fingers of my free hand
lightly to Lodi's lips to still her whisper and to let her know I was now
fully awake.

I swung my bare feet to the floor and stood up. The fact that I was as
naked as one of Mike Angelo's cherubs didn't occur to me then, and even
if it had I wouldn't have wasted time looking for a robe.

Moving on tiptoe, I crossed the room and was careful about shooting the
bolts on the door. I could hear nothing from downstairs, but that didn't
mean no one was down there. Lodi's almost incredibly sharp sense of
hearing was something I had learned long ago not to doubt. Twenty years
among the perils of the jungle develops the senses like nothing else, and
the African jungle was where Lodi had come from.

With the door opened wide enough for me to slip through, I stepped into the upper hall. Still no sound. A tomb would have been noisier. No light either. It was like walking through a bottle of ink.

Still no sound from below. I wasn't surprised. Whoever was down there wouldn't be a common garden-variety burglar. Burglars didn't come out here in the wilderness eighty-odd miles north of New York City in search of loot.

I went down that flight of carpeted steps like a jungle cat stalking its prey. The damp chill of early morning began to flow across my skin, reminding me of my lack of clothing. At the foot of the stairs I froze in my tracks, listening, making sure the safety catch on the .45 was off.

More silence. Nothing stirred, nothing breathed. Had Lodi been mistaken after all? Had her nerves, under a growing strain for almost two months now, finally started to give way? I refused to believe it. . . .

And then I heard it. A sound so slight that only keen ears straining to listen would possibly have caught it. The chink of metal against metal, and that only once.

The study. The wall safe was in there; a vault actually, built by the previous owner. It would be the natural place for an intruder to start his search.

Silently I crossed to the study door, the gun ready in my fist. The door, I discovered, had been left open no more than an inch or two to enable the man in there to catch any sound from outside the room.

Slowly, with almost painful care, I pushed the door inward. As the space between its edge and the jamb widened, I saw a circle of light fixed on the combination knob of the vault. A man was standing there, one ear pressed to the metal surface of the vault door, his fingers slowly manipulating the dial. He was alone.

I leaned forward and groped along the wall until my fingers found the light switch. I flipped it, flooding the room with light, said, "Cheerio, you son of a bitch," and shot him through the head.

The sound of the heavy .45 was like an exploding bomb in the confines of that small room. Blood and brains and bone showered the vault door and the black-clad figure melted into the rug.

"Karl!" It was Lodi calling from the head of the stairs. "Darling, are you all right?"

"I'm fine," I said. "Go on back to bed, baby. I'll be up in a minute."

"Did you . . . did you—?"

"I sure as hell did. I'll tell you about it over grapefruit in the morning."

I crossed the room and knelt beside the body. There wasn't much left of him above the eyebrows, and what was below them was a face I had never seen before. The pockets held nothing personal that might identify him. An oiled-silk packet containing as nice a set of burglar tools as you'd find anywhere, but that and a half-empty pack of Philip Morris made up the total.

I didn't like that. In fact, I liked it so little that I scooped the .45 off the rug and stood up, all in one quick movement.

Too late! Before I could turn around a silken drawl said, "No further, Mr. Terris. Stand perfectly still."

I said a couple words under my breath but that was as far as I went. I heard the rustle of silk and the sound of light steps coming toward my back. "Let the gun drop. . . . Now, kick it away from you."

I could smell her now: the music of an expensive perfume and the nice female smell of a lovely woman. The drawl said, "You may turn around now and lower your hands. Any more than that and I'll shoot you through the knee."

She was wearing black, broken only by a white appliqued design just above the left breast. A pastel mink jacket hung casually from perfect shoulders and she was as blonde as a wheat field. It would have been a shame for her not to be beautiful, and beautiful she was, and not with the standard, nightclub kind of beauty that's almost commonplace these days.

"Which knee?" I said.

"I know all about you, Mr. Terris," she said coolly. "Forty million dollars and a sense of humor. Only I don't want any of either."

"That's a relief," I said. "What *do* you want?"

She was standing in front of me, a gun large in her hand, a slight smile tugging at the corners of an almost sensual mouth. Her eyes went over me frankly and with something more than faint approval. "Do you find the evening oppressively warm?"

I glanced down at my naked body, then back up at her. "I'm sorry. Would you like to wait while I run up and get into my dress suit?"

"I'm afraid we can't spare the time." She walked over to a lamp table and whisked the large scarf off it and tossed it to me. "Do something with this," she said. "I find your—well, your masculinity a little overpowering."

The scarf was on the skimpy side but I made it do. She leaned against the back of a lounge chair and went on pointing the gun at me. "And now back to business, Mr. Terris. I came here for that machine you brought back from Africa.''

''You're not strong enough to lift it.''

''Are you?''

''Just barely.''

''That's fine. My car is waiting. You can carry it out and put it in the trunk.''

I shook my head. ''No dice, Blondie.''

''You'd rather have a bullet through your leg?''

''Any day,'' I said. ''Because some day the leg would heal, the bone would mend. And then I'd find you and I'd kill you. Nice and slow, then use your guts for shoe laces and your spine for a necktie rack.''

She smiled. ''Tough guy. We know all about you. I don't scare, Mr. Terris, but neither do you, unfortunately. Threatening you with personal injury is a waste of time. I told them that, but they wanted me to try it anyway. Well, I tried.''

Without taking her eyes off me, she raised her voice. ''Stephan. Gregory. Come here.''

Two men, one large and bull-necked and with a face like a dropped melon, the other slim and white-faced and black-eyed, appeared in the doorway behind her. Both held guns in their right hands.

''Mr. Terris refuses to frighten, gentlemen,'' the girl said. ''Go up and get Mrs. Terris. Tie and gag her and put her in the car. Let me know when you're ready to leave.''

They turned silently and started out. I said, ''Hold it.'' They kept on going. I said, ''Call off your dogs, Sadie.''

Her quiet voice stopped them as though they'd run into a wall. Her confident smile revealed flawless teeth. ''Yes, Mr. Terris?''

''There is no machine. There never was.''

Her smile now was almost sad. ''Lies won't help. In fact, I'm surprised you even bother to try them on me.''

''I mean it, Sadie. The first time I heard about my having a machine was ten days ago. Two men broke into my apartment in New York and demanded I hand 'the machine' over to them. You may have read about it in the papers.''

The gun in her hand stayed as steady as Mount Hood. ''Yes. You killed them both. With your bare hands, I believe—or was that just tabloid talk?''

"No."

"They were bunglers, Mr. Terris. I am not. Do you give us what we came for, or do we take your wife instead?"

My muscles began to ache from the strain of not jumping straight into the muzzle of her gun. "I'm telling you, Sadie: there is no machine. Somebody's given you a bum steer."

Her sigh was small but unmistakable. "Fifty-three days ago," she said, "you arrived in New York aboard a small steamer which you chartered at Dakar. This was almost exactly two years after your small plane crashed somewhere in the interior of French Equatorial Africa while you were searching for a uranium deposit in that section of the continent. Your government combed the area for weeks without finding any trace of your plane, and you were given up for lost. Am I correct so far?"

"The newspapers carried the story," I said.

"Your arrival in New York," she went on in the same even, unhurried voice, "created a major sensation. The country's richest, handsomest, most eligible bachelor had returned from the dead! Only the bachelor part no longer applied: you had brought back as your bride the world's most beautiful woman. I believe that's how she was described—although no one has been able to see her face clearly through the heavy veil she constantly wears. In fact, no one but you knows what your wife looks like. True, Mr. Terris?"

I shrugged and said nothing.

"You then placed your bride in the penthouse suite of a building you owned in Manhattan. You engaged no servants; you had no callers. No one—I repeat, *no one*—was permitted to enter your apartment. You were called to Washington to report on the success of your search for the uranium deposit. You stated that your mission was a failure. As a loyal and patriotic citizen—as well as one of the wealthiest—your statement was accepted and the matter closed."

She paused to raise an eyebrow at me meaningly. "Closed, that is, until two weeks ago. For it was about that time that a man and his wife were found dead in a small hotel in Nice. The cause of death was so startling that an immediate investigation was made. Do you know what killed those two people, Mr. Terris?"

"Measles?" I hazarded.

Her jaw hardened. "Radiation, Mr. Terris. A kind of radiation sickness not known before. Those two people died of cosmic radiation!"

"Do tell!"

She took a slow breath and her eyes bored into me. "Further investigation established that the dead couple had been exposed to the radiation roughly five weeks earlier. At that time they were occupying a cabin on a small steamer en route to Sweden. By a strange coincidence, Mr. Terris, it was the same steamer that brought you and your wife to America a few days before. By an even stranger coincidence, they had occupied the same cabin used by you and your wife. But the ultimate in coincidences, Mr. Terris, is that you had been in Africa in search of a fissionable material!"

"As you've pointed out," I said, "a matter of coincidence."

She shook her head. "I'm afraid it's not that simple. The inescapable conclusion is that, while in Africa, you discovered some method of trapping and converting the power of cosmic radiation. Either you found some natural substance that would do this, or—more likely—you were able to construct a machine that would do so. The residue from some leakage in the machine's operation was picked up by the unfortunate couple who next engaged that cabin, causing their deaths."

"No machine," I said. "I don't know what you're talking about. Go ahead. Search the house. But tell your goons to keep their hands off my wife. I mean it."

She wasn't listening. "Any country, Mr. Terris, who controls the secret you've learned will own the earth. As usual, your own government has only just learned the facts as I have given them to you. I happen to know that within a few days you'll be summoned to Washington and asked for the secret you hold. My government wants it instead—and we mean to have it!"

"If I had anything like what you're talking about," I said, "why wouldn't I have turned it over to Washington before this?"

She smiled. "I think I can answer that. It's well known that you are against war—that you narrowly escape being called a pacifist. To turn this secret over to the military of your government might very well lead to war."

"And in the hands of *your* government?"

"Peace, Mr. Terris. Peace because no other country or coalition of countries could prevail against us. Universal adherence to the principles of true democracy—the people's democracy."

"You mean communism, Sadie?"

"Exactly."

"Love that people's democracy," I said. "Slave labor, purges, secret police, rigged trials, mass executions. Good-bye, Sadie. Sorry, no machines today."

"You prefer that we take your wife?"

"A word of advice," I said. "Keep your nail polish off my wife. Otherwise I'll spend the rest of my life and forty million dollars, if it takes that long and that much, finding you and your stooges. And when I do, I'll be judge, jury and executioner. You'll die like no one ever died before."

My words were just words, but my tone and my expression were something else again. The color faded in her cheeks and the gun barrel wavered slightly. But her smile was steady enough and faintly mocking.

"I think you mean that," she said quietly. Her free hand moved up and settled the mink jacket closer about her flawless shoulders. "But I've learned long since to pay no attention to threats. . . . Last opportunity. Do you hand over what we came for."

"You talk American real good, Sadie. They must have fine schools in Leningrad."

Her lips twitched. "Westchester, Mr. Terris. And one of the best finish—" She stopped abruptly and all expression faded from her lovely face. "Where is the machine?"

I spread my hands. "You're slipping your clutch, Blondie. No machine. I told you that."

Her patience began to break up. "You fool!" she blazed. "You're actually going to hand us your wife rather than surrender it? You're as cold-blooded as a snake, Mr. Terris!"

"You can call me Karl," I said.

She stepped back and nodded to the two men behind her. They came forward cautiously, guns ready, circled until they were behind me. I went on looking at the blonde, memorizing every line of her face, the lobes of her ears, the curve of her nostrils, the shape of her eyes. Suddenly the muzzle of a gun ground savagely into my back and a hand closed firmly on one of my naked arms. Before I could twist away the needle of a hypodermic lanced into my shoulder, the plunger thudded down and I staggered back.

I stood there panting, still staring at the girl. I could feel my lips curl back in a strained rictus of hatred. A buzzing sound began to crawl into my ears.

"It had better finish me, Sadie," I said around my thickening tongue.

"If I come through this, you'll feed five generations of worms."

She was leaning slightly forward, her eyes glittering, the tip of her tongue touching her parted lips, her breathing quick and shallow, watching the drug take hold of me. The gun in her hand was forgotten.

I tried to lift an arm. Somebody had tied an anvil to it. The City Hall was glued to my feet. The room clouded, wavered, then slowly dissolved. I fell face forward into the ruins. . . .

II

A voice said, "You made two mistakes, Sadie. You let me see your face and you said too much. Just a little too much, but enough."

It was my voice. I was talking out loud, coming out of it. I opened my eyes and rolled over and looked at the ceiling. Back of my eyes somebody had built a fire and left the ashes.

After a while I tried getting to my feet. It seemed to take a long time, but I finally made it. I stood there holding onto the back of a chair and let my eyes move around the room.

Sunlight was fighting to get in through the half-closed Venetian blinds at the two windows. The man I had shot earlier was still dead on the floor, with a pool of almost black blood under what was left of his head. The vault door stood wide open with its contents scattered. The rest of the room had the look of being worked over by a platoon of Marines armed with bayonets. Upholstery had been ripped to shreds, pictures were torn from the walls, drapes were piled in one corner, bookcases had been cleared ruthlessly.

Anger began to rise inside me. I crossed to the ruins of the small bar in one corner of the room, found a bottle of bourbon and drank a solid slug of the contents. The stuff almost put me back on the floor, but when the first shock passed my brain was working again.

I went up the stairs at a wavering run. The bedroom door stood open and Lodi was gone. The room itself was as much a shambles as the study downstairs, and the rest of the house was no better.

"It's all right, Lodi," I muttered. "They won't dare harm you. They'll wait a couple of days for me to get good and worried, then they'll get in touch with me and try to make a deal. Only I'm not going to wait that long."

In the kitchen I ate toast and drank four cups of scalding black coffee.

Then I went back into the study and picked up the phone and called a number in the Lenox Hill section of New York City.

"Eddie? Karl. Now get this. I want all year books for the past ten years put out by all the finishing schools on the East Coast. Have them in your office two hours from now. . . . How the hell do I know? You've got an organization; put it to work. As fast as they come in put people to work going through them to pick out every girl who lived in Westchester County at the time she was attending school. The girl I want is around twenty-five or twenty-six, so tell them to keep that in mind. You've got two hours, and I don't want any excuses."

I slammed down the receiver while he was still talking and looked around for the gun I had dropped on the rug the night before. It was still there, half buried under papers from the vault. I went back upstairs to shave, bathe and dress, then found a shoulder holster for the .45 and slid my suit coat on over it.

I walked out the front door and down the driveway. It was getting on toward ten o'clock and the sun was hot on my shoulders. In the valley a mile down the slope was the nearest highway to New York. Cars and trucks moved along the concrete ribbon, looking like ants on a garden path.

My convertible was where I had left it the day before. I was checking the tires when the sound of an engine coming up the gravel road to the house froze me. I stepped behind the car and unbuttoned my coat and waited.

A gray Plymouth turned into the highway and stopped and a man in his early thirties got out from behind the wheel. There was no one else in the car. He saw me standing there, nodded and started toward me without hurrying. He wasn't anyone I knew.

When he was about twenty feet away I slid my hand under the left lapel of my jacket and said, "That's close enough, friend."

He stopped abruptly and stared at my right arm, a puzzled look on his smooth, not unhandsome face. "I'm afraid I don't understand this. Are you Mr. Terris?"

"That's right."

"I'd like a word with you."

"Sure," I said. "What word would you like?"

He smiled crookedly. "I wish you'd take your hand out of there, Mr. Terris. It gives me the feeling you're about to pull a gun on me."

"That," I said, "is the general idea. Just who the hell are you?"

He kept his hands carefully away from his body. "The name is Granger, Mr. Terris. I'm an agent with the Federal Bureau of Investigation. Would you like to see my credentials?"

"Not especially," I said. "What is it you want?"

He laughed shortly. "Well, to put it bluntly—you! It seems there's a Congressional committee meeting in Washington this afternoon and they want you there. The AEC, to be exact. I was asked to come up and—ah—escort you there."

I recalled that the blonde had said something about that a few hours earlier. Whatever her pipeline, it certainly was reliable. I shook my head. "Sorry, Mr. Granger. I won't be able to make it. Another engagement—a rather pressing one. Good-bye."

He wasn't smiling now. "Afraid you don't understand, sir. I have a subpoena calling for your appearance at that hearing."

"That's different," I said. I took my hand from under my coat and walked over to him. "Can I give you some breakfast before we leave?"

Granger eyed me warily. "No, thanks. I've had breakfast. We'd better be getting into New York. We're catching a twelve-o'clock plane. I suppose you'll want to pack a bag."

"Good idea," I said and turned and started back to the house with him beside me. We went up on the porch and through the front door. Granger took one look at the wreckage from last night's activities and his jaw dropped. "What hap—"

That was as far as he got before the edge of my hand caught him sharply on the back of the neck. He folded like a carpenter's rule, out cold. I caught him before he hit the floor and carried him into the living room. I found some strong cord in the kitchen and bound his hands behind him and his feet to the legs of the couch, careful not to cut off the circulation.

He opened his eyes while I was finishing up. "You're making a serious mistake, Mr. Terris."

I tightened the last knot and straightened up. "You won't be too uncomfortable. Mrs. Morgan, the cleaning woman, should show up about two this afternoon and she'll cut you loose. Incidentally, you'll find a body in the study. My work; I'll tell you about it some day."

I was out the front door before he could protest further. The convertible came alive under my foot and I roared down the curving gravel side-road to where it joined the highway.

III

At eleven-thirty-six I pulled into the curb in front of an office building on Madison Avenue in the Seventies. I rode the elevator to the ninth floor and entered the first door to a suite that took up most of one corridor. The legend on that door read "Edward Treeglos, Investments." The only investment involved was the money I invested to keep the place staffed and functioning. I had set it up, under the management of Eddie Treeglos, a former college friend of mine, five years before, at the time I came into the vast holdings from my father's estate. Its purpose was to handle matters too confidential to be taken care of by the mammoth organization, further downtown, known as The Terris Foundation.

I passed the receptionist before she could get her nose out of a magazine, and charged into Eddie's private office without bothering to knock.

He was behind his desk, his sharp-featured intelligent face bent over a pile of thin, outsize volumes bound in everything from leather to glossy stock. He looked up as I came in.

"Did you know," he said, "that four out of every ten girls attending finishing school on the East Coast come from Westchester County?"

I said, "When I want percentages I'll ask for them. What have you got?"

He gestured toward the pile of volumes. "Help yourself, playboy. The pages with Westchester babes are marked, and I've got six girls in the other offices going through more books. If I never see a sweet innocent school-girl face again it'll be fine with me."

At one o'clock I was still going strong, flipping pages, scanning face after face, as many as thirty to a page. One of the office girls brought in sandwiches and coffee; they cooled and were finally taken away without my even noticing them.

Slowly my hopes were beginning to dim. Maybe that blonde was cleverer than I had supposed. Her seemingly careless remark might have been a deliberate plant to throw me off the track. If so, she was too good for her job; she should have been the head of the entire Russian M.V.B. And then, just when I was about ready to sweep the books to the floor with rage, I spotted the face I was hunting for.

I came close to missing it entirely. She wore her hair different then and her face was fuller. But the angle to her nose and the high cheek bones and the slope of her jaw were unmistakable. She stared up at me from the glossy paper, the eyes wide and direct, the same faint curl to her lips. *Do you find the evening oppressively warm, Mr. Terris?*

Under the photo were several lines of type. They told me her name was Ann Fullerton, that she lived at 327 Old Colony Drive, Larchmont, New York, that she was a political science major. She belonged to a swank sorority, was vice-president of her senior class and had been mixed up in a lot of campus activities that probably would make fascinating reading for her children—if she lived long enough to have any.

My eyes went back to the mocking smile. "Laugh, baby," I muttered. "Laugh while you can. Your belly will make me a fine dart board."

Across the desk, Eddie stared at me open-mouthed. "Take it slow, pal. You sound like a goddam tax collector."

I ripped the page out, shoved a pile of the books to the floor and pulled the phone over in front of me. "Tell the help to forget it. I've found what I'm after."

"Sure, sure. You feel like telling me what's going on?"

"Next week," I said. "You got a Westchester phone directory?"

He shrugged, reached out and flipped a lever on the intercom and told the receptionist to bring one in. I leafed through the Fullertons and found an Eric Fullerton living at the same address in Larchmont shown on the page from the year book. I dialed the number.

"Fullerton residence," a man's voice said.

I made my voice brisk and business-like. "Is this Mr. Fullerton?"

"Mr. Fullerton is not in, sir. Caldwell, the butler, speaking. Is there a message?"

"I'll talk to Ann Fullerton," I said.

The silence at the other end lasted long enough to be shocked. ". . . . I'm afraid there's some mistake, sir. Miss Ann Fullerton died almost a year ago."

"*What!*"

"Yes, sir."

I got my chin up off my necktie. "Look—uh, Caldwell. Is Mrs. Fullerton there?"

"Yes, sir. Who shall I say is calling?"

"My name is . . . Carney. Alan Carney."

"One moment, Mr. Carney."

The receiver went down and I lit a cigarette, getting over the shock.

There wasn't the slightest chance that the girl in the year book and the girl who had held a gun on my a few hours before were not one and the same. I had studied her face much too carefully to be mistaken.

A quiet voice said, "This is Mrs. Fullerton."

I said, "I hate to bother you, Mrs. Fullerton. I had no idea, of course, that your daughter . . ."

"I understand, Mr. Carney."

"You see, it's very important that I get in touch with a former friend of Ann's. A girl named . . . Taylor—Mollie Taylor. I wonder if you could tell me anything about her."

"I'm afraid not, Mr. Carney." Her voice sounded flat, almost weary. "You see, I didn't know Ann's friends. She hadn't lived with us for nearly two years before her death."

I said, "Would you mind giving me her address at the time? It's just possible somebody there could help me."

"We never knew her address, Mr. Carney. Ann was employed by an importing company. Anton & Porkov, I believe it was called."

"In New York?"

"Yes. I don't know the street address."

I wrote the name on a pad. "You've been very patient, Mrs. Fullerton. I know how painful all this has been for you. But would you mind telling me the circumstances of your daughter's death?"

There was a lengthy pause during which I expected her quietly to hang up the receiver. When she finally did speak I could barely hear her. "Ann died in a warehouse fire. I'm afraid that's all I can tell you. Good-bye, Mr. Carney."

A dry click told me the connection had been broken. I hung up and sat there staring at my thumb. All I had to do now was find a girl who had died months before, but who last night had engineered the kidnaping of my wife. Lodi's secret was now known to at least three people other than me. I should never have taken her out of Africa. I thought of her in the hands of those two silent ghouls and the blonde and a cold fury shook me. The mere fact that they had discovered what was behind Lodi's veil meant they must die. How they would die would depend on how they had treated her.

Eddie Treeglos was watching me wide-eyed. I tripped the lever on the intercom and said to the receptionist, "Get me the street address of Anton & Porkov, importers." I closed the key and leaned back in my chair and looked at Eddie through the smoke of my cigarette. "Does that name—

Anton & Porkov—mean anything to you?''

"Can't say it does."

"My wife was snatched last night, Eddie."

"We'll get her back, Karl."

"Yes," I said. "Yes, we'll get her back." I got up and walked across the office and slapped my hand hard against the wall. For no reason. I turned and came back to the desk just as the intercom buzzer sounded. I moved the key again. "Well?"

"There is a listing for Anton & Porkov at 774 West Thirty-first Street, sir. The phone number is Clinton 9-5444. Also a listing for Sergi Porkov at 917 East Sixty-eighth. Butterfield 4-6793. It's the only other Porkov in the book, so it may be the same man."

I wrote it all down and closed the line. "I want a full report on that outfit, Eddie. They're importers; Washington should give you a line on them. No direct inquiries; I don't want them to know they're being checked. You've got half an hour."

"You're the boss."

"Yeah." I tossed the page from the year book across the desk to him. "Ann Fullerton. Check the police files to learn if she's got a record. Call Osborne at the FBI and see if he's got anything on her. And anything else you think of."

"Right."

I moved my hand and the .45 was in it, pointed at him. All he did was blink. "Just finding out if I've still got the speed," I said.

He nodded. "I never even saw your hand move, brother."

"That's nice to know," I said. I picked up the slip with the addresses and phone numbers on it, folded it small and put it behind my display handkerchief. "I'll call you in half an hour. About Anton & Porkov."

"Okay."

I gave him a brief nod and walked over to the door and out.

IV

I stopped off at the Roosevelt Hotel and had lunch in the Men's Grill, then supplied myself with a handful of change and entered one of the phone booths. I put through a person-to-person call to Senator McGill at the Senate Building in Washington. My father had put him in office almost sixteen years before, and kept him there. When you own between forty and fifty million bucks in one form and another you need a loud voice where it can be heard.

His secretary told him who was calling and he came on the wire very excited. "Karl, you young idiot, are you trying to ruin me?"

"That's what I like about you, Senator," I said. "Always worrying about your friends rather than yourself."

"Oh, stop it! Have you any idea what the penalty is for attacking a Federal officer?"

"How did he work it so fast?" I asked. "I figured Mrs. Morgan would be untieing him about now. What's behind all this subpoena business anyway?"

His voice was desperate. "You're in trouble, boy. The AEC says you lied about not getting anything useful out of Africa. They have good reason to think you came out of there with some kind of gadget to do with cosmic energy, whatever the hell that is. You better get down here and straighten things out before it's too late."

"Nuts to that," I said. "I got something a lot more important to take care of. Get them to call off their dogs."

His voice went up four octaves. "You think I'm the President? Not only does the AEC want you for questioning, but you're charged with attacking an FBI man and committing a murder! You grab a plane and get out here in nothing flat. Demarest of the Attorney General's office called me not more than half an hour ago and said they were getting out a general alarm to have you picked up."

"Get it cancelled."

"I tell you I can't! What's more, they've issued a subpoena for your wife. Word's gotten around she's the one who gave you that gadget, and this business of her going around heavily veiled, no one ever seeing what she looks like, is beginning to look mighty suspicious."

"You think I give a damn how it looks? I'm telling you, get these alphabet boys out of my hair. Or are you tired of being a senator?"

"Don't you threaten me, you young upstart! I was making laws in this country while you were still soiling diapers. My record—"

"Stick your record," I cut in. "You get that general alarm withdrawn and those subpoenas held up or I'll plaster the darker side of your precious record over the front pages of every newspaper in the country."

He was still sputtering when I slammed down the receiver. I went into the Rough Rider Room at the Roosevelt and had a couple of bourbons to settle my lunch and get the taste of politicians out of my mouth. My strapwatch showed 2:10. I went out into the hot sun and slid behind the wheel of the convertible and drove through a blue fog of exhaust fumes until I reached the 700 block on West Thirty-first.

It was a crummy neighborhood. Ancient loft buildings and sagging tenements and fly-specked delicatessens and cut-rate liquor stores and wise punks hanging around corner taverns. It stunk of dirt and poverty, with an occasional whiff of stale water and dead fish from the Hudson River a block to the west. A puff of tired air moved through the littered gutters and blew dust in my face.

I parked behind a truck half a block from 774 and waded through dirty-faced brats and sloppy-breasted housewives until I reached a corner drugstore. There were a couple of phone booths at the rear and I called Eddie Treeglos from one of them.

"What've you got, Eddie?"

"A thing or two. One, Sergi Porkov, alias Sam Parks, is one of the top Russian agents in this country. At present he is reported to be somewhere in Mexico. He's a tall blond guy, in his early forties, looks like a Swedish diplomat—at least that's the way my source of information described him—and has three rather large pockmarks on his left cheek. Two, Maurice Anton, his former partner in the importing firm, died of cancer at Morningside General Hospital four months ago. At that time Porkov sold the importing business to a man named Luke Ritter; no record on him but he's suspected of being a front man for Porkov. That's it, Karl."

I breathed in some of the booth's odor of cheap cigars. "Anything on Ann Fullerton?"

"Yeah. Identified by a close friend as one of the victims of a fire nine months ago at a warehouse owned by the Fullbright Radio Company. Body was too badly burned for the parents to make a positive identification, but a purse under the body was hers. It was in the papers at the time."

"Who was the friend that made the I.D.?"

"Nobody seems to know. I'm working on it."

"Anything else on her?"

"Well, she was one of these college pinks. Carried banners on a couple of picket lines, belonged to several commie front outfits and so on. But right after she left school she dropped out of sight and nobody seems to have heard of her until she got too close to the fire. Except for one possible connection."

"Let's have it, Eddie."

"Here about eight, nine months ago, Sergi Porkov came up with a new girl friend—a knockout of a blonde named Arleen Farmer. The similarity in initials could mean something."

"You can bet on it," I said. "Got an address on her?"

"She was living with Porkov at the Sixty-eighth Street address."

"Nothing else?"

He sounded aggrieved. "My God, isn't that enough? You only gave me half an hour."

I cut him off, got out the list of addresses and phone numbers the girl at Eddie's had given me, and looked up Porkov's home phone. I stood there and listened to the buzz come back over the wire. No answer. I let it ring a dozen times before I decided that Anton & Porkov was the place to start.

I hung up and stopped at the cigar counter for cigarettes. Outside, the sun still baked the street. I walked slowly on down to 774, a loft building of battered red brick, four floors, with a hand laundry and a job printer flanking the entrance.

The lobby was narrow and had been swept out shortly before they built the Maginot Line. It smelled like toadstools in the rain, with a binder of soft-coal smoke held over from the previous winter.

A thin flat-faced kid with hornrimmed glasses and a mop of black hair was propped up on a backless kitchen chair outside a freight elevator, buried to the eyebrows in a battered copy of Marx's *Das Kapital*. I brought him out of it by kicking one of the chair legs.

"Fie on you," I said. "You ought to know that stuff's rank bourgois deviationism."

He looked up at me like a pained owl. He couldn't have been much past seventeen, if that. "I *beg* your pardon?"

"Now take Trotsky," I said. "There was a boy you could learn something from. Yes, *sir*. He had the right slant, that boy."

The kid's expression said he was smelling something stronger than toadstools. "Such as?" he snapped coldly.

"Search me. I'm a States Rights man myself." I indicated the cage. "How's about cranking this thing up to the fourth floor?"

He closed the book, leaving a finger in to mark his place. "Whom did you wish to see?"

"You figure on announcing me?"

He sighed, registering patience. "No, sir. That's the offices of Anton & Porkov. They're closed."

"This time of day? What will the stockholders say?"

He came close to saying what was on his mind, but changed it at the last moment. ''Mr. Ritter hasn't come back from lunch yet.''

''What about the rest of the help?''

''There is no one else, sir. Only Mr. Ritter.''

''Certainly no way to run a business. Where does Luke have lunch? At Chambord's?''

''No, sir. At the Eagle Bar & Grill. Around the corner, on Twelfth Avenue.''

I was turning away when he added: ''And for your information, sir, Leon Trotsky was a counter-revolutionary, a tool of Wall Street, a reactionary and a jerk. Good afternoon.''

I was halfway to Twelfth Avenue before I thought of an answer to that.

V

There was the smell of beer and steam-table cuisine, but not much light. I stepped inside and waited until my eyes adjusted to the dim interior. Four men were grouped at the bar discussing something with the man in the white apron, and further down the room another man in a crumpled seersucker suit sat at a small round table wolfing down a sandwich. A tired-looking blonde waitress was folding napkins in a booth at the rear of the room. I leaned across the bar and, during a sudden silence, beckoned to the apron. ''I'm looking for Mr. Ritter.''

A thumb indicated the man at the table. The silence continued while I walked back there and swung a chair around and sat down across from him. His head snapped up and I was looked at out of a pair of narrow dark eyes set in an uneven face that seemed mostly jaw.

''Mr. Ritter?''

''. . . What about it?''

I said, ''We can't talk here. Let's go up to your office.''

He said, 'Hah!'' and bit into his sandwich and put what was left of it down on the plate and leaned back and chewed slowly, with a kind of circular motion. ''What we got to talk about?''

''Not here,'' I said again. ''You never know who's listening.''

''I don't know you. What's your name?''

''My name wouldn't mean a thing to you, Mr. Ritter. Let's say I'm an old friend of Maurice Anton's.''

His jaws ground to a halt and for a moment he seemed not to be breathing. Then he took a slow careful breath and his hands slid off the table and dropped to his knees. "Maurice, hunh?" he grunted. "Well, well. And how is Maurice these days?"

"He hasn't been getting around much," I said. "They buried him four months ago."

He went on staring at me without expression. The waitress got out of the booth and carried the folded napkins over to the bar. Ritter brought up a hand and picked up the heavy water glass beside his plate and emptied it down his throat. When he set it down again he kept his stubby fingers around it.

"Like I said, mister," he growled, "I don't know you. You got something to say, say it here. Otherwise, beat it."

I lifted an eyebrow. "That's no way to talk to a customer, Luke. Let's go up to your office."

"Customer, hell! You smell like a cop to me!"

There was no point in wasting any more time. I moved my hand and the .45 was in it, down low, the muzzle resting on the edge of the table and pointed at him. "Your office, Ritter," I said very quietly.

His whole body twitched spasmodically, then seemed to freeze. Behind me the voices went on at the bar. Ritter's eyes were glued to the gun and his heavy jaw sagged slightly.

"You can stand up now," I murmured. "Then you walk on out the door and straight to 774. I'll be riding in your hip pocket all the way; one wrong move and you'll have bullets for dessert. Get going!"

He wet his lips, still staring at the gun, and started to get up—and an arm and a pair of female breasts came between us. That goddam waitress.

She got as far as "Will that be—?" before Ritter grabbed her with one hand and threw the water glass at my head with the other. I ducked in time, but my gun was useless with the girl between us. Glass broke, somebody cursed, the blonde screamed—and I moved.

I bent and grabbed Ritter's ankle and yanked. He fell straight back, taking the girl with him in a flurry of suntan stockings and white thighs. I tried shoving her aside to ram the .45 against Ritter's ribs, and he clawed out blindly, trying to hold her, caught the neckline of her apron and ripped it and the brassiere beneath completely away. This being July she had dressed for comfort; and any lingering doubt over her being a true blonde was gone forever.

The blonde let out a screech that rattled the glassware and tried to get out from under. Somebody plowed into me from behind and I rammed against her, both of us crashing down on Ritter. I lost the .45 when my hand hit a chair leg, and a second later I was buried under an avalanche of humanity.

Fists, feet and knees banged into me from all angles. I managed to turn on my back and draw my knees up, then snapped my feet into the barman's belly, like the handsome hero of a Western, and threw him halfway across the room into a pinball machine.

It let me get to my feet. Ritter was running for the door, the blonde was trying to crawl under a table, giving me ·a view of her I would never forget, and facing me were the four guys I had first seen at the bar.

No sound but heavy breathing. The screen door banged behind Ritter. The barman began slowly to untangle himself from the ruins of the pinball machine, like a fly pulling loose from a sheet of Tanglefoot.

I said, "Get the hell out of my way," and walked straight at the four of them. The one in front of me looked plenty tough. He put up his fists in the standard boxing position and came up on the balls of his feet and took a couple of dancing steps toward me. I said, "You looke a little pale to be Joe Louis," and slammed a hard right to his chin. He fell straight forward and I sidestepped and caught the next man by his belt and shirtfront and threw him into the pyramided bottles and mirror behind the bar. It sounded like Libby-Owens blowing up.

The remaining pair goggled at me and got out of the way. Not the barman, though. He took one look at the wreckage behind the bar, let out a bellow of rage and pain and charged me head-down. I stepped aside and put out my foot. He tripped and went sprawling into the booth where the blonde was crouched, landing squarely on top of her. I hoped they both would be very happy.

I scooped my gun off the floor and headed for the front door. Just as I got there a blue uniform pushed through a knot of spectators gathered outside and opened the screen. One of New York's finest—big and wide and handsome. He took one look at the gun in my fist and reached for his holster. I yelled and jumped forward and nailed him on the side of the jaw. The blow spun him in a limp circle and he fell halfway into an open phone booth. A few of the hardier members of the mob outside let out a yell and started to come in after me, but sight of the gun melted them like snow in Death Valley. I realized, however, that leaving by the front door would be foolish at best, and more than likely ruinous. That left the back way, if there was one, and I headed in that direction.

A swinging door let me into a combination store room and kitchen, with a bolted door off that. I shot the bolts and opened the door and stuck my head out for a cautious look around. A narrow alley, crowded with torn papers, overflowing garbage cans and bit fat blue-bottle flies buzzing in the hot sun. The stink would have taken top honors from a family of skunks, but it was nothing I couldn't live through.

Nobody in sight. I slid the gun back under my arm and trotted along the uneven bricks toward Eleventh Avenue, a block to the east, past loading platforms and the rear entrances to the buildings fronting on Thirty-first Street. Most of them had street numbers chalked up for the benefit of delivery men, and my mind was already made up by the time I reached 774.

A sagging wooden door with four glass panels, three of them broken, the fourth coated with dust and cobwebs. There had been a lock on it once, but that was a long time ago. I peered through one of the broken panes. A dim and dusty corridor led toward the front of the building, with a closed door at the far end.

There was no time for advance planning. Any moment now cops would be pouring into the alleyway with blood in their eyes and guns in their hands. I pushed the door open, getting a complaining groan from rusty hinges, closed it carefully behind me and went quickly along the passageway to the inner door. I listened for a long moment, heard nothing but the faraway mumble of traffic, then turned the knob and gave it a small even tug. The door swung toward me an inch or two and I put an eye to the crack.

He was still there, no more than twenty feet away, in exactly the same position, still gulping down Marx and looking as though it agreed with him.

And between us, in the same wall as the elevator, was the entrance to the building stairs.

As a cause for rejoicing it left a good deal to be desired. Getting to those stairs without the kid seeing me depended on just how strong a hold Marx had on him. Three or four steps would get me there, but the door had to be opened as well, not to mention the one I was standing behind. Of course, I could always shove my gun in his back, tie and gag him and dump him behind something, and use the elevator. But it would be a hell of a lot better to leave him undisturbed in case the cops came snooping around hunting for me.

I took another minute to study the kid's position. He was facing three quarters away from me, one shoulder propped against the wall, head bent over the book. To see me at all he would have to turn his head halfway around. No reason for him to turn his head unless I stumbled over my feet on the way.

It went off without a hitch. I was across the open stretch of hall and through the stairway door and had it closed again and my back against it within the space of six heartbeats. Now that it was over with, I had the feeling I could have driven an oil truck past the kid without his knowing it.

I climbed the three flights, found the door at the top unlocked and stepped into the hot dry air of a narrow hall with office doors, closed, lining both walls. None of the frosted glass panels had legends painted on them until I got down to the far end of the corridor. Three of the doors there, side by side, had the words "Anton & Porkov—Importers" painted on them in black, with the additional word "Entrance" on the one in the center.

I was standing there eyeing the center door and wondering if the thing to do was knock first, when a telephone suddenly shrilled behind the door on the left. I froze. A second ring broke off in the middle and the heavy voice of Luke Ritter said, "Yeah? . . . Not yet, no. . . . Any minute now. He was due in from Mexico City two hours ago. . . . I doubt it, Max. I called her but nobody answered. She probably met the plane. . . . I'll be right here."

The sound of a phone going back into its cradle. Some more silence behind the door. Then a chair creaked and another voice said, "That eye don't look any too good, Luke." It was a light, smooth voice, almost feminine.

"It hurts like hell," Ritter growled. "I'd like to get my hands on that bastard for about one minute. One minute's all I'd need!"

"You make him for a cop?"

"Naw. A cop would've pushed his badge at me. I figure him for a private dick trying to get a line on Porkov. He'll hear about it when he calls me."

"Any chance of the guy showing up here?"

A dry short laugh. "I sure as hell hope so, brother. The minute he walks into the lobby, the punk downstairs will ring our private buzzer. That's all the notice I want!"

I went on down to the third of the three doors marked Anton & Porkov and tried the knob. Locked. Nothing was easy for me today. This was an old door, fitting the frame loosely after many years. I reached in behind my display handkerchief and got out the nail file I carried there. It was thin enough for my purpose; I hoped it would be long enough. By pressing the knob hard away from the jamb I was able to slip the point of the file against the slope of the spring lock. It moved slightly, then snapped back with a light, almost inaudible, click. I opened the door. Nothing moved inside. I stepped through and closed it tenderly behind me.

It was a large square room, dim in the afternoon light filtering through a single unwashed window. Heavy wooden packing cases were stacked to the ceiling in two of the corners. A roll-top desk held a clutter of invoices, bills and loose papers. A communicating door was unlocked and I passed through it into the center office. This one held metal files, a desk with a typewriter on the shelf, several chairs, a washstand behind a black lacquered screen in one corner. I could smell dust and, very faintly, a touch of cologne. Another door, closed, led to the first office, with the murmur of voices straining through it.

I went over to it, making sure my shadow wouldn't appear on the pebbled glass. The voices went on mumbling. The .45 came out, cool and comforting against my palm. I began a slow turning of the doorknob, the way they take the fuse out of a blockbuster. The door gave just enough to tell me what I wanted to know.

I slammed it all the way open with a hard movement of my knee and said, "Merry Christmas, you sons-a-bitches!"

That was as far as I got. Luke Ritter was behind a desk, tilted back in a swivel chair and looking at me with a twisted grin. He was alone. Even as I realized he couldn't be alone, something swished through the air behind me and the room exploded into a pain-filled void of stars. I felt myself falling as from a great height, then the stars were gone and nothing was left.

VI

Water trickled down my face and under my collar. I swam up from the depths into a pale green world of twisted shapes. Another wave of water poured over me and I sneezed suddenly, sending a lance of pain through my head.

I opened my eyes. I was flat on my back. Up above me floated a pair of pale balloons with grotesque faces painted on them. I blinked a time or two before my eyes focused, and then the balloons were faces after all.

The familiar undershot jaw, slept-in features and dark eyes belonged to
Luke Ritter; but the other was a pale cameo of delicate perfection, the face
of a dreamer, a poet, a faerie prince. Eyes of azure blue widened appealingly, perfect lips parted to show beautiful teeth and a voice like muted
viol strings said, "You want I should rough him up some more, Luke?"

"You did fine, Nekko," Ritter said. He drew back his foot and slammed his toe into my ribs. "All right, snoop. Up you go."

I rolled over and got both knees and one hand under me and tried to
stand up. My head weighed a ton and was as tender as a ten-dollar steak.
A hand came down and took hold of my hair and lifted me three feet in
the air. The pain almost caused me to black out a second time. The edge
of a chair hit me under the knees and I sat down, hard. The room moved
around a time or two, then lurched to a stop. It looked only slightly better
that way.

I could see my gun over on a corner of the desk, much too far away to
reach by any sudden move on my part. Ritter gave me a cold smile and
went around behind the desk and sat down in the swivel chair. He reached
out, lifted the .45 by its trigger guard, swung it idly back and forth between thumb and forefinger and looked at me over it.

"You're kind of a secretive guy, mister," he grumbled. "I kind of went
through your wallet while you were sleeping. Some money, but no identification. Just who the aching Jesus you supposed to be?"

"The name's Trotsky," I said. "My friends call me Cutie-pie."

Ritter stopped swinging the gun and lifted a corner of his lip. "Nekko,"
he said quietly.

A small hard fist came out of nowhere and hit me under the right eye. It
hurt, but not enough to get excited about. I turned my head far enough to
look at the beautiful young man called Nekko. I said, "Hello, honey.
How're the boys down at the Turkish bath?"

His flawless complexion turned scarlet. He lashed out at me again but I
moved my head quickly and he missed. He tried again, instantly, but his
rage made him careless and he got too close to me. I lifted my foot hard
and caught him squarely in the crotch. He screamed like a woman and fell
over a chair.

Ritter bounded to his feet, came quickly around the desk and hit me
high on the cheek with a straight left. No one had ever hit me harder in
my life. My chair went over backwards with me in it. The back of my
head hit the carpet and the light from the desk lamp blurred in my eyes.

Ritter, his mouth twisting in a snarl, followed me down, trying to hit me again, this time with the gun. I took a glancing blow on the shoulder and grabbed the gun hand and tried to bite it off at the wrist. He slammed a fist into my throat and I vomited against the front of my shirt. That was when I got the barrel of the .45 behind my left ear and I went to sleep again. . . .

When I opened my eyes I was back in the same chair. Ritter was over behind the desk mopping his shirt front with a wet handkerchief and swearing in a monotonous undertone that sounded like the buzz of a rattler. Nekko sat in a straight-backed chair tilted against the wall. His azure eyes stared at me with distilled hate through a veil of blue cigarette smoke. A good deal more important was the shortbarrelled .32 revolver he was holding against his thigh.

My head felt like a busted appendix and my throat wasn't any improvement. I sat there and caught up on my breathing and thought bitter thoughts. The room was ominously quiet.

Ritter finally threw the handkerchief savagely into a wastebasket and lifted his eyes to me. "Let's try it again," he snarled. "Give me your name."

"Take it," I said. "I can always get another."

"You come busting in here with a gun, smart guy. All I got to do is call in the cops and you end up behind bars."

"Ha ha," I said.

He stood up casually and came over to me and swung the back of his hand against my face. I rolled with the blow but that didn't help much. I tried to kick him in the shin but missed and it earned me another belt in the face. I felt my teeth cut into the inner surface of my cheek and the salt taste of blood filled my mouth.

Nekko slid out of his chair and jabbed the .32 against the back of my neck. Ritter bent down until his face was inches from mine. His breath was the reason they'd invented chlorophyll.

"Your name, you son of a bitch!"

I spat a mouthful of blood squarely into his eyes. He bellowed like a branded bull and swung a punch that started from the floor. Even though Nekko's gun was boring into my neck I jerked my head aside. The fist whistled past my ear and knocked Nekko's gun clear across the room.

It was my chance—maybe the last one I'd get. Before Ritter could recover his balance I slammed a shoulder into his gut and knocked him across the desk. Nekko was already across the room, bending to pick up the gun. I picked up the chair and threw it. It caught him in the ribs and spun him against a filing case. I jumped for the gun, snatched it up and turned, just as Nekko, his small white even teeth gleaming behind a crazed snarl, sprang at me. I took one step back and hammered the gun barrel full into his half-open mouth. He sprayed broken teeth like a fountain and his scream was half gurgle from the blood filing his mouth. He staggered back a few steps clutching his face, then collapsed into a sobbing heap.

I wheeled, just in time to see Ritter leveling my own gun at me from the opposite side of the desk. The look on his face told me he meant to blast me down and worry about the consequences afterward.

The .32 jumped in my hand with a spiteful *crack*. A red flower seemed to blossom under Ritter's left eye. The .45 dropped from his extended hand and bounced once on the blotter. Ritter turned in a slow half circle, took a wavering step going nowhere, then fell like the First National Bank.

I stood there, listening. Doors didn't slam, no feet came running down the hall, no one yelled for the police. Evidently the rest of the fourth floor was deserted, and from any place else that single shot could have been the slamming of a distant door or the filtered backfire from a car. The only sound was the bubbling sobs from the crumpled and no longer beautiful man known as Nekko.

I went behind the desk and looked at Ritter. He was as dead as Diogenes. I picked up the .45 and slipped it back under my arm and came back to where Nekko lay. Picking him up was like picking up a bucket of mush. I flopped him into a chair and took a handful of his wavy blond hair and shook him.

"Arleen Farmer," I said. "Where do I find her?"

His mouth dripped crimson like a fresh wound. The shattered stumps of teeth winked through the red. A vague mumble ground its way into the open. His eyes were completely mad.

I gave his head another shake. "Arleen Farmer," I said again. "Where is she?" I slapped him across the face and wiped the blood on his coat. "Talk, damn you!"

". . . do'n'know . . ."

I hit him squarely in the nose. More blood spurted. His eyes rolled up and he fell off the chair. I kicked him full in the mouth. Even the stumps went this time. I tore off his necktie and bound his hands behind his back and left him lying there. My only hope was to find an address book that might give me additional leads to the kidnapers of my wife.

I stepped over what was left of Luke Ritter and started through the desk drawers. I was halfway through the junk in the center one when the phone rang.

VII

I stood there staring at the phone under the cone of light from the desk lamp. It rang a second time before I reached out and took up the receiver. "Yeah," I said, trying to pitch my voice to the same dull rumble I'd heard Ritter use.

A soft feminine drawl came over the wire. "Luke? Did Max call you?"

My fingers tightened against the hard rubber and my lips pulled back into an aching grimace. It was the voice of the blonde responsible for snatching my wife. I fought down a wave of pure fury and said, "Yeah. A while ago."

"All right," the soft voice went on. "When he calls back, tell him Sergi wants the woman brought to his apartment at ten o'clock tonight. Use the rear entrance and the service elevator. Got it?"

"Yeah."

"That's all." A click at the other end told me I was alone.

I put down the instrument with slow care, suddenly aware that my hands were shaking slightly. Ten o'clock. I looked at my strapwatch. Six hours yet. Either I had to find out just who this "Max" was and where he had my wife, or I must wait all those hours before I could do anything about getting her back.

A liquid groan reached my ears from across the room. I looked up in time to see Nekko moving weakly on the floor like a dying insect. I walked over and caught him by the collar and yanked him to his feet. "Last chance, sweetheart," I said. "Where do I find Max?"

He hung there, his eyes glazed, his mouth slack, and said nothing. I brought up the .32 and raked the sight across one cheek, laying it open to the bone. "Give, damn you! Where do I find Max?"

Pain took the vacant look from his eyes and brought a groan from his tortured lungs. The battered lips writhed, forming words that were too faint and indistinct for me to interpret. I put my ear close to his mouth. "Tell me again."

". . . warehouse . . . full . . . radio . . ."

Bright blood came spilling from his mouth and he went slack in my grasp. I stared at the blood, realizing it was arterial blood. Something had given way inside of him from the treatment he had taken; perhaps a broken rib had punctured a lung as the result of his being hit by the thrown chair.

He died in my hands. I let the body slip to the floor and went back to the desk. Nekko's last words had been too vague to be useful. "A warehouse full of radios" could have meant anything. I tackled the desk again, looking for a lead.

At the end of half an hour I had gone through those three offices as thoroughly as it is possible to go through anything. No file of private phone numbers, no personal papers of any kind. Only a lot of bills of lading, invoices, etc., on miscellaneous merchandise being shipped abroad.

I was at the washbasin in the center office when the phone rang again. Before it could ring a second time I was in there and lifting the receiver. I took a slow breath and said, "Max?"

"Yeah, Luke." Nothing distinctive about the voice. "You hear from Porkov?"

"Bring her to his apartment. Ten tonight." I tried desperately to think of a question that would help me and not make him suspicious. The slightest doubt in his mind could ruin everything. But before I could come up with something, the voice said, "Check," and I was holding a dead wire.

I returned to the center office and looked at my face in the mirror over the washbasin. There was a bruise on my right cheek and a slight discoloration under one eye. I rinsed the taste of blood from my mouth, washed a few evil-smelling spots from my coat lapel and went back to wipe fingerprints off the furniture and the file cabinets. The two dead men lay where they had fallen. Sight of the man called Nekko brought his words back to me. "Warehouse full of radios." It was entirely possible that Lodi was being held in some warehouse, but the fact that there were radios in that warehouse was no help at all.

A faint memory nagged at the back of my brain. Somewhere in Nekko's last words was a key—a key that tied in with a piece of information I had picked up during the day. I went over it again, word by word. "Warehouse" . . . a blank. "Full" . . . just as blank. "Radios" . . . I frowned. Was it "radios" or "radio"? All right, so it was one radio. That made no more sense than—

And then the missing piece fell into place. Eddie Treeglos had told me earlier in the day that Ann Fullerton had died in a fire at a radio company—the *Full*bright Radio Company!

I grabbed the Manhattan telephone directory and leafed through to the right page. No listing for Fullbright Radio. The classified directory drew the same blank. But there had to be a—wait! The company was supposed to have burned out; the fire that had "killed" Ann Fullerton.

I dialed Eddie Treeglos. "Eddie, that Fullbright Radio outfit you told me about. I can't find them listed in the latest phone books. See what you can find. I'll hang on."

He came back almost immediately. "1220 Huber Street. A few blocks below Canal Street. 1220 would be damn near in the Hudson River."

I put back the receiver, used my handkerchief to wipe away the prints and went out into the corridor. Nobody around. I took the stairs to the third floor, stopped off there and rang for the elevator. The moment I heard the heavy door clang shut on the first floor, I trotted down the steps. The cage was still up there when I went out the front door to the street.

My watch showed the time as 4:45 and the sun was still high and still hot. I walked back through the heat and the stink to where I had left the convertible. It was still there and still intact. Considering the neighborhood, it could have been otherwise. I got in and drove on down to Huber Street.

VIII

It was a small narrow building of ancient red brick crammed in between a cold storage warehouse and a moving and van outfit. The front entrance was boarded up and the smoke-grimed bricks told the story. A wooden sign below the broken second-floor windows read: Fullbright Radio Corp. It looked about ready to fall into the street.

I drove on by and turned the corner. Halfway along was the entrance to an alley. I parked well above it and got out. Sunlight glittered on the river's oily swell across the way. A pair of piers jutted out into the water, pointed like daggers at the Jersey shore. In one of the slips a rusty freighter stood high out of the water, its hold empty of cargo. The reek of hot tar made my nose twitch in protest.

A few doors above the alley was a hole-in-the-wall smoke shop with two shirt-sleeved men in front of it consulting a racing form. I walked past them, turning my head to look at a sunbleached advertisement for La Palina cigars in the window. The two men didn't look up. I would have had to eat oats and run five-and-a-half furlongs in 1:03 first.

This alley was cleaner than my last one. Wire refuse containers were piled high with empty cartons and there was the clean odor of excelsior. A panel truck was backed up to the loading platform of the cold storage plant, but the driver was nowhere in sight. A few steps more and the fire-blackened rear of the Fullbright Radio Corporation was where I could reach it.

Two windows on either side of a strong-looking door. The windows still had their glass and bars besides, and the door had a new look. I went over and leaned against it and delicately tried the latch. My first break. It was unlocked.

After a long succession of bad breaks, a good one makes you suspicious. I chewed a lip, hesitating. I looked both ways along the alley. Empty as a campaign promise. I let the door swing inward a foot or two and peered through. A big room that went all the way to the front of the building, strewn with fire-blackened timbers, wrecked partitions and charred furniture. The acrid odor found after a building burns, no matter how long after, bit into my lungs. I stepped inside and closed the door, breathing lightly, and looked around. A warped metal door in one of the side walls had a floor indicator over it, but I was reasonably sure the elevator would be out of order. Even if it wasn't, the sound would alarm anybody in the place—and I didn't want to alarm anybody. Not even me.

I picked my way gingerly through the wreckage until I was nearly to the front of the building. A narrow staircase hugged one wall, its bannister sagging. What had once been a strip of carpeting covering treads and risers was now little more than flame-chewed threads.

It looked strong enough. I went up one flight, using the balls of my feet only and staying close to the wall. At the top things looked much better than they had downstairs, although the smell was as strong. There was a line of wooden and glass partitions, with a desk, a filing case and three chairs in each where the salesmen took orders from wholesalers. Or so I figured it out. The glass on several of the partitions was broken, but that was the only damage.

I prowled the entire floor and found no sign of life. I moved quietly, opening doors without a sound and closing them the same way. Nothing.

The third floor was split by a wooden partition that extended clear to the ceiling. The half I was in had been completely cleared out, leaving bare boards and a layer of dust you could write your name in if there was nothing better to do. I stood at the top of the steps and eyed a closed door in that partition. I could see no reason for the door being closed. You have a fire and the boys with ladders and the gleaming axes come and put out the flames and back a few holes and go away. Then you haul out what is left and move it down the stairs and away and that's all there is to it. Why go around closing doors?

I took out my gun and went over to the door. No sound came through it. I turned the knob slowly and pushed it open carefully. Not very far open. Just far enough to see the broad back of a man playing solitaire at a table under a shaded light globe hanging from a ceiling cord.

Against a side wall was a daybed and on the bed, her back to me, lay a woman fully dressed. I didn't need to see her face. It was Lodi. Lodi, whose beauty of face and figure was beyond the dreams of man once that initial shock had passed. Lodi, whose secret I had managed to keep from the prying eyes of the civilized world; Lodi, who had given up so much to be with the man she loved.

I slipped into the room and came silently up behind the man at the table. He laid a black seven on a red eight with clumsy care, studied the next card in the pile, then peeled three more from those in his hand.

I said, ''You could use the ace of clubs.''

He jumped a foot and started to rise. I hit him on the back of the head with the gun barrel and he fell face down on the table, out cold.

''Karl!''

Lodi was struggling to sit up, her arms tied at her back. I went over and tore away the ropes and gathered her into my arms and kissed her until she was breathless.

''What have they done to you?'' I demanded finally.

She shook her head, fighting back both tears and laughter. Her long dark hair needed a comb, but for my money it had never looked lovelier. ''Nothing really, Karl. They were stunned, of course, when they saw my face for the first time. I think they were even a little in awe of me. They made me get dressed and brought me directly here.''

''How many of them actually saw you?''

''What does it matter, darling?'' She shivered. ''Let's leave this horrible place. They'll be—''

''No,'' I said. ''I've got to know.''

''Four, Karl. The blonde girl and those two strange men with her and the man you found here.''

''They ask you questions?''

She shrugged. ''Something about a machine, and they seemed to know about the rays. At least the girl did. I pretended I couldn't understand her.''

My own gun was back under my arm. I took the late Mr. Nekko's .32 out of my coat pocket and said, ''Wait for me at the top of the stairs, Lodi. I've got a matter to take care of before I leave.''

Her luminous eyes were troubled. ''You're not going to kill him, Karl?''

''He saw you,'' I said flatly.

''But people will find out some day, darling. They're bound to. You can't go around—''

Her voice faltered and broke. She was staring past me, fear suddenly filling her eyes. A voice said, ''Let the gun fall, my friend.''

The .32 dropped from my hand and I turned slowly. It wasn't the guard after all. Standing in the doorway were the same two men who had accompanied the blonde to my home the night before. Both were holding guns.

I said, ''Relax,'' and showed them my empty hands. The slim one gestured at the man lying half across the table and said, ''Wake him up, Stephan.'' There was a faintly foreign sound to the words.

The burly one of the pair lowered his gun and started toward the table. The other said in the same bored tone, ''Turn around, both of you,'' to Lodi and me, and allowed the gun in his hand to sag slightly.

I moved my hand and the .45 was out from under my arm and speaking with authority. The first slug struck Gergory above the nose and tore away half his head; the second one ripped the entire throat out of the guard, who had chosen that second to sit erect; the third caught Stephan as he was pulling the trigger of his own gun. Something made an angry sound past my ear and buried itself in the wall behind me with a dull *thunk*.

Blood, bodies and the smell of cordite. Lodi was swaying, her face buried in her hands. I picked up her light cape and the hat with the long heavy veil lying on a table next to the bed and said, ''Get into these, quick. We'll have to move fast if we're going to leave before the cops get here.''

She obeyed me numbly and we went quickly through the door and down the two flights of steps. Faces peered through the broken windows at the front of the building and somebody yelled at us.

We ran swiftly through the mounds of rubble to the rear door. I opened it and looked out. The alley appeared as empty of life as before. The panel truck was still backed up to the loading platform next door. I turned and beckoned to Lodi, and when I turned around again, five calm-faced men with drawn guns stepped from behind the truck to face us.

"Take it kind of easy, Mr. Terris," one of them said mildly. "We're government officers."

IX

The committee meeting was called for 10:00 a.m. at one of the hearing rooms in the Senate Building. Lodi and I got there about fifteen minutes early, escorted by a couple of extra-polite agents from the FBI.

Senator McGill was already in the waiting room outside. His mane of white hair didn't look quite as neat as usual and his heavy face was more red than florid.

He was upset enough to forget to shake hands. "Karl! My God, man, do you realize what a bad time you've given me?" He stared curiously at Lodi, who was heavily veiled, her arms covered with white gloves that ended under the sleeves of a long, high-necked dress. "Good morning, Mrs. Terris," he said, civilly enough. "I hear you've had something of a bad time of it. I do hope you're fully recovered."

"Thank you," Lodi said shortly.

He drew me to one side. "Don't hold anything back from them, Karl," he pleaded in an undertone. "They're sore as hell. Unless you can do some mighty tall explaining, you're going to be charged with everything from murder to spitting on the sidewalk! The way you were moving around, I'm surprised they even found you."

"I discovered how they did it," I said. "Granger, the FBI man I tied up out at the house, knew what car I was using. They put the license number on the police radio and some squad spotted it parked near Huber Street. There were a dozen Feds in the block ten minutes later, and the sound of shooting did the rest."

The door to the hearing room opened and a young man beckoned to us. I took Lodi by the arm and we walked in and sat down at a long table. Across from us were several dignified-looking men in conservative business suits. Two of them I already knew; Millard Cavendish, the ranking member of the AEC; and Winston Blake, a sharp-featured bantam-rooster of a man, who wore elevator shoes and sported a black-ribboned pince-nez. Blake and I had taken an instant dislike to each other the first time we met, shortly after my return from Africa, and I knew he would be out for my scalp this time for sure.

Millard Cavendish sounded a gavel and brought the meeting to order. He was a tall, thin man with deep hollows under his cheeks and a shock of iron-gray hair that kept sliding down over his high forehead. He said, "Your name is Karl Terris and you reside in Clinton Township, Catskill County, in the State of New York. Is that correct?"

I looked at the girl behind the stenotype machine and said, "That is correct."

At this point, Winston Blake, who had been staring hard at Lodi, cut in to say, "Mr. Cavendish, will you order this woman to remove her veil? I see no reason why she should keep her face covered during this hearing."

Before Cavendish could open his mouth, I said, "That veil stays on, Blake."

The little man bristled. "Speak when you're spoken to, sir! We're running this hearing."

"Then go ahead and run it. But the veil stays on."

Cavendish said quietly, "This is a hearing, Mr. Blake, not a style symposium. Let's get on with this, shall we?"

"I think Mr. Terris should be reminded," Blake snapped, "that it is within the province of this committee to cite a witness for contempt."

"Let's hope," I said, "that none of its members gives me a reason for being contemptuous."

Behind me somebody smothered a chuckle. Blake's face turned a fiery red. The gavel smacked its block once and Cavendish said, "Mr. Terris, you appeared before this committee some six weeks ago upon your unexpected return from Africa after an absence of two years. At the time of your disappearance you were, as a volunteer, engaged in mapping an area of French Equatorial Africa by air for the United States Government. The purpose of this aerial survey was to locate unusually rich deposits of fissionable material believed to be somewhere in that locality. Am I correct thus far?"

"Yes, sir."

"In your appearance before this committee earlier you stated, under oath, that you failed to locate such deposits, that you had no idea where, if at all, they were located, and that the photographs taken of the locality had been destroyed at the time your plane crashed. This, too, is correct?"

"Yes, sir."

Cavendish fixed me with a not unkindly eye. "Do you, at this time, wish to enlarge on that testimony?"

"No, sir."

The chairman picked up a sheet of paper from a thin sheaf next to his right elbow, studied it briefly, then put it down and looked sharply at me. "Mr. Terris," he said, "twelve days ago a Mr. and Mrs. Clarence Mather died under mysterious circumstances in the south of France. An examination showed both had died of being exposed to cosmic radiation of a highly concentrated form. Exposure took place, it has been established, between thirty and thirty-five days before their deaths. Further investigation revealed that the couple were aboard the tramp steamer *City of Stockholm* at the time of such exposure. Now, it is a matter of record that you chartered the *City of Stockholm* at the port of Dakar, in Africa, for the purpose of transporting you and your wife to America. Furthermore, the cabin you and your wife occupied during the crossing was the one occupied immediately afterward by Mr. and Mrs. Mather. An immediate investigation was made of the ship and your cabin by qualified scientists, and a faint but unmistakeable trace of radiation was found therein. By this time the radiation was far too slight to harm anyone, but the fact remains that it was found therein. In view of these facts, and in view of the purpose behind your original visit to Africa, this committee again asks if you wish to correct your previous testimony."

"No, sir."

There was a general shuffling of feet and shifting of chairs by the rest of the committee. Blake leaned toward the man to his left and whispered something in his ear. The two of them engaged Cavendish in a muttered colloquy pitched too low for me to hear, even if I had wanted to, which I didn't.

Senator McGill bent over me. "Damn it, Karl, what are you trying to pull? They've got enough evidence to pin perjury on you ten times over! This is your country; why aren't you willing to help it?"

I looked up at him. "Senator, if anyone's going to teach me patriotism, it won't be you. Now kindly get the hell away from me!"

Lodi reached over and put a gloved hand on my arm and squeezed it understandingly. Behind the heavy veil she was watching me, I knew, with deep concern.

Millard Cavendish had concluded his discussion with the rest of the committee members. He looked me directly in the eye and the lines of his face were stern.

"I have some questions to ask you, Mr. Terris. Please let me remind you that this committee is empowered to ask these questions and to demand a truthful answer to each. Is that clear?"

"Perfectly."

He nodded shortly. "I will ask you, Mr. Terris, if you brought into this country, at any time, a device or machine having to do with cosmic radiation or energy?"

"No, sir."

A wrinkle deepened between his eyes. "Then how do you explain what happened to the Mathers, and the finding of the experts who examined your cabin on the *City of Stockholm?*"

"That, Mr. Cavendish," I said, "would be a matter of conjecture on my part. I recognize this committee's right to ask me questions, but I do not believe it can demand conjectures."

The wrinkle became a frown. "Then I will ask you, sir: do you know how the cosmic radiation got into that cabin?"

"The question," I said, "is do I *know* how the radiation got into that cabin. The answer is no."

Winston Blake said, "This man is deliberately evasive. I say he should be cited for contempt for his last remark, and for every succeeding remark of its kind."

"Is that supposed to intimidate me?" I asked.

The gavel came down, hard. Cavendish said, "Let's keep our tempers, gentlemen. . . . Mr. Terris, while you were in Africa, did you come into contact with any device, manufactured or natural, that had to do with cosmic radiations or energy?"

"I did."

It took a moment for the reply to get a reaction. There was a sudden babble of voices behind me and the members of the committee stiffened in their chairs. Cavendish rapped several times before order was restored.

He said sternly, "As a patriotic American, Mr. Terris, you must have a sound reason for withholding such information from your country. This committee would like to hear that reason."

I said, "I yield to no one on the strength of my patriotism. But I'm not going to confuse patriotism with chauvinism. By revealing the location of the machines used in controlling and concentrating cosmic energy, I would bring death and destruction not only to a peaceful and innocent people but to the rest of the world."

Millard Cavendish sighed. "This nation is not a warlike one, Mr. Terris. Possession of this secret, judging from what you say, would make America so powerful that no other nation, or coalition of nations, would dare launch a war."

I laughed shortly. "Secret weapons as a deterrent to war are useful only as long as they are controlled by one nation. Need I remind you that spies invariably manage to get their hands on such weapons and peddle them to other nations?"

Winston Blake said, "I'm getting tired of this nonsense." He leaned across the table and stabbed me with his chill blue eyes. "I'll put this in words of one syllable for you, Terris. We want this secret and we want it now. Either you give us the exact location of these devices, or whatever they are, or you'll be branded a traitor to your country in the eyes and ears of every one of your fellow Americans. You're a rich man, I'm told. Well, this is one time your wealth isn't going to save you."

I said, "It's fatheads like you that guarantee my silence."

His face turned a violent crimson and for a moment I thought he was on the verge of a stroke. "I want this man arrested!" he bellowed. "I'll show him he can't vilify a member of this body and get away—"

The banging of the gavel cut him off. Cavendish said frostily, "Mr. Blake is ready for your apology, Mr. Terris."

"Then let him earn it," I said, just as frostily. "I don't have to take that kind of talk from him or anybody else."

By this time Blake was on his feet. "I see no reason to continue questioning this witness. His reasons for refusing to turn over to us such vital information are patently the usual Communist Party line. A man like this deserves to be named a traitor—and if we can't make that stick, let him answer for his unprovoked assault on an agent of the Federal Bureau of Investigation, as well as the brutal slaying of six men in something less than twenty-four hours."

Beside me, Lodi spoke for the first time. "Tell them what they want to know, Karl. It doesn't matter."

I stared at her, aghast. "You don't know what you're saying! Do you want your people to go through what the rest of the world has suffered? Have you forgotten what happened to them that first time?"

Her voice was firm. "You know the kind of protection my people have,

Karl. Ten thousand planes couldn't find our city in hundreds of years if they didn't want to be found. Tell these men the whole story. I don't want the man I love to be hated by his own country.''

I placed a hand lightly on her veil. ''Do you want them to know about you? Do you want this veil stripped away for the world to see? Do you want to be laughed at, shunned, hear every so-called comedian toss off a collection of gag-lines about you?''

''It doesn't matter, Karl. Your real reason for refusing to tell them is your wish to protect me, not my people. I know that, and it must not be that way. All that does matter is your love for me.''

They were listening to us. The room was silent as a morgue. I took a deep slow breath. ''Is that the way you want it, Lodi?''

''Yes.''

I rose from the chair and looked at the men behind the table. ''Okay,'' I said. ''I'm going to tell you a story. It's a story I want the world to hear from my lips, not to learn through a lot of distorted secondhand accounts. Bring in the newsmen and the spectators.''

''We're running this, Terris,'' Winston Blake said coldly. ''I see no reason to—''

''You're not running it now,'' I said. ''Either I tell it my way or you can sweat turpentine and not get a word out of me. It's strictly up to you.''

An almost invisible smile was tugging at Millard Cavendish's fine lips. He said, ''I suggest a compromise. Newsmen, yes; but no spectators. Any part of Mr. Terris' story that can be a threat to our national security will not be published. Is that satisfactory to you, Mr. Terris?''

Once more I looked at Lodi. She nodded ever so slightly. I said, ''Bring 'em in and let's get this over with.''

It required only a few minutes before the press seats were filled. Curious eyes bored into us, but more of them were on the veiled woman next to me than anywhere else. Cavendish rapped his gavel lightly once and said, ''We're ready to hear you, sir.''

I stood there, bending forward slightly, one hand resting on the table. I said:

''Two years ago, I crashed my plane in an African jungle hundreds of miles from civilization. The reason for my being in that part of the world is known to everybody. I was injured in the crash and lay at the edge of a clearing for hours in great pain before I finally blacked out. When I came to, I found myself in a vast underground city, attended by the kindest, most generous people who ever lived. These people nursed me back to health and made me one of them. They trusted me, and when I fell in love with the daughter of their ruling family, they gave her to me as my wife.

"I learned the history of this race. Many thousands of years ago this race lived in four great cities on the surface of the Earth. These were cities of great beauty, of towering spires and luxurious homes. The rest of the Earth was just emerging from the Paleolithic Age, and nothing broke the peace and contentment of their lives.

"And then one day a vast armada of airships swooped down on these peaceful people. Bombs leveled the four cities and those who did not die were taken away as captives. When the enemy finally left, the few survivors sought refuge in underground caves."

Everybody in the room was hanging on my words. A few of the reporters were taking notes, but most of them simply listened with open mouths. I took a couple of steps down the room and came back and stood there, resting a hand lightly on Lodi's shoulder.

"These people I'm telling you about," I went on, "had the knowledge of great power. They knew how to harness cosmic rays—a force sufficient to blow this globe of ours into atoms. They could have constructed weapons that would make the H-bomb something, by comparison, you could shoot off in your fingers!

"But they used this power for more important things. With it they illuminated their caves to the brilliance of sunlight. As the centuries passed, their numbers increased until the population was back to where it had been at the time the attack had come. But they chose to remain underground, so that never again would they be attacked; and except for a few surface guards, none of them ventured out of those caves."

I paused again, this time to look at the three men across the table from me. Cavendish was leaning back in his chair, staring fixedly at my face; Blake was staring down at the pince-nez in his hand; Rasmussen, the third man, sat with his chin resting on one palm. The silence was absolute.

"One of those surface guards found me," I said. "Instead of killing me, he brought me to safety. I grew to love those people, made one of them my wife, and through her and them I knew happiness for the first time in my life.

"But there was one factor I forgot to take into consideration, gentlemen. We call it homesickness. I wanted to go back, to leave that paradise, for the doubtful benefits of what we call civilization. And against my better judgment, knowing exactly what it would mean to her, I brought Lodi with me."

I stopped long enough to pour water into a glass and drink it, then lit a cigarette and went on:

"This brings me to something I failed to mention earlier. These people had learned the secret of longevity. I knew men and women three and four hundred years old who looked and acted younger than I did!"

A murmur of astonishment and open doubt ran through the room. I kept right on talking, getting it all out before my vocal cords gave up:

"Cosmic radiations were the answer. Ages of exposure to those rays had resulted in an inherent immunity to harmful effects. Once every fourteen days each of these people exposed himself to a full charge of the energy; by doing so old age was held back. But after such exposure they gave off for a few days rays that would kill any ordinary man who came in contact with them. They knew this, of course; I was given a series of injections immediately to keep the emanations from harming me.

"There's not much left to tell you, gentlemen. Lodi went with me in my repaired plane. We landed near Dakar the following day; I chartered a ship for our trip to America. Unknown to me, however, Lodi had exposed herself to the customary charge of cosmic energy shortly before we left her people. As long as she wore the proper clothing no one would be harmed; but by undressing in her cabin, she left a concentration of the rays. By the time we reached this country she was no longer a threat to other people; but the Mathers were unfortunate enough to occupy the cabin too soon afterward."

I spread my hands. "Except for one more incident, that's the story. The incident concerns a group of Communist agents who learned what had caused the Mathers' deaths. They assumed I had brought back a machine that produced cosmic energy, and to force me to turn it over to them they kidnaped my wife. In getting her back, I'm afraid, a few people got hurt. It makes for a nice touch: in kidnaping my wife to force me into giving them the 'machine,' they had the machine all along!"

I sat down and knocked the ash from my cigarette gently into a tray. No one said anything for almost a minute. Then Winston Blake carefully lifted his pince-nez and placed it firmly astride his nose.

"Of all the arrant nonsense I ever heard," he snarled, "this concoction I've just listened to takes the prize. By what evolutionary freak did a race of people shoot up ahead of cave men to produce the wonders you told us about? And this air raid; I suppose it came from Saturn!''

I shook my head politely. "No, sir. From Venus. And evolution had nothing to do with the people of the caves, Mr. Blake. They came originally from Mars!''

I got out of my chair and helped Lodi to her feet. "You want proof, Mr. Blake. Then by God you'll get proof!''

Before any of them realized what was happening, I tore away the veil covering Lodi's face; then hooked my fingers under the high neckline of her dress and ripped it and the underclothing beneath completely from her lush and lovely body.

"Go ahead, you lousy ghouls," I said. "Take a good look!''

The collective gasp was like the rustling of a strong breeze. For the skin of the most beautiful woman of two worlds was a rich and luminous green!

X

It was after two o'clock by the time we drove into New York City, and by that time the newspapers were out with the story. At Lodi's insistence I stopped at a stand and bought two of them. The banner head on the *Gazette* said: HOW GREEN WAS MY MARTIAN, and the managing editor had made his bid for a salary increase by having the words printed in green ink. The *Standard* headline was less imaginative but more factual: TERRIS MYSTERY BRIDE FROM MARS!

We were nearly to the Westchester county line before Lodi put aside the papers and leaned back to let the air cool her burning cheeks. I said, "That's only a small sample, baby. They'll crucify you from now on.''

"I don't mind, Karl. If you don't.''

"You'll mind," I said. "You'd have to have the skin of a rhinoceros not to mind. To the rest of the world you're a freak and freaks pay a high price for living.''

"Will it matter so much to you, Karl?''

"It won't get a chance to," I said harshly. "We're going back, Lodi. Back to your people for the rest of our lives. I've had enough of my kind; let them blow themselves to hell and I'll like it fine.''

She laid one of her delicate hands over mine on the wheel. "They are your people, darling. You can't run out on them, on the responsibilities your great wealth gives you. You'd be terribly unhappy before long.''

It was my turn to squeeze *her* hand. "Not as long as we're together, Lodi."

After several miles of silence, Lodi said, "At least they're not going to try to find where my people are."

"Not after they got the details of the power they'd be up against," I said. "The theory of the rest of the world will be: 'Let sleeping dogs lie'—no matter how tempted any nation gets to pull a fast one."

Shortly before five-thirty I swung off the Taconic Parkway and followed the private road on up the hill to the house. The late afternoon sun dappled the lawn through the trees and a tired breeze moved the leaves with a whispering sound. Lodi opened the car door and picked up her veil preparatory to getting out.

I said, "Forget the veil, baby. You'll never wear it again."

She smiled, the slow warm smile that had knocked me for a loop the first time I'd seen it. "You're sure you want it to be that way, Karl?"

"Absolutely."

She left it lying crumpled on the seat and we went up the porch steps together. I unlocked the front door and followed her into the entrance hall—and a tall, slender blond man stepped from behind the short wall of the dining room and pointed a gun at us.

He flashed his teeth and said, "I was beginning to think you hadn't paid the rent. Close the door, please—and keep your hands away from your body."

He looked like a Swedish diplomat, all right, and there were the three pock marks high up on his left cheek. Sergi Porkov. It couldn't have been anyone else. And just to wrap it up for sure, Ann Fullerton, in figured crepe silk that did a lot for her wheat-field hair, appeared in the opening behind him. She was carrying a good-sized patent-leather bag under one arm and she looked cool and neat and very, very lovely.

I started to say something but Porkov cut me off with a small gesture of the gun. From where I stood I judged it to be one of the old model Walther P-38's. Not exactly a cannon, but at the moment he didn't need a cannon. He said, "I think you had better lift your hands quite high and turn around. Both of you. Slowly."

We had a choice. We could turn around or we could refuse—and get shot down on the spot. We turned. He slithered up behind me and let a soft meaty hand prowl my body. He was smart enough to hold the gun so that it actually wasn't against me. He snaked out the .45 from under my arm, made sure it was the only weapon I carried, then went to work on Lodi. She couldn't have hidden a penknife in what she was wearing, but that didn't keep him from trying. I heard her gasp slightly a time or two, and while my muscles crawled I kept them from getting away from me.

He finally stepped back. "I think we will go up the stairs now. In case of unexpected visitors."

We went up the stairs and into the sitting room between the two master bedroosm. Porkov waved us into a couple of the lounge chairs there and then sat down on the edge of one across from Lodi and me. The Fullerton girl remained near the hall door, just standing there looking a little pale, a pinched expression around her full lips.

Lodi leaned back in her chair and folded her hands. She had the Oriental trick of turning completely impassive when things weren't going right. Porkov crossed his legs and wagged the gun carelessly at her. "Green or not," he said admiringly, "you're still the best-looking woman I've ever seen."

I said, "Maybe you'd like to change off for a night or two."

He turned his teeth on again. "It is a thought. Rather a good one. But I'm afraid not. No. I have other plans for your very charming and very beautiful green wife."

I said, "I'd like a cigarette."

"By all means! Perhaps your wife would like a last one also."

From the doorway Ann Fullerton said, "Sergi! You're not—"

Without turning his head he said, "Shut up! Speak when you're spoken to."

I lit a cigarette for Lodi and one for myself. My hands weren't shaking, but not because they didn't want to. I said, "So you're going to pull the string on us. I wonder why. Not for the secret 'machine,' I'm sure. You must have read all about that in the papers by this time."

He swung his crossed leg idly. "No, my friend. Not the machine. We slipped badly on that, Ann and I. No; you took the lives of six of the men associated with me. In effect, you made a fool out of me as well. This last is unforgivable, Mr. Terris."

"Then you won't accept my apology?"

He eyed me almost admiringly. "You are a brave man, sir. I like brave men. . . . Tell me, Mr. Terris, do you love your wife?"

". . . We weren't planning on getting a divorce."

He nodded, satisfied. "I don't intend to kill you, my friend. Not, that is, unless you literally force me to—which you may very well do. It will be an interesting experiment, this—to learn if grief can drive a man to ignoring the law of self-preservation. I know it has done that to some men.''

''I haven't the slightest idea,'' I said, ''what the hell you're talking about.''

He bent forward across his knee. ''Killing you, sir, would accomplish nothing. As they say, your troubles would be over. Dead men feel nothing: no pain, no anguish of soul, no regrets. But when a man loses the one thing he holds most dear, something he has suffered for, endured hardship for, fought for—that loss is, to him, more horrible even than death. In your particular case, Mr. Terris, it would be your wife.''

Something with cold feet walked up my spine. I bit down on my teeth, and it was almost a minute before my throat could form words. ''You can't afford another mistake, Porkov. You'll take a full helping of hell if you so much as start a run in one of my wife's stockings. People who know me will tell you that.''

He said, ''You fascinate me, Mr. Terris,'' and lifted the gun and shot Lodi three times through the left breast.

Through a twisting nightmare of incredulity I watched my wife droop like a tired flower. Then her body sagged forward and she toppled out of the chair to form a pathetic heap on the rug. Death had been instantaneous.

I stood up the way an old, old man stands up. I started toward Porkov. I was in no hurry. I wouldn't live to reach his throat anyway. But that was where I was going.

From the doorway, Ann Fullerton took a gun out of her bag and shot Porkov through the head. Before he hit the floor she was standing over him, pulling the trigger again and again. He caught the full load and even after the gun was empty she went on pulling the trigger in a frenzy of hatred and revulsion until I took it gently out of her fingers.

She turned on me, her eyes burning, her breasts shaking, her body trembling. ''I killed him, Karl. I love you! I want you! Right here! Now! Now!''

You don't explain those things. Not at the time, nor later. Nor ever. The blood sang through me and her body was hotter than any fire and mine was just as hot.

I was sitting on the bed when she came out of the shower. She was as naked as the palm of a baby's hand and she smelled of bath powder. She came over and sat down on the bed beside me and put both arms around me.

"We'll put all those other things out of our minds, Karl, darling." Her voice was like the purr of a cat. "I loved you from the first moment I saw you. We'll go away, Karl, and we'll have each other, and that will be all we'll ever want. Just us two . . ."

I didn't say anything. She got up and went over to the vanity and began to run the comb through her hair. She was what the boys who invented Valhalla were talking about. She had a body that would melt a glacier from across the street. She was everything a man wanted in a woman if all he wanted was a body.

Very slowly I reached under the pillow and took out the .45. I held it loosely in one hand and raised my head and said, "Turn around, Ann."

She turned around and saw the gun and all the color ran out of her face. "No, darling. No! I killed him, Karl. I killed the man who shot your wife. He would have killed you, too. I saved your life!"

I said, "Sure, baby, you did fine," and fired twice. She caught both slugs full in the belly. I could hear them go in from clear across the room.

I put the gun down and smiled a little looking at her. I said, "The worms will love you, darling," and got up and walked over to the telephone.

I wondered what the cops would say about finding her naked that way.

Once, when a television interviewer learned that **Mickey Spillane's** *first seven novels were all among the top 10 fiction best sellers of this century, he said it was a terrible commentary on American reading habits.*

"Ah, shut up!" said the irrepressible Mr. Spillane. "You're lucky I didn't write three more!"

Later on, of course, he did write several more stories, but "The Veiled Woman" may not be one of them. At least that is the claim of Ted White, who currently edits Fantastic, *the magazine in which the story was first published. He attributes authorship to former editor* **Howard Browne** *(1908–   ). Certainly Mr. Browne should have been capable of such a feat, since he had already written an excellent series of hard-boiled mysteries under the pseudonym of John Evans. But did he father this particular work?*

Frankly, we don't know.

What do you think?

INNOVATIONS _____

*It takes **Stanley Ellin** (1916–   ) such a dreadfully long time to write a short story—the opening sentence may take weeks—that he usually does only one a year. But his results are impressive. He has won three Edgar Awards from the Mystery Writers of America. Each of his first seven stories collected an award in the annual Ellery Queen Mystery Magazine contests. In twelve attempts, his prizes included one third, five seconds, two firsts, and one special award of merit. "The Blessington Method," for example, is a clever story about the Society for Gerontology, a go-get-'em company noted for handling problems with dispatch.*

THE BLESSINGTON METHOD

Stanley Ellin

Mr. Treadwell was a small, likeable man who worked for a prosperous company in New York City, and whose position with the company entitled him to an office of his own. Late one afternoon of a fine day in June a visitor entered this office. The visitor was stout, well-dressed, and imposing. His complexion was smooth and pink, his small, near-sighted eyes shone cheerfully behind heavy horn-rimmed eyeglasses.

"My name," he said, after laying aside a bulky portfolio and shaking Mr. Treadwell's hand with a crushing grip, "is Bunce, and I am a representative of the Society for Gerontology. I am here to help you with your problem, Mr. Treadwell."

Mr. Treadwell sighed. "Since you are a total stranger to me, my friend," he said, "and since I have never heard of the outfit you claim to represent, and, above all, since I have no problem which could possibly concern you, I am sorry to say that I am not in the market for whatever you are peddling. Now, if you don't mind—"

"Mind?" said Bunce. "Of course, I mind. The Society for Gerontology does not try to sell anything to anybody, Mr. Treadwell. Its interests are purely philanthropic. It examines case histories, draws up reports, works

325

toward the solution of one of the most tragic situations we face in modern society.''

''Which is?''

''That should have been made obvious by the title of the organization, Mr. Treadwell. Gerontology is the study of old age and the problems concerning it. Do not confuse it with geriatrics, please. Geriatrics is concerned with the diseases of old age. Gerontology deals with old age as the problem itself.''

''I'll try to keep that in mind,'' Mr. Treadwell said impatiently. ''Meanwhile, I suppose, a small donation is in order? Five dollars, say?''

''No, no, Mr. Treadwell, not a penny, not a red cent. I quite understand that this is the traditional way of dealing with various philanthropic organizations, but the Society for Gerontology works in a different way entirely. Our objective is to help you with your problem first. Only then would we feel we have the right to make any claim on you.''

''Fine,'' said Mr. Treadwell more amiably. ''That leaves us all even. I have no problem, so you get no donation. Unless you'd rather reconsider?''

''Reconsider?'' said Bunce in a pained voice. ''It is you, Mr. Treadwell, and not I who must reconsider. Some of the most pitiful cases the Society deals with are those of people who have long refused to recognize or admit their problem. I have worked months on your case, Mr. Treadwell. I never dreamed you would fall into that category.''

Mr. Treadwell took a deep breath. ''Would you mind telling me just what you mean by that nonsense about working on my case? I was never a case for any damned society or organization in the book!''

It was the work of a moment for Bunce to whip open his portfolio and extract several sheets of paper from it.

''If you will bear with me,'' he said, ''I should like to sum up the gist of these reports. You are forty-seven years old and in excellent health. You own a home in East Sconsett, Long Island, on which there are nine years of mortgage payments still due, and you also own a late-model car on which eighteen monthly payments are yet to be made. However, due to an excellent salary you are in prosperous circumstances. Am I correct?''

''As correct as the credit agency which gave you that report,'' said Mr. Treadwell.

Bunce chose to overlook this. ''We will now come to the point. You have been happily married for twenty-three years, and have one daughter who was married last year and now lives with her husband in Chicago.

Upon her departure from your home your father-in-law, a widower and somewhat crotchety gentleman, moved into the house and now resides with you and your wife.''

Bunce's voice dropped to a low, impressive note. ''He's seventy-two years old, and, outside of a touch of bursitis in his right shoulder, admits to exceptional health for his age. He has stated on several occasions that he hopes to live another twenty years, and according to actuarial statistics which my Society has on file *he has every chance of achieving this*. Now do you understand, Mr. Treadwell?''

It took a long time for the answer to come. ''Yes,'' said Mr. Treadwell at last, almost in a whisper. ''Now I understand.''

''Good,'' said Bunce sympathetically. ''Very good. The first step is always a hard one—the admission that there *is* a problem hovering over you, clouding every day that passes. Nor is there any need to ask why you make efforts to conceal it even from yourself. You wish to spare Mrs. Treadwell your unhappiness, don't you?''

Mr. Treadwell nodded.

''Would it make you feel better,'' asked Bunce, ''if I told you that Mrs. Treadwell shared your own feelings? That she, too, feels her father's presence in her home as a burden which grows heavier each day?''

''But she can't!'' said Mr. Treadwell in dismay. ''She was the one who wanted him to live with us in the first place, after Sylvia got married, and we had a spare room. She pointed out how much he had done for us when we first got started, and how easy he was to get along with, and how little expense it would be—it was she who sold me on the idea. I can't believe she didn't mean it!''

''Of course, she meant it. She knew all the traditional emotions at the thought of her old father living alone somewhere, and offered all the traditional arguments on his behalf, and was sincere every moment. The trap she led you both into was the pitfall that awaits anyone who indulges in murky, sentimental thinking. Yes, indeed, I'm sometimes inclined to believe that Eve ate the apple just to make the serpent happy,'' said Bunce, and shook his head grimly at the thought.

''Poor Carol,'' groaned Mr. Treadwell. ''If I had only known that she felt as miserable about this as I did—''

''Yes?'' said Bunce. ''What would you have done?''

Mr. Treadwell frowned. ''I don't know. But there must have been something we could have figured out if we put our heads together.''

''What?'' Bunce asked. ''Drive the man out of the house?''

"Oh, I don't mean exactly like that."

"What then?" persisted Bunce. "Send him to an institution? There are some extremely luxurious institutions for the purpose. You'd have to consider one of them, since he could not possibly be regarded as a charity case; nor, for that matter, could I imagine him taking kindly to the idea of going to a public institution."

"Who would?" said Mr. Treadwell. "And as for the expensive kind, well, I did look into the idea once, but when I found out what they'd cost I knew it was out. It would take a fortune."

"Perhaps," suggested Bunce, "he could be given an apartment of his own—a small, inexpensive place with someone to take care of him."

"As it happens, that's what he moved out of to come live with us. And on that business of someone taking care of him—you'd never believe what it costs. That is, even allowing we could find someone to suit him."

"Right!" Bunce said, and struck the desk sharply with his fist. "Right in every respect, Mr. Treadwell."

Mr. Treadwell looked at him angrily. "What do you mean—right? I had the idea you wanted to help me with this business, but you haven't come up with a thing yet. On top of that you make it sound as if we're making great progress."

"We are, Mr. Treadwell, we are. Although you weren't aware of it we have just completed the second step to your solution. The first step was the admission that there was a problem; the second step was the realization that no matter which way you turn there seems to be no logical or practical solution to the problem. In this way you are not only witnessing, you are actually participating in, the marvelous operation of The Blessington Method which, in the end, places the one possible solution squarely in your hands."

"The Blessington Method?"

"Forgive me," said Bunce. "In my enthusiasm I used a term not yet in scientific vogue. I must explain, therefore, that The Blessington Method is the term my co-workers at the Society for Gerontology have given to its course of procedure. It is so titled in honor of J. G. Blessington, the Society's founder, and one of the great men of our era. He has not achieved his proper acclaim yet, but he will. Mark my words, Mr. Treadwell, some day his name will resound louder than that of Malthus."

"Funny I never heard of him," reflected Mr. Treadwell. "Usually I keep up with the newspapers. And another thing," he added, eyeing Bunce narrowly, "we never did get around to clearing up just how you happened to list me as one of your cases, and how you managed to turn up so much about me."

Bunce laughed delightedly. "It does sound mysterious when you put it like that, doesn't it? Well, there's really no mystery to it at all. You see, Mr. Treadwell, the Society has hundreds of investigators scouting this great land of ours from coast to coast, although the public at large is not aware of this. It is against the rules of the Society for any employee to reveal that he is a professional investigator—he would immediately lose effectiveness.

"Nor do these investigators start off with some specific person as their subject. Their interest lies in *any* aged person who is willing to talk about himself, and you would be astonished at how garrulous most aged people are about their most intimate affairs. That is, of course, as long as they are among strangers.

"These subjects are met at random on park benches, in saloons, in libraries—in any place conducive to comfort and conversation. The investigator befriends the subjects, draws them out—seeks, especially, to learn all he can about the younger people on whom they are dependent."

"You mean," said Mr. Treadwell with growing interest, "the people who support them."

"No, no," said Bunce. "You are making the common error of equating *dependence* and *finances*. In many cases, of course, there is a financial dependence, but that is a minor part of the picture. The important factor is that there is always an *emotional* dependence. Even where a physical distance may separate the older person from the younger, that emotional dependence is always present. It is like a current passing between them. The younger person by the mere realization that the aged exist is burdened by guilt and anger. It was his personal experience with this tragic dilemma of our times that led J. G. Blessington to his great work."

"In other words," said Mr. Treadwell, "you mean that even if the old man were not living with us, things would be just as bad for Carol and me?"

"You seem to doubt that, Mr. Treadwell. But tell me, what makes things bad for you now, to use your own phrase?"

Mr. Treadwell thought this over. "Well," he said, "I suppose it's just a case of having a third person around all the time. It gets on your nerves after a while."

"But your daughter lived as a third person in your home for over twenty years," pointed out Bunce. "Yet, I am sure you didn't have the same reaction to her."

"But that's different," Mr. Treadwell protested. "You can have fun with a kid, play with her, watch her growing up—"

"Stop right there!" said Bunce. "Now you are hitting the mark. All the years your daughter lived with you you could take pleasure in watching her grow, flower like an exciting plant, take form as an adult being. But the old man in your house can only wither and decline now, and watching that process casts a shadow on your life. Isn't that the case?"

"I suppose it is."

"In that case, do you suppose it would make any difference if he lived elsewhere? Would you be any the less aware that he was withering and declining and looking wistfully in your direction from a distance?"

"Of course not. Carol probably wouldn't sleep half the night worrying about him, and I'd have him on my mind all the time because of her. That's perfectly natural, isn't it?"

"It is, indeed, and, I am pleased to say, your recognition of that completes the third step of The Blessington Method. You now realize that it is not the *presence* of the aged subject which creates the problem, but his *existence*."

Mr. Treadwell pursed his lips thoughtfully. "I don't like the sound of that."

"Why not? It merely states the fact, doesn't it?"

"Maybe it does. But there's something about it that leaves a bad taste in the mouth. It's like saying that the only way Carol and I can have our troubles settled is by the old man's dying."

"Yes," Bunce said gravely, "it is like saying that."

"Well, I don't like it—not one bit. Thinking you'd like to see somebody dead can make you feel pretty mean, and as far as I know it's never killed anybody yet."

Bunce smiled. "Hasn't it?" he said gently.

He and Mr. Treadwell studied each other in silence. Then Mr. Treadwell pulled a handkerchief from his pocket with nerveless fingers and patted his forehead with it.

"You," he said with deliberation, "are either a lunatic or a practical joker. Either way, I'd like you to clear out of here. That's fair warning."

Bunce's face was all sympathetic concern. "Mr. Treadwell," he cried, "don't you realize you were on the verge of the fourth step? Don't you see how close you were to your solution?"

Mr. Treadwell pointed to the door. "Out—before I call the police."

The expression on Bunce's face changed from concern to disgust. "Oh, come, Mr. Treadwell, you don't believe anybody would pay attention to whatever garbled and incredible story you'd concoct out of this. Please think it over carefully before you do anything rash, now or later. If the exact nature of our talk were even mentioned, you would be the only one to suffer, believe me. Meanwhile, I'll leave you my card. Anytime you wish to call on me I will be ready to serve you."

"And why should I ever want to call on you?" demanded the white-faced Mr. Treadwell.

"There are various reasons," said Bunce, "but one above all." He gathered his belongings and moved to the door. "Consider, Mr. Treadwell: anyone who has mounted the first three steps of The Blessington Method inevitably mounts the fourth. You have made remarkable progress in a short time, Mr. Treadwell—you should be calling soon."

"I'll see you in hell first," said Mr. Treadwell.

Despite this parting shot, the time that followed was a bad one for Mr. Treadwell. The trouble was that having been introduced to The Blessington Method he couldn't seem to get it out of his mind. It incited thoughts that he had to keep thrusting away with an effort, and it certainly colored his relationship with his father-in-law in an unpleasant way.

Never before had the old man seemed so obtrusive, so much in the way, and so capable of always doing or saying the thing most calculated to stir annoyance. It especially outraged Mr. Treadwell to think of this intruder in his home babbling his private affairs to perfect strangers, eagerly spilling out details of his family life to paid investigators who were only out to make trouble. And, to Mr. Treadwell in his heated state of mind, the fact that the investigators could not be identified as such did not serve as any excuse.

Within very few days Mr. Treadwell, who prided himself on being a sane and level-headed businessman, had to admit he was in a bad way. He began to see evidences of a fantastic conspiracy on every hand. He could visualize hundreds—no, thousands—of Bunces swarming into offices just like his all over the country. He could feel cold sweat starting on his forehead at the thought.

But, he told himself, the whole thing was *too* fantastic. He could prove this to himself by merely reviewing his discussion with Bunce, and so he did, dozens of times. After all, it was no more than an objective look at a social problem. Had anything been said that a *really* intelligent man should shy away from? Not at all. If he had drawn some shocking inferences, it was because the ideas were already in his mind looking for an outlet.

On the other hand—

It was with a vast relief that Mr. Treadwell finally decided to pay a visit to the Society for Gerontology. He knew what he would find there: a dingy room or two, a couple of underpaid clerical workers, the musty odor of a piddling charity operation—all of which would restore matters to their proper perspective again. He went so strongly imbued with this picture that he almost walked past the gigantic glass and aluminum tower which was the address of the Society, rode its softly humming elevator in confusion, and emerged in the anteroom of the Main Office in a daze.

And it was still in a daze that he was ushered through a vast and seemingly endless labyrinth of rooms by a sleek, long-legged young woman, and saw, as he passed, hosts of other young women, no less sleek and long-legged, multitudes of brisk, square-shouldered young men, rows of streamlined machinery clicking and chuckling in electronic glee, mountains of stainless-steel card indexes, and, over all, the bland reflection of modern indirect lighting on plastic and metal—until finally he was led into the presence of Bunce himself, and the door closed behind him.

"Impressive, isn't it?" said Bunce, obviously relishing the sight of Mr. Treadwell's stupefaction.

"Impressive?" croaked Mr. Treadwell hoarsely. "Why, I've never seen anything like it. It's a ten-million-dollar outfit!"

"And why not? Science is working day and night like some Frankenstein, Mr. Treadwell, to increase longevity past all sane limits. There are fourteen million people over sixty-five in this country right now. In twenty years their number will be increased to twenty-one million. Beyond that no one can even estimate what the figures will rise to!

"But the one bright note is that each of these aged people is surrounded by many young donors or potential donors to our Society. As the tide rises higher, we, too, flourish and grow stronger to withstand it."

Mr. Treadwell felt a chill of horror penetrate him. "Then it's true, isn't it?"

"I beg your pardon?"

"This Blessington Method you're always talking about," said Mr.

Treadwell wildly. "The whole idea is just to settle things by getting rid of old people!"

"Right!" said Bunce. "That is the exact idea. And not even J. G. Blessington himself ever phrased it better. You have a way with words, Mr. Treadwell. I always admire a man who can come to the point without sentimental twaddle."

"But you can't get away with it!" said Mr. Treadwell incredulously. "You don't really believe you can get away with it, do you?"

Bunce gestured toward the expanses beyond the closed doors. "Isn't that sufficient evidence of the Society's success?"

"But all those people out there! Do they realize what's going on?"

"Like all well-trained personnel, Mr. Treadwell," said Bunce reproachfully, "they know only their own duties. What you and I are discussing here happens to be upper echelon."

Mr. Treadwell's shoulders drooped. "It's impossible," he said weakly. "It can't work."

"Come, come," Bunce said not unkindly, "you mustn't let yourself be overwhelmed. I imagine that what disturbs you most is what J. G. Blessington sometimes referred to as the Safety Factor. But look at it this way, Mr. Treadwell: isn't it perfectly natural for old people to die? Well, our Society guarantees that the deaths will appear natural. Investigations are rare—not one has ever caused us any trouble.

"More than that, you would be impressed by many of the names on our list of donors. People powerful in the political world as well as the financial world have been flocking to us. One and all, they could give glowing testimonials as to our efficiency. And remember that such important people make the Society for Gerontology invulnerable, no matter at what point it may be attacked, Mr. Treadwell. And such invulnerability extends to every single one of our sponsors, including you, should you choose to place your problem in our hands."

"But I don't have the right," Mr. Treadwell protested despairingly. "Even if I wanted to, who am I to settle things this way for anybody?"

"Aha." Bunce leaned forward intently. "But you do want to settle things?"

"Not this way."

"Can you suggest any other way?"

Mr. Treadwell was silent.

"You see," Bunce said with satisfaction, "the Society for Gerontology offers the one practical answer to the problem. Do you still reject it, Mr. Treadwell?''

''I can't see it,'' Mr. Treadwell said stubbornly. ''It's just not right.''

''Are you sure of that?''

''Of course I am!'' snapped Mr. Treadwell. ''Are you going to tell me that it's right and proper to go around killing people just because they're old?''

''I am telling you that very thing, Mr. Treadwell, and I ask you to look at it this way. We are living today in a world of progress, a world of producers and consumers, all doing their best to improve our common lot. The old are neither producers nor consumers, so they are only barriers to our continued progress.

''If we want to take a brief, sentimental look into the pastoral haze of yesterday we may find that once they did serve a function. While the young were out tilling the fields, the old could tend to the household. But even that function is gone today. We have a hundred better devices for tending the household, and they come far cheaper. Can you dispute that?''

''I don't know,'' Mr. Treadwell said doggedly. ''You're arguing that people are machines, and I don't go along with that at all.''

''Good heavens,'' said Bunce, ''don't tell me that you see them as anything else! Of course, we are machines, Mr. Treadwell, all of us. Unique and wonderful machines, I grant, but machines nevertheless. Why, look at the world around you. It is a vast organism made up of replaceable parts, all striving to produce and consume, produce and consume until worn out. Should one permit the worn-out part to remain where it is? Of course not! It must be cast aside so that the organism will not be made inefficient. It is the whole organism that counts, Mr. Treadwell, not any of its individual parts. Can't you understand that?''

''I don't know,'' said Mr. Treadwell uncertainly. ''I've never thought of it that way. It's hard to take in all at once.''

''I realize that, Mr. Treadwell, but it is part of The Blessington Method that the sponsor fully appreciate the great value of his contribution in all ways—not only as it benefits him, but also in the way it benefits the entire social organism. In signing a pledge to our Society a man is truly performing the most noble act of his life.''

''Pledge?'' said Mr. Treadwell. ''What kind of pledge?''

Bunce removed a printed form from a drawer of his desk and laid it out carefully for Mr. Treadwell's inspection. Mr. Treadwell read it and sat up sharply.

"Why, this says that I'm promising to pay you two thousand dollars in a month from now. You never said anything about that kind of money!''

"There has never been any occasion to raise the subject before this,'' Bunce replied. "But for some time now a committee of the Society has been examining your financial standing, and it reports that you can pay this sum without stress or strain."

"What do you mean, stress or strain?'' Mr. Treadwell retorted. "Two thousand dollars is a lot of money, no matter how you look at it.''

Bunce shrugged. "Every pledge is arranged in terms of the sponsor's ability to pay, Mr. Treadwell. Remember, what may seem expensive to you would certainly seem cheap to many other sponsors I have dealt with.''

"And what do I get for this?''

"Within one month after you sign the pledge, the affair of your father-in-law will be disposed of. Immediately after that you will be expected to pay the pledge in full. Your name is then enrolled on our list of sponsors, and that is all there is to it.''

"I don't like the idea of my name being enrolled on anything.''

"I can appreciate that," said Bunce. "But may I remind you that a donation to a charitable organization such as the Society for Gerontology is tax-deductible?''

Mr. Treadwell's fingers rested lightly on the pledge. "Now just for the sake of argument," he said, "suppose someone signs one of these things and then doesn't pay up. I guess you know that a pledge like this isn't collectible under the law, don't you?''

"Yes," Bunce smiled, "and I know that a great many organizations cannot redeem pledges made to them in apparently good faith. But the Society for Geronotology has never met that difficulty. We avoid it by reminding all sponsors that the young, if they are careless, may die as unexpectedly as the old . . . No, no," he said, steadying the paper, "just your signature at the bottom will do.''

When Mr. Treadwell's father-in-law was found drowned off the foot of East Sconsett pier three weeks later (the old man fished from the pier regularly although he had often been told by various local authorities that the fishing was poor there), the event was duly entered into the East Sconsett records as Death By Accidental Submersion, and Mr. Treadwell himself made the arrangements for an exceptionally elaborate funeral. And it was at the funeral that Mr. Treadwell first had the Thought. It was a fleeting and unpleasant thought, just disturbing enough to make him miss a step as he entered the church. In all the confusion of the moment, however, it was not too difficult to put aside.

A few days later, when he was back at his familiar desk, the Thought suddenly returned. This time it was not to be put aside so easily. It grew steadily larger and larger in his mind, until his waking hours were terrifyingly full of it, and his sleep a series of shuddering nightmares.

There was only one man who could clear up the matter for him, he knew; so he appeared at the offices of the Society for Gerontology burning with anxiety to have Bunce do so. He was hardly aware of handing over his check to Bunce and pocketing the receipt.

"There's something that's been worrying me," said Mr. Treadwell, coming straight to the point.

"Yes?"

"Well, do you remember telling me how many old people there would be around in twenty years?"

"Of course."

Mr. Treadwell loosened his collar to ease the constriction around his throat. "But don't you see? I'm going to be one of them!"

Bunce nodded. "If you take reasonably good care of yourself there's no reason why you shouldn't be," he pointed out.

"You don't get the idea," Mr. Treadwell said urgently. "I'll be in a spot then where I'll have to worry all the time about someone from this Society coming in and giving my daughter or my son-in-law ideas! That's a terrible thing to have to worry about all the rest of your life."

Bunce shook his head slowly. "You can't mean that, Mr. Treadwell."

"And why can't I?"

"Why? Well, think of your daughter, Mr. Treadwell. Are you thinking of her?"

"Yes."

"Do you see her as the lovely child who poured out her love to you in exchange for yours? The fine young woman who has just stepped over the threshold of marriage, but is always eager to visit you, eager to let you know the affection she feels for you?"

"I know that."

"And can you see in your mind's eye that manly young fellow who is her husband? Can you feel the warmth of his handclasp as he greets you? Do you know his gratitude for the financial help you give him regularly?"

"I suppose so."

"Now, honestly, Mr. Treadwell, can you imagine either of these affectionate and devoted youngsters doing a single thing—the slightest thing—to harm you?"

The constriction around Mr. Treadwell's throat miraculously eased; the chill around his heart departed.

"No," he said with conviction, "I can't."

"Splendid," said Bunce. He leaned far back in his chair and smiled with a kindly wisdom. "Hold on to that thought, Mr. Treadwell. Cherish it and keep it close at all times. It will be a solace and comfort to the very end."

Many mystery writers have written about trains, but **Michael Gilbert** *(1912–   ) is probably the only one who writes on them. To avoid disturbing his legal work and his home life, Mr. Gilbert composes as he commutes. Usually the results, while entertaining mysteries, deal only with the work-a-day world. A pleasant exception, however, is the following story, in which those imperturable secret agents, Behrens and Calder, get mixed up with top-secret research, adultery, espionage, radical scientists, bridge clubs, and a new nerve gas called dianthromine.*

THE ONE‑TO‑TEN AFFAIR

Michael Gilbert

THE NOTICE, in firm, black letters on a big white board, read: "War Department Property. Keep to made tracks. If you find anything, leave it alone. IT MAY EXPLODE." Beside it, a much smaller, older, faded green board read: "Hurley Bottom Farm—One Mile."

Mr. Calder read out both notices to Rasselas, and added, "You'd better keep to heel and leave the rabbits alone." Rasselas grinned at him. He thought that Salisbury Plain was a promising sort of place.

Man and dog set off down the path. After half a mile it forked. There was nothing to indicate which fork to take. Mr. Calder decided on the right-hand one, which went uphill and looked more attractive.

It was a windless autumn day. As they reached the top of the rise they could see the Plain spread round them in a broad arc, wave behind wave, all soft greens and browns, running away to the horizon, meeting and melting into the gray of the sky. Two pigeons got up from a clump of trees and circled at a safe distance from the man and the dog. A big flock of fieldfares swung across the sky, thick as black smoke, forming and re-forming and vanishing as mysteriously as they had come.

Mr. Calder unslung his field glasses and made a slow traverse of the area. Rasselas sat beside him, a tip of pink tongue hanging out of the side of his mouth.

When the voice spoke it was unexpectedly harsh, magnified by the loudspeaker. "You there, with the dog!"

Mr. Calder turned slowly.

It was an Army truck, and a blond subaltern in battle dress, with the red and blue flashes of the Artillery, was standing beside the driver.

"If you go much further, you'll be in the target area."

Mr. Calder said, "Well, thanks very much for telling me." By this time he had got close enough to the truck to see the unit signs. "I'm too old to be shot at. Don't you think your people might have put up some sort of warning?"

"The red flags are all flying."

"I must have missed them. I was looking for Hurley Bottom Farm."

"You should have forked left a good quarter of a mile back. We ought to put a notice up there, I suppose. All the locals know it, of course. I take it you're a stranger?"

"That's right," said Mr. Calder. "I'm a stranger, and if it's crossed your mind that I might be a Chinese spy, I could refer you to Colonel Crofter at Porton. He'll give you some sort of character for me, I daresay."

The boy smiled, and said, "I didn't think you were a spy. But I thought you might be going to get your head blown. It causes a lot of trouble when it happens. Courts of inquiry and goodness knows what. That's a lovely dog. What sort is he?"

"He's a Persian deerhound. They need them to hunt wolves, actually."

"He looks as if he could deal with a wolf, too. Are you a friend of Mrs. King-Bassett? Or perhaps you were just going to ride."

Mr. Calder looked blank.

"She owns Hurley Bottom Farm—the place you said you were going to. And runs a riding stable. A lot of our chaps go there."

"To ride?"

"That's right." The boy, who seemed to think he had said too much, added abruptly, "You'll find the turning back there."

Mr. Calder thanked him and trudged off. As he did so, the battery, tucked into a valley to his right, opened up, and a salvo of shells came whistling lazily over, and landed with a familiar *crump-crump* in the dip to his left.

The path to Hurley Bottom took him away from the ranges and into farmland. The soil was Wiltshire chalk with a thin crust of loam. It would not be very productive, he imagined. At a point where the path ran between two thorn hedges he heard a sudden thundering of hoofs behind him, and removing himself with undignified haste to one side, tripped, and landed on all fours.

"What the bloody hell do you think you're doing?" inquired a magnificent female figure, encased in riding breeches, riding boots, a canary yellow turtle-necked sweater, and a hard hat, and mounted on what appeared to Mr. Calder, from his worm's-eye view, to be about thirty foot of chestnut horse.

He climbed to his feet, removed a handful of leaf mold from his right ear, and said, "This is a public footpath, isn't it?"

"It also happens to be a bridle path," said the lady.

Mr. Calder had had time to look at her now. He saw a brick-red but not unhandsome face, sulky eyes, a gash of red mouth, and a firm chin.

"When you come round a corner as fast as that," he said, "you ought to sound your horn. I take it you're Mrs. King-Bassett?"

"Correct. And if you're looking for a ride, I'm afraid all my horses are booked just now."

"Oddly enough, I was simply going for a walk."

"Then let me give you a word of warning. Don't bring your dog too near the Farm. I've got an Alsatian called Prince. He's a killer."

"We will both bear it in mind," said Mr. Calder. Rasselas grinned amiably.

The Cathedral clock sent out its sixteen warning notes into the still, bonfire-scented air, and then started to strike nine times. The radio set in Canon Trumpington's drawing room said:

"This is the nine-o'clock news. Here are the headlines. In Chinese Turkestan an earthquake has destroyed sixteen villages. After a football match in Rio de Janeiro the crowd invaded the field and was dispersed by tear gas. A subsequent bayonet charge resulted in twenty-five casualties. There has been an unexpected rise of twenty-seven percent in the price of copper. The death toll from the as yet unexplained outbreak of cholera at the Al-Maza Military Research Station near Cairo has now risen to seven and includes a number of Egypt's leading scientific experts. Professor Fawazi, head of the establishment, who was seriously ill, is now off the danger list. The death toll in Aden—"

"For heaven's sake," said Mrs. Trumpington. "Turn that voice of doom off, Herbert."

Canon Trumpington stretched out a hand, and peace was restored to the pleasant room in the South Canonry. In the garden outside an owl was serenading the full moon.

"Is it my imagination, or does the news seem to get worse and worse?"

"There wasn't much to cheer anyone up tonight, I agree. What do you say, Behrens? Is the world running down? Are we all on our way out, in a maelstrom of violence and silliness?"

Mr. Behrens said, "Is it the world that's getting old? Or is it us? The older we get, the more we value calm and peace, and a settled routine. Our nerves aren't as strong as they were. Things which look like desperate threats to us—if we were forty years younger they might look like adventures."

"I may be old," said Mrs. Trumpington with spirit, "and I may be nervous, but I can't see how anyone, whatever their age or state of health, could regard a thousand people being wiped out in an earthquake as an adventure."

"Certainly not. But the first reaction of a young man might not be one of horror. It might be a desire to go out and help."

Mrs. Trumpington snorted. The Canon said, "He's quite right, you know." He made a mental note for his next sermon.

"And what about those poor Egyptian scientists?"

"There," said Mr. Behrens, "I must confess that my own reaction was one of incredulity. Cholera, nowadays, is controllable by quite simple forms of immunization. If the outbreak had been in some primitive community where serum was unobtainable—but in a scientific institution—"

"It said an *unexplained* outbreak. Might it be a new and more virulent type?"

"It's possible. I remember when I was in Albania before the war a particularly unpleasant form of skin disease, akin to lupus—"

"If you go on like this," said Mrs. Trumpington, "I'm going to bed."

Mr. Behrens apoligized, and said, "Tell us what you've planned for tomorrow."

"We're going to take coffee at the Deanery. There's a bring-and-buy sale in the afternoon. I'll let you off that. And we're having tea with Marjorie and Albert Rivers—although I don't expect he'll be there. They have that cottage just outside Harnham Gate. He's one of the top scientists out at Porton and she's a bridge fanatic."

"Not a fanatic, my dear. An expert. That's something quite different."

"They're both very good, anyway. No one round here will take them on any more."

"When people say that," said Mr. Behrens, "is usually means they think they're a bit sharp."

"No. Nothing like that. They're simply above our standard. They're both county players. Indeed I'm told that if Marjorie Rivers had the time to devote to it she might be an international player."

"A scientist and a bridge international," said Mr. Behrens. "They sound like an interesting couple."

"If there's one thing I can't abide," said Mrs. Wort, "it's rabbits. And rats. They're both vermin. And as for *eating* them—"

"I'm not very fond of them myself," admitted Mr. Calder. "It was Rasselas who insisted on catching them. I should bury them, and forget about it."

The great dog was stretched out in front of the fire, his amber eyes half shut, the tip of his tail twitching.

"I declare," said Mrs. Wort, "I think he understands every word you say. And isn't he enjoying his holi   The Plain was a grand place for dogs, before the Army messed it up. I remember the time, when I was a girl, there wasn't a soldier in sight. Just a few airmen, in what they called the Balloon School. Now you can't move for 'em."

"You can't indeed," said Mr. Calder. He was as relaxed as Rasselas, full length in an armchair as old and faded and comfortable as everything in the farmhouse kitchen. "I ran into them myself this afternoon. And *I* nearly got run into by a high-spirited female on a horse."

"Swore at you, did she?"

"That's right."

"Then it'd be Missus King-Bassett. Keeps a riding stable out at Hurley Bottom, and kennels, and runs the farm. You know what they call her, up at the Camp? The merry widow."

"Then Mr. King-Bassett is dead?"

"*If* he ever existed."

"I see," said Mr. Calder. "*If* he ever existed. That sort of widow. How long's she been here?"

"She bought the place—oh—three, four years ago. When old man Rudd died. She's pulled it up too. She's a good farmer, they say."

"It's a lonely sort of spot."

Mrs. Wort sniffed, and said, *"She's* not lonely. Not if half the stories you hear are true. There was a Major from Larkhill, made a perfect fool of himself over her. Married too. Now he's been sent abroad. So it's off with the old and on with the new."

"And who's the new?"

"I wouldn't know, and I wouldn't care. There's a lot of men to choose from round here. Soldiers and airmen, and all the scientists at Porton. They say the scientists are the worst of the lot. Would you be wanting anything more?"

"Not a thing," said Mr. Calder sleepily. "As soon as I can bring myself to stir from this beautiful fire, I'll be toddling on up to bed."

When Mrs. Wort had departed, on her nightly round of locking up, he sat for a long time, staring into the red heart of the fire, and wondering why an attractive and capable woman should hide herself away in the wilds of Salisbury Plain. . . .

"I'm sorry Albert couldn't be here this afternoon," said Marjorie Rivers. "They're keeping him very busy out at Porton just now. Some new gas, I think. He doesn't talk to me about his work. Most of it's secret, anyway."

She was a thick, competent-looking, gray-haired woman who reminded Mr. Behrens of the matron at his preparatory school.

"I was telling Mr. Behrens," said Canon Trumpington, "what a formidable record you and your husband had established at the bridge table."

"Are you a player, Mr. Behrens?"

"I'm a rabbit. What I really enjoy about the game is the curious psychological kinks it throws up. I played with a man once who would do *anything* to avoid bidding spades."

"That must have been rather limiting. Did you find out why?"

"I discovered, in the end, that he stuttered very badly on the letter 's'."

Marjorie Rivers gave a sudden guffaw, and said, "You're making the whole thing up. Another cup of tea, Mrs. Trumpington? Mind you, I agree with you about psychology. Albert's a scientist, you know."

"And a very distinguished one," said the Canon politely.

"Oh, I wasn't talking about his work. I meant, at the bridge table. He counts points, adds them up, calculates the probability factor, applies the appropriate formula, presses a button in his head, and expects the answer to come out. And so it might, if the players were automata. But they aren't. They're human beings. Now, I play by instinct, and I think I get better results.''

"I entirely agree," said Mr. Behrens. "I'd back instinct every time."

"Are you in Salisbury for long?"

"The Trumpingtons are kindly putting up with me for a few days."

"We have a little bridge club. Mondays, Wednesdays, and Fridays, at half-past two. Would you care to come along tomorrow?"

"It's quite safe," said Mrs. Trumpington. "Most of us are beginners. I shall be there."

"I can't manage tomorrow, I'm afraid. I have to run up to London. But I might come along on Friday."

"We'll look forward to it," said Marjorie Rivers with what seemed to Mr. Behrens to be rather a grim smile. Or maybe it was his imagination. He carried the question up to London with him on the following day and propounded it to Mr. Fortescue, the manager of the Westminster Branch of the London and Home Counties Bank.

Mr. Fortescue said, "She is certainly a remarkable woman. A top-class bridge player, with the sort of mind which that implies. A competent linguist in half a dozen languages, and the holder of very left-wing views which, to do her justice, she makes no attempt to conceal. But whether she, or her husband, or both of them are traitors is the precise matter which you and Calder have to decide."

"There *is* a leak, then?"

"That is one fact which had been established beyond any reasonable doubt. And it was confirmed by this outbreak at Al-Maza."

"I never really believed in that cholera. What was it?"

"It was the delayed effects of a prototype form of dianthromine."

"Remember, please," said Mr. Behrens, "that you're talking to someone whose scientific education never got beyond making a smell with sulfureted hydrogen."

"Dianthromine is a nonlethal gas. It is light and odorless, and it freezes the nerve centers of the brain, causing sudden and complete unconsciousness which lasts from four to six hours and then wears off without any side effects."

"That sounds like a fairly humane sort of weapon."

"Yes. Unfortunately the prototype had a delayed side effect which did not become apparent for some days. The subject went mad and, in most cases, died."

"How many people did we kill at Porton?"

"We killed a number of rats and guinea pigs. Then the defect was traced and eliminated."

"I see," said Mr. Behrens. "Yes. How very unfortunate. It was the experimental type that our traitor transmitted to Egypt?"

"It would appear so."

"The traitor being Albert Rivers?" Mr. Behrens asked.

"That's an assumption. He was one of four men with the necessary technical knowledge. And his security clearance is low. So low that I think it was a mistake to let him work at Porton at all. He's a compulsive drinker and is known to be having affairs with at least two women in the neighborhood. He's also living well above his means."

"If it's him, how does he get the stuff out?"

"That is the interesting point. He would appear to have devised an entirely novel method."

Mr. Behrens said, "Do you think it could be his wife? She goes abroad a good deal—bridge congresses and things like that."

"It was one of the possibilities, but the Al-Maza incident proved it wrong. Porton knew about the side effects of dianthromine at the beginning of August. We must assume that Rivers would have transmitted a warning as quickly as he could. Yet the fatalities in Egypt did not occur until the third week in August. By the end of the month they, too, had corrected the defect."

"So we're looking for a message which takes two or three weeks to get through. It sounds like a letter to a safe intermediary."

"His post has been very carefully checked."

"Radio?"

"Too fast. He'd have got the news out before the trouble occurred."

"Some form of publication—in code. A weekly or fortnightly periodical?"

"I think that sounds more like it," said Mr. Fortescue. "You'll have to find out what the method is. And you'll have to stop it. There are some things going on at Porton now which we would certainly *not* want the Egyptians to know about. Or anyone else, for that matter."

"I'll have a word with Harry Sands-Douglas. He knows as much about codes and ciphers as anyone in England. I can probably catch him at the Dilly Club."

The Dons-in-London, known to its members as the Dilly, occupies two old houses in St. Johns Wood on the north side of Lords Cricket ground. It has the best cellar and the worst food in London, and a unique collection of classical pornography, bequeathed to it some years before by the Warden of an Oxford College.

Mr. Behrens found it very useful, since he could be sure of meeting there former colleagues from that group of temporary Intelligence operatives who had come, in 1939, from the older Universities and the Bar, had created one of the most unorthodox and effective Intelligence organizations in the world, and had returned in 1945 to their former professions—to the unconcealed relief of their more hidebound professional colleagues.

"The idea which occurred to me," said Mr. Behrens, "was that you might conceal a code in a bridge column."

Harry Sands-Douglas, huge, pink-faced, with a mop of fluffy white hair, considered the suggestion. He said, "Whereabouts in the column? In the hands themselves?"

"That's what I thought. Every self-respecting bridge column contains two or three sample hands."

Old Mr. Happold said, "Most ingenious, Behrens. What put you onto it?"

"Rivers and his wife are both bridge fiends. It's become the rage of Salisbury—so much so that the local paper now runs a bridge column. A *weekly* bridge column, you'll note. If, as I rather suspect, one of the Riverses is contributing it—"

Sands-Douglas had been making some calculations on the back of the menu. He said, "It'd be a devilish difficult code to break."

"I thought nowadays you simply used a computer."

"You talk about using a computer as if it was a can opener," said Sands-Douglas. "It hadn't occurred to you, I suppose, that you'd have to program it first. The fifty-two cards in a pack can be arranged—in how many ways, Happold?"

"One hundred and sixty-five billion billion—that is, approximately. We shall have to do something about this claret."

"It's the 1943. The only wartime vintage they produced in the Medoc."

"I expect the *vignerons* had other things to think about in 1943," agreed Mr. Happold. "It's our fault. We should have drunk it at least ten years ago. What were we talking about?"

"Bridge," said Mr. Behrens. "The possible permutations and combinations of a pack of cards."

"A large computer probably *could* deal with that number. But there's a snag. I don't suppose your chap is sending code messages every week?''

''Almost certainly not. Half a dozen times a year probably. He'd key the column in some way—put an agreed word or expression into the first paragraph so that they'd know a code was coming.''

''Exactly. So if we took, say, fifty-two examples and fed them into a computer, with instructions to detect any repeated correlations between the cards in the hand and known alphabetical and numerical frequencies in the English language and the mathematics of physics—which is roughly how it would have to be done, if you follow me—''

''I didn't understand a word of it,'' said Mr. Behrens. ''But go on.'' He was sipping the claret. It was quite true: gradually, imperceptibly over the years, it had built up to maturity, had climbed from maturity to supermaturity, and was now descending into gentle ineffectiveness. ''Like us,'' thought Mr. Behrens sadly.

''If only ten percent of your examples were true,'' said Sands-Douglas, ''and the others weren't examples at all, but only blinds, even a giant computer would turn white-hot and start screaming.''

''Is that true?'' said Mr. Happold. ''I've often wondered. If you abuse a computer, *does* it really start screaming?''

''Certainly. It's only human!''

''I'm sorry I can't be more definite,'' said Mr. Calder to Colonel Crofter, ''and I do appreciate the awkward position it puts *you* in—as head of the department and Albert Rivers' boss.''

''And it's really only suspicion.''

''Most security work starts like that. Something out of the ordinary—''

''Rivers isn't ordinary. I grant you that. Very few of our scientists are. They've most of them got their little peculiarities. I suppose it's the price you have to pay for exceptional minds. All the same, *if* it's true, it's got to be stopped. The stuff we're working on now is a damned sight more dangerous than One-to-Ten.''

''One-to-Ten?''

''That's our laboratory name for dianthromine. It's not instantaneous. If I gave you a whiff of it, and counted slowly, you'd go out as I reached ten. That's one of its attractions. Imagine a commando raid on enemy headquarters. One of our chaps lets off the stuff in the guard room. Until they start dropping, they'd have no idea anything was wrong. And when they did catch on, it'd be too late to do anything about it.''

"Commandos! It's light enough to be carried around then?"

"Oh, certainly." Colonel Crofter unlocked a steel cabinet in the corner and pulled out something that looked like a small fire extinguisher. "A man could carry two or three of these in a pack. And it's very simple to operate. Just point it, and pull the trigger. Only don't, because it's loaded."

"Fascinating," said Mr. Calder. "Useful bit of kit for a burglar, too." He handed it back with some reluctance. Colonel Crofter locked it away, and said, "Just what are you planning to do next?"

"We're looking for the outlet—the line of communication. For a start we'll have to investigate both his girl friends."

"Both? I only knew about one."

"He's running two at the moment. One's called Doris. She's the wife of an Air Force W.O. at Boscombe Down. The other's Mrs. King-Bassett."

"Yes," said Colonel Crofter. "The merry widow. Quite a character."

"You know her?"

"I know of her," said the Colonel, with some reserve.

"She seems to have had a succession of boy friends in the stations round here. A Major Dunstable at Larkhill, a Captain Strong from the Defensive Weapons Establishment at Netheravon, a light-haired subaltern from the 23rd Field Regiment whom I spoke to the other day—I'm not sure about him yet, so I won't mention his name. And Albert Rivers."

Colonel Crofter said, "Hm—ha. Yes." He turned on his stupid-soldier look for a moment, thought better of it, and became his normal shrewd self. He said, "Have you met Rivers?"

"Not yet. Deliberately."

"When you're ready to meet him I can arrange it. We have a guest night every Friday. Nothing chichi. We're a civilian establishment. But we observe the decencies—black tie. Why don't you come along?"

"When I'm ready," said Mr. Calder, "I'd like to do just that."

After lunch at Mrs. Wort's, Mr. Calder grabbed a stick and set out once again for Hurley Bottom Farm. Rasselas cantered ahead of him, tail cocked. The weather was clearer, ominously so, with the wind swinging round to the north, and great cloud galleons were scudding across the sky.

As he approached the farm Rasselas spotted a chicken and gave a short derisive bark. The chicken squawked. A deeper baying note answered.

"That sounds like the opposition," said Mr. Calder. They rounded the corner and saw the farmhouse and outbuildings. A big, rather top-heavy Alsatian gave tongue from behind the farmhouse gate. Rasselas trotted up to the gate and sat down with his head on one side. The Alsatian jumped up at the top bar of the gate, scrabbled at it, failed to clear it, and fell back. Rasselas said "Fatty," in dog language. The Alsatian's barking became hysterical.

Sheila King-Bassett added her voice to the tumult.

"Call that bloody dog off, or there'll be trouble."

"Good evening," said Mr. Calder.

"I said, call that dog off."

"And I said, good evening."

Mrs. King-Bassett looked baffled.

"Don't worry. They're only exchanging compliments. Yours is saying, 'Come through that gate and I'll eat you.' Mine's saying, 'Be your age, sonny. Don't start something you can't finish.' They won't fight."

"You seem damned certain about it."

"Open the gate and see."

"All right. But don't blame me if—well, I'm damned. That's the first time I've seen *that* happen."

The two dogs had approached each other, until their noses were almost touching. Rasselas had said something, very low down in his throat, and the Alsatian had turned away, and sat down, and started to scratch himself.

"It's probably the first time his bluff's been called," said Mr. Calder.

Mrs. King-Bassett transferred her attention abruptly from the dogs to Mr. Calder and said, "Come inside. I want to talk to you."

She led the way into the front room of the farmhouse and said, "What's your tipple? And, incidentally, what's your game?"

"Whiskey," said Mr. Calder, "and croquet."

Mrs. King-Bassett gave vent to a sort of unwilling half guffaw, somewhere deep down in her throat. It was not at all unlike the noise Rasselas had made. She said, "I've seen you walking round a good deal with that dog of yours. And using a pair of field glasses. What are you? Some sort of security guard?"

"Sort of, you might say."

"And who are you watching?"

"This may be a bit embarrassing," said Mr. Calder slowly. He took a long sip of the whiskey. It was good whiskey. "The man I'm chiefly interested in is, I think, by way of being a friend of yours. Albert Rivers."

Mrs. King-Bassett spat, with force and accuracy, into a vase of ferns in the fireplace. "That's what I think of Albert Rivers," she said. "And if he was here I'd spit in his face."

"What—?"

"He's a slimy, parsimonious two-timer and no friend of mine. If he comes near here again, Prince has got orders to take the seat out of his trousers. And he will."

"But—"

"Look. I didn't mind him inviting himself round here every other day. I didn't mind him drinking all my whiskey. I could even put up with him talking a lot of scientific mishmash—God, how he talked. Talk and drink was all he ever did. All right. But when it comes to trying to run *me* in double harness with a bloody airman's wife—"

"Not very tactful."

"And *if* you're now telling me that he's a damned Russian spy, and you're planning to run him in, all I can say is, bloody good show. In fact, come to think of it, I might be able to help you. Some of what he told me about his work—nerve gases and all that stuff. I can't remember all the details, but I'm pretty sure it was against the Official Secrets Act. What are those damned dogs up to now? Fighting again?"

"I'm afraid they're *both* chasing your chickens."

Mrs. Trumpington put her head round the door after breakfast next morning and told Mr. Behrens that his Bank Manager wanted him on the telephone.

"I expect it's your overdraft," she said. "Mine's quite out of hand these days."

Mr. Fortescue said, "There's some news from Porton which I thought you ought to have. It came to me from the Defense Ministry this morning. They've had a burglary. Someone broke into Colonel Crofter's office last night and stole a fully charged cylinder of dianthromine."

"Why on earth would anyone do that?"

"I've no idea," said Mr. Fortescue. He sounded techy. "You and Calder are the men on the spot. You'd be more likely to know than I would. I think it's time you two got together over this. You've been operating at different ends long enough. Get together."

"I'll arrange a rendezvous," said Mr. Behrens. "Before I ring off, could you pass on a message to Harry Sands-Douglas? The Dilly Club will be able to find him. Tell him that I think I've located the key to the bridge articles. The hot ones have all got a reference to 'science' or 'scientists' in the third sentence.''

"I suppose he'll understand what you're talking about?"

"He'll understand," said Mr. Behrens, and hung up.

After that he did some complicated telephoning, had lunch at the Haunch of Venison, and wandered slowly back, along the High Street, under the crenelated gate and into the Close. Ahead of him loomed the bulk of the Cathedral, like a gray whale asleep in the sun. A pair of falcons, male and female, were flirting in the air currents round the top of the spire.

Mr. Behrens entered the precincts and made his way to the seat by the west front. Mr. Calder was already there. Rasselas was flat on the turf beside him.

Mr. Behrens said, "The old man wanted me to find out how things were going at your end. He's had no report from you for forty-eight hours."

"I've been busy. Clearing the ground. I don't think either of Rivers' girl friends is involved. I'm on rather good terms now with Mrs. King-Bassett."

"How did you fix that?"

"I sent her an anonymous letter, giving her the ripest details of Albert's liaisons with the Sergeant Major's wife at Boscombe Down. Then I called on her, with Rasselas."

"I don't think," said Mr. Behrens, "that he's using either woman as a courier. In fact, I'm pretty certain that we know how he *is* doing it."

"Through the bridge columns?"

"Yes. I had a telephone message after lunch. There's a positive correlation. They should have the code finally broken by this evening. I gather the old man is already thinking about how to use it. He had the idea of sending them out something pretty horrific to try out next."

"*If* the messages are going out through this bridge column, does it mean that his wife's in it too?"

Mr. Behrens paused before answering this. He seemed to be wholly engrossed in watching the falcons. The male had spiraled up to a height above the female and now plummeted down in mock attack. The female sidestepped at the last moment; the male put on the brakes and volplaned down almost to the transept roof.

"No," said Mr. Behrens at last. "I don't. For two reasons. First, because it's Albert Rivers who writes the bridge columns. His wife has no hand in them. I've found that out. By itself, it's not conclusive. But it was a remark by her, about Albert being a scientist, which put me onto the key to the cipher. If she'd been guilty, she'd never have done that.''

''It seems to me,'' said Mr. Calder, ''that *if* we pull in Albert Rivers, simply on the basis of the code messages, we may be in for rather a sticky run. Fancy trying to persuade an average jury that something a computer has worked out on the basis of a few bridge hands constitutes treason.''

Mr. Behrens said, ''I once knew a Baconian. He was convinced that all Shakespeare's plays were full of code messages. He demonstrated to me, very cleverly, that if you applied his formula to Hamlet's soliloquy, 'To be or not to be,' you could produce the sentence: 'F.B. made me for Q.E.'; which meant, of course, 'Francis Bacon wrote the play for Queen Elizabeth.' ''

''Of course.''

''Sands-Douglas applied the same formula to a later speech and produced the message: 'Arsenal for ye cuppe.' ''

Mr. Calder laughed. Then he stopped laughing and said, ''I've got a strange feeling we may have to consider an alternative solution.''

''Was that why you broke into Colonel Crofter's office and stole the dianthromine?''

''How do you know I stole it?''

''It had to be either you or Rivers. You were the only two disreputable characters in the neighborhood. He had no need to steal it. He could have got some legitimately. So it must have been you.''

''What a nasty horrible mind you've got,'' said Mr. Calder.

Albert Rivers leaned back in his chair in the mess anteroom, lit a cigarette which he extracted from a pack, and returned the pack to his pocket. As an afterthought he took it out again and offered it to the two men sitting with him. Both shook their heads.

''You're a civilian yourself, Corker,'' he said.

''It's Calder, actually.''

''Calder. I beg yours. I never remember a name for five minutes. Never forget a formula, but never remember a name.''

''Perhaps that's because formulas are often more important than names.''

Rivers squinted at Mr. Calder, as though he suspected the remark of some deep double meaning, then laughed, and said, "You're damned right they are. What was I saying?"

"You were pointing out that I was a civilian. I imagine that goes for the majority of the people here, too." As he said this Mr. Calder looked round the room. Most of the diners had disappeared to their own quarters, but there was a hard core left. Four were playing bridge with silent concentration. Two younger men were drinking beer. A man with a beard was finishing a crossword puzzle and a large port.

"That's just my point. Why do we have to confuse scientific research and the para-paraphernalia of military life? All that nonsense after dinner—sitting round for half an hour in our best bibs and tuckers, drinking port, when we'd all rather be down at the local, or enjoying a bit of slap and tickle in the car park."

"Really, Rivers," said Colonel Crofter. "I don't think—"

"That's all right, Colonel. You can't shock old Corker. I've seen him sneaking off down to Hurley Bottom Farm. Lechery Lodge, we call it round here. What do you think of the merry widow, Corker?"

Mr. Calder appeared untroubled by this revelation. He said, "I had a very interesting talk with Mrs. King-Bassett."

"I bet. Did she tell you she thought I was a prize skunk?"

"Yes."

Albert Rivers burst into a hearty guffaw of laughter which drew glances of disapproval from the bridge players.

"That's what I like about you, Corker. You tell the truth. Waiter! . . . What's your tipple, Corker?"

"Scotch and water."

"And yours, Colonel?"

"Nothing more for me, thank you."

"Oh, come along, Colonel. It won't do you any harm. Bring us three large whiskeys. In fact, it'll save a lot of time in the long run if you bring the bottle."

"Bring the bottle, sir?"

"The bottle, Moxon. The whole bottle, and nothing but the bottle."

The waiter shot a sideways look at Colonel Crofter, but getting no help there, pottered off. Albert Rivers stretched himself even more comfortably in his chair and prepared to ride one of his favorite hobby horses. "As I was saying, it always seems odd to me that we have to mix up militarism and science."

"This happens," said Colonel Crofter, "to be a military establishment."

"Sure, Colonel. But you don't parade your scientists in the morning." Rivers threw his head back and roared out, "Scientists form fours. By the right. Quick march."

One of the bridge players said angrily, "This is impossible. We'll have to move." They carried the table and chairs into the next room as Moxon arrived with the whiskey.

The two beer drinkers had left and the port drinker had fallen asleep over his crossword. Mr. Calder knew very well that if he himself made the least move to depart, Colonel Crofter would take himself off as well. As long as he stayed, the Colonel, as his host, had to stay too. He watched Rivers pouring out the drinks. A double for each of them, and pretty nearly half a tumblerful for himself. Mr. Calder reckoned that this one would do the trick.

"Let's face it, Colonel," said Rivers. "Cheers! Let's face it. You can't conduct scientific research by numbers. Science can't be drilled, or court-martialed." He had added a little water, and now knocked back nearly half the contents of the glass in three gulps. "Science is universal, and international."

"I hope you're bearing in mind," said Colonel Crofter, "that you've got to drive home tonight."

"I've got my car trained. It finds its own way home. What was I saying?"

Mr. Calder said, "You were telling us that since science was international it no longer observes national boundaries. That the days when nations conducted their own private, selfish scientific research were over, and that the results of one should be freely communicated to all."

The room was very quiet. Rivers seemed to be thinking. The cool and cautious part of his mind was fighting with the fumes of the whiskey. Colonel Crofter sat watching him, his gray eyes wary.

Rivers said, "I don't think I like you, Corker."

"That makes it mutual."

"You're a crafty old buzzard. You've been leading me on. I'm going home."

"It's time we all went home," said the Colonel. They got up. Rivers seemed to be steady enough.

"You're not going to waste that lovely drink, surely," said Mr. Calder.

Rivers glared at him, picked the glass up, swallowed what was left in it, and put it back where he thought the table was. The glass fell on the carpet, without breaking. While the Colonel was picking up the glass, Mr. Calder moved to the door. He didn't appear to hurry, but he wasted no time. He had something to do.

Rivers' car was parked in front of his. It was pitch-dark, and he had to work quickly, making no mistakes. First he took some things out of his own car, went back to Rivers' car, then back to his own car, then back to the front steps again.

He was standing there buttoning up his overcoat when Rivers and the Colonel came out. Rivers was his jaunty self again. He said, "Good night, Colonel. Up guards and at 'em, as Wellington didn't say at the battle of Waterloo. Good night, Corker, you crafty old buzzard."

"He's not often as bad as this," said the Colonel apologetically.

"Don't apologize. It was a most enlightening evening."

"Do you think I ought to have let him take that last drink?"

"He had so much alcohol in his bloodstream already that I don't suppose it made any difference."

"He's got to get home." They heard the car start up. "Luckily it's a fairly straight road." The car started to move. "And there isn't likely to be a lot of traffic about."

"One," said Mr. Calder softly, "two, three, four."

"I beg your pardon?"

"Five, six, seven."

"Watch that ditch—"

"Eight, nine."

"Slow down, you bloody fool! He'll never—"

"Ten."

There was an appalling crash. The Colonel and Mr. Calder started to run.

"At the adjourned inquest," said the news commentator, "on the well-known scientist and bridge player, Albert Rivers, Inspector Walsh said that, in view of the evidence that the car drove straight out into the main road without making any attempt to slow down, he could only surmise that at some stage Rivers had completely lost consciousness. Inquiries are still proceeding. A further outbreak has been reported from the Egyptian Military Research Station at Al-Maza. Victims include the Director, Professor Fawazi. Among other alarming symptoms he had lost all the hair on his body, and his skin has wrinkled and turned bright yellow—"

"For goodness' sake," said Mrs. Trumptington, "turn it off."

Of all contemporary mystery writers, **Jack Ritchie** *(1922–   )*
is perhaps the most underrated. His stories are masterpieces of
style, humor, and imagination. For example, in the annual
Best Detective Stories of the Year *series he appears more often*
than any other author. Yet, because Mr. Ritchie concentrates
exclusively on short stories, he is ignored by both
Contemporary Authors *and the otherwise excellent*
Encyclopedia of Mystery and Detection. *Fortunately, he seems*
temperamentally able to handle such neglect; for otherwise, as
his story indicates, some of us might be in big trouble.

FOR ALL THE RUDE PEOPLE

Jack Ritchie

"How old are you?" I asked.

His eyes were on the revolver I was holding. "Look, mister, there's not much in the cash register, but take it all. I won't make no trouble."

"I am not interested in your filthy money. How old are you?"

He was puzzled. "Forty-two."

I clucked my tongue. "What a pity. From your point of view, at least. You might have lived another twenty or thirty years if you had just taken the very slight pains to be polite."

He didn't understand.

"I am going to kill you," I said, "Because of the four-cent stamp and because of the cherry candy."

He did not know what I meant by the cherry candy, but he did know about the stamp.

Panic raced into his face. "You must be crazy. You can't kill me just because of that."

"But I can."

And I did.

When Dr. Briller told me that I had but four months to live, I was, of course, perturbed. "Are you positive you haven't mixed up the X-rays? I've heard of such things."

"I'm afraid not, Mr. Turner."

I gave it more earnest thought. "The laboratory reports. Perhaps my name was accidentally attached to the wrong . . ."

He shook his head slowly. "I double-checked. I always do that in cases like these. Sound medical practice, you know."

It was late afternoon and the time when the sun is tired. I rather hoped that when my time came to actually die, it might be in the morning. Certainly more cheerful.

"In cases like this," Dr. Briller said, "a doctor is faced with a dilemma. Shall he or shall he not tell his patient? I always tell mine. That enables them to settle their affairs and to have a fling, so to speak." He pulled a pad of paper toward him. "Also I'm writing a book. What do you intend doing with your remaining time?"

"I really don't know. I've just been thinking about it for a minute or two, you know."

"Of course," Briller said. "No immediate rush. But when you do decide, you will let me know, won't you? My book concerns the things that people do with their remaining time when they know just when they're going to die."

He pushed aside the pad. "See me every two or three weeks. That way we'll be able to measure the progress of your decline."

Briller saw me to the door. "I already have written up twenty-two cases like yours." He seemed to gaze into the future. "Could be a best seller, you know."

I have always lived a bland life. Not an unintelligent one, but bland.

I have contributed nothing to the world—and in that I have much in common with almost every soul on earth—but on the other hand I have not taken away anything either. I have, in short, asked merely to be left alone. Life is difficult enough without undue association with people.

What can one do with the remaining four months of a bland life?

I have no idea how long I walked and thought on that subject, but eventually I found myself on the long curving bridge that sweeps down to join the lake drive. The sounds of mechanical music intruded themselves upon my mind and I looked down.

A circus, or very large carnival, lay below.

It was the world of shabby magic, where the gold is gilt, where the top-hatted ringmaster is as much a gentleman as the medals on his chest are authentic, and where the pink ladies on horseback are hard-faced and narrow-eyed. It was the domain of the harsh-voiced vendors and the short-change.

I have always felt that the demise of the big circus may be counted as one of the cultural advances of the twentieth century, yet I found myself descending the footbridge and in a few moments I was on the midway between the rows of stands where human mutations are exploited and exhibited for the entertainment of all children.

Eventually, I reached the big top and idly watched the bored ticket-taker in his elevated box at one side of the main entrance.

A pleasant-faced man leading two little girls approached him and presented several cardboard rectangles which appeared to be passes.

The ticket-taker ran his finger down a printed list at his side. His eyes hardened and he scowled down at the man and the children for a moment. Then slowly and deliberately he tore the passes to bits and let the fragments drift to the ground. "These are no damn good," he said.

The man below him flushed. "I don't understand."

"You didn't leave the posters up," the ticket-taker snapped. "Beat it, crumb!"

The children looked up at their father, their faces puzzled. Would he do something about this?

He stood there and the white of anger appeared on his face. He seemed about to say something, but then he looked down at the children. He closed his eyes for a moment as though to control his anger, and then he said, "Come on, kids. Let's go home."

He led them away, down the midway, and the children looked back, bewildered, but saying nothing.

I approached the ticket-taker. "Why did you do that?"

He glanced down. "What's it to you?"

"Perhaps a great deal."

He studied me irritably. "Because he didn't leave up the posters."

"I heard that before. Now explain it."

He exhaled as though it cost him money. "Our advance man goes through a town two weeks before we get there. He leaves posters advertising the show any place he can—grocery stores, shoe shops, meat markets—any place that will paste them in the window and keep them there until the show comes to town. He hands out two or three passes for that. But what some of these jokers don't know is that we check up. If the posters aren't still up when we hit town, the passes are no good.''

''I see,'' I said dryly. ''And so you tear up the passes in their faces and in front of their children. Evidently that man removed the posters from the window of his little shop too soon. Or perhaps he had those passes given to him by a man who removed the posters from his window.''

''What's the difference? The passes are no good.''

''Perhaps there is no difference in that respect. But do you realize what you have done?''

His eyes were narrow, trying to estimate me and any power I might have.

''You have committed one of the most cruel of human acts,'' I said stiffly. ''You have humiliated a man before his children. You have inflicted a scar that will remain with him and them as long as they live. He will take those children home and it will be a long, long way. And what can he say to them?''

''Are you a cop?''

''I am not a cop. Children of that age regard their father as the finest man in the world. The kindest, the bravest. And now they will remember that a man had been bad to their father—and he had been unable to do anything about it.''

''So I tore up his passes. Why didn't he buy tickets? Are you a city inspector?''

''I am not a city inspector. Did you expect him to *buy* tickets after that humiliation? You left the man with no recourse whatsoever. He could not buy tickets and he could not create a well-justified scene because the children were with him. He could do nothing. Nothing at all, but retreat with two children who wanted to see your miserable circus and now they cannot.''

I looked down at the foot of his stand. There were the fragments of many more dreams—the debris of other men who had committed the capital crime of not leaving their posters up long enough. ''You could at least have said, 'I'm sorry, sir. But your passes are not valid.' And then you could have explained politely and quietly why.'

''I'm not paid to be polite.'' He showed yellow teeth. ''And, mister, I *like* tearing up passes. It gives me a kick.''

And there it was. He was a little man who had been given a little power and he used it like a Caesar.

He half rose. ''Now get the hell out of here, *mister*, before I come down there and chase you all over the lot.''

Yes. He was a man of cruelty, a two-dimensional animal born without feeling and sensitivity and fated to do harm as long as he existed. He was a creature who should be eliminated from the face of the earth.

If only I had the power to . . .

I stared up at the twisted face for a moment more and then turned on my heel and left. At the top of the bridge I got a bus and rode to the sports shop at Thirty-seventh.

I purchased a .32 caliber revolver and a box of cartridges.

Why do we *not* murder? Is it because we do not feel the moral justification for such a final act? Or is it more because we fear the consequences if we are caught—the cost to us, to our families, to our children?

And so we suffer wrongs with meekness, we endure them because to eliminate them might cause us even more pain than we already have.

But I had no family, no close friends. And four months to live.

The sun had set and the carnival lights were bright when I got off the bus at the bridge. I looked down at the midway and he was still in his box.

How should I do it? I wondered. Just march up to him and shoot him as he sat on his little throne?

The problem was solved for me. I saw him replaced by another man— apparently his relief. He lit a cigarette and strolled off the midway toward the dark lake front.

I caught up with him around a bend concealed by bushes. It was a lonely place, but close enough to the carnival so that its sounds could still reach me.

He heard my footsteps and turned. A tight smile came to his lips and he rubbed the knuckles of one hand. ''You're asking for it, mister.''

His eyes widened when he saw my revolver.

''How old are you?'' I asked.

''Look, mister,'' he said swiftly. ''I only got a couple of tens in my pocket.''

''How old are you?'' I repeated.

His eyes flicked nervously. ''Thirty-two.''

I shook my head sadly. ''You could have lived into your seventies. Perhaps forty more years of life, if only you had taken the simple trouble to act like a human being.''

His face whitened. "Are you off your rocker, or something?"

"A possibility."

I pulled the trigger.

The sound of the shot was not as loud as I expected, or perhaps it was lost against the background of the carnival noises.

He staggered and dropped to the edge of the path and he was quite dead.

I sat down on a nearby park bench and waited.

Five minutes. Ten. Had no one heard the shot?

I became suddenly conscious of hunger. I hadn't eaten since noon. The thought of being taken to a police station and being questioned for any length of time seemed unbearable. And I had a headache, too.

I tore a page from my pocket notebook and began writing.

A careless word may be forgiven. But a lifetime of cruel rudeness cannot. This man deserves to die.

I was about to sign my name, but then I decided that my initials would be sufficient for the time being. I did not want to be apprehended before I had a good meal and some aspirins.

I folded the page and put it into the dead ticket-taker's breast pocket.

I met no one as I returned up the path and ascended the footbridge. I walked to Weschler's, probably the finest restaurant in the city. The prices are, under normal circumstances, beyond me, but I thought that this time I could indulge myself.

After dinner, I decided an evening bus ride might be in order. I rather enjoyed that form of city excursion and, after all, my freedom of movement would soon become restricted.

The driver of the bus was an impatient man and clearly his passengers were his enemies. However, it was a beautiful night and the bus was not crowded.

At Sixty-eighth Street, a fragile white-haired woman with cameo features waited at the curb. The driver grudgingly brought his vehicle to a stop and opened the door.

She smiled and nodded to the passengers as she put her foot on the first step, and one could see that her life was one of gentle happiness and very few bus rides.

"Well!" the driver snapped. "Is it going to take you all day to get in?"

She flushed and stammered. "I'm sorry." She presented him with a five-dollar bill.

He glared. "Don't you have any change?"

The flush deepened. "I don't think so. But I'll look."

The driver was evidently ahead on his schedule and he waited.

And one other thing was clear. He was enjoying this.

She found a quarter and held it up timorously.

"In the box!" he snapped.

She dropped it into the box.

The driver moved his vehicle forward jerkily and she almost fell. Just in time, she managed to catch hold of a strap.

Her eyes went to the passengers, as though to apologize for herself—for not having moved faster, but not having immediate change, for almost falling. The smile trembled and she sat down.

At Eighty-second, she pulled the buzzer cord, rose, and made her way forward.

The driver scowled over his shoulder as he came to a stop.

"Use the rear door. Don't you people ever learn to use the rear door?"

I am all in favor of using the rear door. Especially when a bus is crowded. But there were only half a dozen passengers on this bus and they read their newspapers with frightened neutrality.

She turned, her face pale, and left by the rear door.

The evening she had had, or the evening she was going to have, had now been ruined. Perhaps many more evenings with the thought of it.

I rode the bus to the end of the line.

I was the only passenger when the driver turned it around and parked.

It was a deserted, dimly-lit corner, and there were no waiting passengers at the small shelter at the curb. The driver glanced at his watch, lit a cigarette, and then noticed me. "If you're taking the ride back, mister, put another quarter in the box. No free riders here."

I rose from my seat and walked slowly to the front of the bus. "How old are you?"

His eyes narrowed. "That's none of your business."

"About thirty-five, I'd imagine," I said. "You'd have had another thirty years or more ahead of you." I produced the revolver.

He dropped the cigarette. "Take the money," he said.

"I'm not interested in money. I'm thinking about a gentle lady and perhaps the hundreds of other gentle ladies and the kind, harmless men and the smiling children. You are a criminal. There is no justification for what you do to them. There is no justification for your existence."

And I killed him.

I sat down and waited.

After ten minutes, I was still alone with the corpse.

I realized that I was sleepy. Incredibly sleepy. It might be better if I turned myself in to the police after a good night's sleep.

I wrote my justification for the driver's demise on a sheet of note paper, added my initials, and put the page in his pocket.

I walked four blocks before I found a taxi and took it to my apartment building.

I slept soundly and perhaps I dreamed. But if I did, my dreams were pleasant and innocuous, and it was almost nine before I woke.

After a shower and a leisurely breakfast, I selected my best suit. I remembered I had not yet paid that month's telephone bill. I made out a check and addressed an envelope. I discovered that I was out of stamps. But no matter, I would get one on the way to the police station.

I was almost there when I remembered the stamp. I stopped in at a corner drugstore. It was a place I had never entered before.

The proprietor, in a semi-medical jacket, sat behind the soda fountain reading a newspaper and a salesman was making notations in a large order book.

The proprietor did not look up when I entered and he spoke to the salesman. "They've got his fingerprints on the notes, they've got his handwriting, and they've got his initials. What's wrong with the police?"

The salesman shrugged. "What good are fingerprints if the murderer doesn't have his in the police files? The same goes for the handwriting if you got nothing to compare it with. And how many thousand people in the city got the initials L. T.?" He closed his book. "I'll be back next week."

When he was gone, the druggist continued reading the newspaper.

I cleared my throat.

He finished reading a long paragraph and then looked up. "Well?"

"I'd like a four-cent stamp, please."

It appeared almost as though I had struck him. He stared at me for fifteen seconds and then he left his stool and slowly made his way to the rear of the store toward a small barred window.

I was about to follow him, but a display of pipes at my elbow caught my attention.

After a while I felt eyes upon me and looked up.

The druggist stood at the far end of the store, and one hand on his hip and the other disdainfully holding the single stamp. "Do you expect me to bring it to you?"

And now I remembered a small boy of six who had had five pennies. Not just one this time, but five, and this was in the days of penny candies.

He had been entranced at the display in the showcase—the fifty varieties of sweet things, and his mind had revolved in a pleasant indecision. The red whips? The licorice? The grab bags? But not the candy cherries. He didn't like those.

And then he had become conscious of the druggist standing beside the display case—tapping one foot. The druggist's eyes had smouldered with irritation—no, more than that—with anger. "Are you going to take all day for your lousy nickel?"

He had been a sensitive boy and he had felt as though he had received a blow. His precious five pennies were now nothing. This man despised them. And this man despised him.

He pointed numbly and blindly. "Five cents of that."

When he left the store he had found that he had the candy cherries.

But that didn't really matter. Whatever it had been, he couldn't have eaten it.

Now I stared at the druggist and the four-cent stamp and the narrow hatred for anyone who did not contribute directly to his profits. I had no doubt that he would fawn if I purchased one of his pipes.

But I thought of the four-cent stamp and the bag of cherry candy I had thrown away so many years ago.

I moved toward the rear of the store and took the revolver out of my pocket. "How old are you?"

When he was dead, I did not wait longer than necessary to write a note. I had killed for myself this time and I felt the need of a drink.

I went several doors down the street and entered a small bar. I ordered a brandy and water.

After ten minutes, I heard the siren of a squad car.

The bartender went to the window. "It's just down the street." He took off his jacket. "Got to see what this is all about. If anybody comes in, tell them I'll be right back." He put the bottle of brandy on the bar. "Help yourself, but tell me how many."

I sipped the brandy slowly and watched the additional squad cars and finally the ambulance appear.

The bartender returned after ten minutes and a customer followed at his heels. "A short beer, Joe."

"This is my second brandy," I said.

Joe collected my change. "The druggist down the street got himself murdered. Looks like it was by the man who kills people because they're not polite."

The customer watched him draw a beer. "How do you figure that? Could have been just a hold-up."

Joe shook his head. "No. Fred Masters—he's got the TV shop across the street—found the body and he read the note."

The customer put a dime on the bar. "I'm not going to cry about it. I always took my business someplace else. He acted as though he was doing you a favor every time he waited on you."

Joe nodded. "I don't think anybody in the neighborhood's going to miss him. He always made a lot of trouble."

I had been about to leave and return to the drug store to give myself up, but now I ordered another brandy and took out my notebook. I began making a list of names.

It was surprising how one followed another. They were bitter memories, some large, some small, some I had experienced and many more that I had witnessed—and perhaps felt more than the victims.

Names. And that warehouseman. I didn't know his name, but I must include him.

I remembered the day and Miss Newman. We were her sixth graders and she had taken us on another one of her excursions—this time to the warehouses along the river, where she was going to show us "how industry works."

She always planned her tours and she always asked permission of the places we visited, but this time she strayed or became lost and we arrived at the warehouse—she and the thirty children who adored her.

And the warehouseman had ordered her out. He had used language which we did not understand, but sensed its intent, and he directed it against us and Miss Newman.

She was small and she had been frightened and we retreated. And Miss Newman did not report to school the next day or any day after that and we learned that she had asked for a transfer.

And I who loved her, too, knew why. She could not face us after that.

Was he still alive? He had been in his twenties then, I imagined.

When I left the bar a half an hour later, I realized I had a great deal of work to do.

The succeeding days were busy ones and, among others, I found the warehouseman. I told him why he was dying because he did not even remember.

And when that was done, I dropped into a restaurant not far away.

The waitress eventually broke off her conversation with the cashier and strode to my table. "What do you want?"

I ordered a steak and tomatoes.

The steak proved to be just about what one could expect in such a neighborhood. As I reached for my coffee spoon, I accidentally dropped it to the floor. I picked it up. "Waitress, would you mind bringing me another spoon, please?"

She stalked angrily to my table and snatched the spoon from my hand. "You got the shakes, or something?"

She returned in a few moments and was about to deposit a spoon, with considerable emphasis, upon my table.

But then a sudden thought altered the harsh expression on her face. The descent of the arm diminuendoed, and then the spoon touched the tablecloth, it touched gently. Very gently.

She laughed nervously. "I'm sorry if I was sharp, mister."

It was an apology, and so I said, "That's quite all right."

"I mean that you can drop a spoon any time you want to. I'll be glad to get you another."

"Thank you." I turned to my coffee.

"You're not offended, are you, mister?" she asked eagerly.

"No. Not at all."

She snatched a newspaper from an empty neighboring table. "Here, sir, you can read this while you eat. I mean it's on the house. Free."

When she left me, the wide-eyed cashier stared at her. "What's with all that, Mable?"

Mable glanced back at me with a trace of uneasiness. "You can never tell who he might be. You better be polite these days."

As I ate I read, and an item caught my eye. A grown man had heated pennies in a frying pan and tossed them out to some children who were making trick-or-treat rounds before Halloween. He had been fined a miserable twenty dollars.

I made a note of his name and address.

Dr. Briller finished his examination. "You can get dressed now, Mr. Turner."

I picked up my shirt. "I don't suppose some new miracle drug has been developed since I was here last?"

He laughed with self-enjoyed good nature. "No, I'm afraid not." He watched me button the shirt. "By the way, have you decided what you're going to do with your remaining time?"

I had, but I thought I'd say, "Not yet."

He was faintly perturbed. "You really should, you know. Only about three months left. And be sure to let me know when you do."

While I finished dressing, he sat down at his desk and glanced at the newspaper lying there. "The killer seems to be rather busy, doesn't he?"

He turned the page. "But really the most surprising thing about the crimes seems to be the public's reaction. Have you read the Letters From the People column recently?"

"No."

"These murders appear to be meeting with almost universal approval. Some of the letter writers even hint that they might be able to supply the murderer with a few choice names themselves."

I would have to get a paper.

"Not only that," Dr. Briller said, "but a wave of politeness has struck the city."

I put on my coat. "Shall I come back in two weeks?"

He put aside the paper. "Yes, and try to look at this whole thing as cheerfully as possible. We all have to go someday."

But his day was indeterminate and presumably in the distant future.

My appointment with Dr. Briller had been in the evening, and it was nearly ten by the time I left my bus and began the short walk to my apartment building.

As I approached the last corner, I heard a shot. I turned into Milding Lane and found a little man with a revolver standing over a newly-dead body on the quiet and deserted sidewalk.

I looked down at the corpse. "Goodness, a policeman."

The little man nodded. "Yes, what I've done does seem a little extreme, but you see he was using a variety of language that was entirely unnecessary."

"Ah," I said.

The little man nodded. "I'd parked my car in front of this fire hydrant. Entirely inadvertently, I assure you. And this policeman was waiting when I returned to my car. And also he discovered that I'd forgotten my driver's license. I would not have acted as I did if he had simply written out a ticket—for I was guilty, sir, and I readily admit it—but he was not content with that. He made embarrassing observations concerning my intelligence, my eyesight, the possibility that I'd stolen the car, and finally on the legitimacy of my birth." He blinked at a fond memory. "And my mother was an angel, sir. An angel."

I remembered a time when I'd been apprehended while absent-mindedly jaywalking. I would contritely have accepted the customary warning, or even a ticket, but the officer insisted upon a profane lecture before a grinning assemblage of interested pedestrians. Most humiliating.

The little man looked at the gun in his hand. "I bought this just today and actually I'd intended to use it on the superintendent of my apartment building. A bully."

I agreed. "Surly fellows."

He sighed. "But now I suppose I'll have to turn myself over to the police?"

I gave it thought. He watched me.

He cleared his throat. "Or perhaps I should just leave a note? You see I've been reading in the newspapers about . . ."

I lent him my notebook.

He wrote a few lines, signed his initials, and deposited the slip of paper between two buttons of the dead officer's jacket.

He handed the notebook to me. "I must remember to get one of these."

He opened the door of his car. "Can I drop you off anywhere?"

"No, thank you," I said. "It's a nice evening. I'd rather walk."

Pleasant fellow, I reflected, as I left him.

Too bad there weren't more like him.

DANGEROUS
MADMEN _____

Donald Westlake *(1933–   ) is an accomplished and prolific novelist who has won an Edgar Award for his 1967 novel,* God Save the Mark. *While he writes tough-guy stories under the pseudonym of Richard Stark, he usually reserves his own moniker for hilarious farces such as* The Hot Rock. *It should be quite apparent, however, that for "The Winner," a parable about prisons and aversive conditioning, he has made a shocking exception.*

THE WINNER

Donald Westlake

WORDMAN stood at the window, looking out, and saw Revell walk away from the compound. "Come here," he said to the interviewer. "You'll see the Guardian in action."

The interviewer came around the desk and stood beside Wordman at the window. He said, "That's one of them?"

"Right." Wordman smiled, feeling pleasure. "You're lucky," he said. "It's rare when one of them even makes the attempt. Maybe he's doing it for your benefit."

The interviewer looked troubled. He said, "Doesn't he know what it will do?"

"Of course. Some of them don't believe it, not till they've tried it once. Watch."

They both watched. Revell walked without apparent haste, directly across the field toward the woods on the other side. After he'd gone about two hundred yards from the edge of the compound he began to bend forward slightly at the middle, and a few yards farther on he folded his arms across his stomach as though it ached him. He tottered, but kept moving forward, staggering more and more, appearing to be in great pain. He managed to stay on his feet nearly all the way to the trees, but finally crumpled to the ground, where he lay unmoving.

Wordman no longer felt pleasure. He liked the theory of the Guardian better than its application. Turning to his desk, he called the infirmary and said, "Send a stretcher out to the east, near the woods. Revell's out there."

The interviewer turned at the sound of the name, saying, "Revell? Is that who that is? The poet?"

"If you can call it poetry." Wordman's lips curled in disgust. He'd read some of Revell's so-called poems; garbage, garbage.

The interviewer looked back out the window. "I'd heard he was arrested," he said thoughtfully.

Looking over the interviewer's shoulder, Wordman saw that Revell had managed to get back up onto hands and knees, was now crawling slowly and painfully toward the woods. But a stretcher team was already trotting toward him and Wordman watched as they reached him, picked up the pain-weakened body, strapped it to the stretcher, and carried it back to the compound.

As they moved out of sight, the interviewer said, "Will he be all right?"

"After a few days in the infirmary. He'll have strained some muscles."

The interviewer turned away from the window. "That was very graphic," he said carefully.

"You're the first outsider to see it," Wordman told him, and smiled, feeling good again. "What do they call that? A scoop?"

"Yes," agreed the interviewer, sitting back down in his chair. "A scoop."

They returned to the interview, just the most recent of dozens Wordman had given in the year since this pilot project of the Guardian had been set up. For perhaps the fiftieth time he explained what the Guardian did and how it was of value to society.

The essence of the Guardian was the miniature black box, actually a tiny radio receiver, which was surgically inserted into the body of every prisoner. In the center of this prison compound was the Guardian transmitter, perpetually sending its message to these receivers. As long as a prisoner stayed within the hundred-and-fifty-yard range of that transmitter, all was well. Should he move beyond that range, the black box inside his skin would begin to send messages of pain throughout his nervous system. This pain increased as the prisoner moved farther from the transmitter, until at its peak it was totally immobilizing.

"The prisoner can't hide, you see," Wordman explained. "Even if Revell had reached the woods, we'd have found him. His screams would have led us to him."

The Guardian had been initially suggested by Wordman himself, at that time serving as assistant warden at a more ordinary penitentiary in the Federal system. Objections, mostly from sentimentalists, had delayed its acceptance for several years, but now at last this pilot project had been established, with a guaranteed five-year trial period, and Wordman had been placed in charge.

"If the results are as good as I'm sure they will be," Wordman said, "all prisons in the Federal system will be converted to the Guardian method."

The Guardian method had made jailbreaks impossible, riots easy to quell—by merely turning off the transmitter for a minute or two—and prisons simplicity to guard. "We have no guards here as such," Wordman pointed out. "Service employees only are needed here, people for the mess hall, infirmary and so on."

For the pilot project, prisoners were only those who had committed crimes against the State rather than against individuals. "You might say," Wordman said, smiling, "that here are gathered the Disloyal Opposition."

"You mean, political prisoners," suggested the interviewer.

"We don't like that phrase here," Wordman said, his manner suddenly icy. "It sounds Commie."

The interviewer apologized for his sloppy use of terminology, ended the interview shortly afterward, and Wordman, once again in a good mood, escorted him out of the building. "You see," he said, gesturing. "No walls. No machine guns in towers. Here at last is the model prison."

The interviewer thanked him again for his time, and went away to his car. Wordman watched him leave, then went over to the infirmary to see Revell. But he'd been given a shot, and was already asleep.

Revell lay flat on his back and stared at the ceiling. He kept thinking, over and over again, "I didn't know it would be as bad as that. I didn't know it would be as bad as that." Mentally, he took a big brush of black paint and wrote the words on the spotless white ceiling: "*I didn't know it would be as bad as that.*"

"Revell."

He turned his head slightly and saw Wordman standing beside the bed. He watched Wordman, but made no sign.

Wordman said, "They told me you were awake."

Revell waited.

"I tried to tell you when you first came," Wordman reminded him. "I told you there was no point trying to get away."

Revell opened his mouth and said, "It's all right, don't feel bad. You do what you have to do, I do what I have to do."

"Don't *feel* bad!" Wordman stared at him. "What have *I* got to feel bad about?"

Revell looked up at the ceiling, and the words he had painted there just a minute ago were gone already. He wished he had paper and pencil. Words were leaking out of him like water through a sieve. He needed paper and pencil to catch them in. He said, "May I have paper and pencil?"

"To write more obscenity? Of course not."

"Of course not," echoed Revell. He closed his eyes and watched the words leaking away. A man doesn't have time both to invent and memorize, he has to choose, and long ago Revell had chosen invention. But now there was no way to put the inventions down on paper and they trickled through his mind like water and eroded away into the great outside world. "Twinkle, twinkle, little pain," Revell said softly, "in my groin and in my brain, down so low and up so high, will you live or will I die?"

"The pain goes away," said Wordman. "It's been three days. It should be gone already."

"It will come back," Revell said. He opened his eyes and wrote the words on the ceiling. "It will come back."

Wordman said, "Don't be silly. It's gone for good, unless you run away again."

Revell was silent.

Wordman waited, half-smiling, and then frowned. "You aren't," he said.

Revell looked at him in some surprise. "Of course I am," he said. "Didn't you know I would?"

"No one tries it twice."

"I'll never stop leaving. Don't you know that? I'll never stop leaving. I'll never stop being, I'll not stop believing I'm who I must be. You had to know that."

Wordman stared at him. "You'll go through it *again?*"

"Ever and ever," Revell said.

"It's a bluff." Wordman pointed an angry finger at Revell, saying, "If you want to die, I'll let you die. Do you know if we don't bring you back you'll die out there?"

"That's escape, too," Revell said.

"Is that what you want? All right. Go out there again, and I won't send anyone after you, that's a promise."

"Then you lose," Revell said. He looked at Wordman finally, seeing the blunt angry face. "They're your rules," Revell told him, "and by your own rules you're going to lose. You say your black box will make me stay, and that means the black box will make me stop being me. I say you're wrong. I say as long as I'm leaving you're losing, and if the black box kills me you've lost forever."

Spreading his arms, Wordman shouted, "Do you think this is a *game?*"

"Of course," said Revell. "That's why you invented it."

"You're insane," Wordman said. He started for the door. "You shouldn't be here, you should be in an asylum."

"That's losing, too," Revell shouted after him, but Wordman had slammed the door and gone.

Revell lay back on the pillow. Alone again, he could dwell once more on his terrors. He was afraid of the black box, much more now that he knew what it could do to him, afraid to the point where his fear made him sick to his stomach. But he was afraid of losing himself, too, this a more abstract and intellectual fear but just as strong. No, it was even stronger, because it was driving him to go out again.

"But I didn't know it would be as bad as that," he whispered. He painted it once more on the ceiling, this time in red.

Wordman had been told when Revell would be released from the infirmary, and he made a point of being at the door when Revell came out. Revell seemed somewhat leaner, perhaps a little older. He shielded his eyes from the sun with his hand, looked at Wordman, and said, "Goodbye, Wordman." He started walking east.

Wordman didn't believe it. He said, "You're bluffing, Revell."

Revell kept walking.

Wordman couldn't remember when he'd ever felt such anger. He wanted to run after Revell and kill him with his bare hands. He clenched his hands into fists and told himself he was a reasonable man, a rational man, a merciful man. As the Guardian was reasonable, was rational, was merciful. It required only obedience, and so did he. It punished only such purposeless defiance as Revell's, and so did he. Revell was antisocial, self-destructive, he had to learn. For his own sake, as well as for the sake of society, Revell had to be taught.

Wordman shouted, "What are you trying to *get* out of this?" He glared at Revell's moving back, listened to Revell's silence. He shouted, "I won't send anyone after you! You'll crawl back *yourself!*"

He kept watching until Revell was far out from the compound, staggering across the field toward the trees, his arms folded across his stomach, his legs stumbling, his head bent forward. Wordman watched, and then gritted his teeth, and turned his back, and returned to his office to work on the monthly report. Only two attempted escapes last month.

Two or three times in the course of the afternoon he looked out the window. The first time, he saw Revell far across the field, on hands and knees, crawling toward the trees. The last time, Revell was out of sight, but he could be heard screaming. Wordman had a great deal of trouble concentrating his attention on the report.

Toward evening he went outside again. Revell's screams sounded from the woods, faint but continuous. Wordman stood listening, his fists clenching and relaxing at his sides. Grimly he forced himself not to feel pity. For Revell's own good he had to be taught.

A staff doctor came to him a while later and said, "Mr. Wordman, we've got to bring him in."

Wordman nodded. "I know. But I want to be sure he's learned."

"For God's sake," said the doctor, "*listen* to him."

Wordman looked bleak. "All right, bring him in."

As the doctor started away, the screaming stopped. Wordman and the doctor both turned their heads, listened—silence. The doctor ran for the infirmary.

Revell lay screaming. All he could think of was the pain, and the need to scream. But sometimes, when he managed a scream of the very loudest, it was possible for him to have a fraction of a second for himself, and in those fractions of seconds he still kept moving away from the prison, inching along the ground, so that in the last hour he had moved approximately seven feet. His head and right arm were now visible from the country road that passed through these woods.

On one level, he was conscious of nothing but the pain and his own screaming. On another level, he was totally, even insistently, aware of everything around him, the blades of grass near his eyes, the stillness of the woods, the tree branches high overhead. And the small pickup truck, when it stopped on the road beyond him.

The man who came over from the truck and squatted beside Revell had a lined and weathered face and the rough clothing of a farmer. He touched Revell's shoulder and said, "You hurt, fella?"

"Eeeeast!" screamed Revell. "Eeeeast!"

"Is it okay to move you?" asked the man.

"Yesssss!" shrieked Revell. "Eeeeast!"

"I'd best take you to a doctor."

There was no change in the pain when the man lifted him and carried him to the truck and lay him down on the floor in back. He was already at optimum distance from the transmitter; the pain now was as bad as it could get.

The farmer tucked a rolled-up wad of cloth into Revell's open mouth. "Bite on this," he said. "It'll make it easier."

It made nothing easier, but it muffled his screams. He was grateful for that; the screams embarrassed him.

He was aware of it all, the drive through increasing darkness, the farmer carrying him into a building that was of colonial design on the outside but looked like the infirmary on the inside, and a doctor who looked down at him and touched his forehead and then went to one side to thank the farmer for bringing him. They spoke briefly over there, and then the farmer went away and the doctor came back to look at Revell again. He was young, dressed in laboratory white, with a pudgy face and red hair. He seemed sick and angry. He said, "You're from that prison, aren't you?"

Revell was still screaming through the cloth. He managed a head-spasm which he meant to be a nod. His armpits felt as though they were being cut open with knives of ice. The sides of his neck were being scraped by sandpaper. All of his joints were being ground back and forth, back and forth, the way a man at dinner separates the bones of a chicken wing. The interior of his stomach was full of acid. His body was stuck with needles, sprayed with fire. His skin was being peeled off, his nerves cut with razor blades, his muscles pounded with hammers. Thumbs were pushing his eyes out from inside his head. And yet, the genius of this pain, the brilliance that had gone into its construction, it permitted his mind to work, to remain constantly aware. There was no unconsciousness for him, no oblivion.

The doctor said, "What beasts some men are. I'll try to get it out of you. I don't know what will happen, we aren't supposed to know how it works, but I'll try to take the box out of you."

He went away, and came back with a needle. "Here. This will put you to sleep."

Ahhhhh.

"He isn't there. He just isn't anywhere in the woods."

Wordman glared at the doctor, but knew he had to accept what the man reported. "All right," he said. "Someone took him away. He had a confederate out there, someone who helped him get away."

"No one would dare," said the doctor. "Anyone who helped him would wind up here themselves."

"Nevertheless," said Wordman. "I'll call the State Police," he said, and went on into his office.

Two hours later the State Police called back. They'd checked the normal users of that road, local people who might have seen or heard something, and had found a farmer who'd picked up an injured man near the prison and taken him to a Dr. Allyn in Boonetown. The State Police were convinced the farmer had acted innocently.

"But not the doctor," Wordman said grimly. "He'd have to know the truth almost immediately."

"Yes, sir, I should think so."

"And he hasn't reported Revell."

"No, sir."

"Have you gone to pick him up yet?"

"Not yet. We just got the report."

"I'll want to come with you. Wait for me."

"Yes, sir."

Wordman traveled in the ambulance in which they'd bring Revell back. They arrived without siren at Dr. Allyn's with two cars of state troopers, marched into the tiny operating room, and found Allyn washing instruments at the sink.

Allyn looked at them all calmly and said, "I thought you might be along."

Wordman pointed at the man who lay, unconscious, on the table in the middle of the room. "There's Revell," he said.

Allyn glanced at the operating table in surprise. "Revell? The poet?"

"You didn't know? Then why help him?"

Instead of answering, Allyn studied his face and said, "Would you be Wordman himself?"

Wordman said, "Yes, I am."

"Then I believe this is yours," Allyn said, and put into Wordman's hands a small and bloody black box.

The ceiling was persistently bare. Revell's eyes wrote on it words that should have singed the paint away, but nothing ever happened. He shut his eyes against the white at last and wrote in spidery letters on the inside of his lids the single word *oblivion*.

He heard someone come into the room, but the effort of making a change was so great that for a moment longer he permitted his eyes to remain closed. When he did open them he saw Wordman there, standing grim and mundane at the foot of the bed.

Wordman said, "How are you, Revell?"

"I was thinking about oblivion," Revell told him. "Writing a poem on the subject." He looked up at the ceiling, but it was empty.

Wordman said, "You asked, one time, you asked for pencil and paper. We've decided you can have them."

Revell looked at him in sudden hope, but then understood, "Oh," he said. "Oh, *that*."

Wordman frowned and said, "What's wrong? I said you can have pencil and paper."

"If I promise not to leave any more."

Wordman's hands gripped the foot of the bed. He said, "What's the matter with you? You can't get away, you have to know that by now."

"You mean I can't win. But I won't lose. It's your game, your rules, your home ground, your equipment; if I can manage a stalemate, that's pretty good."

Wordman said, "You still think it's a game. You think none of it matters. Do you want to see what you've done?" He stepped back to the door, opened it, made a motion, and Dr. Allyn was led in. Wordman said to Revell, "You remember this man?"

"I remember," said Revell.

Wordman said, "He just arrived. They'll be putting the Guardian in him in about an hour. Does it make you proud, Revell?"

Looking at Allyn, Revell said, "I'm sorry."

Allyn smiled and shook his head. "Don't be. I had the idea the publicity of a trial might help rid the world of things like the Guardian." His smile turned sour. "There wasn't very much publicity."

Wordman said, "You two are cut out of the same cloth. The emotions of the mob, that's all you can think of. Revell in those so-called poems of his, and you in that speech you made in court."

Revell, smiling, said, "Oh? You made a speech? I'm sorry I didn't get to hear it."

"It wasn't very good," Allyn said. "I hadn't known the trial would only be one day long, so I didn't have much time to prepare it."

Wordman said, "All right, that's enough. You two can talk later, you'll have years."

At the door Allyn turned back and said, "Don't go anywhere till I'm up and around, will you? After my operation."

Revell said, "You want to come along next time?"

"Naturally," said Allyn.

*Erle Stanley Gardner (1889–1970) is king of the paperbacks.
His books about Doug Selby, the firm of Lam and Cool, and
Perry Mason have sold over 200 million copies, and are still
selling over 20,000 per day. But few people realize that early
in his career, he wrote several outstanding novelettes of the
fantastic, and that at least two of these are also mysteries. In
"The Human Zero," for example, there is a locked room
puzzle, a mad scientist, an incipient super-criminal, and a
series of chilling murders.*

THE HUMAN ZERO

Erle Stanley Gardner

1. A Mysterious Kidnaping

Bob Sands took the letter from the hands of the captain of police, read it,
and pursed his lips in a whistle.

Four pairs of eyes studied the secretary of the kidnaped man as he read.
Two pencils scribbled notes on pads of scratch paper, of the type used by
newspaper reporters.

Bob Sands showed that he had been aroused from sleep, and had rushed
to headquarters. His collar was soiled. His tie was awry. The eyes were
still red from rubbing, and his chin was covered with a bristling stubble.

"Good Heavens," he said, "the Old Man was sure given a scare when
he wrote that!"

Captain Harder noted the sleep-reddened eyes of the secretary.

"Then it's his writing?"

"Undoubtedly."

Ruby Orman, "sob-sister" writer of the *Clarion*, added to her penciled
notes. "Tears streamed down the cheeks of the loyal secretary as he identified the writing as being that of the man by whom he was employed."

Charles Ealy, reporter for the more conservative *Star*, scribbled sketchy notes. "Sands summoned—Identifies writing as being that of P. H. Dangerfield—Dramatic scene enacted in office of Captain Harder at an early hour this morning—Letter, written by kidnaped millionaire, urges police to drop case and bank to pay the half million demanded in cash as ransom—Letter hints at a scientist as being the captor and mentions fate 'so horrible I shudder to contemplate it.' "

Sid Rodney, the other occupant of the room, wrote nothing. He didn't believe in making notes. And, since he was the star detective of a nationally known agency, he was free to do pretty much as he pleased.

Rodney didn't make detailed reports. He got results. He had seen them come and seen them go. Ordinary circumstances found him cool and unexcited. It took something in the nature of a calamity to arouse him.

Now he teetered back on the two legs of his chair and his eyes scanned the faces of the others.

It was three o'clock in the morning. It was the second day following the mysterious abduction of P. H. Dangerfield, a millionaire member of the stock exchange. Demands had been made for a cool half million as ransom. The demands had been okayed by the millionaire himself, but the bank refused to honor the request. Dangerfield had not over two hundred thousand in his account. The bank was willing to loan the balance, but only when it should be absolutely satisfied that it was the wish of the millionaire, and that the police were powerless.

Rodney was employed by the bank as a special investigator. In addition, the bank had called in the police. The investigation had gone through all routine steps and arrived nowhere. Dangerfield had been at his house. He had vanished. There was no trace of him other than the demands of the kidnapers, and the penciled notations upon the bottom of those letters, purporting to be in the writing of the missing millionaire.

Then had come this last letter, completely written in pen and ink by Dangerfield, himself. It was a letter addressed directly to Captain Harder, who was assuming charge of the case, and implored him to let the bank pay.

Captain Harder turned to Rodney.

"How will the bank take this?" he asked.

Rodney took a deep drag at his cigarette. He spoke in a matter-of-fact tone, and, as he spoke, the smoke seeped out of the corners of his mouth, clothing the words in a smoky halo.

"Far as the newspapers are concerned," he said, "I have nothing to say. As a private tip, I have an idea the bank will regard this as sufficient authorization, and pay the money.''

Captain Harder opened a drawer, took out photostatic copies of the other demands which had been received.

''They want five hundred thousand dollars in gold certificates, put in a suitcase, sent by the secretary of the kidnaped man, to the alley back of Quong Mow's place in Chinatown. It's to be deposited in an ash can that sits just in front of the back door of Quong Mow's place. Then Sands is to drive away.

''The condition is that the police must not try to shadow Sands or watch the barrel, that Sands must go alone, and that there must be no effort to trace the numbers of the bills. When that has been done, Dangerfield will go free. Otherwise he'll be murdered. The notes point out that, even if the money is deposited in the ash can, but the other conditions are violated, Dangerfield will die.''

There was silence in the room when the captain finished speaking. All of those present knew the purport of those messages. The newspaper reporters had even gone so far as to photograph the ash can.

There was a knock at the door.

Captain Harder jerked it open.

The man who stood on the threshold of the room, surveying the occupants through clear, gray, emotionless eyes, was Arthur L. Solomon, the president of the bank.

He was freshly shaved, well dressed, cool, collected.

''I obeyed your summons, captain,'' he said in a dry, husky voice that was as devoid of moisture as a dead leaf scuttling across a cement sidewalk on the wings of a March wind.

Captain Harder grunted.

''*I* came without waiting to shave or change,'' said Sands, his voice showing a trace of contempt. ''They said it was life or death.''

The banker's fish-like eyes rested upon the flushed face of Bob Sands.

''I shaved,'' said Solomon. ''I never go out in the morning without shaving. What is the trouble, captain?''

Harder handed over the letter.

The banker took a vacant chair, took spectacles from his pocket, rubbed the lenses with a handkerchief, held them to the light, breathed upon the lenses and polished them again, then finally adjusted the spectacles and read the letter.

His face remained absolutely void of expression.

"Indeed," he said, when he had finished.

"What we want to know," said Captain Harder, "is whether the bank feels it should honor that request, make a loan upon the strength of it and pay that ransom."

The banker put the tips of his fingers together and spoke coldly.

"One-half a million dollars is a very great deal of money. It is altogether too much to ask by way of ransom. It would, indeed, be a dangerous precedent for the more prominent business men of this community, were any such ransom to be paid."

"We've been all over that before, Mr. Soloman. What I want to know is what do you want the police to do? If we're to try and find this man, we'd better keep busy. If we're going to sit back and let you ransom him, and then try and catch the kidnapers afterward, we don't want to get our wires crossed."

The banker's tone dripped sarcasm.

"Your efforts so far have seemed to be futile enough. The police system seems inadequate to cope with these criminals."

Captain Harder flushed. "We do the best we can with what we've got. Our salary allowances don't enable us to employ guys that have got the brains of bank presidents to pound our pavements."

Ruby Orman snickered.

The banker's face remained gray and impassive.

"Precisely," he said coldly.

"Nothin' personal," said Harder.

The banker turned to Sid Rodney.

"Has your firm anything to report, Mr. Rodney?"

Rodney continued to sit back in his chair, his thumbs hooked into the arm holes of his vest, his cigarette hanging at a drooping angle.

"Nothin' that I know of," he said, smoke seeping from his lips with the words.

"Well?" asked Charles Ealy.

Captain Harder looked at the banker meaningly.

"Well?" he said.

Ruby Orman held her pencil poised over her paper.

"The *Clarion* readers will be *so* much interested in your answer, Mr. Soloman."

The banker's mouth tightened.

"The answer," he said, still speaking in the same husky voice, "is *no!*"

The reporters scribbled.

Bob Sands, secretary of the missing man, got to his feet. His manner was belligerent. He seemed to be controlling himself with an effort.

"You admit Mr. Dangerfield could sell enough securities within half an hour of the time he got back on the job to liquidate the entire amount!" he said accusingly.

"I believe he could."

"And this letter is in his handwriting?"

"Yes. I would say it was."

"And he authorizes you to do anything that needs to be done, gives you his power of attorney and all that, doesn't he?"

"Yes." Soloman nodded.

"Then why not trust his judgment in the matter and do what he says?"

The banker smiled, and the smile was cold and tight-lipped.

"Because the bank is under no obligations to do so. Mr. Dangerfield has a checking account of about two hundred thousand dollars. The bank would honor his check in that amount, provided our attorney could advise us that the information we have received through the press and the police would not be tantamount to knowledge that such check was obtained by duress and menace.

"But as far as loaning any such additional sum to be paid as ransom, the bank does not care to encourage kidnapings by establishing any such precedent. The demand, gentlemen, is unreasonable."

"What," yelled Sands, "has the bank got to say about how much kidnapers demand?"

"Nothing. Nothing at all, Mr. Sands. Mr. Rodney, I trust your firm will uncover some clue which will be of value. The bank values Mr. Dangerfield's account very much. We are leaving no stone unturned to assist the police. But we cannot subscribe to the payment of such an unheard-of ransom."

"A human life is at stake!" yelled Sands.

The banker paused, his hand on the door, and firmly said:

"The safety of the business world is also at stake, gentlemen. Good morning!"

2. Who is Albert Crome?

The door slammed shut.

Captain Harder sighed.

Sid Rodney tossed away the stub of his cigarette, groped for a fresh one.

"Such is life," mused Charles Ealy.

"The dirty pirate!" snapped Sands. "He's made thousands off of the Dangerfield account. He doesn't care a fig what happens to Dangerfield. He's just afraid of establishing a precedent that will inspire other criminals."

Sid Rodney lit his fresh cigarette.

Ruby Orman's pencil scribbled across the paper.

"Scene one of greatest consternation," she wrote. "Men glanced at each other in an ecstasy of futility. Sands gave the impression of fighting back tears. Even strong men may weep when the life of a friend is at stake. Police promise renewed activity . . ."

Bob Sands reached for his hat.

"I'll go crazy if I hang around here. Is there anything I can do?"

Captain Harder shook his head.

"We'll have this letter gone over by the handwriting department," he said.

Sands walked from the room.

"Good morning," he said wearily.

"Nothing new, Harry?"

"Not a thing, other than that letter," said Captain Harder. "This is one case where we can't get a toe-hold to work on."

Charles Ealy nodded sympathetically.

"Anything for publication?" he asked.

"Yes," snapped Captain Harder. "You can state that I am working on a brand new lead, and that within the next twenty-four hours we feel certain we will have the criminals in custody. You may state that we already have a cordon of police guarding against an escape from the city, and that, momentarily, the dragnet is tightening . . . Oh, you folks know, say the usual thing that may put the fear of God into the kidnapers and make the public think we aren't sitting here with arms folded."

Charles Ealy scraped back his chair.

"Wait a minute," said Rodney, the cigarette in his mouth wabbling in a smoky zigzag as he talked. "I may have a hunch that's worth while. Will you give me a break on it, captain, if it's a lead?"

The police captain nodded wearily.

"Shoot," he said.

Rodney grinned at the two reporters.

"This stuff is off the record," he admonished. "You two can scoop it if anything comes of it. Right now it's on the q.t."

The reporters nodded.

They were there, in the first place, because the two papers were "in right" with the administration. And they kept in right with the police department by printing what the police were willing they should print, and by keeping that confidential which was given to them in confidence.

Sid Rodney went to the trouble of removing his cigarette from the corner of his mouth, sure sign of earnestness.

"I've got a funny angle on this thing. I didn't say anything before, because I think it's a whole lot more grave than many people think. I have a hunch we're doing business with a man who has a lot more sense than the average kidnaper. I have a hunch he's dangerous. And if there was any chance of the bank coming to the front, then letting us try to recover the money afterward, I wanted to play it that way.

"But the bank's out, so it's everything to gain and nothing to lose. Now here's the situation. I ran down every one I could find who might have a motive. One of the things the agency did, which the police also did, was to run down every one who might profit by the disappearance or death of P. H. Dangerfield.

"But one thing our agency did that the police didn't do, was to try and find out whether or not any person had been trying to interest Dangerfield in a business deal and been turned down.

"We found a dozen leads and ran 'em down. It happened I was to run down a list of three or four, and the fourth person on the list was a chap named Albert Crome. Ever hear of him?"

He paused.

Captain Harder shook his head.

Ruby Orman looked blank. Charles Ealy puckered his brows.

"You mean the scientist that claimed he had some sort of a radium method of disrupting ether waves and forming an etheric screen?"

Rodney nodded. "That's the chap."

"Sort of cuckoo, isn't he? He tried to peddle his invention to the government, but they never took any particular notice of him. Sent a man, I believe, and Crome claimed the man they sent didn't even know elemental physics."

Sid Rodney nodded again.

There was a rap at the door.

Captain Harder frowned, reached back a huge arm, twisted the knob, and opened the door a crack.

"I left orders . . ." He paused in mid-sentence as he saw the face of Bob Sands.

"Oh, come in, Sands. I left orders only five people could come in here, and then I didn't want to be disturbed . . . Lord, man, what's the matter? You look as though you'd seen a ghost!"

Sands nodded.

"Look what happened. I started for home. My roadster was parked out in front of headquarters. I got in and drove it out Claremont Street, and was just turning into Washington when another car came forging alongside of me.

"I thought it would go on past, but it kept crowding me over. Then I thought of all the talk I'd heard of gangsters, and I wondered if there was any chance I was going to be abducted, too.

"I slammed on the brakes. The other car pushed right in beside me. There was a man sitting next to the driver, sort of a foreign looking fellow, and he tossed something.

"I thought it was a bomb, and I yelled and put my hand over my eyes. The thing thudded right into the seat beside me. When I grabbed it to throw it out, I saw it was a leather sack, weighted, and that there was crumpled paper on the inside. I opened the sack and found—this!"

Dramatically he handed over the piece of typewritten paper.

"Read it aloud," begged Ealy.

"Take a look," invited Captain Harder, spreading the sheet of paper on the desk.

They clustered about in a compact group, read the contents of that single spaced sheet of typewriting.

SANDS:

You are a damned fool. The banker would have given in if you hadn't been so hostile. And the police bungled the affair, as they nearly always do. I've got a method of hearing and seeing what goes on in Captain Harder's office. I'm going to tell you folks right now that you didn't do Dangerfield any good. When I showed him on the screen what was taking place, and he heard your words, he was beside himself with rage.

You've got one more chance to reach that banker. If he doesn't pay the sum within twelve hours there won't be any more Dangerfield.

And the next time I kidnap a man and hold him for ransom I don't want so much powwow about it. Just to show my power, I am going to abduct you, Sands, after I kill Dangerfield, and then I'm going to get Arthur Soloman, the banker. Both of you will be held for a fair ransom. Soloman's ransom will be seven hundred and fifty thousand dollars. So he'd better get ready to pay.

This is the final and last warning.   X.

Captain Harder's eyes were wide.

"Good Lord, has that man got a dictograph running into this office?"

Sands made a helpless gesture with the palms of his hands. He was white, his teeth were chattering, and his knees seemed utterly devoid of strength.

"I don't know. He's a devil. He's always seemed to know just what was going on. And he surely must have known Dangerfield's habits from A to Z. I'm frightened."

Captain Harder walked to the door.

"Send in a couple of men to search this place for a dictograph," he said. Then he turned on his heel, gave a swing of his arm. "Come on in another room, you folks. We'll go into this thing."

The little group trooped into one of the other offices.

"All right, Rodney. You were mentioning a scientist. What of him?"

"I went to his office," said Rodney, "and tried to engage him in conversation. He wouldn't talk. I asked him what he knew about Dangerfield, and he all but frothed at the mouth. He said Dangerfield was a crook, a pirate, a robber. Then he slammed the door.

"But, here's the point. I got a peep at the inside of his office. There was a Royal portable in there, and these letters that were received demanding ransom were written on a Royal portable.

"It's not much of a lead, and it's one that the police will have to run down—now. If it's a matter of life and death, and working against time, then it's too big for our agency to handle. But my opinion is that Albert Crome was violently insane, at least upon the subject of Dangerfield."

The police captain whirled to Sands.

"What sort of a car were these men using?"

"You mean the men who tossed the letter?"

"Yes."

"I can't tell you. I know it's stupid of me, but I just got too rattled to notice. It was a big car, and it looked as though it might have been a Cadillac, or a Buick, or a Packard. It might even have been some other make."

The captain snorted.

"What do you know about Crome?"

Sands blinked.

"I know Mr. Dangerfield was negotiating for the purchase of some patent rights, or the financing of some formula or something, but that's about all. The deal fell through."

"Ever meet Crome?"

The secretary hesitated, knitted his brows.

"You'll have to let me think . . . Yes, yes, of course I did. I met him several times. Some of the negotiations were carried on through me."

"Impress you as being a little off?" asked Sid Rodney, drawling the question, his inevitable cigarette dangling loosely from the corner of his mouth as he talked.

"No. He impressed me as being a pretty wide awake sort of a chap, very much of a gentleman, with a high sense of honor."

Captain Harder, pressed a button.

"Take these letters. Have 'em photographed," he told the man who answered the buzzer. "Check the typewriting with the others. Then get me everything you can get on Albert Crome. I want to know what he's been doing with his time the last few days, who he associates with, who's seen him lately, where he lives, what he's doing with his work, everything about him.

"And if you can get a man into his offices and laboratory, I want a specimen of the typewriting that comes from the portable machine he's got—a Royal."

The man nodded, withdrew.

Captain Harder grinned at the little group.

"Well, we might go down to T-Bone Frank's and have a cup of coffee and some eats. Maybe we'll have something new when we get back."

Sands fidgeted.

"I don't want anything to eat."

"Well, you'd better wait a little while, Sands. You know that threat may mean nothing. Then again, it may mean a lot."

Sands nodded.

"Are you going to tell Soloman?"

"Yes. I'll give him a ring, I guess. Maybe I'd better do it before he gets home and to bed. Let's see, I've got his number here. I'll give him a buzz and break the glad tidings and then put a couple of the boys on guard in front of the place. It'll make him think a little. Didn't like his attitude, myself . . . Oh, well!"

He gave the exchange operator the number, replaced the receiver, fished a cigar from his pocket and scraped a noisy match along the sole of his shoe.

Ruby Orman scribbled on her pad of paper: "In tense silence, these men waited grimly for the dawn."

Charles Ealy put a matter-of-fact question.

"Can we get these letters for the noon editions, Harry?"

"What's deadline?" asked the captain.

"We'd have to have them by eight o'clock in order to get the plates ready."

"I guess so. It ain't eight o'clock yet."

Ealy perked up his ears.

"You speak as though you had something up your sleeve," he said.

The officer nodded grimly.

"I have," he said.

The telephone rang. Captain Harder cupped his ear to the receiver.

"Funny," he said, "Soloman's residence says he's not home yet." Then: "Keep calling. Tell him I want to speak to him. It's important."

They went to the all-night restaurant, lingered over coffee and sandwiches. They were all nervous, with the exception of Sid Rodney. That individual seemed to be utterly relaxed, but it was the inactivity of a cat who is sprawled in the sun, keeping a lazy eye upon a fluttering bird, trying to locate the nest.

Charles Ealy watched Sid Rodney narrowly. Once he nodded, slowly.

They finished their meal, returned to headquarters.

Heard from Soloman?" asked Captain Harder.

Sergeant Green, at the desk, shook his head.

"They keep saying he hasn't returned. But we've unearthed some stuff about Crome from our department files. He wanted a permit to establish an experimenting station in a loft building down town. Had the lease on the place and was all ready to go ahead when he found out he had to have a permit to operate the sort of a place he wanted.

"He was turned down on the permit after it appeared that his experiments were likely to increase the fire hazard, and he was bitter about it."

Captain Harder grunted.

"That doesn't help much."

"Did he sent in any typewritten letters?" asked Sid Rodney.

"Maybe. I'll look in the files. Most of those things would be in another file."

"Got the address of the loft building?"

"Yes—632 Grant Street. That's down near the wholesale district, a little side street."

Sid nodded.

"Yeah. I know. What say we take a run down there, captain?"

"Why? He was turned down on his permit. There's nothing there for us."

Rodney lit a fresh cigarette and resumed.

"The man's a scientist. He hates Dangerfield. He impresses me as being very much unbalanced. He's got a loft that isn't being used. Now *if* he should happen to be mixed up in the kidnaping, where would be a better place to keep a prisoner than in an unused loft building, that had been taken over and fitted up as an experimental laboratory?"

Captain Harder grinned.

"You win," he said. "Get me half a dozen of the boys out, sergeant. I'm going down there myself and give it a once over. Better take along a bunch of keys."

"Do we go along?" asked Ealy, his eyes twinkling.

Captain Harder grinned.

"Certainly not," he said.

Sands took him seriously.

"I'm glad of that. I'm simply all in. I want to go and get some sleep, a bath and a shave."

Captain Harder looked sympathetic.

"I know, Sands. Ealy and I were kidding. But if you feel all in, go on home and get some sleep. We've got your number. We'll call you if there's anything there.''

''How about an escort?'' asked Rodney. ''Those threats, you know . . .''

Sands vehemently shook his head.

''No. I don't want to advertise to the neighborhood that I'm afraid. I'll go on home and sleep. I'm safe for twelve hours yet, anyway. If you think there's any danger at the end of that time, I'll move into a hotel and you can give me a guard.''

Captain Harder nodded in agreement.

''Okay.''

3. Into Thin Air

The two police cars slid smoothly to the curb before the loft building.

The first streaks of dawn were tingeing the buildings in the concrete cañon of loft buildings, wholesale houses and nondescript apartments.

Captain Harder jerked his thumb.

''This is the place. No use standin' on formality. Let's go up. He had the whole building leased. Looks vacant now.''

The men moved across the echoing sidewalk in a compact group. There was the jingle of keys against the brass lock plate, and then the click of a bolt. The door opened. A flight of stairs, an automatic elevator, a small lobby, showed in the reddish light of early morning. There was a musty smell about the place.

''Take the elevator,'' said Captain Harder. ''Then we won't have so much trouble . . . funny he leased the whole building in advance of a permit. This lease cost him money.''

No one said anything. They opened the door of the elevator. Then they drew back with an exclamation.

''Look there!'' said one of the men.

There was a stool in the elevator. Upon that stool was a tray, and upon the tray was some food, remnants of sandwhiches, a cup of coffee, the sides stained where trickles of the liquid had slopped over the side of the cup.

Captain Harder smelled the cup, jabbed a finger into the crust of the sandwiches.

''Looks like it's less than twenty-four hours old,'' he said.

The men examined the tray.

Captain Harder snapped into swift activity. It was plainly apparent that the curiosity which had sent him down to the loft building for a "look around" merely because there were no other clues to run down, had given place to well-defined suspicion.

"Here, Bill. You take one of the boys with you and watch the steps. Frank, get out your gun and watch the fire escape. Go around the back way, through the alley. We'll keep quiet and give you three minutes to get stationed. Then we're going up.

"If you see any one, order him to stop. If he doesn't obey, shoot to kill. George, you go with Frank. The rest of us are going up in the elevator."

He took out his watch.

"Three minutes," he said.

The men snapped into action.

Captain Harder held a thumb nail upon the dial of his big watch, marking the time.

"Okay," he said, at length. "Let's go. You two birds on the stairs, make sure you don't get above the first floor without covering every inch of ground you pass. We don't want any one to duck out on us. If you hear any commotion, don't come unless I blow my whistle. Watch those stairs!"

He closed the door of the elevator, jabbed the button marked by the figure "1."

The elevator creaked and swayed upward at a snail's pace, came to the first floor and stopped. Captain Harder propped the door open, emerged into a hallway, found himself facing two doors.

Both were unlocked. He opened first one, and then the other.

There were disclosed two empty lofts, littered with papers and rubbish. They were bare of furniture, untenanted. Even the closet doors were open, and they could see into the interiors of them.

"Nothing doing," said the officer. "Guess it's a false alarm, but we'll go on up."

They returned to the elevator, pressed the next button.

"There were three floors, narrow, but deep.

The second floor was like the first as far as the doors were concerned. But as soon as Captain Harder opened the first door, it was at once apparent they were on a warm trail.

The place was fitted up with benches, with a few glass jars, test tubes, some rather complicated apparatus enclosed in a glass case. There were a few jars of chemical, and there were some more trays with food remnants upon them.

"Somebody," said Captain Harder grimly, making sure his service revolver was loose in its holster, "is living here. Wonder what's in that room on the corner. Door looks solid enough."

He pushed his way forward through the litter on the floor, twisted the knob of the door.

"Locked," he said, "and feels solid as stone."

And, at that moment, sounding weak and faint, as though coming from a great distance, came a cry, seeping through the door from the room beyond, giving some inkling of the thickness of the door.

"Help, help, help! This is Paul Dangerfield. Help me! Help me!"

Captain Harder threw his weight against the door. As well have thrown his weight against the solid masonry of a wall.

"Hello," he called. "Are you safe, Dangerfield? This is the police!"

The men could hear the sound of frantic blows on the opposite side of the door.

"Thank God! Quick, get me out of here. Smash in the door. It's a foot thick!"

The words were faint, muffled. The blows which sounded upon the other side of the door gave evidence of the thickness and strength of the mortal.

Captain Harder turned to one of the men.

"How about keys?"

"I've got 'em, captain, but where do we put 'em?"

The officer stepped back to look at the door.

There was not a sign of a lock or keyhole in it. There was a massive knob, but nothing else to show that the door differed from the side of the wall, save the hairline of its borders.

"Smash it in! All together!"

They flung themselves against the door.

Their efforts were utterly unavailing.

"Hurry, hurry!" yelled the voice on the other side of the door. "He's going to . . . No, no! Don't. Oh! Go away! Don't touch that door. Oh . . . Oh . . . Not that!"

The voice rose to a piercing wail of terror, and then was silent. The squad pounded on the door, received no answer.

Captain Harder whirled to examine the loft.

"There's a bar over there. Let's get this door down."

He raised the whistle to his lips, blew a shrill blast. The two men who had been guarding the stairs came up on the run.

"Get this door down!" snapped the police captain, "and let's make it snappy."

They held a block of wood so that it formed a fulcrum for the bar, inserted the curved end, started to pry. The door was as solid as though it had been an integral part of the wall. Slowly, however the men managed to get the bar inserted to a point where the leverage started to spring the bolts.

Yet it was a matter of minutes, during which time there was no sound whatever from that mysterious inner room.

At length the door swayed, creaked, pried unevenly, sprung closed as the men shifted their grips on the bar to get a fresh purchase.

"Now, then, boys!" said Captain Harder, perspiration streaming down from his forehead and into his eyes. "Let's go!"

They flung themselves into the work. The door tottered, creaked, slowly pried loose and then banged open.

The squad stared at a room built without windows. There was ventilation which came through a grating in the roof. This grating was barred with inch-thick iron bars. The air sucked out through one section, came blowing through another. The air seemed fresh enough, yet there was an odor in that room which was a stale stench of death. It was the peculiar, sickeningly sweet odor which hangs about a house which has been touched by death.

There was a table, a reclining chair, a carpet, a tray of food, a bed. The room gave evidence of having been lived in.

But it was vacant, so far as any living thing was concerned.

On the floor, near the door which had been forced, was a pile of clothing. The clothing was sprawled out as though it had covered the form of a man who had toppled backward to the door, stretched his full length upon the floor, and then been withdrawn from his garments.

Captain Harder bent to an examination of the garments. There was a watch in the pocket which had stopped. The stopping of the watch was exactly five minutes before, at about the time the officers had begun pounding at the door.

There was a suit of silk underwear inside of the outer garments. The tie was neatly knotted about the empty collar. The sleeves of the shirt were down inside the sleeves of the coat. There were socks which nested down inside the shoes, as though thrust there by some invisible foot.

There was no word spoken.

Those officers, reporters, detectives, hardened by years of experience, to behold the gruesome, stared speechlessly at that vacant bundle of clothing.

Charles Ealy was the one who broke the silence.

"Good Heavens! There's been a man in these clothes and he's been sucked out, like a bit of dirt being sucked up into a vacuum cleaner!"

Captain Harder regained control of himself with an effort. His skin was still damp with perspiration, but that perspiration had cooled until it presented an oily slime which accentuated the glistening pallor of his skin.

"It's a trap, boys. It's a damned clever trap, but it's just a trap. There couldn't have been . . ."

He didn't finish, for Ruby Orman, speaking in a hushed voice, pointed to one of the shoes.

"Try," she said, "just try fitting a sock into the toe of that shoe the way this one is fitted, and try doing it while the shoe's laced, or do it, and then lace the shoe afterward, and see where you get."

"Humph," said Ealy, "as far as that's concerned, try getting a necktie around the collar of a shirt and then fitting a coat and vest around the shirt."

Captain Harder cleared his throat and addressed them all.

"Now listen, you guys, you're actin' like a bunch of kids. Even supposing there was some one in this room, where could he have gone? There ain't any opening. He couldn't have slid through those bars in the ventilator."

Some of the detectives nodded sagely, but it remained for Rodney to ask the question which left them baffled.

"How," he asked, "was it possible to get the foot out of that laced shoe?"

Captain Harder turned away.

"Let's not get stampeded," he said.

He started to look around him.

"Cooked food's been brought in here at regular intervals . . . the man that was here was Dangerfield, all right. Those are his clothes. There's the mark of the tailor, and there's his goldscrolled fountain pen. His watch has his initials on, even his check book is in the pocket.

"I tell you, boys, we're on the right track. This is the place Dangerfield's been kept, and it's that inventor who's at the bottom of the whole thing. We'll go knock his place over, and we'll probably find where Dangerfield is right now. He was spirited away from here, somehow.

"Those clothes were left here for a blind. Don't get stampeded. Here, feel the inside of the cloth. It's plumb cold, awfully cold. If anybody'd been inside those clothes within five minutes, the clothes'd be warm."

One of the officers nodded. His face gave an exhibition of sudden relief which was almost ludicrous. He grinned shamefacedly.

"By George, captain, that's so! Do you know, for a minute, this thing had me goofy. But you can see how cool the clothes are, and this watch is like a chunk of ice. It's be warm if anybody had been inside those clothes."

"Who," asked Sid Rodney, "was it that was calling to us through the door?"

Captain Harder stepped to the door, dragged in the bar.

"I don't know. It may have been a trick of ventriloquism, or it may have been a sound that was projected through the ventilating system. But, anyhow, I'm going to find out. If there's a secret entrance to this room, I'm going to find it if I have to rip off every board of the walls one at a time."

He started with the bar, biting it into the tongue and groove which walled the sides of the room. Almost instantly the ripping bar disclosed the unique construction of that room.

It consisted of tongue and groove, back of which was a layer of thick insulation that looked like asbestos. Back of that was a layer of thick steel, and the steel seemed to be backed with concrete, so solid was it.

By examining the outside of the room, they were able to judge the depth of the walls. They seemed to be at least three feet thick. The room was a veritable sound-proof chamber.

Evidently the door was operated by some electro-magnetic control. There were thick bars which went from the interior of the door down into sockets built in the floor, steel faced, bedded in concrete.

Captain Harder whistled.

"Looks like there was no secret exit there. It must have been some sort of ventriloquism."

Sid Rodney grunted.

"Well, it wasn't ventriloquism that made the jars on that door. It was some one pounding and kicking on the other side. And, if you'll notice the toes of those shoes, you'll see where there are fragments of wood splinters, little flakes of paint, adhering to the soles right where they point out into the uppers.

"Now, then, if you'll take the trouble to look at the door, you'll find little marks in the wood which correspond to the marks on the toes of the shoes. In other words, whether those shoes were occupied or not, they were hammering against that door a few minutes ago."

Captain Harder shook his head impatiently.

"The trouble with all that reasoning is that it leads into impossibilities."

Sid Rodney stooped to the vest pocket, looked once more at the gold embossed fountain pen.

"Has any one tried this to see if it writes?" he asked.

"What difference would that make?" asked the police captain.

"He might have left us a message," said Sid.

He abstracted the pen, removed the cap, tried the end of the pen upon his thumb nail. Then he took a sheet of paper from his notebook, tried the pen again.

"Listen, you guys, all this stuff isn't getting us anywhere. The facts are that Dangerfield was here. He ain't here now. Albert Crome has this place rented. He has a grudge against Dangerfield. It's an odds-on bet that we're going to get the whole fiendish scheme out of him—if we get there soon enough."

There was a mutter of affirmation from the officers, even men who were more accustomed to rely upon direct action and swift accusation than upon the slower method of deduction.

"Wait a minute," said Sid Rodney. His eyes were flaming with the fire of an inner excitement. He unscrewed the portion of the pen which contained the tip, from the barrel, drew out the long rubber tube which held the ink.

Captain Harder regarded him with interest, but with impatience.

"Just like any ordinary self-filling pen the world over," said the police captain.

Sid Rodney made no comment. He took a knife from his pocket, slit open the rubber sac. A few sluggish drops of black liquid trickled slowly down his thumb, then he pulled out a jet black rod of solid material.

He was breathing rapidly now, and the men, attracted by the fierce earnestness of his manner, crowded about him.

"What is it?" asked one.

Rodney did not answer the question directly. He broke the thing in half, peered at the ends.

These ends glistened like some polished, black jewel which had been broken open. The light reflected from little tiny points, giving an odd appearance of sheen and luster.

Slowly a black stain spread along the palm of the detective's hand.

Sid Rodney set the long rod of black, broken into two pieces, down upon the tray of food.

"Is that ink?" demanded Harder.

"Yes."

"What makes it look so funny?"

"It's frozen."

"Frozen!"

"Yes."

"But how could ink be frozen in a room of this sort? The room isn't cold."

Sid Rodney shrugged his shoulders.

"I'm not advancing any theories—yet. I'm simply remarking that it's frozen ink. You'll notice that the rubber covering and the air which was in the barrel of the pen acted as something of a thermal insulation. Therefore, it was slower to thaw out than some things."

Captain Harder stared at Rodney with a puckered forehead and puzzled eyes.

"What things do you mean?"

"The watch, for instance. You notice that it's started to run again."

"By George, it has!" said Charles Ealy. "It's started ticking right along just as though nothing had happened, but it's about six and a half or seven minutes slow."

Sid nodded silent affirmation.

Captain Harder snorted.

"You birds can run all the clues that you want to. I'm going to get a confession out of the bird that's responsible for this.

"Two of you stay here and see that no one comes in or goes out. Guard this place. Shoot to kill any one who disobeys your orders. This thing is serious, and there's murder at the bottom of it, or I miss my guess."

He whirled and stamped from the room, walking with that aggressive swing of the shoulders, that forward thrust of his sturdy legs, which betokened no good for the crack-brained scientist.

4. A Madman's Laboratory

They hammered on the door. After a matter of minutes there was an answer, a thin, cracked voice which echoed through the thick partitions of a door which seemed every bit as substantial as the door which Captain Harder had forced in order to enter that curious room where an empty suit of clothes had mocked him.

"Who is it?"

Captain Harder tried a subterfuge.

"Captain Harder, come to see about the purchase of an invention. I'm representing the War Department."

The man on the other side of that door crackled into a cackling chuckle. "It's about time. Let's have a look at you."

Captain Harder nodded to the squad of grim-visaged men who were grouped just back of him.

"All ready, boys," he said.

They lowered their shoulders, ready to rush the door as soon as it should be opened.

But, to their surprise, there was a slight scraping noise, and a man's face peered malevolently at them from a rectangular slit in the door.

Captain Harder jerked back.

The face was only partially visible through the narrow peephole. But there was a section of wrinkled forehead, shaggy, unkempt eyebrows, the bridge of a bony nose, and two eyes.

The eyes compelled interest.

They were red rimmed. They seemed to be perpetually irritated, until the irritation had seeped into the brain itself. And they glittered with a feverish light of unwholesome cunning.

"Psh! The police!" said the voice, sounding startlingly clear through the opening of the door.

"Open in the name of the law!" snapped Captain Harder.

"Psh!" said the man again.

There was the faintest flicker of motion from behind the little peephole in the door, and a sudden coughing explosion. A little cloud of white smoke mushroomed slowly out from the corner of the opening.

The panel slid into place with the smooth efficiency of a well oiled piece of machinery.

Captain Harder jerked out his service revolver.

"All together, boys. Take that door down!"

He gathered himself, then coughed, flung up his hand to his eyes.

"Gas!" he yelled. "Look out!"

The warning came too late for most of the squad of officers who were grouped about that door. The tear gas, a new and deadly kind which seemed so volatile as to make it mix instantly with the atmosphere, spread through the corridor. Men were blinded, staggering about, groping their way, crashing into one another.

The panel in the door slid back again. The leering, malevolent features twisted into a hoarse laugh.

Captain Harder flung up his revolver and fired at the sound of that demoniac laughter.

The bullet thudded into the door.

The panel slid shut.

Sid Rodney had flung his arm about the waist of Ruby Orman at the first faint suggestion of mushrooming fumes.

"Back! It may be deadly!"

She fought against him.

"Let me go! I've got to cover this!"

But he swept her from her feet, flung her to his shoulder, sprinted down the hallways of the house. A servant gazed at them from a lower floor, scowling. Men were running, shouting questions at each other, stamping up and down stairs. The entire atmosphere of the house took on a peculiarly acrid odor.

Sid Rodney got the girl to an upper window on the windward side of the house. Fresh air was blowing in in a cooling stream.

"Did it get your eyes?"

"No. I'm going back."

Sid held her.

"Don't be foolish. There's going to be something doing around here, and you and I have got to have our eyes where they can see something."

She fought against him.

"Oh, I *hate* you! You're so domineering, so cocksure of yourself."

Abruptly, he let her go.

"If you feel that way," he said, "go ahead."

She jerked back and away. She looked at him with eyes that were flaming with emotion. Sid Rodney turned back toward the window. Her eyes softened in expression, but there was a flaming spot in each cheek.

"Why *will* you persist in treating me like a child?"

He made no effort to answer the question.

She turned back toward the end of the hallway, where the scientist had maintained his secret laboratory with the door that held the sliding panel.

Men were struggling blindly about that door. Others were wrapping their eyes in wet towels. Here and there a figure groped its way about the corridor, clutching at the sides of the banister at the head of the stairs, feeling of the edges of the walls.

Suddenly, the entire vision swam before her eyes, grew blurred. She felt something warm trickling down her cheek. Abruptly her vision left her. Her eyes streamed moisture.

"Sid!" she called. "Oh, Sid!"

He was at her side in an instant. She felt the strong tendons of his arm, the supporting bulk of his shoulder, and then she was swung toward the window where the fresh air streamed into the house.

"I'm sorry," she said. "Now it's got me."

"It probably won't bother you very long. You didn't get much of a dose of it. Hold your eyes open if you can, and face the breeze. They'll have the house cleared of the fumes in a few minutes."

There was the sound of a siren from the outer street, the clang of a gong.

"Firemen to clear the house," said Sid.

They stood there, shoulder to shoulder, cheek to cheek, letting the fresh morning breeze fan their faces. Out in the yard were hurrying shadows. Men came running to stations of vantage, carrying sawed-off shotguns. More cars sirened their way to the curb. Spectators gathered.

Electric fans were used to clear the corridor of the gas. Men were brought up carrying bars and jimmies. They attacked the door. Captain Harder's eyes were still disabled, as were the eyes of the others who had stood before that door.

Sid Rodney touched the girl's shoulder.

"They're getting ready to smash in the door. Can you see now?"

She nodded.

"I think they've got the hallway pretty well cleared of gas. Let's go and see what happens."

She patted his arm.

"Sid, you're just like a big brother—some one to take care of me, some one to scold; but I like you a lot."

"Just as you would a brother?" he asked.

"Just exactly."

"Thanks," he said, and the disappointment of his voice was lost in the sound of splintering wood as the door swung back on its hinges.

They stared into a great laboratory and experimenting room. It was a scene of havoc. Wreckage of bottles, equipment and apparatus was strewn about the room. It looked as though some one had taken an ax and ruthlessly smashed everything.

Here, too, was another room without windows. Such light as there was in the room was artificial. The ventilation came through grilles which were barred with heavy iron. It was a room upon which it was impossible to spy.

There was no trace of Albert Crome, the man whose malevolent face had been thrust through the aperture in the doorway.

The police crowded into the room.

Bottles of various acids had been smashed, and the pools upon the floor seethed and bubbled, gave forth acrid, throat-stinging fumes. In a cage by the door there were three white rats. These rats were scampering about, shrilling squeaky protests.

There was no other sign of life left in that room, save the hulking shoulders of the policemen who moved about in a dazed manner.

Captain Harder's voice bellowed instructions. He was blinded, but he was receiving reports from a detective who stood at his side and giving a rapid summary of conditions in the room.

"He's escaped some way. There's a secret passage out of this room. Get the guards about the place to establish a dead-line. Let no man through unless he has a pass signed by me. Those instructions are not to be varied or changed under any circumstances . . ."

A man approached the officer.

"You're wanted on the telephone, captain. I can plug in an extension here in the laboratory."

A servant, surly-faced, resentful, impassively placed a telephone extension in the hand of Captain Harder, plugged in the wires.

The blinded officer raised the receiver to his ear.

"Yeah?" he said.

There came a rasping series of raucous notes, then the shrill cackle of metallic laughter and the click which announced the party at the other end of the line had hung up.

Captain Harder started fiddling with the hook of the receiver in a frantic effort to get central.

"Hello, hello. This is Captain Harder. There was a call just came through to me on this line. Trace it. Try and locate it . . . What's that? No call? He said he was calling from a down town drug store . . . All right."

The captain hung up the receiver.

"Well, boys, I guess he's given us the slip. That was his voice, all right. He was calling from a down town drug store, he said. Told me to look in the northeast corner of the room and I'd find a secret passage leading down into his garage. Said he ran right out in his car without any trouble at all. He's laughing at us."

One of the men picked his way through the wreckage of the room to the northeast corner. The others shuffled forward. Broken glass crunched under the soles of their feet as they moved.

5. A Fantastic Secret

The man who was bending over the wainscoting emitted a triumphant shout.

"Here it is!"

He gave a pull, and a section of the wall slid back, disclosing an oblong opening.

Captain Harder was cursing as a detective led him toward this oblong.

"I'm blinded . . . the outer guard let him slip through! What sort of boobs are we, anyhow? I thought I had this place guarded. Who was watching the outside? Herman, wasn't it? Get me that guy. I've got things to say to him!"

Men went down the steep flight of stairs which led from that secret exit, and came to the garage. Here were several cars, neatly lined up, ready for instant use, also several vacant spaces where additional cars could be kept.

"Big enough!" grunted one of the men.

Sid Rodney had an idea.

"Look here, captain, it took time to smash up that laboratory."

Captain Harder was in no mood for theories.

"Not so much! What if it did?"

"Nothing. Only it took some little time. I don't believe a man could have looked out of the door, recognized the police, turned loose the tear gas, and then smashed up this laboratory and still have time enough to make his escape by automobile from the garage.

"I happened to be looking out of a window after that tear gas was released, and I saw your additional guards start to arrive . . ."

Captain Harder interrupted. He was bellowing like a bull.

"What a bunch of boobs we are!" he yelled at the men who had clustered around him in a circle. "He didn't get away at all. He stayed behind to smash up the laboratory! Then he sneaked out and telephoned me from some place in the house. No wonder central couldn't trace the call.

"Look around, you guys, for another exit from this laboratory. And keep those electric fans going. I don't trust this bird. He's likely to flood a lot of poison gas through that ventilating system of his . . . I'm commencing to get so I can see a little bit. Be all right in a few minutes, I hope."

The men scattered, examining the wainscoting.

"Here we are, captain!" called one of the men. "Take a look at this. Something here, right enough, but I just can't figure how it works . . . Wait a minute. That's it!"

Something clicked as the officer stepped back. A section of the wainscoting swung open, revealing a passage the height of a man crawling on all fours.

"Volunteers," said Captain Harder. "Damn these eyes! I'm going myself."

And he approached the passageway.

There was a stabbing burst of flame, the rattle of a machine gun, and a withering hail of bullets vomited from out of the passageway.

Captain Harder staggered backward, his right arm dangling at his side. The man who had been next to him dropped to the floor, and it needed no second glance to tell that the man was dead, even before he hit the floor.

The walls of the laboratory echoed to the crash of gunfire. Policemen, flinging themselves upon the floor, fired into the yawning darkness of that oblong hole in the wall. Here and there, riot guns belched their buckshot into the passageway.

There was the sound of the mocking laughter, another spurt of machine gun fire, then silence.

Captain Harder had his coat off, was groping with his left hand for the location of the two bullet holes in his right arm and shoulder.

"Reckon I'm going to be an ambulance case, boys. Don't risk anything in there. Try gas."

The captain turned, groped for the door, staggered, fell. Blood spurted from the upper wound, which had evidently severed an artery.

Men grabbed him, carried him to the head of the stairs where ambulance men met them with a stretcher. Officers continued to keep up a fire upon the passageway. A man brought in a basket containing hand grenades and tear gas bombs. The pin was pulled from a tear gas bomb. The hissing of the escaping gas sounded plainly while the men on the floor held their fire.

The man who carried the gas bomb ran along the side of the wainscoting, flung the bomb into the opening. It hit with a thud, rolled over and over.

There was no sound emanating from the passageway, save the faint hiss of the gas.

"Give him a dose of it and see how he likes it," said one of the men.

As though to answer his question, from the very vicinity of the tear gas bomb, came a glittering succession of ruddy flashes, the rattle of a machine gun.

One of the men who was on the floor gave a convulsive leap, then quivered and was still. A hail of bullets splintered through the glass equipment which had been broken and scattered about. An officer tried to roll out of the way. The stream of bullets overtook him. He jumped, twitched, shivered, and the deadly stream passed on.

Sid Rodney grasped a hand grenade from the basket, pulled the pin, jumped to his feet.

The machine gun whirled in his direction.

"He's got a gas mask!" yelled one of the men who was crouched behind the shelter of an overturned bench.

Sid Rodney threw the grenade with all of the hurtling force of a professional baseball pitcher.

The missile hit squarely in the center of the opening, thudded against something that emitted a yell of pain.

The machine gun became silent, then stuttered into another burst of firing.

A livid sheet of orange flame seared its way out into the room. The whole side of the place seemed to lift, then settle. A deafening report ripped out the glass of windows in one side of the house. Plaster dust sprayed the air.

The oblong hole from which the machine gun had been coughing its message of death vanished into a tumbled mass of wreckage.

Men coughed from the acrid powder fumes, the irritating plaster dust.

"Believe that got him," said one of the men, rolling out from the shelter, holding a riot gun at ready as he rushed toward the tumbled mass of wreckage.

A human foot was protruding from between a couple of splintered two-by-fours. About it eddied wisps of smoke.

The officer was pined by others. Hands pulled the rafters and studs to one side. The body of a mangled man came sliding out.

From the blackness of that hole came the orange flicker of ruddy flame, the first faint cracklings of fire.

The mangled body had on what was left of a gas mask. The torso was torn by the force of the explosion. Parts of a machine gun were buried in the quivering flesh. But the features could be recognized.

Albert Crome, the crack-brained scientist, had gone to his doom.

Men rushed up with fire-fighting apparatus. The flames were swiftly extinguished. The wreckage was cleared away. Men crawled into that little cubicle where the scientist had prepared a place of refuge.

It was a little room, steel-lined, fitted with a desk, a table and a cot. Also there was a telephone extension in the room, and an electrical transformer, wires from which ran to a box-like affair, from the interior of which came a peculiar humming sound.

"Leave it alone until the bombing squad gets here. They'll know if it's some sort of an infernal machine. In the meantime let's get out of here."

The sergeant who gave the orders started pushing the men back.

Even as he spoke, there was a glow of ruddy red light from the interior of the box-like affair into which the electric wires ran.

"Better disconnect those wires," called one of the men.

The sergeant nodded, stepped forward, located the point of contact, reached to jerk one of the wires loose.

"Look out, don't short circuit 'em!"

Sid Rodney had crawled back out of the passage. The sergeant was tugging at the wires, they came loose, touched. There was a flash from the interior of the box-like machine, a humming, and then a burst of flame that died away and left a dense white smoke trailing out in sizzling clouds.

"You've short circuited the thing. That other wire must have been a ground and a button . . ."

But Sid Rodney was not listening.

His eyes happened to have been upon the cage of white rats as the voice called its warning. Those rats were scampering about the cage in the hysteria of panic.

Abruptly they ceased all motion, stood for a split fraction of a second as though they had been cast in porcelain. Then they shrank upon themselves.

Sid Rodney screamed a warning.

Men looked at him, followed the direction of his pointing forefinger, and saw an empty cage.

"What is it?" asked a detective.

Sid Rodney's face was white, the eyes bulging.

"The rats!"

"They got away. Somebody turned 'em loose, or the explosion knocked the cage around or blew a door open," said the officer. "Don't worry about them."

"No, no. I saw them melt and disappear. They just dissolved into the atmosphere."

The officer snickered.

"Don't bother yourself about rats," he said. "We've got work to do. Gotta find out what's going on here, and we've gotta locate Dangerfield."

He turned away.

Sid Rodney went over to the cage. He grasped the metal wires. They were so cold to his touch that the slight moisture on the tips of his fingers stuck to them.

He jerked one hand, and a bit of skin from the tips of his fingers pulled away.

He noticed a little pan of water which had been in the cage. It was filmed with ice. He touched the wires of the cage again. They were not so cold this time.

The film of ice was dissolving from the pan of water in the cage.

But there were no more white rats. They had disappeared, gone, utterly vanished.

Sid Rodney examined the cage. The door was tightly closed, held in place with a catch. There was no possible loophole of escape for those white rats. They had been caged, and the cage held them until, suddenly, they had gone into thin air.

There was a touch on his shoulder.

"What is it, Sid?"

Sid Rodney had to lick his dry lips before he dared to trust his voice.

"Look here, Ruby, did you ever hear of absolute zero?"

She looked at him with a puzzled frown, eyes that were dark with concern.

"Sid, are you sure you're all right?"

"Yes, yes! I'm talking about things scientific. Did you ever hear of absolute zero?"

She nodded.

"Yes, of course. I remember we had it in school. It's the point at which there is absolutely no temperature. Negative two hundred and seventy-three degrees centigrade, isn't it? Seems to me I had to remember a lot of stuff about it at one time. But what has it got to do with what's been going on here?"

"A lot," said Sid Rodney. "Listen to this:

"Dangerfield disappears. He's located in a room. There's no such thing as escape from that room. Yet, before our eyes—or, rather, before our ears—he vanishes. His watch is stopped. The ink in his fountain pen is frozen. His clothes remain behind.

"All right, that's an item for us to remember.

"Then next come these white rats. I'm actually looking at them when they cease to move, dwindle in size and are gone, as though they'd been simply snuffed out of existence.

"Now you can see the ice film still on the water there. You can see what the wires of the cage did to my fingers. Of course, it happened so quickly that these things didn't get so awfully cold . . . but I've an idea we've seen a demonstration of absolute zero. And if we have, thank heavens, that dastardly criminal is dead!"

The girl looked at him, blinked her eyes, looked away, then back at him.

"Sid," she said, "you're talking nonsense. There's something wrong with you. You're upset."

"Nothing of the sort! Just because it's never been done, you think it can't be done. Suppose, twenty years ago, someone had led you into a room and showed you a modern radio. You'd have sworn it was a fake because the thing was simply impossible. As it was, your mind was prepared for the radio and what it would do. You accepted it gradually, until it became a part of your everyday life.

"Now, look at this thing scientifically.

"We know that heat is merely the result of internal molecular motion. The more heat, the more motion. Therefore, the more heat, the more volume. For instance, a piece of red-hot metal takes up more space than a piece of ice-cold metal. Heat expands. Cold contracts.

"Now, ever since these things began to be known, scientists have tried to determine what is known as *absolute* zero. It's the place at which all molecular motion would cease. Then we begin to wonder what would happen to matter at that temperature.

"It's certain that the molecules themselves are composed of atoms, the atoms of electrons, that the amount of actual solid in any given bit of matter is negligible if we could lump it all together. It's the motion of the atoms, electrons and molecules that gives what we see as substance.

"Now, we have only to stop that motion and matter would utterly disappear, as we are accustomed to see it."

The girl was interested, but failed to grasp the full import of what Rodney was telling her.

"But when the body started to shrink it would generate a heat of its own," she objected. "Push a gas into a smaller space and it gets hotter than it was. That temperature runs up fast. I remember having a man explain artificial refrigeration. He said . . ."

"Of course," interrupted Sid impatiently. "That's elemental. And no one has ever reached an absolute zero as yet. But suppose one did? And remember this, all living matter is composed of cells.

"Now, this man hasn't made inanimate matter disappear. But he seems to have worked out some method, perhaps by a radio wave or some etheric disturbance, by which certain specially prepared bodies vanish into thin air, leaving behind very low temperatures.

"Probably there is something in the very life force itself which combines with this ray to eliminate life, temperature, substance. Think of what that means!"

She sighed and shook her head.

"I'm sorry, Sid, but I just can't follow you. They'll find Dangerfield somewhere or other. Probably there was some secret passage in that room. The fact that there were two here indicates that there must be others in that room.

"You've been working on this thing until it's got you groggy. Go home and roll in for a few hours' sleep—please."

He grimly shook his head.

"I know I'm working on a live lead."

She moved away from him.

"Be good, Sid. I've got to telephone in a story to the rewrite, and I've got to write some sob-sister articles. They will be putting out extras. I think this is all that's going to develop here."

Sid Rodney watched her move away.

He shrugged his shoulders, turned his attention to the empty cage in which the white rats had been playing about.

His jaw was thrust forward, his lips clamped in a firm, straight line.

6. Still They Vanish

Captain Harder lay on the hospital bed, his grizzled face drawn and gray. The skin seemed strangely milky and the eyes were tired. But the indomitable spirit of the man kept him driving forward.

Sid Rodney sat on the foot of the bed, smoking a cigarette.

Captain Harder had a telephone receiver strapped to his left ear. The line was connected directly with headquarters. Over it, he detailed such orders as he had to his men.

Betweentimes he talked with the detective.

The receiver rattled with metallic noises. Captain Harder ceased talking to listen to the message, grunted.

He turned to Sid Rodney.

"They've literally torn the interior out of that room where we found the empty clothes," he said. "There isn't the faintest sign of a passageway. There isn't any exit, not a one. It's solid steel, lined with asbestos, backed with concrete. Evidently a room for experiments . . . Oh, Lord, that shoulder feels cold!

"Hello, here's something else."

The telephone receiver again rattled forth a message.

Captain Harder's eyes seemed to bulge from their sockets.

"What?" he yelled.

The receiver continued to rattle forth words.

"Well, don't touch a thing. Take photographs. Get the fingerprint men to work on the case. Look at the watch and see if it stopped, and, if it did, find out what time it stopped."

He sighed, turned from the mouthpiece of the telephone to stare at Sid Rodney with eyes that held something akin to panic in them.

"They've found the clothes of Arthur Soloman, the banker!"

Sid Rodney frowned.

"The clothes?"

The officer sighed, nodded, weakly.

"Yes, the clothes."

"Where?"

"They were sitting at the steering wheel of Soloman's roadster. The car had skidded into the curb. The clothes are all filled out just as though there'd been a human occupant that had slipped out of them by melting into the thin air. The shoes are laced. One of the feet, or, rather, one of the empty shoes is on the brake pedal of the machine. The sleeves of the coat are hung over the wooden rim of the steering wheel. The collar's got a tie in it . . . just the same as the way we found Dangerfield's clothes.

"One of the men found the roadster and reported. The squad that handled the Dangerfield case went out there on the jump . . ."

He broke off as the receiver started to rattle again.

He listened, frowned, grunted.

"Okay, go over everything with a fine-toothed comb," he said, and turned once more to Sid Rodney.

"The watch," he said, "had stopped, and didn't start running again until the officer took it out of the pocket and gave it just a little jar in so doing. The hands pointed to exactly thirteen minutes past ten o'clock."

"That," observed Rodney, "was more than two hours after Albert Crome had died, more than two hours after the disappearance of the white rats."

Captain Harder rolled his head from side to side on the propped-up pile of pillows.

"Forget those white rats, Rodney. You're just making a spectacular something that will frighten the public to death. God knows they're going to be panicky enough as it is. I'd feel different about the thing if I thought there was anything to it."

Rodney nodded, got up from the bed.

"Well, captain, when they told me you were keeping your finger on the job, I decided to run in and tell you, so you'd know as much about it as I do. But I tell you I *saw* those white rats vanish."

The captain grinned.

"Seen 'em myself, Rodney, in a magician's show. I've seen a woman vanish, seen another one sawed in two. I've even seen pink elephants walking along the foot of the bed—but that was in the old days.''

Sid Rodney matched his grin, patted the captain's foot beneath the spotless white of the hospital bedspread.

''Take care of yourself, old timer, and don't let this thing keep you from getting some sleep. You've lost some blood and you'll need it. Where were the banker's clothes found?''

''Out on Seventy-first and Boyle Streets.''

''They leaving them there?''

''For the time being. I'm going to have the car finger-printed from hood to gas tank. And I'm having the boys form a line and close off the street. We're going to go all over the thing with a fine-toothed comb, looking for clues.

''If you want to run out there you'll find Selby in charge. Tell him I said you were to have any of the news, and if you find out anything more, you'll tell me, won't you?''

''Sure, Cap. Sure.''

''Okay. So long.''

And Captain Harder heaved a tremulous sigh.

Sid Rodney walked rapidly down the corridor of the hospital, entered his car, drove at once to Seventy-first near where it intersected Boyle.

There was a curious crowd, being kept back by uniformed officers.

Sid showed his credentials, went through the lines, found Detective Sergeant Selby, and received all of the latest news.

''We kept trying to locate Soloman at his home. He came in, all right, and his wife told him we were trying to get him. He went to the telephone, presumably to call police headquarters, and the telephone rang just as he was reaching for the receiver.

''He said 'hello,' and then said a doubtful 'yes.' His wife heard that much of the conversation. Then she went into another room. After that she heard Soloman hang up the receiver, and walk into the hall where he reached for his hat and coat.

''He didn't tell her a word about where he was going. Just walked out, got in his car, and drove away. She supposed he was coming to police headquarters.''

Sid lit a cigarette.

''Find out who he called?''

''Can't seem to get a lead on it.''

''Was he excited?''

"His wife thought he was mad at something. He slammed the door as he went out."

"These the clothes he was wearing?"

"Yes."

Sid Rodney nodded.

"Looks just like another of those things. Thanks, Selby. I'll be seeing you."

"Keep sober," said the police detective.

Sid Rodney drove to Arthur Soloman's residence.

Newspaper reporters, photographers, and detectives were there before him. Mrs. Soloman was staring in dazed confusion, answering questions mechanically, posing for photographs.

She was a dried-out wisp of a woman, tired-eyed, docile with that docility which comes to one whose spirit has been completely crushed by the constant inhibitions imposed by a domineering mate.

Sid Rodney asked routine questions and received routine answers. He went through the formula of investigation, but there was a gnawing uneasiness in his mind. Some message seemed to be hammering at the borderline of his consciousness, as elusive as a dream, as important as a forgotten appointment.

Sid Rodney walked slightly to one side, tried to get away from the rattle of voices, the sputter of flash lights as various photographs were made.

So far there were only a few who appreciated the full significance of those vacant clothes, propped up behind the steering wheel of the empty automobile.

The telephone rang, rang with the insistent repetition of mechanical disinterest. Some one finally answered. There was a swirl of motion, a beckoning finger.

"Rodney, it's for you."

Vaguely wondering, Rodney placed the receiver to his ear. There was something he wanted to think about, something he wanted to do, and do at once. Yet it was evading his mind. The telephone call was just another interruption which would prevent sufficient concentration to get the answer he sought.

"Hello!" he rasped, and his voice did not conceal his irritation.

It was Ruby Orman on the line, and at the first sound of her voice Sid snapped to attention.

He knew, suddenly, what was bothering him.

Ruby should have been present at the Soloman house, getting sob-sister stuff on the fatherless children, the dazed widow who was trying to carry on, hoping against hope.

"What is it, Ruby?"

Her words rattled swiftly over the wire, sounded as a barrage of machine gunfire.

"Listen, Sid; get this straight, because I think it's important. I'm not over there at Soloman's because I'm running down something that I think is a hot lead. I want you to tell me something, and it may be frightfully important. What would a powder, rubbed in the hair, have to do with the disappearance, if it was the sort of disappearance you meant?"

Sid Rodney grunted and registered irritation.

"What are you doing, Ruby—kidding me?"

"No, no. Tell me. It's a matter of life and death."

"I don't know, Ruby. Why?"

"Because I happen to know that Soloman had a little powder dusted on his hair. It was just a flick of the wrist that put it there. I didn't think much of it at the time. It looked like a cigarette ash, but I noticed that it seemed to irritate him, and he kept scratching at his head. Did you notice?"

"No," snapped Sid, interested. "What makes you think it had anything to do with what happened afterward?"

"Because I got to investigating about that powder, and wondering, and I casually mentioned the theory you had, and I felt a prickling in my scalp, and then I knew that some of that same powder had been put in my hair. I wonder if . . ."

Sid Rodney was at instant attention.

"Where are you now?"

"Over in my apartment. I've got an appointment. It's important. You can't come over. If it's what I think it is, the mystery is going to be solved. You're right. It's absolute zero, and—My God, Sid, it's getting cold . . ."

And there was nothing further, nothing save the faint sounds of something thump-thump-thumping—the receiver, dangling from the cord, thumping against the wall.

Rodney didn't stop for his hat. He left the room on the run. A newspaper reporter saw him, called to him, ran to follow. Sid didn't stop. He vaulted into his car, and his foot was pressing the starter before he had grabbed the wheel.

He floor-boarded the throttle, and skidded at the corner with the car lurching far over against the springs, the tires shrieking a protest.

He drove like a crazy man, getting to the apartment where Ruby Orman spent the time when she was not sob-sistering for her newspaper. He knew he could beat the elevator up the three flights of stairs, and took them two at a time.

The door of the apartment was closed. Sid banged his fist upon it in a peremptory knock and then rattled the knob.

"Oh, Ruby!" he called softly.

A canary was singing in the apartment. Aside from that, there was no faintest suggestion of sound.

Sid turned the knob, pushed his shoulder against the door. It was unlocked. He walked into the apartment. The canary perked its head upon one side, chirped a welcome, then fluttered nervously to the other side of the cage.

Sid strode through the little sitting room to the dining room and kitchenette. The telephone was fastened to the wall here.

But the receiver was not dangling. It had been neatly replaced on its hook. But there was a pile of garments just below the telephone which made Sid stagger against the wall for a brief second before he dared to examine them.

He knew that skirt, that businesslike jacket, knew the sash, the shoes . . . He stepped forward.

They were Ruby's clothes, all right, lying there in a crumpled heap on the floor.

And at the sight Sid Rodney went berserk.

He flung himself from room to room, ripping open closet doors. For a wild moment he fought back his desire to smash things, tear clothes, rip doors from hinges.

Then he got a grip on himself, sank into a chair at the table, lit a cigarette with trembling hand. He must think.

Soloman had had something put in his hair, a powder which irritated . . . Ruby had seen that powder, flicked there—a casual gesture, probably, like a cigarette ash. The powder had irritated . . . Ruby had told some one person something of Rodney's theory. Powder had been applied to her hair. . . . She had known of it . . . She had telephoned . . . She had an appointment . . . And it had become cold . . . Then the clothes at the foot of the telephone . . .

And the chair in which Sid Rodney had been sitting was flung back upon its shivering legs as he leaped from the table—flung back by the violence of the motion with which he had gone into action.

He gained the door in three strides, took the stairs on the run, climbed into his automobile and drove like some mythical dust jinni scurrying forward on the crest of a March wind.

He whizzed through street intersections, disregarded alike traffic laws and arterial stops, swung down a wide street given over to exclusive residences, and came to a stop before a large house constructed along the conventional lines of English architecture.

He jumped from the machine, ran rapidly up the steps, held his finger against the doorbell.

A man in livery came to the door, regarded him with grave yet passive disapproval.

"This is the residence of P. H. Dangerfield?"

"Yes."

"His secretary, Mr. Sands, is here?"

"Yes."

"I want to see him," said Sid, and started to walk into the door.

The servant's impassive face changed expression by not so much as a flicker, but he moved his broad bulk in such a manner as to stand between the detective and the stairs.

"If you'll pardon me, sir, the library to the left is the reception room. If you will give me your name and wait there I'll tell Mr. Sands that you are here. Then, *if* he wishes to see you, you will be notified."

There was a very perceptible emphasis upon the word "if."

Sid Rodney glanced over the man's shoulder at the stairs.

"He's upstairs, I take it?"

"Yes, sir, in the office, sir."

Sid Rodney started up.

The servant moved with swiftness, once more blocking the way.

"I beg your pardon, sir!"

His eyes were hard, his voice firm.

Sid Rodney shook his head impatiently, as a fighter shakes the perspiration out of his eyes, as a charging bull shakes aside some minor obstruction.

"To hell with that stuff! I haven't got time!"

And Sid Rodney pushed the servant to one side.

The man made a futile grab at Sid's coat.

"Not so fast . . ."

Sid didn't even look back. "Faster, then!" he said, with a cold grin.

The arm flashed around and down. The liveried servant spun, clutched at the cloth, missed, and went backward down the few steps to the landing.

Rodney was halfways up the stairs by the time the servant had scrambled over to hands and knees.

"Oh, Sands!" called Rodney.

There was no answer.

Rodney grunted, tried a door—a bedroom; another door—a bath; another door—the office.

It seemed vacant. A desk, a swivel chair, a leather-covered couch, several sectional bookcases, some luxuriously comfortable chairs, a filing case or two . . . and Sid Rodney jumped back with a startled exclamation.

A suit of clothes was spread out on the couch.

He ran toward it.

It was the checkered suit Sands had been wearing at the time of the interview at police headquarters. It was quite empty, was arranged after the manner of a suit spread out upon the couch in the same position a man would have assumed had he been resting.

Rodney bent over it.

There was no necktie around the collar of the shirt. The sleeves of the shirt were in the coat. The vest was buttoned over the shirt. The shoes were on the floor by the side of the couch, arranged as though they had been taken off by some man about to lie down.

7. A Fiend is Unmasked

Sid Rodney went through the pockets with swift fingers. He found a typewritten note upon a bit of folded paper. It bore his name and he opened and read it with staring eyes.

Sid Rodney, Ruby Orman, and Bob Sands, each one to be visited by the mysterious agency which has removed the others. This is no demand for money. This is a sentence of death.

Sid Rodney put the paper in his own pocket, took the watch from the suit, checked the time with the time of his own watch. They were identical as far as the position of the hands was concerned.

Sid Rodney replaced the watch, started through the rest of the pockets, found a cigarette case, an automatic lighter, a knife, fountain pen and pencil, a ring of keys, a wallet.

He opened the wallet.

It was crammed with bills, bills of large denomination. There were some papers as well, a letter in feminine handwriting, evidently written by an old friend, a railroad folder, a prospectus of an Oriental tour.

There was another object, an oblong of yellow paper, printed upon, with blanks left for data and signature. It was backed with carbon compound so as to enable a duplicate impression to be made, and written upon with pencil.

Sid studied it.

It was an express receipt for the shipment of a crate of machinery from George Huntley to Samuel Grove at 6372 Milpas Street. The address of the sender was given as 753 Washington Boulevard.

Sid puckered his forehead.

No. 753 Washington Boulevard was the address of Albert Crome.

Sid opened the cigarette case. Rather a peculiar odor struck his nostrils. There was a tobacco odor, also another odor, a peculiar, nostril-puckering odor.

He broke open one of the cigarettes.

So far as he could determine, the tobacco was of the ordinary variety, although there was a peculiar smell to it.

The lighter functioned perfectly. The fountain pen gave no hint of having been out of condition. Yet the clothes were as empty as an empty meal sack.

Sid Rodney walked to the door.

He found himself staring into the black muzzle of a huge revolver.

"Stand back, sir. I'm sorry, sir, but there have been strange goings on here, sir, and you'll get your hands up, or, by the Lord, sir, I shall let you have it, right where you're thickest, sir."

It was the grim-faced servant, his eyes like steel, his mouth stretched across his face in a taut line of razor-thin determination.

Sid laughed.

"Forget it. I'm in a hurry, and . . ."

"When I count three, sir, I shall shoot . . ."

There was a leather cushion upon one of the chairs. Sid sat down upon that leather cushion, abruptly.

"Oh, come, let's be reasonable."

"Get your hands up."

"Shucks, what harm can I do. I haven't got a gun, and I only came here to see if I couldn't . . ."

"One . . . two . . ."

Rodney raised his weight, flung himself to one side, reached around, grasped the leather cushion and flung it. He did it all in one sweeping, scrambling motion.

The gun roared for the first time as he flung himself to one side. It roared the second time as the spinning cushion hurtled through the air.

Sid was conscious of the mushrooming of the cushion, the scattering of hair, the blowing of bits of leather. The cushion smacked squarely upon the end of the gun, blocking the third shot. Before there could have been a fourth, Sid had gone forward, tackling low. The servant crashed to the floor.

It was no time for etiquette, the hunting of neutral corners, or any niceties of sportsmanship. The stomach of the servant showed for a moment, below the rim of the leather cushion, and Sid's fist was planted with nice precision and a degree of force which was sufficiently adequate, right in the middle of that stomach.

The man doubled.

Sid Rodney took the gun from the nerveless fingers, scaled it down the hall where it could do no harm, and made for the front door. He went out on the run.

Once in his car, he started for the address which had been given on the receipt of the express company as the destination of the parcel of machinery, Samuel Grove at 6372 Milpas Street. It was a slender clue, yet it was the only one that Sid possessed.

He made the journey at the same breakneck speed that had characterized his other trips. The car skidded to the curb in front of a rather sedate looking house which was in a section of the city where exclusive residences had slowly given way to cleaning establishments, tailor shops, small industries, cheap boarding houses.

Sid ran up the steps, tried the bell.

There was no response. He turned the knob of the door. It was locked. He started to turn away when his ears caught the light flutter of running steps upon an upper floor.

The steps were as swiftly agile as those of a fleeing rabbit. There followed, after a brief interval, the sound of pounding feet, a smothered scream, then silence.

Sid rang the bell again.

Again there was no answer.

There was a window to one side of the door. Sid tried to raise it, and found that it was unlocked. The sash slid up, and sid clambered over the sill, dropped to the floor of a cheaply furnished living room.

He could hear the drone of voices from the upper floor, and he walked to the door, jerked it open, started up the stairs. Some instinct made him proceed cautiously, yet the stairs creaked under the weight of his feet.

He was halfway up the stairs when the talking ceased.

Once more he heard the sounds of a brief struggle, a struggle that was terminated almost as soon as it had begun. Such a struggle might come from a cat that has caught a mouse, lets it almost get away, then swoops down upon it with arched back and needle-pointed claws.

Then there was a man's voice, and he could hear the words:

"Just a little of the powder on your hair, my sweet, and it will be almost painless . . . You know too much, you and your friend. But it'll all be over now. I knew he would be suspecting me, so I left my clothes where they'd fool him. And I came and got you.

"You washed that first powder out of your hair, didn't you, sweet? But this time you won't do it. Yes, my sweet, I knew Crome was mad. But I played on his madness to make him do the things I wanted done. And then, when he had become quite mad, I stole one of his machines.

"He killed Dangerfield for me, and that death covered up my own short accounts. I killed the banker because he was such a cold-blooded fish . . . Cold-blooded, that's good."

There was a chuckle, rasping, mirthless, the sound of scraping objects upon the floor, as though some one tried to struggle ineffectively. Then the voice again.

"I left a note in my clothes, warning of the deaths of you, of myself, and of that paragon of virtue, Sid Rodney, who gave you the idea in the first place. Later on, I'll start shaking down the millionaires, but no one will suspect me. They'll think I'm dead.

"It's painless. Just the first chill, then death. Then the cells dissolve, shrink into a smaller and smaller space, and then disappear. I didn't get too much of it from Crome, just enough to know generally how it works. It's sort of an etheric wave, like radio and X-ray, and the living cells are the only ones that respond so far. When you've rubbed this powder into the hair . . ."

Sid Rodney had been slowly advancing. A slight shadow of his progress moved along the baseboard of the hall.

"What's that?" snapped the voice, losing its gloating monotone, crisply aggressive.

Sid Rodney stepped boldly up the last of the stairs, into the upper corridor.

A man was coming toward him. It was Sands.

"Hello, Sands," he said. "What's the trouble here?"

Sands was quick to take advantage of the lead offered. His right hand dropped to the concealment of his hip, but he smiled affably.

"Well, well, if it isn't my friend Sid Rodney, the detective! Tell me, Rodney, have you got anything new? If you haven't, I have. Look here. I want you to see something . . ."

And he jumped forward.

But Rodney was prepared. In place of being caught off guard and balance, he pivoted on the balls of his feet and snapped home a swift right.

The blow jarred Sands back. The revolver which he had been whipping from his pocket shot from his hand in a glittering arc and whirled to the floor.

Rodney sprang forward.

The staggering man flung up his hands, lashed out a vicious kick. Then, as he got his senses cleared from the effects of the blow, he whirled and ran down the hall, dashed into a room and closed the door.

Rodney heard the click of the bolt as the lock was turned.

"Ruby!" he called. "Ruby!"

She ran toward him, attired in flowing garments of colored silk, her hair streaming, eyes glistening.

"Quick!" she shouted. "Is there any of that powder in your hair? Do you feel an itching of the scalp?"

He shook his head.

"Tell me what's happened."

"Get him first," she said.

Sid Rodney picked up the revolver which he had knocked from the hand of the man he hunted, advanced toward the door.

"Keep clear!" yelled Sands from behind that door.

Rodney stepped forward.

"Surrender, or I'll start shooting through the door!" he threatened.

There was a mocking laugh, and something in that laugh warned Rodney; for he leaped back, just as the panels of the door splintered under a hail of lead which came crashing from the muzzle of a sawed-off shotgun.

"I'm calling the police!" shouted Ruby Orman.

Sid saw that she was at a telephone, placing a call.

Then he heard a humming noise from behind the door where Sands had barricaded himself. It was a high, buzzing note, such as is made by a high-frequency current meeting with resistance.

"Quick, Ruby! Are you all right?"

"Yes," she said, and came to him. "I've called the police."

"What is it?" he asked.

"Just what you thought—absolute zero. Crome perfected the process by which any form of cell life could be made receptive to a certain peculiar etheric current. But there had to be a certain chemical affinity first.

"He achieved this by putting a powder in the hair of his victims. The powder irritated the scalp, but it did something to the nerve ends which made them receptive to the current.

"I mentioned your theory to Sands. At the time I didn't know about the powder. But I had noticed that when the banker was talking with Captain Harder, Sands had flipped some ashes from the end of his cigarette so that they had lit on the hair on the back of Soloman's head, and that Soloman had started to rub at his head shortly afterward as though he had been irritated by an itching of the scalp.

"Then Sands made the same gesture while he was talking with me. He left. I felt an itching, and wondered. So I washed my head thoroughly. Then I thought I would leave my clothes where Sands could find them, make him think he'd eliminated me. I was not certain my suspicions were correct, but I was willing to take a chance. I called you to tell you, and then I felt a most awful chill. It started at the roots of my hair and seemed to drain the very warmth right out of my nerves.

"I guess the washing hadn't removed all of that powder, just enough to keep me from being killed. I became unconscious. When I came to, I was in Sands's car. I supposed he had dropped in to make certain his machine had done the work.

"You know the rest . . . But how did you know where to look for me?"

Rodney shook his head dubiously.

"I guess my brains must have been dead, or I'd have known long before. You see, the man who wrote the letters seemed to know everything that had taken place in Captain Harder's office when we were called in to identify that last letter from Dangerfield.

"Yet there was no dictograph found there. It might have been something connected with television, or, more likely, it might have been because someone who was there was the one who was writing those letters.

"If the story Sands had told had been true, the man who was writing the letters had listened in on what was going on in the captain's office, had written the warning note, had known just where Sands was going to be in his automobile, and had tossed it in.

"That was pretty improbable. It was much more likely that Sands had slipped out long enough to have written the letter and then brought it in with that wild story about men crowding him to the curb.

"Then, again, Sands carefully managed to sneak away when Harder raided that loft building. He really did it to notify the crazy scientist that the hiding place had been discovered.

"Even before you telephoned, I should have known Sands was in with the scientist. Afterward, it was, of course, apparent. You had seen some powder placed in Soloman's hair. That meant it must have been done when you were present. That narrowed the list of suspects to those who were also present.

"There were literally dozens of clues pointing to Sands. He was naturally sore at the banker for not coming through with the money. If they'd received it, they'd have killed Dangerfield anyhow. And Sands was to deliver that money. Simple enough for him to have pretended to drop the package into the receptacle, and simply gone on . . ."

A siren wailed.

There was a pound of surging feet on the stairs, blue-coated figures swarming over the place.

"He's behind that door, boys," Rodney, "and he's armed."

"No use getting killed, men," said the officer in charge. "Shoot the door down."

Guns boomed into action. The lock twisted. The wood splintered and shattered. The door quivered, then slowly swung open as the wood was literally torn away from the lock.

Guns at ready, the men moved into the room.

They found a machine, very similar to the machine which had been found in the laboratory of the scientist. It had been riddled with gunfire.

They found an empty suit of clothes.

Rodney identified them as being the clothes Sands had worn when he last saw the man. The clothes were empty, and were cold to the touch. Around the collar, where there had been a little moisture, there was a rim of frost.

There was no outlet from the room, no chance for escape.

Ruby looked at Sid Rodney, nodded.

"He's gone," she said.

Rodney took her hand.

"Anyhow, sister, I got here in time."

"Gee, Sid, let's tie a can to that brother-and-sister stuff. I thought I had to fight love to make a career, but when I heard your steps on the stairs, just when I'd given up hope . . ."

"Can you make a report on what happened?" asked the sergeant, still looking at the cold clothes on the floor.

Sid Rodney answered in muffled tones.

"Not right now," he said. "I'm busy."

EXTRAORDINARY
DETECTIVES_____

*For over 50 years and 40 volumes, Simon Templar's escapades
have been reported by* **Leslie Charteris** *(1907–   ). From
sampling these Saintly chronicles most people would probably
regard Templar as the consummate man of the world. Yet, on
the average of every six years, he encounters decidedly
out-of-this-world phenomena such as mad scientists, startling
inventions, dream worlds, and zombies. In "The Convenient
Monster," for example, he wanders into a classic who-done-it
in which the finger of guilt seems to point toward the Loch
Ness monster.*

THE CONVENIENT MONSTER

Leslie Charteris

"OF COURSE," said Inspector Robert Mackenzie, of the Invernessshire
Constabulary, with a burr as broad as his boots seeming to add an extra R
to the word, "I know ye're only in Scotland as an ordinary visitor, and no'
expectin' to be mixed up in any criminal business."

"That's right," said the Saint cheerfully.

He was so used to this sort of thing that the monotony sometimes became irritating, but Inspector Mackenzie made the conventional gambit
with such courteous geniality that it almost sounded like an official welcome. He was a large and homely man with large red hands and small
twinkling grey eyes and sandy hair carefully plastered over the bare patch
above his forehead, and so very obviously and traditionally a policeman
that Simon Templar actually felt a kind of nostalgic affection for him.
Short of a call from Chief Inspector Claud Eustace Teal in person, nothing
could have brought back more sharply what the Saint often thought of as
the good days; and he took it as a compliment that even after so many
years, and even as far away as Scotland itself, he was not lost to the tele-
scopic eye of Scotland Yard.

"And I suppose," Mackenzie continued, "ye couldna even be bothered
with a wee bit of a local mystery."

"What's your problem?" Simon asked. "Has somebody stolen the haggis you were fattening for the annual Police Banquet?"

The Inspector ignored this with the same stony dignity with which he would have greeted the hoary question about what a Scotsman wore under his kilt.

"It might be involvin' the Loch Ness Monster," he said with the utmost gravity.

"All right," said the Saint good-humoredly. "I started this. I suppose I had it coming. But you're the first policeman who ever tried to pull my leg. Didn't they tell you that I'm the guy who's supposed to do the pulling?"

"I'm no' makin' a joke," Mackenzie persisted aggrievedly, and the Saint stared at him.

It was in the spring of 1933 that a remarkable succession of sober and reputable witnesses began to testify that they had seen in Loch Ness a monstrous creature whose existence had been a legend of region since ancient times, but which few persons in this century had claimed to have seen for themselves. The descriptions varied in detail, as human observations are prone to do, but they seemed generally to agree that the beast was roughly 30 feet long and could swim at about the same number of miles per hour; it was a dark grey in colour, with a small horse-like head on a long tapering neck, which it turned from side to side with the quick movements of an alert hen. There were divergencies as to whether it had one or more humps in its back, and whether it churned the water with flippers or a powerful tail; but all agreed that it could not be classified with anything known to modern natural history.

The reports culminated in December with a photograph showing a strange reptilian shape thrashing in the water, taken by a senior employee of the British Aluminum Company, which has a plant nearby. A number of experts certified the negative to be unretouched and unfaked, and the headline writers took it from there.

Within a fortnight a London newspaper had a correspondent on the scene with a highly publicized big-game authority in tow; some footprints were found and casts made of them—which before the New Year was three days old had been pronounced by the chief zoologists of the British Museum to have all been made by the right hind foot of a hippopotamus, and a stuffed hippopotamus at that. In the nation-wide guffaw which followed the exposure of this hoax, the whole matter exploded into a theme for cartoonists and comedians, and that aura of hilarious incredulity still colored the Saint's vague recollections of the subject.

It took a little while for him to convince himself that the Inspector's straight face was not part of an elaborate exercise in Highland humor.

"What has the Monster done that's illegal?" Simon inquired at length, with a gravity to match Mackenzie's own.

"A few weeks ago, it's thocht to h' eaten a sheep. And last night it may ha' killed a dog."

"Where was this?"

"The sheep belonged to Fergus Clanraith, who has a farm by the loch beyond Foyers, and the dog belongs to his neighbors, a couple named Bastion from doon in England who settled here last summer. 'Tis only aboot twenty miles away, if ye could spairr the time with me."

The Saint sighed. In certain interludes, he thought that everything had already happened to him that could befall a man even with his exceptional gift for stumbling into fantastic situations and being offered bizarre assignments, but apparently there was always some still more preposterous imbroglio waiting to entangle him.

"Okay," he said resignedly. "I've been slugged with practically every other improbability you could raise an eyebrow at, so why should I draw the line at dog-slaying monsters. Lay on, Macduff."

"The name is Mackenzie," said the Inspector seriously.

Simon paid his hotel bill and took his own car, for he had been intending to continue his pleasantly aimless wandering that day anyhow, and it would not make much difference to him where he stopped along the way. He followed Mackenzie's somewhat venerable chariot out of Inverness on the road that takes the east bank of the Ness River, and in a few minutes the slaty grimness of the town had been gratefully forgotten in the green and gold loveliness of the countryside.

The road ran at a fairly straight tangent to the curves of the river and the Caledonian Canal, giving only infrequent glimpses of the seven locks built to lift shipping to the level of the lake, until at Dores he had his first view of Loch Ness at its full breadth.

The Great Glen of Scotland transects the country diagonally from northeast to southwest, as if a giant had tried to break off the upper end of the land between the deep natural notches formed by Loch Linnhe and the Beauly Firth. On the map which Simon had seen, the chain of lochs stretched in an almost crow-flight line that had made him look twice to be sure that there was not in fact a clear channel across from the Eastern to the Western Sea. Loch Ness itself, a tremendous trough 24 miles long but only averaging about a mile in width, suggested nothing more than an enlargement of the Canal system which gave access to it at both ends.

But not many vessels seemed to avail themselves of the passage, for there was no boat in sight on the lake that afternoon. With the water as calm as a millpond and the fields and trees rising from its shores to a blue sky dappled with soft woolly clouds, it was as pretty as a picture postcard and utterly unconvincing to think of as a place which might be haunted by some outlandish horror from the mists of antiquity.

For a drive of twenty minutes, at the sedate pace set by Mackenzie the highway paralleled the edge of the loch a little way up its steep stony banks. The opposite shore widened slightly into the tranquil beauty of Urquhart Bay with its ancient castle standing out grey and stately on the far point, and then returned to the original almost uniform breadth. Then, within fortunately brief sight of the unpicturesque aluminium works, it bore away to the south through the small stark village of Foyers and went winding up the glen of one of the tumbling streams that feed the lake.

Several minutes further on, Mackenzie turned off into a narrow side road that twisted around and over a hill and swung down again, until suddenly the loch was spread out squarely before them once more and the lane curled past the first of two houses that could be seen standing solitarily apart from each other but each within a bowshot of the loch. Both of them stood out with equal harshness against the gentle curves and colors of the landscape with the same dark graceless austerity as the last village or the last town or any other buildings Simon had seen in Scotland, a country whose unbounded natural beauty seemed to have inspired no corresponding artistry in its architects, but rather to have goaded them into competition to offset it with the most contrasting ugliness into which bricks and stone and tile could be assembled. This was a paradox to which he had failed to fit a plausible theory for so long that he had finally given up trying.

Beside the first house a man in a stained shirt and corduroy trousers tucked into muddy canvas leggings was digging in a vegetable garden. He looked up as Mackenzie brought his rattletrap to a stop, and walked slowly over to the hedge. He was short but powerfully built, and his hair flamed like a stormy sunset.

Mackenzie climbed out and beckoned to the Saint. As Simon reached them, the red-haired man was saying: ''Aye, I've been over and seen what's left o' the dog. It's more than they found of my sheep, I can tell ye.''

''But could it ha' been the same thing that did it?'' asked the Inspector.

''That' no' for me to say, Mackenzie. I'm no' a detective. But remember, it wasna me who said the Monster took my sheep. It was the Bastions who thocht o' that, it might be to head me off from askin' if *they* hadn't been the last to see it—pairhaps on their Sunday dinner table. There's nae such trick I wouldna put beyond the Sassenach.''

MacKenzie introduced them: ''This is Mr. Clanraith, whom I was tellin' ye aboot. Fergus, I'd like ye to meet Mr. Templar, who may be helpin' me to investigate.''

Clanraith gave Simon a muscular and horny grip across the untrimmed hedge, appraising him shrewdly from under shaggy ginger brows.

''Ye dinna look like a policeman, Mr. Templar.''

''I try not to,'' said Saint expressionlessly. ''Did you mean by what you were just saying that you don't believe in the Monster at all?''

''I didna say that.''

''Then apart from anything else, you think there might actually be such a thing.''

''There might.''

''Living where you do, I should think you'd have as good a chance as anyone of seeing it yourself—if it does exist.''

The farmer peered at Simon suspiciously.

''Wad ye be a reporrter, Mr. Templar, pairhaps?''

''No, I'm not,'' Simon assured him; but the other remained wary.

''When a man tells o' seein' monsters, his best friends are apt to wonder if he may ha' taken a wee drop too much. If I had seen anything, ever, I wadna be talkin' aboot it to every stranger, to be made a laughin'-stock of.''

''But ye'll admit,'' Mackenzie put in, ''it's no' exactly norrmal for a dog to be chewed up an' killed the way this one was.''

''I wull say this,'' Clanraith conceded guardedly. ''It's strange that nobody hairrd the dog bark, or e'en whimper.''

Through the Saint's mind flickered an eerie vision of something amorphous and loathsome oozing soundlessly out of night-blackened water, flowing with obscene stealth towards a hound that slept unwarned by any of its senses.

''Do you mean it mightn't've had a chance to let out even a yip?''

"I'm no' sayin'," Clanraith maintained cautiously. "But it was a guid watchdog, if naught else."

A girl had stepped out of the house and come closer while they talked. She had Fergus Clanraith's fiery hair and greenish eyes, but her skin was pink and white where his was weather-beaten and her lips were full where his were tight. She was a half a head taller than he, and her figure was slim where it should be.

Now she said: "That's right. He even barked whenever he heard me coming, although he saw me every day."

Her voice was low and well modulated, with only an attractive trace of her father's accent.

"Then if it was a pairrson wha' killed him, Annie, 'twad only mean it was a body he was still more used to."

"But you can't really believe that any human being would do a thing like that to a dog that knew them—least of all to their own dog!"

"That's the trouble wi' lettin' a lass be brocht up an' schooled on the wrong side o' the Tweed," Clanraith said darkly. "She forgets what the English ha' done to honest Scotsmen no' so lang syne."

The girl's eyes had kept returning to the Saint with candid interest, and it was to him that she explained, smiling: "Father still wishes he could fight for Bonnie Prince Charlie. He's glad to let me do part-time secretarial work for Mr. Bastion because I can live at home and keep house as well, but he still feels I'm guilty of fraternizing with the Enemy."

"We'd best be gettin' on and talk to them ourselves," Mackenzie said. "And then we'll see if Mr. Templar has any more questions to ask."

There was something in Annie Clanraith's glance which seemed to say that she hoped that he would, and the Saint was inclined to be of the same sentiment. He had certainly not expected to find anyone so decorative in the cast of characters, and he began to feel a tentative quickening of optimism about this interruption in his travels. He could see her in his rear-view mirror, still standing by the hedge and following with her gaze after her father had turned back to his digging.

About three hundred yards and a few bends farther on, Mackenzie veered between a pair of stone gateposts and chugged to a standstill on the circular driveway in front of the second house. Simon stopped behind him and then strolled after him to the front door, which was opened almost at once by a tall thin man in a pullover and baggy grey flannel slacks.

"Good afternoon, sir," said the detective courteously. "I'm Inspector Mackenzie from Inverness. Are ye Mr. Bastion?"

"Yes."

Bastion had a bony face with a long aquiline nose, lank black hair flecked with grey, and a broad toothbrush moustache that gave him an indeterminately military appearance. His black eyes flickered to the Saint inquiringly.

"This is Mr. Templar, who may be assistin' me," Mackenzie said. "The constable who was here this morning told me all aboot what ye showed him, on the telephone, but could we ha' a wee look for ourselves?"

"Oh, yes, certainly. Will you come this way?"

The way was around the house, across an uninspired formal garden at the back which looked overdue for the attention of a gardener, and through a small orchard beyond which a stretch of rough grass sloped quickly down to the water. As the meadow fell away, a pebbly beach came into view, and Simon saw that this was one of the rare breaches in the steep average angle of the loch's sides. On either side of the little beach the ground swelled up again to form a shallow bowl that gave an easy natural access to the lake. The path that they traced led to a short rustic pier with a shabby skiff tied to it, and on the ground to one side of the pier was something covered with potato sacking.

"I haven't touched anything, as the constable asked me," Bastion said. "Except to cover him up."

He bent down and carefully lifted off the burlap.

They looked down in silence at what was uncovered.

"The puir beastie," Mackenzie said at last.

It had been a large dog of confused parentage in which the Alsatian may have predominated. What had happened to it was no nicer to look at than it is to catalogue. Its head and hindquarters were partly mashed to a red pulp; and plainly traceable across its chest was a row of slot-like gashes, each about an inch long and close together, from which blood had run and clotted in the short fur. Mackenzie squatted and stretched the skin with gentle fingers to see the slits more clearly. The Saint also felt the chest: it had an unnatural contour where the line of punctures crossed it, and his probing touch found only sponginess where there should have been a hard cage of ribs.

His eyes met Mackenzie's across the pitifully mangled form.

"That would be quite a row of teeth," he remarked.

"Aye," said the Inspector grimly. "But what lives here that has a mouth like that?"

They straightened up and surveyed the immediate surroundings. The ground here, only a stride or two from the beach, which in turn was less than a yard wide, was so moist that it was soggy, and pockets of muddy liquid stood in the deeper indentations with which it was plentifully rumpled. The carpet of coarse grass made individual impressions difficult to identify, but three or four shoe-heel prints could be positively distinguished.

"I'm afraid I made a lot of those tracks," Bastion said. "I know you're not supposed to go near anything, but all I could think of at the time was seeing if *he* was still alive and if I could do anything for him. The constable tramped around a bit too, when he was here." He pointed past the body. "But neither of us had anything to do with those marks there."

Close to the beach was a place where the turf looked as if it had been raked by something with three gigantic claws. One talon had caught in the roots of a tuft of grass and torn it up bodily: the clump lay on the pebbles at the water's edge. Aside from that, the claws had left three parallel grooves, about four inches apart and each about half an inch wide. They dug into the ground at their upper ends to a depth of more than two inches, and dragged back towards the lake for a length of about ten inches as they tapered up.

Simon and Mackenzie stood on the pebbles to study the marks. Simon spanning them experimentally with his fingers while the detective took exact measurements with a tape and entered them in his notebook.

"Anything wi' a foot big enough to carry claws like that," Mackenzie said, "I'd no' wish to ha' comin' after me."

"Well, they call it a Monster, don't they?" said the Saint dryly. "It wouldn't impress anyone if it made tracks like a mouse."

Mackenzie unbent his knees stiffly, shooting the Saint a distrustful glance, and turned to Bastion.

"When did ye find all this, sir?" he asked.

"I suppose it was about six o'clock," Bastion said. "I woke up before dawn and couldn't get to sleep again, so I decided to try a little early fishing. I got up as soon as it was light—"

"Ye didna hear any noise before that?"

"No."

"It couldna ha' been the dog barkin' that woke ye?"

"Not that I'm aware of. And my wife is a very light sleeper, and she didn't hear anything. But I was rather surprised when I didn't see the dog outside. He doesn't sleep in the house, but he's always waiting on the doorstep in the morning. However, I came on down here—and that's how I found him.''

"And you didn't see anything else?" Simon asked. "In the lake, I mean."

"No. I didn't see the Monster. And when I looked for it, there wasn't a ripple on the water. Of course, the dog may have been killed some time before, though his body was still warm.''

"Mr. Bastion," Mackenzie said, "do *ye* believe it was the Monster that killed him?''

Bastion looked at him and at the Saint.

"I'm not a superstitious man," he replied. "But if it wasn't a monster of some kind, what else could it have been?''

The Inspector closed his notebook with a snap that seemed to be echoed by his clamping lips. It was evident that he felt that the situation was wandering far outside his professional province. He scowled at the Saint as though he expected Simon to do something about it.

"It might be interesting," Simon said thoughtfully, "if we get a vet to do a post-mortem.''

"What for?" Bastion demanded brusquely.

"Let's face it," said the Saint. "Those claw marks *could* be fakes. And the dog *could* have been mashed up with some sort of club—even a club with spikes set in it to leave wounds that'd look as if they were made by teeth. But by all accounts, no one could have got near enough to the dog to do that without him barking. *Unless the dog was doped first.* So before we go overboard on this Monster theory, I'd like to rule everything else out. An autopsy would do that.''

Bastion rubbed his scrubby moustache.

"I see your point. Yes, that might be a good idea.''

He helped them to shift the dog on to the sack which had previously covered it, and Simon and Mackenzie carried it between them back to the driveway and laid it in the boot of the detective's car.

"D'ye think we could ha' a wurrd wi' Mrs. Bastion, sir?" Mackenzie asked, wiping his hands on a clean rag and passing it to the Saint.

"I suppose so," Bastion assented dubiously. "Although she's pretty upset about this, as you can imagine. It was really her dog more than mine. But come in, and I'll see if she'll talk to you for a minute.''

But Mrs. Bastion herself settled that by meeting them in the hall, and she made it obvious that she had been watching them from a window.

"What are they doing with Golly, Noel?" she greeted her husband wildly. "Why are they taking him away?"

"They want to have him examined by a doctor, dear."

Bastion went on to explain why, until she interrupted him again:

"Then don't let them bring him back. It's bad enough to have seen him the way he is, without having to look at him dissected." She turned to Simon and Mackenzie. "You must understand how I feel. Golly was like a son to me. His name was really Goliath—I called him that because he was so big and fierce, but actually he was a pushover when you got on the right side of him."

Words came from her in a driving torrent that suggested the corollary of a power-house. She was a big-boned, strong-featured woman who made no attempt to minimize any of her probable forty-five years. Her blonde hair was unwaved and pulled back into a tight bun, and her blue eyes were set in a nest of wrinkles that would have been called characterful on an outdoor man. Her lipstick, which needed renewing, had a slapdash air of being her one impatient concession to feminine artifice. But Bastion put a soothing arm around her as solicitously as if she had been a dimpled bride.

"I'm sure these officers will have him buried for us, Eleanor," he said. "But while they're here I think they wanted to ask you something."

"Only to comfairrm what Mr. Bastion told us, ma'am," said Mackenzie. "That ye didna hear an disturrbance last night."

"Absolutely not. And if Golly had made a sound, I should have heard him. I always do. Why are you trying so hard to get around the facts? It's as plain as a pikestaff that the Monster did it."

"Some monsters have two legs," Simon remarked.

"And I suppose you're taught not to believe in any other kind. Even with the evidence under your very eyes."

"I mind a time when some other footprints were found, ma'am," Mackenzie put in deferentially, "which turned oot to be a fraud."

"I know exactly what you're referring to. And that stupid hoax made a lot of idiots disbelieve the authentic photograph which was taken just before it, and refuse to accept an even better picture that was taken by a thoroughly reputable London surgeon about four months later. I know what I'm talking about. As a matter of fact, the reason we took this house was mainly because I'm hoping to discover the Monster."

Two pairs of eyebrows shot up and lowered almost in unison, but it was the Saint who spoke for Mackenzie as well as himself.

"How would you do that, Mrs. Bastion?" he inquired with some circumspection. "If the Monster has been well known around here for a few centuries, at least to everyone who believes in him—"

"It still hasn't been scientifically and officially established. I'd like to have the credit for doing that, beyond any shadow of doubt, and naming it *Monstrum eleanoris.*"

"Probably you gentlemen don't know it," Bastion elucidated, with a kind of quaintly protective pride, "but Mrs. Bastion is a rather distinguished naturalist. She's hunted every kind of big game there is, and even holds a couple of world's records."

"But I never had a trophy as important as this would be," his better half took over again. "I expect you think I'm a little cracked—that there couldn't really be any animal of any size in the world that hasn't been discovered by this time. Tell them the facts of life, Noel."

Bastion cleared his throat like a schoolboy preparing to recite, and said with much the same awkward air: "The gorilla was only discovered in 1847, the giant panda in 1869, and the okapi wasn't discovered till 1901. Of course explorers brought back rumours of them, but people thought they were just native fairy tales. And you yourselves probably remember reading about the first coelacanth being caught. That was only in 1938."

"So why shouldn't there still be something else left that I could be the first to prove?" Eleanor Bastion concluded for him. "The obvious thing to go after, I suppose, was the Abominable Snowman; but Mr. Bastion can't stand high altitudes. So I'm making do with the Loch Ness Monster."

Inspector Mackenzie, who had for some time been looking progressively more confused and impatient in spite of his politely valiant efforts to conceal the fact, finally managed to interrupt the antiphonal barrage of what he could only be expected to regard as delirious irrelevancies.

"All that I'm consairned wi', ma'am," he said heavily, "is tryin' to detairrmine whether there's a human felon to be apprehended. If it should turn oot to be a monster, as ye're thinkin', it wadna be in my jurisdeection. However, in that case, pairhaps Mr. Templar, who is no' a police officer, could be o' more help to ye."

"Templar," Bastion repeated slowly. "I feel as if I ought to recognize that name, now, but I was rather preoccupied with something else when I first heard it."

"Do you have a halo on you somewhere?" quizzed Mrs. Bastion, the huntress, in a tone which somehow suggested the aiming of a gun.

"Sometimes."

"Well, by Jove!" Bastion said. "I should've guessed it, of course, if I'd been thinking about it. You didn't sound like a policeman."

Mackenzie winced faintly, but both the Bastions were too openly absorbed in reappraising the Saint to notice it.

Simon Templar should have been hardened to that kind of scrutiny, but as the years went on it was beginning to cause him a mixture of embarrassment and petty irritation. He wished that new acquaintances could dispense with the reactions and stay with their original problems.

He said, rather roughly: "It's just my bad luck that Mackenzie caught me as I was leaving Inverness. I was on my way to Loch Lomond, like any innocent tourist, to find out how bonnie the banks actually are. He talked me into taking the low road instead of the high road, and stopping here to stick my nose into your problem."

"But that's perfectly wonderful!" Mrs. Bastion announced like a bugle. "Noel, ask him to stay the night. I mean, for the weekend. Or for the rest of the week, if he can spare the time."

"Why—er—yes," Bastion concurred obediently. "Yes, of course. We'd be delighted. The Saint ought to have some good ideas about catching a monster."

Simon regarded him coolly, aware of the invisible glow of slightly malicious expectation emanating from Mackenzie, and made a reckless instant decision.

"Thank you," he said. "I'd love it. I'll bring in my things, and Mac can be on his way."

He sauntered out without further palaver, happily conscious that only Mrs. Bastion had not been moderately rocked by his casual acceptance.

They all ask for it, he thought. Cops and civilians alike, as soon as they hear the name. Well, let's oblige them. And see how they like whatever comes of it.

Mackenzie followed him outside, with a certain ponderous dubiety which indicated that some of the joke had already evaporated.

"Ye'll ha' no authorrity in this, ye underrstand," he emphasized, "except the rights o' any private investigator—which are no' the same in Scotland as in America, to judge by some o' the books I've read."

"I shall try very hard not to gang agley," Simon assured him. "Just phone me the result of the P.M. as soon as you possibly can. And while you're waiting for it, you might look up the law about shooting monsters. See if one has to take out a special licence, or anything like that."

He watched the detective drive away, and went back in with his two-suiter. He felt better already, with no official eyes and ears absorbing his most trivial responses. And it would be highly misleading to say that he found the bare facts of the case, as they had been presented to him, utterly banal and boring.

Noel Bastion showed him to a small but comfortable room upstairs, with a window that faced towards the home of Fergus Clanraith but which also afforded a sidelong glimpse of the loch. Mrs. Bastion was already busy there, making up the bed.

"You can't get any servants in a place like this," she explained. "I'm lucky to have a woman who bicycles up from Fort Augustus once a week to do the heavy cleaning. They all want to stay in the towns where they can have what they think of as a bit of life."

Simon looked at Bastion innocuously and remarked: "You're lucky to find a secretary right on the spot like the one I met up the road."

"Oh, you mean Annie Clanraith." Bastion scrubbed a knuckle on his upper lip. "Yes. She was working in Liverpool, but she came home at Christmas to spend the holidays with her father. I had to get some typing done in a hurry, and she helped me out. It was Clanraith who talked her into staying. I couldn't pay her as much as she'd been earning in Liverpool, but he pointed out that she'd end up with just as much in her pocket if she didn't have to pay for board and lodging, which he'd give her if she kept house. He's a widower, so it's not a bad deal for him."

"Noel's a writer," Mrs. Bastion said. "His big book isn't finished yet, but he works on it all the time."

"It's a life of Wellington," said the writer. "It's never been done, as I think it should be, by a professional soldier."

"Mackenzie didn't tell me anything about your background," said the Saint. "What should he have called you—Colonel?"

"Only Major. But that was in the Regular Army."

Simon did not miss the faintly defensive tone of the addendum. But the silent calculation he made was that the pension of a retired British Army Major, unless augmented by some more commercial form of authorship than an unfinished biography of distinctly limited appeal, would not finance enough big-game safaris to earn an ambitious huntress a great reputation.

"There," said Mrs. Bastion finally. "Now, if you'd like to settle in and make yourself at home, I'll have some tea ready in five minutes."

The Saint had embarked on his Scottish trip with an open mind and an attitude of benevolent optimism, but if anyone had prophesied that it would lead to him sipping tea in the drawing-room of two practically total strangers, with his valise unpacked in their guest bedroom, and solemnly chatting about a monster as if it were as real as a monkey, he would probably have been mildly derisive. His hostess, however, was obsessed with the topic.

"Listen to this," she said, fetching a well-worn volume from a bookcase. "It's a quotation from the biography of St. Columba, written about the middle of the seventh century. It tells about his visit to Inverness some hundred years before, and it says *he was obliged to cross the water of Nesa; and when he had come to the bank he sees some of the inhabitants bringing an unfortunate fellow whom, as those who were bringing him related, a little while before some aquatic monster seized and savagely bit while he was swimming. . . . The blessed man orders one of his companions to swim out and bring him from over the water a coble . . . Lugne Mocumin without delay takes off his clothes except his tunic and casts himself into the water. But the monster comes up and moves towards the man as he swam. . . . The blessed man, seeing it, commanded the ferocious monster saying, 'Go thou no further nor touch the man; go back at once.' Then on hearing his word of the Saint the monster was terrified and fled away again more quickly than if it had been dragged off by ropes.*"

"I must try to remember that formula," Simon murmured, "and hope the Monster can't tell one Saint from another."

" 'Monster' is really a rather stupid name for it," Mrs. Bastion said. "It encourages people to be illogical about it. Actually, in the old days the local people called it *an Niseag*, which is simply the name 'Ness' in Gaelic with a feminine diminutive ending. You could literally translate it as 'Nessie'."

"That does sound a lot cuter," Simon agreed. "If you forget how it plays with dogs."

Eleanor Bastion's weathered face went pale, but the muscles under the skin did not flinch.

"I haven't forgotten Golly. But I was trying to keep my mind off him."

"Assuming this beastie does exist," said the Saint, "how did it get here?"

"Why did it have to 'get' here at all? I find it easier to believe that it always was here. The loch is 750 feet deep, which is twice the mean depth of the North Sea. *An Niseag* is a creature that obviously prefers the depths and only comes to the surface occasionally. I think its original home was always at the bottom of the loch, and it was trapped there when some prehistoric geological upheaval cut off the loch from the sea.''

"And it's lived there ever since—for how many million years?''

"Not the original ones—I suppose we must assume at least a couple. But their descendants. Like many primitive creatures, it probably lives to a tremendous age.''

"What do you think it is?''

"Most likely something of the plesiosaurus family. The descriptions sound more like that than anything—large body, long neck, paddle-like legs. Some people claim to have seen stumpy projections on its head, rather like the horns of a snail, which aren't part of the usual reconstruction of a plesiosaurus. But after all, we've never seen much of a pleiosaurus except its skeleton. You wouldn't know exactly what a snail looked like if you'd only seen its shell.''

"But if Nessie has been here all this time, why wasn't she reported much longer ago?''

"She was. You heard that story about St. Columba. And if you think only modern observations are worth paying attention to, several reliable sightings were recorded from 1871 onwards.''

"But there was no motor road along the loch until 1933,'' Bastion managed to contribute at last, "and a trip like you made today would have been quite an expedition. So there weren't many witnesses about until fairly recently, of the type that scientists would take seriously.''

Simon lighted a cigarette. The picture was clear enough. Like the flying saucers, it depended on what you wanted to believe—and whom.

Except that here there was not only fantasy to be thought of. There could be felony.

"What would you have to do to make it an official discovery?''

"We have movie and still cameras with the most powerful telephoto lenses you can buy,'' said the woman. "I spend eight hours a day simply watching the lake, just like anyone might put in at a regular job, but I vary the times of day systematically. Noel sometimes puts in a few hours as well. We have a view for several miles in both directions, and by the law of averages *an Niseag* must come up eventually in the area we're covering. Whenever that happens, our lenses will get close-up pictures that'll show every detail beyond any possibility of argument. It's simply a matter of patience, and when I came here I made up my mind that I'd spend ten years on it if necessary.''

"And now," said the Saint, "I guess you're more convinced than ever that you're on the right track and the scent is hot.''

Mrs. Bastion looked him in the eyes with terrifying equanimity.

"Now," she said, "I'm going to watch with a Weatherby Magnum as well as the cameras. *An Niseag* can't be much bigger than en elephant, and it isn't any more bulletproof. I used to think it'd be a crime to kill the last survivor of a species, but since I saw what it did to poor Golly, I'd like to have it as a trophy as well as a picture.''

There was much more of this conversation, but nothing that would not seem repetitious in verbatim quotation. Mrs. Bastion had accumulated numerous other books on the subject, from any of which she was prepared to read excerpts in support of her convictions.

It was hardly eight-thirty, however, after a supper of cold meat and salad, when she announced that she was going to bed.

"I want to get up at two o'clock and be out at the loch well before daylight—the same time when that thing must have been there this morning.''

"Okay," said the Saint. "Knock on my door, and I'll go with you.''

He remained to accept a nightcap of Peter Dawson, which seemed to taste especially rich and smooth in the land where they made it. Probably this was his imagination, but it gave him a pleasant feeling of drinking the wine of the country on its own home ground.

"If you're going to be kind enough to look after her, I may sleep a bit later," Bastion said. "I must get some work done on my book tonight, while there's a little peace and quiet. Not that Eleanor can't take care of herself better than most women, but I wouldn't like her being out there alone after what's happened.''

"You're thoroughly sold on this monster yourself, are you?''

The other stared into his glass.

"It's the sort of thing that all my instincts and experience would take with a grain of salt. But you've seen for yourself that it isn't easy to argue with Eleanor. And I must admit that she makes a terrific case for it. But until this morning I was keeping an open mind.''

"And now it isn't so open?''

"Quite frankly, I'm pretty shaken. I feel it's got to be settled now, one way or the other. Perhaps you'll have some luck tomorrow."

It did in fact turn out to be a vigil that gave Simon goose pimples, but they were caused almost entirely by the pre-dawn chill of the air. Daylight came slowly, through a grey and leaky-looking overcast. The lake remained unruffled, guarding its secrets under a pale pearly glaze.

"I wonder what we did wrong," Mrs. Bastion said at last, when the daylight was as broad as the clouds evidently intended to let it become. "The thing should have come back to where it made its last kill. Perhaps if we hadn't been so sentimental we should have left Golly right where he was and built a *machan* over him where we could have stood watch in turns."

Simon was not so disappointed. Indeed, if a monster had actually appeared almost on schedule under their expectant eyes, he would have been inclined to sense the hand of a Hollywood B-picture producer rather than the finger of Fate.

"As you said yesterday, it's a matter of patience," he observed philosophically. "But the odds are that the rest of your eight hours, now, will be just routine. So if you're not nervous I'll ramble around a while."

His rambling had brought him no nearer to the house than the orchard when the sight of a coppery-rosy head on top of a shapely free-swinging figure made his pulse fluctuate enjoyably with a reminder of the remotely possible promise of romantic compensation that had started to warm his interest the day before.

Annie Clanraith's smile was so eager and happy to see him that he might have been an old and close friend who had been away for a long time.

"Inspector Mackenzie told my father he'd left you here. I'm so glad you stayed!"

"I'm glad you're glad," said the Saint, and against her ingenuous sincerity it was impossible to make the reply sound even vestigially sceptical. "But what made it so important?"

"Just having someone new and alive to talk to. You haven't stayed long enough to find out how bored you can be here."

"But you've got a job that must be a little more attractive than going back to an office in Liverpool."

"Oh, it's not bad. And it helps to make father comfortable. And it's nice to live in such beautiful scenery, I expect you'll say. But I read books and I look at the TV, and I can't stop having my silly dreams.''

"A gal like you," he said teasingly, "should have her hands full, fighting off other dreamers.''

"All I get my hands full of is pages and pages of military strategy, about a man who only managed to beat Napoleon. But at least Napoleon had Josephine. The only thing Wellington gave his name to was an old boot.''

Simon clucked sympathetically.

"He may have had moments with his boots off, you know. Or has your father taught you to believe nothing good of anyone who was ever born south of the Tweed?''

"You must have thought it was terrible, the way he talked about Mr. Bastion. And he's so nice, isn't he? It's too bad he's married!''

"Maybe his wife doesn't think so.''

"I mean, I'm a normal girl and I'm not old-fashioned, and the one thing I do miss here is a man to fight off. In fact, I'm beginning to feel that if one did come along I wouldn't even struggle.''

"You sound as if that Scottish song was written about you," said the Saint, and he sang softly:

"Ilka lassie has her laddie,
Ne'er a ane ha' I;
But all the lads they smile at me,
Comin' through the rye.''

She laughed.

"Well, at least you smiled at me, and that makes today look a little better.''

"Where were you going?''

"To work. I just walked over across the fields—it's much shorter than by the lane.''

Now that she mentioned it, he could see a glimpse of the Clanraith house between the trees. He turned and walked with her through the untidy little garden towards the Bastion's entrance.

"I'm sorry that stops me offering to take you on a picnic.''

"I don't have any luck, do I? There's a dance in Fort Augustus tomorrow night, and I haven't been dancing for months, but I don't know a soul who'd take me.''

"I'd like to do something about that," he said. "But it rather depends on what develops around here. Don't give up hope yet, though."

As they entered the hall, Bastion came out of a back room and said: "Ah, good morning, Annie. There are some pages I was revising last night on my desk. I'll be with you in a moment."

She went on into the room he had just come from, and he turned to the Saint.

"I suppose you didn't see anything."

"If we had, you'd've heard plenty of gunfire and hollering."

"Did you leave Eleanor down there?"

"Yes. But I don't think she's in any danger in broad daylight. Did Mackenzie call?"

"Not yet. I expect you're anxious to hear from him. The telephone's in the drawing room—why don't you settle down there? You might like to browse through some of Eleanor's collection of books about the Monster."

Simon accepted the suggestion, and soon found himself so absorbed that only his empty stomach was conscious of the time when Bastion came in and told him that lunch was ready. Mrs. Bastion had already returned and was dishing up an agreeably aromatic lamb stew which she apologized for having only warmed up.

"You were right, it was just routine," she said. "A lot of waiting for nothing. But one of these days it won't be for nothing."

"I was thinking about it myself, dear," Bastion said, "and it seems to me that there's one bad weakness in your eight-hour-a-day system. There are enough odds against you already in only being able to see about a quarter of the loch, which leaves the Monster another three-quarters where it could just as easily pop up. But on top of that, watching only eight hours out of the twenty-four only gives us a one-third chance of being there even if it does pop up within range of our observation post. That doesn't add to the odds against us, it multiplies them."

"I know; but what can we do about it?"

"Since Mr. Templar pointed out that anyone should really be safe enough with a high-powered rifle in their hands and everyone else within call, I thought that three of us could divide up the watches and cover the whole day from before dawn till after dusk, as long as one could possibly see anything. That is, if Mr. Templar would help out. I know he can't stay here indefinitely, but—"

"If it'll make anybody feel better, I'd be glad to take a turn that way,"

Simon said indifferently.

It might have been more polite to sound more enthusiastic, but he could not make himself believe that the Monster would actually be caught by any such system. He was impatient for Mackenzie's report, which he thought was the essential detail.

The call came about two o'clock, and it was climactically negative.

"The doctor canna find a trrace o' drugs or poison in the puir animal."

Simon took a deep breath.

"What did he think of its injuries?"

"He said he'd ne'er seen the like o' them. He dinna ken anything in the wurruld wi' such crrushin' power in its jaws as yon Monster must have. If 'twas no' for the teeth marrks, he wad ha' thocht it was done wi' a club. But the autopsy mak's that impossible."

"So I take it you figure that rules you officially out," said the Saint bluntly. "But give me a number where I can call you if the picture changes again."

He wrote it down on a pad beside the telephone before he turned and relayed the report.

"That settles it," said Mrs. Bastion. "It can't be anything else but *an Niseag*. And we've got all the more reason to try Noel's idea of keeping watch all day."

"I had a good sleep this morning, so I'll start right away," Bastion volunteered. "You're entitled to a siesta."

"I'll take over after that," she said. "I want to be out there again at twilight. I know I'm monopolizing the most promising times, but this matters more to me than to anyone else."

Simon helped her with the dishes after they had had coffee, and then she excused herself.

"I'll be fresher later if I do take a little nap. Why don't you do the same? It was awfully good of you to get up in the middle of the night with me."

"It sounds as if I won't be needed again until later tomorrow morning," said the Saint. "But I'll be reading and brooding. I'm almost as interested in *an Niseag* now as you are."

He went back to the book he had left in the drawing-room as the house settled into stillness. Annie Clanraith had already departed, before lunch, taking a sheaf of papers with her to type at home.

Presently he put the volume down on his thighs and lay passively thinking, stretched out on the couch. It was his uniquely personal method of tackling profound problems, to let himself relax into a state of blank receptiveness in which half-subconscious impressions could grow and flow together in delicately fluid adjustments that could presently mold a conclusion almost as concrete as knowledge. For some time he gazed sightlessly at the ceiling, and then he continued to meditate with his eyes closed.

He was awakened by Noel Bastion entering the room, humming tunelessly. The biographer of Wellington was instantly apologetic.

"I'm sorry, Templar—I thought you'd be in your room."

"That's all right." Simon glanced at his watch, and was mildly surprised to discover how sleepy he must have been. "I was doing some thinking, and the strain must have been too much for me."

"Eleanor relieved me an hour ago. I hadn't seen anything, I'm afraid."

"I didn't hear you come in."

"I'm pretty quiet on my feet. Must be a habit I got from commando training. Eleanor often says that if she could stalk like me she'd have a lot more trophies." Bastion went to the bookcase, took down a book, and thumbed through it for some reference. "I've been trying to do some work, but it isn't easy to concentrate."

Simon stood up and stretched himself.

"I guess you'll have to get used to working under difficulties if you're going to be a part-time monster hunter for ten years—isn't that how long Eleanor said she was ready to spend at it?"

"I'm hoping it'll be a good deal less than that."

"I was reading in this book *More Than A Legend* that in 1934, when the excitement about the Monster was at its height, a chap named Sir Edward Mountain hired a bunch of men and organized a systematic watch like you were suggesting, but spacing them all around the lake. It went on for a month or two, and they got a few pictures of distant splashings, but nothing that was scientifically accepted."

Bastion put his volume back on the shelf. "You're still skeptical, aren't you?"

"What I've been wondering," said the Saint, "is why this savage behemoth with the big sharp teeth and the nutcracker jaws chomped up a dog but didn't swallow even a little nibble of it."

"Perhaps it isn't carnivorous. An angry elephant will mash a man to a pulp, but it won't eat him. And that dog could be very irritating, barking at everything—"

"According to what I heard, there wasn't any barking. And I'm sure the sheep it's supposed to have taken didn't bark. But the sheep disappeared entirely, didn't it?''

''That's what Clanraith says. But for all we know, the sheep may have been stolen.''

''But that could have given somebody the idea of building up the Monster legend from there.''

Bastion shook his head.

''But the dog *did* bark at everyone,'' he insisted stubbornly.

''Except the people he knew,'' said the Saint, no less persistently. ''Every dog is vulnerable to a few people. You yourself, for instance, if you'd wanted to, could have come along, and if he felt lazy he'd've opened one eye and then shut it again and gone back to sleep. Now, are you absolutely sure that nobody else was on those terms with him? Could a postman or a milkman have made friends with him? Or anyone else at all?''

The other man massaged his moustache.

''I don't know. . . . Well, perhaps Fergus Clanraith might.''

Simon blinked.

''But it sounded to me as if he didn't exactly love the dog.''

''Perhaps he didn't. But it must have known him pretty well. Eleanor likes to go hiking across country, and the dog always used to go with her. She's always crossing Clanraith's property and stopping to talk to him, she tells me. She gets on very well with him.''

''What, that old curmudgeon?''

''I know, he's full of that Scottish Nationalist nonsense. But Eleanor is half Scots herself, and that makes her almost human in his estimation. I believe they talk for hours about salmon fishing and grouse shooting.''

''I wondered if he had an appealing side hidden away somewhere,'' said the Saint thoughtfully, ''or if Annie got it all from her mother.''

Bastion's deep-set sooty eyes flickered over his appraisingly.

''She's rather an attractive filly, isn't she?''

''I have a feeling that to a certain type of man, in certain circumstances, and perhaps at a certain age, her appeal might be quite dangerous.''

Noel Bastion had an odd expression of balancing some answer on the tip of his tongue, weighing it for advisability, changing his mind a couple of times about it, and finally swallowing it. He then tried to recover from the pause by making a business of consulting the clock on the mantelpiece.

''Will you excuse me? Eleanor asked me to bring her a thermos of tea about now. She hates to miss that, even for *an Niseag.*"

"Sure."

Simon followed him into the kitchen, where a kettle was already simmering on the black coal stove. He watched while his host carefully scalded a teapot and measured leaves into it from a canister.

"You know, Major," he said, "I'm not a detective by nature, even of the private variety."

"I know. In fact, I think you used to be just the opposite."

"That's true, too, I do get into situations, though, where I have to do a bit of deducing, and sometimes I startle everyone by coming up with a brilliant hunch. But as a general rule, I'd rather prevent a crime than solve one. As it says in your kind of textbooks, a little preventive action can save a lot of counterattacks."

The Major had poured boiling water into the pot with a steady hand, and was opening a vacuum flask while he waited for the brew.

"You're a bit late to prevent this one, aren't you?—if it *was* a crime."

"Not necessarily. Not if the death of Golly was only a steppingstone—something to build on the story of a missing sheep, and pave the way for the Monster's next victim to be a person. If a person were killed in a similar way now, the Monster explanation would get a lot more believers than if it had just happened out of the blue."

Bastion put sugar and milk into the flask, without measuring, with the unhesitating positiveness of practice, and took the lid off the teapot to sniff and stir it.

"But, good heavens, Templar, who could treat a dog like that, except a sadistic maniac?"

Simon lighted a cigarette. He was very certain now, and the certainty made him very calm.

"A professional killer," he said. "There are quite a lot of them around who don't have police records. People whose temperament and habits have developed a great callousness about death. But they're not sadists. They're normally kind to animals and even to human beings, when it's normally useful to be. But fundamentally they see them as expendable, and when the time comes they can sacrifice them quite impersonally."

"I know Clanraith's a farmer, and he raises animals only to have them butchered," Bastion said slowly. "But it's hard to imagine him doing what you're talking about, much as I dislike him."

"Then you think we should discard him as a red herring?"

Bastion filled the thermos from the teapot, and capped it.

"I'm hanged if I know. I'd want to think some more about it. But first I've got to take this to Eleanor."

"I'll go with you," said the Saint.

He followed the other out of the back door. Outside, the dusk was deepening with a mistiness that was beginning to do more than the failing light to reduce visibility. From the garden, one could see into the orchard but not beyond it.

"It's equally hard for the ordinary man," Simon continued relentlessly, "to imagine anyone who's lived with another person as man and wife, making love and sharing the closest moments, suddenly turning around and killing the other one. But the prison cemeteries are full of 'em. And there are plenty more on the outside who didn't get caught—or who are still planning it. At least half the time, the marriage has been getting a bit dull, and someone more attractive has come along. And then, for some idiotic reason, often connected with money, murder begins to seem cleverer than divorce."

Bastion slackened his steps, half turning to peer at Simon from under heavily contracted brows, then spoke slowly.

"I'm not utterly dense, Templar, and I don't like what you seem to be hinting at."

"I don't expect you to, chum. But I'm trying to stop a murder. Let me make a confession. When you and Eleanor have been out or in bed at various times, I've done quite a lot of prying. Which may be a breach of hospitality, but it's less trouble than search warrants. You remember those scratches in the ground near the dead dog which I said could've been made with something that wasn't claws? Well, I found a gaff among somebody's fishing tackle that could've made them, and the point had fresh shiny scratches and even some mud smeared on it which can be analyzed. I haven't been in the attic and found an embalmed shark's head with several teeth missing, but I'll bet Mackenzie could find one. And I haven't yet found the club with the teeth set in it, because I haven't yet been allowed down by the lake alone; but I think it's there somewhere, probably stuffed under a bush, and just waiting to be hauled out when the right head is turned the wrong way."

Major Bastion had come to a complete halt by that time.

"You unmitigated bounder," he said shakily. "Are you going to have the impertinence to suggest that I'm trying to murder my wife, to come into her money and run off with a farmer's daughter? Let me tell you that I'm the one who has the private income, and—''

''You poor feeble egotist,'' Simon retorted harshly. ''I didn't suspect that for one second after she made herself rather cutely available to me, a guest in your house. She obviously wasn't stupid, and no girl who wasn't would have gambled a solid understanding with you against a transient flirtation. But didn't you ever read *Lady Chatterly's Lover*? Or the Kinsey Report? And hasn't it dawned on you that a forceful woman like Eleanor, just because she isn't a glamour girl, couldn't be bored to frenzy with a husband who only cares about the campaigns of Wellington?''

Noel Bastion opened his mouth, and his fists clenched, but whatever was intended to come from either never materialized. For at that moment came the scream.

Shrill with unearthly terror and agony, it split the darkening haze with an eldritch intensity that seemed to turn every hair on the Saint's nape into an individual icicle. And it did not stop, but ululated again and again in weird cadences of hysteria.

For an immeasurable span then were both petrified; and then Bastion turned and began to run wildly across the meadow, towards the sound.

''*Eleanor!*'' he yelled, insanely, in a voice almost as piercing as the screams.

He ran so frantically that the Saint had to call on all his reserves to make up for Bastion's split-second start. But he did close the gap as Bastion stumbled and almost fell over something that lay squarely across their path. Simon had seen it an instant sooner, and swerved, mechanically identifying the steely glint that had caught his eye as a reflection from a long gunbarrel.

And then, looking ahead and upwards, he saw through the blue fogginess something for which he would never completely believe his eyes, yet which would haunt him for the rest of his life. Something grey-black and scaly-slimy, an immense amorphous mass from which a reptilian neck and head with strange protuberances reared and swayed far up over him. And in the hideous dripping jaws something of human shape, from which the screams came, that writhed and flailed ineffectually with a peculiar-looking club. . . .

With a sort of incoherent sob, Bastion scooped up the rifle at his feet and fired it. The horrendous mass convulsed; and into Simon's eardrums, still buzzing from the heavy blast, came a sickening crunch that cut off the last shriek in the middle of a note.

The towering neck corkscrewed with frightful power, and the thing that had been human was flung dreadfully towards them. It fell with a kind of soggy limpness almost at their feet, as whatever had spat it out lurched backwards and was blotted out by the vaporous dimness with the sound of a gigantic splash while Bastion was still firing again at the place where it had been. . . .

As Bastion finally dropped the gun and sank slowly to his knees beside the body of his wife, Simon also looked down and saw that her hand was still spasmodically locked around the thinner end of the crude bludgeon in which had been set a row of shark's teeth. Now that he saw it better, he saw that it was no home-made affair, but probably a souvenir of some expedition to the South Pacific. But you couldn't be right all the time, about every last detail. Just as a few seconds ago, and until he saw Bastion with his head bowed like that over the woman who had plotted to murder him, he had never expected to be restrained in his comment by the irrational compassion that finally moved him.

"By God," he thought, "now I know I'm ageing."

But aloud he said: "She worked awful hard to sell everyone on the Monster. If you like, we can leave it that way. Luckily I'm a witness to what happened just now. But I don't have to say anything about—this."

He released the club gently from the grip of the dead fingers, and carried it away with him as he went to telephone Mackenzie.

Perhaps no other villain sent as many chills up and down adolescent spines as that sinister master criminal, Dr. Fu Manchu. But **Sax Rohmer** *(a pseudonym for Arthur Henry Ward: 1883–1959) also wrote many other fine fantastic mysteries such as* The Moon is Red, Brood of the Witch Queen, *and* The Dream Detective. *Indeed, this last book introduces one of Mr. Rohmer's most interesting creations, psychic detective Moris Klaw, who solves the bizarre puzzle of "The Tragedies in the Greek Room" by falling asleep on the job.*

THE TRAGEDIES IN THE GREEK ROOM

Sax Rohmer

Chapter I

When did Moris Klaw first appear in London? It is a question which I am asked sometimes and to which I reply, "To the best of my knowledge, shortly before the commencement of the strange happenings at the Menzies Museum."

What I know of him I have gathered from various sources; and in these papers, which represent an attempt to justify the methods of one frequently accused of being an insane theorist, I propose to recount all the facts which have come to my knowledge. In some few of the cases I was personally though slightly concerned; but regard me merely as the historian and on no account as the principal or even minor character in the story. My friendship with Martin Coram led, then, to my first meeting with Moris Klaw—a meeting which resulted in my becoming his biographer, inadequate though my information unfortunately remains.

It was some three months after the appointment of Coram to the curatorship of the Menzies Museum that the first of a series of singular occurrences took place there.

This occurrence befell one night in August, and the matter was brought to my ears by Coram himself on the following morning. I had, in fact, just taken my seat at the breakfast table, when he walked in unexpectedly and sank into an armchair. His dark, clean-shaven face looked more gaunt than usual and I saw, as he lighted the cigarette which I proffered, that his hand shook nervously.

"There's trouble at the Museum!" he said, abruptly. "I want you to run around."

I looked at him for a moment without replying, and, knowing the responsibility of his position, feared that he referred to a theft from the collection.

"Something gone?" I asked.

"No; worse!" was his reply.

"What do you mean, Coram?"

He threw the cigarette, unsmoked, into the hearth. "You know Conway?" he said; "Conway, the night attendant? Well—he's dead!"

I stood up from the table, my breakfast forgotten, and stared incredulously. "Do you mean that he died in the night?" I inquired.

"Yes. Done for, poor devil!"

"What! murdered?"

"Without a doubt, Searles! He's had his neck broken!"

I waited for no further explanations, but hastily dressing, accompanied Coram to the Museum. It consists, I should mention, of four long, rectangular rooms, the windows of two overlooking South Grafton Square, those of the third giving upon the court that leads to the curator's private entrance, and the fourth adjoining an enclosed garden attached to the building. This fourth room is on the ground floor and is entered through the hall from the Square, the other three, containing the principal and more valuable exhibits, are upon the first floor and are reached by a flight of stairs from the hall. The remainder of the building is occupied by an office and the curator's private apartments, and is completely shut off from that portion open to the public, the only communicating door—an iron one—being kept locked.

The room described in the catalogue as the "Greek Room" proved to be the scene of the tragedy. This room is one of the two overlooking the Square and contains some of the finest items of the collection. The Museum is not open to the public until ten o'clock, and I found, upon arriving there, that the only occupants of the Greek Room were the commissionaire on duty, two constables, a plain-clothes officer and an inspector—that is if I except the body of poor Conway.

He had not been touched but lay as he was found by Beale, the commissionaire who took charge of the upper rooms during the day, and, indeed, it was patent that he was beyond medical aid. In fact, the position of his body was so extraordinary as almost to defy description.

There are three windows in the Greek Room, with wall cases between, and, in the gap corresponding to the east window and just by the door opening into the next room, is a chair for the attendant. Conway lay downward on the polished floor with his limbs partly under this chair and his clenched fists thrust straight out before him. His head, turned partially to one side, was doubled underneath his breast in a most dreadful manner, indisputably pointing to a broken neck, and his commissionaire's cap lay some distance away, under a table supporting a heavy case of vases.

So much was revealed at a glance, and I immediately turned blankly to Coram.

"What do you make of it?" he said.

I shook my head in silence. I could scarce grasp the reality of the thing; indeed, I was still staring at the huddled figure when the doctor arrived. At his request we laid the dead man flat upon the floor to facilitate an examination, and we then saw that he was greatly cut and bruised about the head and face, and that his features were distorted in a most extraordinary manner, almost as though he had been suffocated.

The doctor did not fail to notice this expression. "Made a hard fight of it!" he said. "He must have been in the last stages of exhaustion when his neck was broken!"

"My dear fellow!" cried Coram, somewhat irritably, "what do you mean when you say that he made a hard fight? There could not possibly have been any one else in these rooms last night!"

"Excuse me, sir!" said the inspector, "but there certainly was something going on here. Have you seen the glass case in the next room?"

"Glass case?" muttered Coram, running his hand distractedly through his thick black hair. "No; what of a glass case?"

"In here, sir," explained the inspector, leading the way into the adjoining apartment.

At his words, we all followed, and found that he referred to the glass front of a wall case containing statuettes and images of Egyptian deities. The centre pane of this was smashed into fragments, the broken glass strewing the floor and the shelves inside the case.

"That looks like a struggle, sir, doesn't it?" said the inspector.

"Heaven help us! What does it mean?" groaned poor Coram. "Who could possibly have gained access to the building in the night, or, having done so, quitted it again, when all the doors remained locked?"

"That we must try and find out!" replied the inspector. "Meanwhile, here are his keys. They lay on the floor in a corner of the Greek Room."

Coram took them, mechanically. "Beale," he said to the comissionaire, "see if any of the cases are unlocked."

The man proceeded to go around the rooms. He had progressed no farther than the Greek Room when he made a discovery. "Here's the top of this unfastened, sir!" he suddenly cried, excitedly.

We hurriedly joined him, to find that he stood before a marble pedestal surmounted by a thick glass case containing what Coram had frequently assured me was the gem of the collection—the Athenean Harp.

It was alleged to be of very ancient Greek workmanship and was constructed of fine gold inlaid with jewels. It represented two reclining female figures their arms thrown above their heads, their hands meeting; and the strings several of which were still intact were of incredibly fine gold wire. The instrument was said to have belonged to a Temple of Pallas in an extremely remote age, and at the time it was brought to light much controversy had waged concerning its claims to authenticity, several connoisseurs proclaiming it the work of a famous goldsmith of mediæval Florence, and nothing but a clever forgery. However, Greek or Florentine, amazingly ancient or comparatively modern, it was a beautiful piece of workmanship and of very great intrinsic value, apart from its artistic worth and unique character.

"I thought so!" said the plain-clothes man. "A clever museum thief!"

Coram sighed wearily. "My good fellow," he replied, "can you explain, by any earthly hypothesis, how a man could get into these apartments and leave them again during the night?"

"Regarding that, sir," remarked the detective, "there are a few questions I should like to ask you. In the first place, at what time does the Museum close?"

"At six o'clock in the summer."

"What do you do when the last visitor has gone?"

"Having locked the outside door, Beale, here, thoroughly examines every room to make certain that no one remains concealed. He next locks the communicating doors and comes down into the hall. It was then his custom to hand me the keys. I gave them into poor Conway's keeping when he came on duty at half-past six, and every hour he went through the Museum, relocking all the doors behind him."

"I understand that there is a tell-tale watch in each room?"

"Yes. That in the Greek Room registers 4 A.M., so that it was about then that he met his death. He had evidently opened the door communicating with the next room—that containing the broken glass case, but he did not touch the detector and the door was found open this morning."

"Someone must have laid concealed there and sprung upon him as he entered."

"Impossible! There is no other means of entrance or exit. The three windows are iron-barred and they have not been tampered with. Moreover, the watch shows that he was there at three o'clock, and nothing larger than a mouse could find shelter in the place; there is nowhere a man could hide."

"Then the murderer followed him into the Greek Room."

"Might I venture to point out that, had he done so, he would have been there this morning when Beale arrived? The door of the Greek Room was locked and the keys were found inside upon the floor!"

"The thief might have had a duplicate set."

"Quite impossible; but, granting the impossible, how did he get in, since the hall door was bolted and barred?"

"We must assume that he succeeded in concealing himself before the Museum was closed."

"The assumption is not permissible, in view of the fact that Beale and I both examined the rooms last night prior to handing the keys to Conway. However, again granting the impossible, how did he get out?"

The Scotland Yard man removed his hat and mopped his forehead with his handkerchief. "I must say, sir, it is a very strange thing," he said; "but how about the iron door here?"

"It leads to my own apartments. I, alone, hold a key. It was locked."

A brief examination served to show that exit from any of the barred windows was impossible.

"Well, sir," said the detective, "if the man had keys he could have come down into the hall and the lower room."

"Step down and look," was Coram's invitation.

The windows of the room on the ground floor were also heavily protected, and it was easy to see that none of them had been opened.

"Upon my word," exclaimed the inspector, "it's uncanny! He couldn't have gone out by the hall door, because you say it was bolted and barred on the inside."

"It was," replied Coram.

"One moment, sir," interrupted the plain-clothes man. "If that was so, how did you get in this morning?"

"It was Beale's custom," said Coram, "to come around by the private entrance to my apartments. We then entered the Museum together by the iron door into the Greek Room and relieved Conway of the keys. There are several little matters to be attended to in the morning before admitting the public, and the other door is never unlocked before ten o'clock."

"Did you lock the door behind you when you came through this morning?"

"Immediately on finding poor Conway."

"Could any one have come through this door in the night, provided he had a duplicate key?"

"No. There is a bolt on the private side."

"And you were in your rooms all last night?"

"From twelve o'clock, yes."

The police looked at one another silently; then the inspector gave an embarrassed laugh. "Frankly sir," he said, "I'm completely puzzled!"

We passed upstairs again and Coram turned to the door. "Anything else to report about poor Conway?" he asked.

"His face is all cut by the broken glass and he seems to have had a desperate struggle, although, curiously enough, his body bears no other marks of violence. The direct cause of death was of course a broken neck."

"And how should you think he came by it?"

"I should say that he was hurled upon the floor by an opponent possessing more than ordinary strength!"

Thus the physician, and was about to depart when there came a knocking upon the iron door.

"It is Hilda," said Coram, slipping the key in the lock—"my daughter," he added, turning to the detective.

Chapter II

The heavy door swinging open, there entered Hilda Coram, a slim, classical figure, with the regular features of her father and the pale gold hair of her dead mother. She looked unwell, and stared about her apprehensively.

"Good morning, Mr. Searles," she greeted me. "Is it not dreadful about poor Conway!"—and then glanced at Coram. I saw that she held a card in her hand. "Father, there is such a singular old man asking to see you."

She handed the card to Coram, who in turn passed it to me. It was that of Douglas Glade of the *Daily Cable*, and had written upon it in Glade's hand the words, "To introduce Mr. Moris Klaw."

"I suppose it is all right if Mr. Glade vouches for him," said Coram. "But does anybody here know Moris Klaw?"

"I do" replied the Scotland Yard man, smiling shortly. "He's an antique dealer or something of the kind; got a ramshackle old place by Wapping Old Stairs—sort of a cross between Jamrach's and a rag shop. He's lately been hanging about the Central Criminal Court a lot. Seems to fancy his luck as an amateur investigator. He's certainly smart," he added, grudgingly, "but cranky."

"Ask Mr. Klaw to come through, Hilda," said Coram.

Shortly after entered a strange figure. It was that of a tall man who stooped so that his apparent height was diminished—a very old man who carried his many years lightly, or a younger man prematurely aged; none could say which. His skin had the hue of dirty vellum and his hair, his shaggy brows, his scanty beard were so toneless as to defy classification in terms of colour. He wore an archaic brown bowler, smart, gold-rimmed pince-nez, and a black silk muffler. A long, caped black cloak completely enveloped the stooping figure; from beneath its mud-spattered edge peeped long-toed continental boots.

He removed his hat.

"Good morning, Mr. Coram," he said. His voice reminded me of the distant rumbling of empty casks; his accent was wholly indescribable. "Good morning" (to the detective), "Mr. Grimsby. Good morning, Mr. Searles. Your friend, Mr. Glade tells me I shall find you here. Good morning, Inspector. To Miss Coram I already have said good morning."

From the lining of the flat-topped hat he took out one of those small cylindrical scent sprays and played its contents upon his high, bald brow. An odour of verbena filled the air. He replaced the spray in the hat, the hat upon his scantily thatched crown.

"There is here a smell of dead men!" he explained.

I turned aside to hide my smiles, so grotesque was my first impression of the amazing individual known as Moris Klaw.

"Mr. Coram," he continued, "I am an old fool who sometimes has wise dreams. Crime has been the hobby of a busy life. I have seen crime upon the Gold Coast, where the black fever it danced in the air above the murdered one like a lingering soul, and I have seen blood flow in Arctic Lapland, where it was frozen up into red ice almost before it left the veins. Have I your permit to see if I can help?"

All of us, the police included, were strangely impressed now.

"Certainly," said Coram; "will you step this way?"

Moris Klaw bent over the dead man.

"You have moved him!" he said sharply.

It was explained that this had been for the purpose of a medical examination. He nodded absently. With the aid of a large magnifying glass he was scrutinizing poor Conway. He examined his hair, his hands, his fingernails. He rubbed long, flexible fingers upon the floor beside the body—and sniffed at the dust.

"Someone so kindly will tell me all about it," he said, turning out the dead man's pockets.

Coram briefly recounted much of the foregoing, and replied to the oddly chosen questions which from time to time Moris Klaw put to him. Throughout the duologue, the singular old man conducted a detailed search of every square inch, I think, of the Greek Room. Before the case containing the harp he stood, peering.

"It is here that the trouble centres," he muttered. "What do I know of such a Grecian instrument? Let me think."

He threw back his head, closing his eyes.

"Such valuable curios," he rumbled, "have histories—and the crimes they occasion operate in cycles." He waved his hand in a slow circle. "If I but knew the history of this harp! Mr. Coram!"

He glanced toward my friend.

"Thoughts are things Mr. Coram. If I might spend a night here—upon the very spot of floor where the poor Conway fell—I could from the surrounding atmosphere (it is a sensitive plate) recover a picture of the thing in his mind''—indicating Conway—''at the last!''

The Scotland Yard man blew down his nose.

''You snort, my friend,'' said Moris Klaw, turning upon him. ''You would snort less if you had waked screaming, out in the desert; screaming out with fear of the dripping beaks of the vultures—the last dreadful fear which the mind had known of him who had died of thirst upon that haunted spot!''

The words and the manner of their delivery thrilled us all. ''What is it,'' continued the weird old man, ''but the odic force, the ether—say it how you please—which carries the wireless message, the lightning? It is a huge, subtile, sensitive plate. Inspiration, what you call bad luck and good luck—all are but reflections from it. The supreme thought preceding death is imprinted on the surrounding atmosphere like a photograph. I have trained this''—he tapped his brow—''to reproduct those photographs! May I sleep here to-night, Mr. Coram?''

Somewhere beneath the ramshackle exterior we had caught a glimpse of a man of power. From behind the thick pebbles momentarily had shone out the light of a tremendous and original mind.

''I should be most glad of your assistance,'' answered my friend.

''No police must be here to-night,'' rumbled Moris Klaw. ''No heavy-footed constables, filling the room with thoughts of large cooks and small Basses, must fog my negative!''

''Can that be arranged?'' asked Coram of the inspector.

''The men on duty can remain in the hall, if you wish it, sir.''

''Good!'' rumbled Moris Klaw.

He moistened his brow with verbena, bowed uncouthly, and shuffled from the Greek Room.

Chapter III

Moris Klaw reappeared in the evening, accompanied by a strikingly beautiful brunette.

The change of face upon the part of Mr. Grimsby of New Scotland Yard was singular.

''My daughter—Isis,'' explained Moris Klaw. ''She assists to develop my negatives.''

Grimsby became all attention. Leaving two men on duty in the hall, Moris Klaw, his daughter, Grimsby, Coram and I went up to the Greek Room. Its darkness was relieved by a single lamp.

"I've had the stones in the Athenean Harp examined by a lapidary," said Coram. "It occurred to me that they might have been removed and paste substituted. It was not so, however."

"No," rumbled Klaw. "I thought of that, too. No visitors have been admitted here during the day?"

"The Greek Room has been closed."

"It is well, Mr. Coram. Let no one disturb me until my daughter comes in the morning."

Isis Klaw placed a red silk cushion upon the spot where the dead man had lain.

"Some pillows and a blanket, Mr. Klaw?" suggested the suddenly attentive Mr. Grimsby.

"I thank you, no," was the reply. "They would be saturated with alien impressions. My cushion it is odically sterilized! The 'etheric storm' created by Conway's last mental emotion reaches my brain unpolluted. Good-night, gentlemen. Good-night, Isis!"

We withdrew, leaving Moris Klaw to his ghostly vigil.

"I suppose Mr. Klaw is quite trustworthy?" whispered Coram to the detective.

"Oh, undoubtedly!" was the reply. "In any case, he can do no harm. My men will be on duty downstairs here all night."

"Do you speak of my father, Mr. Grimsby?" came a soft, thrilling voice.

Grimsby turned, and met the flashing black eyes of Isis Klaw.

"I was assuring Mr. Coram," he answered, readily, "that Mr. Klaw's methods have several times proved successful!"

"Several times!" she cried, scornfully. "What! has he ever failed?"

Her accent was certainly French, I determined; her voice, her entire person, as certainly charming—to which the detective's manner bore witness.

"I'm afraid I'm not familiar with all his cases, miss," he said. "Can I call you a cab?"

"I thank you, no." She rewarded him with a dazzling smile. "Good-night."

Coram opened the doors of the Museum, and she passed out. Leaving the men on duty in the hall, Coram and I shortly afterward also quitted the Museum by the main entrance, in order to avoid disturbing Moris Klaw by using the curator's private door.

To my friend's study Hilda Coram brought us coffee. She was unnaturally pale, and her eyes were feverishly bright. I concluded that the tragedy was responsible.

"Perhaps, to an extent" said Coram; "but she is studying music and, I fear, overworking in order to pass a stiff exam."

Coram and I surveyed the Greek Room problem from every conceivable standpoint, but were unable to surmise how the thief had entered, how left, and why he had fled without his booty.

"I don't mind confessing," said Coram "that I am very ill at ease. We haven't the remotest idea how the murderer got into the Greek Room or how he got out again. Bolts and bars, it is evident, do not prevail against him, so that we may expect a repetition of the dreadful business at any time!"

"What precautions do you propose to take?"

"Well, there will be a couple of police on duty in the Museum for the next week or so, but, after that, we shall have to rely upon a night watchman. The funds only allow of the appointment of four attendants: three for day and one for night duty."

"Do you think you'll find any difficulty in getting a man?"

"No," replied Coram. "I know of a steady man who will come as soon as we are ready for him."

I slept but little that night, and was early afoot and around to the Museum. Isis Klaw was there before me, carrying the red cushion, and her father was deep in conversation with Coram.

Detective-Inspector Grimsby approached me.

"I see you're looking at the cushion, sir!" he said, smilingly. "But it's not a 'plant.' He's not an up-to-date cracksman. Nothing's missing!"

"You need not assure me of that," I replied. "I do not doubt Mr. Klaw's honesty of purpose."

"Wait till you hear his mad theory, though!" he said, with a glance aside at the girl.

"Mr. Coram," Moris Klaw was saying, in his odd, rumbling tones, "my psychic photograph is of a woman! A woman dressed all in white!"

Grimsby coughed—then flushed as he caught the eye of Isis.

"Poor Conway's mind," continued Klaw, "is filled with such a picture when he breathes his last—great wonder he has for the white woman and great fear for the Athenean Harp, which she carries!"

"Which she carries!" cried Coram.

"Some woman took the harp from its case a few minutes before Conway died!" affirmed Moris Klaw. "I have much research to make now, and with aid from Isis shall develop my negative! Yesterday I learnt from the constable who was on night duty at the corner of the Square that a heavy pantechnicon van went driving round at four o'clock. It was shortly after four o'clock that the tragedy occurred. The driver was unaware that there was no way out, you understand. Is it important? I cannot say. It often is such points that matter. We must, however, waste no time. Until you hear from me again you will lay dry plaster of Paris all around the stand of the Athenean Harp each night. Good morning, gentlemen!"

His arm linked in his daughter's, he left the Museum.

Chapter IV

For some weeks after this mysterious affair, all went well at the Menzies Museum. The new night watchman, a big Scot, by name John Macalister, seemed to have fallen thoroughly into his duties, and everything was proceeding smoothly. No clue concerning the previous outrage had come to light, the police being clearly at a loss. From Moris Klaw we heard not a word. But Macalister did not appear to suffer from nervousness, saying that he was quite big enough to look after himself.

Poor Macalister! His bulk did not save him from a dreadful fate. He was found, one fine morning, lying flat on his back in the Greek Room—*dead!*

As in the case of Conway, the place showed unmistakable signs of a furious struggle. The attendant's chair had been dashed upon the floor with such violence as to break three of the legs; a bust of Pallas, that had occupied a corner position upon a marble pedestal was found to be hurled down; and the top of the case which usually contained the Athenean Harp had been unlocked, and the priceless antique lay close by, upon the floor!

The cause of death, in Macalister's case, was heart failure, an unsuspected weakness of that organ being brought to light at the inquest; but, according to the medical testimony, deceased must have undergone unnaturally violent exertions to bring about death. In other respects, the circumstances of the two cases were almost identical. The door of the Greek

Room was locked upon the inside and the keys were found on the floor. From the detector watches in the other rooms it was evident that his death must have taken place about three o'clock. Nothing was missing, and the jewels in the harp had not been tampered with.

But, most amazing circumstance of all, imprinted upon the dry plaster of Paris which in accordance with the instructions of the mysteriously absent Moris Klaw, had nightly been placed around the case containing the harp *were the marks of little bare feet!*

A message sent, through the willing agency of Inspector Grimsby, to the Wapping abode of the old curio dealer, resulted in the discovery that Moris Klaw was abroad. His daughter, however, reported having received a letter from her father which contained the words—

"Let Mr. Coram keep the key of the case containing the Athenean Harp under his pillow at night."

"What does she mean?" asked Coram. "That I am to detach that particular key from the bunch or place them all beneath my pillow?"

Grimsby shrugged his shoulders.

"I'm simply telling you what she told me, sir."

"I should suspect the man to be an impostor," said Coram, "if it were not for the extraordinary confirmation of his theory furnished by the footprints. They certainly looked like those of a woman!"

Remembering how Moris Klaw had acted, I sought out the constable who had been on duty at the corner of South Grafton Square on the night of the second tragedy. From him I elicited a fact which, though insignificant in itself, was, when associated with another circumstance, certainly singular.

A Pickford traction engine, drawing two heavy wagons, had been driven round the Square at 3 A.M., the driver thinking that he could get out on the other side.

That was practically all I learned from the constable, but it served to set me thinking. Was it merely a coincidence that, at almost the exact hour of the previous tragedy, a heavy pantechnicon had passed the Museum?

"It's not once in six months," the man assured me, "that any venicle but a tradesman's cart goes round the Square. You see, it doesn't lead anywhere, but this Pickford chap he was rattling by before I could stop him, and though I shouted he couldn't hear me, the engine making such a noise, so I just let him drive round and find out for himself."

I now come to the event which concluded this extraordinary case, and, that it may be clearly understood, I must explain the positions which we took up during the nights of the following week; for Coram had asked me to take a night watch, with himself, Grimsby, and Beale, in the Museum.

Beale, the commissionaire, remained in the hall and lower room—it was catalogued as the "Bronze Room"—Coram patrolled the room at the top of the stairs, Grimsby the next, or Greek Room, and I the Egyptian Room. None of the doors was locked, and Grimsby, by his own special request, held the keys of the cases in the Greek Room.

We commenced our vigil on the Saturday, and I, for one, found it a lugubrious business. One electric lamp was usually left burning in each apartment throughout the night, and I sat as near to that in the Egyptian Room as possible and endeavoured to distract my thoughts with a bundle of papers with which I had provided myself.

In the next room I could hear Grimsby walking about incessantly, and, at regular intervals, the scratching of a match as he lighted a cigar. He was an inveterate cheroot smoker.

Our first night's watching then, was productive of no result, and the five that followed were equally monotonous.

Upon Grimsby's suggestion we observed great secrecy in the matter of these dispositions. Even Coram's small household was kept in ignorance of this midnight watching. Grimsby, following out some theory of his own, now determined to dispense altogether with light in the Greek Room. Friday was intensely hot, and occasional fitful breezes brought with them banks of black thundercloud, which, however, did not break; and, up to the time that we assumed our posts at the Museum, no rain had fallen. At about twelve o'clock I looked out into South Grafton Square and saw that the sky was entirely obscured by a heavy mass of inky cloud, ominous of a gathering storm.

Returning to my chair beneath the electric lamp, I took up a work of Mark Twain's, which I had brought as a likely antidote to melancholy or nervousness. As I commenced to read, for the twentieth time, "The Jumping Frog," I heard the scratch of Grimsby's match in the next room and knew that he had lighted his fifth cigar.

It must have been about one o'clock when the rain came. I heard the big drops on the glass roof, followed by the steady pouring of the deluge. For perhaps five minutes it rained steadily, and then ceased as abruptly as it had begun. Above the noise of the water rushing down the metal gutters, I distinctly detected the sound of Grimsby striking another match. Then, with a mighty crash, came the thunder.

Directly above the Museum it seemed as though the very heavens had burst, and the glass roof rattled as if a shower of stones had fallen, the thunderous report echoing and reverberating hollowly through the building.

As the lightning flashed with dazzling brilliance, I started from my chair and stood, breathless, with every sense on the alert; for, strangely intermingling with the patter of the rain that now commenced to fall again came a low wailing, like nothing so much as the voice of a patient succumbing to an anæsthetic. There was something indefinably sweet, but indescribably weird, in the low and mysterious music.

Not knowing from whence it proceeded, I stood undetermined what to do; but, just as the thunder boomed again, I heard a wild cry—undoubtedly proceeding from the Greek Room! Springing to the door, I threw it open.

All was in darkness, but, as I entered, a vivid flash of lightning illuminated the place.

I saw a sight which I can never forget. Grimsby lay flat upon the floor by the farther door. But, dreadful as that spectacle was, it scarce engaged my attention; nor did I waste a second glance upon the Athenean Harp, which lay close beside its empty case.

For the figure of a woman, draped in flimsy white, was passing across the Greek Room!

Grim fear took me by the throat, since I could not doubt that what I saw was a supernatural manifestation. Darkness followed. I heard a loud wailing cry and a sound as of a fall.

Then Coram came running through the Greek Room.

Trembling violently, I joined him; and together we stood looking down at Grimsby.

"Good God!" whispered Coram; "this is awful. It cannot be the work of mortal hands! Poor Grimsby is dead!"

"Did you—see—the woman?" I muttered. I will confess it: my courage had completely deserted me.

He shook his head; but, as Beale came running to join us, glanced fearfully into the shadows of the Greek Room. The storm seemed to have passed, and, as we three frightened men stood around Grimsby's recumbent body we could almost hear the beating of each other's hearts.

Suddenly, giving a great start, Coram clutched my arm. "Listen!" he said. "What's that?"

I held my breath and listened. "It's the thunder in the distance," said Beale.

"You are wrong," I answered. "It is someone knocking the hall entrance! There goes the bell, now!''

Coram gave a sigh of relief. ''Heavens!'' he said; ''I've no nerves left! Come on and see who it is.''

The three of us, keeping very close together, passed quickly through the Greek Room and down into the hall. As the ringing continued, Coram unbolted the door—and there, on the steps, stood Moris Klaw!

Some vague idea of his mission flashed through my mind. ''You are too late!'' I cried. ''Grimsby has gone!''

I saw a look of something like anger pass over his large pale features, and then he had darted past us and vanished up the stairs.

Chapter V

Having rebolted the door, we rejoined Moris Klaw in the Greek Room. He was kneeling beside Grimsby in the dim light—and Grimsby, his face ghastly pale, was sitting up and drinking from a flask!

''I am in time!'' said Moris Klaw. ''He has only fainted!''

''It was the ghost!'' whispered the Scotland Yard man. ''My God! I'm prepared for anything human—but when the lightning came and I saw that white thing—playing the harp—''

Coram turned aside and was about to pick up the harp, which lay upon the floor near, when—

''Ah!'' cried Moris Klaw, ''do not touch it! It is death!''

Coram started back as though he had been stung as Grimsby very unsteadily got upon his feet.

''Turn up lights,'' directed Moris Klaw, ''and I will show you!''

The curator went out to the switchboard and the Greek Room became brightly illuminated. The ramshackle figure of Moris Klaw seemed to be invested with triumphant majesty. Behind the pebbles his eyes gleamed.

''Observe,'' he said, ''I raise the harp from the floor.'' He did so. ''And I live. For why? Because I do not take hold upon it in a natural manner—*by the top!* I take it by the side! Conway and Macalister took hold upon it at the top; and where are they—Conway and Macalister?''

''Mr. Klaw,'' said Coram, ''I cannot doubt that this black business is all clear to your very unusual intelligence; but to me it is a profound mystery. I have, myself, in the past, taken up the harp in the way you describe as fatal, and without injury—''

''But not immediately after it had been played upon!'' interrupted Moris Klaw.

"Played upon! I have never attempted to play upon it!"

"Even had you done so you might yet have escaped, provided you *set it down* before touching the top part! Note, please!"

He ran his long white fingers over the golden strings. Instantly there stole upon my ears that weird, wailing music which had heralded the strange happenings of the night!

"And now," continued our mentor, "whilst I who am cunning hold it where the ladies' gold feet join, observe the stop—where the hand would in ordinary rest in holding it."

We gathered around him.

"A *needle-point*," he rumbled, impressively, "protruding! The player touches it not! But who takes it from the hand of the player *dies!* By placing the harp again upon its base the point again retires! Shall I say what is upon that point, to drive a man mad like a dog with rabies, to stay potent for generations? I can not. It is a secret buried with the ugly body of Cæsar Borgia!"

"Cæsar Borgia!" we cried in chorus.

"Ah!" rumbled Moris Klaw, "your Athenean Harp was indeed made by Paduano Zelloni, the Florentine! It is a clever forge! I have been in Rome until yesterday. You are surprised? I am sorry, for the poor Macalister died. Having perfected, with the aid of Isis, my mind photograph of the lady who plays the harp, I go to Rome to perfect the story of the harp. For why? At my house I have records, but incomplete, useless. In Rome I have a friend, of so old a family, and once so wicked, I shall not name it!

"He has recourse to the great Vatican Library—to the annals of his race. There he finds me an account of such a harp. In those priceless parchments it is called 'a Greek lyre of gold.' It is described. I am convinced. I am sure!

"Once the beautiful Lucrece Borgia play upon his harp. To one who is distasteful to her she says: 'Replace for me my harp.' He does so. He is a dead man! God! what cleverness!

"Where has it lain for generations before your Sir Menzies find it? No man knows. But it has still its virtues! How did the poor Menzies die? Throw himself from his room window, I recently learn. This harp certainly was in his room. Conway, after dashing, mad, about the place, springs head downward from the attendant's chair. Macalister dies in exhaustion and convulsions!"

A silence; when—

"What caused the harp to play?" asked Coram.

Moris Klaw looked hard at him. Then a thrill of new horror ran through my veins. A low moan came from somewhere hard by! Coram turned in a flash!

"Why, my private door is open!" he whispered.

"Where do you keep your private keys?" rumbled Klaw.

"In my study." Coram was staring at the open door but seemed afraid to approach it. "We have been using the attendant's keys at night. My own are on my study mantelpiece now."

"I think not," continued the thick voice. "Your daughter has them!"

"My daughter!" cried Coram and sprang to the open door. "Heavens! Hilda! Hilda!"

"She is somnambulistic!" whispered Moris Klaw in my ear. "When certain unusual sounds—such as heavy vehicles at night—reach her in her sleep (ah! how little we know of the phenomenon of sleep!), she arises, and, in common with many sleepwalkers, always acts the same. Something in the case of Miss Hilda, attracts her to the golden harp—"

"She is studying music!"

"She must rest from it. Her brain is overwrought! She unlocks the case and strikes the cords of the harp, relocking the door, replacing the keys—I before have known such cases—then retires as she came. Who takes the harp from her hands, or raises it, if she has laid it down upon its side, dies! These dead attendants were brave fellows both, for, hearing the music, they came running, saw how the matter was, and did not waken the sleeping player. Conway was poisoned as he returned the harp to its case; Macalister, as he took it up from where it lay. Something to-night awoke her ere she could relock the door. The fright of so awaking made her to swoon."

Coram's kindly voice and the sound of a girl sobbing affrightedly reached us.

"It was my yell of fear, Mr. Klaw!" said Grimsby, shamefully. "She looked like a ghost!"

"I understand," rumbled Moris Klaw, soothingly. "As I see her in my sleep she is very awesome! I will show you the picture Isis has made from my etheric photograph. I saw it, finished, earlier to-night. It confirmed me that the Miss Hilda with the harp in her hand was poor Conway's last thought in life!"

"Mr. Klaw," said Grimsby, earnestly, "you are a very remarkable man!"

"Yes?" he rumbled, and gingerly placed in its case the "Greek lyre of gold" which Paduano Zelloni had wrought for Cæsar Borgia.

From the brown hat he took out his scent spray and squirted verbena upon his heated forehead.

"That harp," he explained, "it smells of dead men!"

FUTURE VISIONS _____

Edward D. Hoch *(1930–   ) is a very familiar name to mystery readers. For the last eight years, his stories have appeared in every issue of* Ellery Queen's Mystery Magazine. *From his first story on, however, he has written a great many fantastic mysteries such as* The Fellowship of the Hand, The Frankenstein Factory, *and* The Judges of Hades. *"The Forbidden Word," a typical example of his craftsmanship, is an arresting story that leaves you speechless.*

THE FORBIDDEN WORD

Edward D. Hoch

GREGORY had not visited Los Angeles since the summer of 1978, and the changes he now found were a bit unnerving. True, the reconstruction was almost complete, the signs of disaster had nearly vanished; but there was about the city a certain strangeness which he could not at first pinpoint.

Driving in from the airport in his rented electric car, he was aware that the freeway traffic was thinner than he had remembered. At one stretch, just before turning onto Slauson Avenue, he counted only five cars ahead of him—at a time of day when he used to see hundreds.

He asked Browder about it at the office and the grayhaired regional sales manager merely shrugged. "Oh, they're trying to keep it quiet, but we all know it's happening. This building is only half occupied and nearly all the houses on my block have *For Sale* signs out. People are leaving by the thousands."

"But why?" Gregory, a stolid midwesterner, found it difficult to understand.

"The last one was the worst, really bad. People just decided they'd had enough."

"You mean the earthquake?"

Browder held up a hand. "We don't talk about it in public. God, Gregory, it's been bad out here! Haven't you read about the California Enabling Act back east?"

"I might have seen something in the newspapers," Gregory said.

"They're trying everything to minimize the danger, to get people to stay." Browder chuckled dryly. "I'm old enough to remember the depression days when I was a boy. Then they put up roadblocks to keep people *out* of the state. Now they try to keep 'em *in!*"

"Times change," Gregory agreed. "But what about business? The home office sent me out because sales have fallen off so badly. What's been happening?"

The grayhaired man shrugged again. "You need people to buy things."

"Surely it's not that bad!"

"What have I just been telling you? Wait till the census in 1990. They can fake a lot of things, but they can't fake that. That'll tell the story. Some say it'll show a population drop of close to fifty percent."

"But the states back east are booming—they haven't room for all the people!"

"That's back east. This is out here. They have their problems and we have ours."

Gregory glanced down at the sheet of sales figures. "What should I tell the home office?"

"Just that. I can't sell to people who aren't here."

They talked longer, of many things, but when Gregory left the office he was troubled and unhappy. Los Angeles had always been one of their best markets, and if it really was dying as Browder believed, the company was in trouble.

It was the lunch hour, but the downtown streets were pleasantly uncrowded. Gregory found himself able to walk along easily without being pushed off the sidewalk—so unlike the midtown pedestrian jams in New York and Chicago. He almost wondered if this might be a good, uncluttered place to live—but then he remembered the people who were leaving, and the reason they were leaving.

"Hello, there," a girl's voice said at his side. He turned and saw a pretty blonde who seemed vaguely familiar. When she noted his uncertainty she explained, "I'm Mr. Browder's secretary. You probably didn't notice me in the outer office."

"As a matter of fact, I didn't. My name is Gregory."

"I know. I'm Lola Miller. Are you going somewhere for lunch?"

"Do you know a good place?"

"The office girls usually eat at the Sunset Lounge. It's only a block away."

"Sounds good. Would you join me?"

"Glad to. I enjoy company while I eat."

Lola Miller was in her midtwenties, with that sunny California beauty that recalled the movie queens of the 1950s. He liked her smile and the way she had of showing one dimple in her left cheek in a sort of lopsided grin.

"It's nearly ten years since I've visited L.A.," he said, seating himself opposite her at one of the little tables.

"It's almost rebuilt now, isn't it? You wouldn't know anything had happened."

"Apparently the people know. I understand they're leaving."

She nodded. "Terrible for business, isn't it? Pretty soon we'll be a ghost state. I suppose that's why they had to pass all those laws."

"The California Enabling Act? Browder mentioned it."

"It's terrible, but necessary. Something had to be done after the last disaster." She pressed the button for the waitress. "All those scare headlines in the papers, everybody talking so much—that's when the real panic started."

"You mean after the earthquake?" he asked just as the waitress appeared. Across the table Lola Miller's face suddenly drained of color. The waitress took their order and hurried back to the counter.

"You shouldn't have said that," Lola cautioned him. "Not in public. She might turn you in."

"Said what? The word earthquake? Well, that's what it was, wasn't it?"

"Yes, but we're forbidden to—"

She was cut off in midsentence by the appearance of a tall young man dressed in the style of the '70s. There was no mistaking his appearance or the tone of his voice. "Would you step outside for a moment, sir?" he asked.

"What for?"

The newcomer gave a little frozen smile and pressed a button on his flipcase, showing the gold card. "California State Police, sir. I'll have to ask you to come along quietly."

"But what have I done?"

"Greg—" Lola began, trying to interrupt.

"Reported violation of Section 45431 of the Criminal Code, sir. The California Enabling Act."

Gregory got shakily to his feet, still not believing it was really happening. "You'll have to explain it more clearly than that."

"You were heard to utter a word that it is forbidden to speak in public, sir."

"Word? What word?"

A hand of steel closed around his wrist. "Just come along quietly, sir."

Gregory looked back in despair at Lola. "I think I need a lawyer," he said.

The officer in charge was a towering hulk of a man who came right to the point. "You're in big trouble, Gregory. Conviction on a violation of 45431 carries a prison sentence of five years."

"All because I used the word *earthquake?*"

"Exactly. You used it in a public place and thereby violated the law. The word cannot be used in any periodical printed within the state of California or uttered in any public place."

"But that's ridiculous! You can't simply wipe a word out of the language!"

"Mr. Gregory, the future of our state is at stake here. Believe me, we're not the only place that has passed laws about what can or cannot be said in public."

"The Supreme Court—"

"The Supreme Court itself once stated that no one had the right to yell 'Fire' in a crowded theater. Likewise, during the airplane bombings and hijackings some twenty years ago, no one had the right to talk about bombs while flying on a plane. Men were arrested for joking about a bomb in their luggage or saying they were going to take the plane to Cuba."

"But—"

The officer, whose name was Vitroll, cut him off with a wave of the hand. "It's the same thing here. The state is in an emergency situation. The only way to control it is to blot out all mention of what happened a few years back. After a time people will forget, and start to return."

"I'm from out of state," Gregory argued. "I had only the vaguest idea of the law here."

"Ignorance of the law has never been recognized as an excuse in a court of law. In fact, it might go harder on you being from the east. It's all that eastern propaganda causing us the trouble in the first place. Eastern magazines and newspapers and television, always talking about things out here, about the disaster and how it's sure to happen again."

"I'm not exactly an easterner. I'm from a suburb of Chicago."

"That's east to us," Vitroll said, moving his hulk from the edge of the desk. "I'll have to book you."

"How much will the bail be?"

"That's up to the judge. In cases where it seems likely the offense will be repeated, no bail is granted."

"All this for just saying a word?"

"These are troubled times, Mr. Gregory. The survival of the state is at stake."

He went away then, leaving Gregory alone in the room. For a time there was nothing to do but ponder the position in which he found himself. Surely a call to the home office would bring him the best of legal aid. This sort of thing could not go on unnoticed.

The door opened and a uniformed guard said, "Follow me, sir."

"Are you taking me to the judge?"

"No, sir. To a cell. You'll have to wait there until it's time for your hearing."

Gregory followed reluctantly, noticing that a second guard had come up behind him. They were treating him exactly like a criminal, taking no chances. "I'm harmless," he said. "Really."

"In here."

The cell door slid shut automatically behind him and he was left alone with the gray metal walls. He walked over to the bunk and tested its lumpy surface, wondering how many had occupied it before him and for how long. Sitting there, trying to collect his thoughts, he took out his pen to make a few notes. It slipped from his numb fingers, clattering on the steel floor, and he bent to retrieve it.

That was when he noticed the word scrawled under the bunk, where the guards would not see it. Though he might have expected some obscenity in such a place, the word was much more frightening.

There, beneath the bunk, some earlier prisoner had scrawled: *earthquake*.

They took him to the courtroom, between two guards, and he looked up at the frozenfaced judge who seemed almost unaware of his presence.

"Violation of Section 45431 of the Criminal Code, your Honor. California Enabling Act," a voice behind him said.

The judge nodded slightly. "How do you plead?"

"Not guilty, your Honor. I'm from out of state. I knew nothing of this law."

"I would have thought it had been well publicized," the judge commented dryly. "Will you waive your right to a trial?"

"No, sir, I will not! I haven't even consulted a lawyer yet."

"Very well. I'll schedule the trial for October 15th—two weeks from today. Bail is set at five thousand dollars, and you are ordered not to leave the state."

"Five thousand—"

Behind him Vitroll cleared his throat. "Bail has been raised by a friend of the defendant, your Honor."

Gregory turned and saw Lola Miller standing behind the railing. He walked toward her, feeling at once the need for fresh outside air. "Thank you," he said simply.

"The company put it up," she explained, "but they didn't want their name involved."

"Thanks, anyway. I know you had a hand in it."

"I was with you when it happened. I felt some responsibility. Come on, my car is outside."

They drove back to the office where a distracted Browder was waiting. He rose as they entered and hurried over to shake Gregory's hand. "My God, I'd thought we'd lost you! The home office would never have forgiven me! When Lola told me what happened—"

"I wasn't aware of the details of your laws out here. What happens now? I'm supposed to stay here for two weeks."

"What happens?" Browder repeated. "Why, you'll jump bail, of course! The company will stand the loss. Otherwise, believe me, it means a jail sentence."

"They've actually sent people to prison for this?"

"Dozens of them, for terms up to five years. It's not worth taking the chance, Gregory."

"No, indeed," he agreed. "I'll catch the next plane out of here."

"It might not be that easy," Lola cautioned. "They watch the airports—they have electronic surveillance systems of all sorts. Your photograph is already stored in the memory bank.''

He turned to Browder. ''Any suggestions?''

''Drive your rented car out of the state. To Las Vegas, maybe. Then get a plane from there.''

''They don't watch the highways?''

''Only for people moving out of the state—furniture vans, things like that. You'd be safe, especially if Lola traveled with you.''

''Then that's it,'' Gregory decided.

An hour later they were headed out of Los Angeles in the little electric car.

''I know so little about you,'' she said, once the car had cleared the city limits.

''There's not much to know. I'm just a man who cried earthquake and got arrested for it.''

''I mean—well, are you married?''

''I was once.'' He gazed out at the passing landscape of cactus, thinking how little it had changed in the past hundred years. Civilization had not yet reached the back roads of eastern California. ''But that was a long time ago.''

''You don't like to talk about it.''

''Does anyone like to talk about failures?'' He was silent for a time, then said, ''You're taking a chance traveling with me. If we're caught you could end up in prison, too.''

''You'd never find your way alone on these back roads. Either you'd get lost or one of the copter patrol would spot you.''

''Copter patrol?''

She pointed to the sky. ''There's one now. They watch mainly for trucks and vans heading out of the state, but they could make trouble if they spotted you.''

The copter, painted gold, dipped low, catching the sun, as it came in for a closer look. Apparently it saw nothing amiss, for it headed away again at once. ''How far to the state line?'' he asked.

''Less than an hour.'' Like all Californians, she gave distances in time rather than miles.

''You're sure there'll be no roadblocks?''

''Not on these back roads. And once you're across it'll be difficult for them to put their hands on you. Most states won't grant extradition for crimes committed under the California Enabling Act.''

Some 45 minutes later, as they topped a rise of desert land, he saw the first billboard. *"Settle here!"* it proclaimed. *"Free from earthquake danger!''*

''That's it,'' Lola said, giving a little sigh. ''We're across the line—in Nevada now.''

''Will you be going back to California after you drop me in Vegas?''

She turned in her seat, looking at him, ''You know something? I'm scared of those damned earthquakes, too. I was always afraid to admit it till now, but since I'm safely out of that place I don't think I'll be hurrying back.''

''Come east with me,'' he said.

''I've never been east.''

''All the more reason for you to go.''

''Could you get me a job at the home office?''

He considered that for a moment. ''There's too much of my past scattered around Chicago. Besides, they might just come looking for me for jumping bail. Maybe the company doesn't think I'm worth five thousand.''

''Where, then?''

''Farther east—New York.''

''With all those people?''

''It's not so bad. A lot of it is California propaganda.''

They passed more billboards and presently the gleaming towers of Las Vegas came into view, like some mythic kingdom in the desert. ''All right,'' she said finally. ''I'll go east with you.''

He took one hand off the steering wheel and touched her, lightly. ''I'm glad.''

They turned in the rented car at the Vegas airport, even though he knew it would indicate the direction of his flight. He was not a criminal, and had not yet learned to act like one. He was merely a man in flight, with no reason for covering his tracks.

On the plane east they held hands like teenagers of some era of long ago, and he told her what he remembered of the crowded streets of Manhattan. ''There are people, sure, and sometimes it's difficult to stay on the sidewalk, but it's all worth it. The last time I was there, New York really got to me. The smallest event brings out thousands of people. It's a people's town—people everywhere!''

''And they all drive cars.''

''Little electrics, smaller than in California. Traffic is still bad, though, I'll admit that. With so many people in the New York area there are times when nothing moves.''

It was night when they landed at Kennedy International Airport, and close to midnight by the time they took the express subway into Manhattan. Lola was hungry, so they had something to eat in the hotel coffee shop before going up to their rooms.

''Tomorrow we'll look for an apartment, and jobs,'' he said.

''It's good to be here with you.''

''Even with all the people?''

''Even with all the people. That other, in California—it seems like a nightmare now.''

''It does, in a way,'' he agreed. ''We've gone back a long way in this country when words can be so dangerous they have to be banned. And it's no longer the obscenities that frighten people, but a simple word like earthquake. I feel like standing up and shouting it here. Earthquake! *Earthquake!*''

She took his hand. ''You know, I think I could learn to love you.''

He was touched by her gentleness. ''I guess I already do love you.''

Later, after they'd finished eating, they left the coffee shop and headed across the lobby to the elevators. Gregory saw the two men first, waiting for them, and he was reminded of Vitroll and the others in California.

''Lola, those men!''

''What?''

But then it was too late to run. ''Sorry, sir, I'll have to ask you and the lady to accompany us.''

''Not her,'' Gregory said. ''I'm the one you want.''

''It's both of you we want.''

Lola tried to move away, but the second man seized her arm. ''Will you take us back to California?'' she asked, and her voice was close to a sob.

The first man frowned. ''We don't know anything about California. Here's my identification. George Bates of the Population Control Board, New York City Police.''

''New York? But we—''

"You were overheard using a certain word that is not in keeping with the laws of this city. A word that could be harmful, or lead to harmful acts."

"What word?" Gregory demanded, feeling his heart sink.

The man named Bates consulted a notebook. "I believe the word was . . . love."

Joe Gores *(1931–   ) worked as hod carrier, stock clerk,
laborer, assistant motel manager, truck driver, logger, carnival
worker, gymnasium instructor, and private eye before Anthony
Boucher convinced him to begin writing mysteries in 1967.
Since then his tough-minded tales (three Edgar Awards) have
become famous for their verisimilitude. But he also possesses a
fine imagination, as is apparent in such works as the following
why-done-it about the criminal of the future.*

THE CRIMINAL

Joe Gores

IT BEGAN with the routine reporting of an individual transmitter failure.
These are not common, but component fatigue does sometimes develop.
When there is such a failure in the miniaturized circuitry of some citizen's
subcutaneous transmitter, the monitor computer reports loss of contact and
a minimal security drill is gone through. I tele'd Sergeant 1418; in a moment his image flashed on my screen.

"Contacting on transmitter failure report number 31. Do you have the
suspect's personnel tape up yet?"

"I just was about to tele it to you, Controller, sir."

The statistical segment of a personnel tape flashed on the screen. The
suspect was repulsively muscular, dark-haired and dark-eyed, with a square
face and ugly thick neck. Weight, 85 kilos; height, 1.87 meters: name 36/
204/GS/8219. A citizen of State 36, City 204, employed by Communica-
tions Center.

"What is his ComCen Station, Sergeant?"

The sergeant's face was worried. "Ah . . . Controller, sir, he . . . ah
. . . Artifacts, sir."

"*Artifacts?* Did he work in Audio-Visual, 1418, or was—"

"Negative, Controller, sir. He was a . . . a Reading Material Indexer, sir."

"He had access to the book storage tapes?"

"Affirmative, Controller, sir."

"Has 8219 been warned that he has one hour to report to a medical center for replacement of his transmitter?"

"We . . . Negative, sir. 8219 did not report to his work station today, Controller, sir."

This was rapidly becoming very serious. "Has he reported ill, 1418?"

"Negative, Controller, sir. We sent a Helitrans to his dwelling unit, but their report also was negative."

My palms suddenly were wet. We *were out of contact with Citizen 8219!* A faulty individual transmitter was one thing, a misdemeanor only; but a *deliberate* break in contact was a felony because it might possibly involve Norm Deviation.

"Orders in two minutes," I barked crisply.

I blanked the screen and, drenched in sweat, pushed the computer control combination for the applicable action manual. While waiting, I estimated my anxiety level and took the psychotropic tranquilizer dosage recommended by manual for that degree of agitation. The microtapes were fed into my audioscanner; as instructions crackled in my earphones, I reactived the telecom screen and relayed them to Sergeant 1418.

"Cordon suspect's dwelling unit immediately, but delay the search of his individual premises until my arrival. Detain incommunicado all residents present, apprehend all others at work stations, and initiate Action Plan Yellow: all-points, intensive, all-ground coordinated search for Suspect 8219."

"Understood, Controller, sir."

"All individuals in his work station will be charged under section 18.9 of the Criminal Code: Failure to Report an Absence."

"Affirmative, Controller, sir."

My tranquilizers were steading my voice. "I will report to NORMDEV Control for further instructions. Have a Helitrans ready for my use at Port Seven."

I rode the personnel transport belt down broad, restfully pale halls, my hands tremoring slightly. We had not had a case of Norm Deviation in City 204 since I had taken over as security controller five years before. What if Higher Authority found there had been security negligence in clearing the suspect for access to the book storage tapes? It was unpleasant to contemplate. I enjoyed the perquisites of my office: my tele, my supervised sexual activities, my chemical enjoyment aids; I even had been considering a sperm submission to the Genes Bank so that a satisfactory wife could be selected for me.

At NORMDEV Control, I reported name and rank to the telescreen; when a responding image appeared, my fists clenched and acrid sweat started under my arms: it was Medic One himself, head of NORMDEV Research Section and a member of Higher Authority.

"Come in, Controller." He smiled genially from the screen. "Security has been through on tele concerning your mission."

His inner office had picture windows overlooking the dazzling white towers of the city. Far away, toward the ocean and the broad plankton farms, was the green slash of Park Three. Medic One himself was a small, quick, active man, bald and wearing heavy eyeglasses. These and his slight limp would in themselves have marked him as Higher Authority: only in someone born of genetically uncontrolled parents could such physical idiosyncracies have occurred, and only one in Higher Authority could have been allowed to reach maturity with them.

He motioned me to a chair by his heavy plastic desk, fixed me with piercing eyes from behind the thick glasses, and showed yellowed teeth in a smile.

"You have shown considerable dispatch in reacting to this security breach, Controller. If Criminal 8219 is quickly apprehended, you will receive nothing more serious than a reprimand."

Relief flooded through me as he turned again from the window, so disks of reflected light flashed in his glasses.

"Several points are suggestive. Genes Bank records indicate his father was a decent, hard-working fellow in spaceship telemetry; but his mother died of a massive overdose of chemical aids after *deliberately smashing her home telescreen.*"

"I . . . can see the significance of that, sir. She—"

"Can you, Controller?" His mood suddenly had changed. "I doubt that, the overdose . . . destruction of the telescreen . . ."

"Misdemeanor first offense, felony second," I said automatically. My hands were tremoring again after his outburst. But Medic One's brief rage seemed spent.

"Quite so, since four hours' viewing a night is of course mandatory.

Now, despite the mother's criminal instability, 8219 was a brilliant child: brilliant. And since he showed absolutely no Norm Deviation tendencies himself, eventually he was *cleared by Security* and given the Reading Material Index position he requested. *Requested*, Controller: a position which is hardly one for which workers clamor, eh? We should have been suspicious.''

Taking advantage of his apparently lightened mood, I began, ''Yes, sir, I can see that, sir. I—''

''I sincerely hope you can, Controller.''

''Sir?'' My stomach had begun churning again.

''Your department turned him loose with *books. Your* department has so miserably mishandled the investigation up to this point.'' His malevolent gaze drained the blood from my face. ''There is nothing, for example, in your preliminary report concerning the physician who performed the illegal operation.''

''Illegal operation, sir? I don't—''

''Removing 8219's transmitter!'' he shrieked. A fleck of foam appeared at one corner of his mouth. But then he abruptly smiled again, and clicked his yellow teeth together. In an academic voice, he said, ''There are three possibilities concerning the Criminal, Controller. Enumerate, please.''

I stammered, ''First, sir I . . . I think an overdose of a high methamphetamine-content chemical aid.'' His benign nod made the words flow more easily. ''Second: mental or emotional derangement, sir—both common. Third . . .''

I stopped. There was no third possibility.

But Medic One's face paled visibly; his slight, malformed body seemed to swell. Behind the thick lenses his eyes grew large and round.

''Idiot!'' he shrieked. Foam again flecked the corners of his mouth and his body became momentarily rigid, as if he were about to have a catatonic seizure. ''A genetic sport, you fool! He may be a genetic sport! Find him! Seize him!''

I fled down echoing halls toward the heliport, his maledictions ringing in my ears. The tension made me want to throw up. What could I do? How could I cope? Somehow, en route in the Helitrans, I managed to swallow some tranquilizers and so arrived at 8219's dwelling unit in some semblance of control. Those residents present, mostly wives and children, already had been tranquilized and were chatting gaily with the security police detaining them in their individual premises. I could hear them as I was elevated in the man lift to the correct dwelling tier level.

The silence of the criminal's premises was broken only by the hum of the environmental control unit. Per regulation, the central unit's long wall was taken up by the telescreen and the other walls were bare. There were no windows, of course; they are allowed only for Higher Authority. It was pathetically easy to uncache the Norm Deviation material: it was in the criminal's sleeping room, in the tunic drawer. A notebook removed from ComCen suppies—itself a misdemeanor—and neatly filled with quotes and aphorisms illegally copied from the book tapes.

I believe there are more instances of the abridgment of the freedom of the people by gradual and silent encroachments of those in power than by violent and sudden usurpations.

The people never give up their liberties but under some delusion.

We, and all others who believe as deeply as we do, would rather die on our feet than live on our knees.

What sane man in our enlightened and totally free society would risk Deprivation of Existence merely to dwell on such maunderings? Well, I knew, I would soon find out. But it was not to be that easy. The criminal proved most difficult to apprehend.

For one thing, other cases intervened to make security's work more difficult. A berserk plankton farm laborer killed a dozen of his fellow workers, and there was a series of rapes in Map Sectors 11.4 and 11.5. Murder and rape, of course, are not serious crimes like Norm Deviation; but investigating them and recommending the proper fines tied up field agents. Also, to show Medic One where the laxity in the department had existed, I had recommended that Sergeant 1418 be castrated and reassigned to the plankton farms for his dereliction of duty in connection with Criminal 8219's escape. Training his replacement had taken time.

But on the fifteenth day after 8219's escape, Sergeant 1419's calm efficient face appeared on my telescreen. "Controller, sir, Criminal 8219 has been surrounded. Map Sector 11.6, coordinates Ac, Bf."

My visualscanner flashed this sector on my screen. Park Three, that dense wooded area approximating our primitive ancestors' "natural environment," which I had seen from Medic One's window. No wonder we hadn't found him before now! How had he ever survived in there? Park Three does not even have power connections for setting up a portable environmental control unit!

"We will go directly, Sergeant."

Manual states that Norm Deviation Criminals must be taken unharmed to serve as subjècts for NORMDEV medics' diagnostic experiments, so we had a few tense moments. At one point the criminal, a physically powerful brute with rippling, unsightly muscles, broke through the cordon, felled the Helitrans Unit Guard, and was halfway up the boarding ladder before a net rifle was fired and he was rendered helpless.

I began preliminary examination the next day under telescreen monitoring by high NORMDEV officials including, perhaps, even Medic One himself.

"Criminal 8219, once this preliminary examination has established your guilt of Norm Deviation, NORMDEV officials will examine you to determine whether you can be made fit for society again by leucotomy, or whether you will be subject to experimental dissection instead."

"*Sans* anesthesia, of course?" He did not seem disturbed by the prospect; he even grinned engagingly when he said it.

"Unfortunately, that is the scientific necessity. For the moment, forcible detranquilization will begin today—"

"I'm not on the psychotropics anyway."

I glanced at his Physical Examination Data Sheet; it confirmed the almost incredible fact that he did not use any chemical aids. How was he able to stand it? But this fact made him a much more formidable opponent. I began to bear down.

"Criminal 8219, we must have the name of your accomplice: the corrupt medic who surgically removed the individual transmitter from your back."

He gave me that oddly engaging grin again. "I did it myself, Con, with a food preparation knife and two mirrors."

I quickly checked the laboratory reports from his premises. Two small hand mirrors had been found, and a knife had borne a trace of his blood on the blade. A fragment of individual transmitter circuitry component had been found beside the base of his excrement disposal unit. But how to withstand the pain?

"How much pain is there in removing something the size of a baby's fingernail from beneath the epidermal layer, Con?"

"My name is Controller," I said coldly.

He jerked a thumb at the telescreen monitor. "Afraid you'll get in trouble with the boys from NORMDEV?" He shook his head. "They know you're incorruptible, Con. Generations of genetic control have made sure of that. Of course the inbred little band of psychopaths called Higher Authority is scared of me for just that reason: they're afraid I might have genetically uncontrolled—"

"Genetic controls were initiated for the best of reasons!" I snapped, stung by his vicious slander of Higher Authority.

"Because population levels a dozen generations ago were so high, human overcrowding so intense, that a humanity with its aggressions intact probably would have exploded into continual violence? Sure. But how much control can you exercise before people stop being people and become . . . something else?"

I terminated the interrogation abruptly; the man sickened me. And I *was* a little apprehensive, with NORMDEV medics looking in on us. But the next day he started right in again.

"You know, Con, the controls have made the vast mass of humanity a mass of intelligent but unwilled cattle, no more important to Higher Authority than individual dinoflagellates and coelenterates in those plankton farms out there. Of course no one fools around with the genetic structure of those in Higher Authority . . ."

"There are good and sufficient reasons—"

"Sure. Without his aggressions, his competitive spirit, man can't make decisions; to run things, Higher Authority has to be uncontrolled. But even more, men in Higher Authority need those aggressions for the power struggle which has to rage among them at all times."

Though he sickened me, I kept trying to draw him out. "We hear no reports on such a struggle . . ."

"Of course not," he grinned. "But I'll bet the losers are stripped of power, offspring, and the ability to make any more. So . . . that makes me unique: the only person with uncontrolled genes outside the power structure. You can see why I had to be apprehended."

"Indeed? How did you come by these 'uncontrolled genes' as you call them?"

"Mutation. Had to be. I'm a natural sport, a throwback. My parents, like everyone's parents, were themselves products of the Genes Bank, so that's the only explanation for the differences I observed between myself and everyone else."

"And as soon as you observed these differences, you traitorously removed classified material from the book tapes; you deliberately broke contact with Computor Control; you destroyed—"

He spread his arms wide and laughed. "See, Con? A classic example of Norm Deviation. As for *why* I did it: who knows?"

Who knew indeed? My interrogation was complete. I escorted him to NORMDEV Control on the personal transport belt. Since we were free from audio monitoring in the corridor, I asked him a personal question.

"You have done all of this deliberately, Criminal 8219; yet you are not a madman. Why didn't you just remain a Reading Material Indexer, even though you hid Norm Deviation impulses in your brain?"

He flashed that sudden grin and clapped me on the shoulder. "Read my final notebook entry, Con. Think about minor crimes and map sectors. And then read up on the physical properties of mutants. And then, if you figure it out: happy nightmares. Because you won't do anything to stop it."

As Apprehending Official, I had to be watching from behind the observation window at the NORMDEV Experimental Laboratory when they brought him in to strap down on the dissection table. How could any man, completely untranquilized, face so coolly the systematic surgical removal, without anesthesia, of his bodily organs one at a time?

Yet the criminal was oddly jolly, even jumping up to perch on the edge of the operating table, swinging his feet like a little child. And for that critical moment, he held the eyes, the minds, of all in that room with his defiance. It was enough.

"Bet you don't make me say 'ouch,' " he said, grinning.

And then his hand swept up a gleaming scalpel from the instrument tray and jerked it across his throat with a flashing movement. Scarlet arterial blood jumped out, splattering guards, medics, and Higher Authority impartially.

That self-murder triggered a series of tragic events. The NORMDEV agents responsible were sentenced to Deprivation of Existence in the geriatric disposal crematoria; but that was only justice. They had been lax. But a bare two days after Criminal 8219's death, a Helitrans Unit accident between the City and Medic One's country estate left him without wife and children. And before he could recover from the terrible loss—the very next day, in fact—he inadvertently was locked in the NORMDEV radiation room and accidentally sterilized. Higher Authority, with great sorrow, announced his permanent, premature retirement.

So it was not until several days later that I could prepare to close Criminal File 36/204/GS/8219. I idly leafed through that infamous notebook to the final entry. It was nothing: one of those silly sentiments I had noted the day I'd found the notebook. *We, and all others who believe as deeply as we do, would rather die on our feet than live on our knees.*

I supposed it was indeed an explanation, of sorts, for a disturbed mind. But what else was it? Minor crimes. And map sectors. And . . . the physical properties of mutants? Yes.

Curious now, I fed the map sector grid into the visualscanner, at the same time directing the computer to run an information tape on mutants through my audioscanner.

He had been apprehended in map sector . . . what? 11.4? 11.5? No. There had been that series of rapes in those sectors. Park Three was in the adjoining 11.6. But wait a minute. Rape was a minor crime. And the map sectors were adjoining. And the rapes had occurred *during the same fifteen days* that Criminal 8219 had been hiding in Park Three. And—

Sport or Mutant, intoned my earphones. *A sudden departure from the parent type in one or more heritable characteristics, caused by a change in a gene or chromosome with an individual or new species resulting.*

Sudden terror bent me, moaning, over the desk, sent my hand scrabbling for a tranquilizer. Heritable characteristics: *mutants could reproduce their own mutations by breeding with females of the parent species!* Nightmares, had he said? Stark terror!

How many raped and impregnated women had *not* reported? Married women, perhaps, from whom even genetic control has never been able to completely eradicate the protective motherhood urge? Or teenage girls who would not mind the abortion, but who would not want to be sterilized as is automatic with reporting rape victims? Girls who could name a boyfriend as father, thus assuring that the child would be born and then reared by the State?

How many women?

My tranquilizer was letting me breathe again, letting me think, consider. If even *one* offspring resulted and lived, the very fabric of the State would be threatened. A whole strain of the old, unruly men might result. My duty was clear. Report to NORMDEV. Then, an immediate sweep through the affected sectors, aborting all pregnancies, sterilizing all women.

I tele'd NORMDEV. "Medic One, at once. Security Control."

"He is in conference, Controller. He will be alerted."

I waited. And then new terror struck. Criminal 8219 had been *my* responsibility! His suicide had made me his unwitting partner in this monstrous crime of Norm Deviation. As an accessory to Criminal 8219's crime, I would be Deprived of Existence!

"Yes, Controller?" The new Medic One glared at me from the screen, eyes slightly bulging, lank hair plastered across his cranium like strands of beached kelp.

"I . . . sir . . ." But it wasn't *fair!* "Sir, I . . . is further action contemplated on Criminal File 36/204/GS/8219?"

"Closed file," he barked. "Reprimand going into *your* personal folder, Controller, for requesting information on a closed file."

The screen was blanked, and I released my pent breath. A reprimand only, instead of death. What harm, really? Higher Authority had *decreed* that all was well: the file was closed. And Higher Authority *always* is correct. And yet . . . And yet . . .

Higher Authority, even now, did not know of the criminal's diabolic plot. That he, knowing it would mean his own death, had plotted to reproduce himself and his genetic aberrations in the sole way he could without there being genetic scrutiny of the offspring. Nor had Higher Authority foreseen, as the criminal had, that *my* genetic code with its built-in apprehensions made me *incapable* of denouncing his foul plot against the State. Higher Authority was *always* correct?

My hands shook so badly that I could hardly open my desk drawer and remove from it what I needed; I performed the only action which was possible for me.

I took a tranquilizer.

Phyllis Dorothy James *(1920–   ) has been highly regarded by mystery afficionados since she began writing in the early 1960's. Critics favorably compare her to Agatha Christie and Ngaio Marsh, writers shower her with awards, and fans fatten her bank account. The following fantastic mystery demonstrates the strength of her backgrounds, plotting, characterization, and style, and makes us hope she will soon give us yet another one.*

MURDER, 1986

P. D. James

THE GIRL lay naked on the bed with a knife through her heart. That was the one simple and inescapable fact. No, not simple. It was a fact horrible in its complications. Sergeant Dolby, fighting nausea, steadied his shaking thighs against the foot of the bed and forced his mind into coherence— arranging his thoughts in order, like a child piling brick on colored brick and holding its breath against the inevitable tumble into chaos. He mustn't panic. He must take things slowly. There was a proper procedure laid down for this kind of crisis. There was a procedure laid down for everything.

Dead. That, at least, was certain. Despite the heat of the June morning the slim, girlish body was quite cold, the rigor mortis already well advanced in face and arms. What had they taught him in Detective School about the onset of rigor mortis, that inexorable if erratic stiffening of the muscles, the body's last protest against disintegration and decay? He couldn't remember. He had never been any good at the more academic studies. He had been lucky to be accepted for the Criminal Investigation Department; they had made that clear enough to him at the time. They had never ceased to make it clear. A lost car; a small breaking and entering; a purse snatch. Send Dolby. He had never rated anything more interesting or important than the petty crimes of inadequate men. If it was something no one else wanted to be bothered with, send Dolby. If it was something the C.I.D. would rather not be told about, send Dolby.

And that was exactly how this death would rate. He would have to report it, of course. But it wouldn't be popular news at Headquarters. They were overworked already, depleted in strength, inadequately equipped, forced even to employ him six years after his normal retirement age. No, they wouldn't exactly welcome this spot of trouble. And the reason, as if he didn't know it, was fixed there on the wall for him to read. The statutory notice was pasted precisely over the head of her bed.

He wondered why she had chosen that spot. There was no rule about where it had to be displayed. Why, he wondered, had she chosen to sleep under it as people once slept under a Crucifix. An affirmation? But the wording was the same as he would find on the notice in the downstairs hall, in the elevator, on every corridor wall, in every room in the Colony. The Act to which it referred was already two years old:

PRESERVATION OF THE RACE ACT—1984
Control of Interplanetary Disease
Infection Carriers

All registered carriers of the Disease, whether or not they are yet manifesting symptoms, are required under Section 2 of the above Act to conform to the following regulations. . . .

He didn't need to read further. He knew the regulations by heart—the rules by which the Ipdics lived, if you could call it living. The desperate defense of the few healthy against the menace of the many condemned. The small injustices which might prevent the greatest injustice of all, the extinction of man. The stigmata of the Diseased: the registered number tattooed on the left forearm; the regulation Ipdic suit of yellow cotton in summer, blue serge in winter; the compulsory sterilization, since an Ipdic bred only monsters; the rule prohibiting marriage or any close contact with a Normal; the few manual jobs they were permitted to do; the registered Colonies where they were allowed to live.

He knew what they would say at Headquarters. If Dolby had to discover a murder, it would have to be of an Ipdic. And trust him to be fool enough to report it.

But there was no hurry. He could wait until he was calmer, until he could face with confidence whomever they chose to send. And there were things they would expect him to have noticed. He had better make an examination of the scene before he reported. Then, even if they came at once, he would have something sensible to say.

He forced himself to look again at the body. She was lying on her back, eyes closed as if asleep, light brown hair streaming over the pillow. Her arms were crossed over her chest as if in a last innocent gesture of modesty. Below the left breast the handle of a knife stuck out like an obscene horn.

He bent low to examine it. An ordinary handle, probably an ordinary knife. A short-bladed kitchen knife of the kind used to peel vegetables. Her right palm was curved around it, but not touching it, as if about to pluck it out. On her left forearm the registered Ipdic number glowed almost luminous against the delicate skin.

She was neatly covered by a single sheet pulled smooth and taut so that it looked as if the body had been ritually prepared for examination—an intensification of the horror. He did not believe that this childish hand could have driven in the blade with such precision or that, in her last spasms, she had drawn the sheet so tidily over her nakedness. The linen was only a shade whiter than her skin. There had been two months now of almost continuous sunshine. But this body had been muffled in the high-necked tunic and baggy trousers of an Ipdic suit. Only her face had been open to the sun. It was a delicate nut-brown and there was a faint spatter of freckles across the forehead.

He walked slowly around the room. It was sparsely furnished but pleasant enough. The world had no shortage of living space, even for Ipdics. They could live in comfort, even in some opulence, until the electricity, the television, the domestic computer, the micro-oven broke down. Then these things remained broken. The precious skills of electricians and engineers were not wasted on Ipdics. And it was extraordinary how quickly squalor could replace luxury.

A breakdown of electricity in a building like this could mean no hot food, no light, no heating. He had known Ipdics who had frozen or starved to death in apartments which, back in 1980, only six years ago, must have cost a fortune to rent. Somehow the will to survive died quickly in them. It was easier to wrap themselves in blankets and reach for that small white capsule so thoughtfully provided by the Government, the simple painless way out which the whole healthy community was willing for them to take.

But this girl, this female Ipdic PXN 07926431, wasn't living in squalor. The apartment was clean and almost obsessively neat. The micro-oven was out of order, but there was an old-fashioned electric cooker in the kitchen and when he turned it on the hot plate glowed red. There were even a few personal possessions—a little clutch of seashells carefully arranged on the window ledge, a Staffordshire porcelain figurine of a shepherdess, a child's tea service on a papier-mâché tray.

Her yellow Ipdic suit was neatly folded over the back of a chair. He took it up and saw that she had altered it to fit her. The darts under the breasts had been taken in, the side seams carefully shaped. The hand stitching was neat and regular, an affirmation of individuality, or self-respect. A proud girl. A girl undemoralized by hopelessness. He turned the harsh cotton over and over in his hands and felt the tears stinging the back of his eyes.

He knew that this strange and half-remembered sweetness was pity. He let himself feel it, willing himself not to shrink from the pain. Just so, in his boyhood, he had tentatively placed his full weight on an injured leg after football, relishing the pain in the knowledge that he could bear it, that he was still essentially whole.

But he must waste no more time. Turning on his pocket radio he made his report.

"Sergeant Dolby here. I'm speaking from Ipdic Colony 865. Female Ipdic PXN 07926431 found dead. Room 18. Looks like murder."

It was received as he had expected.

"Oh, God! Are you sure? All right. Hang around. Someone will be over."

While he waited he gave his attention to the flowers. They had struck his senses as soon as he opened the door of the room, but the first sight of the dead girl had driven them from his mind. Now he let their gentle presence drift back into his consciousness. She had died amid such beauty.

The apartment was a bower of wild flowers, their delicate sweetness permeating the warm air so that every breath was an intimation of childhood summers, an evocation of the old innocent days. Wild flowers were his hobby. The slow brain corrected itself, patiently, mechanically: wild flowers had been his hobby. But that was before the Sickness, when the words flower and beauty seemed to have meaning. He hadn't looked at a flower with any joy since 1980.

1980. The year of the Disease. The year with the hottest summer for 21 years. That summer when the sheer weight of people had pressed against the concrete bastions of the city like an intolerable force, had thronged its burning pavements, had almost brought its transport system to a stop, had sprawled in checkered ranks across its parks until the sweet grass was pressed into pale straw.

1980. The year when there were too many people. Too many happy, busy, healthy human beings. The year when his wife had been alive; when his daughter Tessa had been alive. The year when brave men, traveling far beyond the moon, had brought back to earth the Sickness—the Sickness which had decimated mankind on every continent of the globe. The Sickness which had robbed him, Arthur Dolby, of his wife and daughter.

Tessa. She had been only 14 that spring. It was a wonderful age for a daughter, the sweetest daughter in the world. And Tessa had been intelligent as well as sweet. Both women in his life, his wife and daughter, had been cleverer than Dolby. He had known it, but it hadn't worried him or made him feel inadequate. They had loved him so unreservedly, had relied so much on his manhood, been so satisfied with what little he could provide. They had seen in him qualities he could never discern in himself, virtues which he knew he no longer possessed. His flame of life was meagre; it had needed their warm breaths to keep it burning bright. He wondered what they would think of him now. Arthur Dolby in 1986, looking once more at wild flowers.

He moved among them as if in a dream, like a man recognizing with wonder a treasure given up for lost. There had been no attempt at formal arrangement. She had obviously made use of any suitable container in the apartment and had bunched the plants together naturally and simply, each with its own kind. He could still identify them. There were brown earthenware jars of Herb Robert, the rose-pink flowers set delicately on their reddish stems. There were cracked teacups holding bunches of red clover meadow buttercups, and long-stemmed daisies; jam jars of white campion and cuckoo flowers; egg cups of birdsfoot trefoil—"eggs and bacon," Tessa used to call it—and even smaller jars of rueleaved saxifrage and the soft pink spurs of haresfoot. But, above all, there were the tall vases of cow-parsley, huge bunches of strong hollow-grooved stems supporting their umbels of white flowers, delicate as bridal lace, yet pungent and strong, shedding a white dust on the table, bed, and floor.

And then, in the last jar of all, the only one which held a posy of mixed flowers, he saw the Lady Orchid. It took his breath away. There it stood, alien and exotic, lifting its sumptuous head proudly among the common flowers of the roadside, the white clover, campion, and sweet wild roses. The Lady Orchid. *Orchis Purpurea.*

He stood very still and gazed at it. The decorative spike rose from its shining foliage, elegant and distinctive, seeming to know its rarity. The divisions of the helmet were wine-red, delicately veined and spotted with purple, their somber tint setting off the clear white beauty of the lip. The Lady Orchid. Dolby knew of only one spot, the fringe of a wood in old Kent County in the Southeast Province, where this flower grew wild. The Sickness had changed the whole of human life. But he doubted if it had changed that.

It was then that he heard the roar of the helicopter. He went to the window. The red machine, like a huge angry insect, was just bouncing down onto the roof landing pad. He watched, puzzled. Why should they send a chopper? Then he understood. The tall figure in the all-white uniform with its gleaming braid swung himself down from the cockpit and was lost to view behind the parapet of the roof. But Dolby recognized at once that helmet of black hair, the confident poise of the head. C. J. Kalvert. The Commissioner of the Home Security Force in person.

He told himself that it couldn't be true—that Kalvert wouldn't concern himself with the death of an Ipdic, that he must have some other business in the Colony. But what business? Dolby waited in fear, his hands clenched so that the nails pierced his palms, waited in an agony of hope that it might not be true. But it was true. A minute later he heard the strong footsteps advancing along the corridor. The door opened. The Commissioner had arrived.

He nodded an acknowledgement to Dolby and, without speaking, went over to the bed. For a moment he stood in silence, looking down at the girl. Then he said, "How did you get in, Sergeant?"

The accent was on the third word.

"The door was unlocked, sir."

"Naturally. Ipdics are forbidden to lock their doors. I was asking what you were doing here."

"I was making a search, sir."

That at least was true. He had been making a private search.

"And you discovered that one more female Ipdic had taken the sensible way out of her troubles. Why didn't you call the Sanitary Squad? It's unwise to leave a body longer than necessary in this weather. Haven't we all had enough of the stench of decay?"

"I think she was murdered, sir."

"Do you indeed, Sergeant. And why?"

Dolby moistened his dry lips and made his cramped fingers relax. He mustn't let himself be intimidated, mustn't permit himself to get flustered. The important thing was to stick to the facts and present them cogently.

"It's the knife, sir. If she were going to stab herself, I think she would have fallen on the blade, letting her weight drive it in. Then the body would have been found face downwards. That way, the blade would have done all the work. I don't think she would have had the strength or the skill to pierce her heart lying in that position. It looks almost surgical. It's too neat. The man who drove that knife in knew what he was doing. And then there's the sheet. She couldn't have placed it over herself so neatly."

"A valid point, Sergeant. But the fact that someone considerately tidied her up after death doesn't necessarily mean that he killed her. Anything else?"

He was walking restlessly about the room as he talked, touching nothing, his hands clasped behind his back. Dolby wished that he would stand still. He said, "But why use a knife at all, sir? She must have been issued her euthanasia capsule."

"Not a very dramatic was to go, Dolby. The commonest door for an Ipdic to let life out. She may have exercised a feminine preference for a more individualistic death. Look around this room, Sergeant. Does she strike you as having been an ordinary girl?"

No, she hadn't struck Dolby as ordinary. But this was ground he dare not tread. He said doggedly, "And why should she be naked, sir? Why take all her clothes off to kill herself?"

"Why, indeed. That shocks you, does it, Dolby? It implies an unpleasant touch of exhibitionism. It offends your modesty. But perhaps she was an exhibitionist. The flowers would suggest it. She made her room into a bower of fragrance and beauty. Then, naked, as unencumbered as the flowers, she stretched herself out like a sacrifice, and drove a knife through her heart. Can you, Sergeant, with your limited imagination, understand that a woman might wish to die like that?"

Kalvert swung round and strode over to him. The fierce black eyes burned into Dolby's. The Sergeant felt frightened, at a loss. The conversation was bizarre. He felt they were playing some private game, but that only one of them knew the rules.

What did Kalvert want of him? In a normal world, in the world before the Sickness when the old police force was at full strength, the Commissioner wouldn't even have known that Dolby existed. Yet here they both were, engaged, it seemed, in some private animus, sparring over the body of an unimportant dead Ipdic.

It was very hot in the room now and the scent of the flowers had been growing stronger. Dolby could feel the beads of sweat on his brow. Whatever happened he must hold on to the facts. He said, "The flowers needn't be funeral flowers. Perhaps they were for a celebration."

"That would suggest the presence of more than one person. Even Ipdics don't celebrate alone. Have you found any evidence that someone was with her when she died?"

He wanted to reply, "Only the knife in her breast." But he was silent. Kalvert was pacing the room again. Suddenly he stopped and glanced at his watch. Then, without speaking, he turned on the television. Dolby remembered. Of course. The Leader was due to speak after the midday news. It was already 12:32. He would be almost finished.

The screen flickered and the too familiar face appeared. The Leader looked very tired. Even the makeup artist hadn't been able to disguise the heavy shadows under the eyes or the hollows beneath the cheekbones. With that beard and the melancholy, pain-filled face, he looked like an ascetic prophet. But he always had. His face hadn't changed much since the days of his student protest. People said that, even then, he had only really been interested in personal power. Well, he was still under thirty but he had it now. All the power he could possibly want. The speech was nearly over.

"And so we must find our own solution. We have a tradition in this country of humanity and justice. But how far can we let tradition hamper us in the great task of preserving our race? We know what is happening in other countries, the organized and ceremonial mass suicides of thousands of Ipdics at a time, the humane Disposal Squads, the compulsory matings between computer-selected Normals. Some compulsory measures against the Ipdics we must now take. As far as possible we have relied on gentle and voluntary methods. But can we afford to fall behind while other less scrupulous nations are breeding faster and more selectively, disposing of their Ipdics, re-establishing their technology, looking with covetous eyes at the great denuded spaces of the world. One day they will be repopulated. It is our duty to take part in this great process. The world needs our race. The time has come for every one of us, particularly our Ipdics, to ask ourselves with every breath we draw: have I the right to be alive?"

Kalvert turned off the set.

"I think we can forego the pleasure of seeing once again Mrs. Sartori nursing her fifth healthy daughter. Odd to think that the most valuable human being in the world is a healthy fecund female. But you got the message I hope, Sergeant. This Ipdic had the wisdom to take her own way out while she still had a choice. And if somebody helped her, who are we to quibble?"

"It was still murder, sir. I know that killing an Ipdic isn't a capital crime. But the Law hasn't been altered yet. It's still a felony to kill any human being."

"Ah, yes. A felony. And you, of course, are dedicated to the detection and punishment of felonies. The first duty of a policeman is to prevent crime; the second is to detect and punish the criminal. You learned all that when you were in Detective School, didn't you? Learned it all by heart. I remember reading the first report on you, Dolby. It was almost identical with the last. 'Lacking in initiative. Deficient in imagination. Tends to make errors of judgment. Should make a reliable subordinate. Lacks self-confidence.' But it did admit that, when you manage to get an idea into your head, it sticks there. And you have an idea in your head. Murder. And murder is a felony. Well, what do you propose to do about it?"

"In cases of murder the body is first examined by the forensic pathologist."

"Not this body, Dolby. Do you know how many pathologists this country now has? We have other uses for them than to cut up dead Ipdics. She was a young female. She was not pregnant. She was stabbed through the heart. What more do we need to know?"

"Whether or not a man was with her before she died."

"I think you can take it there was. Male Ipdics are not yet being sterilized. So we add another fact. She probably had a lover. What else do you want to know?"

"Whether or not there are prints on the knife, sir, and, if so, whose they are."

Kalvert laughed aloud. "We were short of forensic scientists before the Sickness. How many do you suppose we have now? There was another case of capital murder reported this morning. An Ipdic has killed his former wife because she obeyed the Law and kept away from him. We can't afford to lose a single healthy woman, can we, Dolby? There's the rumor of armed bands of Ipdics roaming the Southeast Province. There's the case of the atomic scientist with the back of his skull smashed in. A scientist, Dolby! Now, do you really want to bother the lab with this petty trouble?''

Dolby said obstinately, ''I know that someone was with her when she picked the flowers. That must have been yesterday—they're still fresh even in this heat, and wild flowers fade quickly. I think he probably came back here with her and was with her when she died.''

''Then find him, Sergeant, if you must. But don't ask for help I can' give.''

He walked over to the door without another glance at the room or at the dead girl, as if neither of them held any further interest for him. Then he turned: ''You aren't on the official list of men encouraged to breed daughters in the interest of the race, are you, Sergeant?''

Dolby wanted to reply that he once had a daughter. She was dead and he wanted no other.

''No, sir. They thought I was too old. And then there was the adverse psychologist's report.''

''A pity. One would have thought that the brave new world could have made room for just one or two people who were unintelligent, lacking in imagination, unambitious, inclined to errors of judgment. People will persist in going their own obstinate way. Goodbye, Dolby. Report to me personally on this case, will you? I shall be interested to hear how you progress. Who knows, you may reveal unsuspected talents.''

He was gone. Dolby waited for a minute as if to cleanse his mind of that disturbing presence. As the confident footsteps died away, even the room seemed to settle itself into peace. Then Dolby began the few tasks which still remained.

There weren't many. First, he took the dead girl's fingerprints. He worked with infinite care, murmuring to her as he gently pressed the pad against each fingertip, like a doctor reassuring a child. It would be pointless, he thought, to compare them with the prints on any of the ordinary objects in the room. That would prove nothing except that another person had been there. The only prints of importance would be those on the knife. But there were no prints on the knife—only an amorphous smudge of whorls and composites as if someone had attempted to fold her hand around the shaft but had lacked the courage to press the fingers firm.

But the best clue was still there—the Lady Orchid, splendid in its purity and beauty, the flower which told him where she had spent the previous day, the flower which might lead him to the man who had been with her.

And there was another clue, something he had noticed when he had first examined the body closely. He had said nothing to Kalvert. Perhaps Kalvert hadn't noticed it or hadn't recognized its significance. Perhaps he had been cleverer than Kalvert. He told himself that he wasn't really as stupid as people sometimes thought. It was just that his mind was so easily flustered into incoherence when stronger men bullied or taunted him. Only his wife and daughter had really understood that, had given him the confidence to fight it.

It was time to get started. They might deny him the services of the pathologist and the laboratory, but they still permitted him the use of his car. It would be little more than an hour's drive.

But, before leaving, he bent once more over the body. The Disposal Squad would soon be here for it. He would never see it again. So he studied the clue for the last time—the faint, almost imperceptible circle of paler skin round the third finger of her left hand. The finger that could have worn a ring through the whole of a hot summer day . . .

He drove through the wide streets and sun-filled squares, through the deserted suburbs, until the tentacles of the city fell away and he was in open country. The roads were pitted and unmended, the hedges high and unkempt, the fields a turbulent sea of vegetation threatening to engulf the unpeopled farmlands. But the sun was pleasant on his face. He could almost persuade himself that this was one of the old happy jaunts into the familiar and well-loved countryside of Old Kent.

He had crossed the boundary into the Southeast Province and was already looking for the remembered landmarks of hillside and church spire when it happened. There was an explosion, a crack like a pistol shot, and the windshield shattered in his face. He felt splinters of glass stinging his cheeks. Instinctively he guarded his face with his arms. The car swerved out of control and lurched onto the grass verge. He felt for the ignition key and turned off the engine. Then he tentatively opened his eyes. They were uninjured. And it was then he saw the Ipdics.

They came out of the opposite ditch and moved toward him, with stones still in their hands. There were half a dozen of them. One, the tallest, seemed to be their leader. The others shuffled at his heels, lumpy figures in their illfitting yellow suits, their feet brown and bare, their hair matted like animals', their greedy eyes fixed on the car. They stood still, looking at him. And then the leader drew his right hand from behind his back, and Dolby saw that it held a gun.

His heart missed a beat. So it was true! Somehow the Ipdics were getting hold of weapons. He got out of the car, trying to recall the exact instructions of such an emergency. Never show fear. Keep calm. Exert authority. Remember that they are inferior, unorganized, easily cowed. Never drop your eyes. But his voice, even to him, sounded feeble, pitched unnaturally high.

"The possession of a weapon by an Ipdic is a capital crime. The punishment is death. Give me that gun."

The voice that replied was quiet, authoritative, the kind of voice one used to call educated.

"No. First you give me the keys to the car. Then I give you something in return. A cartridge in your belly!"

His followers cackled their appreciation. It was one of the most horrible sounds in the world—the laughter of an Ipdic.

The Ipdic pointed the gun at Dolby, moving it slowly from side to side as if selecting his precise target. He was enjoying his power, drunk with elation and triumph. But he waited a second too long. Suddenly his arm jerked upward, the gun leaped from his grasp, and he gave one high desolate scream, falling into the dust of the road. He was in the first spasm of an Ipdic fit. His body writhed and twisted, arched and contracted, until the bones could be heard snapping.

Dolby looked on impassively. There was nothing he could do. He had seen it thousands of times before. It had happened to his wife, to Tessa, to all those who had died of the disease. It happened in the end to every Ipdic. It would have happened to that girl on the bed, at peace now with a knife in her heart.

The attack would leave this Ipdic broken and exhausted. If he survived, he would be a mindless idiot, probably for months. And then the fits would come more frequently. It was this feature of the Disease which made the Ipdics so impossible to train or employ, even for the simplest of jobs.

Dolby walked up to the writhing figure and kicked away the gun, then picked it up. It was a revolver, a Smith and Wesson .38, old but in good condition. He saw that it was loaded. After a second's thought he slipped it into the pocket of his jacket.

The remaining Ipdics had disappeared, scrambling back into the hedges with cries of anguish and fear. The whole incident was over so quickly that it already seemed like a dream. Only the tortured figure in the dust and the cold metal in his pocket were witnesses to its reality. He should report it at once, of course. The suppression of armed Ipdics was the first duty of the Home Security Force.

He backed the car onto the road. Then, on an impulse, he got out again and went over to the Ipdic. He bent to drag the writhing figure off the road and into the shade of the hedge. But it was no good. Revolted, he drew back. He couldn't bear to touch him. Perhaps the Ipdic's friends would creep back later to carry him away and tend to him. Perhaps. But he, Dolby, had his own problem. He had a murder to solve.

Fifteen minutes later he drove slowly through the village. The main street was deserted but he could glimpse, through the open cottage doors, the garish yellow of an Ipdic suit moving in the dim interior and he could see other yellow-clad figures bending at work in the gardens and fields. None of them looked up as he passed. He guessed that this was one of the settlements which had grown up in the country, where groups of Ipdics attempted to support themselves and each other, growing their own food, nursing their sick, burying their dead. Since they made no demands on the Normals they were usually left in peace. But it couldn't last long. There was no real hope for them.

As more and more of them were overtaken by the last inevitable symptoms, the burden on those left grew intolerable. Soon they too would be helpless and mad. Then the Security Force, the Health Authorities, and the Sanitary Squads would move in, and another colony of the dispossessed would be cleaned up. And it was a question of cleaning up. Dolby had taken part in one such operation. He knew what the final horror would be. But now in the heat of this sun-scented afternoon, he might be driving through the village as he had known it in the days before the Sickness, prosperious, peaceful, sleepy, with the men still busy on the farms.

He left the car at the churchyard gate and slipping the strap of his murder bag over his shoulder, walked up the dappled avenue of elms to the south entrance. The heavy oak door with its carved panels, its massive hinges of hammered iron creaked open at his touch. He stepped into the cool dimness and smelled again the familiar scent of flowers, musty hymn books, and wood polish, saw once again the medieval pillars soaring high to the hammer beams of the room, and, straining his eyes through the dimness he glimpsed the carving on the rood screen and the far gleam of the sanctuary lamp.

The church was full of wild flowers. They were the same flowers as those in the dead girl's apartment but here their frail delicacy was almost lost against the massive pillars and the richly carved oak. But the huge vases of cow-parsley set on each side of the chancel steps made a brave show, floating like twin clouds of whiteness in the dim air. It was a church decked for a bride.

He saw a female Ipdic polishing the brass lectern. He made his way up the aisle toward her and she beamed a gentle welcome as if his appearance were the most ordinary event in the world. Her baggy Ipdic suit was stained with polish and she wore a pair of old sandals, the soles peeling away from the uppers. Her graying hair was drawn back into a loose bun from which wisps of hair had escaped to frame the anxious, sun-stained face.

She reminded him of someone. He let his mind probe once again, painfully, into the past. Then he remembered. Of course. Miss Caroline Martin, his Sunday School superintendent. It wasn't she, of course. Miss Martin would have been over 70 at the time of the Sickness. No one as old as that had survived, except those few Tasmanian aborigines who so interested the scientists. Miss Martin, standing beside the old piano as her younger sister thumped out the opening hymn and beating time with her gloved hand as if hearing some private and quite different music. Afterward, the students had gone to their different classes and had sat in a circle around their teachers. Miss Martin had taught the older children, himself among them. Some of the boys had been unruly, but never Arthur Dolby. Even in those days he had been obedient, law-abiding. The good boy. Not particularly bright, but well-behaved. Good, dull, ineffectual. Teacher's pet.

And when she spoke it was with a voice like Miss Martin's.

"Can I help you? If you've come for Evensong services, I'm afraid it isn't until five-thirty today. If you're looking for Father Reeves, he's at the Rectory. But perhaps you're just a visitor. It's a lovely church, isn't it? Have you see our sixteenth-century reredos?"

"I hoped I would be in time for the wedding."

She gave a little girlish cry of laughter.

"Dear me, you are late! I'm afraid that was yesterday! But I thought no one was supposed to know about it. Father Reeves said that it was to be quite secret really. But I'm afraid I was very naughty. I did so want to see the bride. After all, we haven't had a wedding here since—"

"Since the Act?"

She corrected him gently, like Miss Martin rebuking the good boy of the class.

"Since 1980. So yesterday was quite an occasion for us. And I did want to see what the bride looked like in Emma's veil."

"In what?"

"A bride has to have a veil, you know." She spoke with gentle reproof, taking pity on his masculine ignorance. "Emma was my niece. I lost her and her parents in 1981. Emma was the last bride to be married here. That was on April 28, 1980. I've always kept her veil and headdress. She was such a lovely bride."

Dolby asked with sudden harshness the irrelevant but necessary question.

"What happened to her bridegroom?"

"Oh, John was one of the lucky ones. I believe he has married again and has three daughters. Just one daughter more and they'll be allowed to have a son. We don't see him, of course. It wasn't to be expected. After all, it is the Law."

How despicable it was, this need to be reassured that there were other traitors.

"Yes," he said. "It is the Law."

She began polishing the already burnished lectern, chatting to him as she worked.

"But I've kept Emma's veil and headdress. So I thought I'd just place them on a chair beside the font so that this new bride would see them when she came into church. Just in case she wanted to borrow them, you know. And she did. I was so glad. The bridegroom placed the veil over her head and fixed the headdress for her himself, and she walked up the aisle looking so beautiful."

"Yes," said Dolby. "She would have looked very beautiful."

"I watched them from behind this pillar. Neither of them noticed me. But it was right for me to be here. There ought to be someone in the church. It says in the prayer book, 'In the sight of God and of this congregation.' She had a small bouquet of wild flowers, just a simple mixed bunch but very charming. I think they must have picked it together."

"She carried a Lady Orchid," said Dolby. "A Lady Orchid picked by her bridegroom and surrounded by daisies, clover, white campion, and wild roses."

"How clever of you to guess! Are you a friend, perhaps?"

"No," said Dolby. "Not a friend. Can you describe the bridegroom?"

"I thought that you must know him. Very tall, very dark. He wore a plain white suit. Oh, they were such a handsome couple! I wished Father Reeves could have seen them."

"I thought he married them."

"So he did. But Father Reeves, poor man, is blind."

So that was why he risked it, thought Dolby. But what a risk!

"Which prayer book did he use?"

She gazed at him, the milky eyes perplexed. "Father Reeves?"

"No, the bridegroom. He did handle a prayer book, I suppose?"

"Oh, yes. I put one out for each of them. Father Reeves asked me to get things ready. It was I who decorated the church. Poor dears, it wasn' as if they could have the usual printed service sheets. Emma's were so pretty, her initials intertwined with the bridegroom's. But yesterday they had to use ordinary prayer books. I chose them specially from the pews and put them on the two prayer stools. I found a very pretty white one for the bride and this splendid old book with the brass clasp for the bridegroom. I looked masculine, I thought."

It lay on the book ledge of the front pew. She made a move to pick i up, but he shot out his hand. Then he dropped his handkerchief over the book and lifted it by the sharp edges of the binding. Brass and leather Good for a print. And this man's palm would be moist, clammy, perhaps with perspiration and fear. A hot day; an illegal ceremony; his mind or murder. To love and to cherish until death us do part. Yes, this bride groom would have been nervous. But Dolby had one more question.

"How did they get here? Do you know?"

"They came by foot. At least, they walked up to the church together. I think they had walked quite a long way. They were quite hot and dusty when they arrived. But I know how they really came."

She nodded her unkempt head and gave a little conspiratorial nod.

"I've got very good ears, you know. They came by helicopter. I heard it."

A helicopter. He knew almost without thinking exactly who was permitted the use of a helicopter. Members of the Central Committee of Government; high ranking scientists and technicians; doctors; the Commissioner of the Home Security Force, and his Deputy. That was all.

He took the prayer book out into the sun and sat on one of the flat topped gravestones. He set up the prayer book on its end, then unzipped his murder bag. His hands shook so that he could hardly manage the brush and some of the gray powder was spilt and blew away in the breeze. He willed himself to keep calm, to take his time. Carefully, like a child with a new toy, he dusted the book and clasp with powder gently blowing off the

rplus with a small rubber nozzle. It was an old procedure, first practiced
hen he was a young Detective Constable. But it still worked. It always
ould. The arches, whorls, and composites came clearly into view.

He was right. It was a beautiful print. The man had made no effort to
ipe it clean. Why should he? How could he imagine that this particular
ook would ever be identified among the many scattered around the
urch? How could he suspect that he would ever be traced to this de-
ised and unregarded place? Dolby took out his camera and photographed
e print. There must be continuity of evidence. He must leave no room
r doubt. Then he classified its characteristics, ready for checking.

There was a little delay at the National Identification Computer Center
hen he phoned, and he had to wait his turn. When it came he gave his
ame, rank, secret code, and the classification of the print. There was a
oment's silence. Then a surprised voice asked, "Is that you, Dolby? Will
ou confirm your code."

He did so. Another silence.

"Okay. But what on earth are you up to? Are you sure of your print
lassification?"

"Yes. I want the identification for elimination purposes."

"Then you can eliminate, all right. That's the Commissioner. Kalvert,
. J. Hard luck, Dolby! Better start again."

He switched off the receiver and sat in silence. He had known it, of
ourse. But for how long? Perhaps from the beginning. Kalvert. Kalvert,
ho had an excuse for visiting an Ipdic Colony. Kalvert, who had the use
f a helicopter. Kalvert, who had known without asking that the television
et in her room was in working order. Kalvert, who had been too sure of
imself to take the most elementary precautions against discovery, because
e knew that it didn't matter, because he knew no one would dare touch
im. Kalvert, one of the four most powerful men in the country. And it
as he, the despised Sergeant Dolby, who had solved the case.

He heard the angry purr of the approaching helicopter without surprise.
le had reported the armed attack by the Ipdics. It was certain that Head-
uarters would have immediately summoned a Squad from the nearest sta-
on to hunt them down. But Kalvert would know about the message. He
ad no doubt that the Commissioner was keeping a watch on him. He
ould know which way Dolby was heading, would realize that he was
angerously close to the truth. The armed Squad would be here in time.
ut Kalvert would arrive first.

He waited for five minutes, still sitting quietly on the gravestone. The air was sweet with the smell of grasses and vibrating with the high-treble midsummer chant of blackbird and thrush. He shut his eyes for a moment breathing in the beauty, taking courage from its peace. Then he got to his feet and stood at the head of the avenue of elms to wait for Kalvert.

The gold braid on the all-white uniform gleamed in the sun. The tall figure, arrogant with confidence and power, walked unhesitatingly toward him, unsmiling, making no sign. When they were three feet apart, Kalvert stopped. They stood confronting each other. It was Dolby who spoke first His voice was little more than a whisper.

"You killed her."

He could not meet Kalvert's eyes. But he heard his reply.

"Yes, I killed her. Shall I tell you about it, Sergeant? You seem to have shown some initiative. You deserve to know part of the truth. I was her friend. That is prohibited by Regulation. She became my mistress. That against the Law. We decided to get married. That is a serious crime. killed her. That, as you earlier explained, is a felony. And what are you going to do about it, Sergeant?"

Dolby couldn't speak. Suddenly he took out the revolver. It seemed ridiculous to point it at Kalvert. He wasn't even sure that he would be able to fire it. But he held it close to his side and the curved stock fitted comfortably to his palm, giving him courage. He made himself meet Kalvert eyes, and heard the Commissioner laugh.

"To kill a Normal is also against the Law. But it's something more Capital murder, Dolby. Is that what you have in mind?"

Dolby spoke out of cracked lips, "But why? *Why?*"

"I don't have to explain to you. But I'll try. Have you the imagination to understand that we might have loved each other, that I might have married her because it seemed a small risk for me and would give her pleasure, that I might have promised to kill her when her last symptoms began? Can you, Sergeant Dolby, enter into the mind of a girl like that She was an Ipdic. And she was more alive in her condemned cell than you have ever been in your life. Female Ipdic PXN 07926431 found dead Looks like murder. Remember how you reported it, Dolby? A felony Something to be investigated. Against the Law. That's all it meant to you isn't it?"

He had taken out his own revolver now. He held it easily, like a man casually dangling a familiar toy. He stood there, magnificent in the sun hine, the breeze lifting his black hair. He said quietly, "Do you think I'd et any Law on earth keep me from the woman I loved?"

Dolby wanted to cry out that it hadn't been like that at all. That Kalvert didn't understand. That he, Dolby, had cared about the girl. But the contempt in those cold black eyes kept him silent. There was nothing they could say to each other. Nothing. And Kalvert would kill him.

The Squad would be here soon. Kalvert couldn't let him live to tell his story. He gazed with fascinated horror at the revolver held so easily, so confidently, in the Commissioner's hand. And he tightened the grip on his own, feeling with a shaking finger for the trigger.

The armored car roared up to the churchyard gate. The Squad were here. Kalvert lifted his revolver to replace it in the holster. Dolby, misunderstanding the gesture, whipped up his own gun and, closing his eyes, fired until the last cartridge was spent. Numbed by misery and panic, he didn't hear the shots or the thud of Kalvert's fall. The first sound to pierce his consciousness was a wild screaming and beating of wings as the terrified birds flew high. Then he was aware of an unnatural silence, and of an acrid smell tainting the summer air.

His right hand ached. It felt empty, slippery with sweat. He saw that he had dropped the gun. There was a long mournful cry of distress. It came from behind him. He turned the glimpsed the yellow-clad figure of the female Ipdic, hand to her mouth, watching him from the shadow of the church. Then she faded back into the dimness.

He dropped on his knees beside Kalvert. The torn arteries were pumping their blood onto the white tunic. The crimson stain burst open like a flower. Dolby took off his jacket with shaking hands and thrust it under Kalvert's head. He wanted to say that he was sorry, to cry out like a child that he hadn't really meant it, that it was all a mistake.

Kalvert looked at him. Was there really pity in those dulling eyes? He was trying to speak. "Poor Dolby! Your final error of judgment."

The last word was hiccupped in a gush of blood. Kalvert turned his head away from Dolby and drew up his knees as if easing himself into sleep. And Dolby knew that it was too late to explain now, that there was no one there to hear him.

He stood up. The Squad were very close now, three of them, walking abreast, guns at hip, moving inexorably forward in the pool of their own shadows. And so he waited, all fear past, with Kalvert's body at his feet. And he thought for the first time of his daughter. Tessa, whom he had allowed to hide from him because that was the Law. Tessa, whom he had deserted and betrayed. Tessa, whom he had sought at last, but had found too late. Tessa, who had led him unwittingly to her lover and murderer. Tessa who would never have picked that Lady Orchid. Hadn't he taught her when she was a child that if you picked a wild orchid it can never bloom again?